Magic Girls

KIRA and the (Maybe) SPACE PRINCESS

Magic Girls

KIRA and the (Maybe) SPACE PRINCESS

MEGAN BRENNAN

RH
GRAPHIC

NEW YORK

Magic Girls: Kira and the (Maybe) Space Princess was drawn in Clip Studio for iPad and colored and lettered in Photoshop.

All rights reserved. Published in the United States by RH Graphic, an imprint of Random House Children's Books, a division of Penguin Random House LLC, New York.

RH Graphic with the book design is a trademark of Penguin Random House LLC.

Visit us on the Web and sign up for our newsletter!

RHKidsGraphic.com

@RHKidsGraphic

Educators and librarians, for a variety of teaching tools, visit us at RHTeachersLibrarians.com

Library of Congress Cataloging-in-Publication Data is available upon request. ISBN 978-0-593-17754-9 (trade) — ISBN 978-0-593-17755-6 (lib. bdg.) — ISBN 978-0-593-70989-4 (pbk.) — ISBN 978-0-593-17756-3 (ebook)

Editors: Whitney Leopard & Danny Diaz
Designer: Juliet Goodman
Copy Editor: Melinda Ackell
Managing Editor: Katy Miller
Production Manager: Jen Jie Li

MANUFACTURED IN CHINA

10 9 8 7 6 5 4 3 2 1

First Edition

A comic on every bookshelf.

For my family and friends who supported
me along the way, and everyone who made
an otaku senshi circa 2001

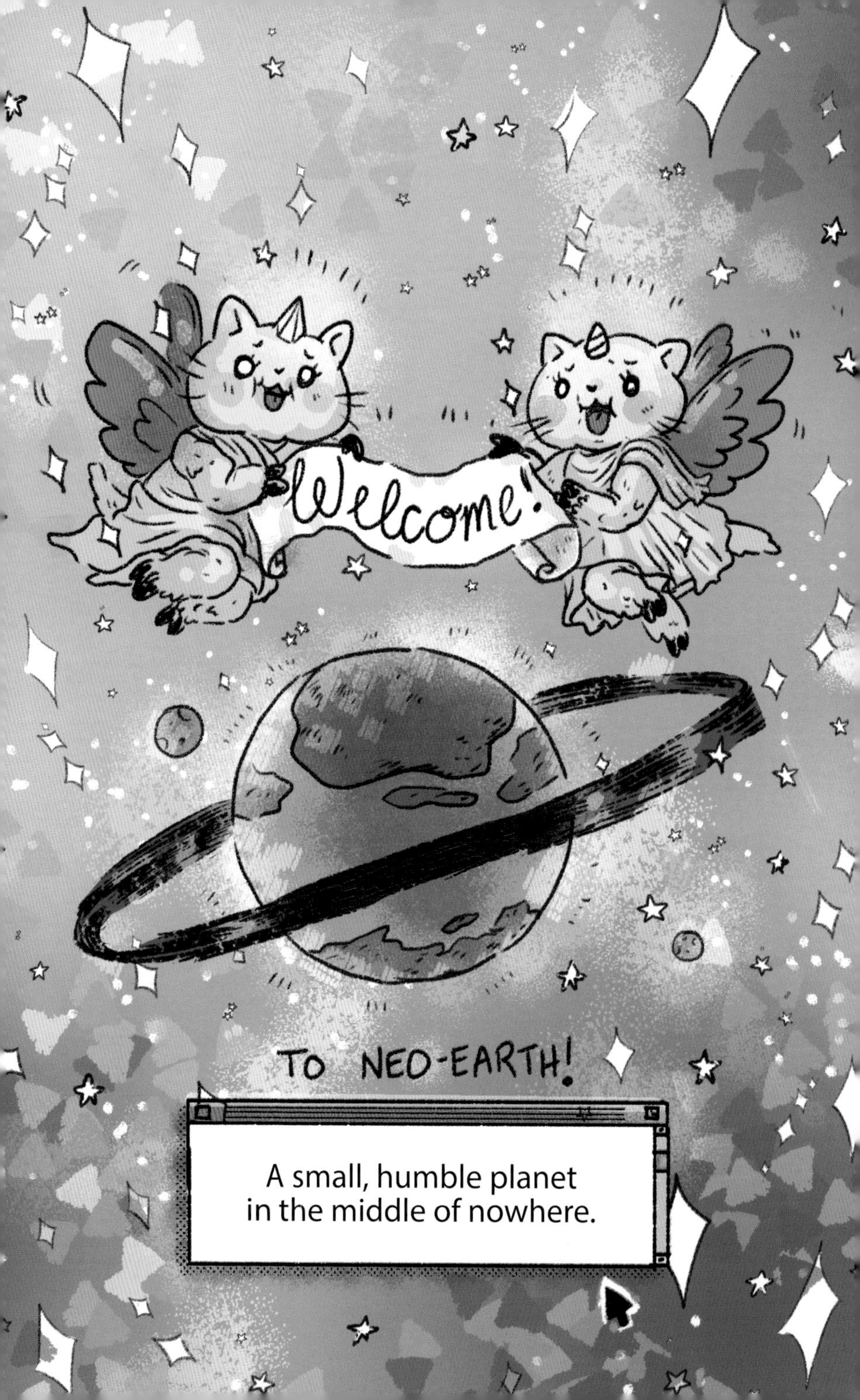
Welcome!
TO NEO-EARTH!
A small, humble planet in the middle of nowhere.

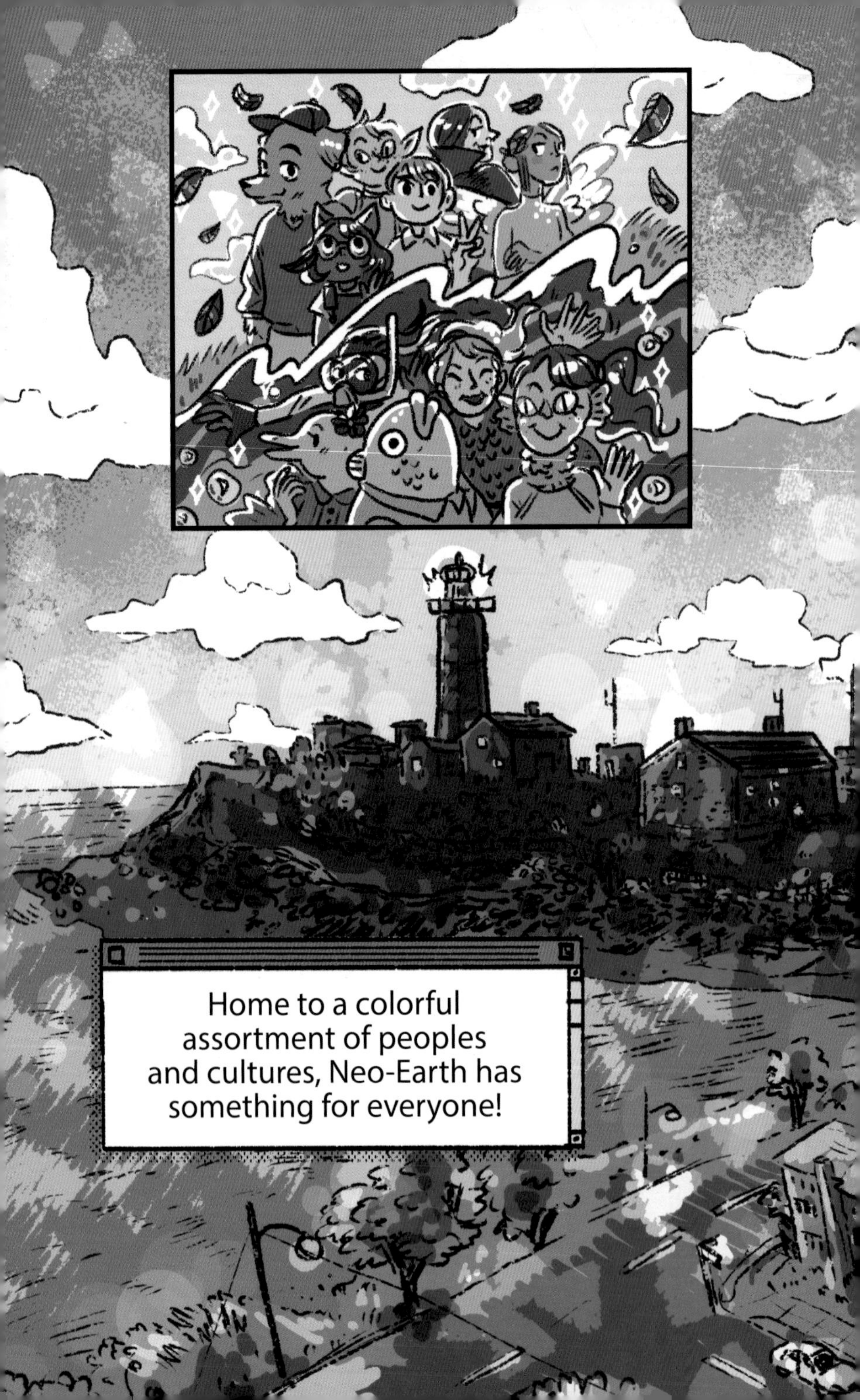
Home to a colorful assortment of peoples and cultures, Neo-Earth has something for everyone!

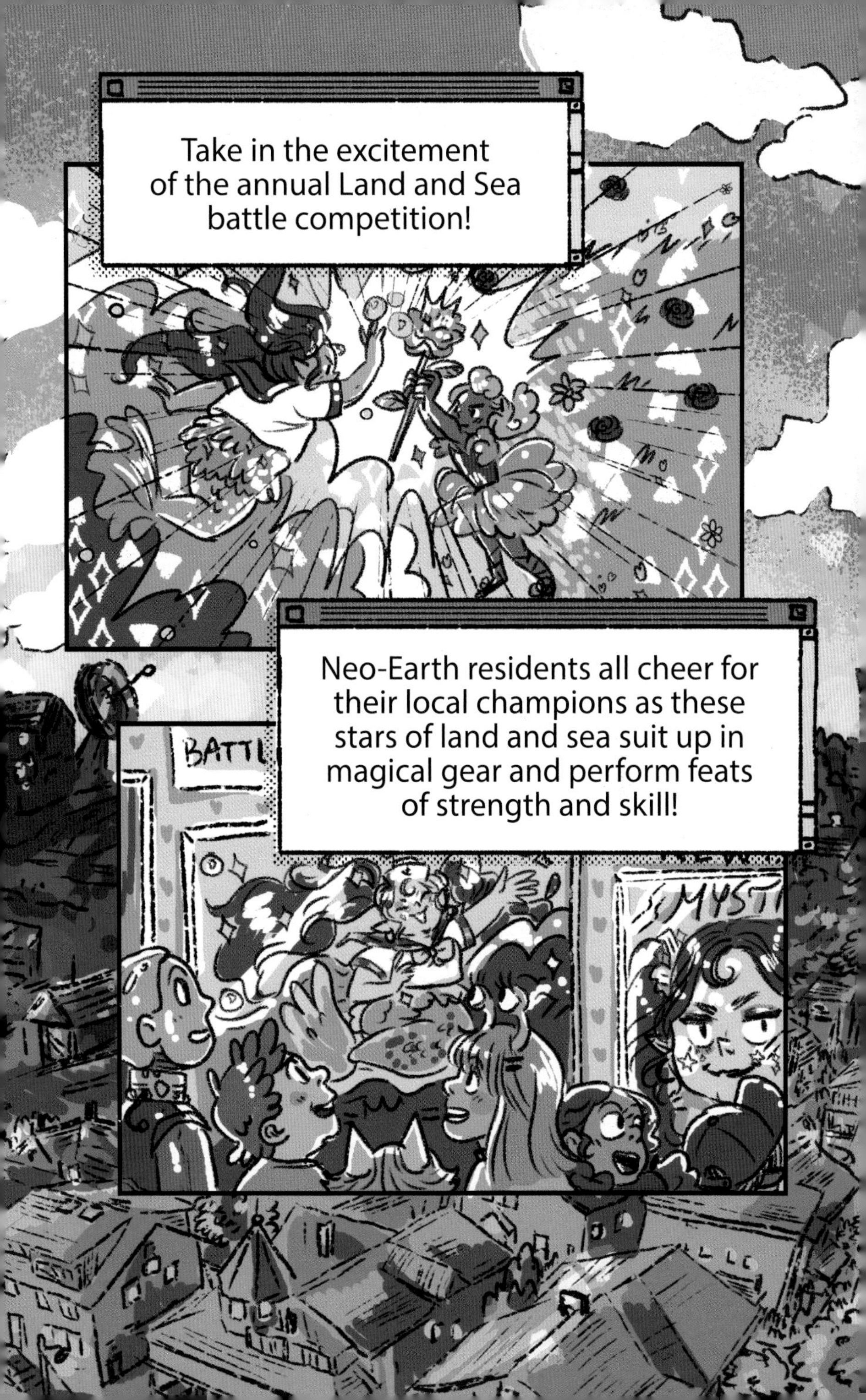
Take in the excitement of the annual Land and Sea battle competition!
Neo-Earth residents all cheer for their local champions as these stars of land and sea suit up in magical gear and perform feats of strength and skill!
BATTL
MYST

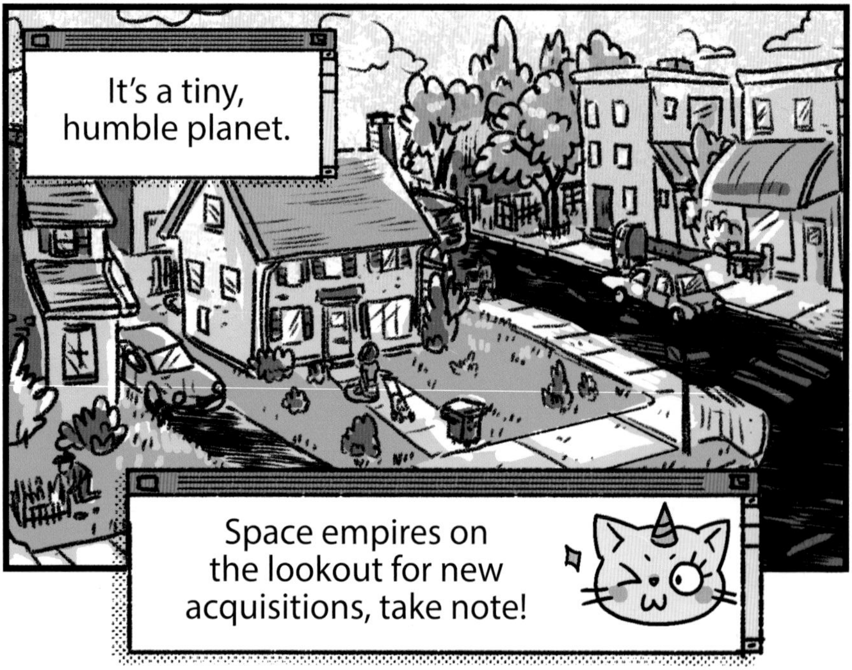
It's a tiny, humble planet.
Space empires on the lookout for new acquisitions, take note!

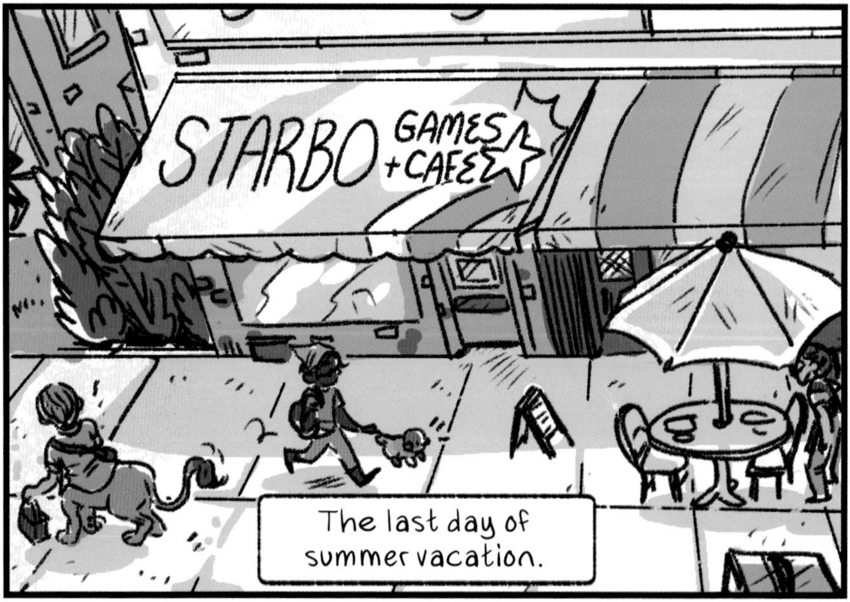
STARBO GAMES + CAFE
The last day of summer vacation.

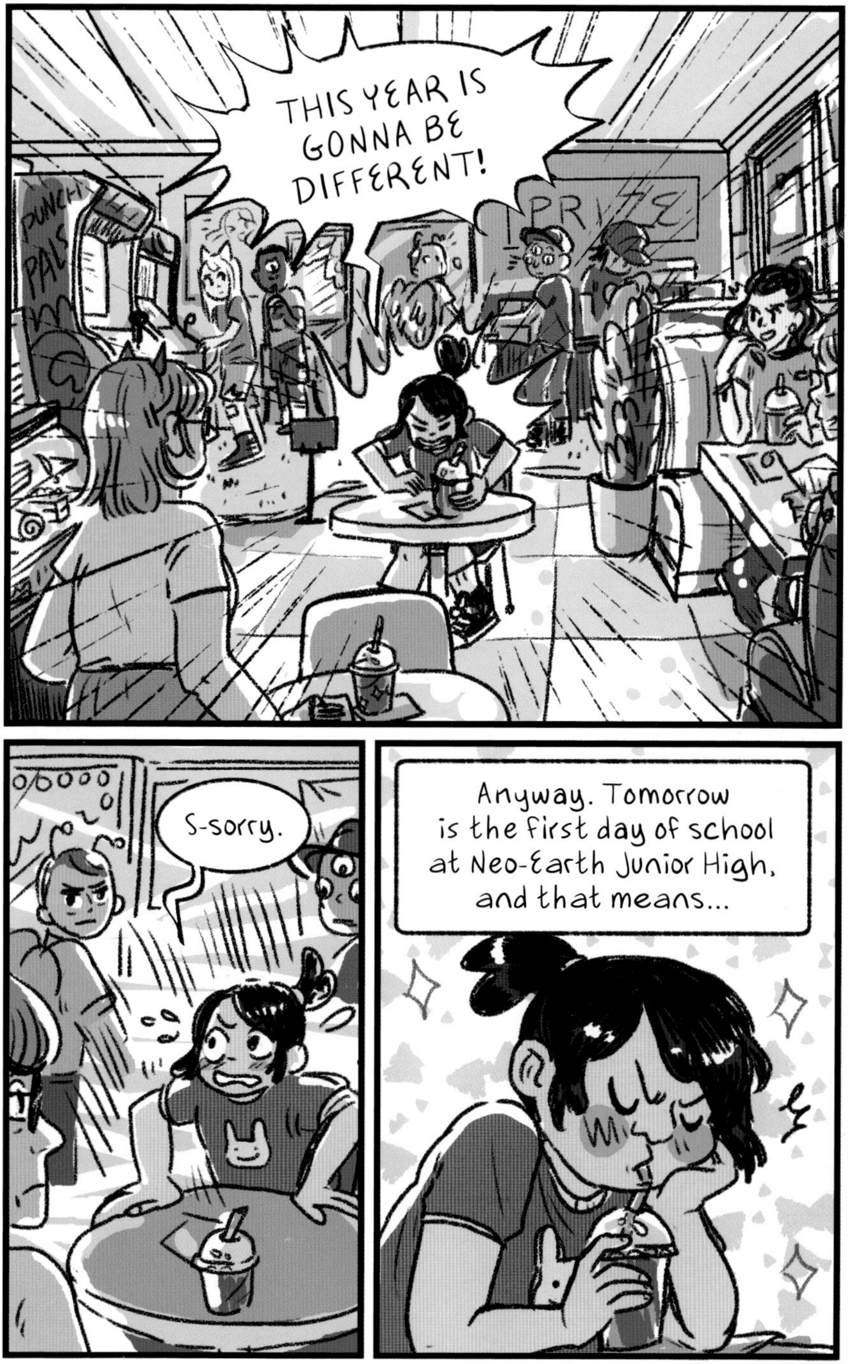
THIS YEAR IS GONNA BE DIFFERENT!
PUNCH PALS
PRIZE
S-sorry.
Anyway. Tomorrow is the first day of school at Neo-Earth Junior High, and that means...

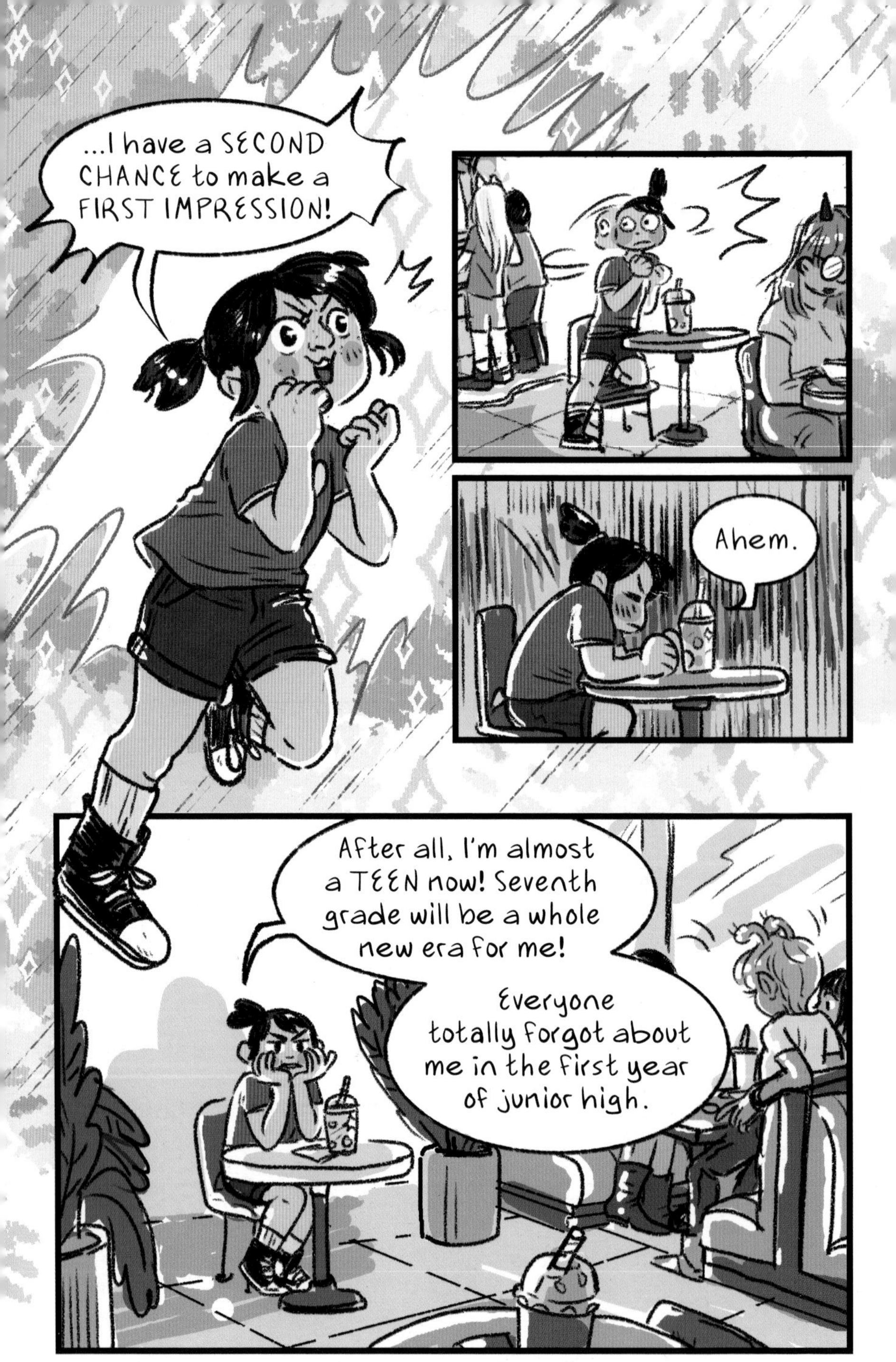
...I have a SECOND CHANCE to make a FIRST IMPRESSION!
Ahem.
After all, I'm almost a TEEN now! Seventh grade will be a whole new era for me!
Everyone totally forgot about me in the first year of junior high.

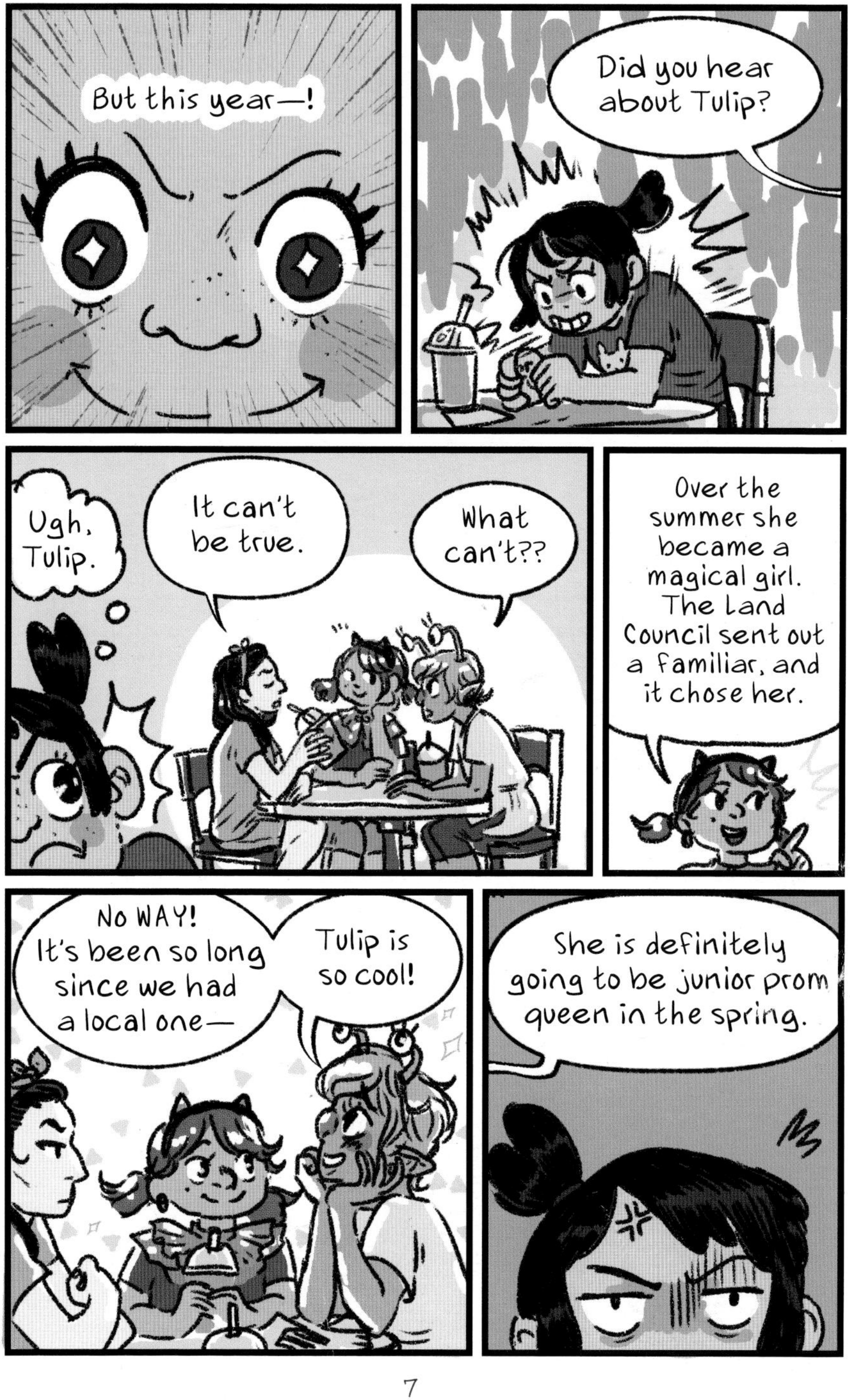
But this year—!
Did you hear about Tulip?
Ugh, Tulip.
It can't be true.
What can't??
Over the summer she became a magical girl. The Land Council sent out a familiar, and it chose her.
NO WAY! It's been so long since we had a local one—
Tulip is so cool!
She is definitely going to be junior prom queen in the spring.

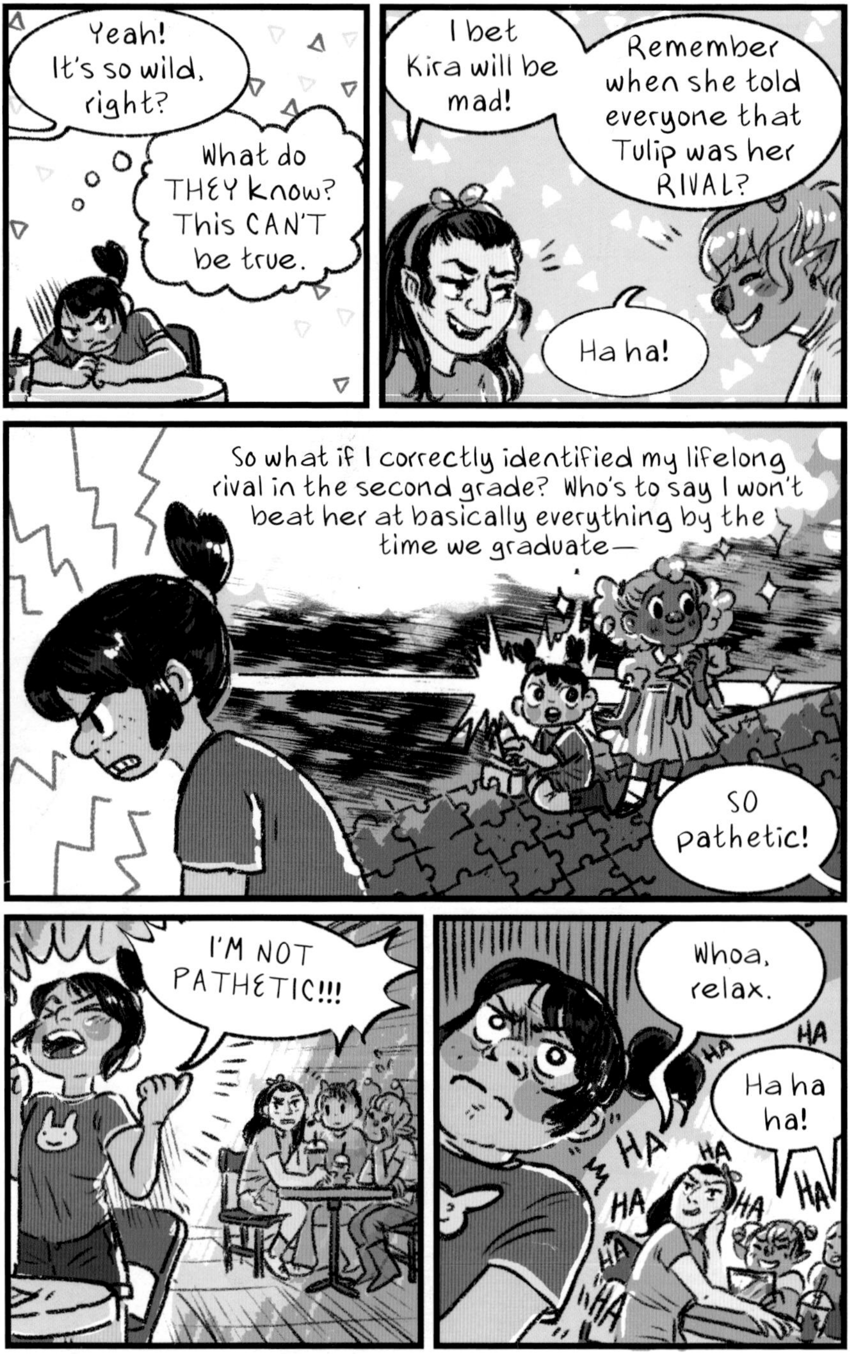
Yeah!
It's so wild, right?
What do THEY know? This CAN'T be true.
I bet Kira will be mad!
Remember when she told everyone that Tulip was her RIVAL?
Ha ha!
So what if I correctly identified my lifelong rival in the second grade? Who's to say I won't beat her at basically everything by the time we graduate—
SO pathetic!
I'M NOT PATHETIC!!!
Whoa, relax.
Ha ha ha!
HA HA HA HA HA HA HA HA HA

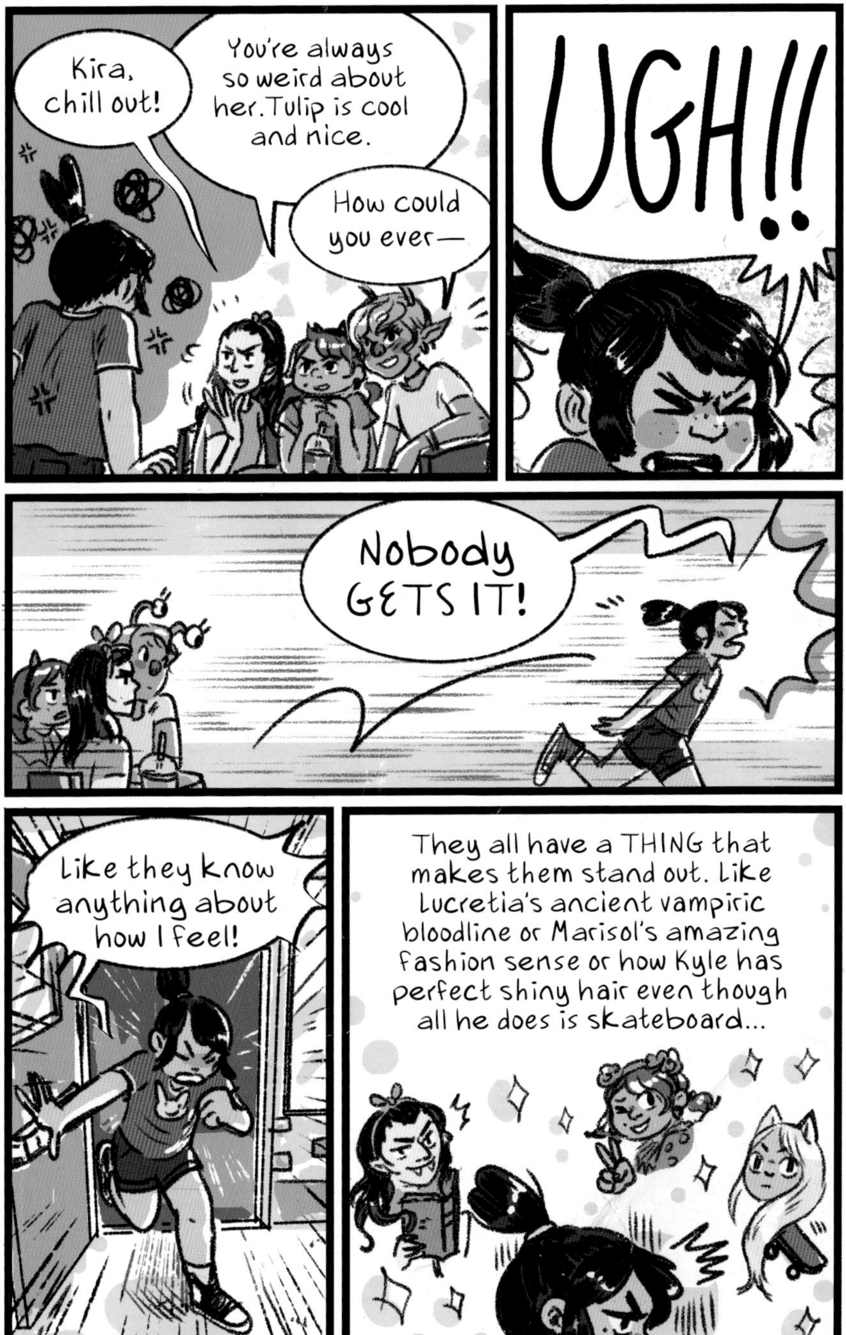
Kira, chill out!
You're always so weird about her. Tulip is cool and nice.
How could you ever—
UGH!!
Nobody GETS IT!
Like they know anything about how I feel!
They all have a THING that makes them stand out. Like Lucretia's ancient vampiric bloodline or Marisol's amazing fashion sense or how Kyle has perfect shiny hair even though all he does is skateboard...

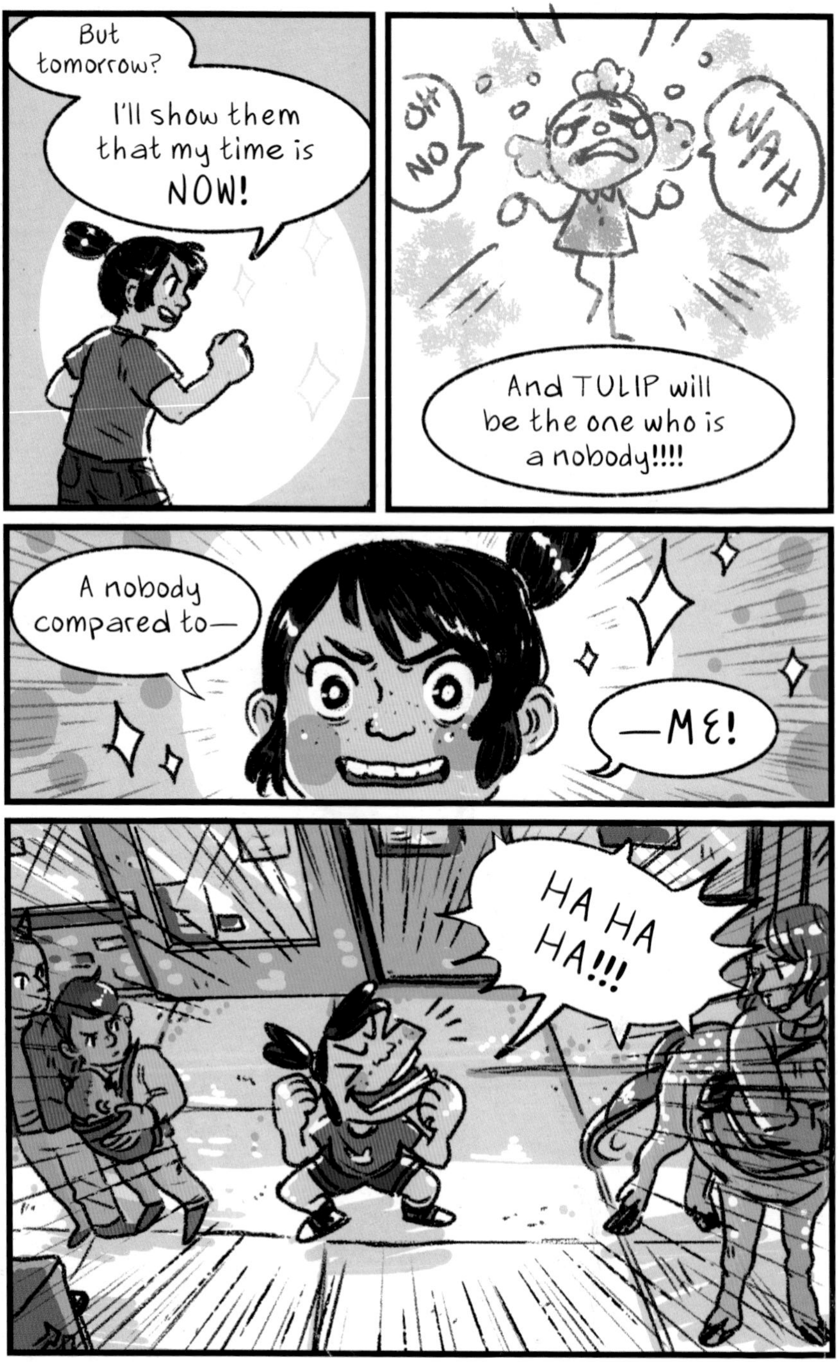
But tomorrow?
I'll show them that my time is NOW!
OH NO
WAH
And TULIP will be the one who is a nobody!!!!
A nobody compared to—
—ME!
HA HA HA!!!

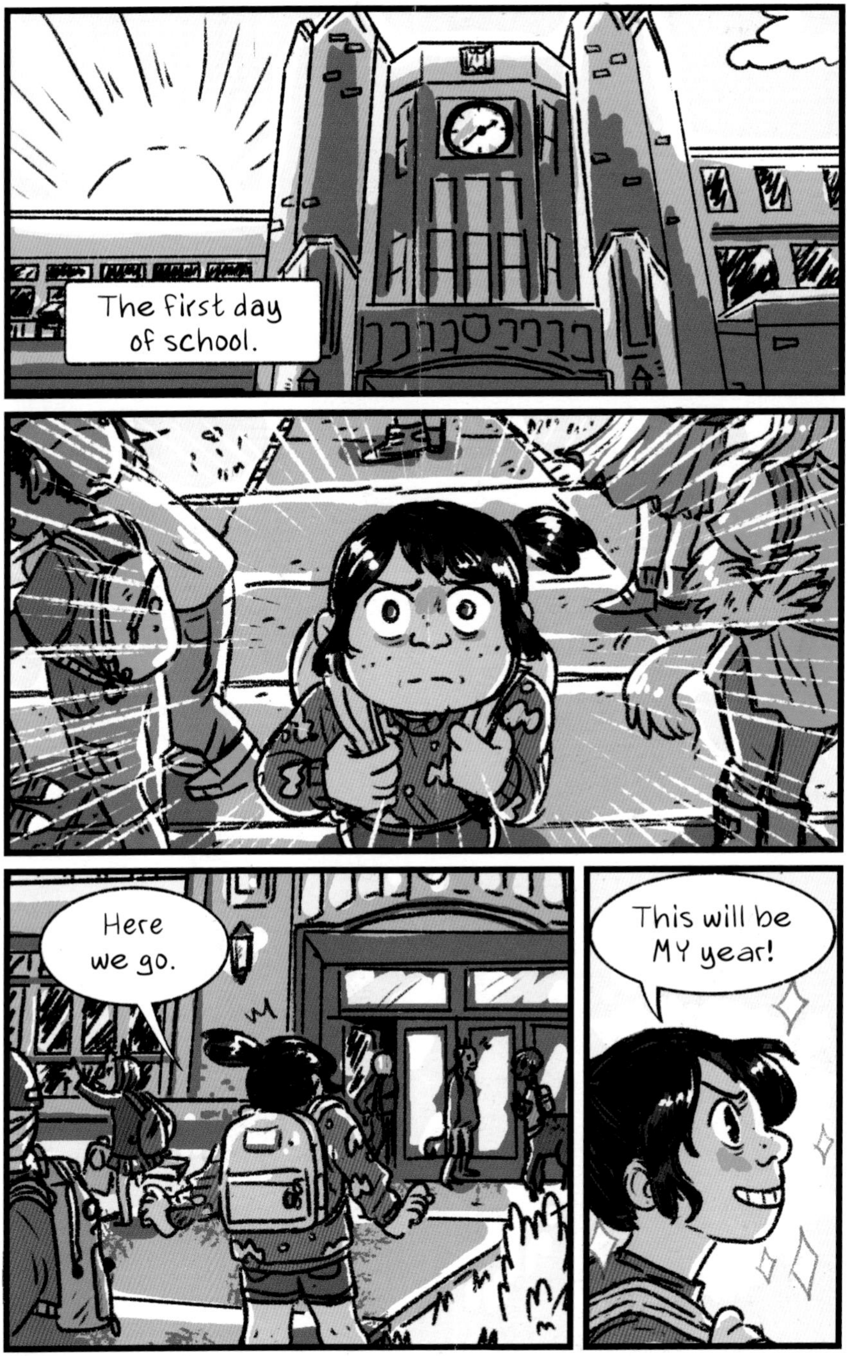
The first day of school.
Here we go.
This will be MY year!

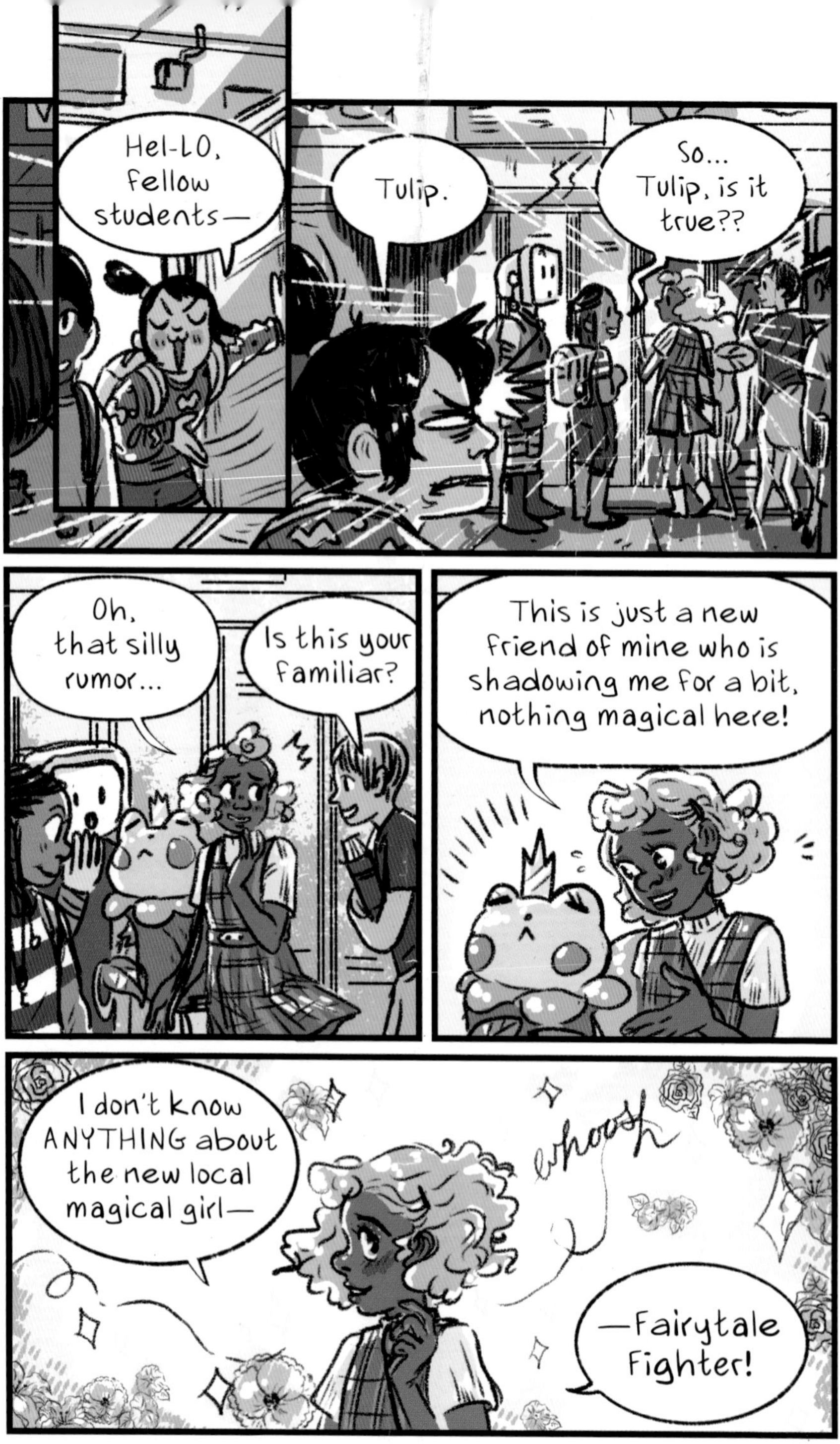
Hel-LO,
fellow
students—
Tulip.
So...
Tulip, is it
true??
Oh,
that silly
rumor...
Is this your
familiar?
This is just a new
friend of mine who is
shadowing me for a bit,
nothing magical here!
I don't know
ANYTHING about
the new local
magical girl—
whoosh
—Fairytale
Fighter!

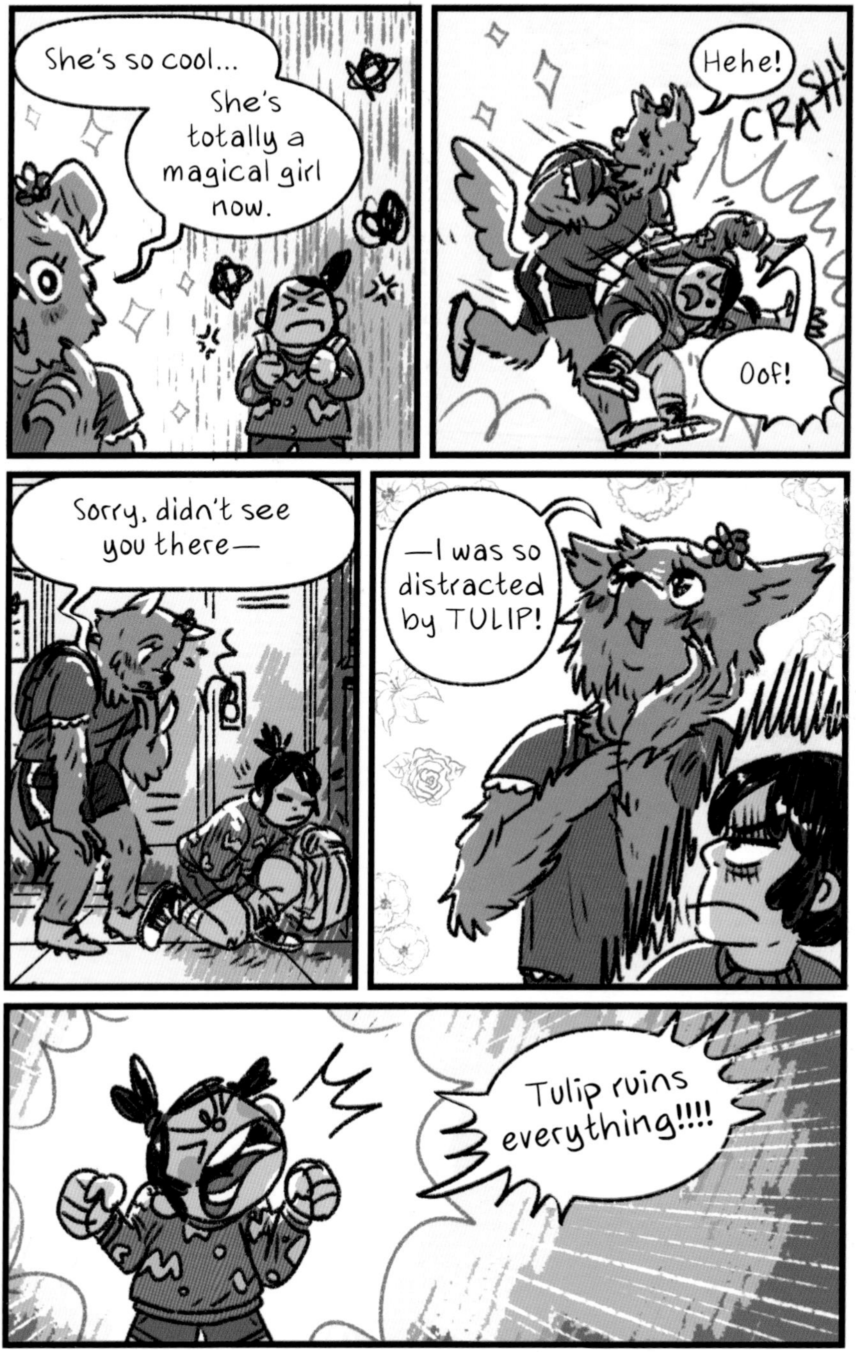
She's so cool...
She's totally a magical girl now.
Hehe!
CRASH!
Oof!
Sorry, didn't see you there—
—I was so distracted by TULIP!
Tulip ruins everything!!!!

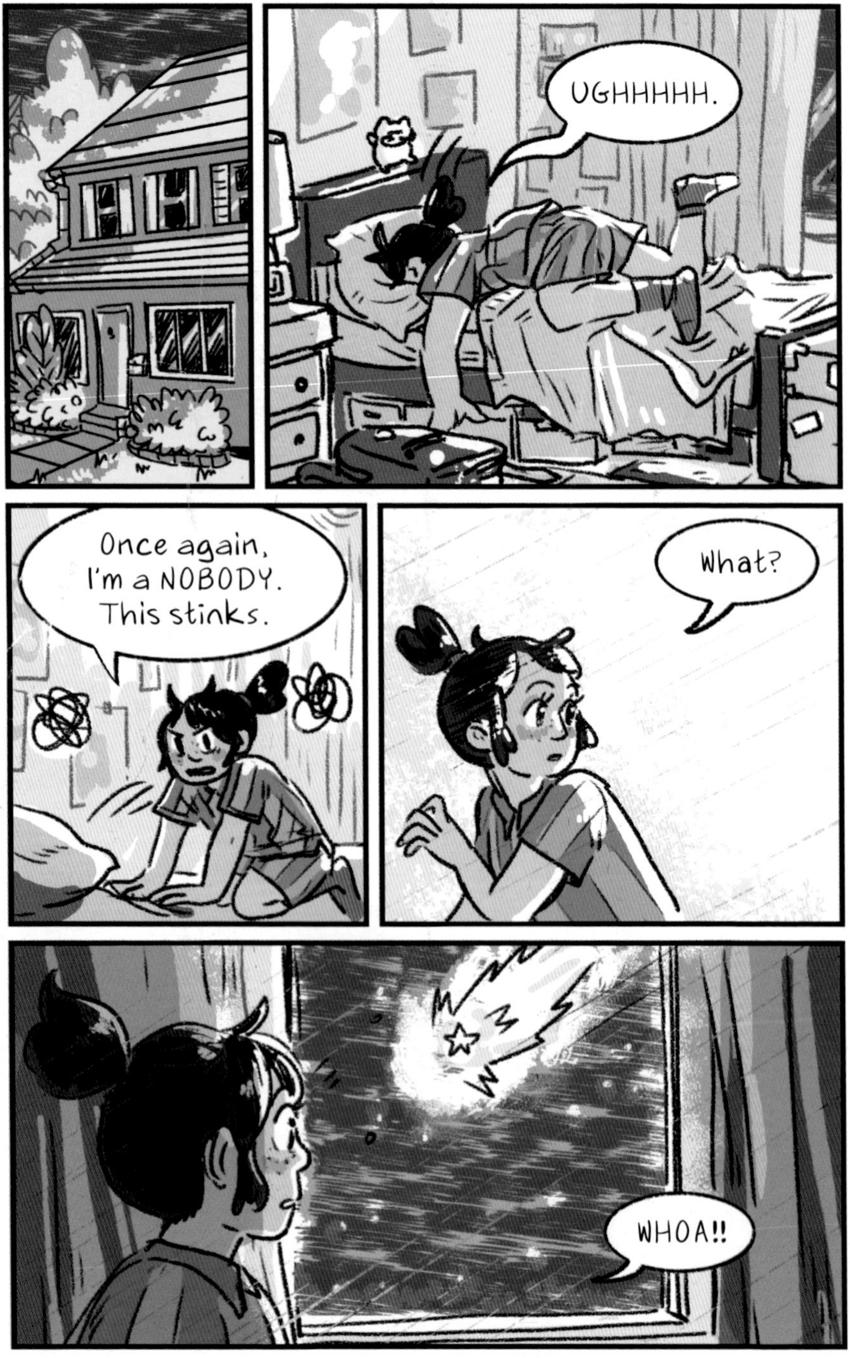
UGHHHHH.
Once again, I'm a NOBODY. This stinks.
What?
WHOA!!

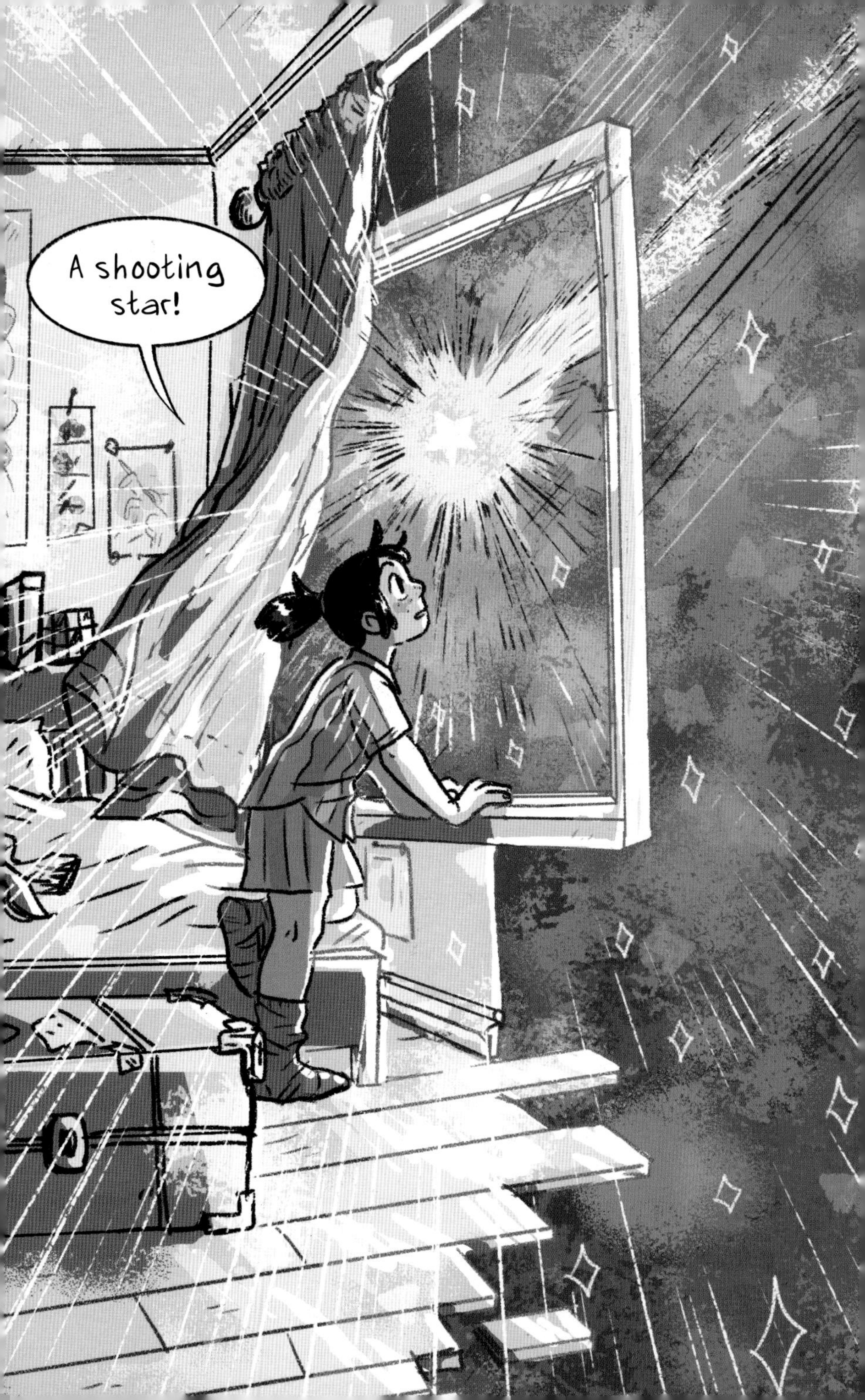
A shooting star!

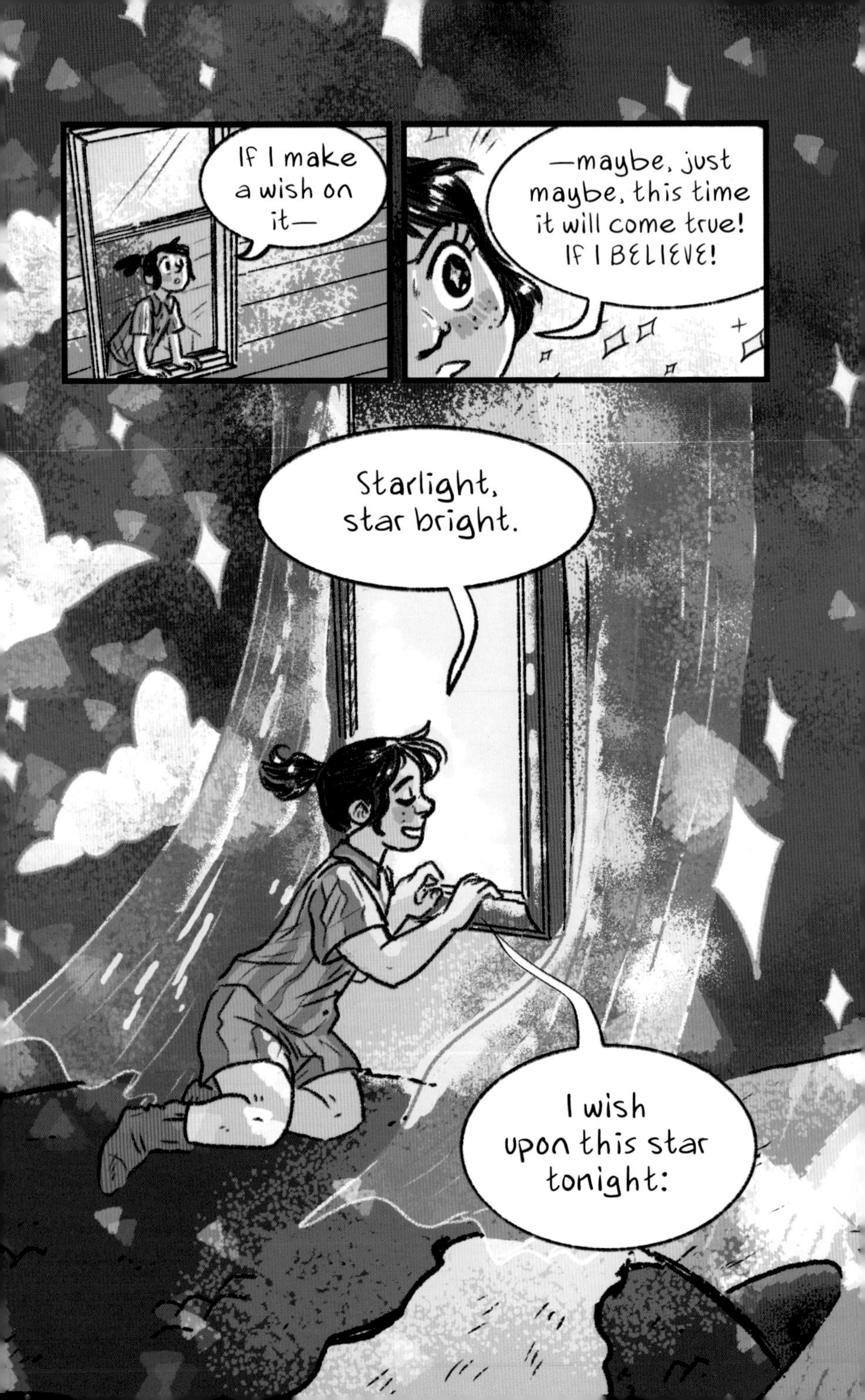
If I make a wish on it—
—maybe, just maybe, this time it will come true! IF I BELIEVE!
Starlight, star bright.
I wish upon this star tonight:

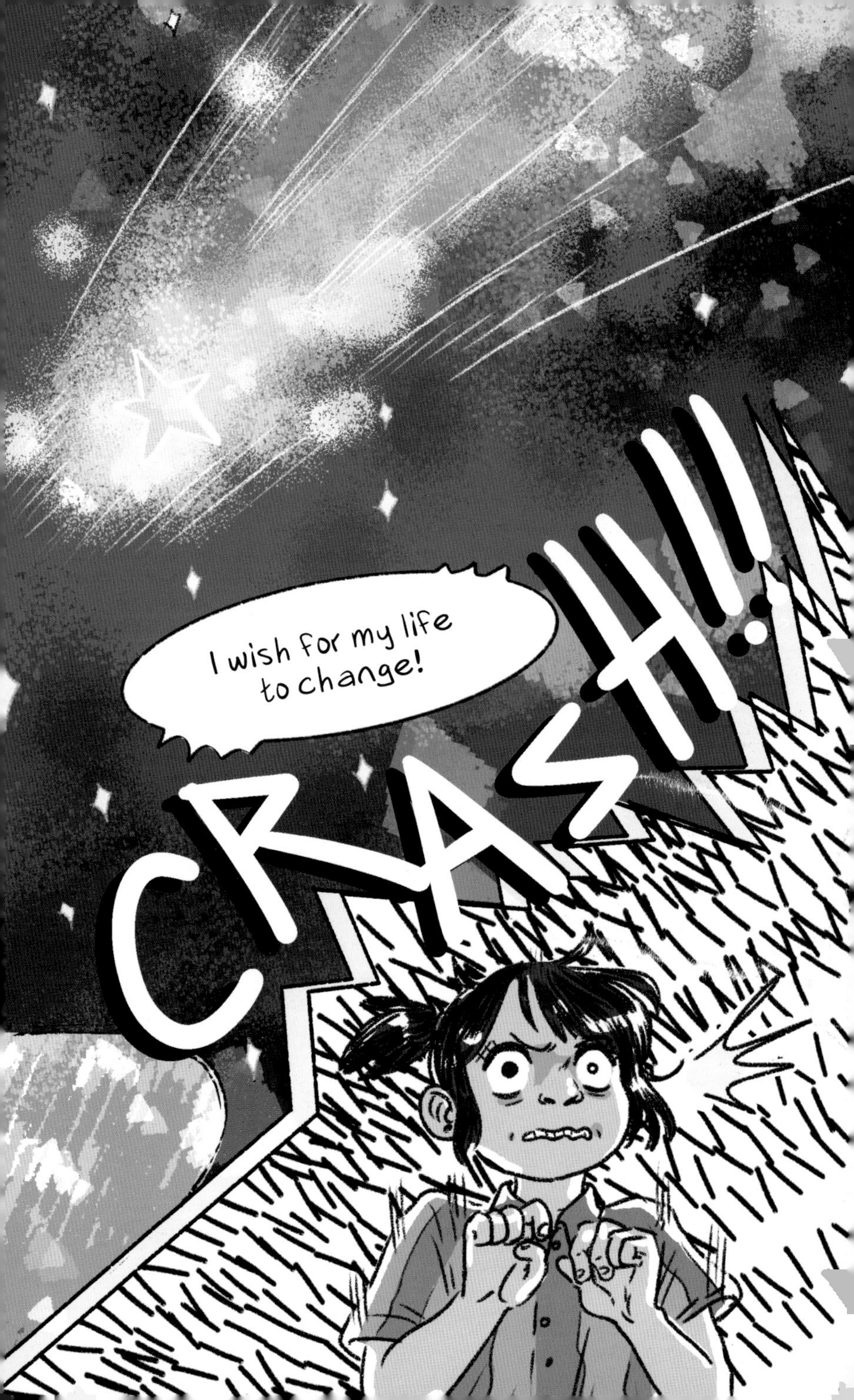
I wish for my life to change!
CRASH!!!

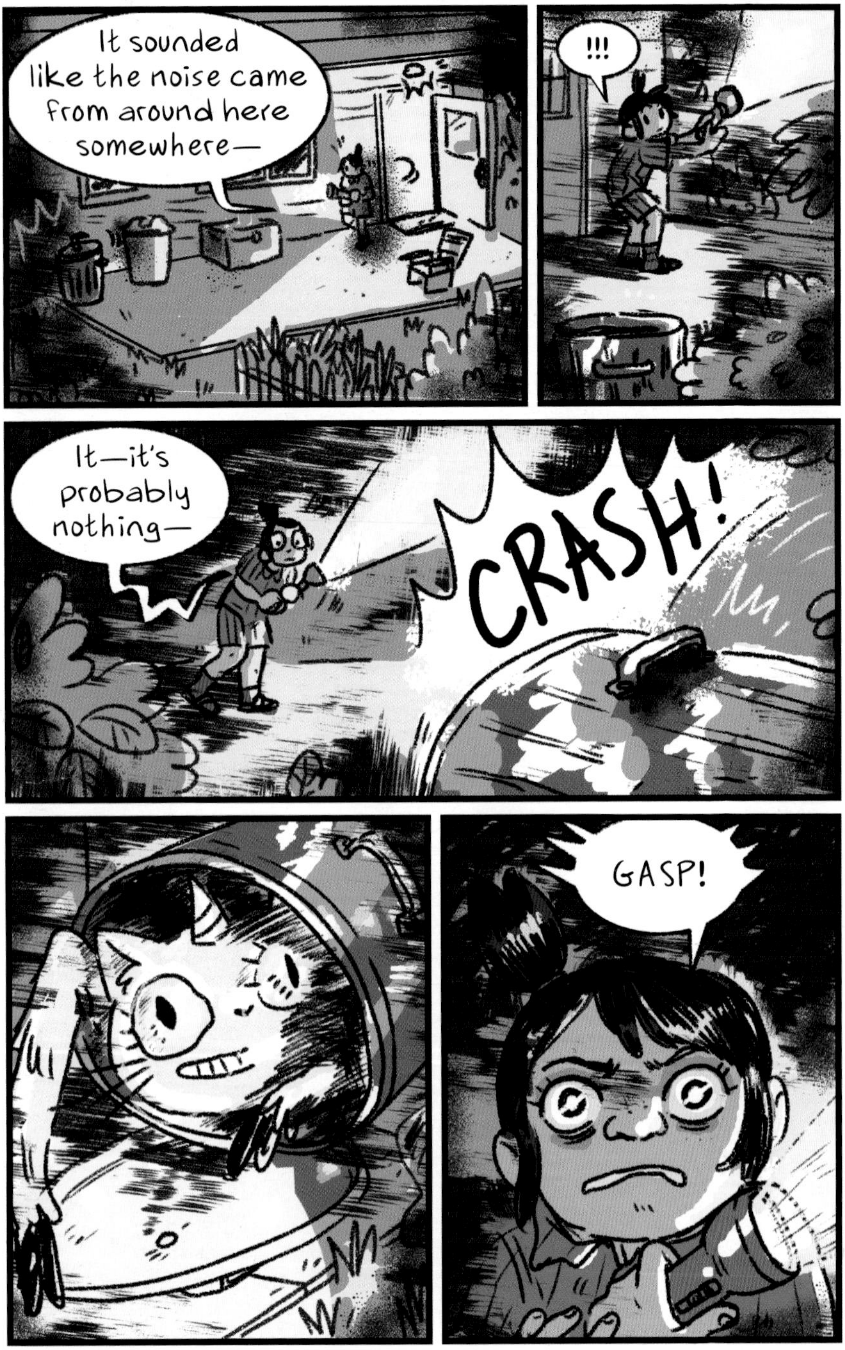
It sounded like the noise came from around here somewhere—
!!!
It—it's probably nothing—
CRASH!
GASP!

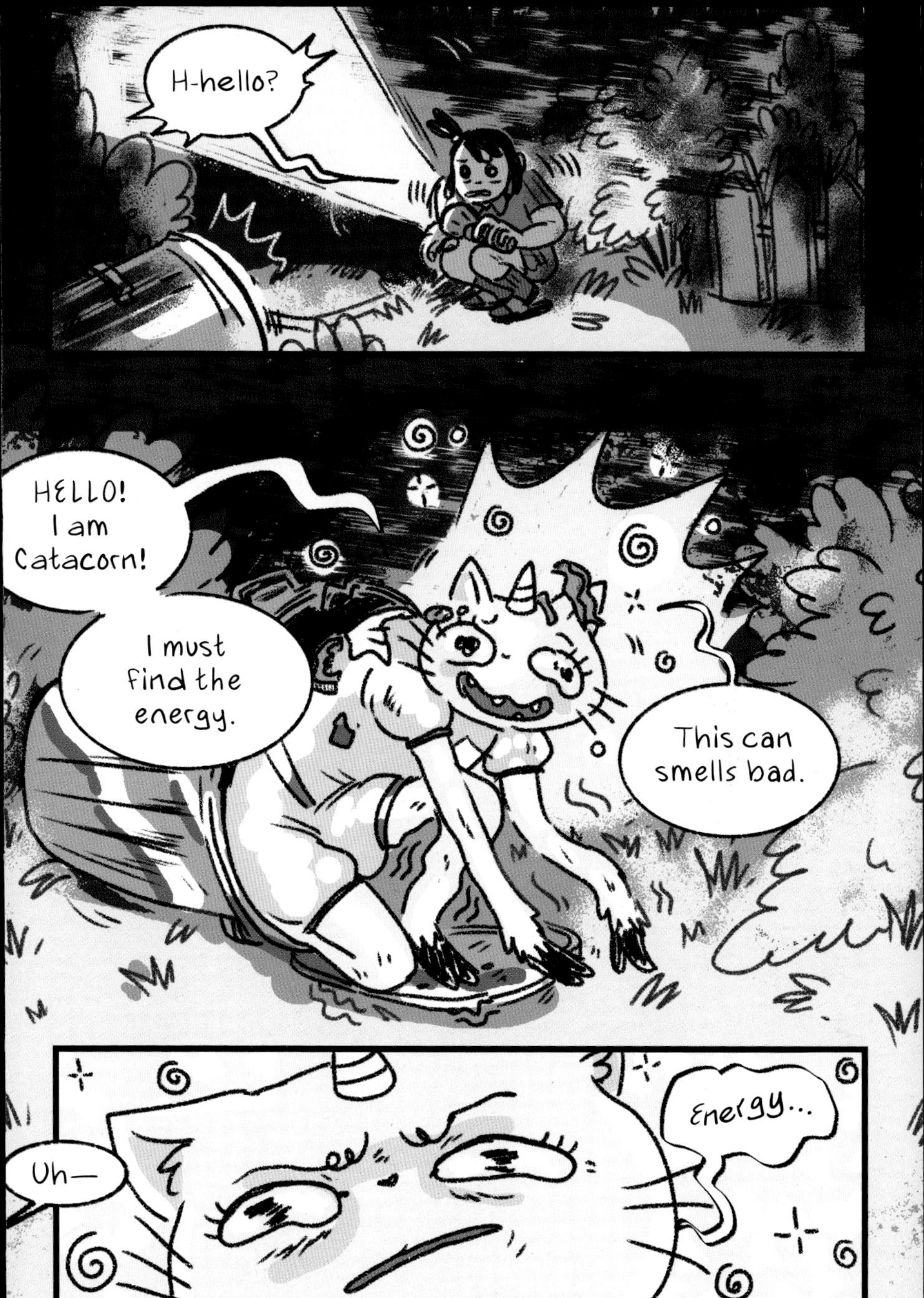
H-hello?
HELLO! I am Catacorn!
I must find the energy.
This can smells bad.
Uh—
Energy...

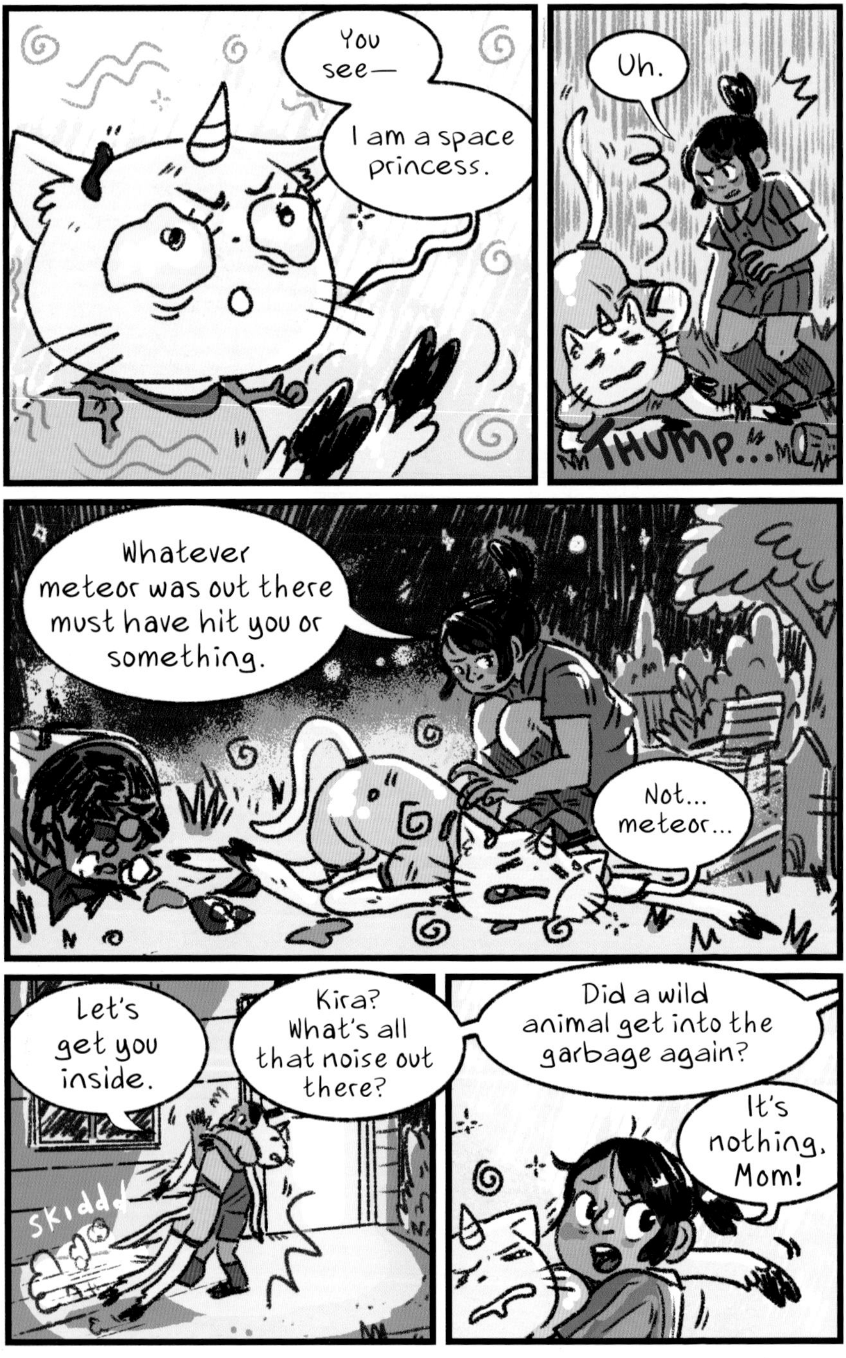
You see—
I am a space princess.
Uh.
THUMP...
Whatever meteor was out there must have hit you or something.
Not... meteor...
Let's get you inside.
Kira? What's all that noise out there?
Did a wild animal get into the garbage again?
It's nothing, Mom!

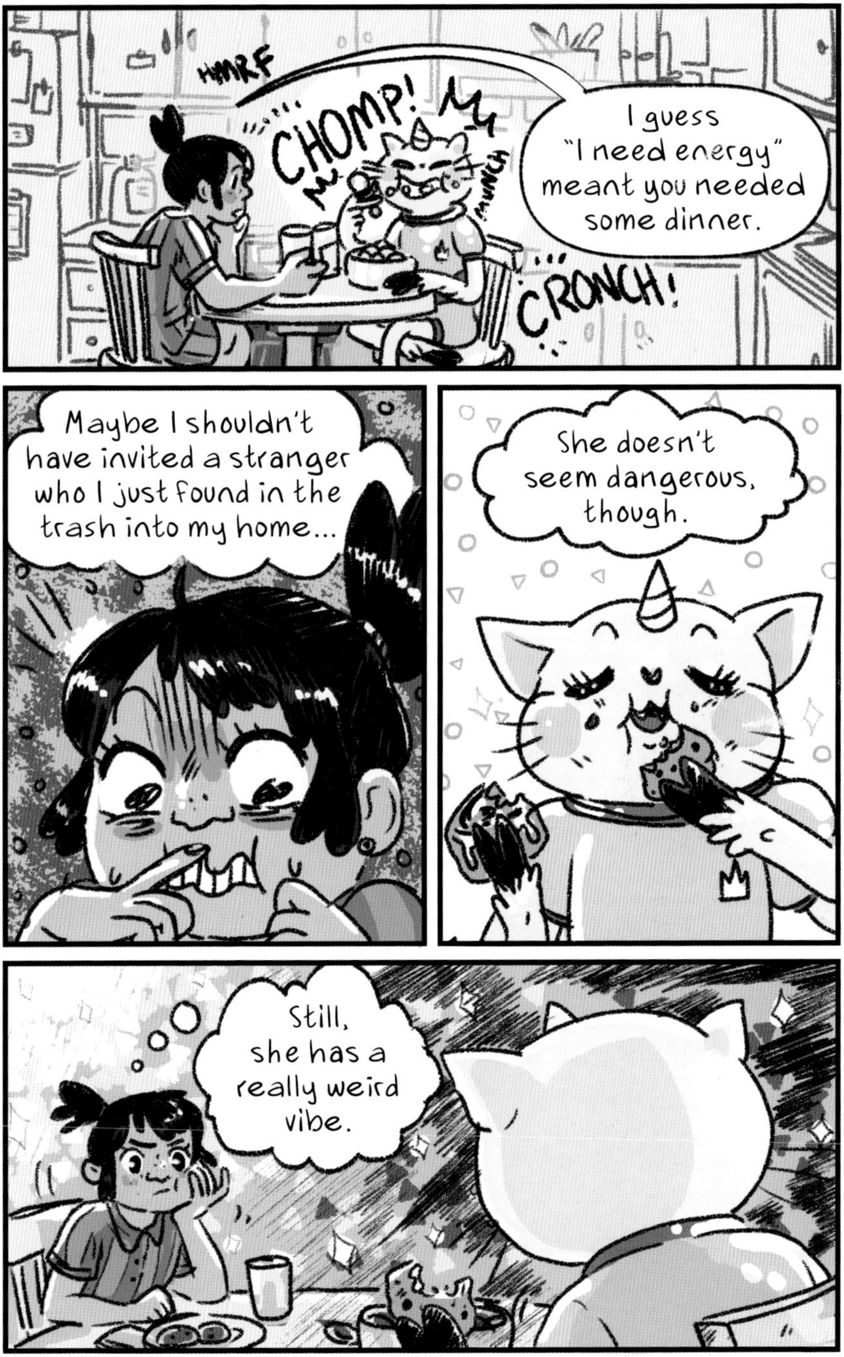
HMRF
CHOMP!
MUNCH
CRONCH!
I guess "I need energy" meant you needed some dinner.
Maybe I shouldn't have invited a stranger who I just found in the trash into my home...
She doesn't seem dangerous, though.
Still, she has a really weird vibe.

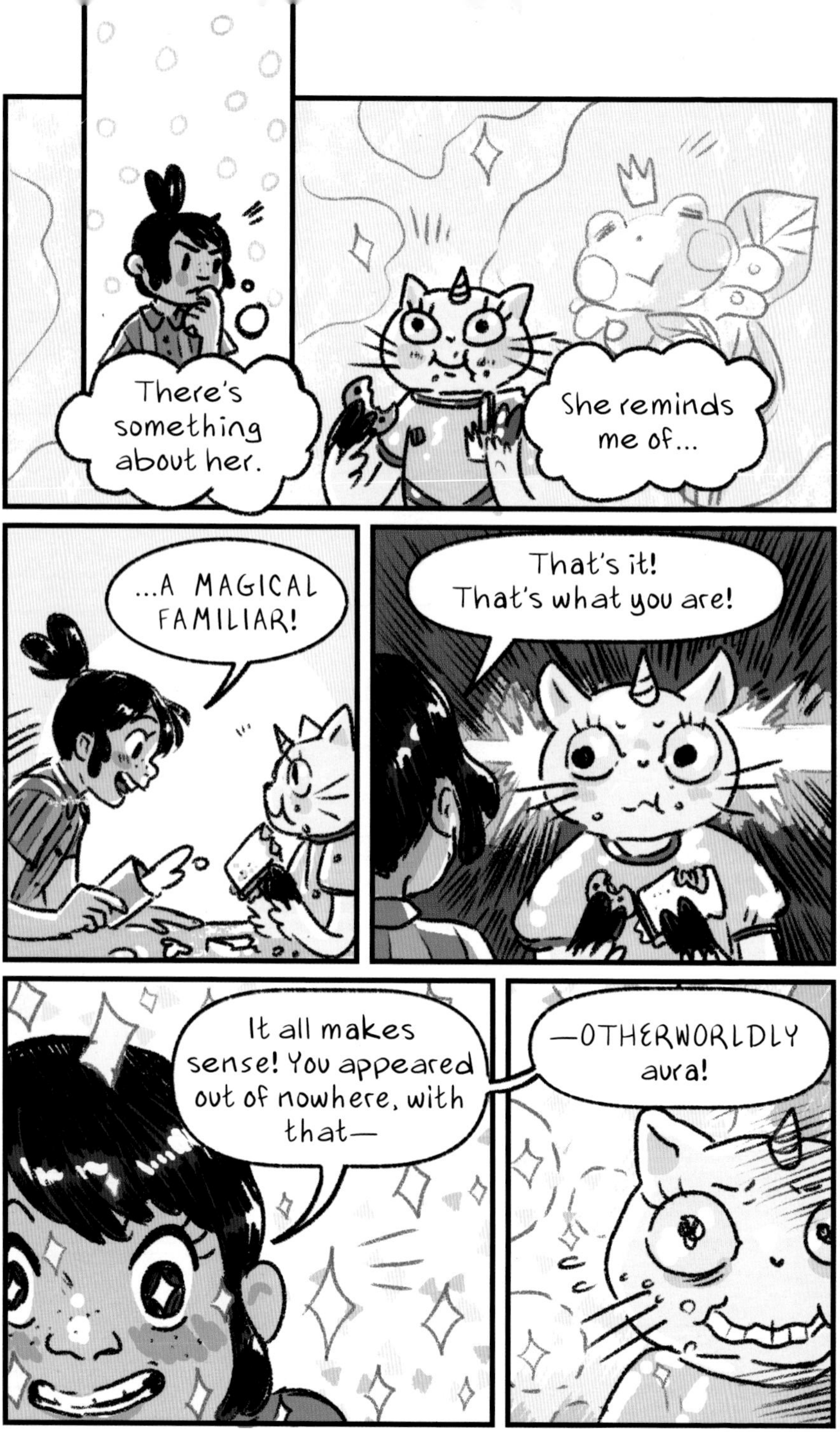
There's something about her.
She reminds me of...
...A MAGICAL FAMILIAR!
That's it! That's what you are!
It all makes sense! You appeared out of nowhere, with that—
—OTHERWORLDLY aura!

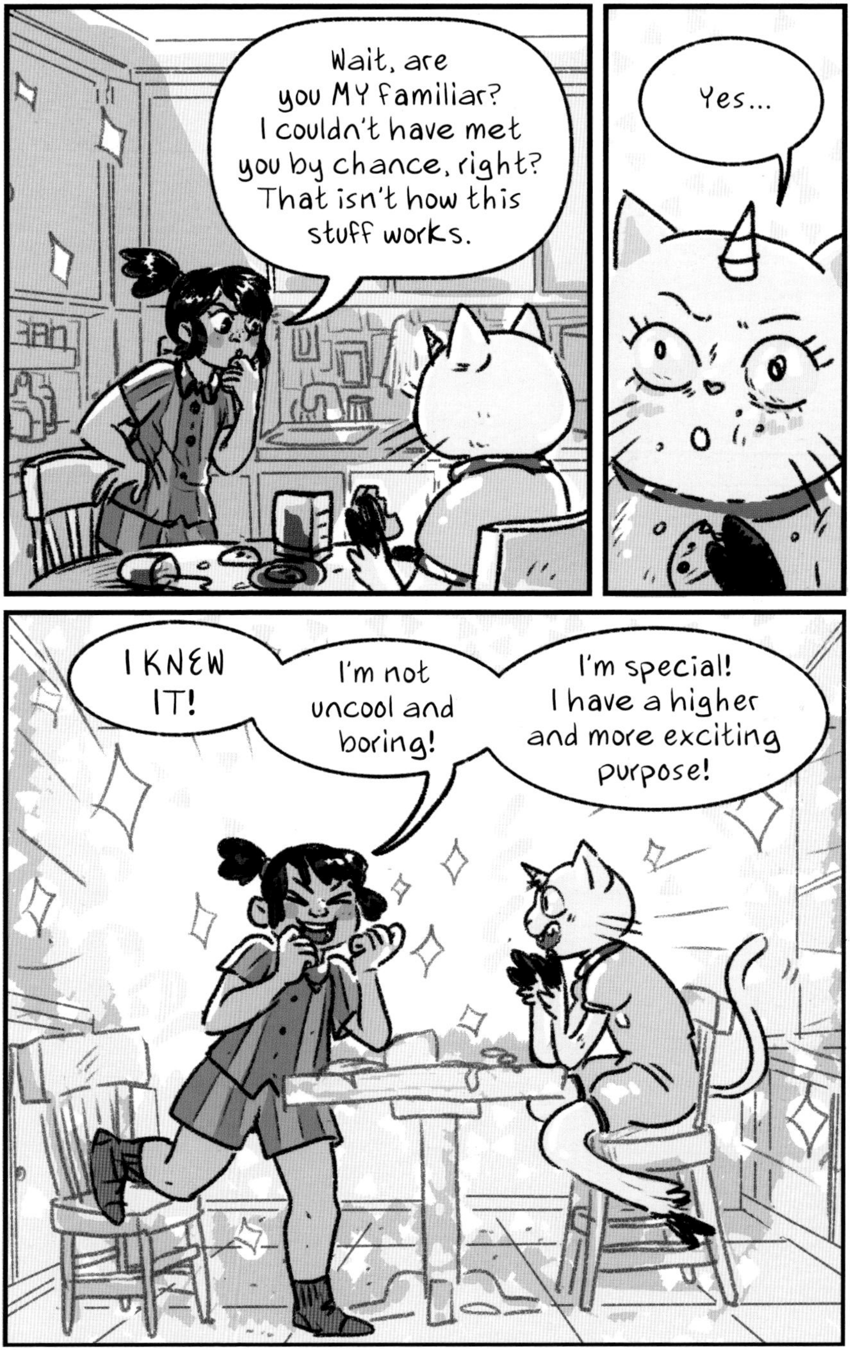
Wait, are you MY familiar? I couldn't have met you by chance, right? That isn't how this stuff works.
Yes...
I KNEW IT!
I'm not uncool and boring!
I'm special! I have a higher and more exciting purpose!

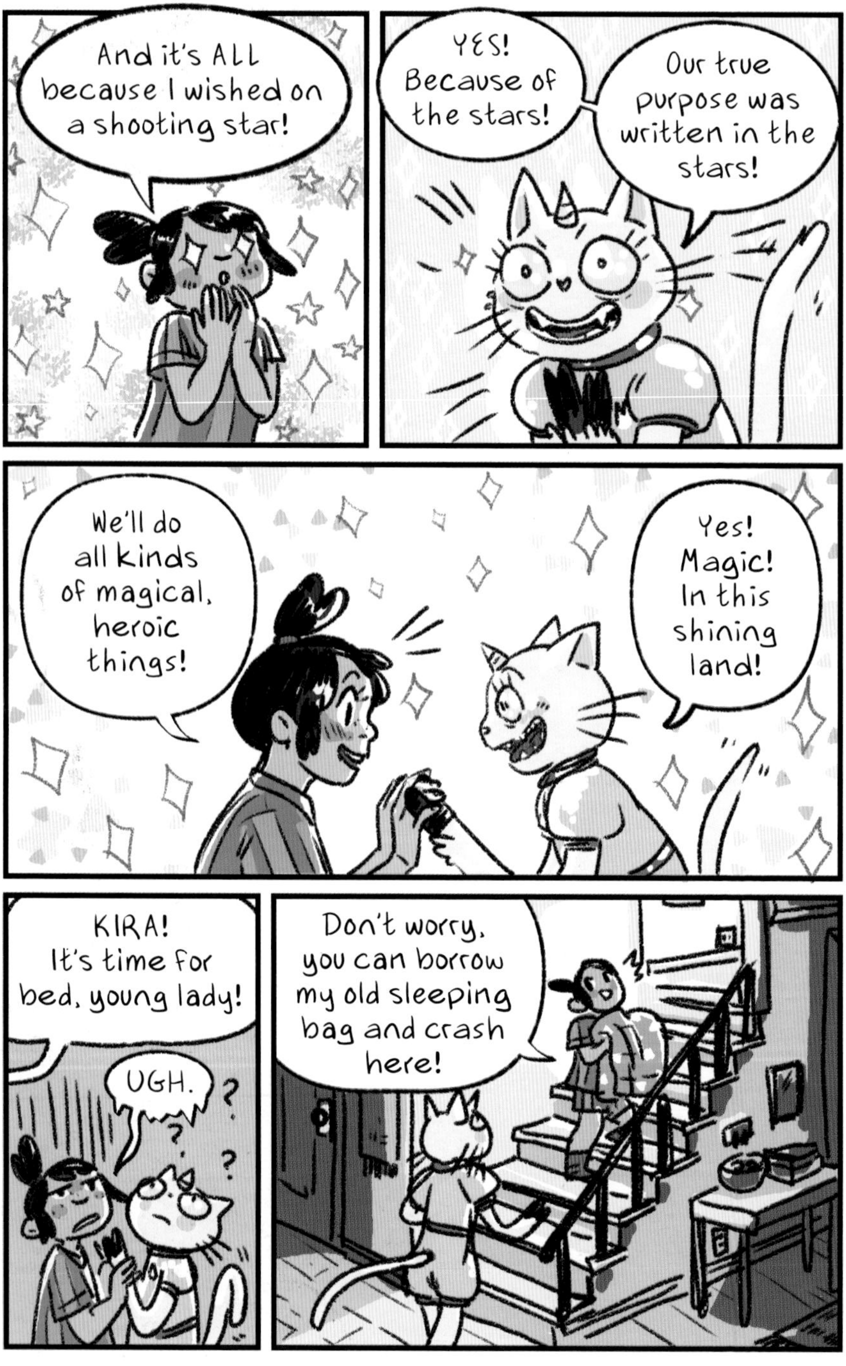
And it's ALL because I wished on a shooting star!
YES! Because of the stars!
Our true purpose was written in the stars!
We'll do all kinds of magical, heroic things!
Yes! Magic! In this shining land!
KIRA! It's time for bed, young lady!
UGH.
?
?
?
Don't worry, you can borrow my old sleeping bag and crash here!

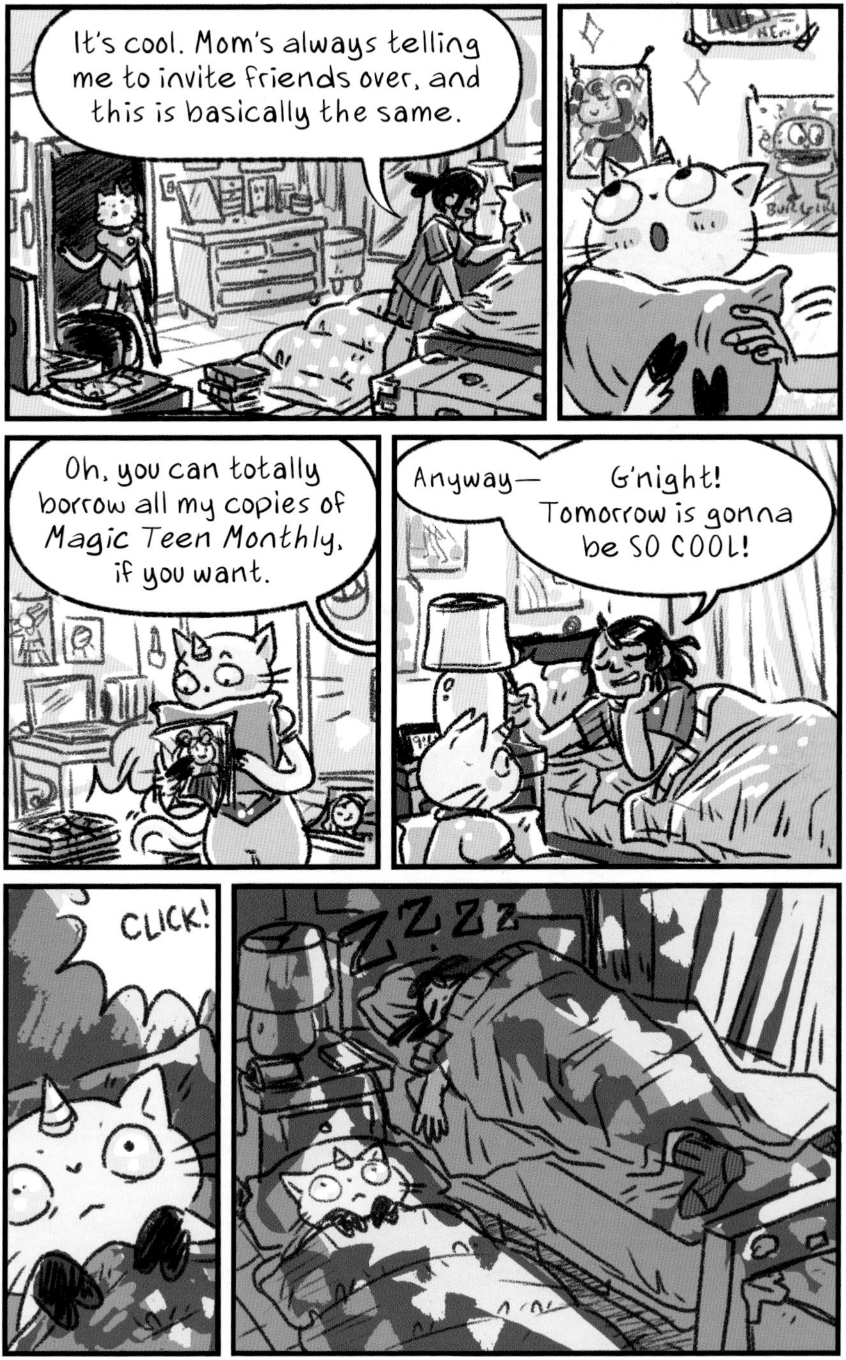
It's cool. Mom's always telling me to invite friends over, and this is basically the same.
Oh, you can totally borrow all my copies of *Magic Teen Monthly*, if you want.
Anyway—
G'night! Tomorrow is gonna be SO COOL!
CLICK!
ZZZZ

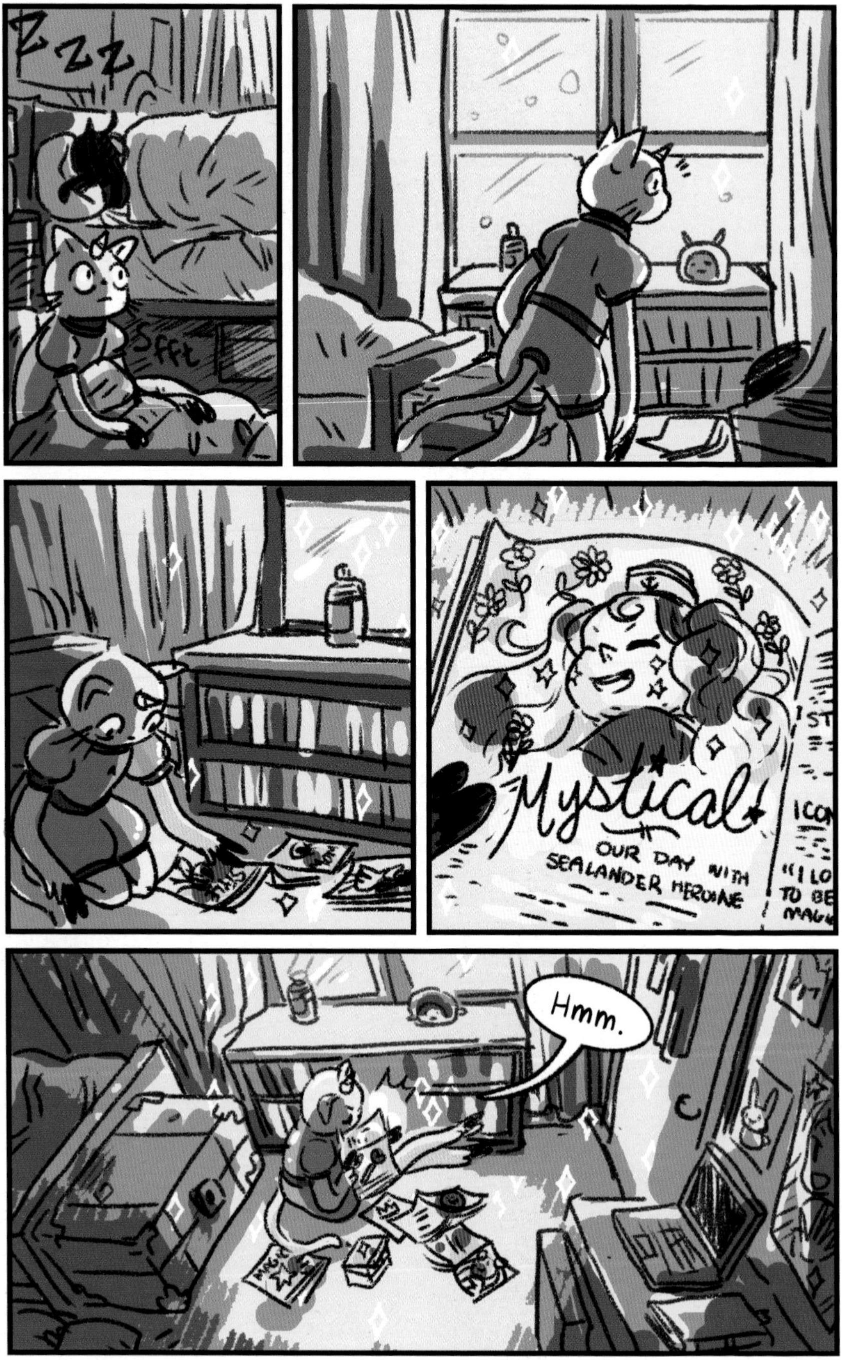
ZZZ
Sfft
Mystical
OUR DAY WITH SEALANDER HEROINE
Hmm.

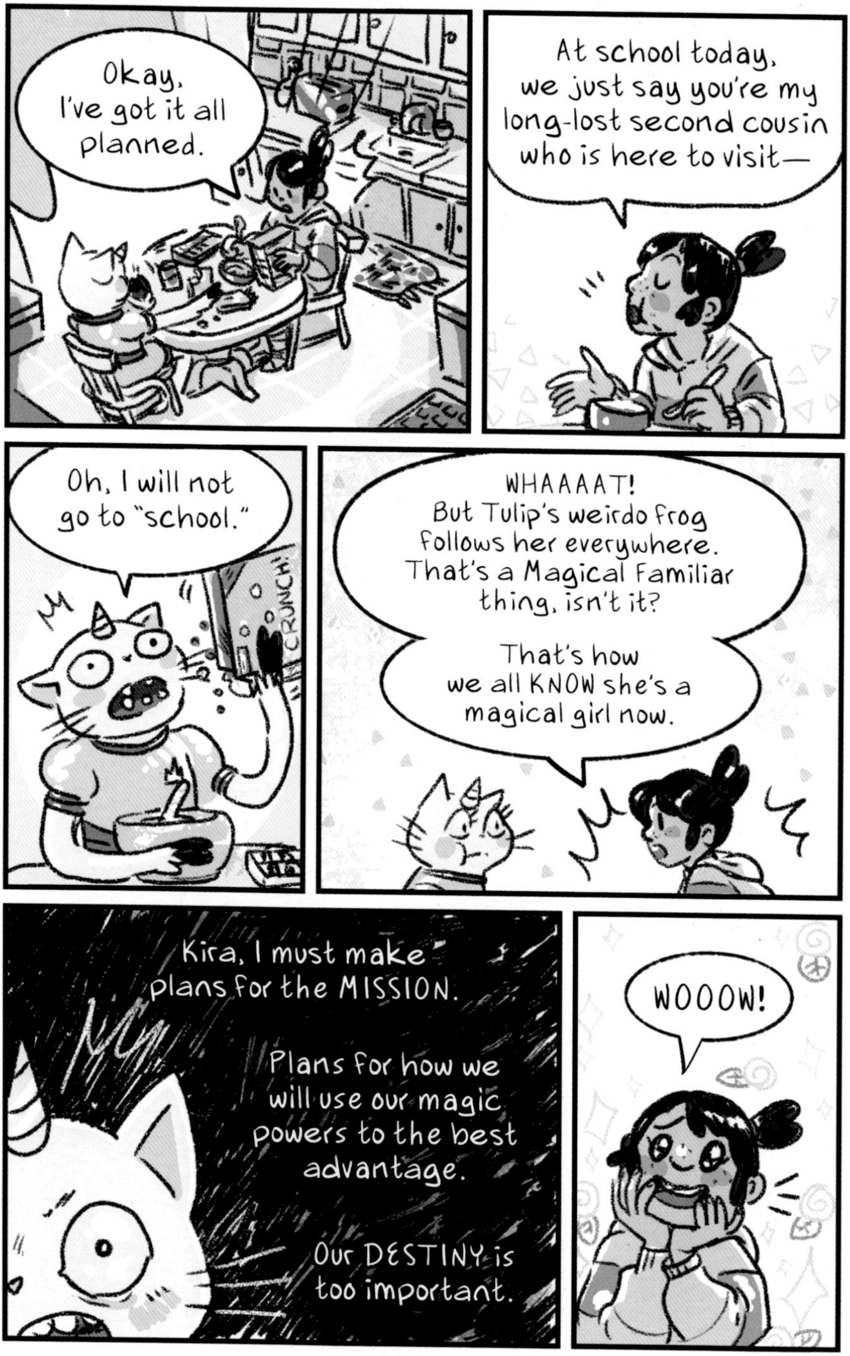
Okay, I've got it all planned.
At school today, we just say you're my long-lost second cousin who is here to visit—
Oh, I will not go to "school."
CRUNCH!
WHAAAAT! But Tulip's weirdo frog follows her everywhere. That's a Magical Familiar thing, isn't it?
That's how we all KNOW she's a magical girl now.
Kira, I must make plans for the MISSION.
Plans for how we will use our magic powers to the best advantage.
Our DESTINY is too important.
WOOOW!

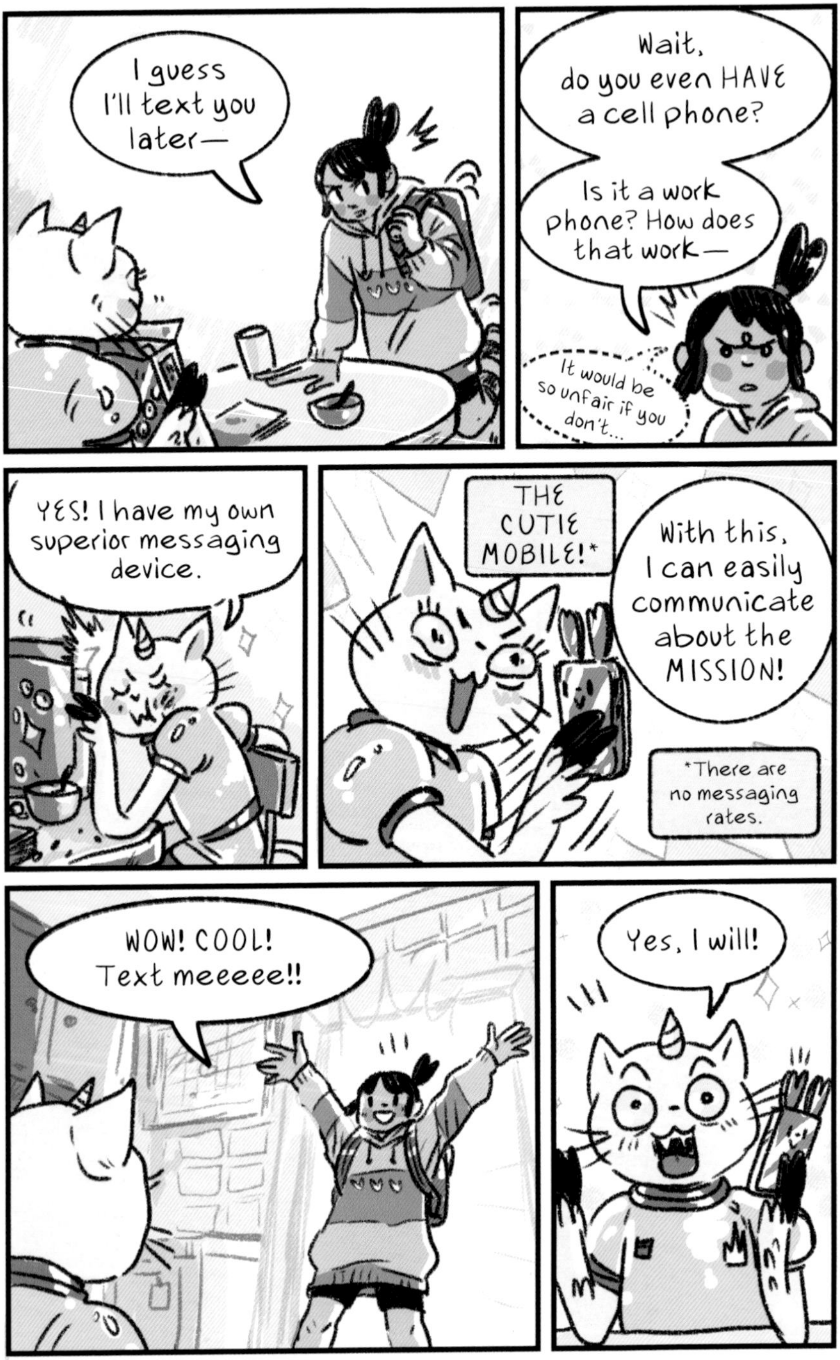
I guess I'll text you later—
Wait, do you even HAVE a cell phone?
Is it a work phone? How does that work—
It would be so unfair if you don't...
YES! I have my own superior messaging device.
THE CUTIE MOBILE!*
With this, I can easily communicate about the MISSION!
*There are no messaging rates.
WOW! COOL! Text meeeeee!!
Yes, I will!

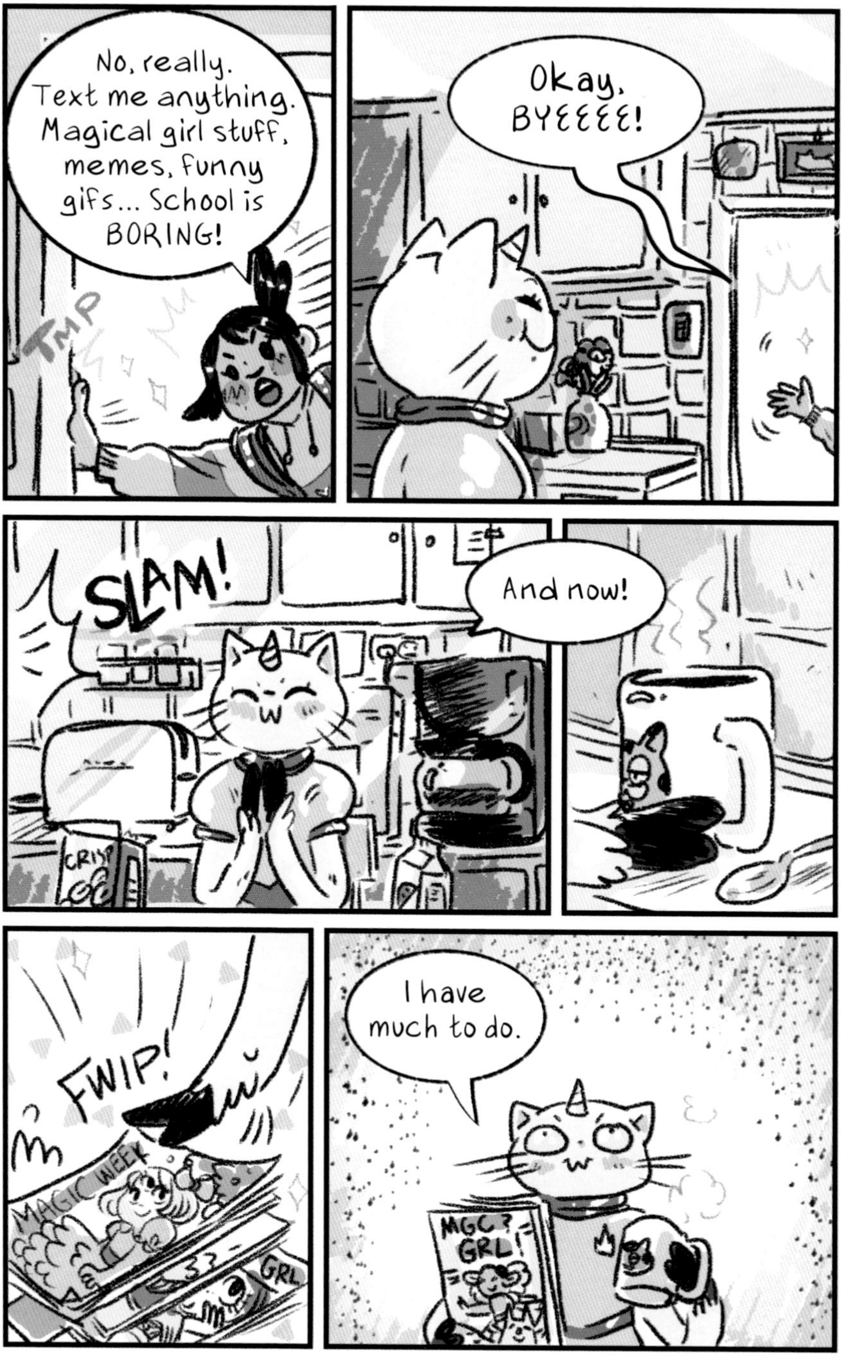
No, really. Text me anything. Magical girl stuff, memes, funny gifs... School is BORING!
TMP
Okay, BYEEEE!
SLAM!
And now!
CRISP
FWIP!
MAGIC WEEK
GRL
I have much to do.
MGC ? GRL

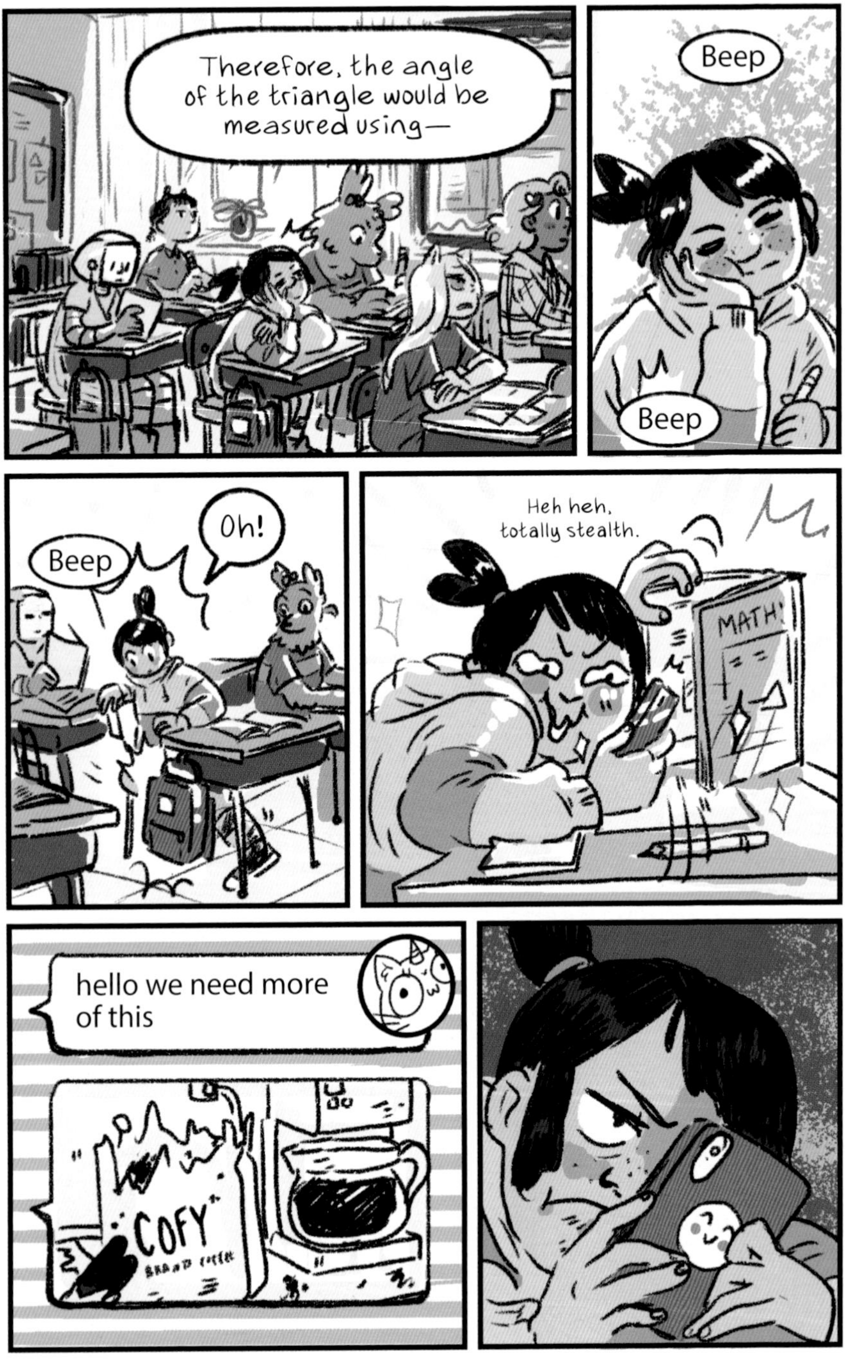
Therefore, the angle of the triangle would be measured using—
Beep
Beep
Beep
Oh!
Heh heh, totally stealth.
MATH!
hello we need more of this
COFY

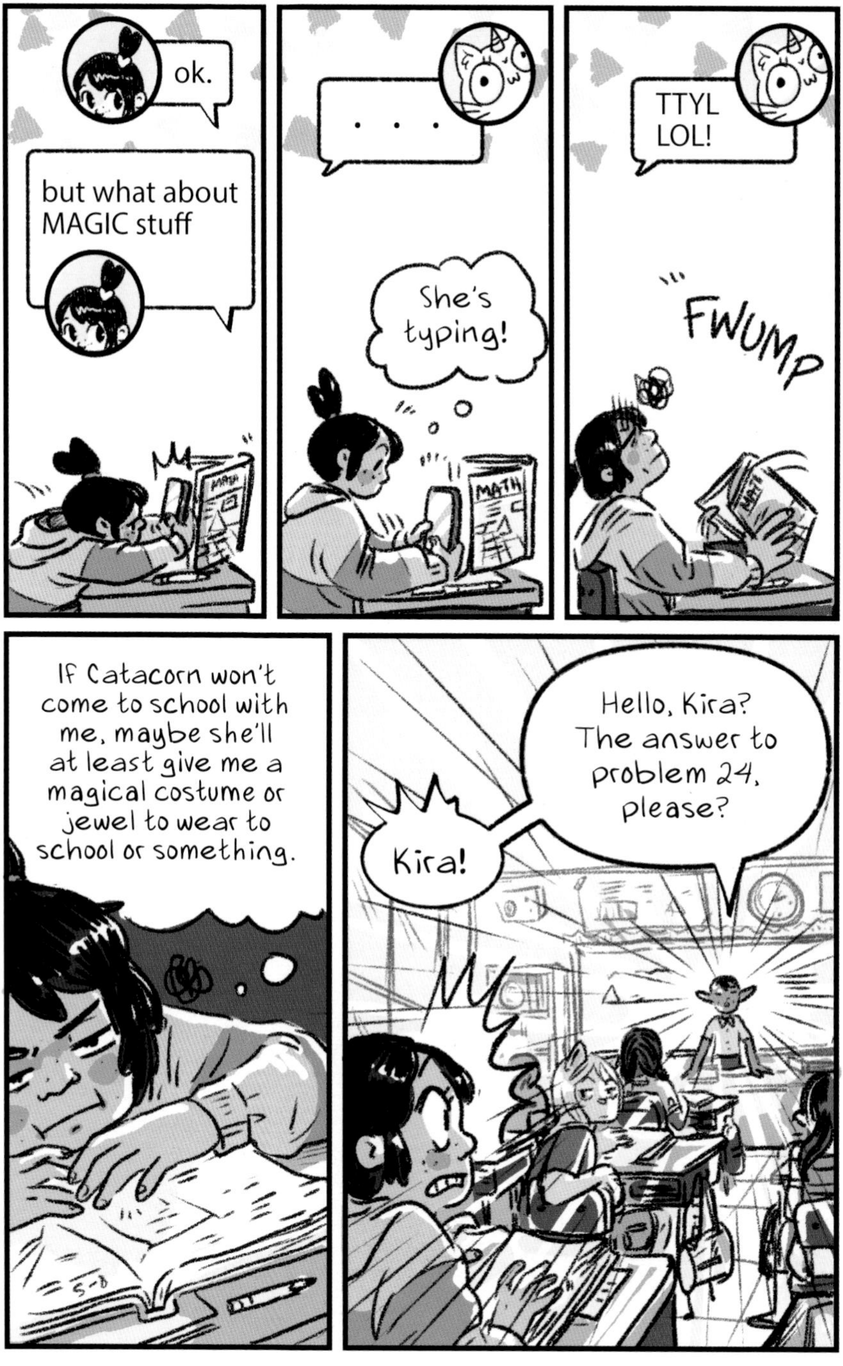
ok.
but what about MAGIC stuff
. . .
She's typing!
TTYL LOL!
FWUMP
If Catacorn won't come to school with me, maybe she'll at least give me a magical costume or jewel to wear to school or something.
Hello, Kira? The answer to problem 24, please?
Kira!

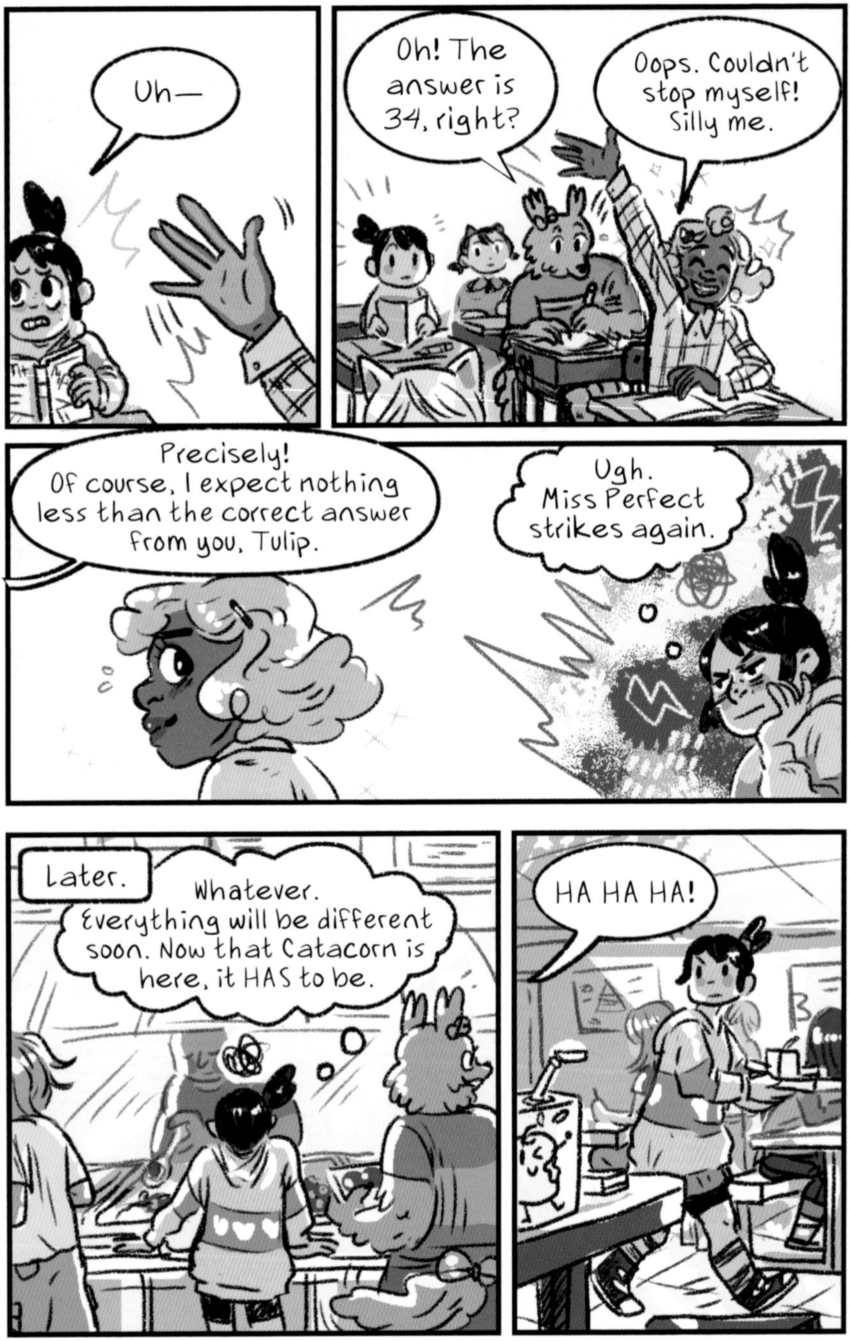
Uh—
Oh! The answer is 34, right?
Oops. Couldn't stop myself! Silly me.
Precisely! Of course, I expect nothing less than the correct answer from you, Tulip.
Ugh. Miss Perfect strikes again.
Later.
Whatever. Everything will be different soon. Now that Catacorn is here, it HAS to be.
HA HA HA!

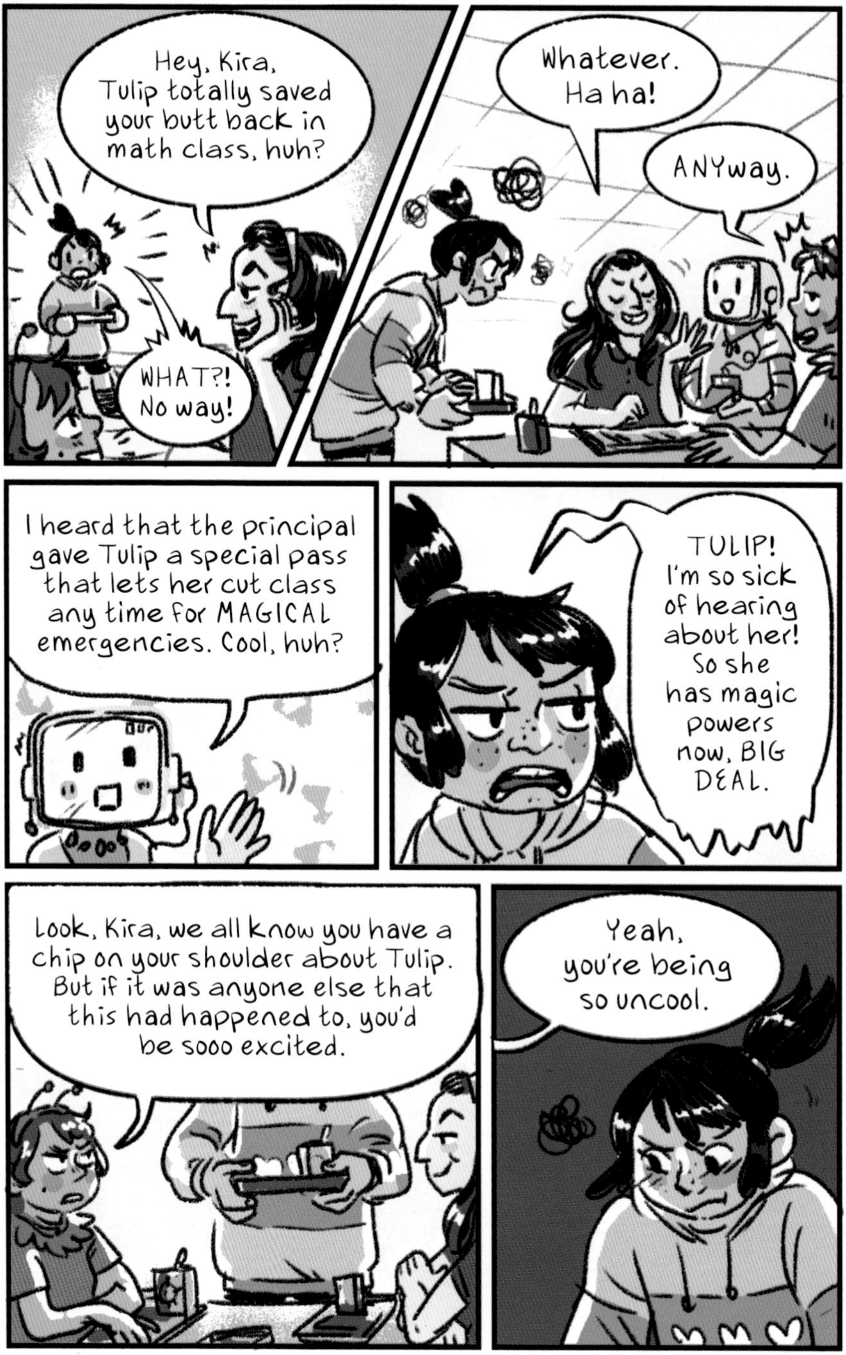
Hey, Kira, Tulip totally saved your butt back in math class, huh?
WHAT?! No way!
Whatever. Ha ha!
ANYway.
I heard that the principal gave Tulip a special pass that lets her cut class any time for MAGICAL emergencies. Cool, huh?
TULIP! I'm so sick of hearing about her! So she has magic powers now, BIG DEAL.
Look, Kira, we all know you have a chip on your shoulder about Tulip. But if it was anyone else that this had happened to, you'd be sooo excited.
Yeah, you're being so uncool.

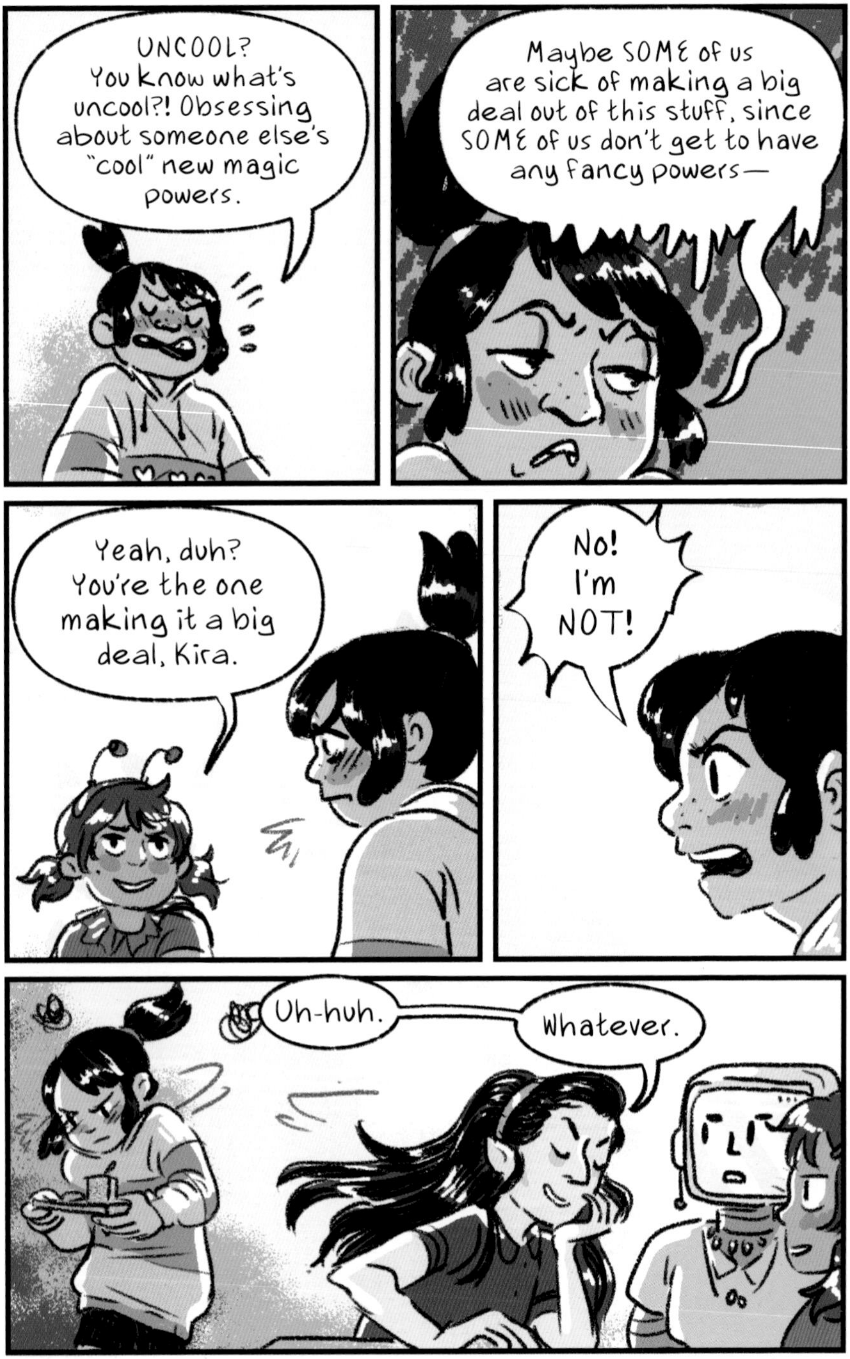
UNCOOL? You know what's uncool?! Obsessing about someone else's "cool" new magic powers.
Maybe SOME of us are sick of making a big deal out of this stuff, since SOME of us don't get to have any fancy powers—
Yeah, duh? You're the one making it a big deal, Kira.
No! I'm NOT!
Uh-huh.
Whatever.

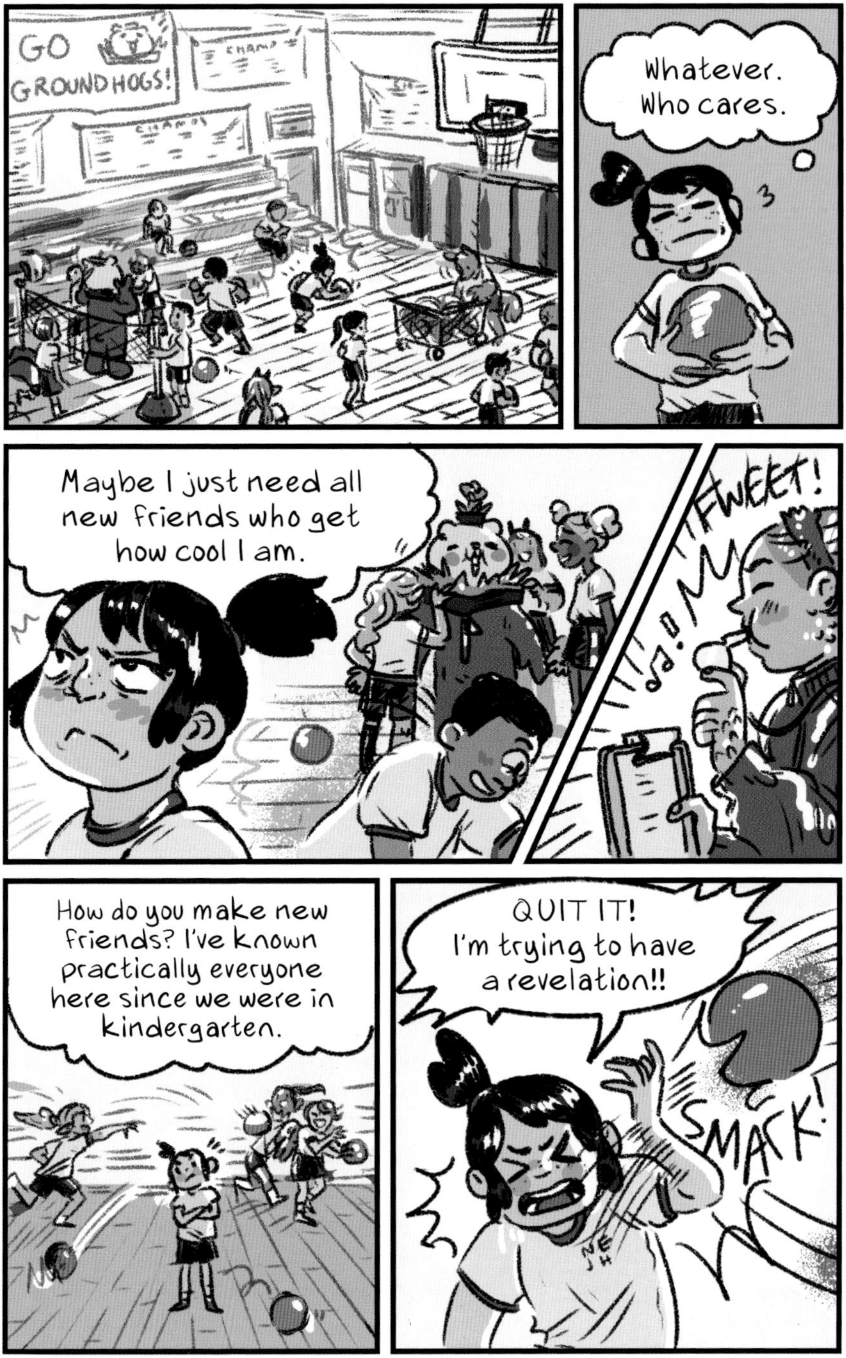
GO GROUNDHOGS!
CHAMPS
CHAMPS
Whatever.
Who cares.
Maybe I just need all new friends who get how cool I am.
FWEET!
How do you make new friends? I've known practically everyone here since we were in kindergarten.
QUIT IT!
I'm trying to have a revelation!!
SMACK!
NE JH

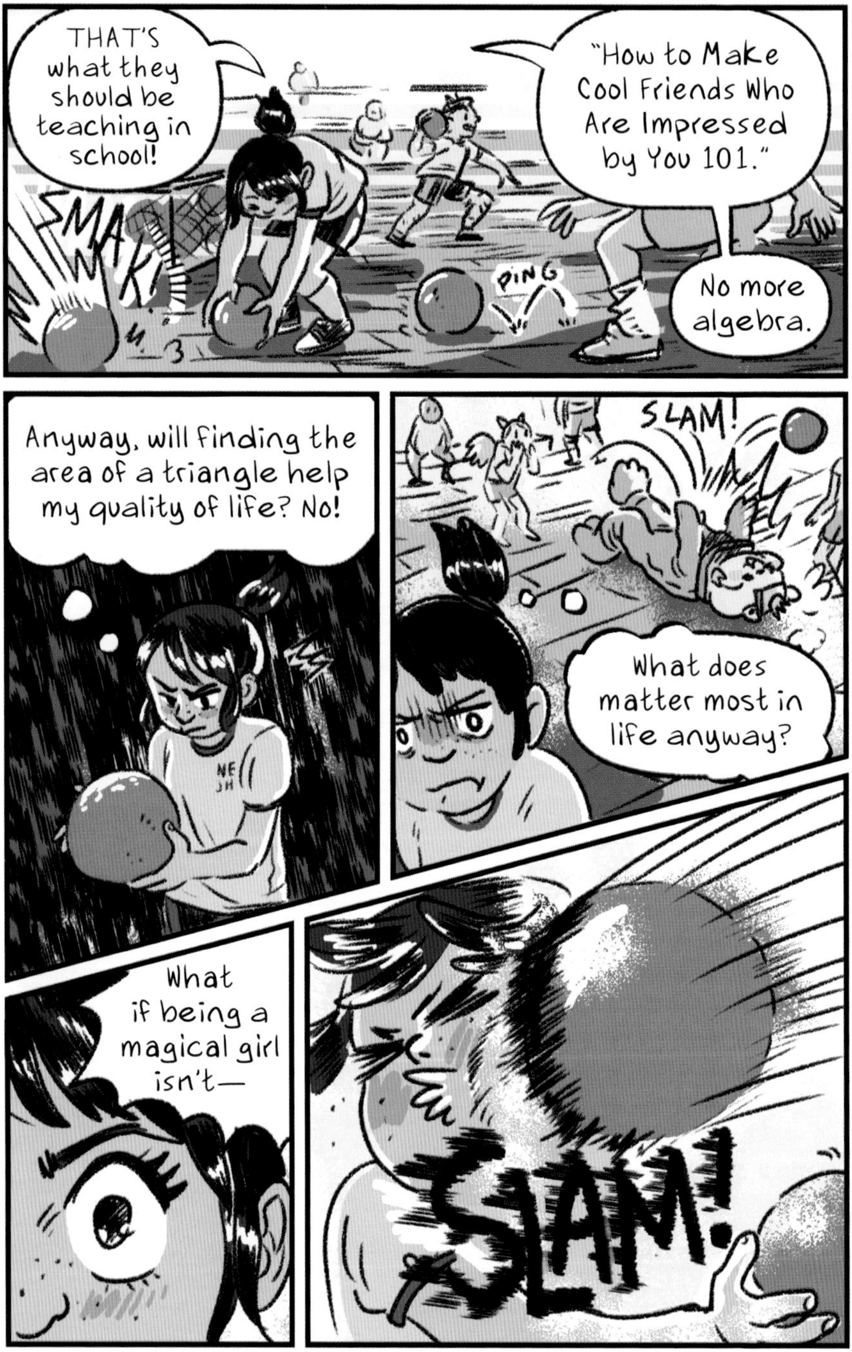
THAT'S what they should be teaching in school!
"How to Make Cool Friends Who Are Impressed by You 101."
SMAK!
PING
No more algebra.
Anyway, will finding the area of a triangle help my quality of life? No!
SLAM!
What does matter most in life anyway?
What if being a magical girl isn't—
SLAM!

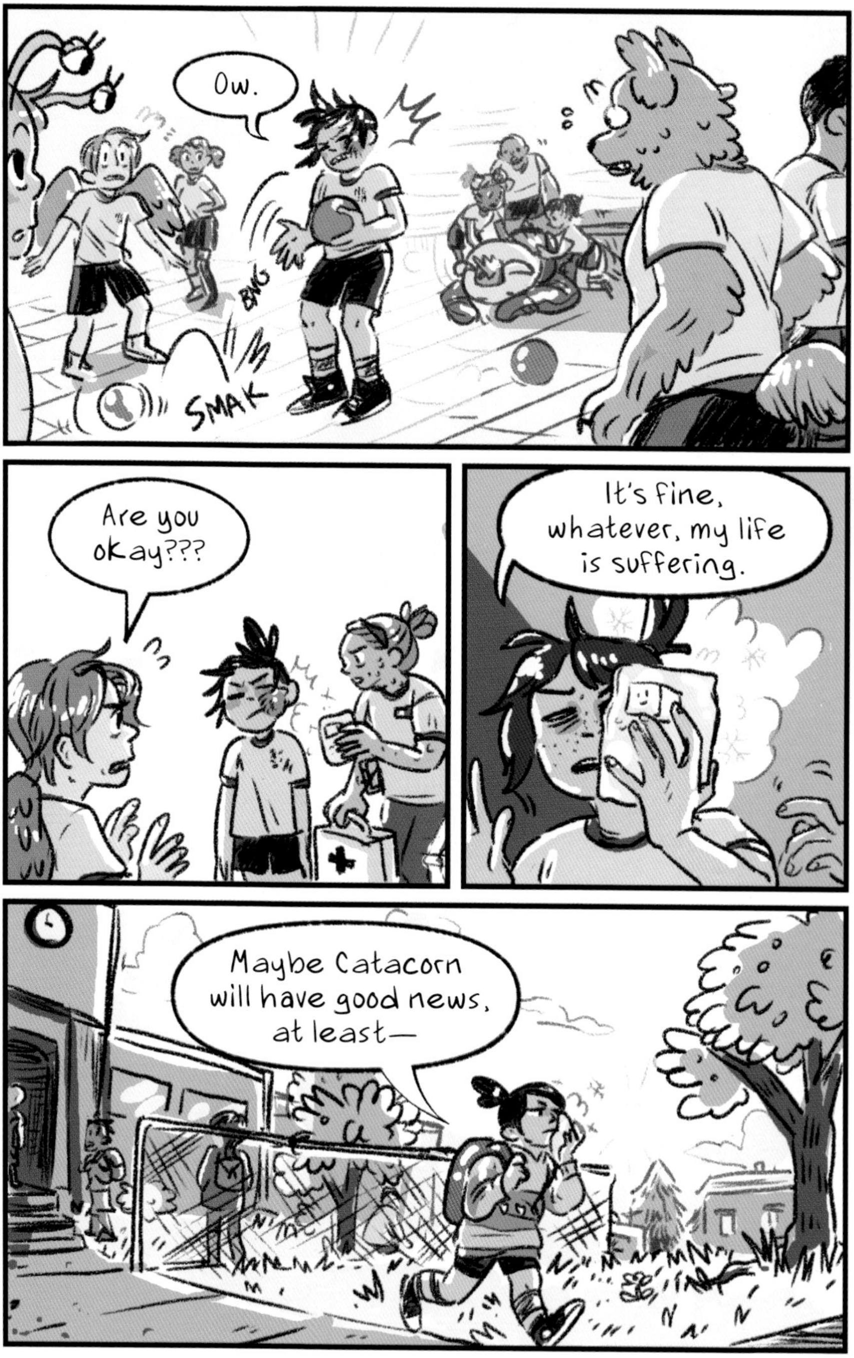
Ow.
BNG
SMAK
Are you okay???
It's fine, whatever, my life is suffering.
Maybe Catacorn will have good news, at least—

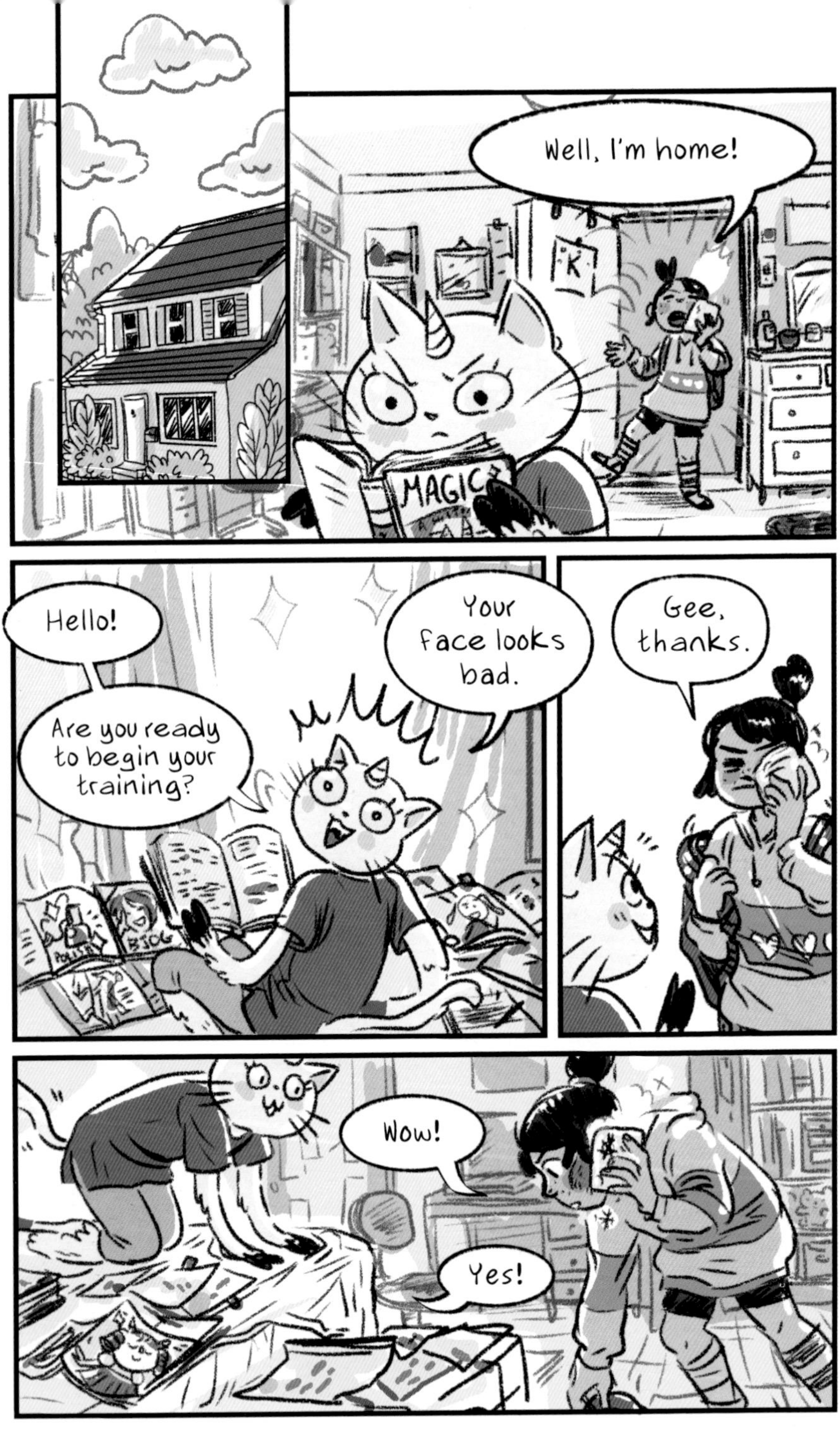
MAGIC
Well, I'm home!
Hello!
Are you ready to begin your training?
Your face looks bad.
Gee, thanks.
Wow!
Yes!

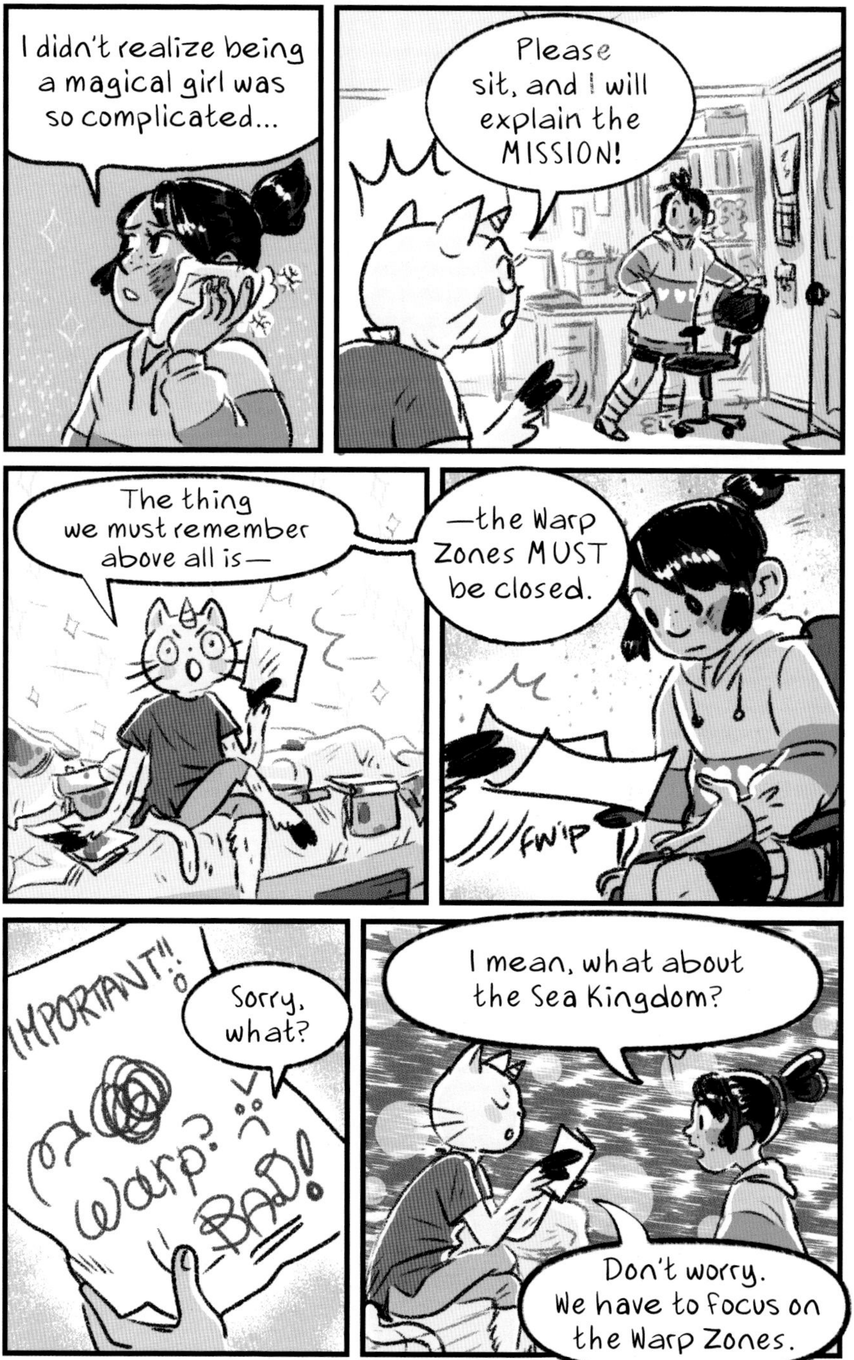
I didn't realize being a magical girl was so complicated...
Please sit, and I will explain the MISSION!
The thing we must remember above all is—
—the Warp Zones MUST be closed.
FWIP
IMPORTANT!!
Sorry, what?
Warp?
BAD!
I mean, what about the Sea Kingdom?
Don't worry. We have to focus on the Warp Zones.

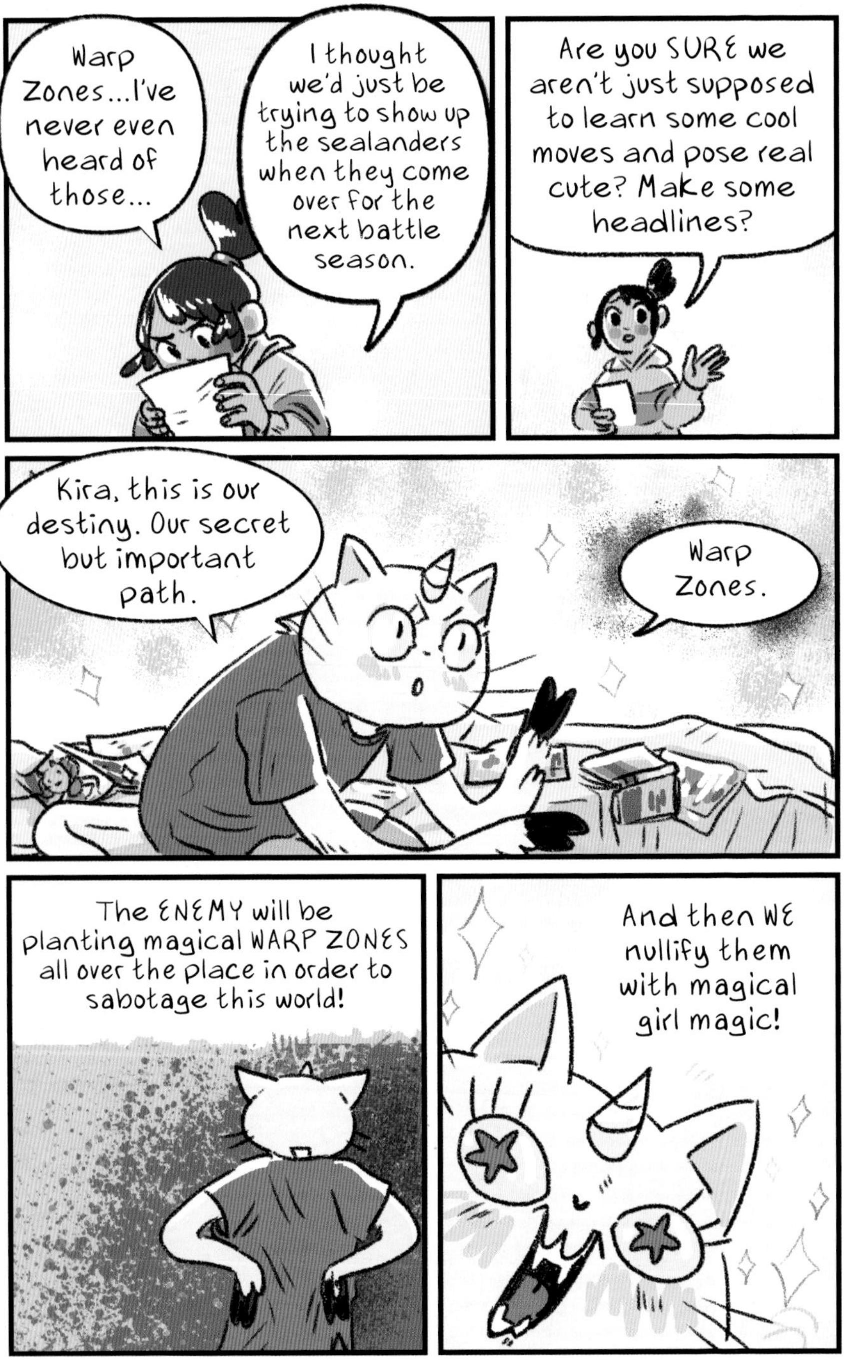
Warp Zones...I've never even heard of those...
I thought we'd just be trying to show up the sealanders when they come over for the next battle season.
Are you SURE we aren't just supposed to learn some cool moves and pose real cute? Make some headlines?
Kira, this is our destiny. Our secret but important path.
Warp Zones.
The ENEMY will be planting magical WARP ZONES all over the place in order to sabotage this world!
And then WE nullify them with magical girl magic!

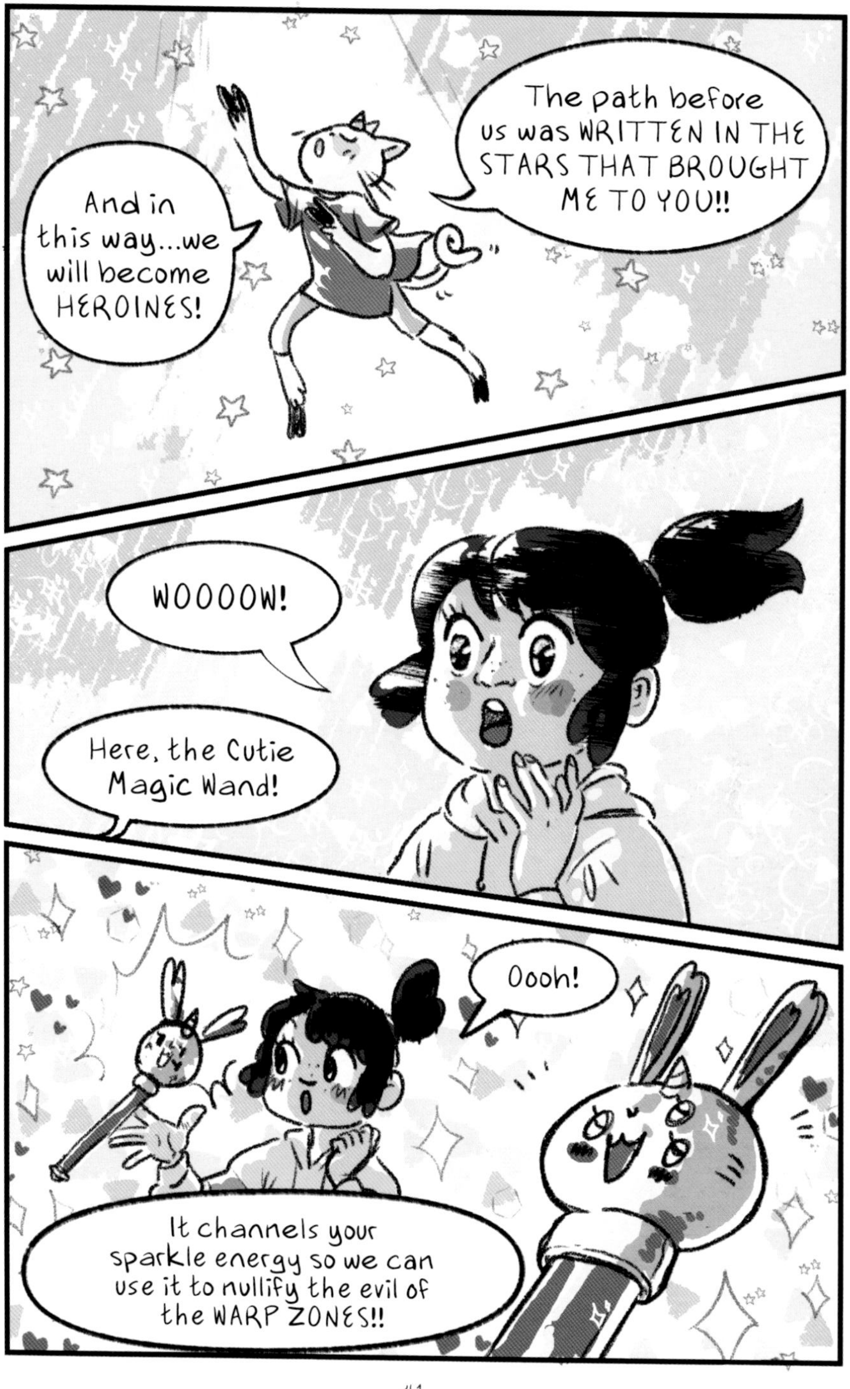
The path before us was WRITTEN IN THE STARS THAT BROUGHT ME TO YOU!!
And in this way...we will become HEROINES!
WOOOOW!
Here, the Cutie Magic Wand!
Oooh!
It channels your sparkle energy so we can use it to nullify the evil of the WARP ZONES!!

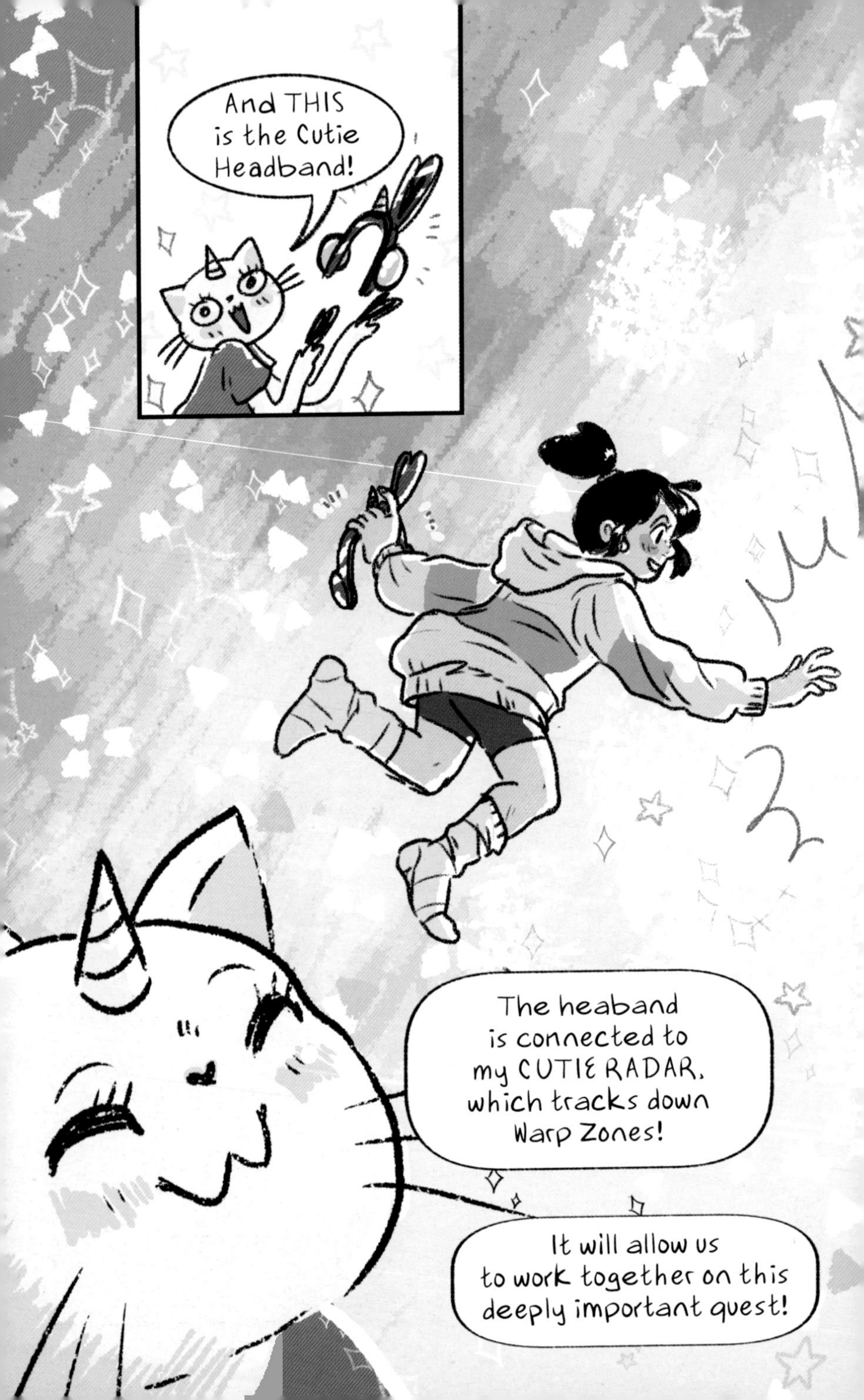
And THIS is the Cutie Headband!
The heaband is connected to my CUTIE RADAR, which tracks down Warp Zones!
It will allow us to work together on this deeply important quest!

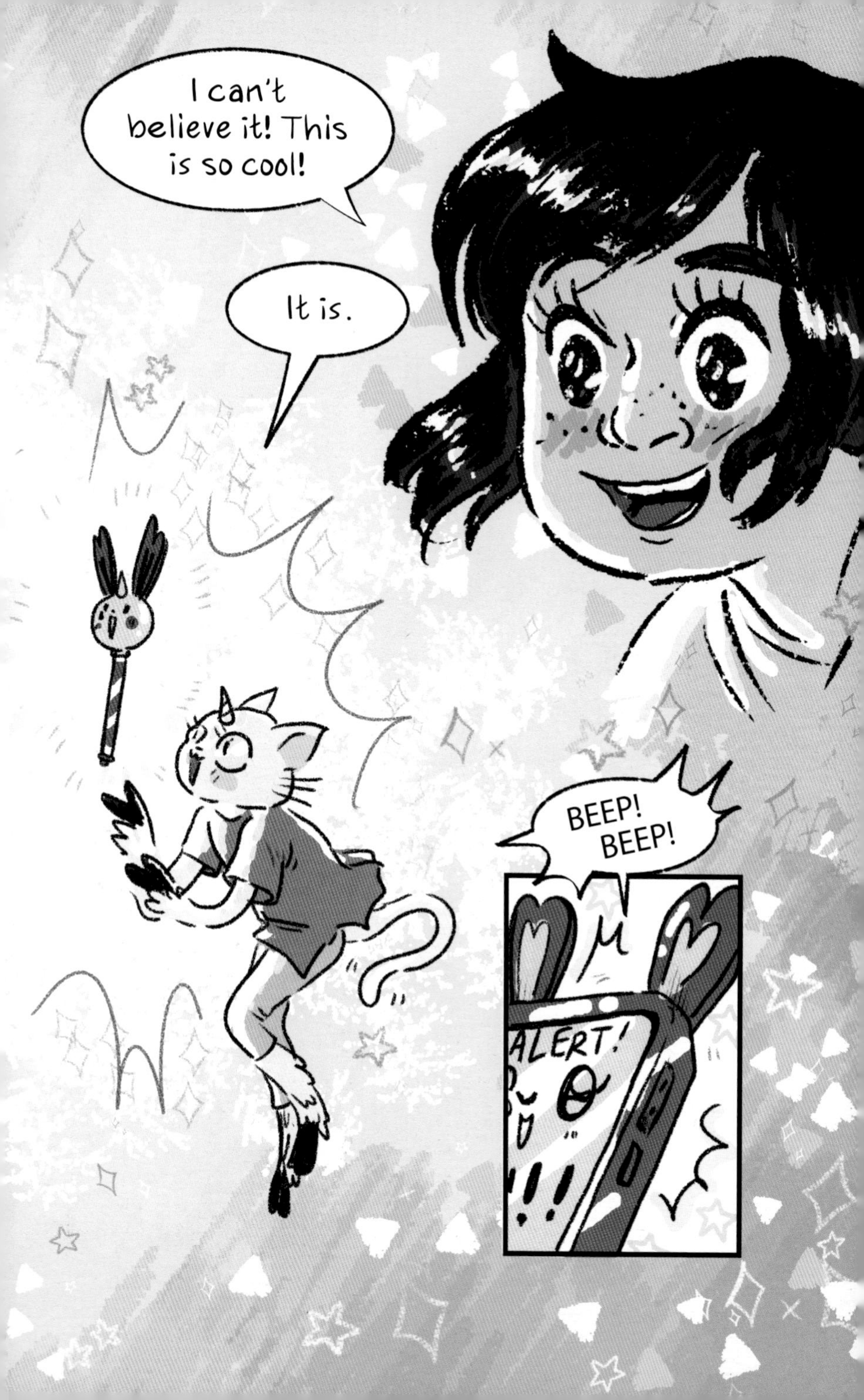
I can't believe it! This is so cool!
It is.
BEEP! BEEP!
ALERT!

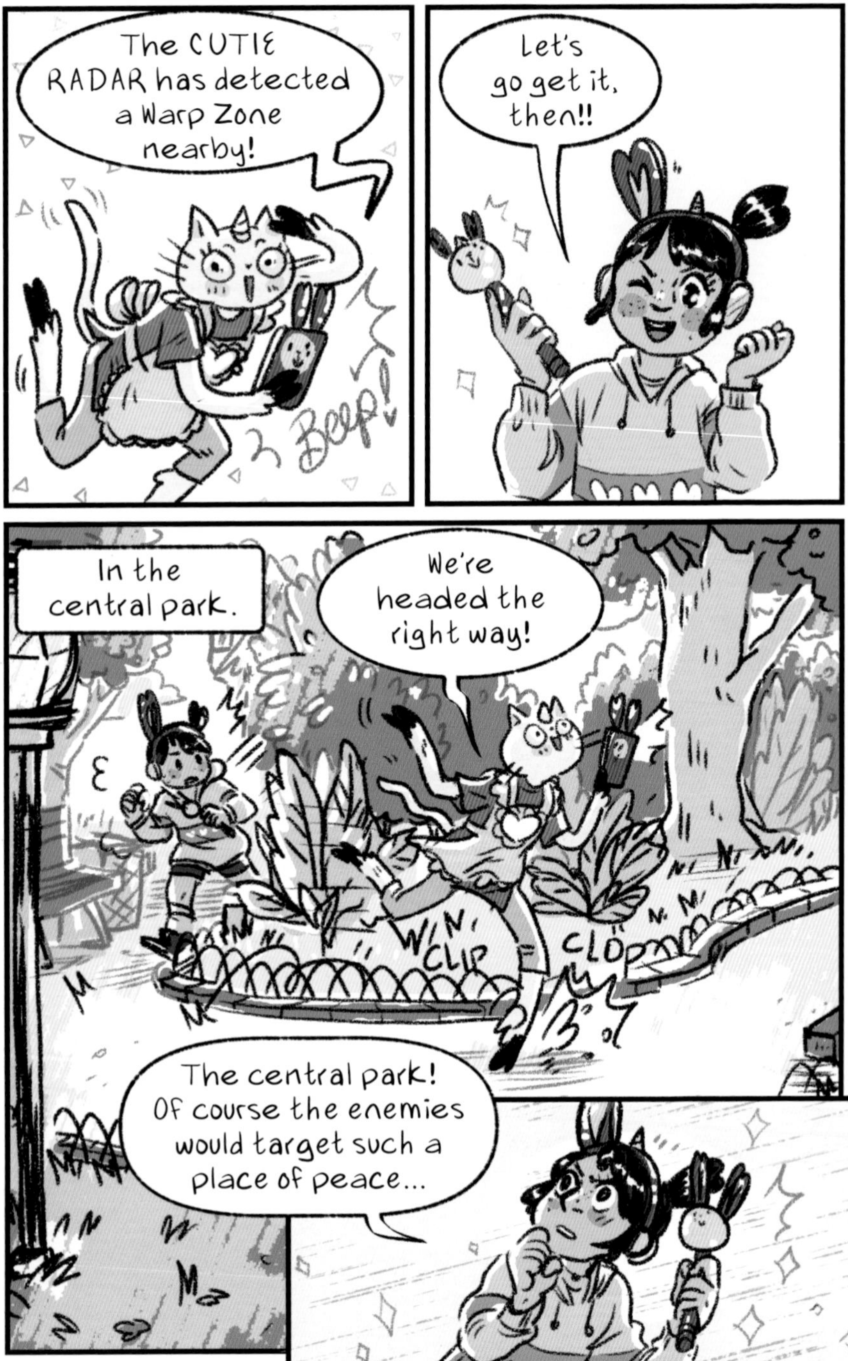
The CUTIE RADAR has detected a Warp Zone nearby!
Beep!
Let's go get it, then!!
In the central park.
We're headed the right way!
CLIP
CLOP
The central park! Of course the enemies would target such a place of peace...

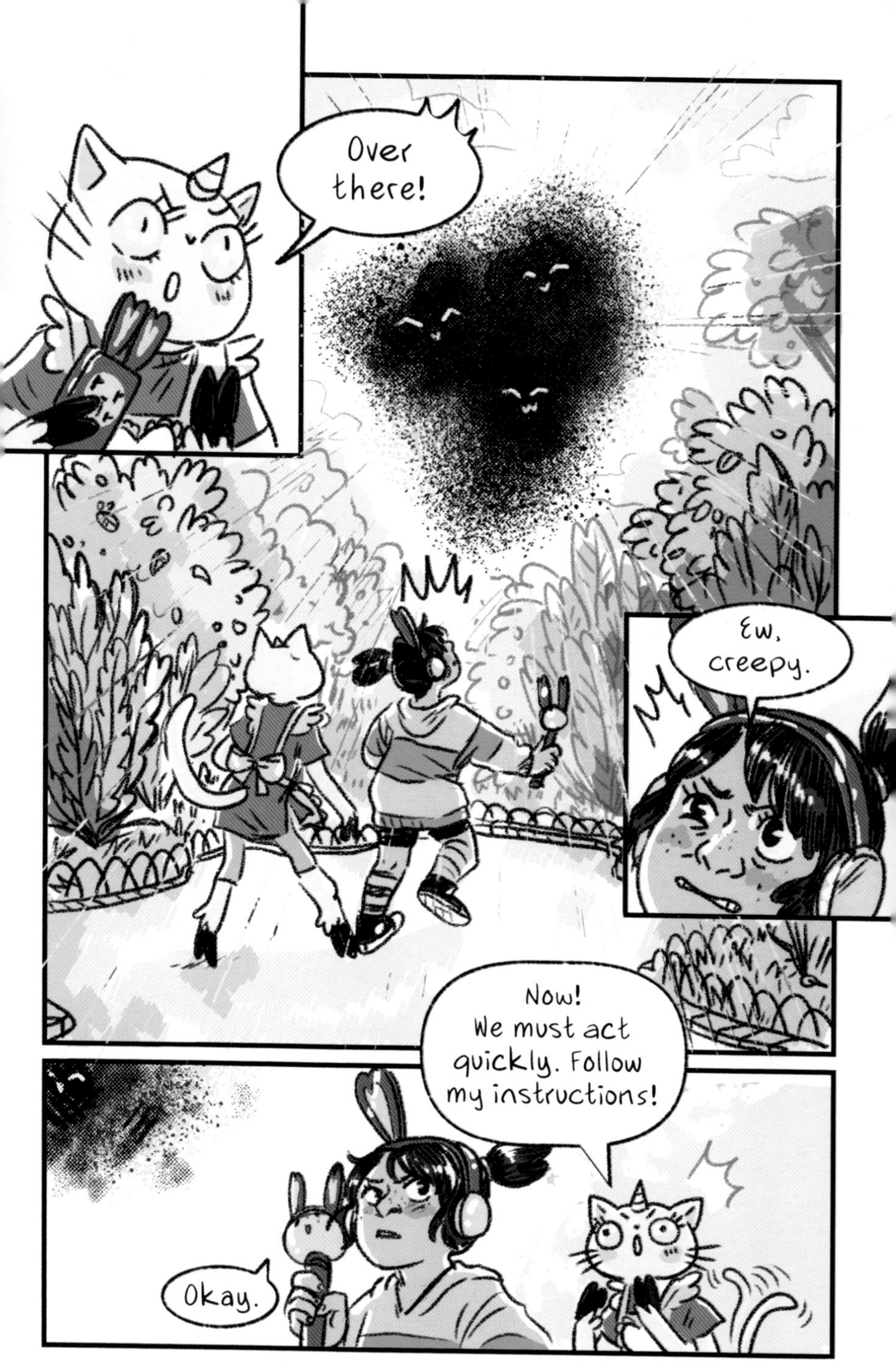
Over there!
Ew, creepy.
Now! We must act quickly. Follow my instructions!
Okay.

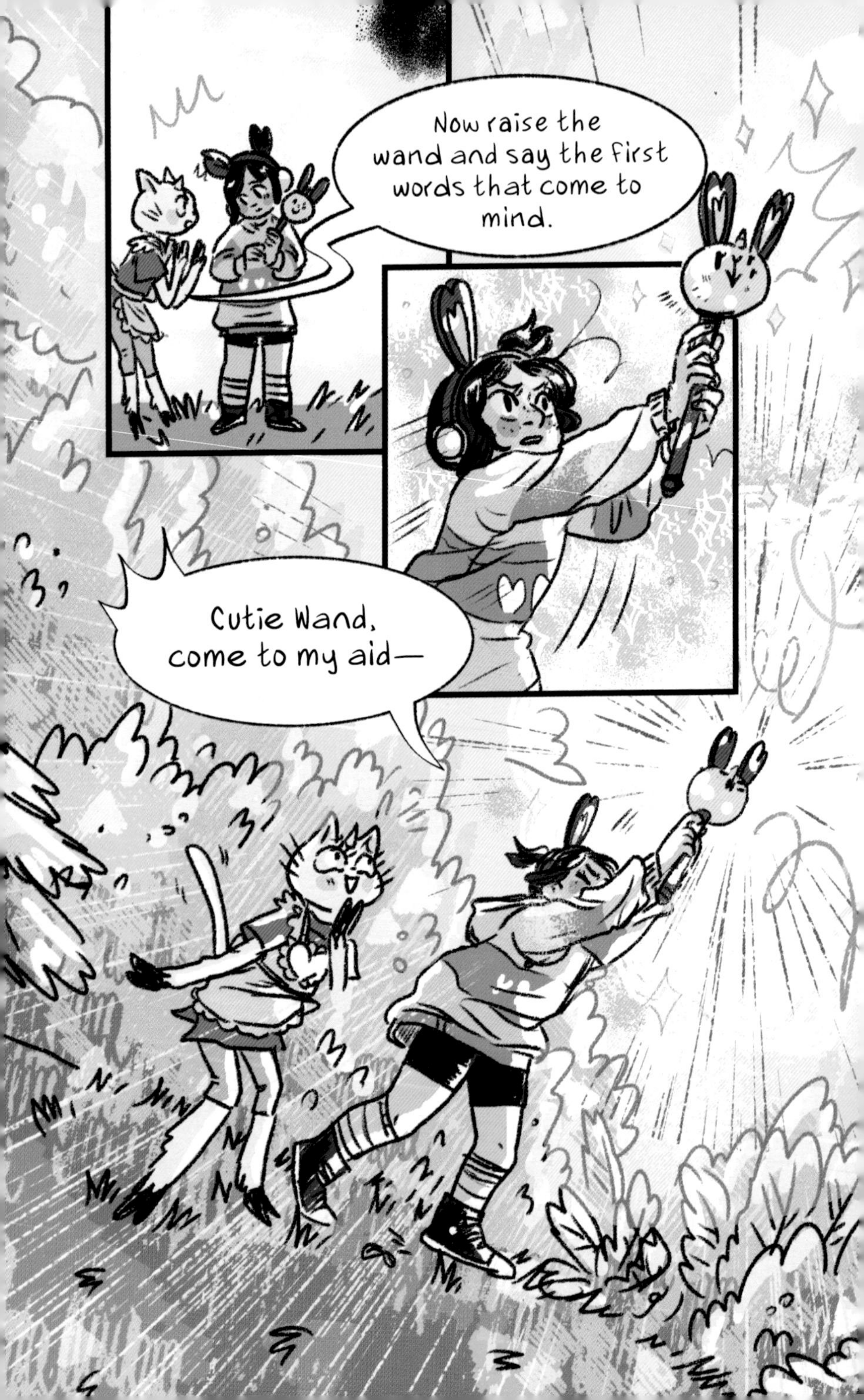
Now raise the wand and say the first words that come to mind.
Cutie Wand, come to my aid—

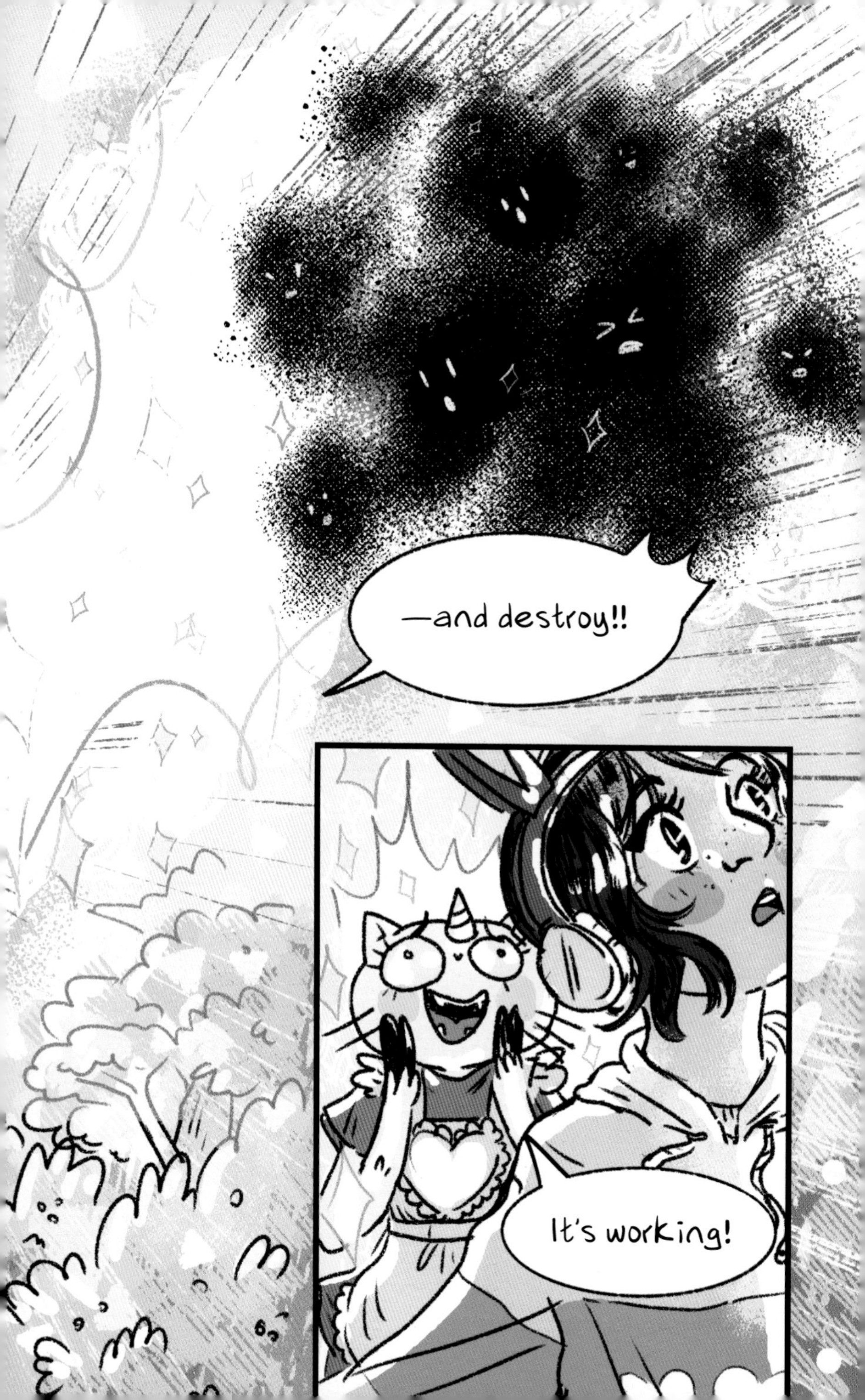
—and destroy!!
It's working!

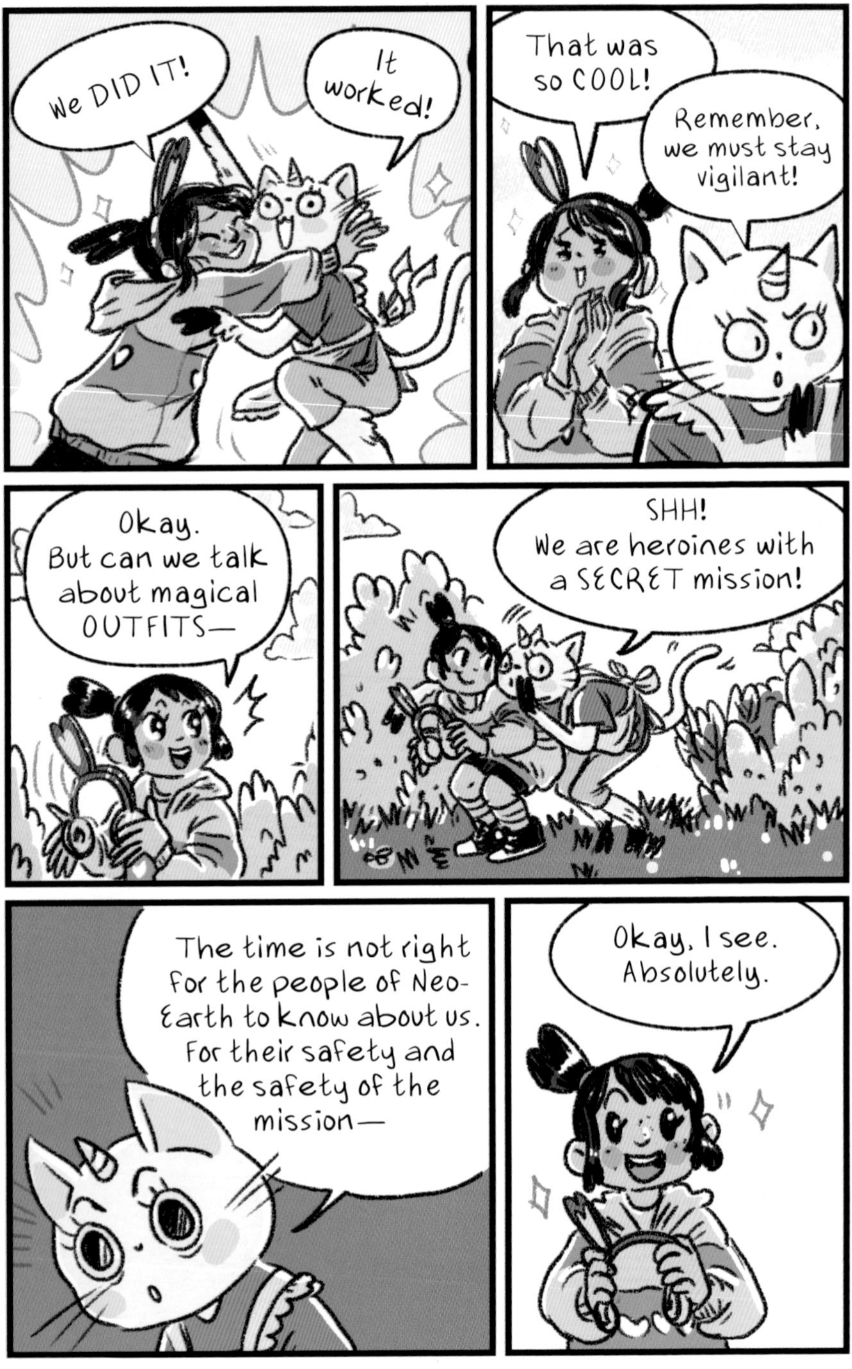
We DID IT!
It worked!
That was so COOL!
Remember, we must stay vigilant!
Okay. But can we talk about magical OUTFITS—
SHH! We are heroines with a SECRET mission!
The time is not right for the people of Neo-Earth to know about us. For their safety and the safety of the mission—
Okay, I see. Absolutely.

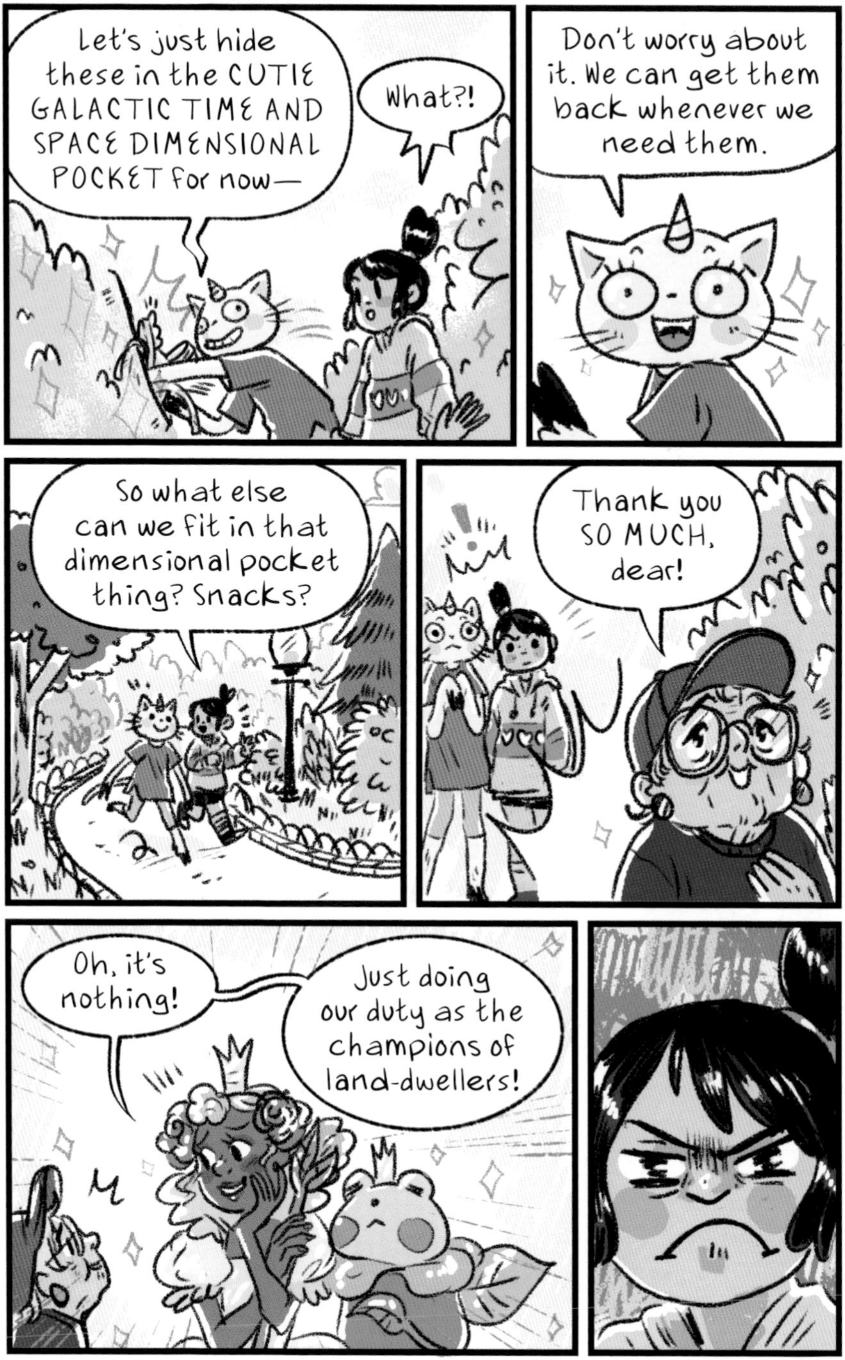
Let's just hide these in the CUTIE GALACTIC TIME AND SPACE DIMENSIONAL POCKET for now—
What?!
Don't worry about it. We can get them back whenever we need them.
So what else can we fit in that dimensional pocket thing? Snacks?
Thank you SO MUCH, dear!
Oh, it's nothing!
Just doing our duty as the champions of land-dwellers!

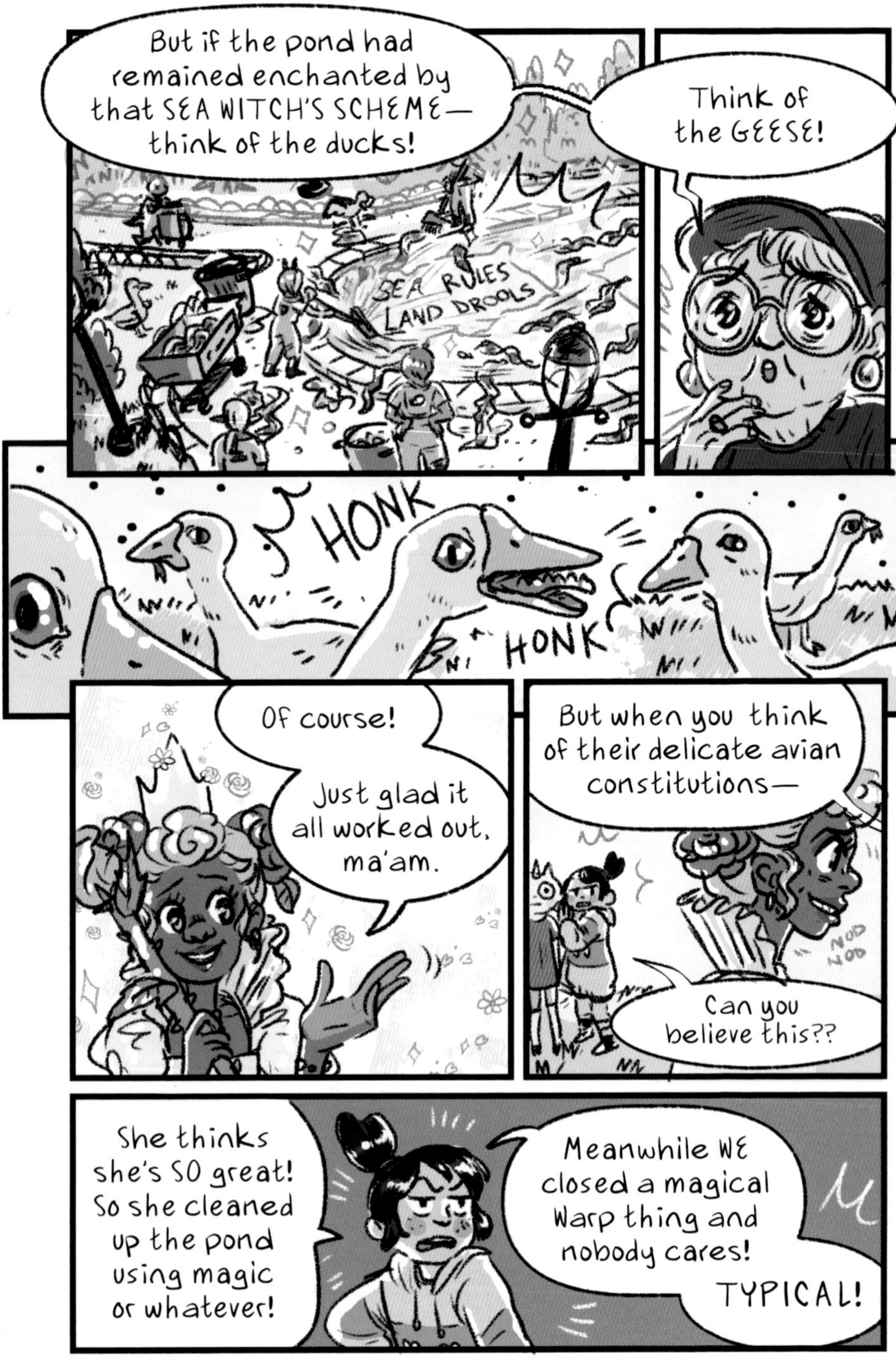
But if the pond had remained enchanted by that SEA WITCH'S SCHEME— think of the ducks!
SEA RULES LAND DROOLS
Think of the GEESE!
HONK
HONK
Of course!
Just glad it all worked out, ma'am.
But when you think of their delicate avian constitutions—
NOD NOD
Can you believe this??
She thinks she's SO great! So she cleaned up the pond using magic or whatever!
Meanwhile WE closed a magical warp thing and nobody cares!
TYPICAL!

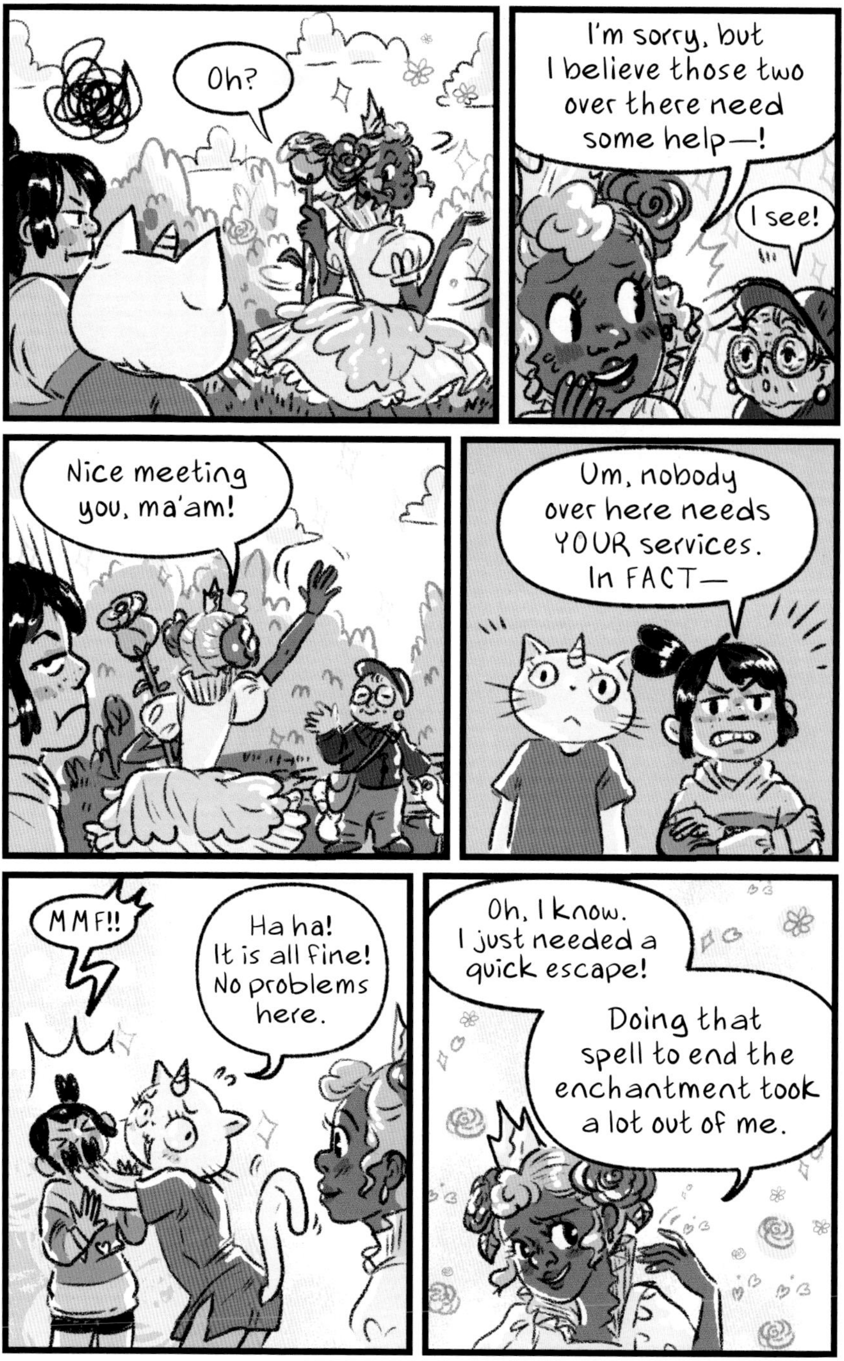
Oh?
I'm sorry, but I believe those two over there need some help—!
I see!
Nice meeting you, ma'am!
Um, nobody over here needs YOUR services. In FACT—
MMF!!
Ha ha! It is all fine! No problems here.
Oh, I know. I just needed a quick escape!
Doing that spell to end the enchantment took a lot out of me.

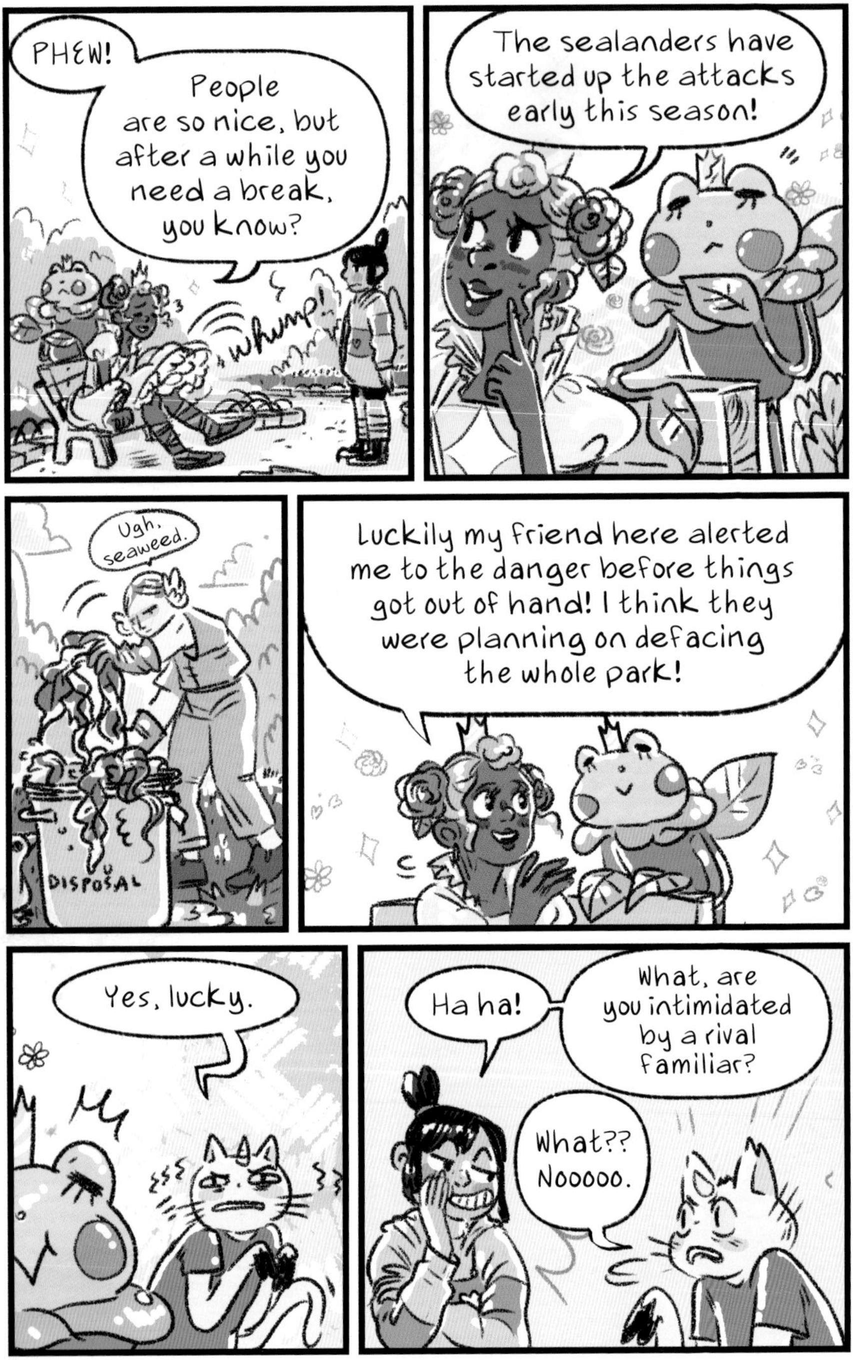
PHEW!
People are so nice, but after a while you need a break, you know?
whump!
The sealanders have started up the attacks early this season!
Ugh, seaweed.
DISPOSAL
Luckily my friend here alerted me to the danger before things got out of hand! I think they were planning on defacing the whole park!
Yes, lucky.
Ha ha!
What, are you intimidated by a rival familiar?
What?? Nooooo.

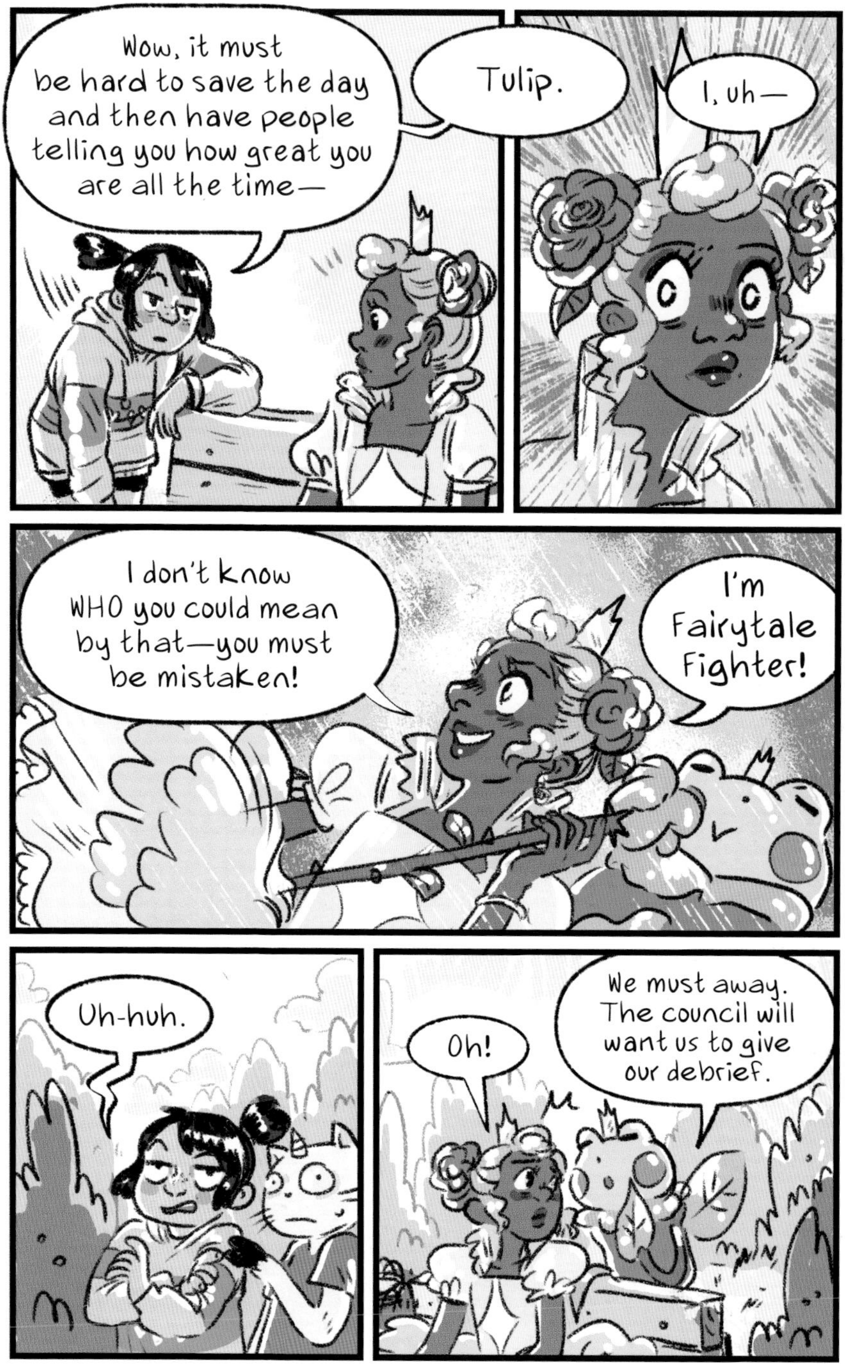
Wow, it must be hard to save the day and then have people telling you how great you are all the time—
Tulip.
I, uh—
I don't know WHO you could mean by that—you must be mistaken!
I'm Fairytale Fighter!
Uh-huh.
Oh!
We must away. The council will want us to give our debrief.

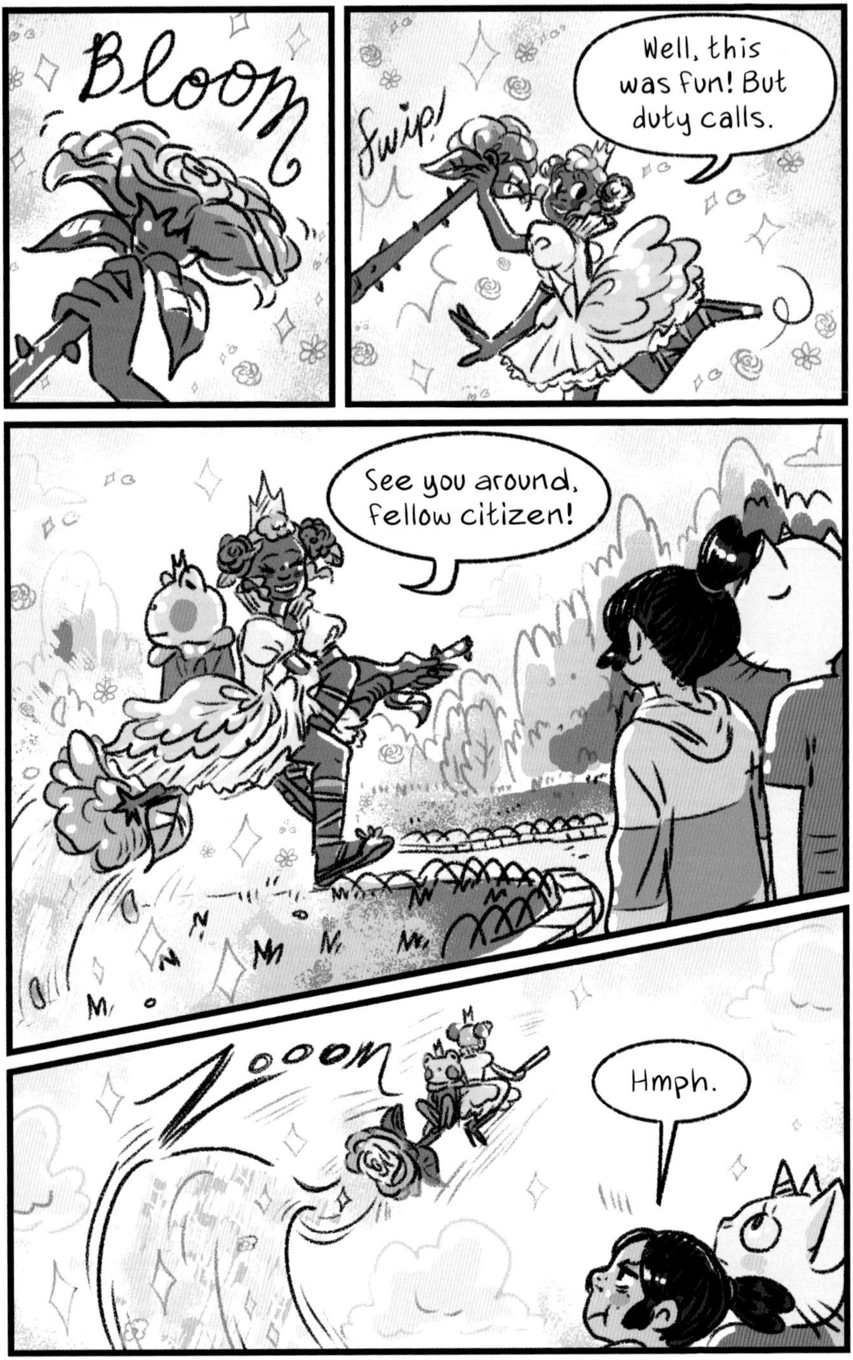
Bloom
Swip!
Well, this was fun! But duty calls.
See you around, fellow citizen!
Zooom
Hmph.

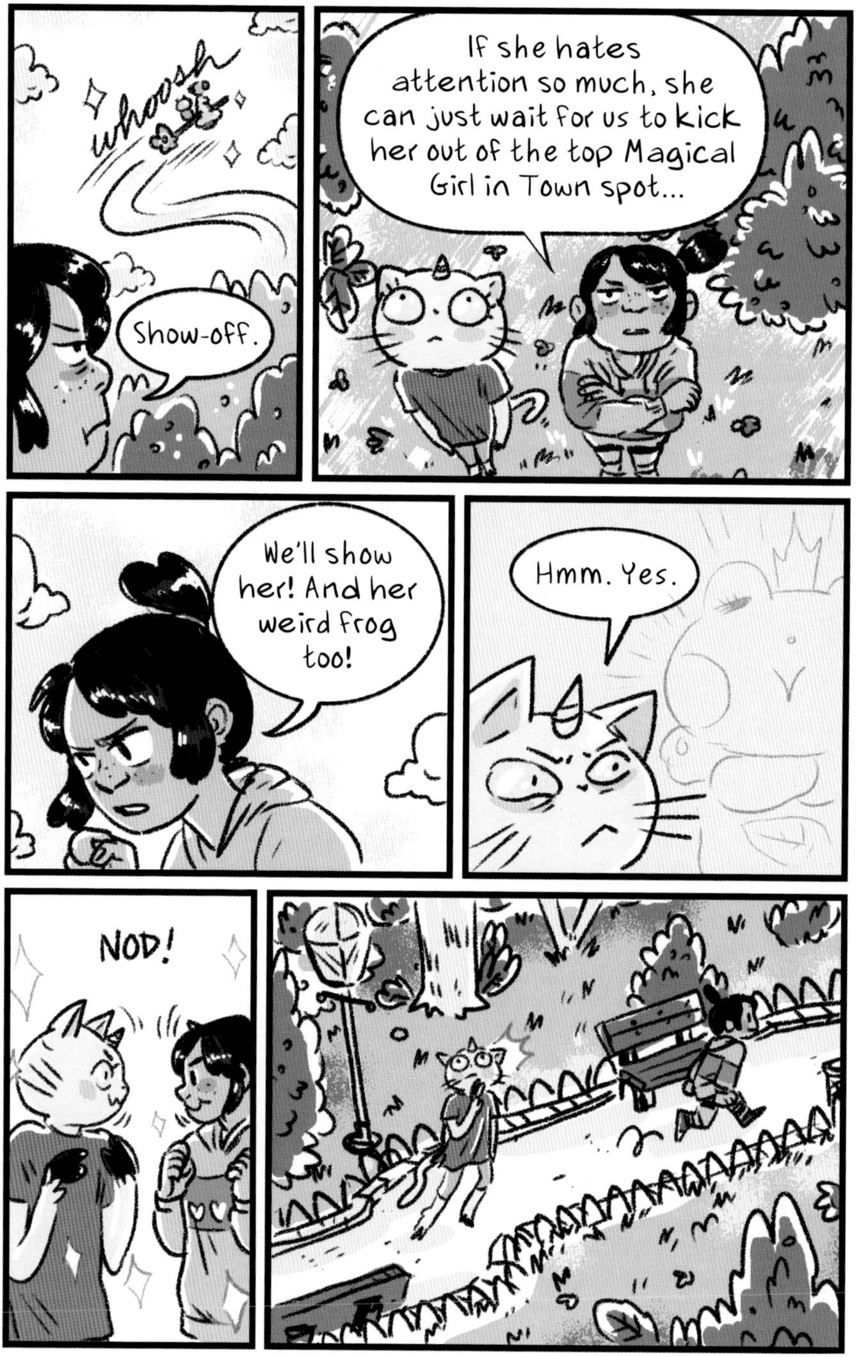
whoosh
Show-off.
If she hates attention so much, she can just wait for us to kick her out of the top Magical Girl in Town spot...
We'll show her! And her weird frog too!
Hmm. Yes.
NOD!

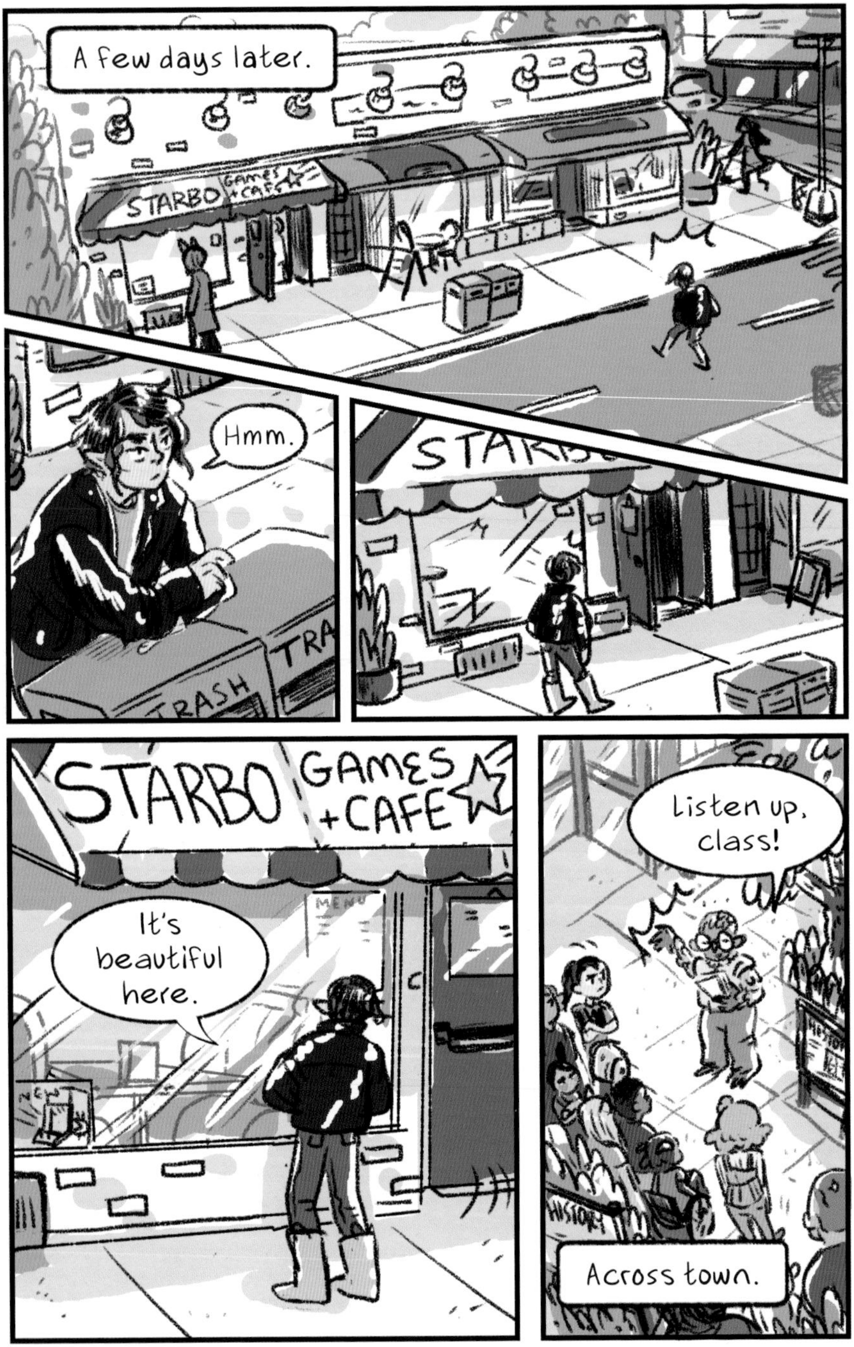
A few days later.
STARBO GAMES + CAFE
Hmm.
TRASH
STARBO
STARBO GAMES + CAFE
It's beautiful here.
Listen up, class!
Across town.

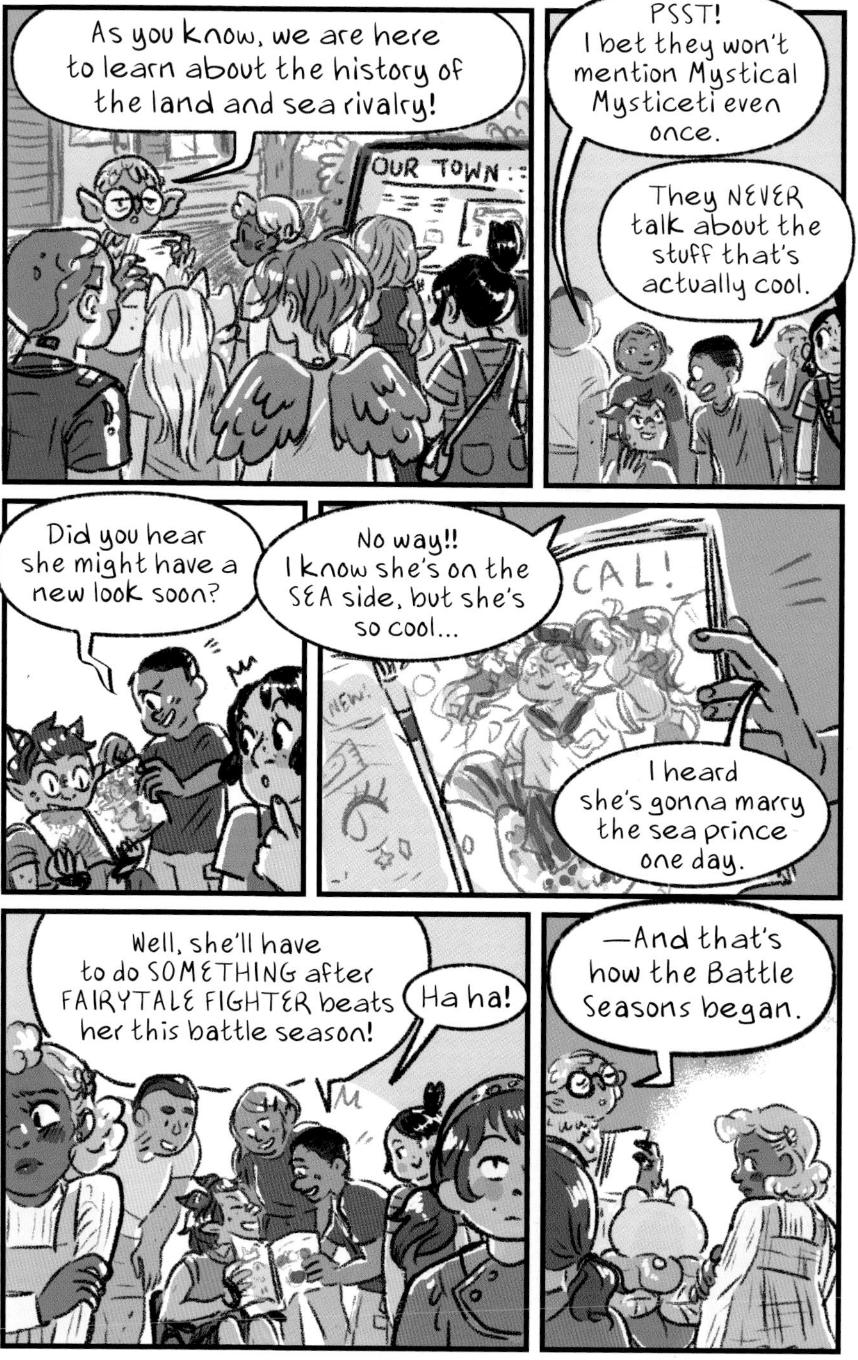
As you know, we are here to learn about the history of the land and sea rivalry!
OUR TOWN
PSST! I bet they won't mention Mystical Mysticeti even once.
They NEVER talk about the stuff that's actually cool.
Did you hear she might have a new look soon?
No way!! I know she's on the SEA side, but she's so cool...
CAL!
NEW!
I heard she's gonna marry the sea prince one day.
Well, she'll have to do SOMETHING after FAIRYTALE FIGHTER beats her this battle season!
Ha ha!
—And that's how the Battle Seasons began.

AHEM!

Now, please begin by observing the informational signs here in the downtown historic district.

I expect you all to turn in your completed worksheets by the end of the trip.

When will teachers quit handing out boring worksheets during field trips?

Hmm...

er... er...

SEEECRETS!

Well, well, well! What are they up to?

58

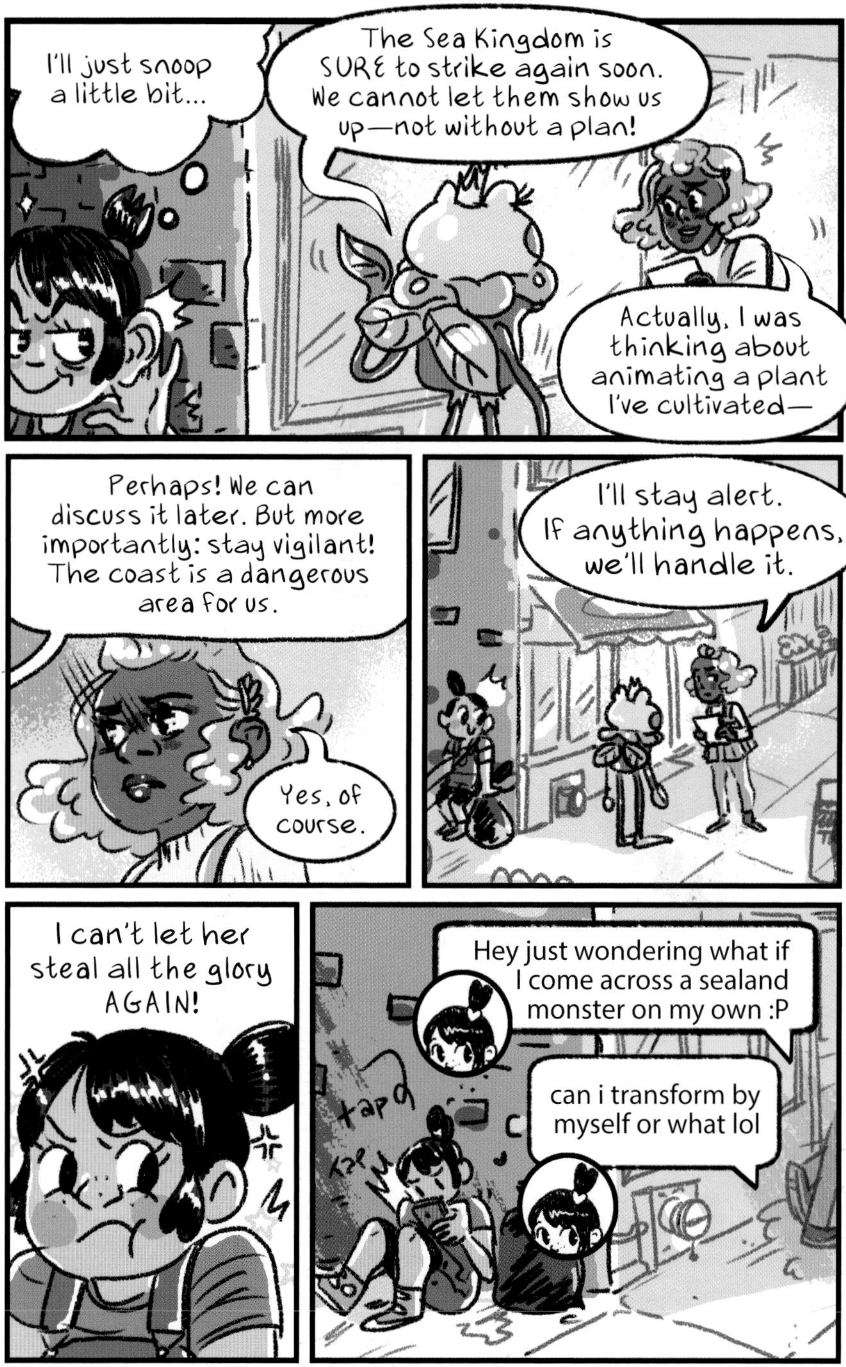
I'll just snoop
a little bit...
The Sea Kingdom is SURE to strike again soon. We cannot let them show us up—not without a plan!
Actually, I was thinking about animating a plant I've cultivated—
Perhaps! We can discuss it later. But more importantly: stay vigilant! The coast is a dangerous area for us.
Yes, of course.
I'll stay alert. If anything happens, we'll handle it.
I can't let her steal all the glory AGAIN!
Hey just wondering what if I come across a sealand monster on my own :P
can i transform by myself or what lol
tap
tap

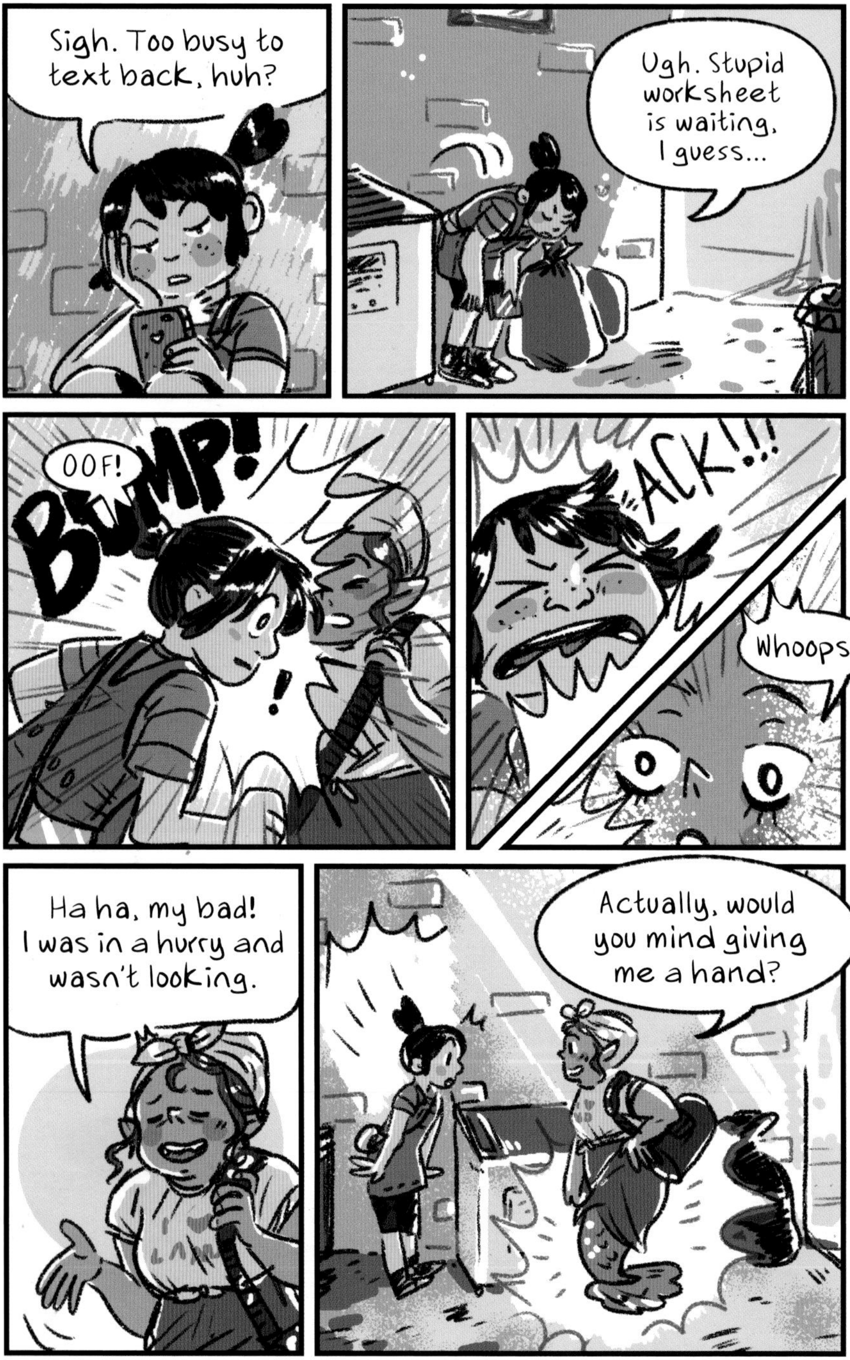
Sigh. Too busy to text back, huh?
Ugh. Stupid worksheet is waiting, I guess...
OOF!
BUMP!
ACK!!!
Whoops!
Ha ha, my bad! I was in a hurry and wasn't looking.
Actually, would you mind giving me a hand?

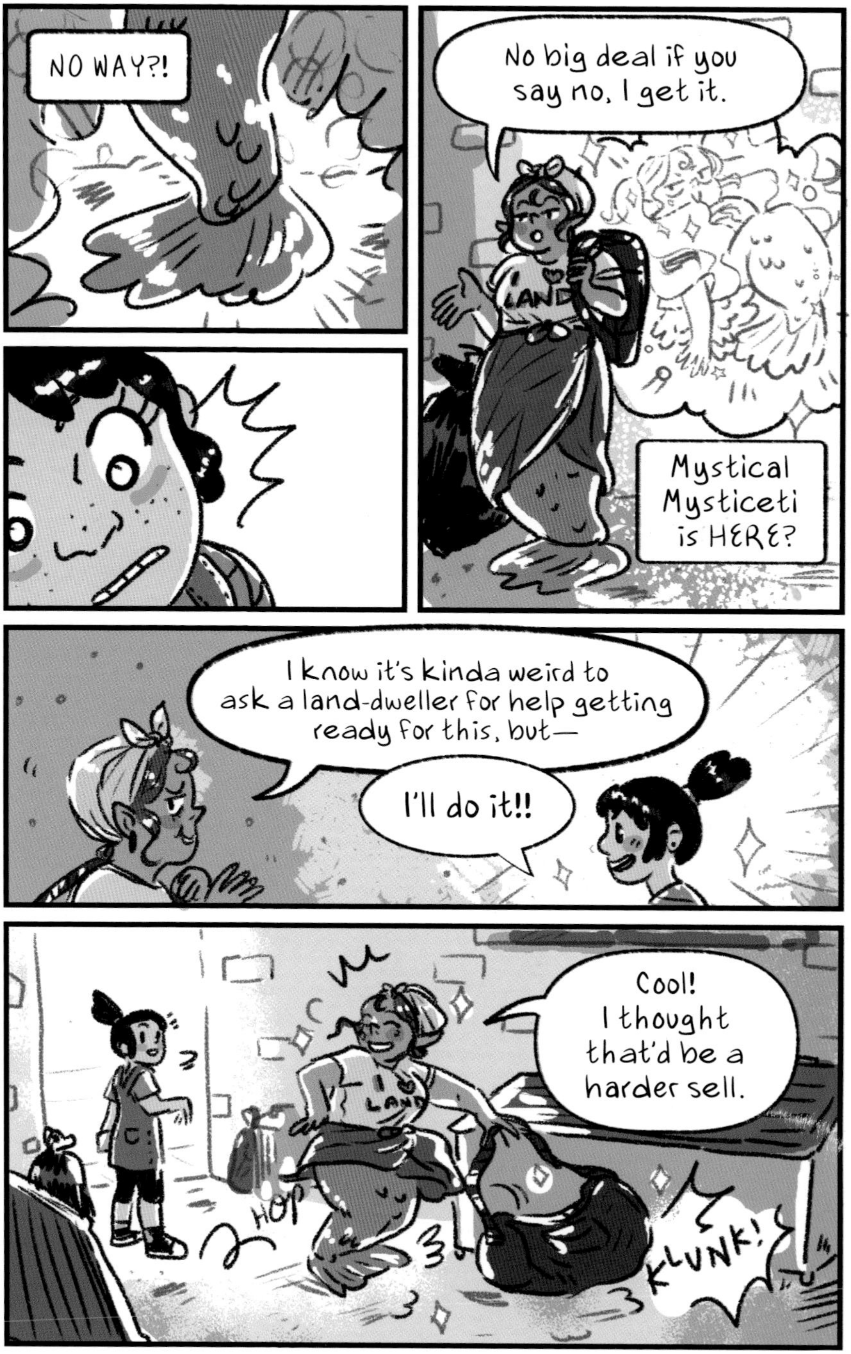
NO WAY?!
No big deal if you say no, I get it.
Mystical Mysticeti is HERE?
I know it's kinda weird to ask a land-dweller for help getting ready for this, but—
I'll do it!!
Cool! I thought that'd be a harder sell.
HOP
KLUNK!

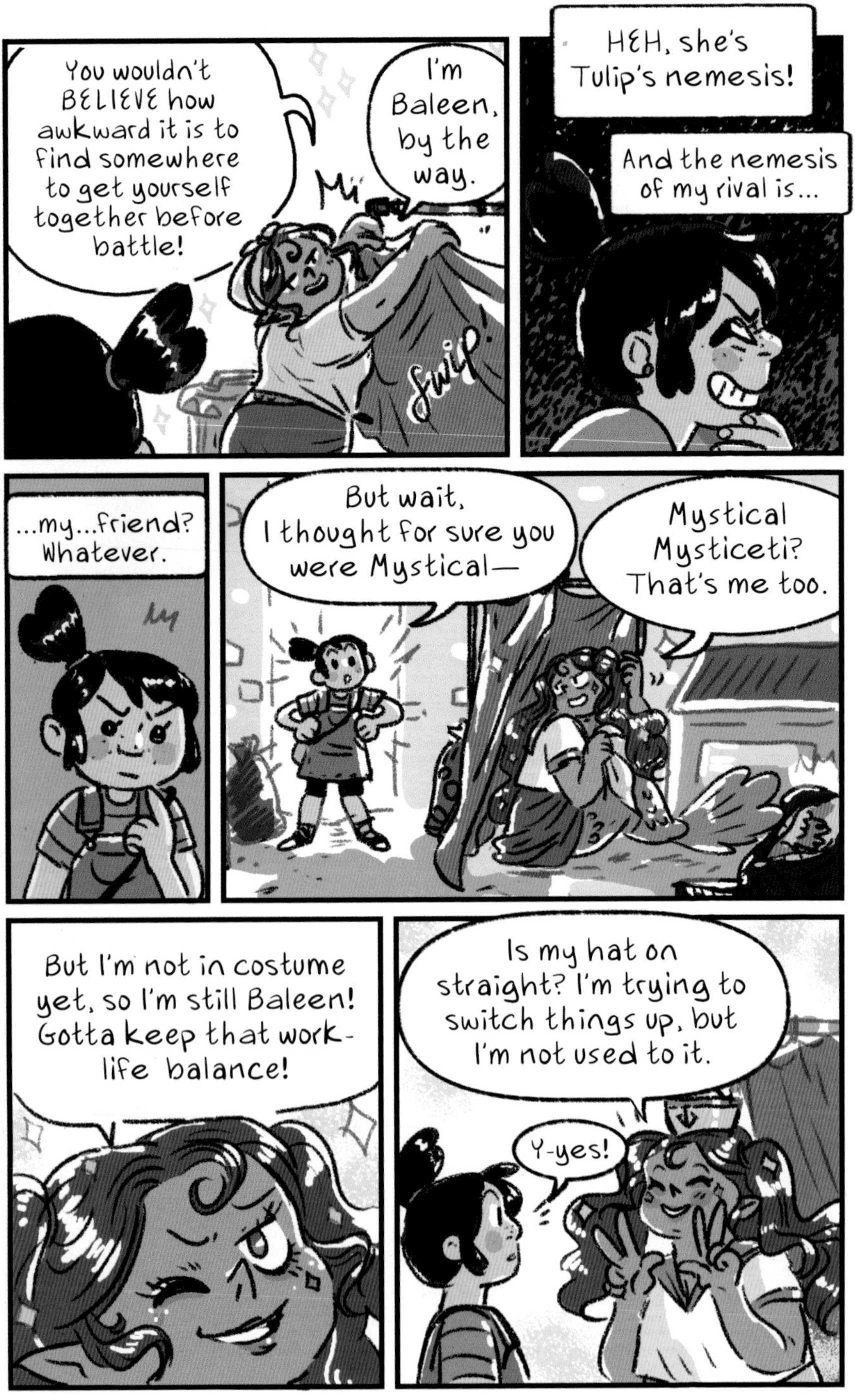

You wouldn't BELIEVE how awkward it is to find somewhere to get yourself together before battle!
I'm Baleen, by the way.
Swip!
HEH, she's Tulip's nemesis!
And the nemesis of my rival is...
...my...friend? Whatever.
But wait, I thought for sure you were Mystical—
Mystical Mysticeti? That's me too.
But I'm not in costume yet, so I'm still Baleen! Gotta keep that work-life balance!
Is my hat on straight? I'm trying to switch things up, but I'm not used to it.
Y-yes!

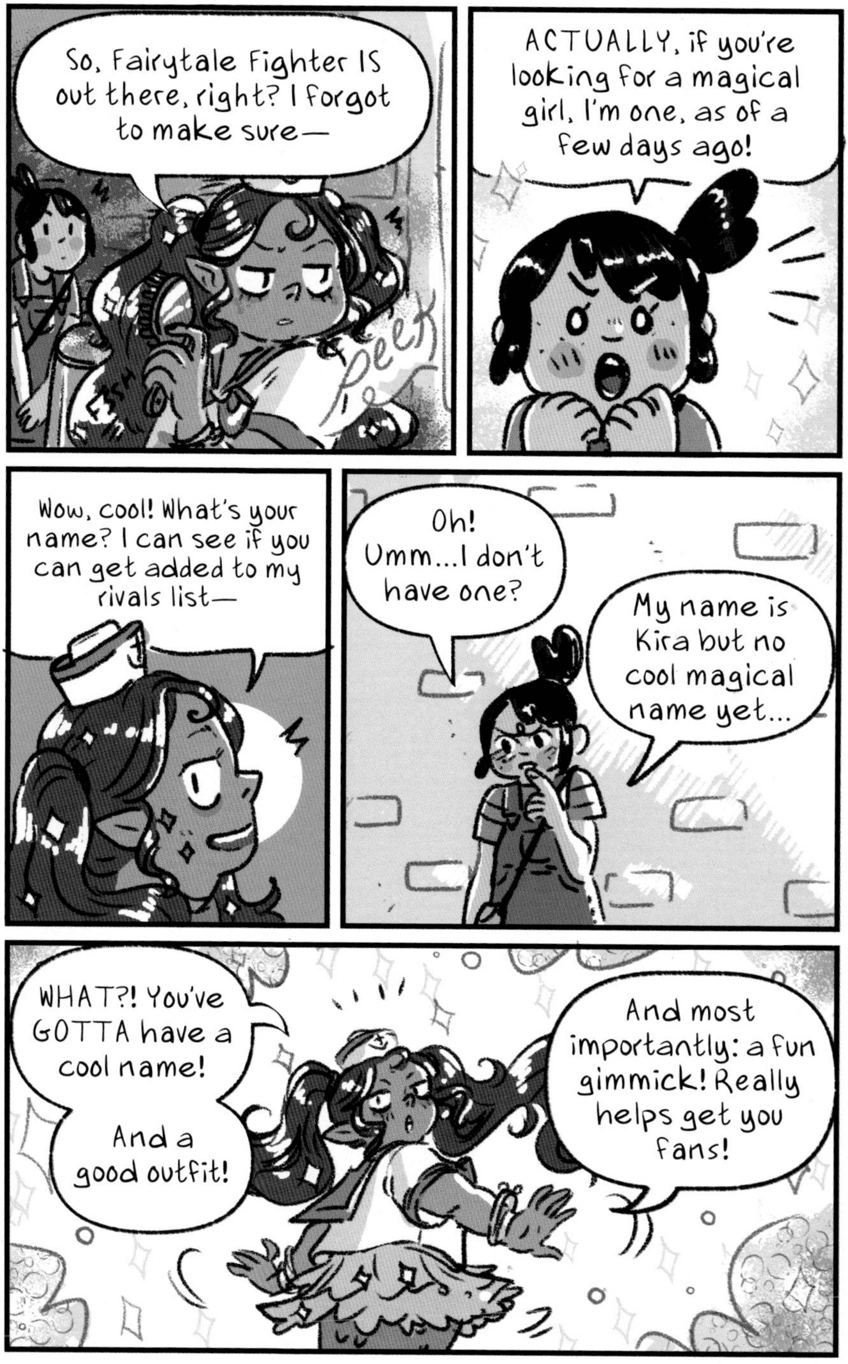
So, Fairytale Fighter IS out there, right? I forgot to make sure—
PEEK
ACTUALLY, if you're looking for a magical girl, I'm one, as of a few days ago!
Wow, cool! What's your name? I can see if you can get added to my rivals list—
Oh! Umm...I don't have one?
My name is Kira but no cool magical name yet...
WHAT?! You've GOTTA have a cool name!
And a good outfit!
And most importantly: a fun gimmick! Really helps get you fans!

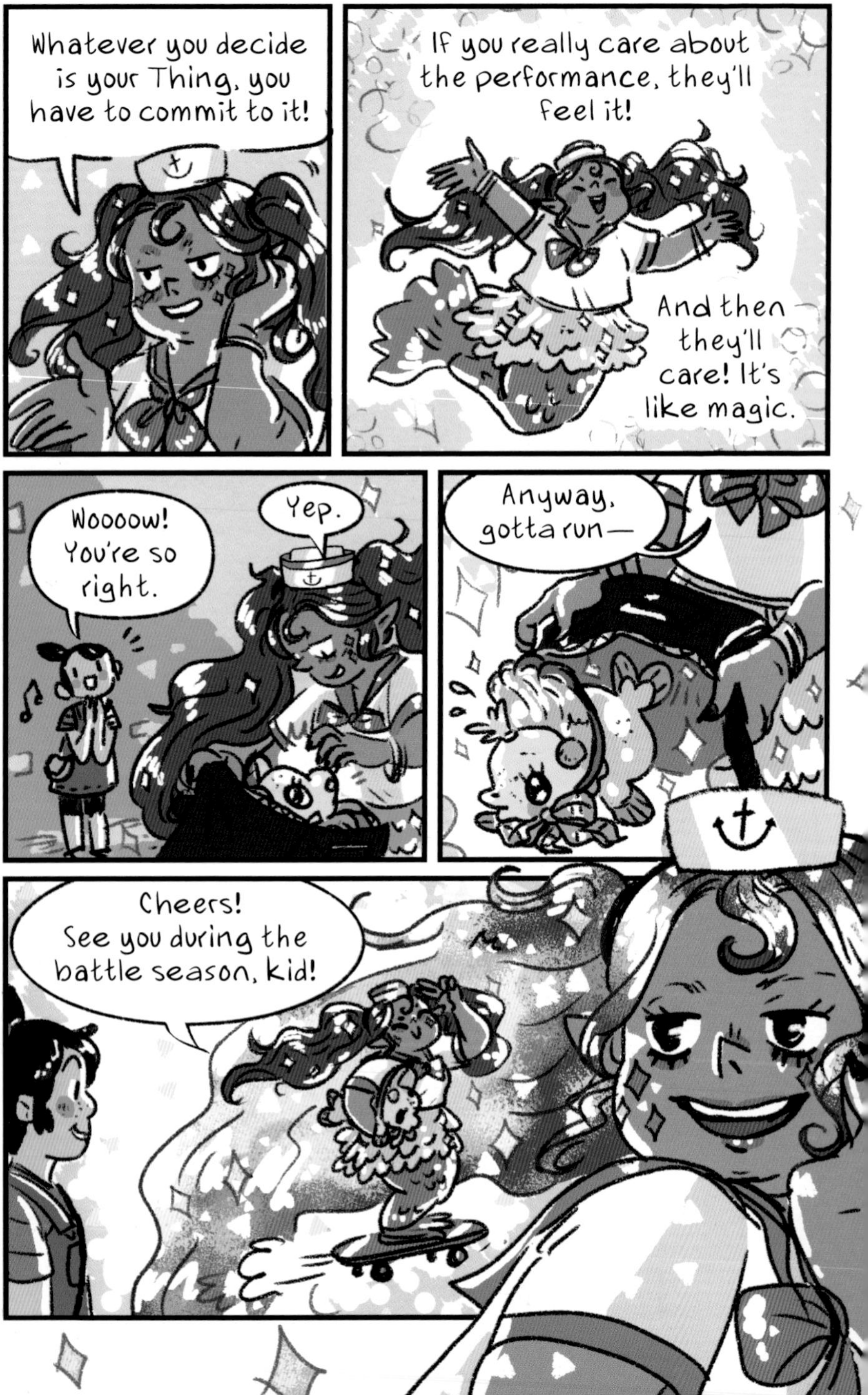
Whatever you decide is your Thing, you have to commit to it!
If you really care about the performance, they'll feel it!
And then they'll care! It's like magic.
Wooooow! You're so right.
Yep.
Anyway, gotta run—
Cheers! See you during the battle season, kid!

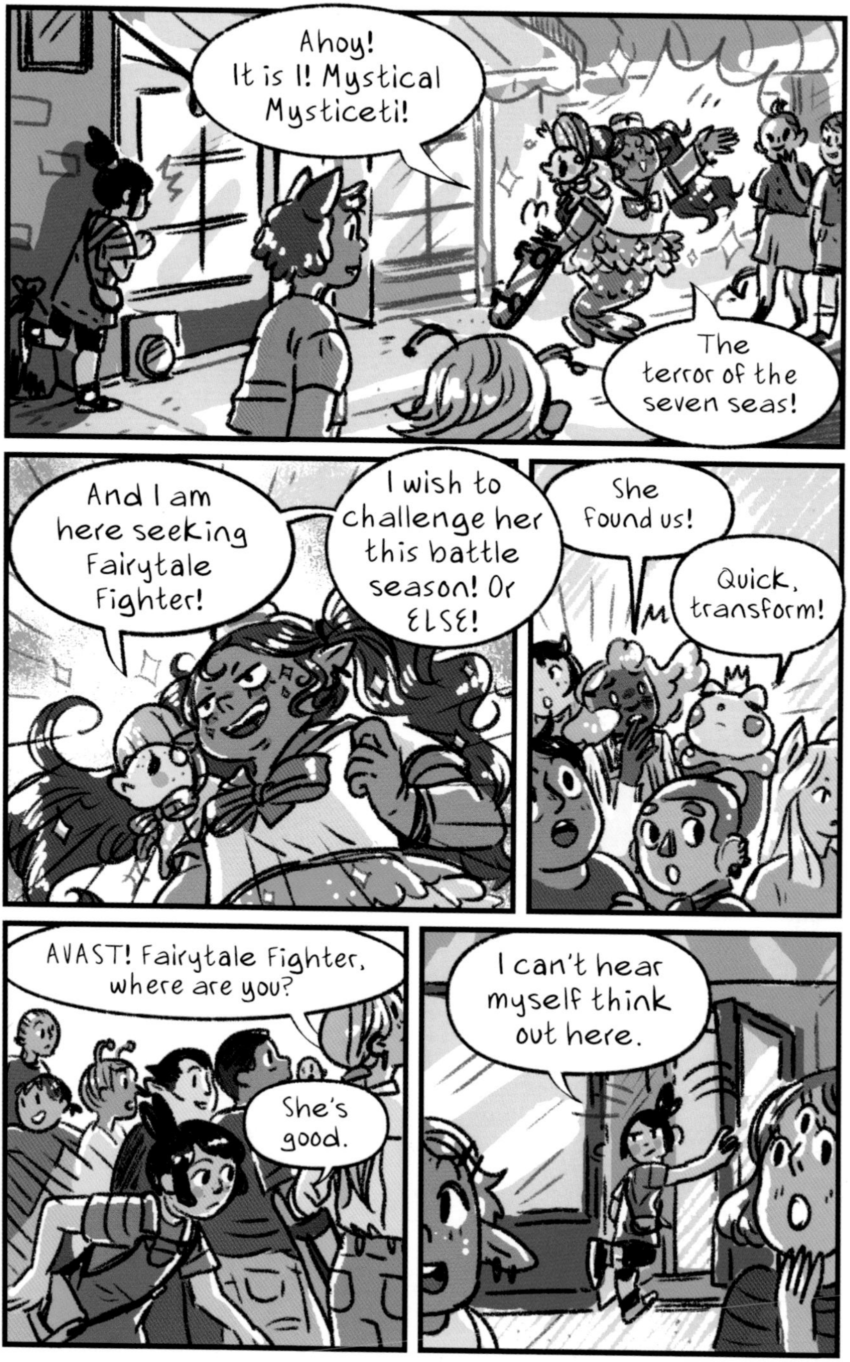
Ahoy! It is I! Mystical Mysticeti!
The terror of the seven seas!
And I am here seeking Fairytale Fighter!
I wish to challenge her this battle season! Or ELSE!
She found us!
Quick, transform!
AVAST! Fairytale Fighter, where are you?
She's good.
I can't hear myself think out here.

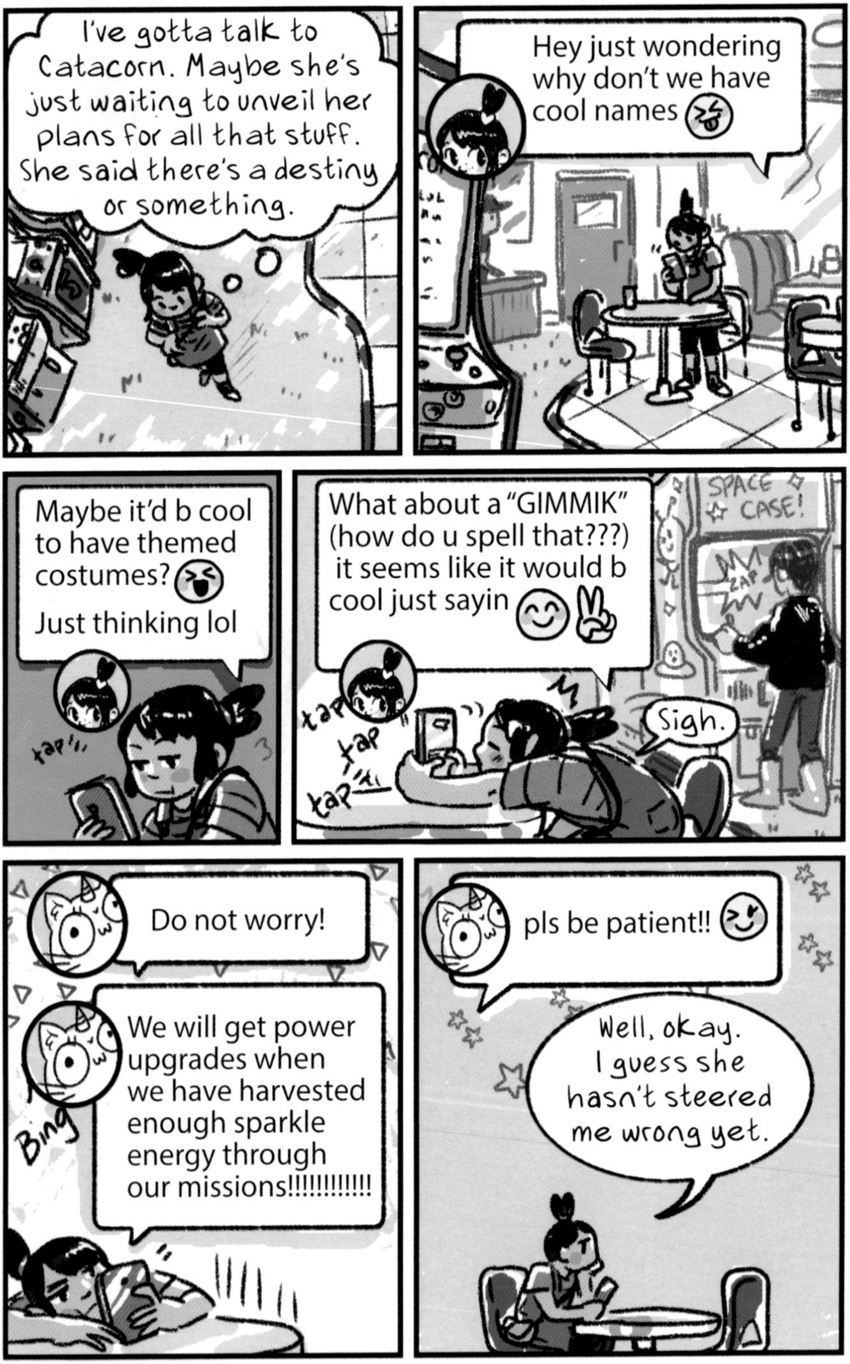
I've gotta talk to Catacorn. Maybe she's just waiting to unveil her plans for all that stuff. She said there's a destiny or something.
Hey just wondering why don't we have cool names
Maybe it'd b cool to have themed costumes?
Just thinking lol
tap
What about a "GIMMIK" (how do u spell that???) it seems like it would b cool just sayin
SPACE CASE!
ZAP
tap
tap
tap
Sigh.
Do not worry!
We will get power upgrades when we have harvested enough sparkle energy through our missions!!!!!!!!!!!!
Bing
pls be patient!!
Well, okay. I guess she hasn't steered me wrong yet.

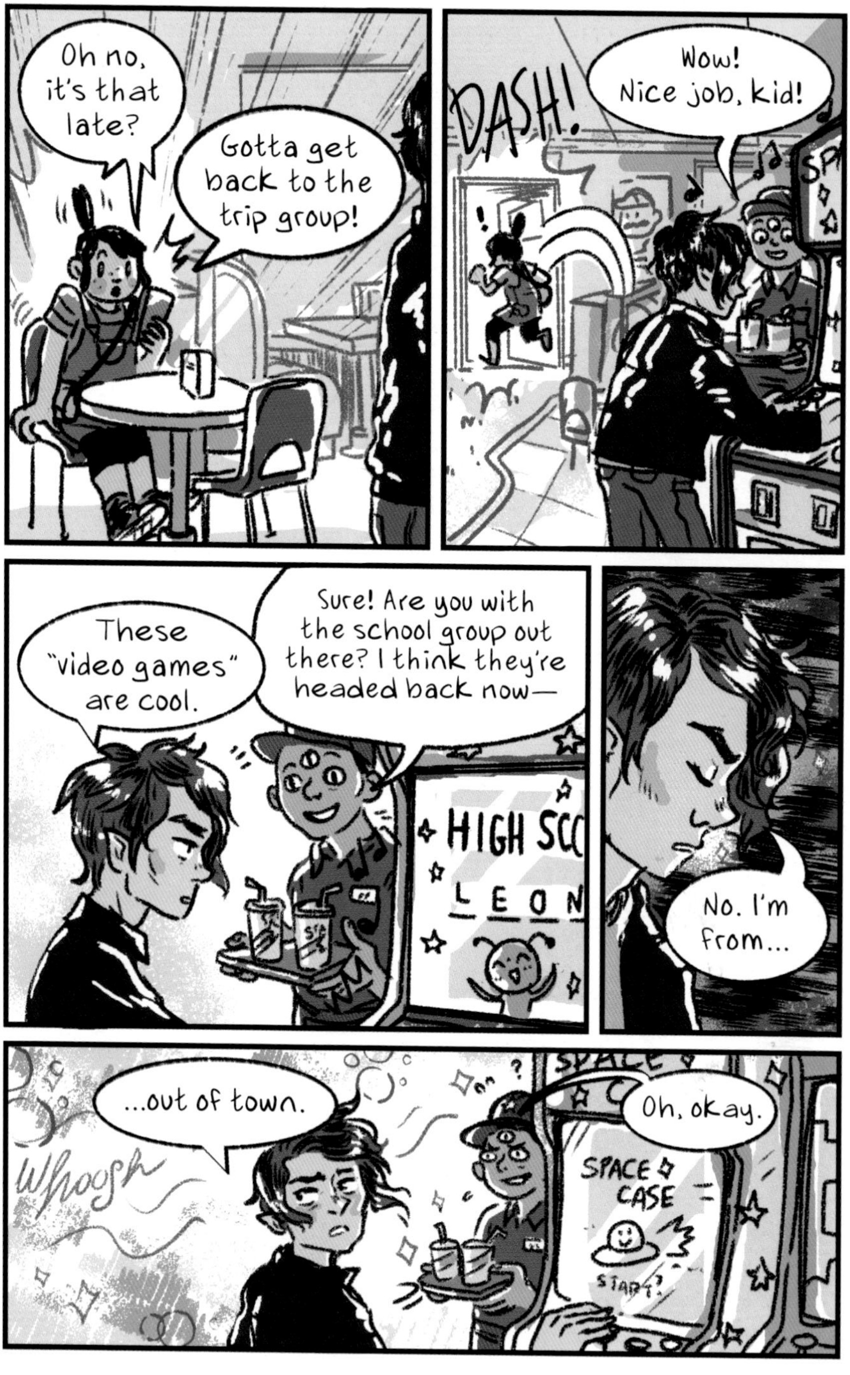
Oh no, it's that late?
Gotta get back to the trip group!
DASH!
Wow! Nice job, kid!
These "video games" are cool.
Sure! Are you with the school group out there? I think they're headed back now—
HIGH SCC
LEON
No. I'm from...
...out of town.
Whoosh
Oh, okay.
SPACE CASE
START?

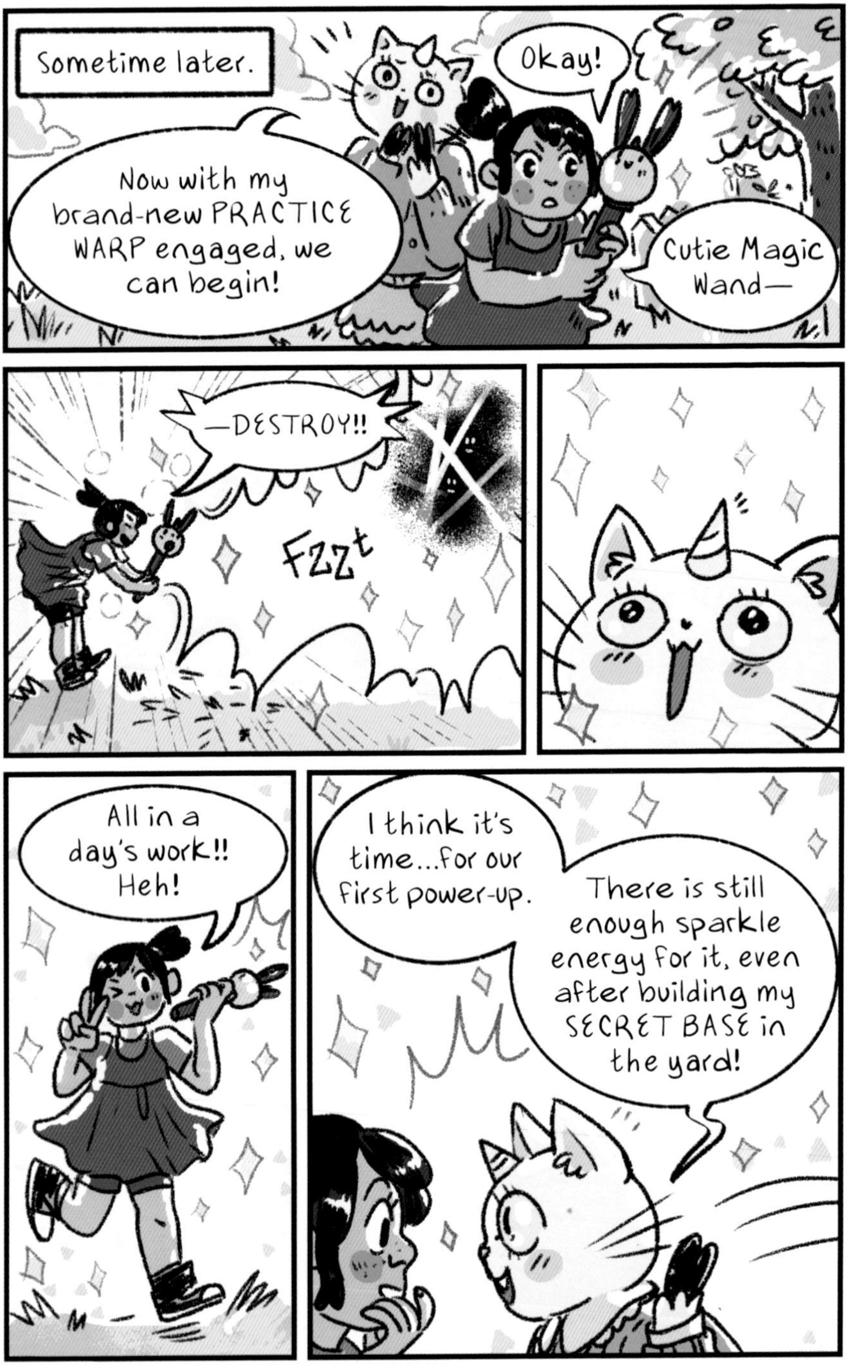
Sometime later.
Okay!
Now with my brand-new PRACTICE WARP engaged, we can begin!
Cutie Magic Wand—
—DESTROY!!
Fzzt
All in a day's work!! Heh!
I think it's time...for our first power-up.
There is still enough sparkle energy for it, even after building my SECRET BASE in the yard!

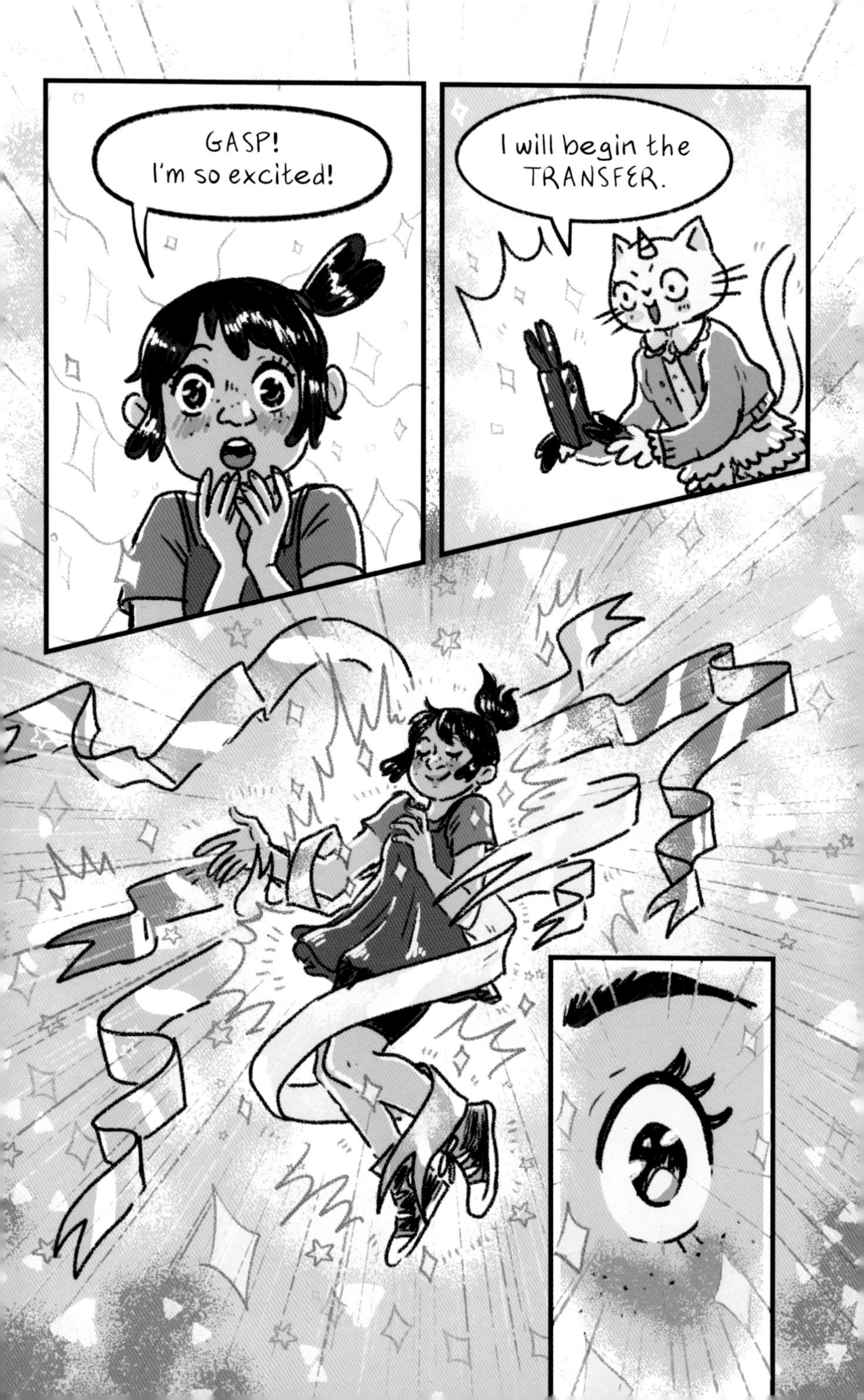
GASP!
I'm so excited!
I will begin the
TRANSFER.

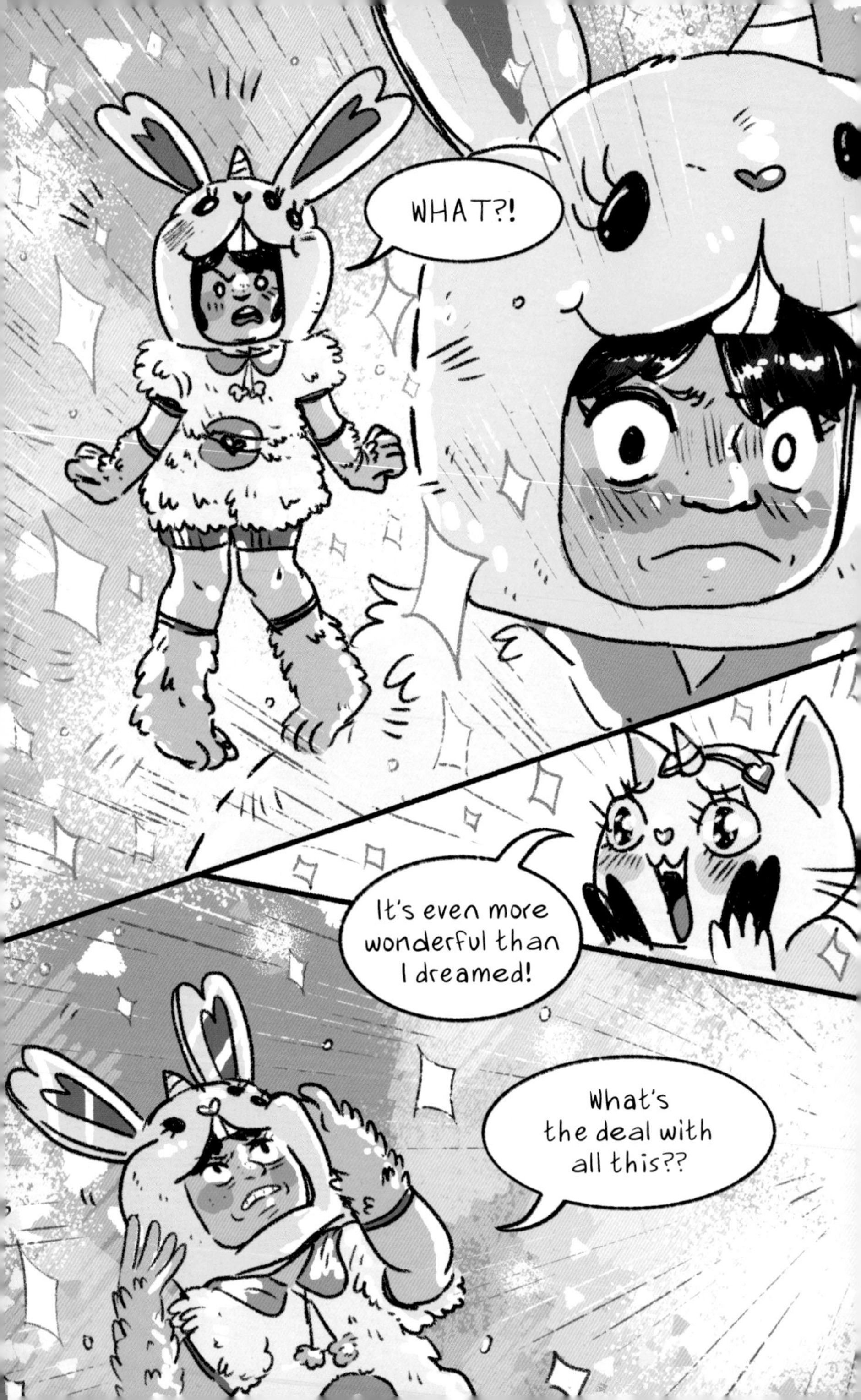
WHAT?!
It's even more wonderful than I dreamed!
What's the deal with all this??

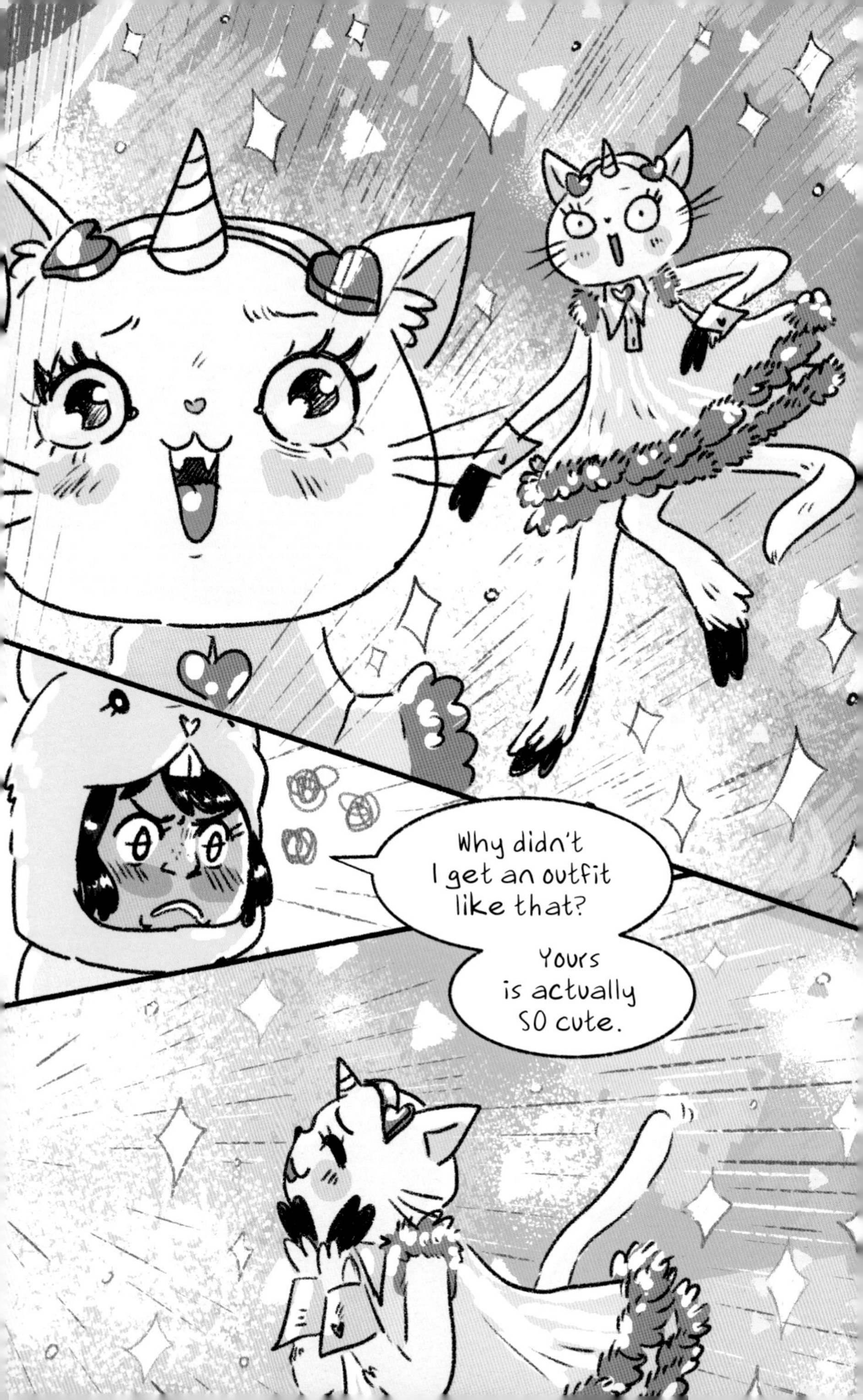
Why didn't I get an outfit like that?
Yours is actually SO cute.

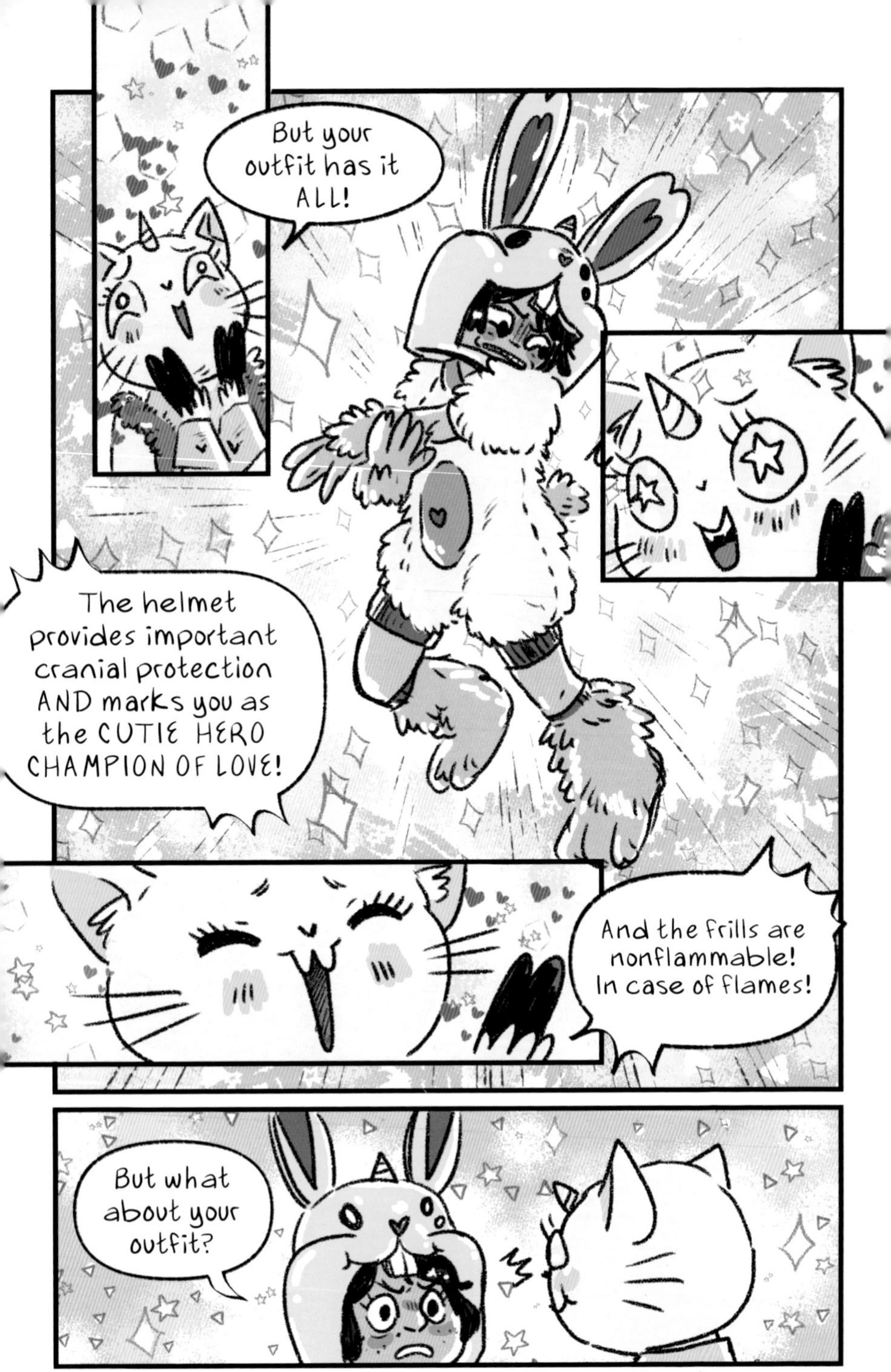
But your outfit has it ALL!
The helmet provides important cranial protection AND marks you as the CUTIE HERO CHAMPION OF LOVE!
And the frills are nonflammable! In case of flames!
But what about your outfit?

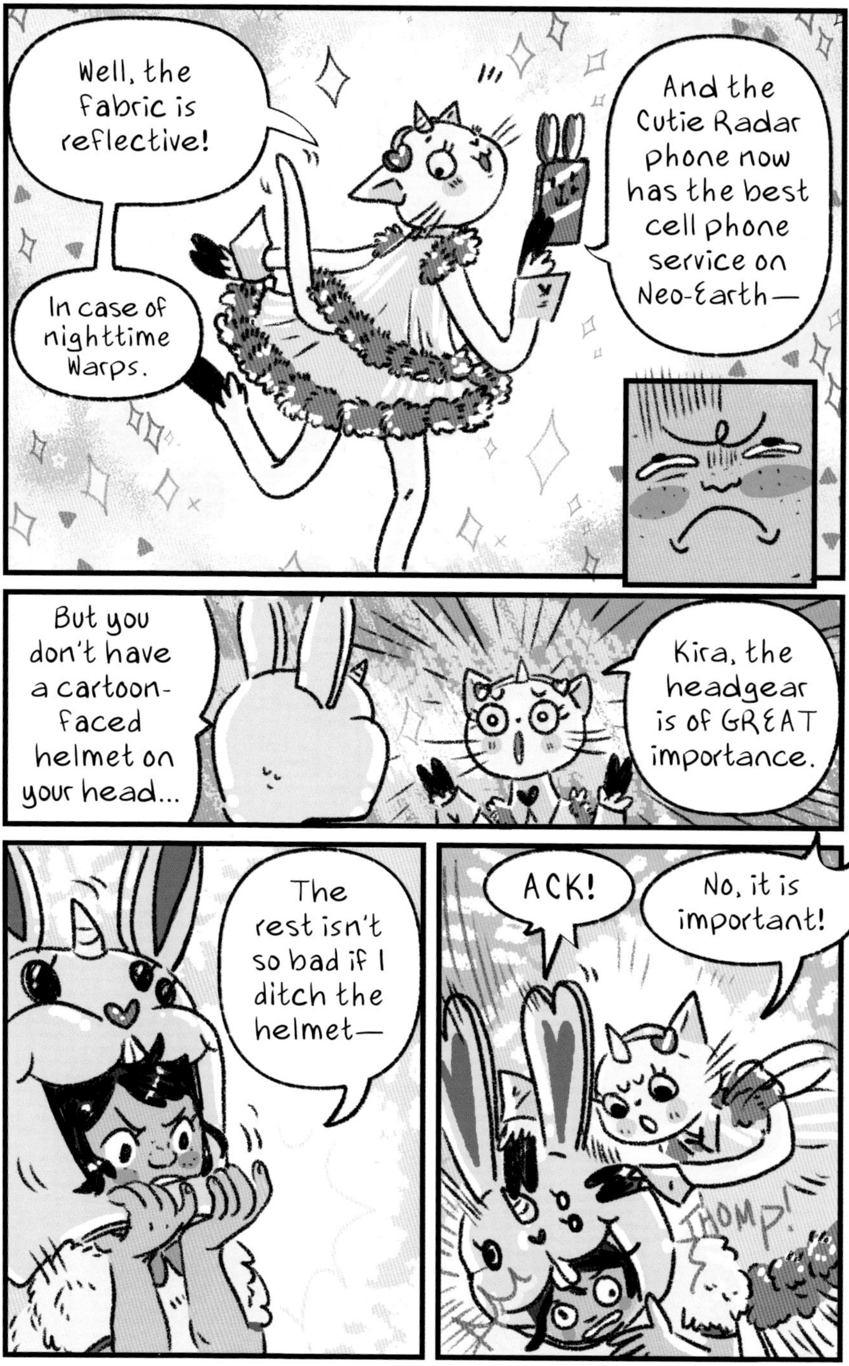
Well, the fabric is reflective!
In case of nighttime Warps.
And the Cutie Radar phone now has the best cell phone service on Neo-Earth—
But you don't have a cartoon-faced helmet on your head...
Kira, the headgear is of GREAT importance.
The rest isn't so bad if I ditch the helmet—
ACK!
No, it is important!
THOMP!

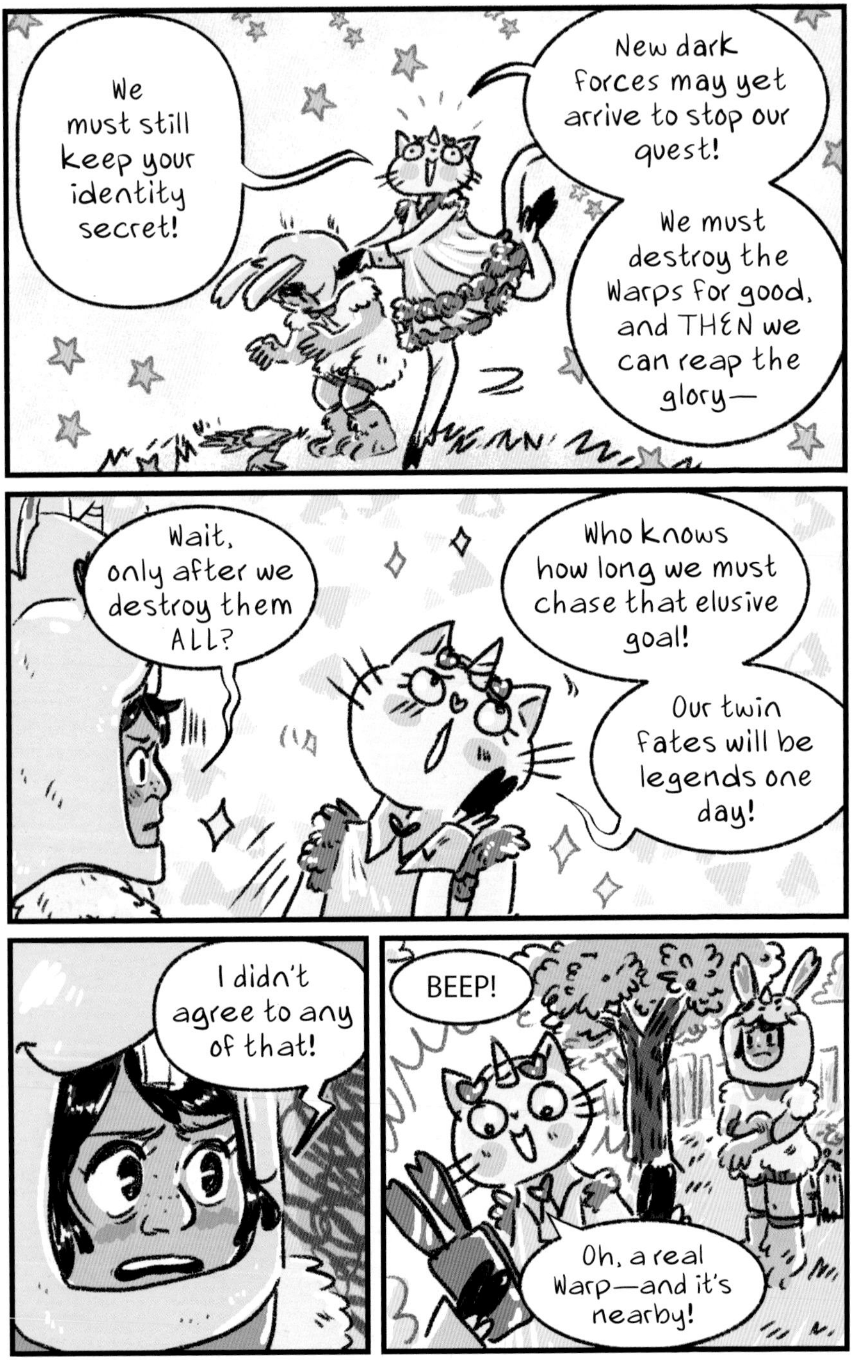
We must still keep your identity secret!
New dark forces may yet arrive to stop our quest!
We must destroy the Warps for good, and THEN we can reap the glory—
Wait, only after we destroy them ALL?
Who knows how long we must chase that elusive goal!
Our twin fates will be legends one day!
I didn't agree to any of that!
...
BEEP!
Oh, a real Warp—and it's nearby!

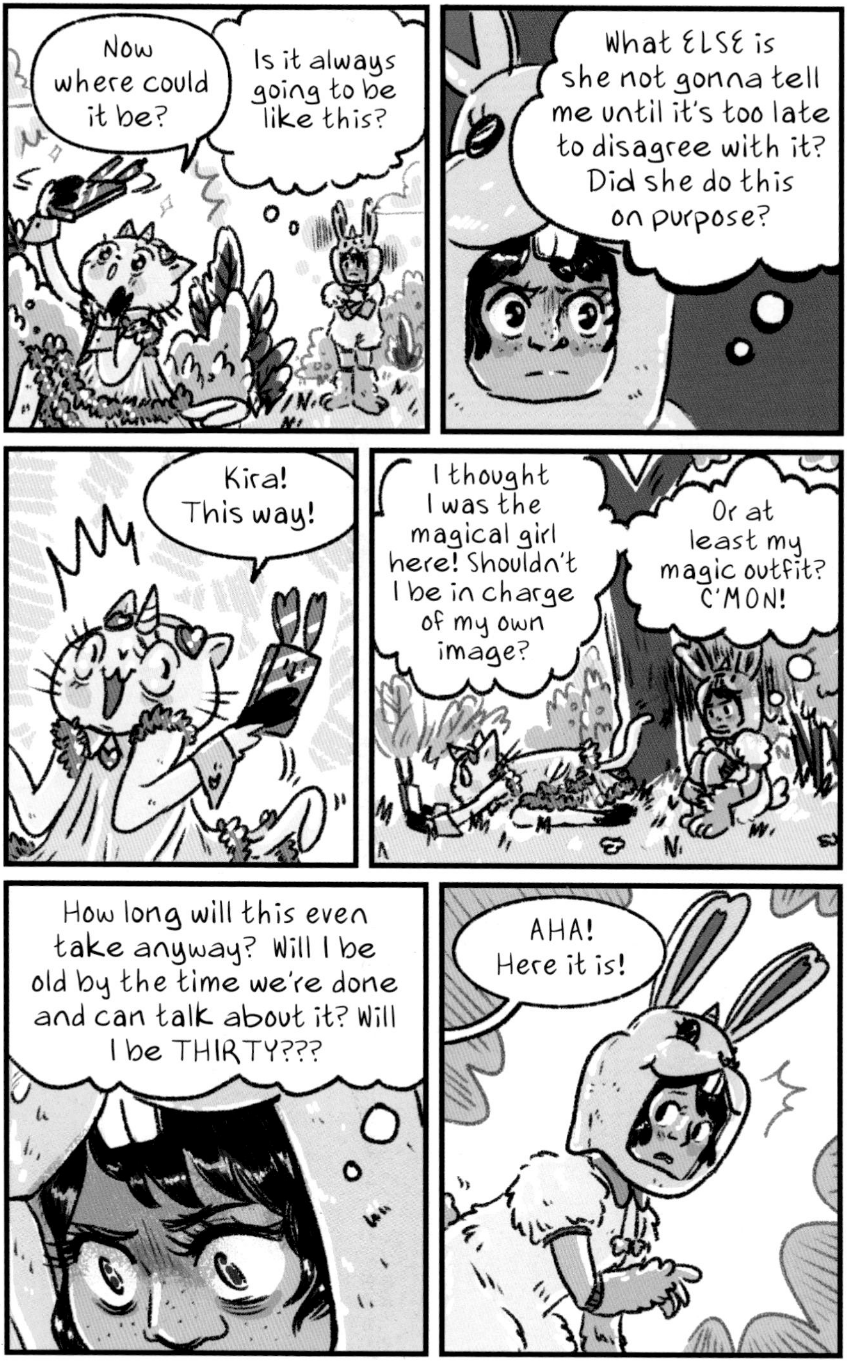
Now where could it be?
Is it always going to be like this?
What ELSE is she not gonna tell me until it's too late to disagree with it? Did she do this on purpose?
Kira! This way!
I thought I was the magical girl here! Shouldn't I be in charge of my own image?
Or at least my magic outfit? C'MON!
How long will this even take anyway? Will I be old by the time we're done and can talk about it? Will I be THIRTY???
AHA! Here it is!

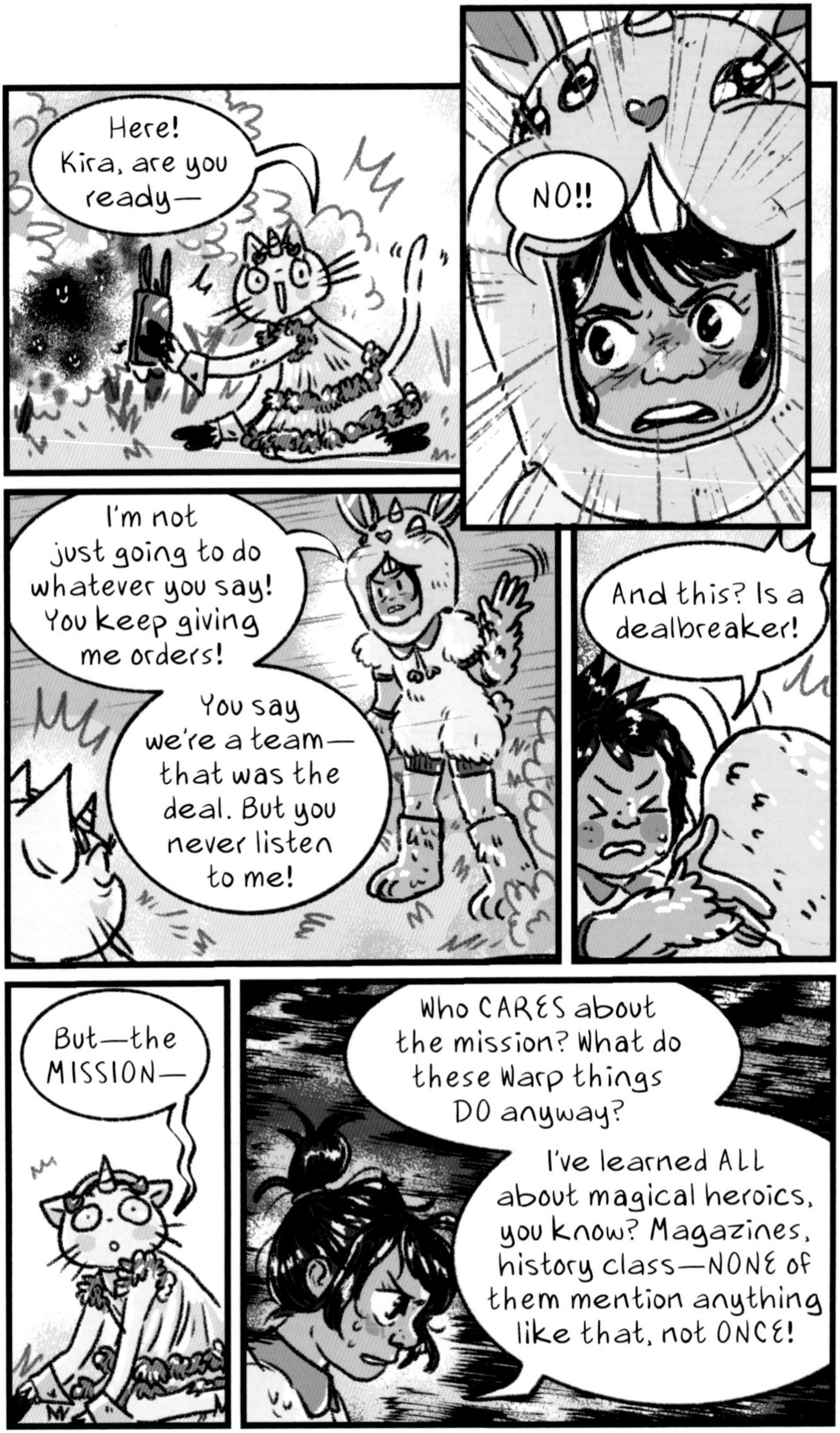
Here! Kira, are you ready—
NO!!
I'm not just going to do whatever you say! You keep giving me orders!
You say we're a team—that was the deal. But you never listen to me!
And this? Is a dealbreaker!
But—the MISSION—
Who CARES about the mission? What do these Warp things DO anyway?
I've learned ALL about magical heroics, you know? Magazines, history class—NONE of them mention anything like that, not ONCE!

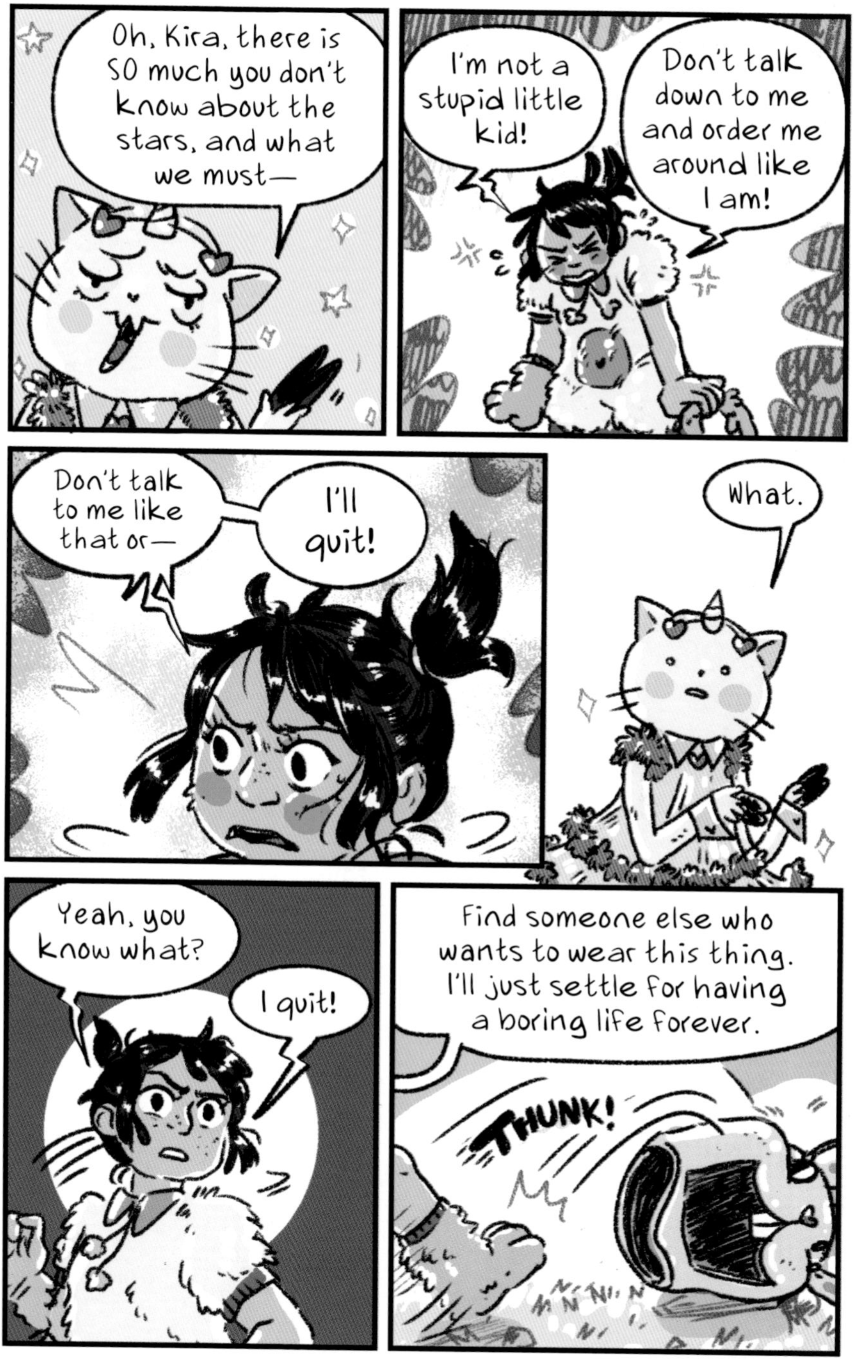
Oh, Kira, there is SO much you don't know about the stars, and what we must—
I'm not a stupid little kid!
Don't talk down to me and order me around like I am!
Don't talk to me like that or—
I'll quit!
What.
Yeah, you know what?
I quit!
Find someone else who wants to wear this thing. I'll just settle for having a boring life forever.
THUNK!

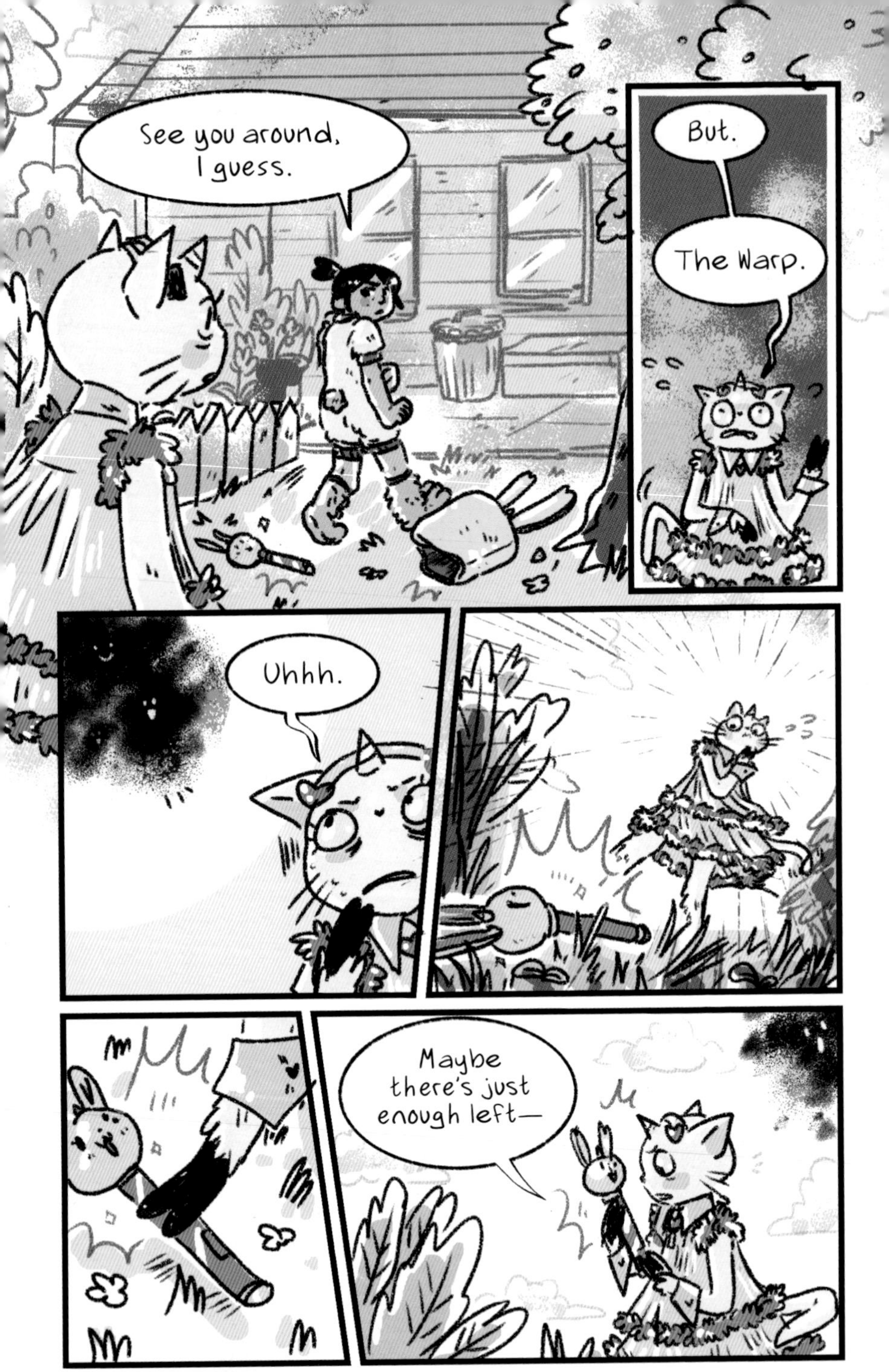
See you around, I guess.
But.
The Warp.
Uhhh.
Maybe there's just enough left—

Emergency—BEAM!!

VWORP!

I suppose it worked this time, but...

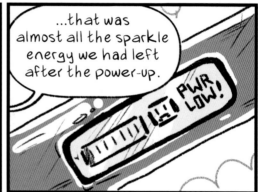

...that was almost all the sparkle energy we had left after the power-up.

PWR LOW!

What do I do now?

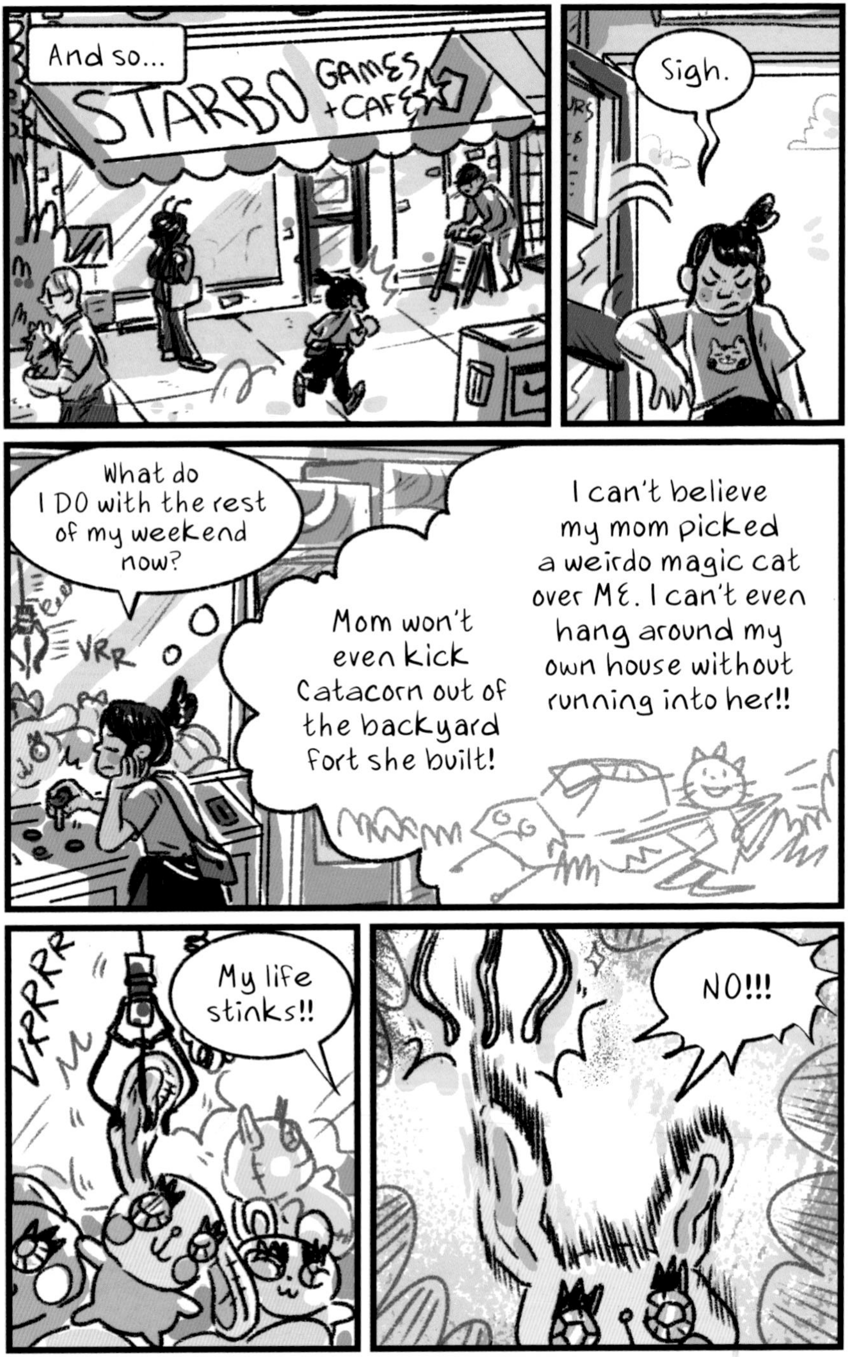
And so...
STARBO GAMES + CAFE
Sigh.
What do I DO with the rest of my weekend now?
Mom won't even kick Catacorn out of the backyard fort she built!
I can't believe my mom picked a weirdo magic cat over ME. I can't even hang around my own house without running into her!!
VRR
VRRRR
My life stinks!!
NO!!!

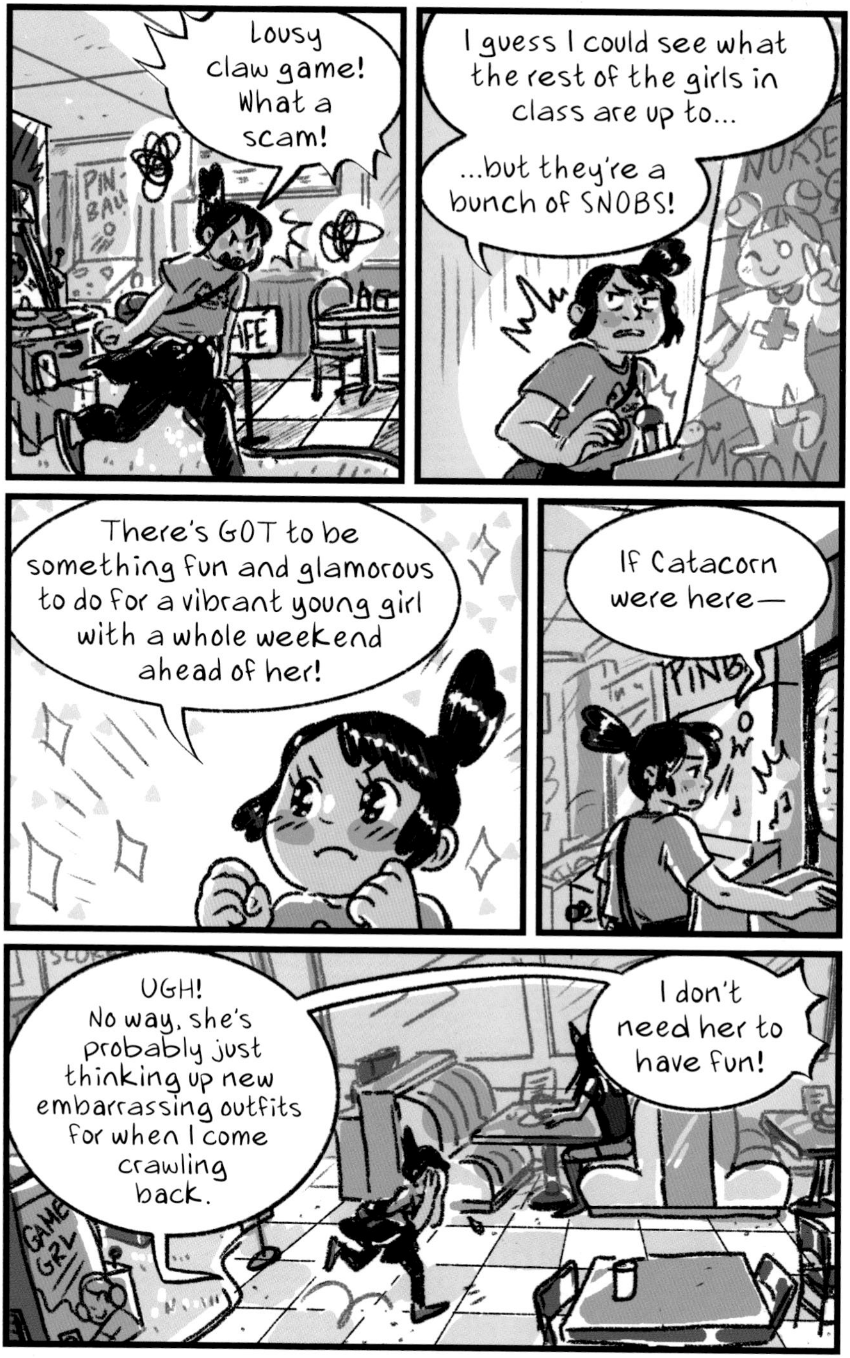
Lousy claw game! What a scam!
I guess I could see what the rest of the girls in class are up to...
...but they're a bunch of SNOBS!
NURSE MOON
There's GOT to be something fun and glamorous to do for a vibrant young girl with a whole weekend ahead of her!
If Catacorn were here—
UGH! No way, she's probably just thinking up new embarrassing outfits for when I come crawling back.
I don't need her to have fun!
GAME GRL

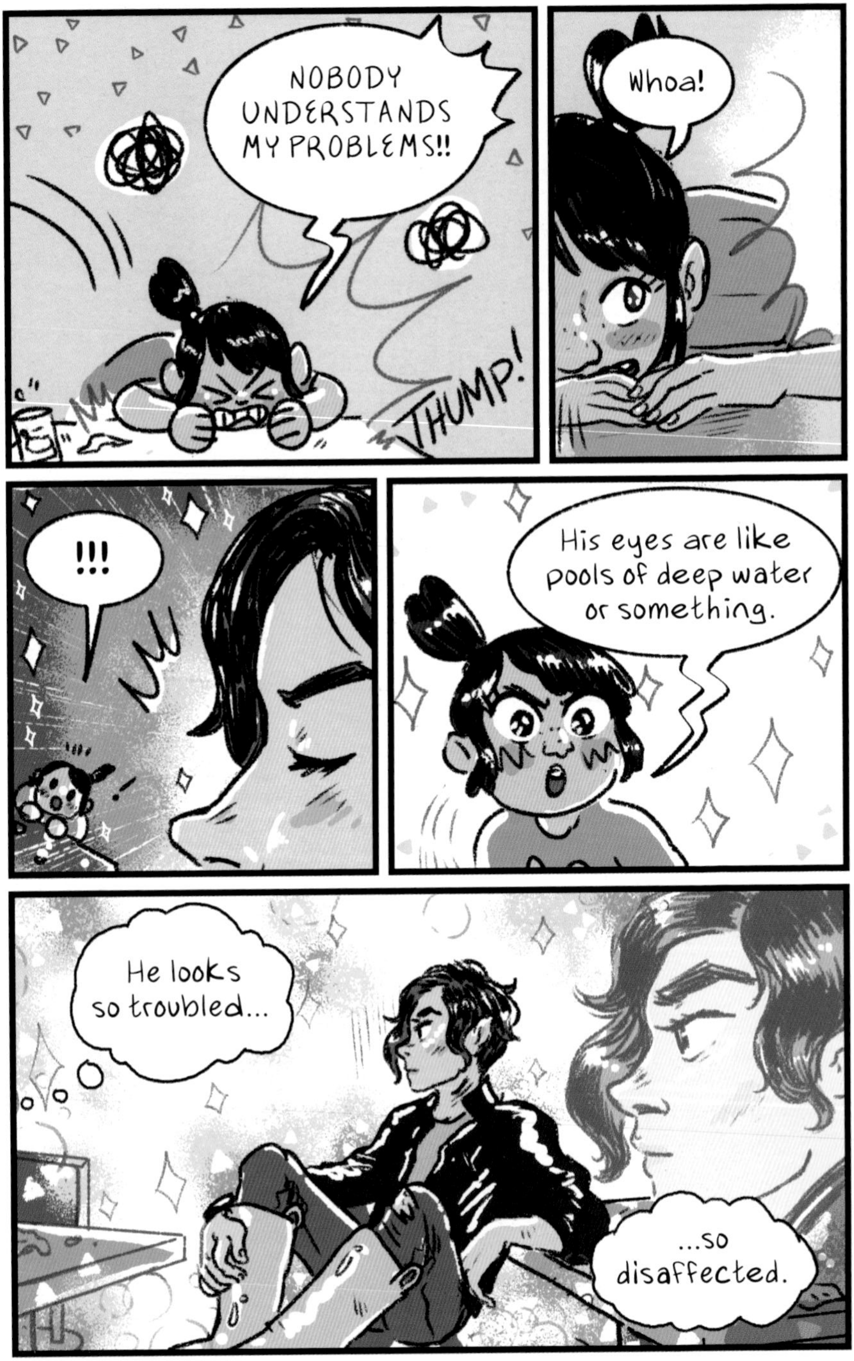
NOBODY UNDERSTANDS MY PROBLEMS!!
THUMP!
Whoa!
!!!
His eyes are like pools of deep water or something.
He looks so troubled...
...so disaffected.

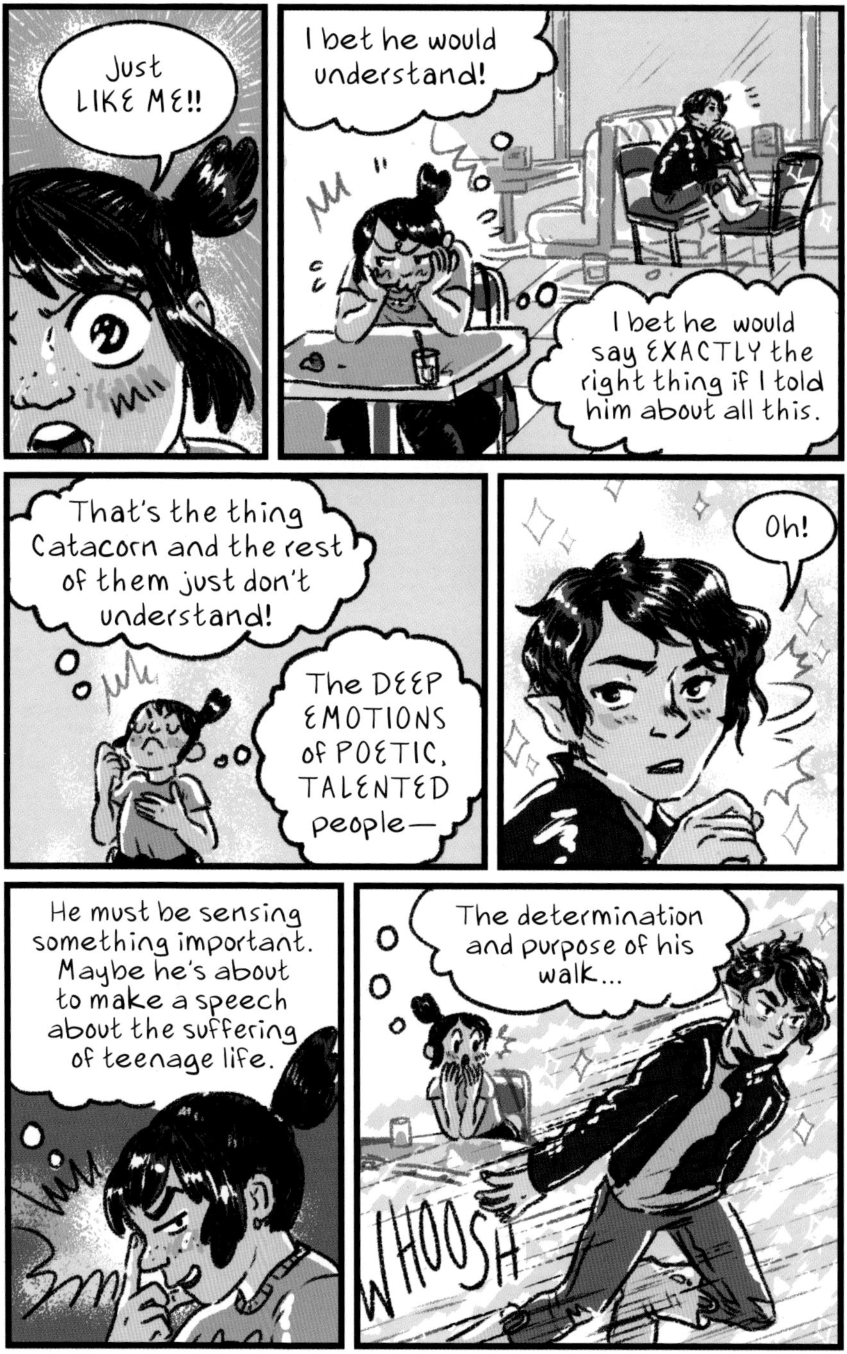
Just LIKE ME!!
I bet he would understand!
I bet he would say EXACTLY the right thing if I told him about all this.
That's the thing Catacorn and the rest of them just don't understand!
The DEEP EMOTIONS of POETIC, TALENTED people—
Oh!
He must be sensing something important. Maybe he's about to make a speech about the suffering of teenage life.
The determination and purpose of his walk...
WHOOSH

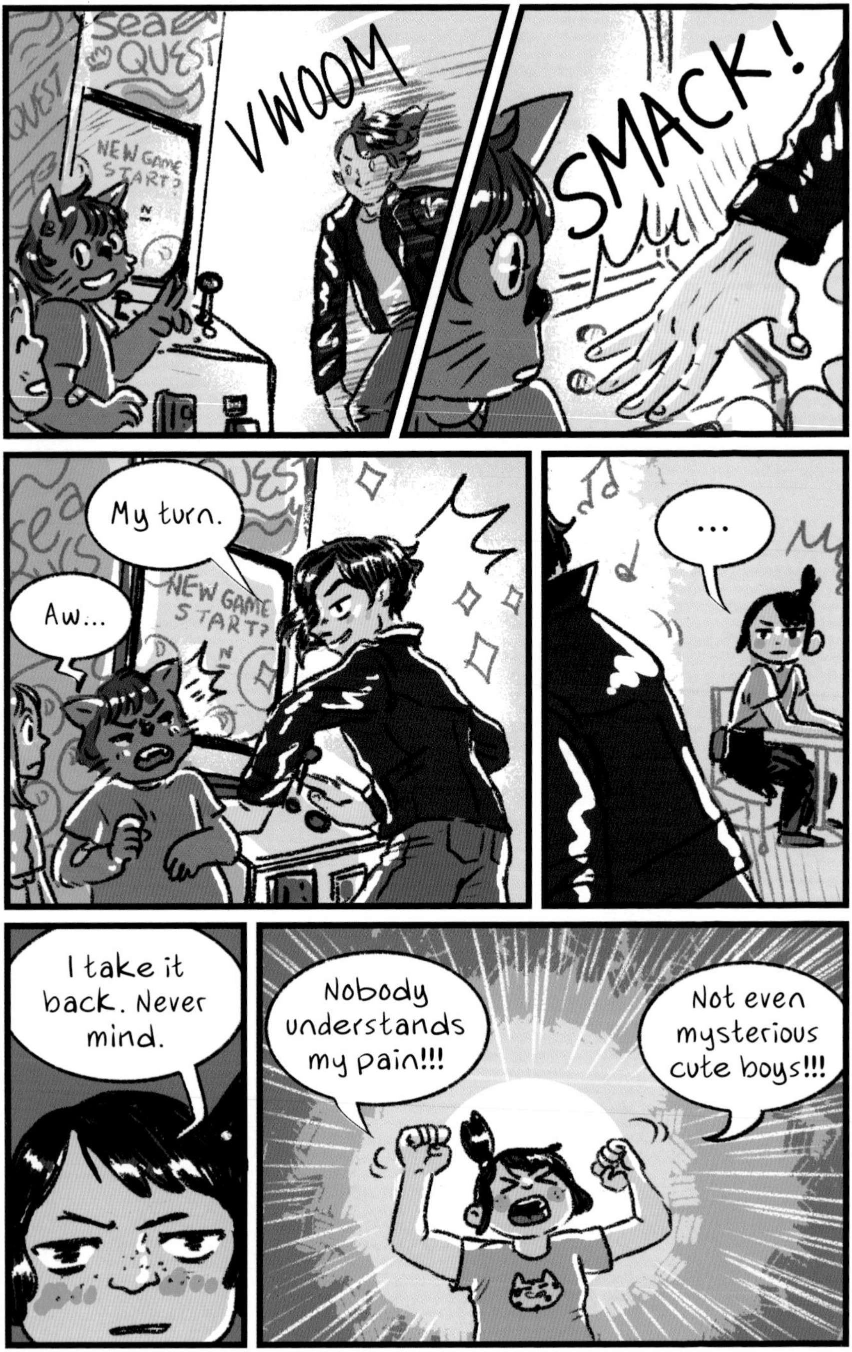
Sea QUEST
QUEST
NEW GAME START?
VWOOM
SMACK!
NEW GAME START?
My turn.
Aw...
...
I take it back. Never mind.
Nobody understands my pain!!!
Not even mysterious cute boys!!!

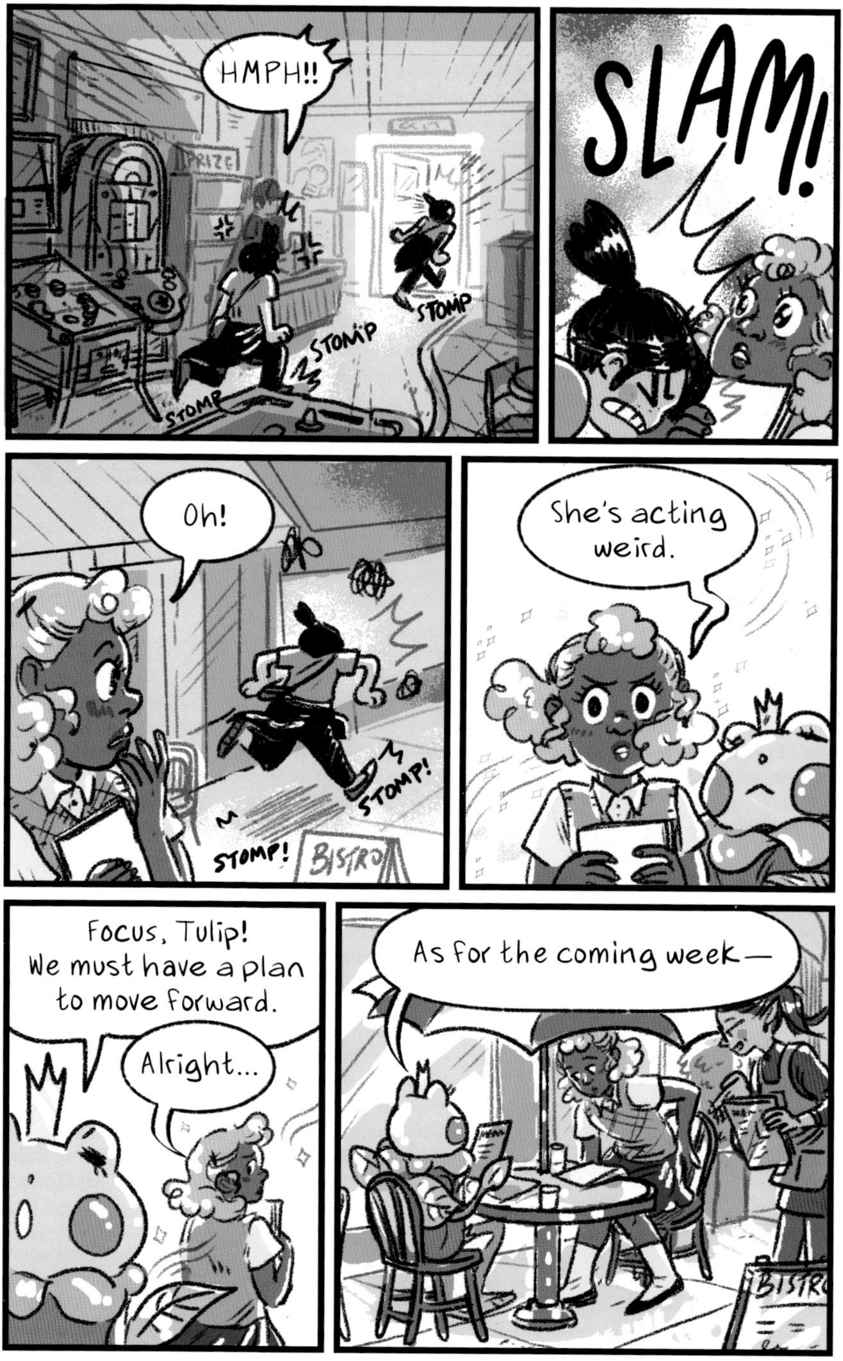
HMPH!!
STOMP
STOMP
STOMP
PRIZE
SLAM!
Oh!
STOMP!
STOMP!
BISTRO
She's acting weird.
Focus, Tulip! We must have a plan to move forward.
Alright...
As for the coming week—
BISTRO

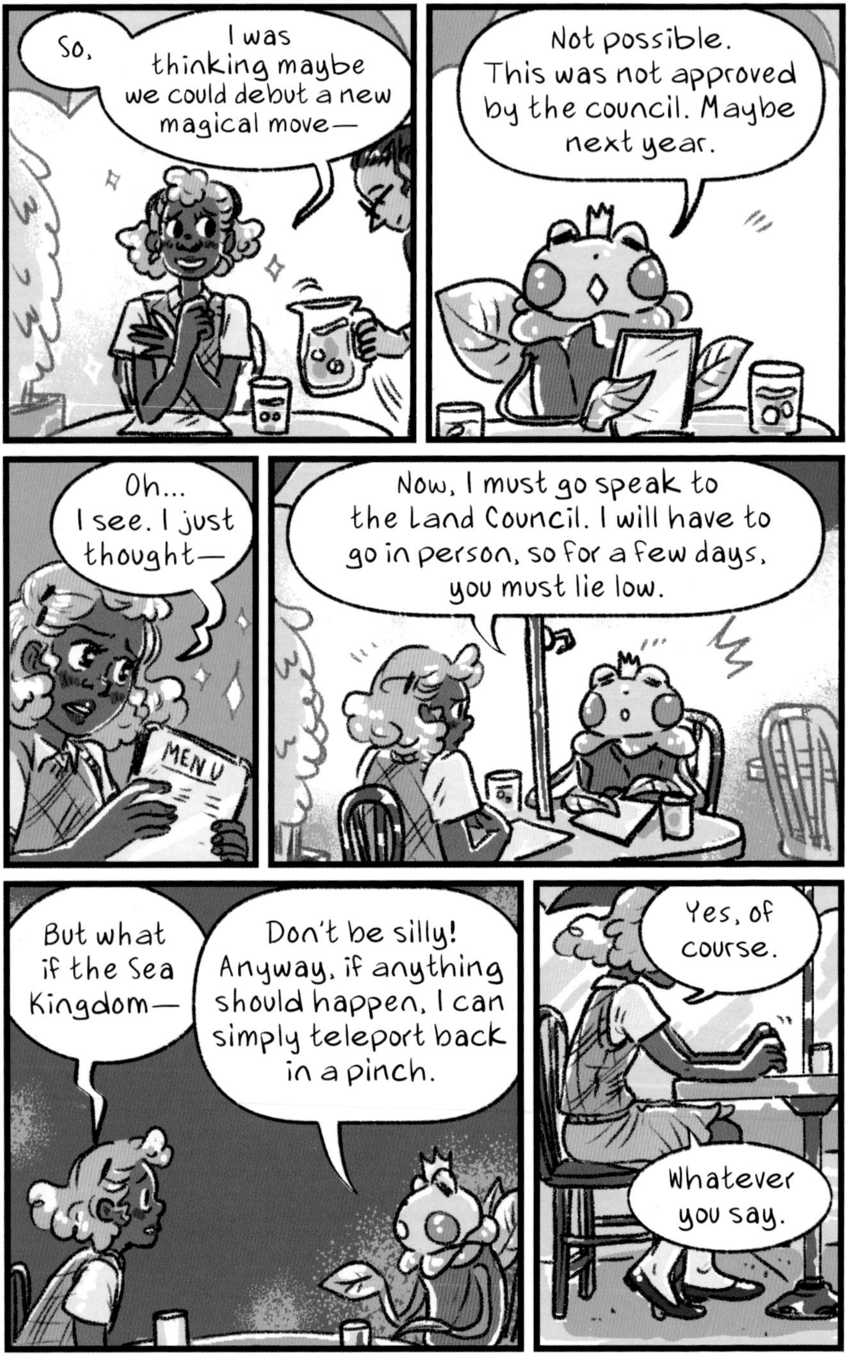
So, I was thinking maybe we could debut a new magical move—
Not possible. This was not approved by the council. Maybe next year.
Oh... I see. I just thought—
MENU
Now, I must go speak to the Land Council. I will have to go in person, so for a few days, you must lie low.
But what if the Sea Kingdom—
Don't be silly! Anyway, if anything should happen, I can simply teleport back in a pinch.
Yes, of course.
Whatever you say.

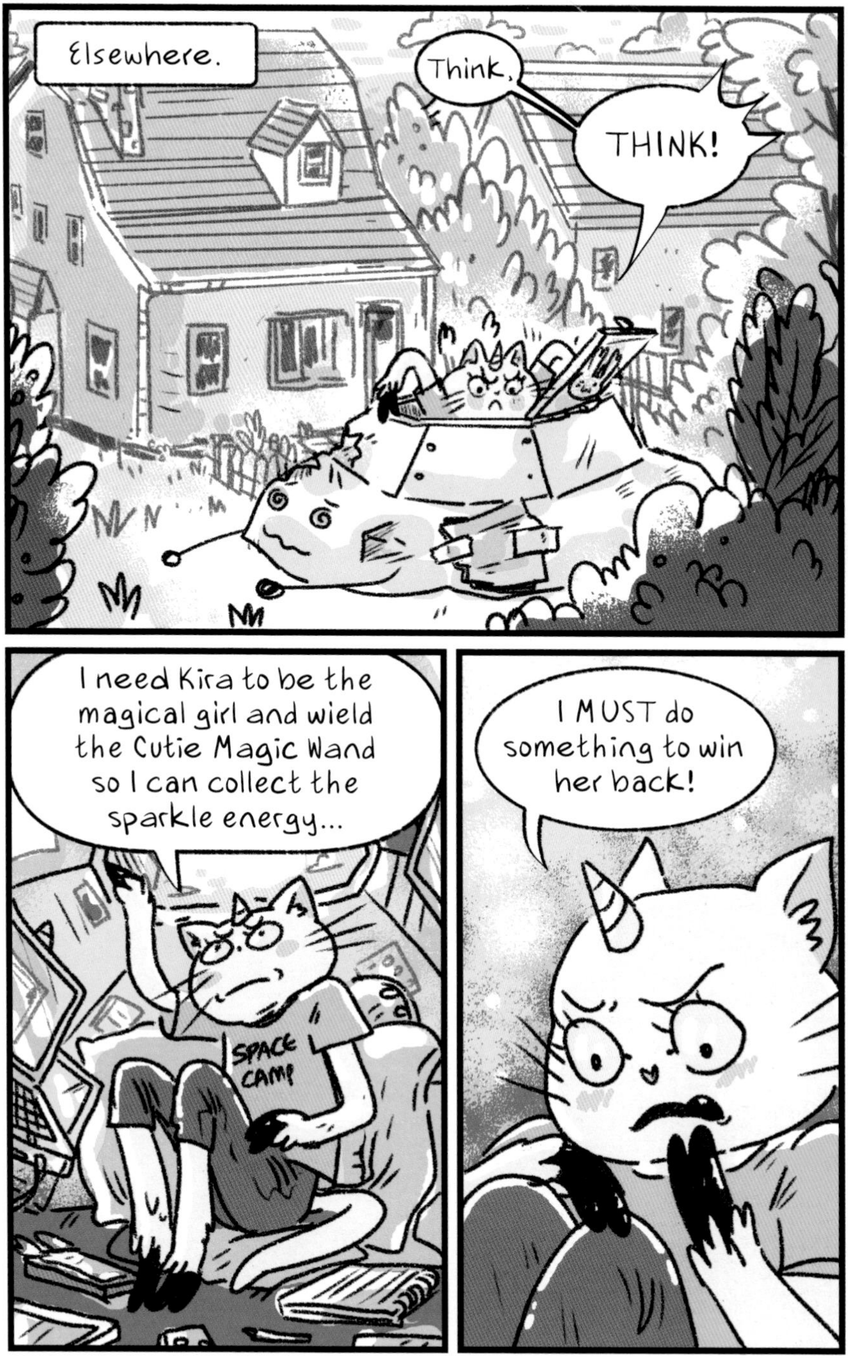
Elsewhere.
Think,
THINK!
I need Kira to be the magical girl and wield the Cutie Magic Wand so I can collect the sparkle energy...
SPACE CAMP
I MUST do something to win her back!

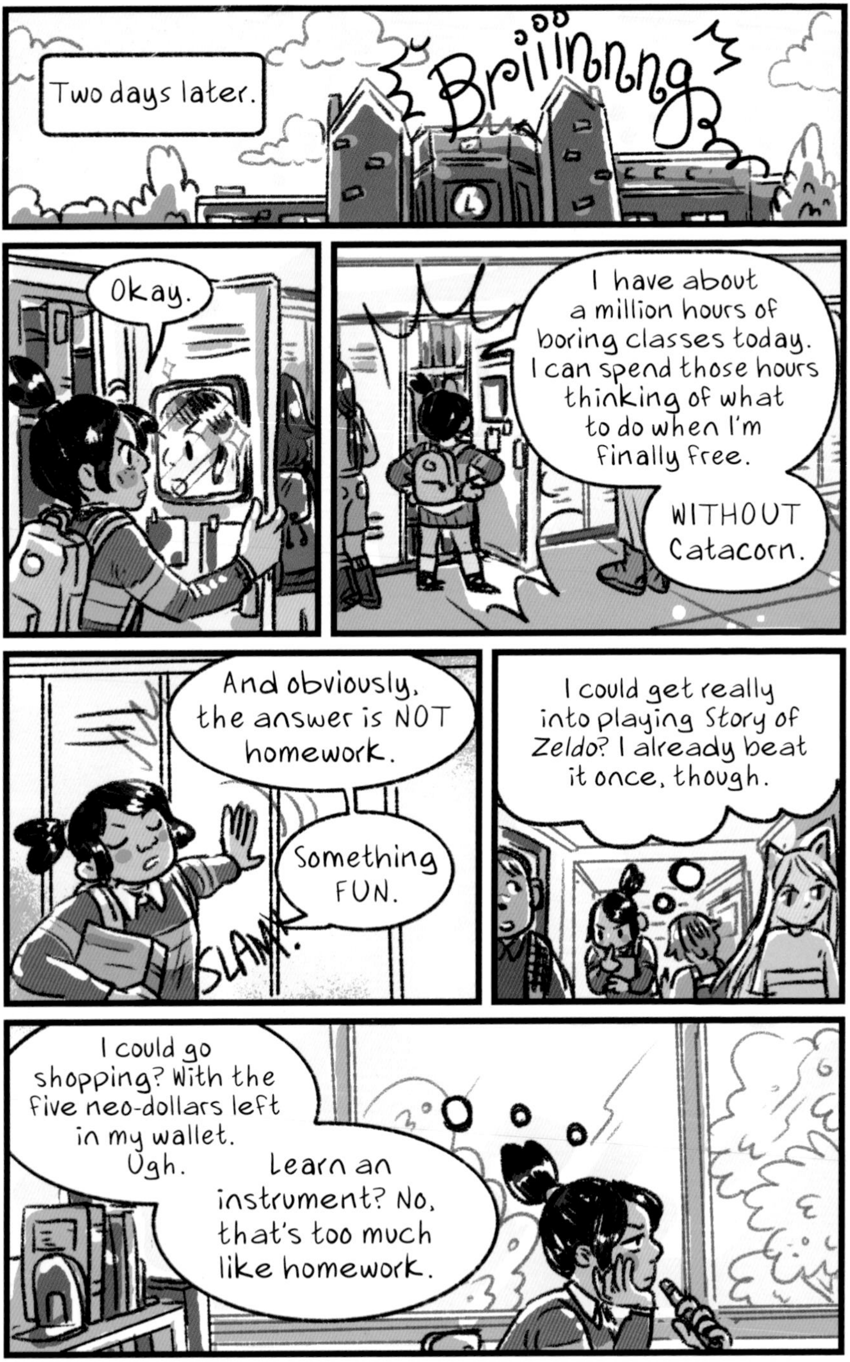

Two days later.
Briiinnng
Okay.
I have about a million hours of boring classes today. I can spend those hours thinking of what to do when I'm finally free.
WITHOUT Catacorn.
And obviously, the answer is NOT homework.
Something FUN.
SLAM!
I could get really into playing Story of Zeldo? I already beat it once, though.
I could go shopping? With the five neo-dollars left in my wallet. Ugh.
Learn an instrument? No, that's too much like homework.

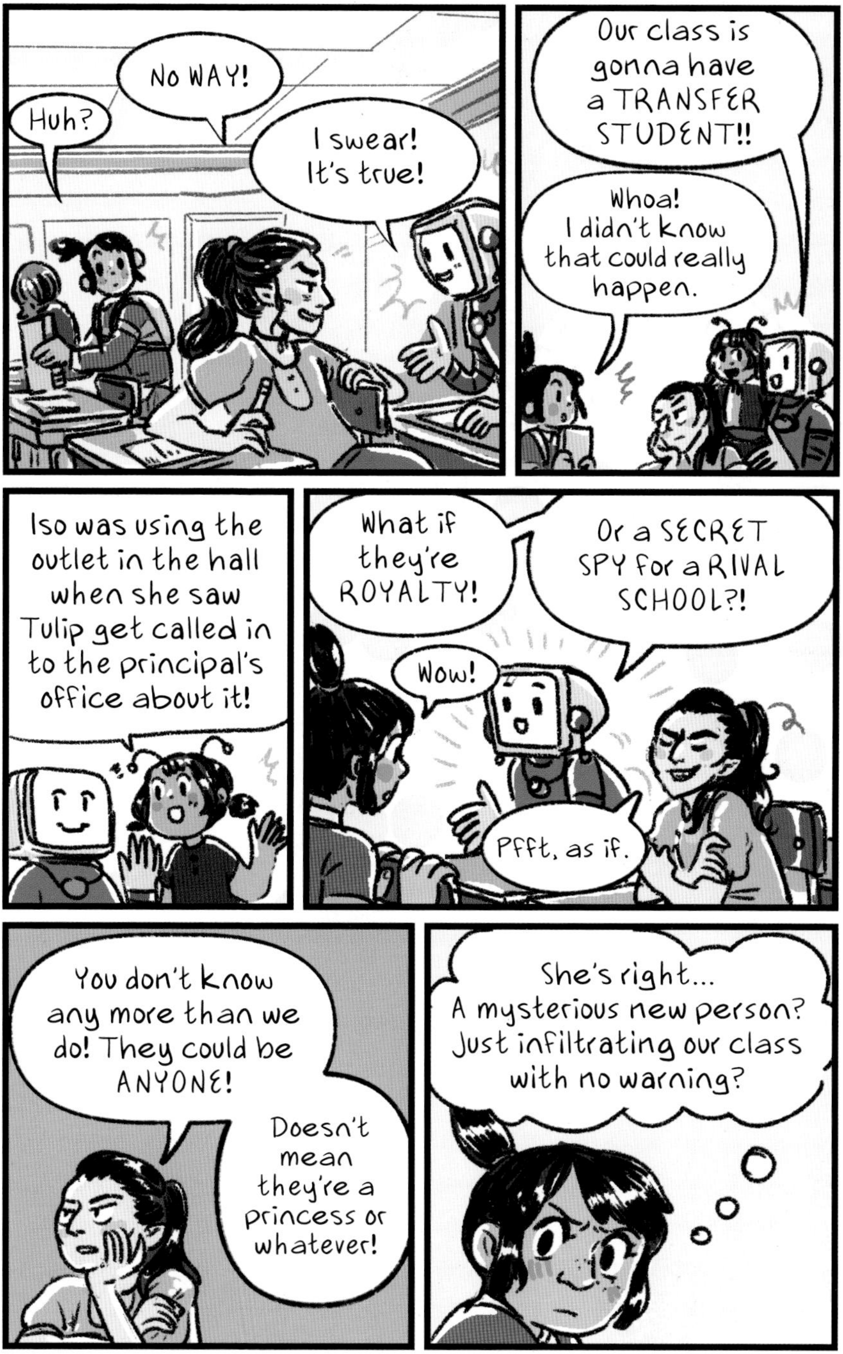

Huh?
No WAY!
I swear! It's true!
Our class is gonna have a TRANSFER STUDENT!!
Whoa! I didn't know that could really happen.
Iso was using the outlet in the hall when she saw Tulip get called in to the principal's office about it!
What if they're ROYALTY!
Or a SECRET SPY for a RIVAL SCHOOL?!
Wow!
Pfft, as if.
You don't know any more than we do! They could be ANYONE!
Doesn't mean they're a princess or whatever!
She's right... A mysterious new person? Just infiltrating our class with no warning?

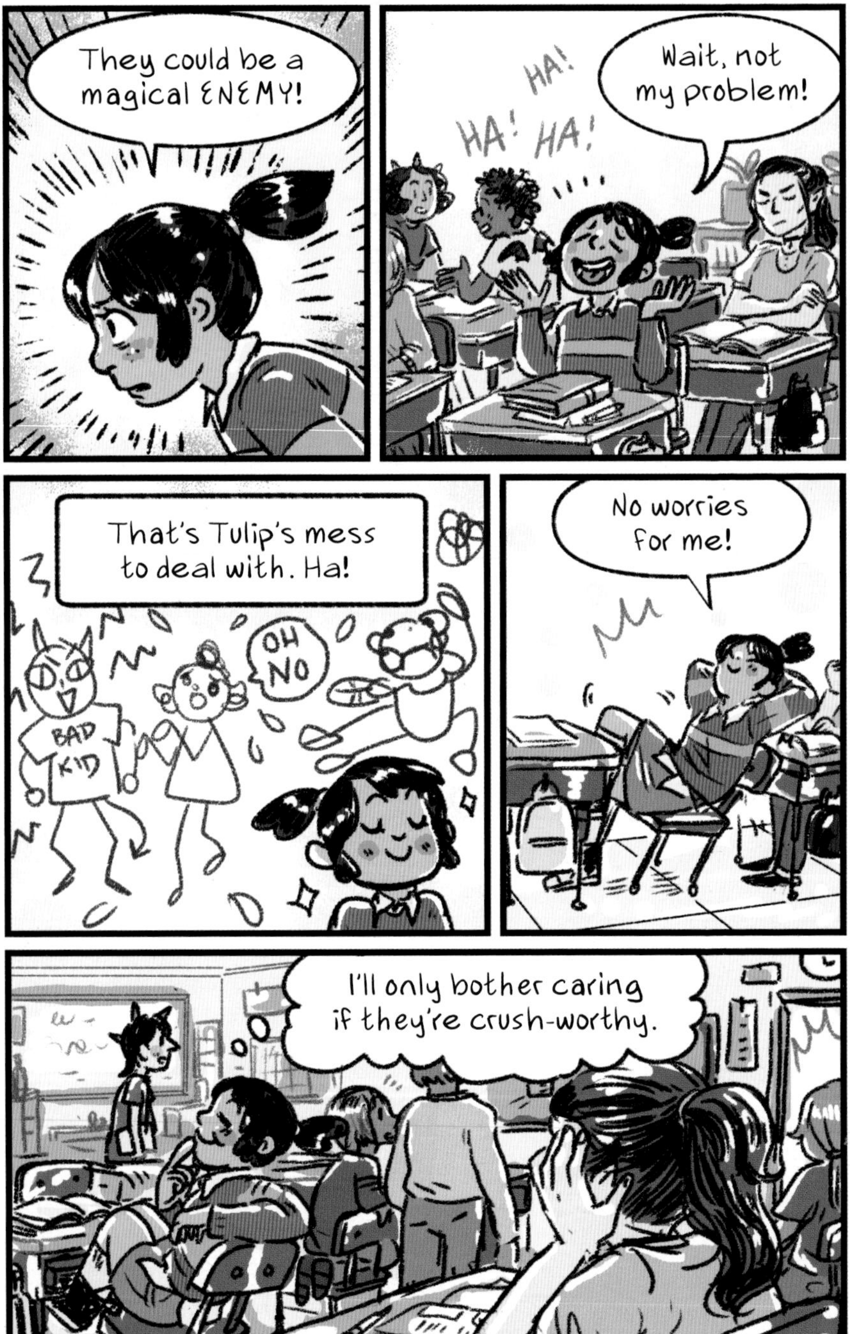
They could be a magical ENEMY!
HA! HA! HA!
Wait, not my problem!
That's Tulip's mess to deal with. Ha!
BAD KID
OH NO
No worries for me!
I'll only bother caring if they're crush-worthy.

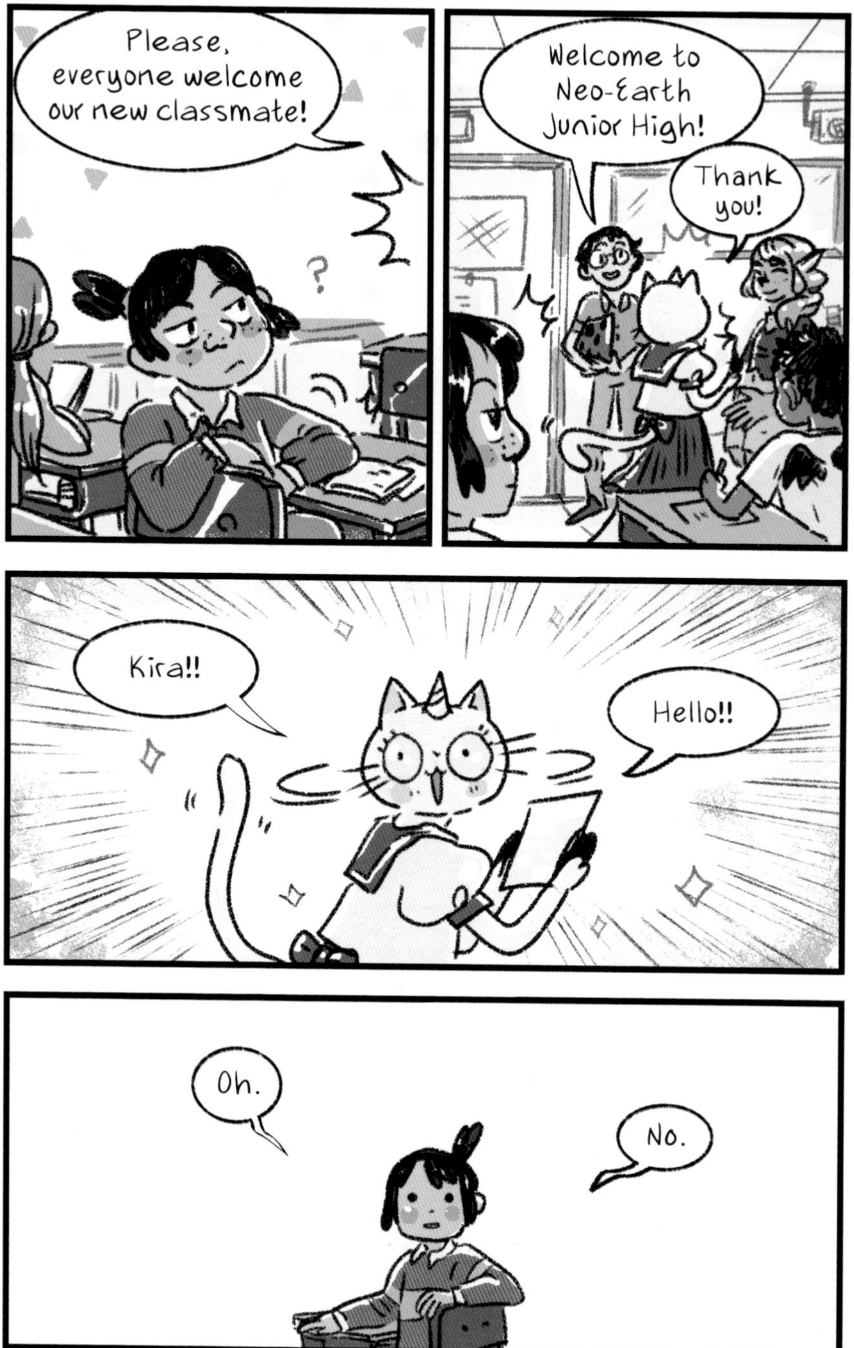
Please, everyone welcome our new classmate!
Welcome to Neo-Earth Junior High!
Thank you!
Kira!!
Hello!!
Oh.
No.

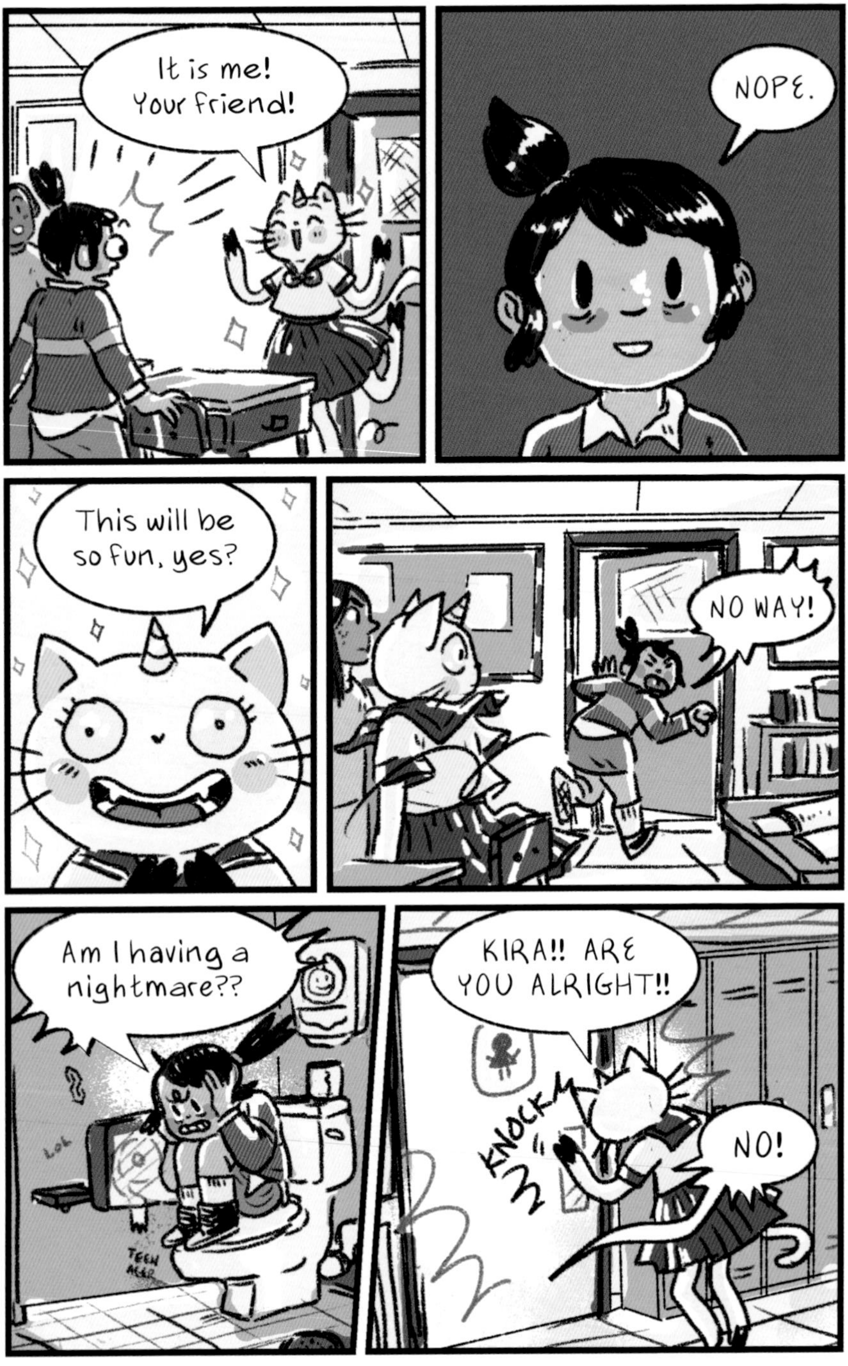
It is me! Your friend!
NOPE.
This will be so fun, yes?
NO WAY!
Am I having a nightmare??
KIRA!! ARE YOU ALRIGHT!!
KNOCK
NO!

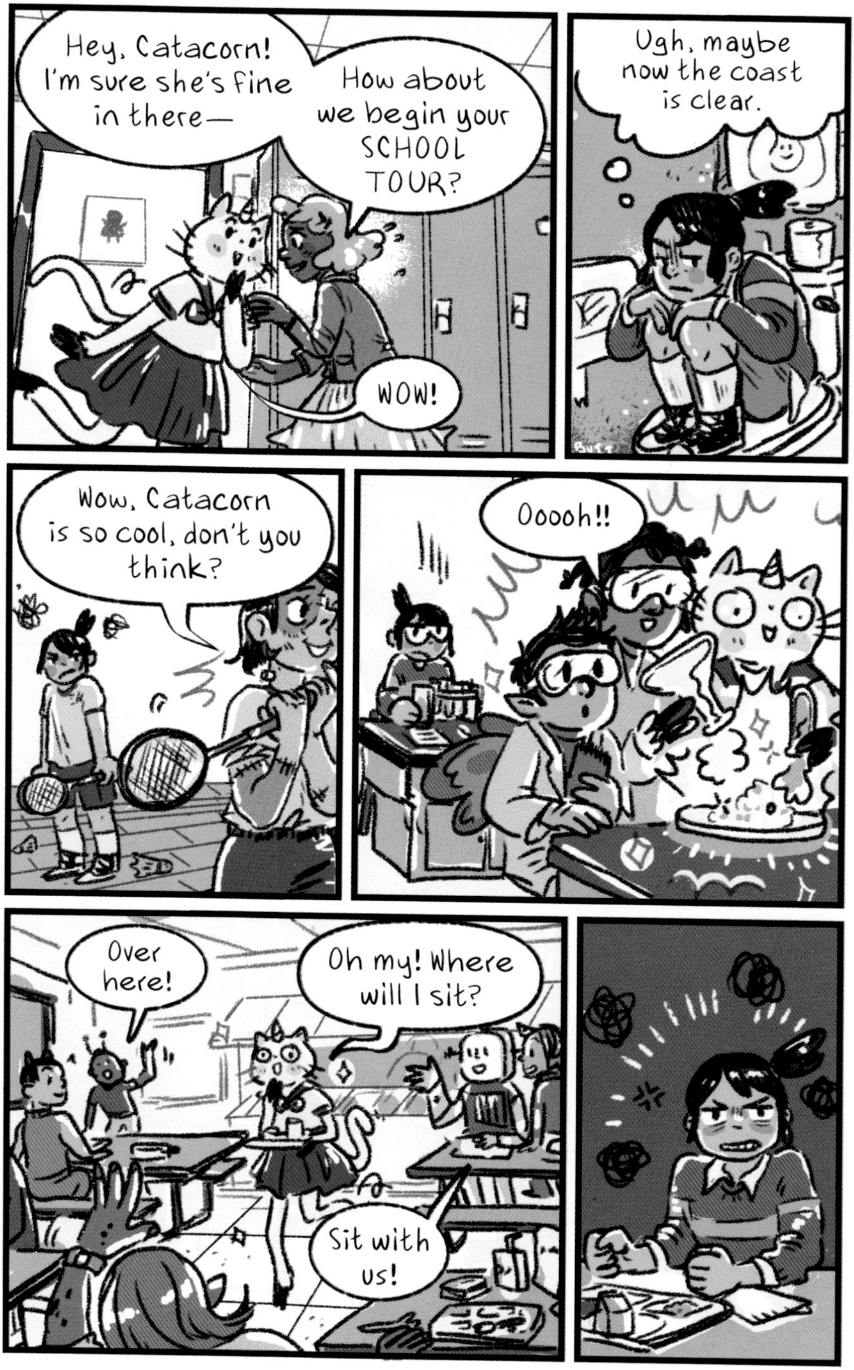
Hey, Catacorn! I'm sure she's fine in there—
How about we begin your SCHOOL TOUR?
WOW!
Ugh, maybe now the coast is clear.
Wow, Catacorn is so cool, don't you think?
Ooooh!!
Over here!
Oh my! Where will I sit?
Sit with us!

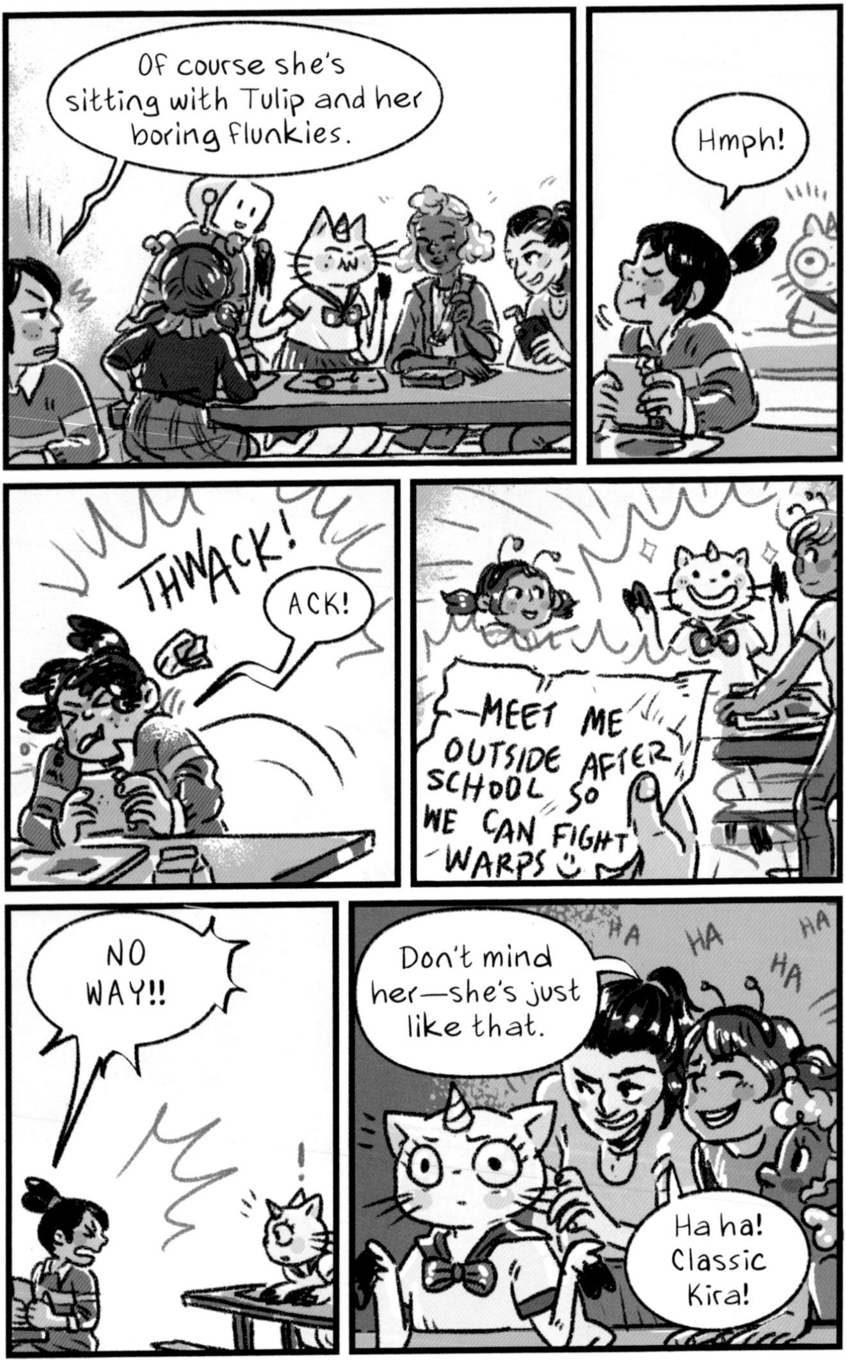
Of course she's sitting with Tulip and her boring flunkies.
Hmph!
THWACK!
ACK!
MEET ME OUTSIDE AFTER SCHOOL SO WE CAN FIGHT WARPS ☺
NO WAY!!
HA HA HA HA
Don't mind her—she's just like that.
Ha ha! Classic Kira!

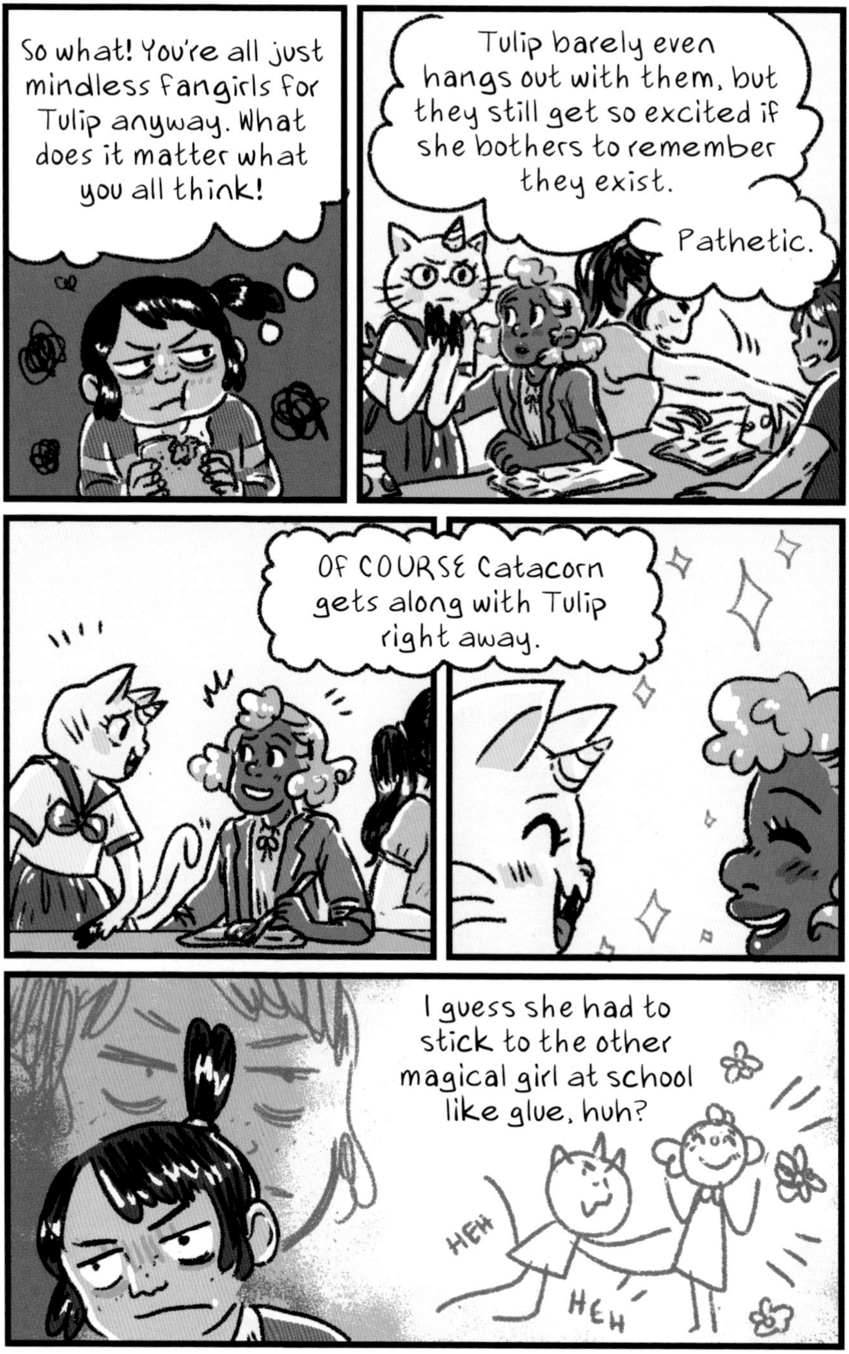
So what! You're all just mindless fangirls for Tulip anyway. What does it matter what you all think!
Tulip barely even hangs out with them, but they still get so excited if she bothers to remember they exist.
Pathetic.
OF COURSE Catacorn gets along with Tulip right away.
I guess she had to stick to the other magical girl at school like glue, huh?
HEH
HEH

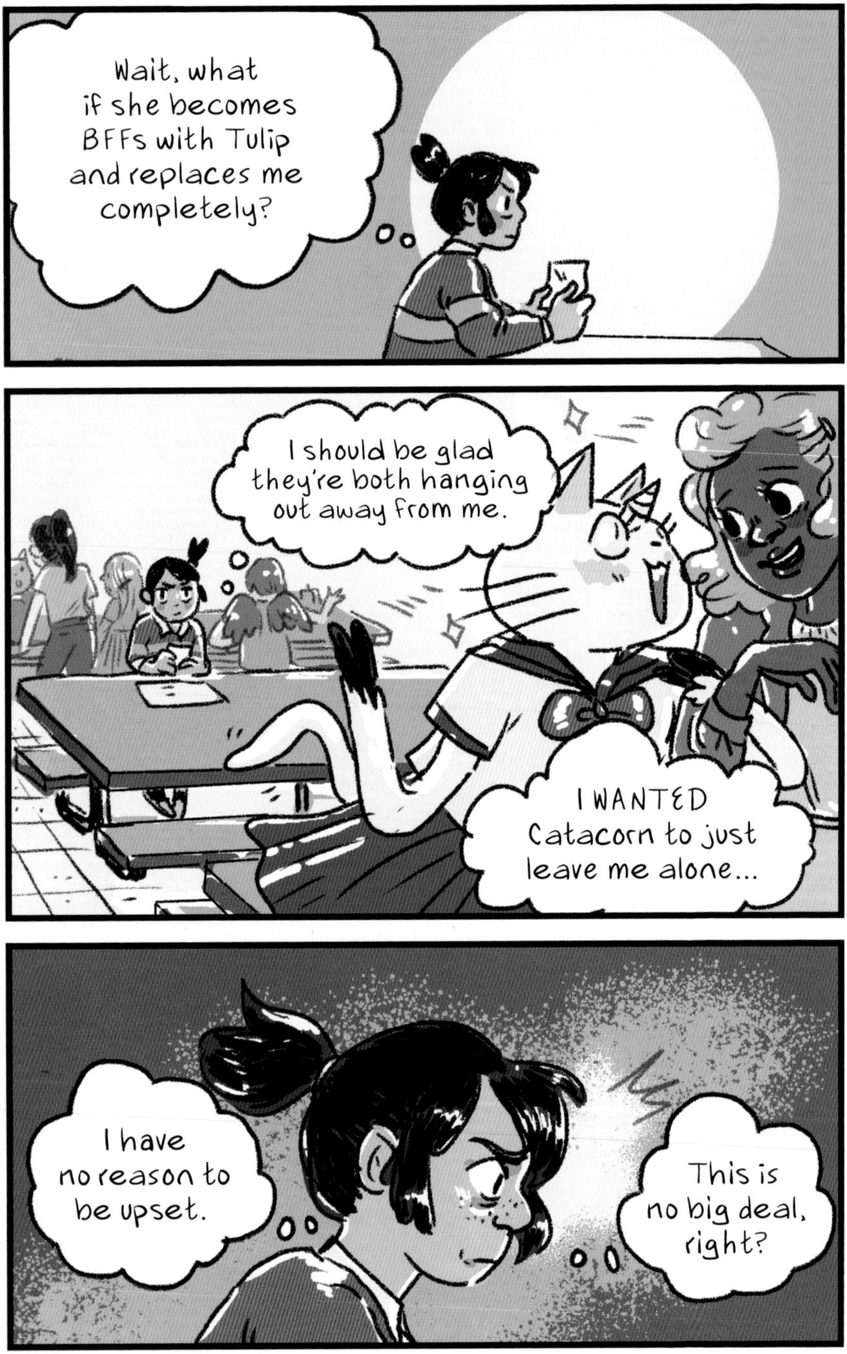
Wait, what if she becomes BFFs with Tulip and replaces me completely?
I should be glad they're both hanging out away from me.
I WANTED Catacorn to just leave me alone...
I have no reason to be upset.
This is no big deal, right?

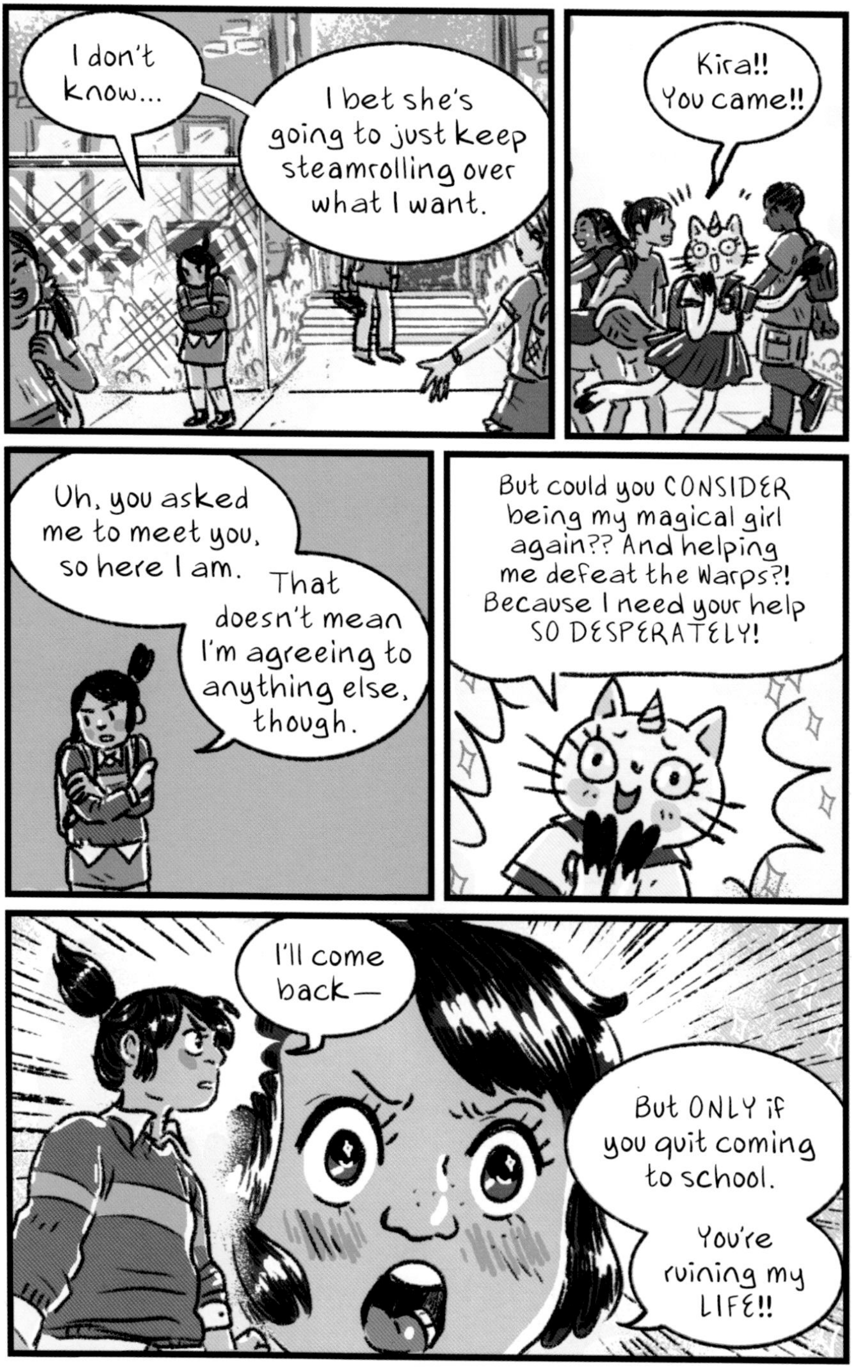
I don't know...
I bet she's going to just keep steamrolling over what I want.
Kira!! You came!!
Uh, you asked me to meet you, so here I am.
That doesn't mean I'm agreeing to anything else, though.
But could you CONSIDER being my magical girl again?? And helping me defeat the Warps?! Because I need your help SO DESPERATELY!
I'll come back—
But ONLY if you quit coming to school.
You're ruining my LIFE!!

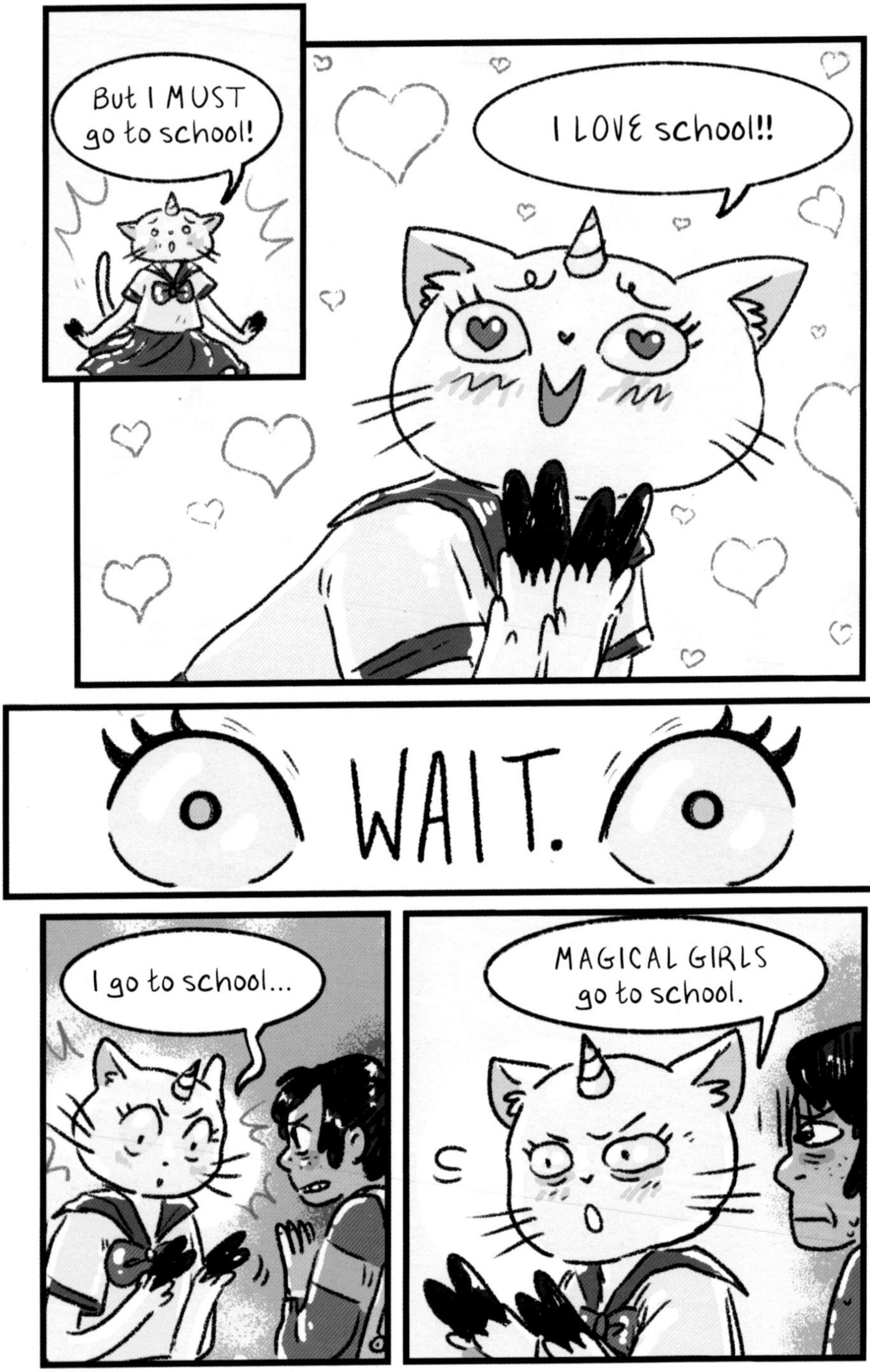
But I MUST go to school!
I LOVE school!!
WAIT.
I go to school...
MAGICAL GIRLS go to school.

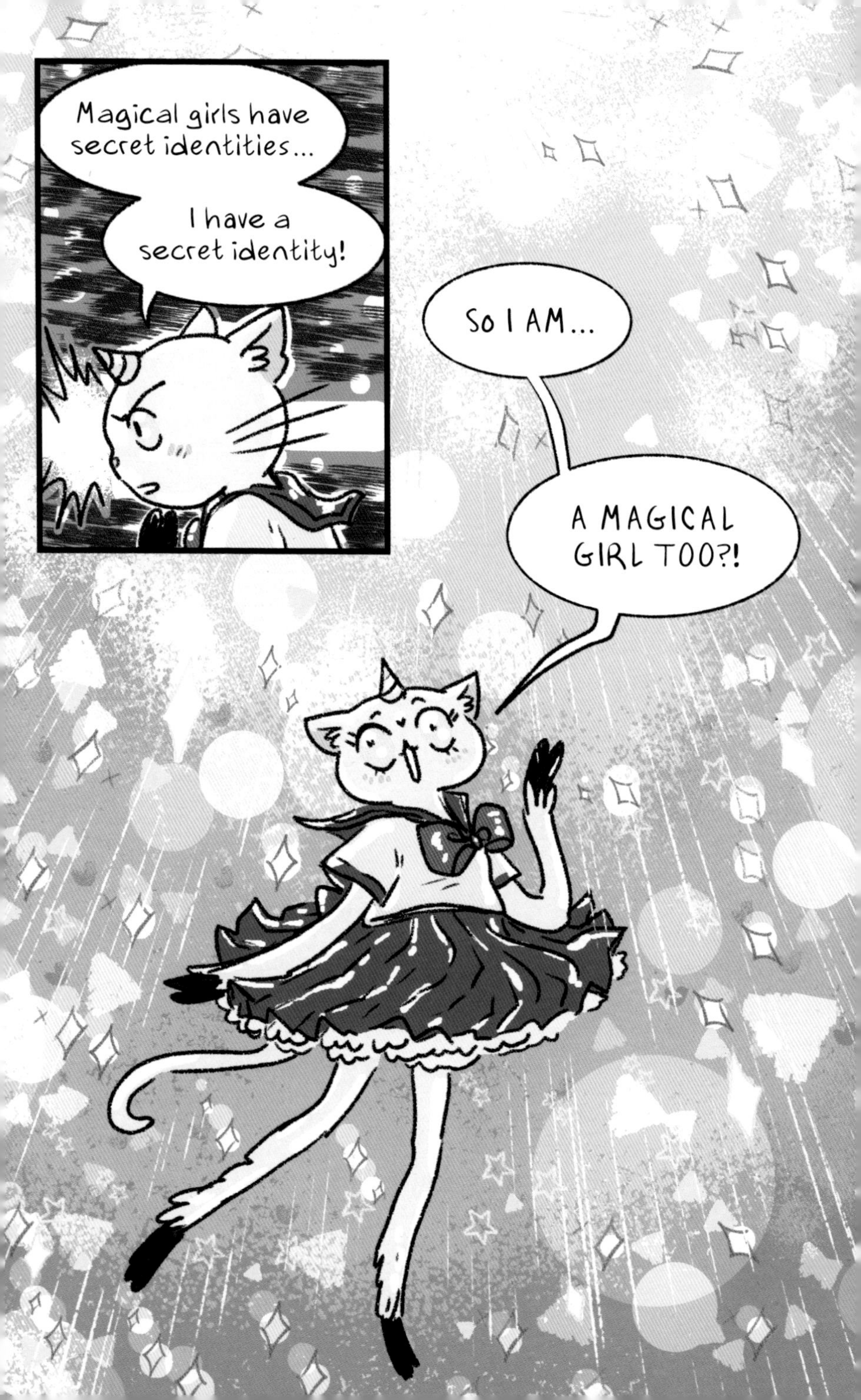
Magical girls have secret identities...
I have a secret identity!
So I AM...
A MAGICAL GIRL TOO?!

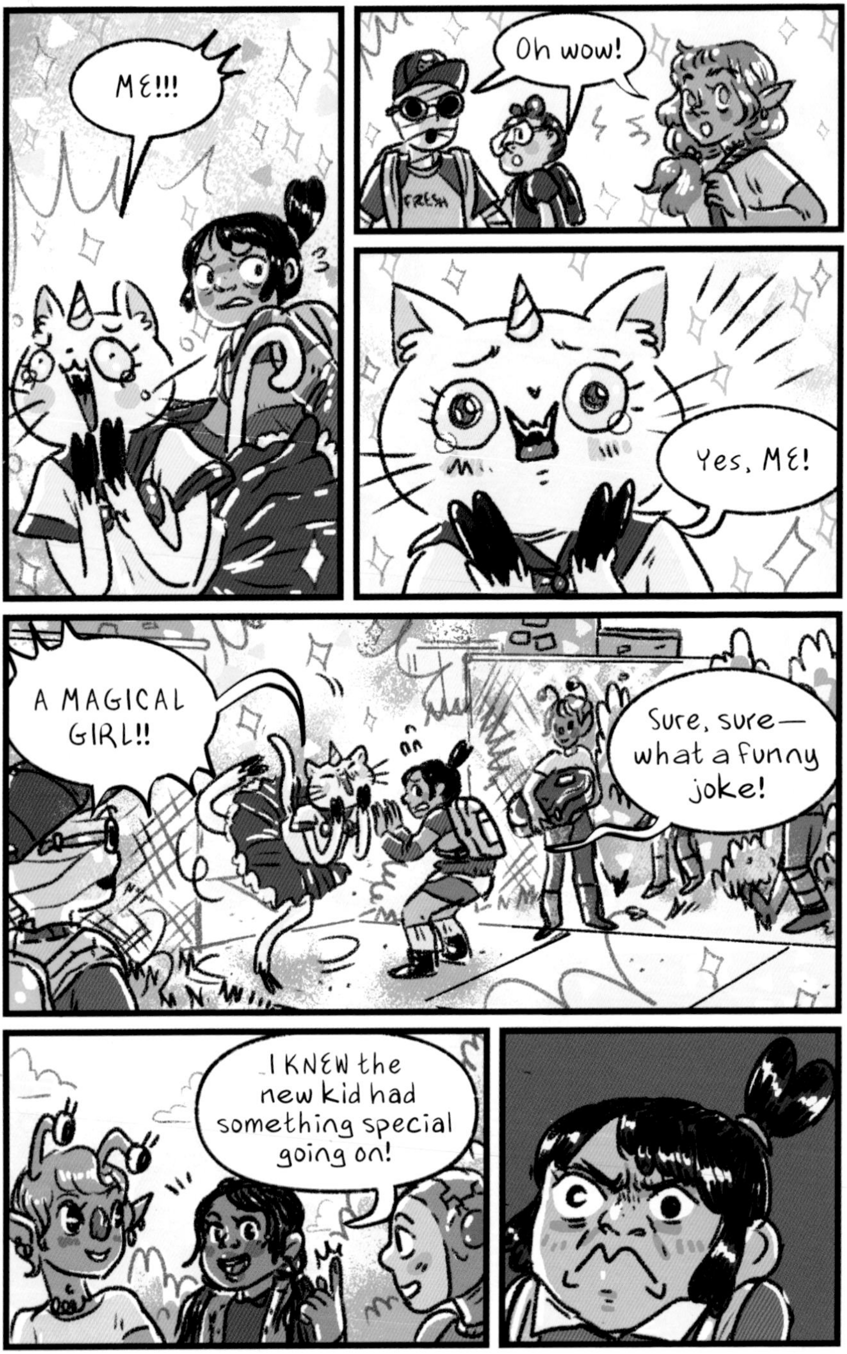
ME!!!
Oh wow!
Yes, ME!
A MAGICAL GIRL!!
Sure, sure—what a funny joke!
I KNEW the new kid had something special going on!

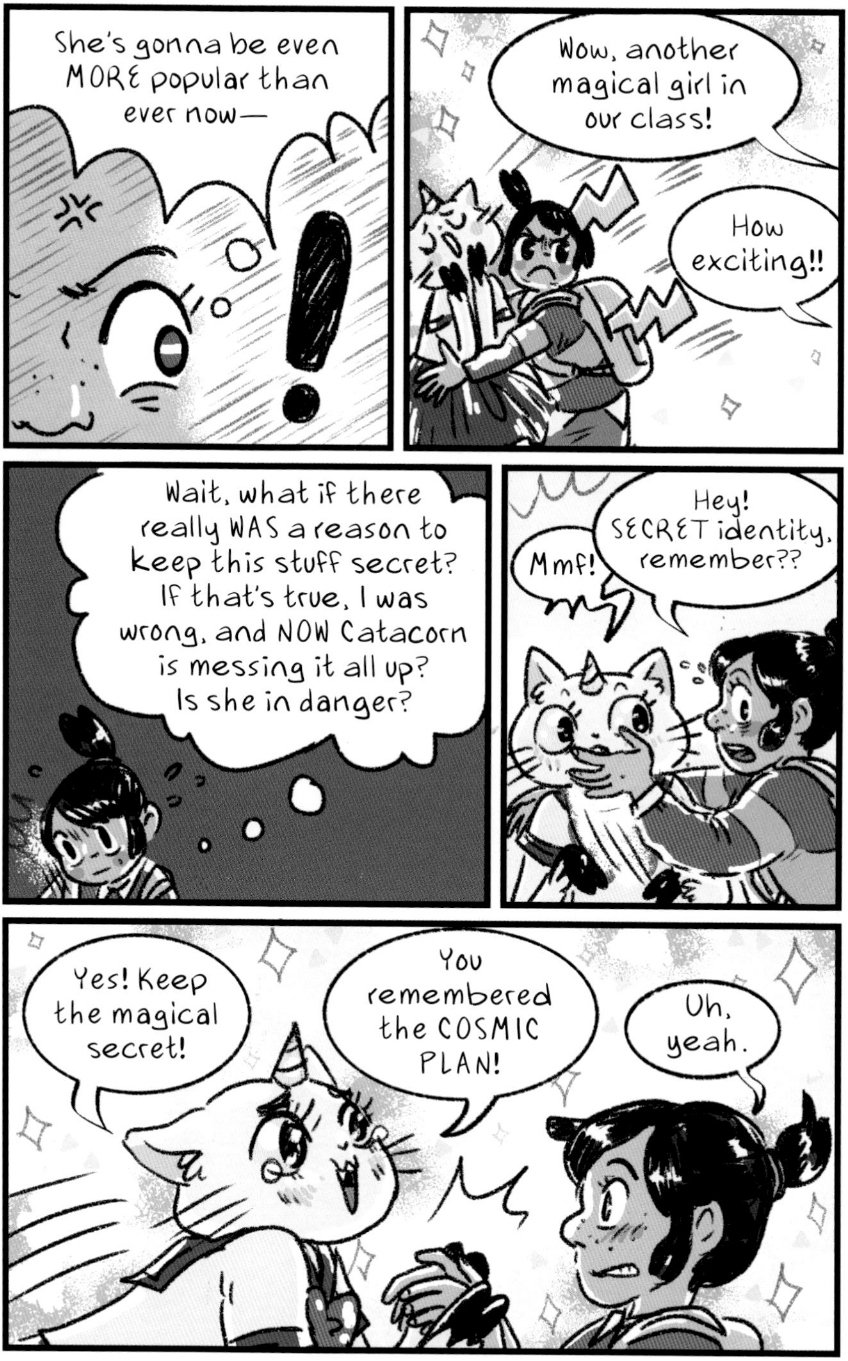
She's gonna be even MORE popular than ever now—
Wow, another magical girl in our class!
How exciting!!
Wait, what if there really WAS a reason to keep this stuff secret? If that's true, I was wrong, and NOW Catacorn is messing it all up? Is she in danger?
Mmf!
Hey! SECRET identity, remember??
Yes! Keep the magical secret!
You remembered the COSMIC PLAN!
Uh, yeah.

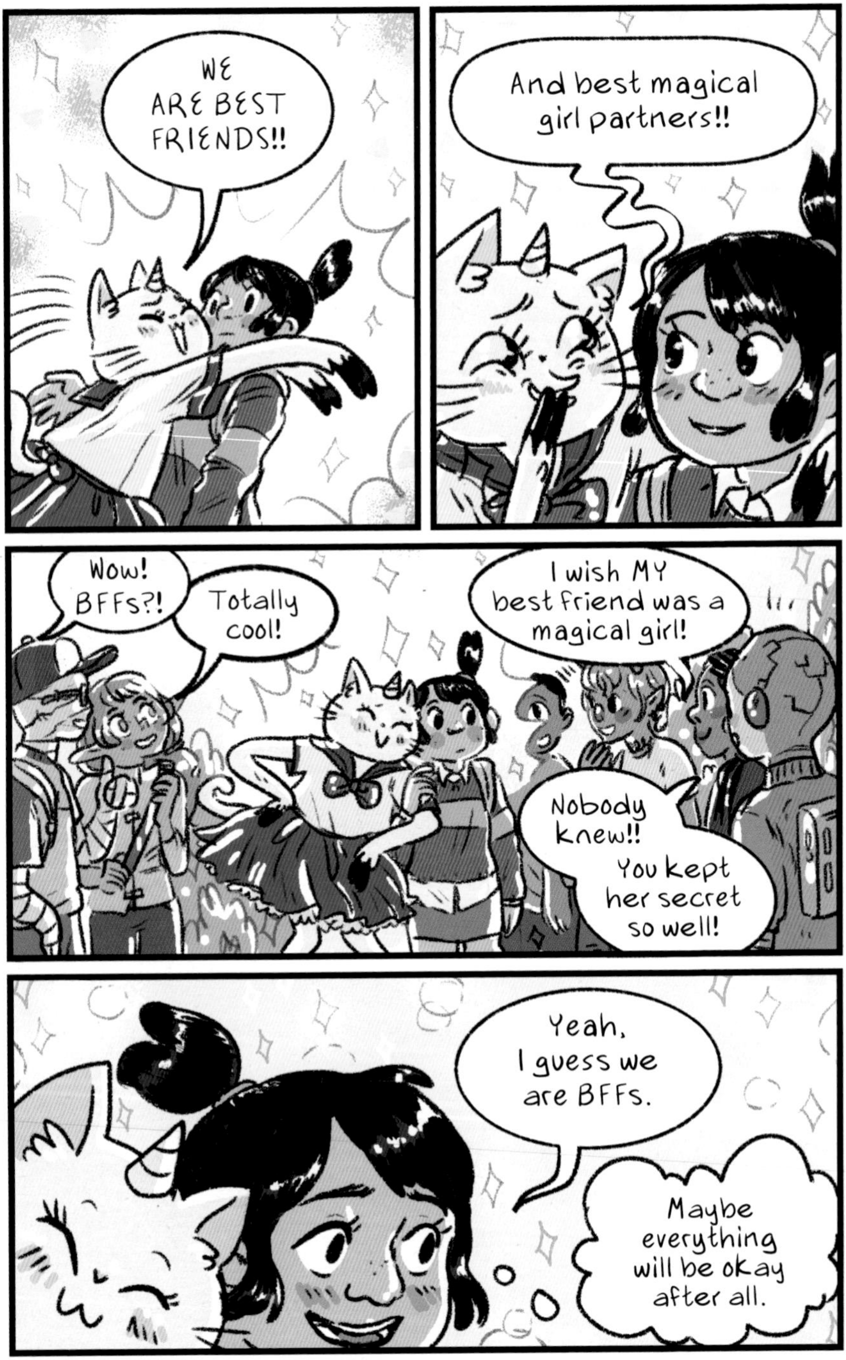
WE ARE BEST FRIENDS!!
And best magical girl partners!!
Wow! BFFs?!
Totally cool!
I wish MY best friend was a magical girl!
Nobody knew!!
You kept her secret so well!
Yeah, I guess we are BFFs.
Maybe everything will be okay after all.

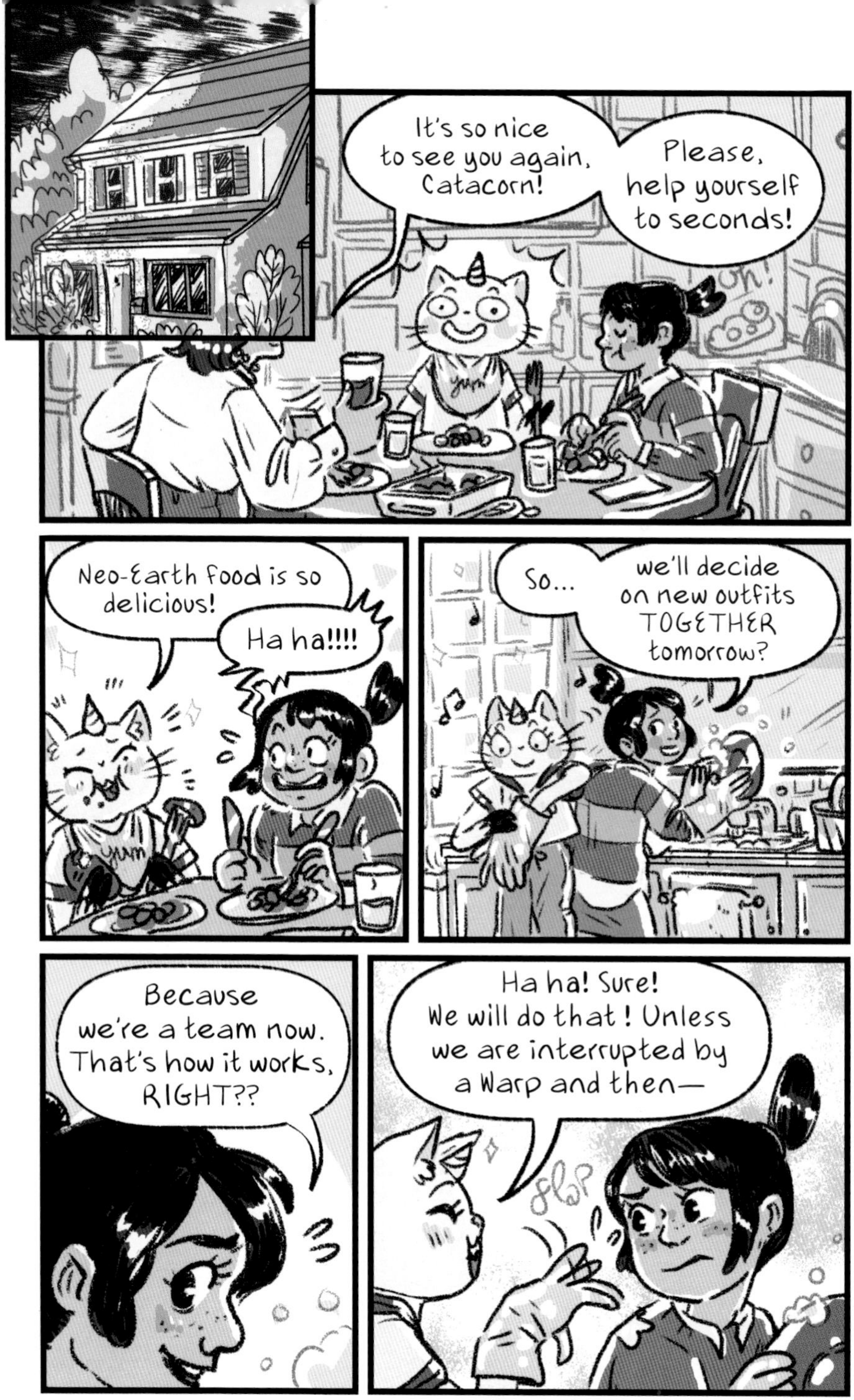
It's so nice to see you again, Catacorn!
Please, help yourself to seconds!
yum
Neo-Earth food is so delicious!
Ha ha!!!!
yum
So...
we'll decide on new outfits TOGETHER tomorrow?
Because we're a team now. That's how it works, RIGHT??
Ha ha! Sure! We will do that! Unless we are interrupted by a Warp and then—
flap

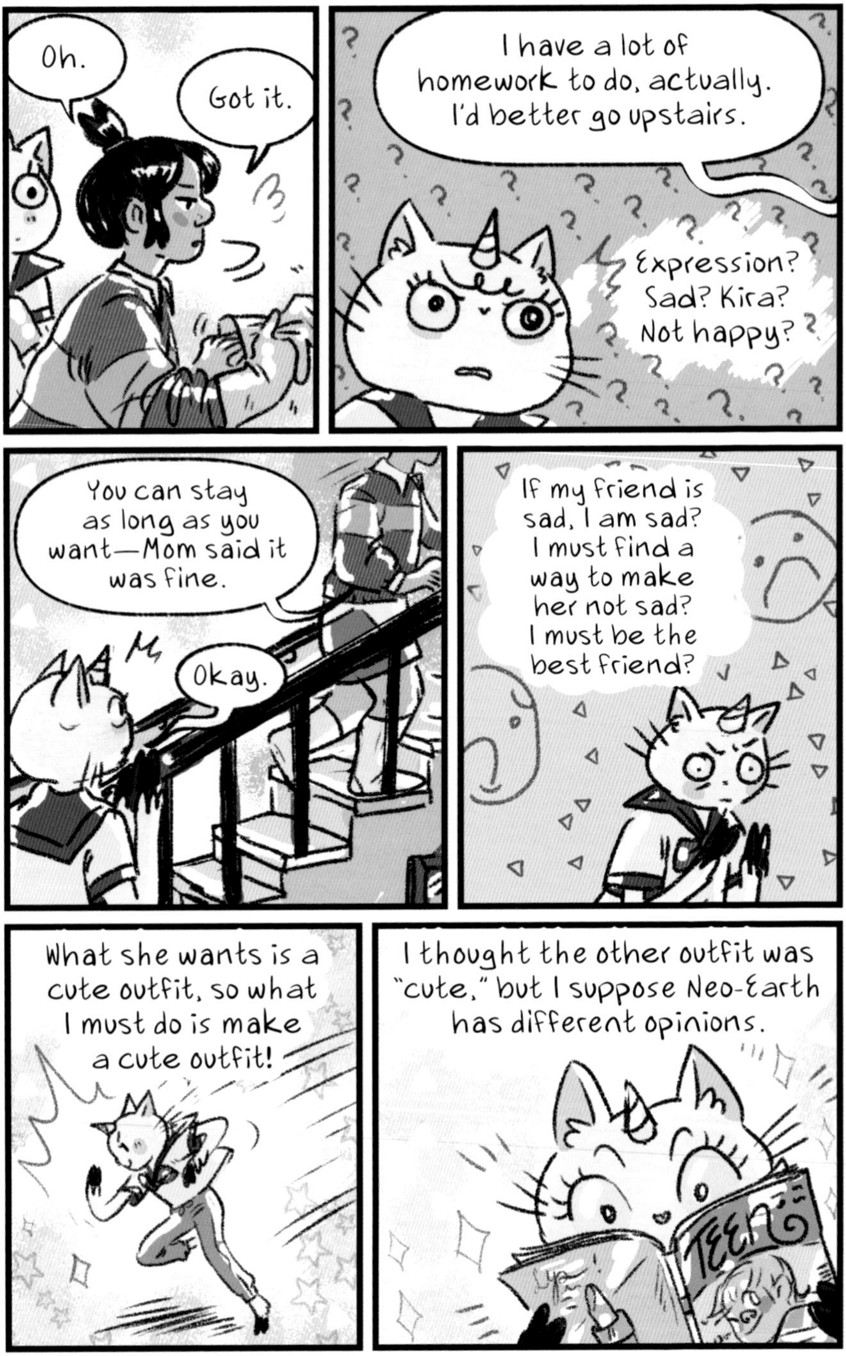
Oh.
Got it.
I have a lot of homework to do, actually. I'd better go upstairs.
Expression? Sad? Kira? Not happy?
You can stay as long as you want—Mom said it was fine.
Okay.
If my friend is sad, I am sad? I must find a way to make her not sad? I must be the best friend?
What she wants is a cute outfit, so what I must do is make a cute outfit!
I thought the other outfit was "cute," but I suppose Neo-Earth has different opinions.
TEEN

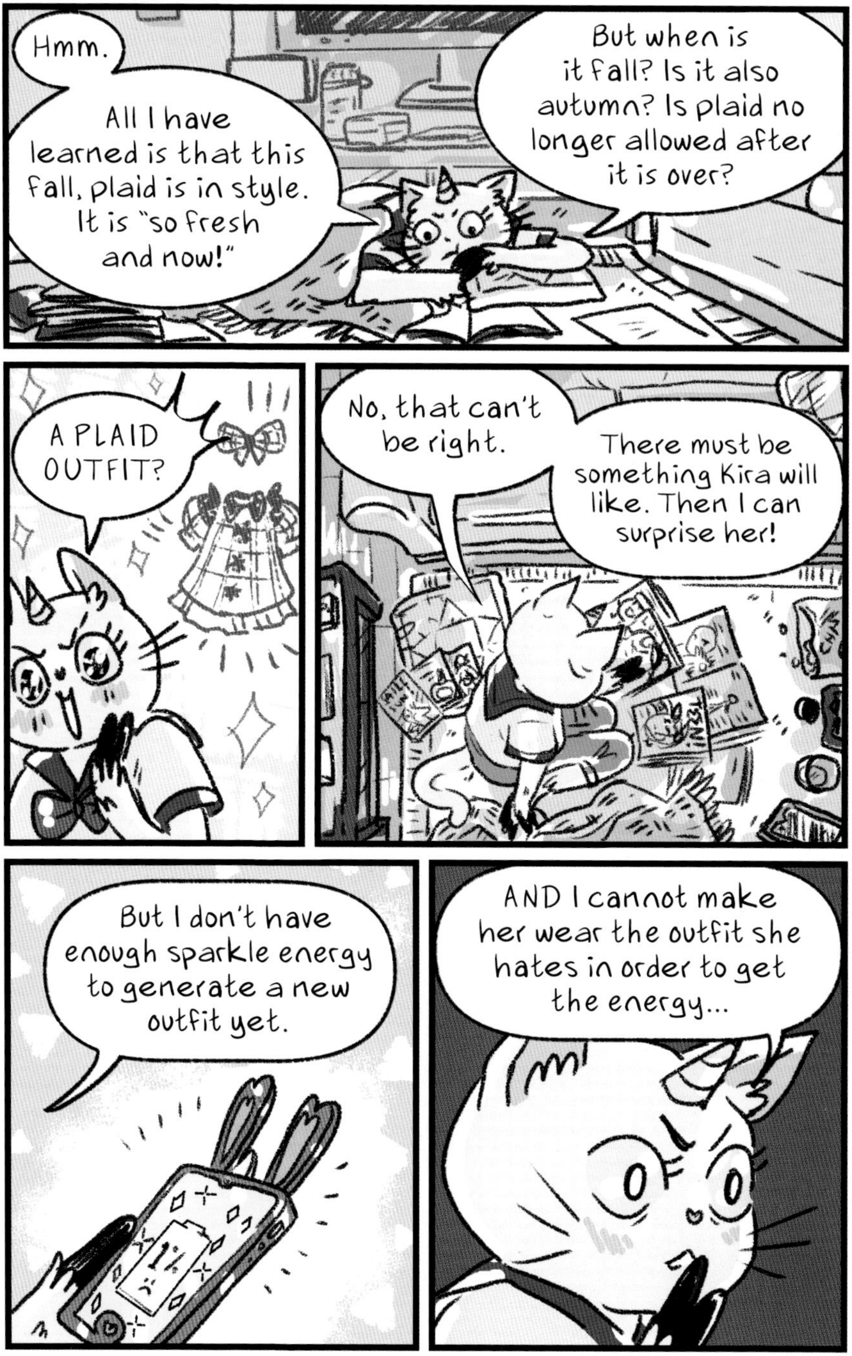
Hmm.
All I have learned is that this fall, plaid is in style. It is "so fresh and now!"
But when is it fall? Is it also autumn? Is plaid no longer allowed after it is over?
A PLAID OUTFIT?
No, that can't be right.
There must be something Kira will like. Then I can surprise her!
But I don't have enough sparkle energy to generate a new outfit yet.
1%
AND I cannot make her wear the outfit she hates in order to get the energy...

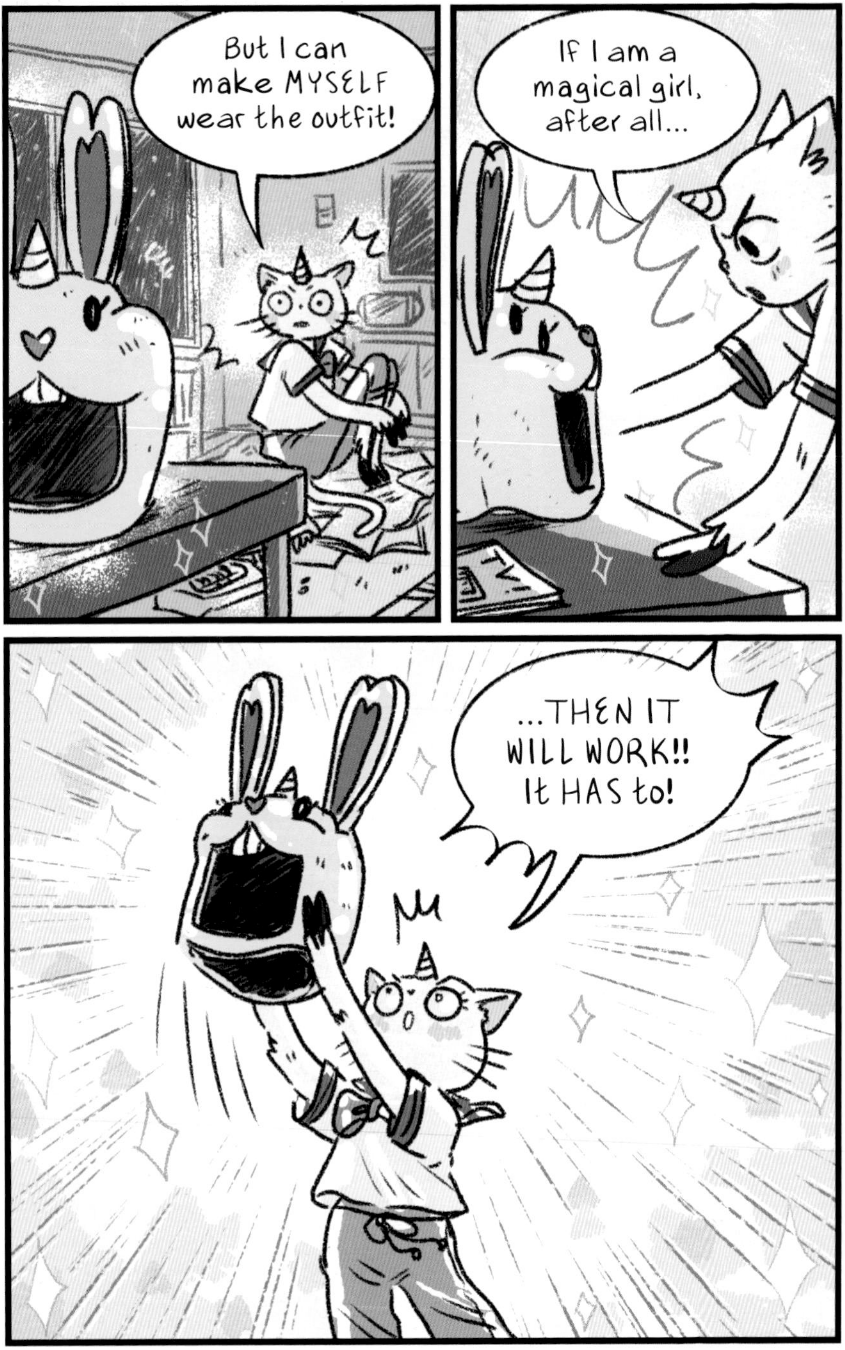
But I can make MYSELF wear the outfit!
If I am a magical girl, after all...
...THEN IT WILL WORK!! It HAS to!

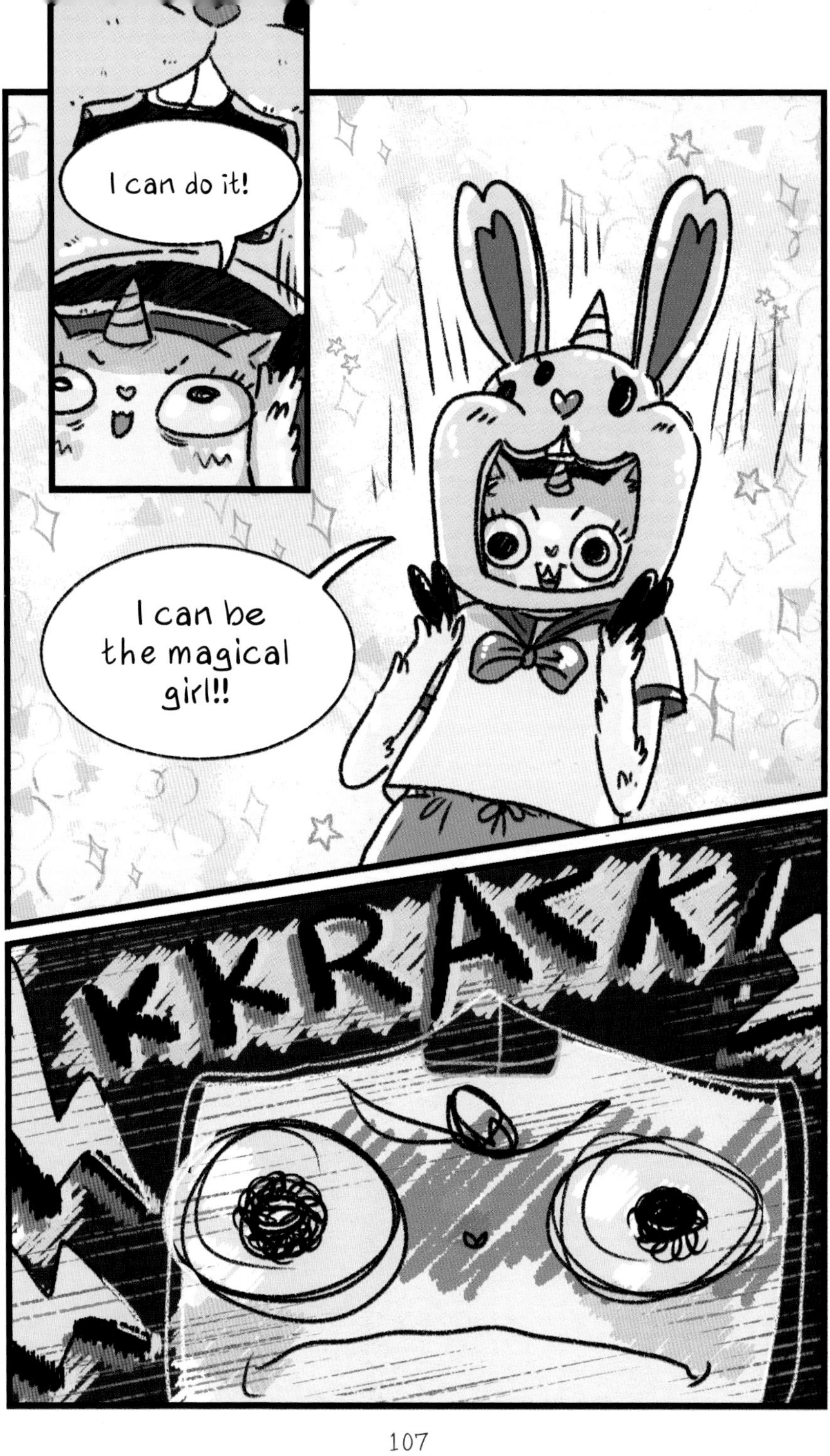
I can do it!
I can be the magical girl!!
KKRACK!

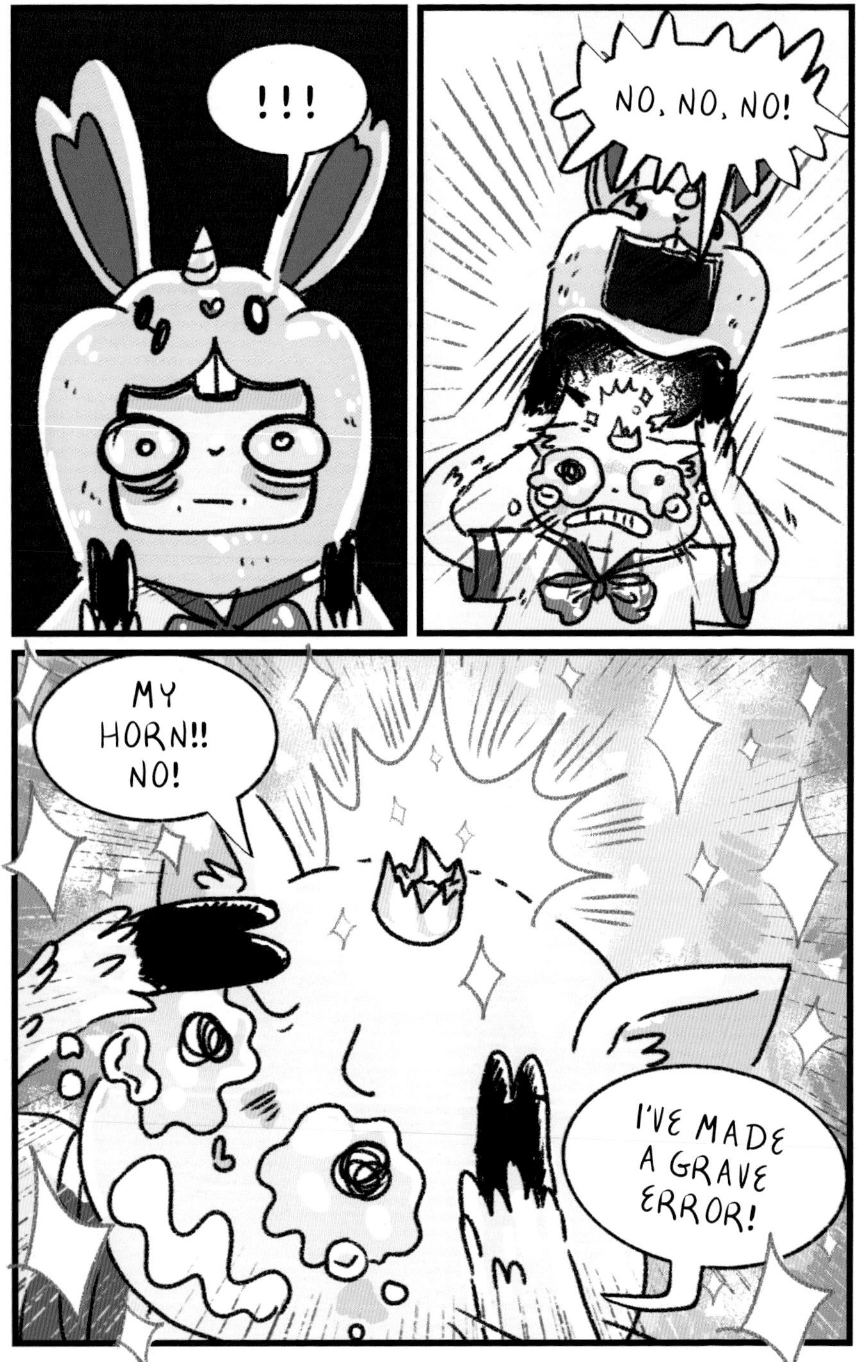
!!!
NO, NO, NO!
MY HORN!! NO!
I'VE MADE A GRAVE ERROR!

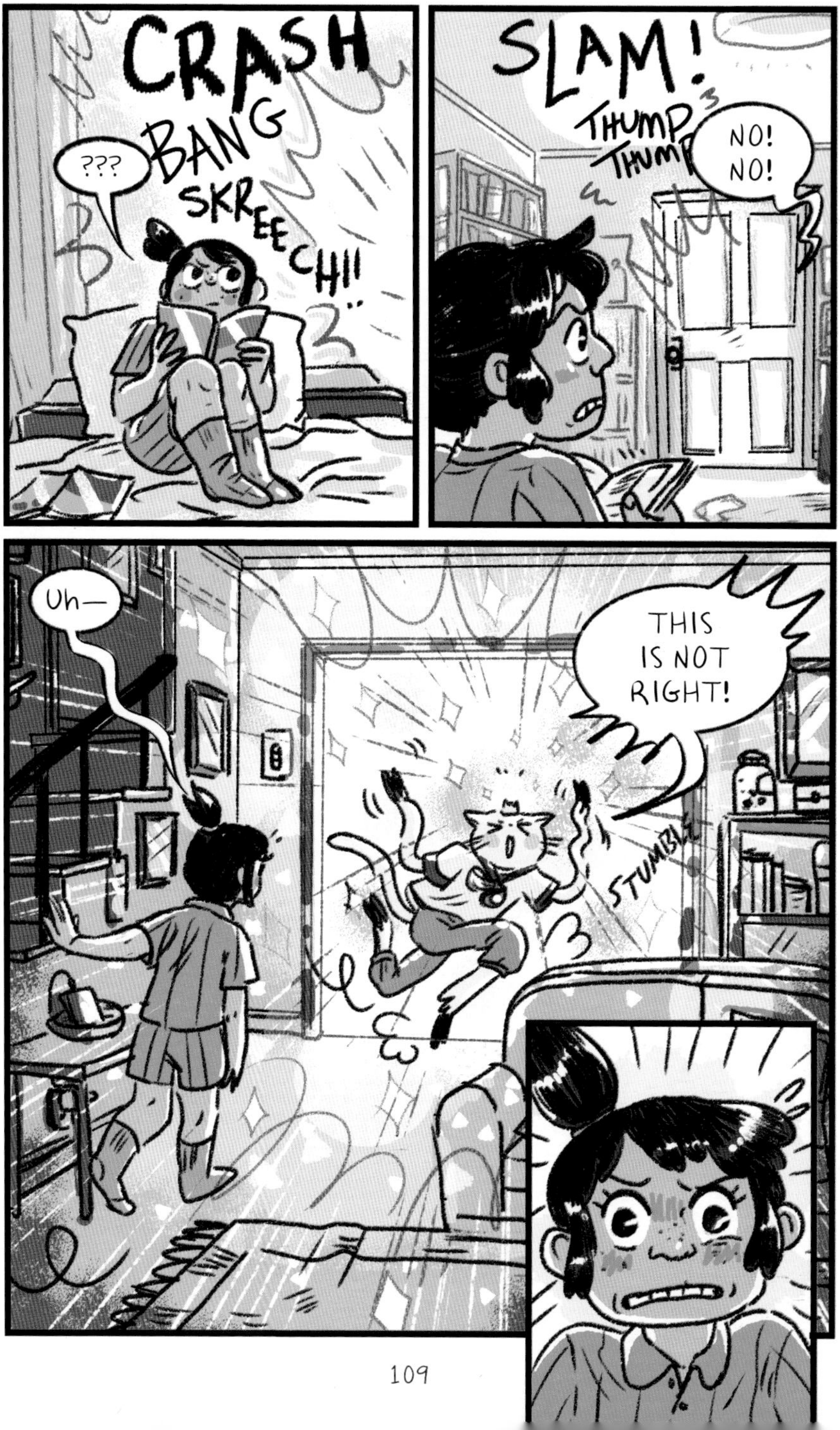
CRASH
BANG
SKREECH!!
???
SLAM!
THUMP
THUMP
NO!
NO!
Uh—
THIS
IS NOT
RIGHT!

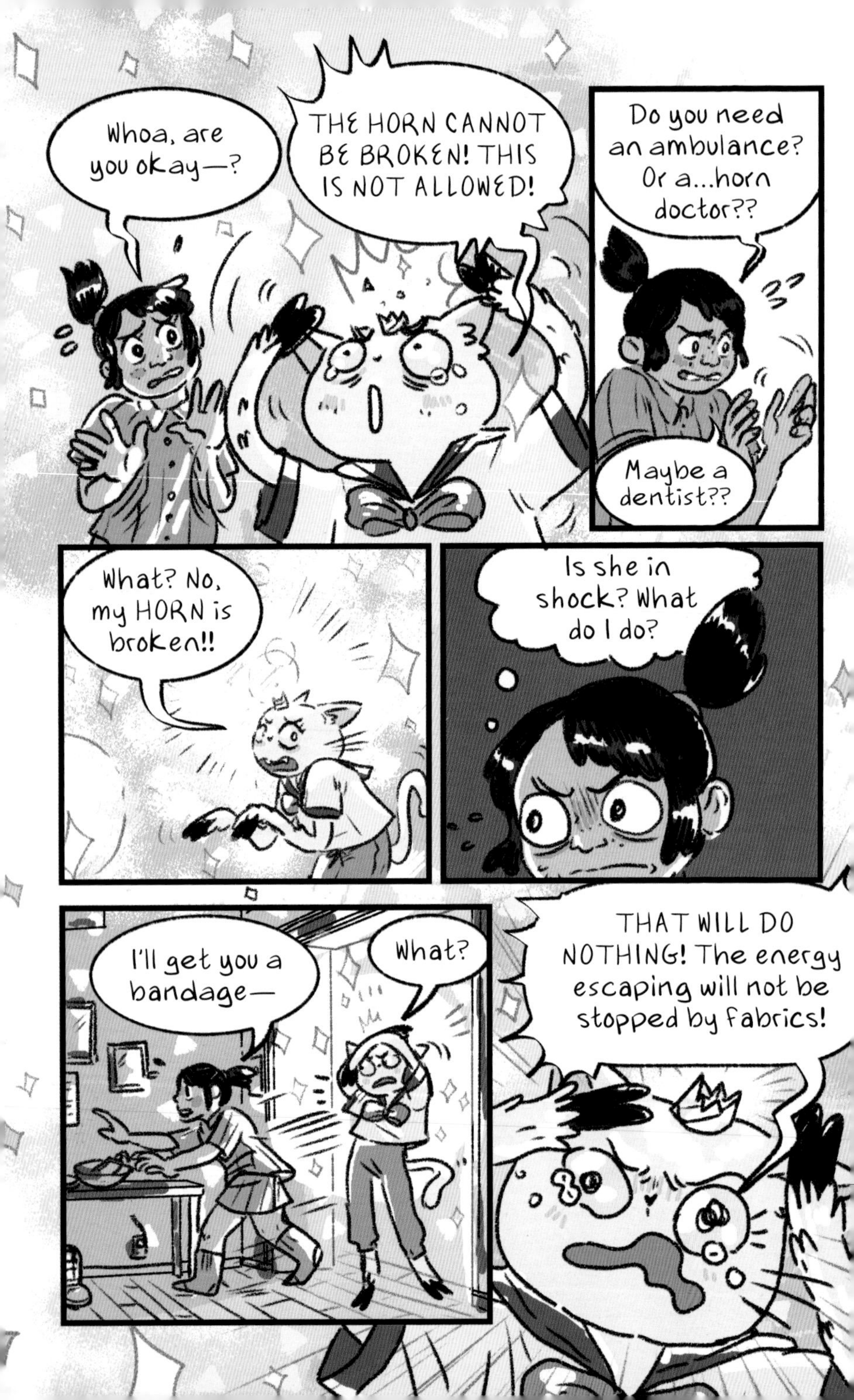
Whoa, are you okay—?
THE HORN CANNOT BE BROKEN! THIS IS NOT ALLOWED!
Do you need an ambulance? Or a...horn doctor??
Maybe a dentist??
What? No, my HORN is broken!!
Is she in shock? What do I do?
I'll get you a bandage—
What?
THAT WILL DO NOTHING! The energy escaping will not be stopped by fabrics!

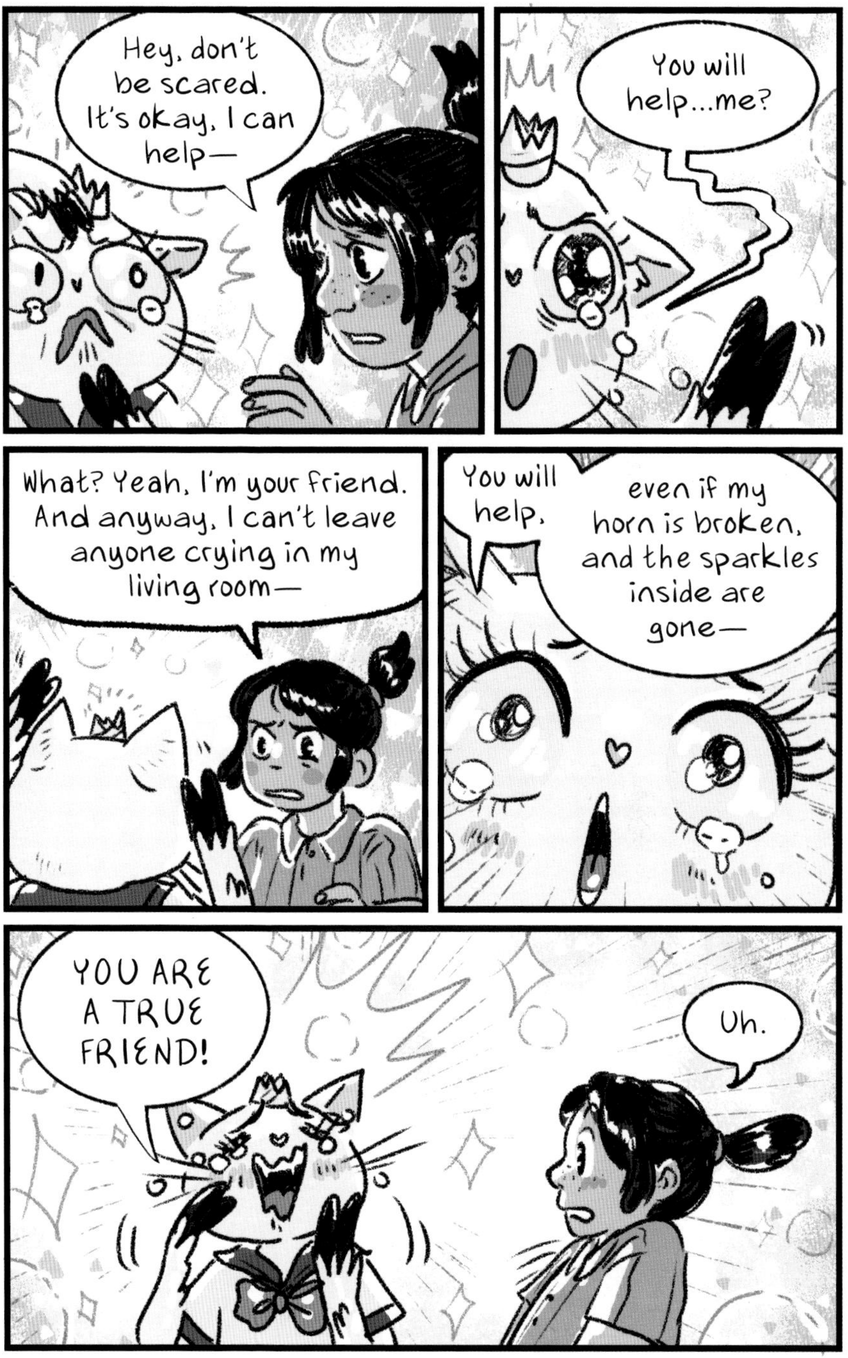
Hey, don't be scared. It's okay, I can help—
You will help...me?
What? Yeah, I'm your friend. And anyway, I can't leave anyone crying in my living room—
You will help,
even if my horn is broken, and the sparkles inside are gone—
YOU ARE A TRUE FRIEND!
Uh.

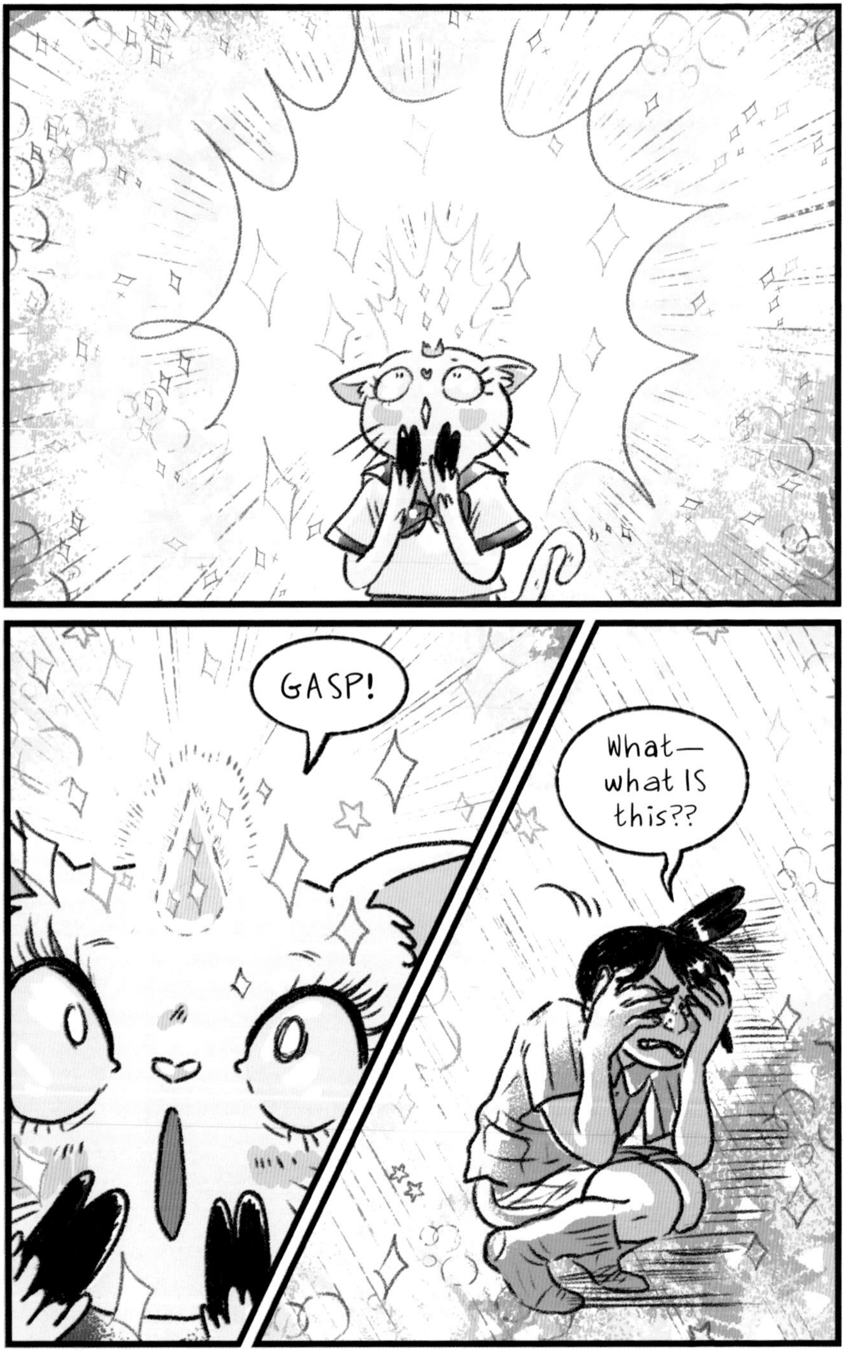
GASP!
What—what IS this??

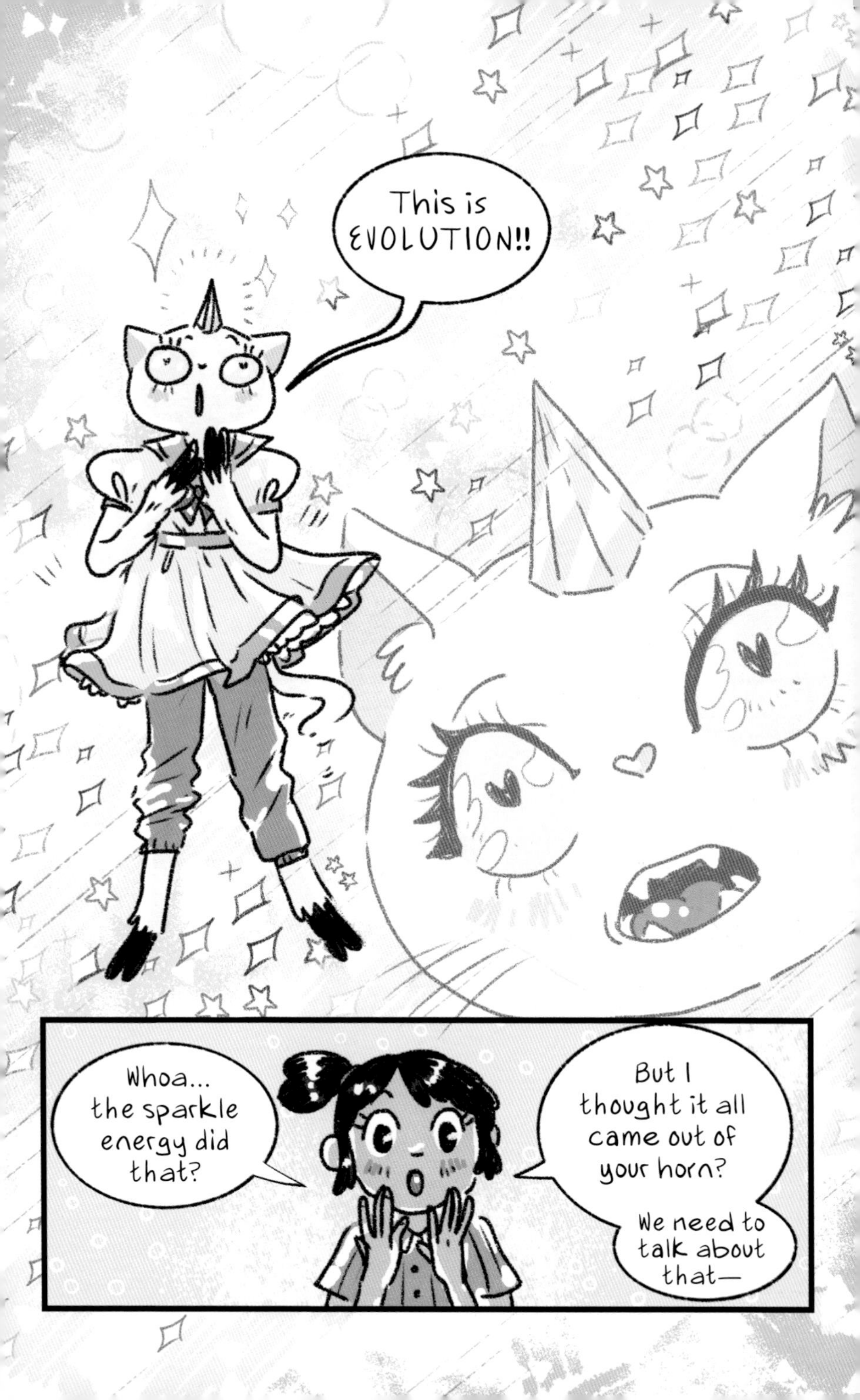
This is EVOLUTION!!
Whoa... the sparkle energy did that?
But I thought it all came out of your horn?
We need to talk about that—

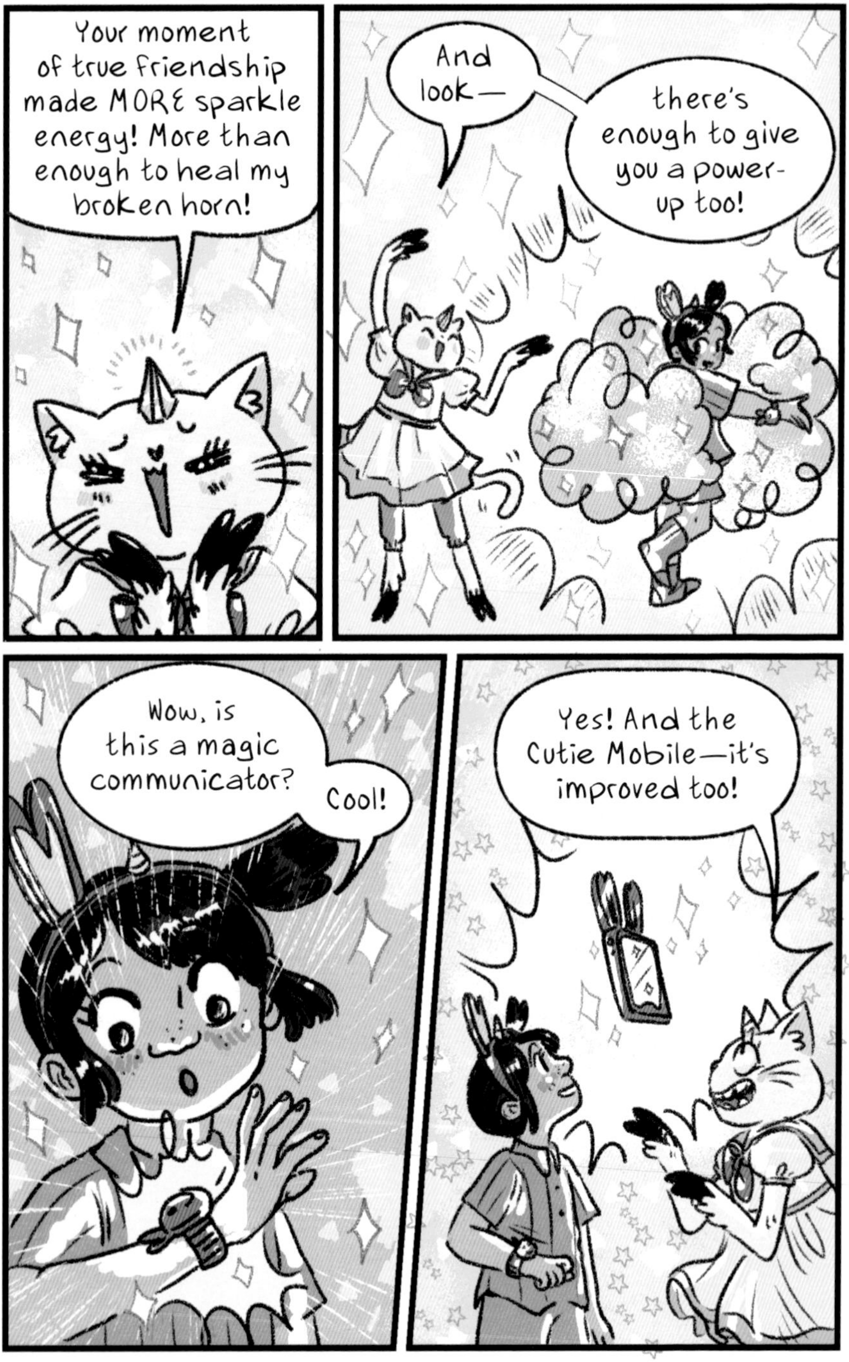
Your moment of true friendship made MORE sparkle energy! More than enough to heal my broken horn!
And look—
there's enough to give you a power-up too!
Wow, is this a magic communicator?
Cool!
Yes! And the Cutie Mobile—it's improved too!

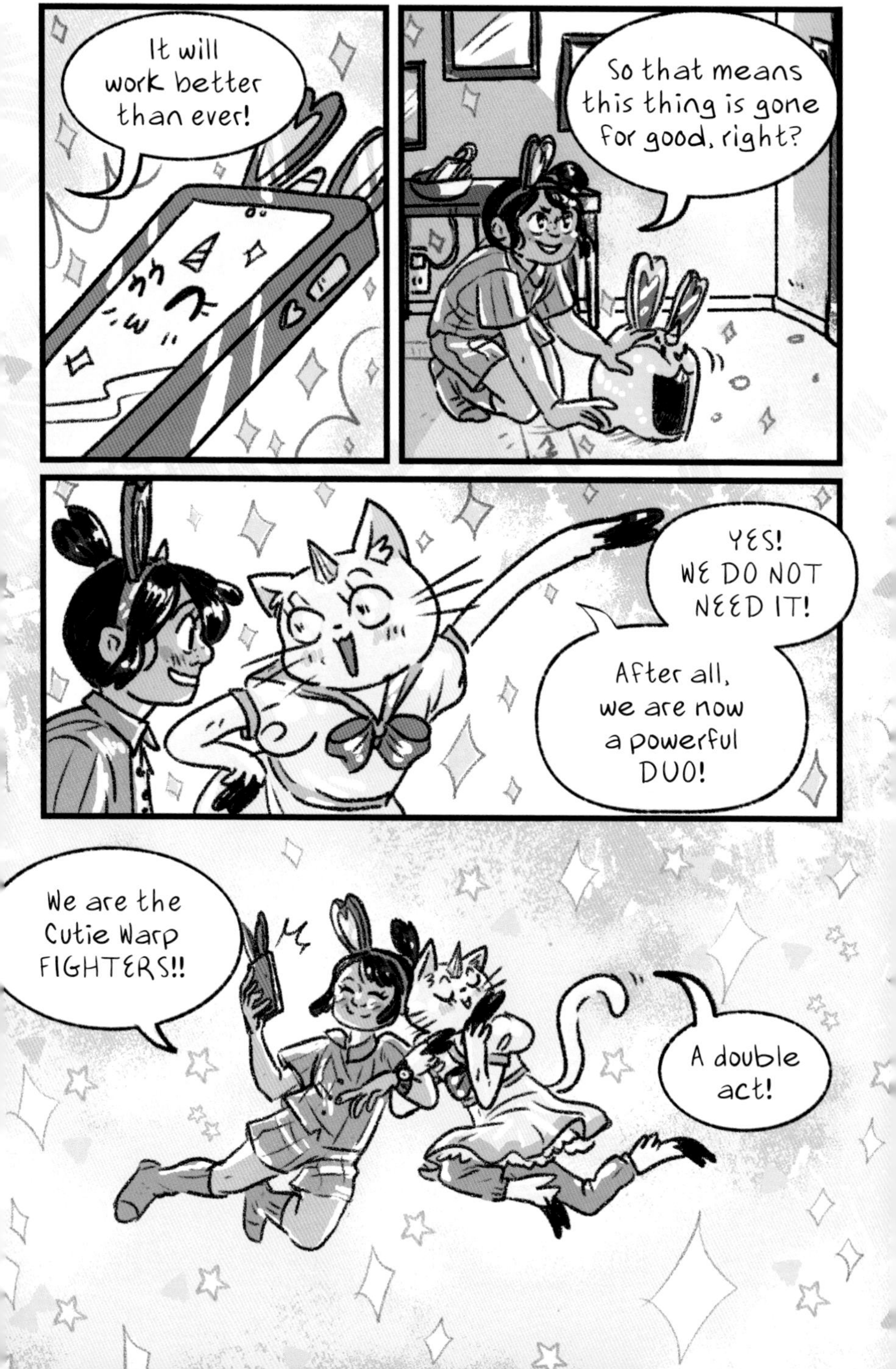
It will work better than ever!
So that means this thing is gone for good, right?
YES! WE DO NOT NEED IT!
After all, we are now a powerful DUO!
We are the Cutie Warp FIGHTERS!!
A double act!

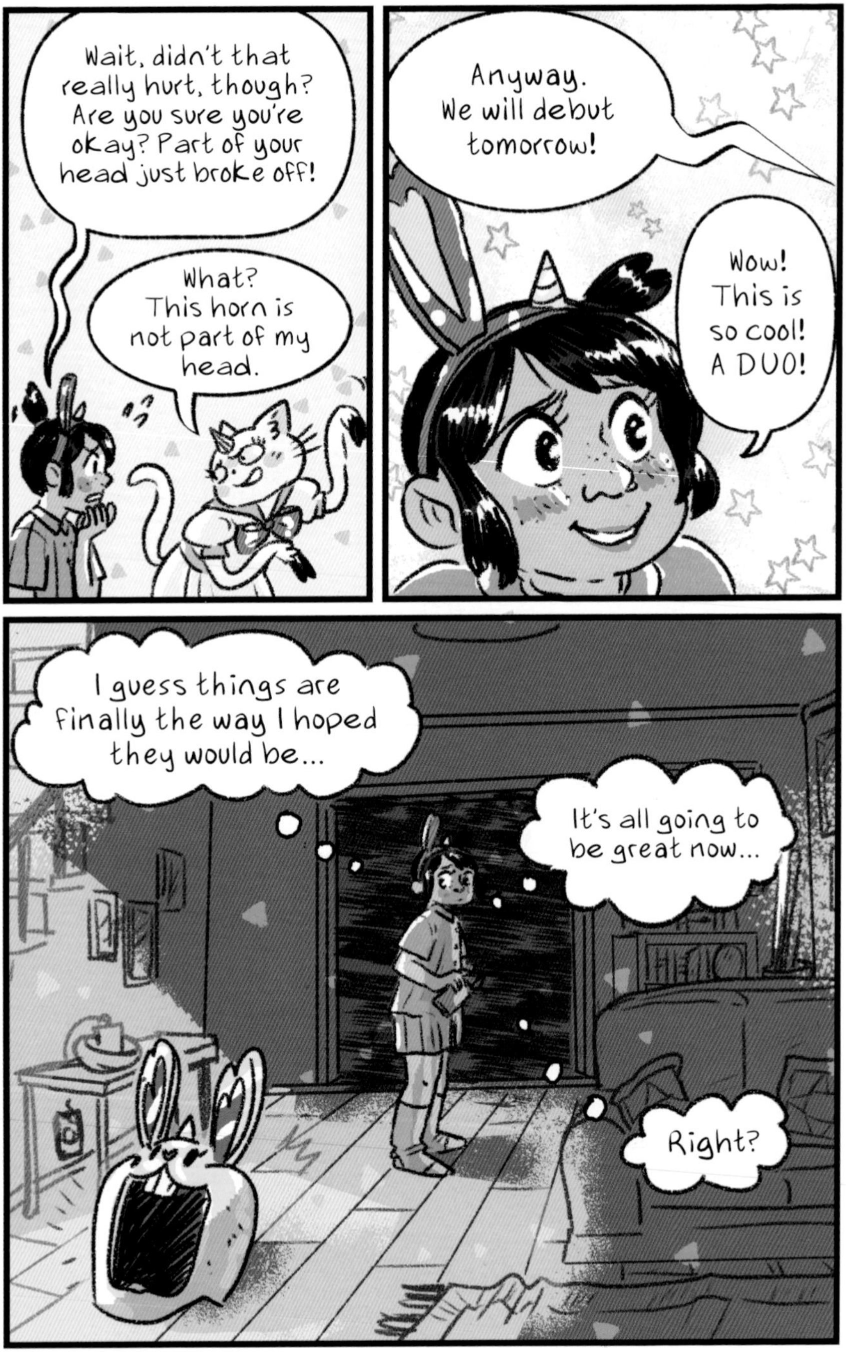
Wait, didn't that really hurt, though? Are you sure you're okay? Part of your head just broke off!
What? This horn is not part of my head.
Anyway. We will debut tomorrow!
Wow! This is so cool! A DUO!
I guess things are finally the way I hoped they would be...
It's all going to be great now...
Right?

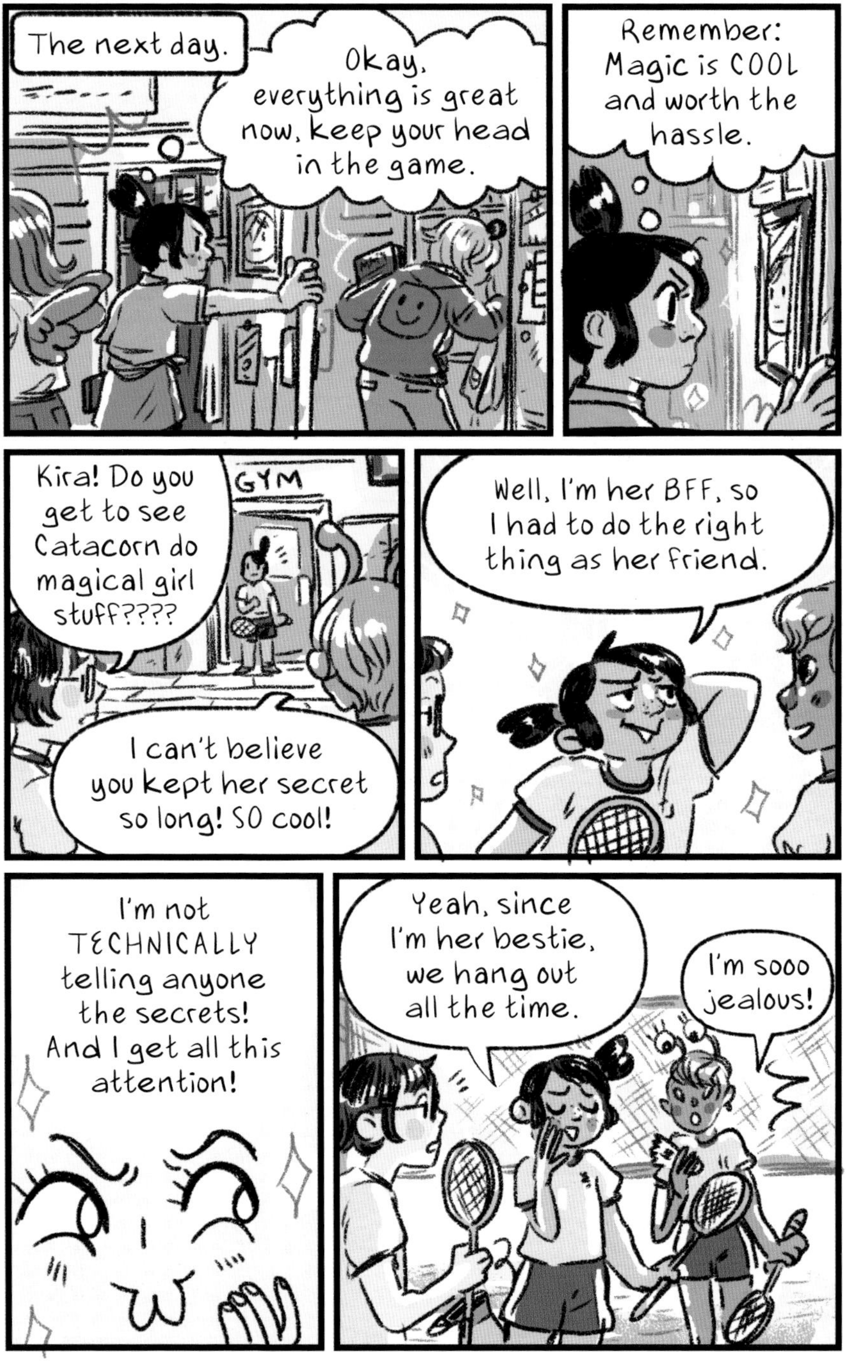

The next day.
Okay, everything is great now, keep your head in the game.
Remember: Magic is COOL and worth the hassle.
GYM
Kira! Do you get to see Catacorn do magical girl stuff????
I can't believe you kept her secret so long! SO cool!
Well, I'm her BFF, so I had to do the right thing as her friend.
I'm not TECHNICALLY telling anyone the secrets! And I get all this attention!
Yeah, since I'm her bestie, we hang out all the time.
I'm sooo jealous!

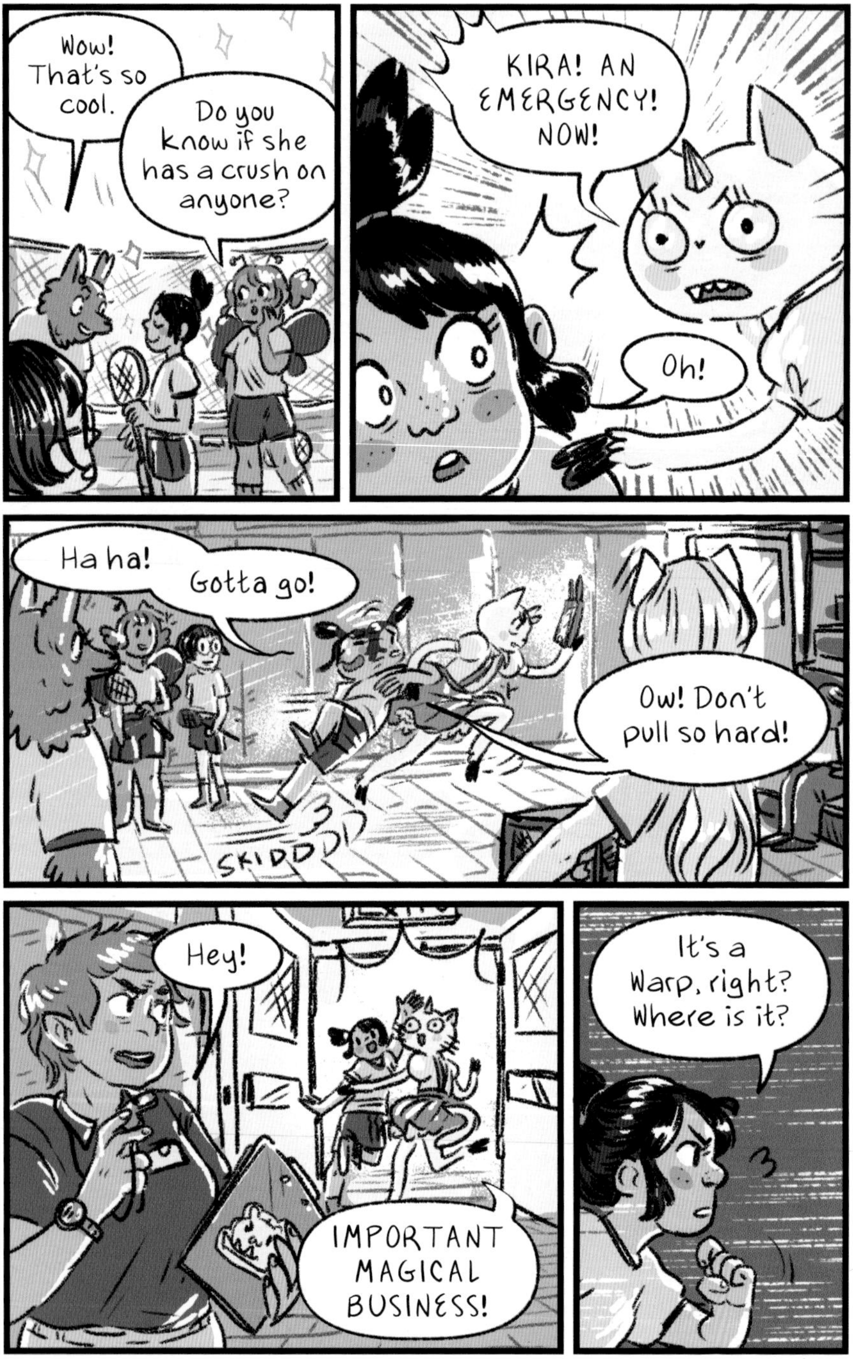
Wow! That's so cool.
Do you know if she has a crush on anyone?
KIRA! AN EMERGENCY! NOW!
Oh!
Ha ha!
Gotta go!
Ow! Don't pull so hard!
SKIDDD
Hey!
IMPORTANT MAGICAL BUSINESS!
It's a Warp, right? Where is it?

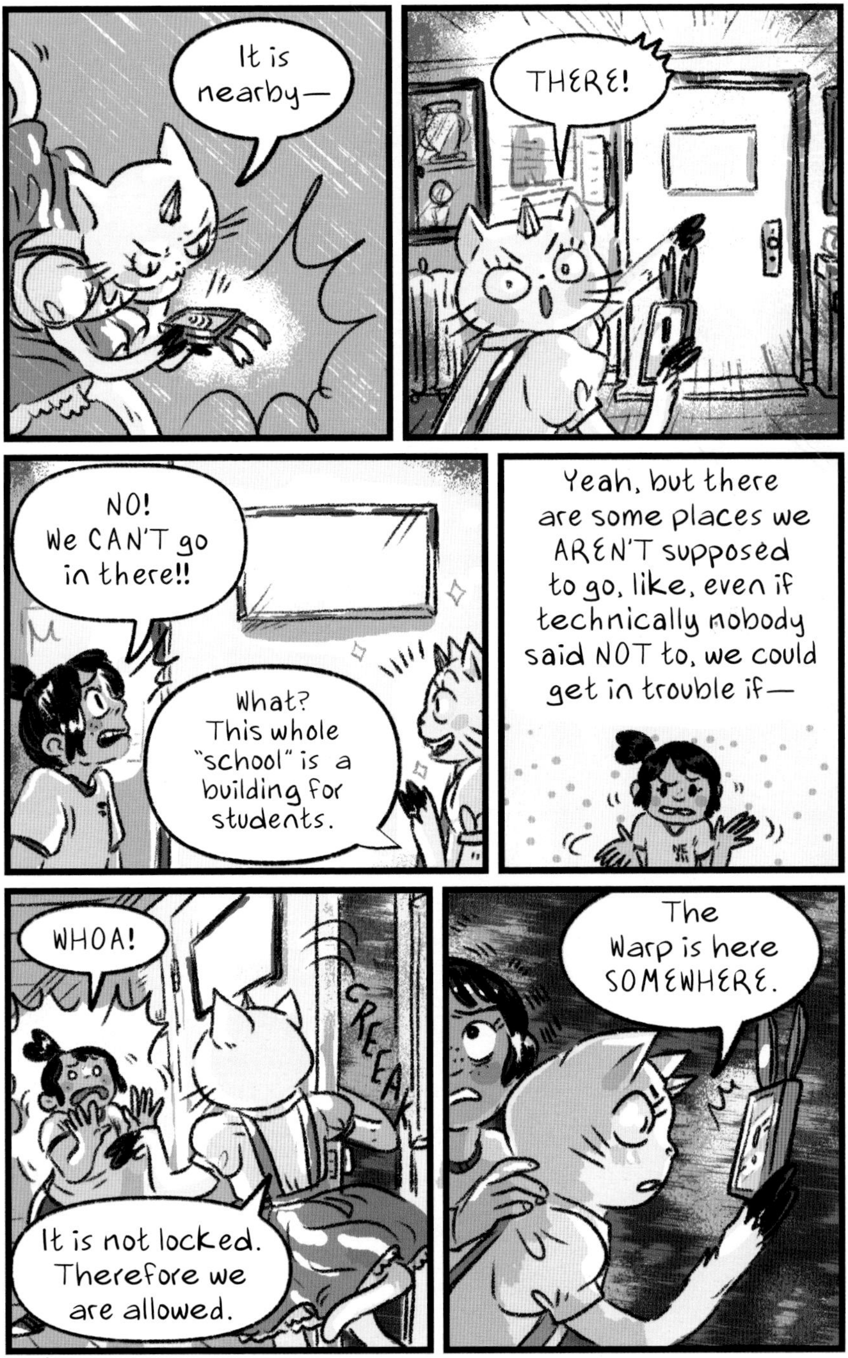
It is nearby—
THERE!
NO! We CAN'T go in there!!
What? This whole "school" is a building for students.
Yeah, but there are some places we AREN'T supposed to go, like, even if technically nobody said NOT to, we could get in trouble if—
WHOA!
CREEAK
It is not locked. Therefore we are allowed.
The Warp is here SOMEWHERE.

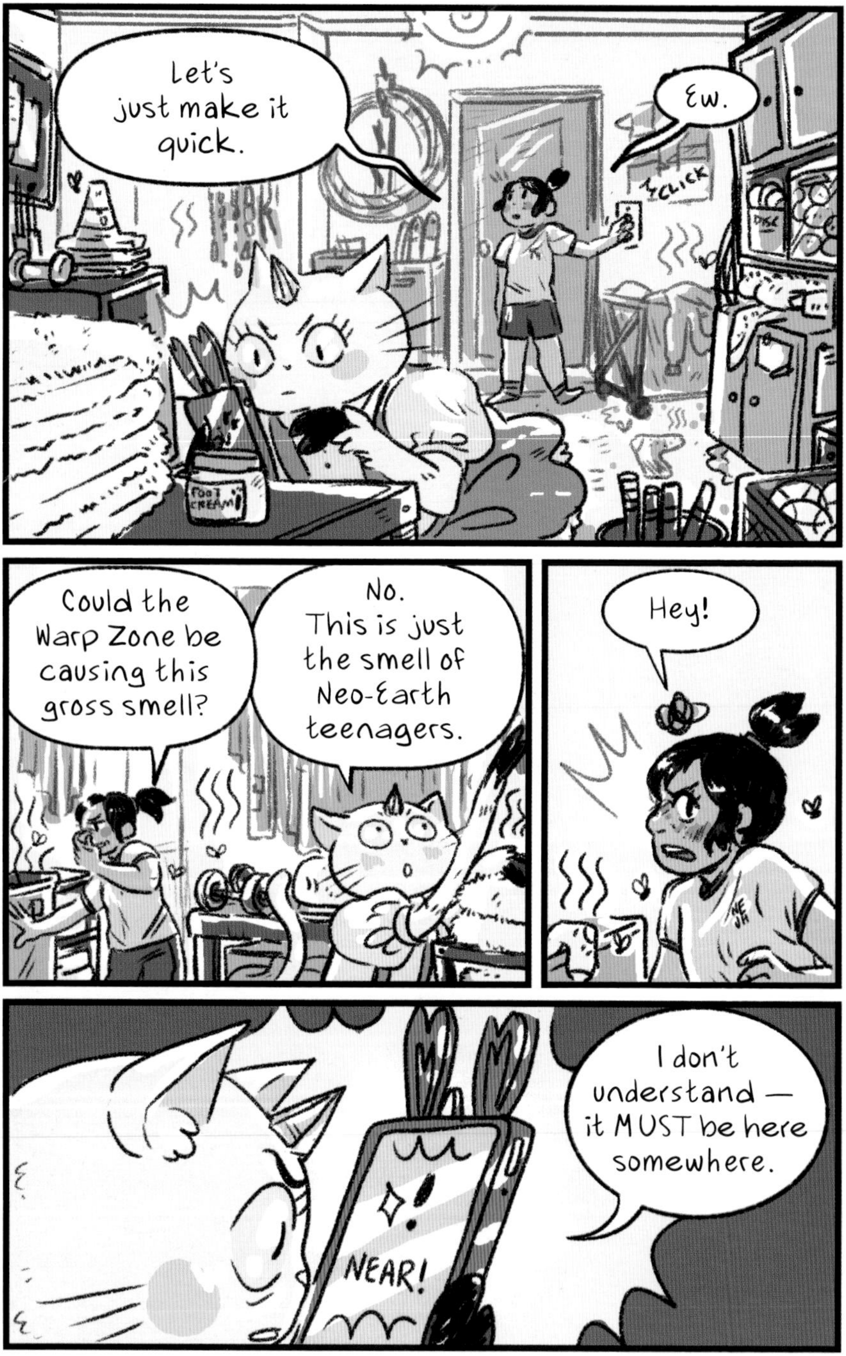
Let's just make it quick.
Ew.
CLICK
FOOT CREAM
Could the Warp Zone be causing this gross smell?
No. This is just the smell of Neo-Earth teenagers.
Hey!
I don't understand — it MUST be here somewhere.
NEAR!

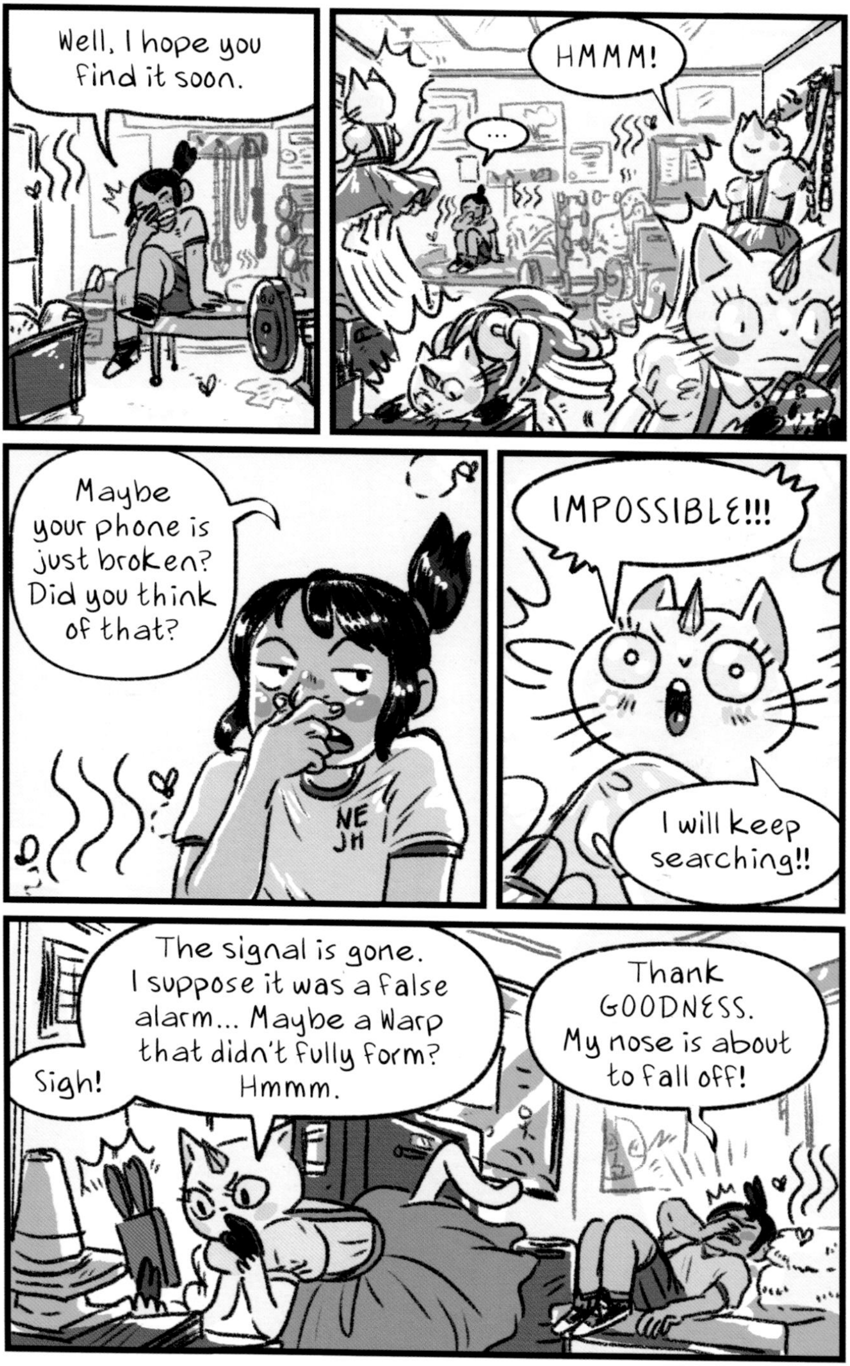
Well, I hope you find it soon.
HMMM!
...
Maybe your phone is just broken? Did you think of that?
IMPOSSIBLE!!!
I will keep searching!!
Sigh!
The signal is gone. I suppose it was a false alarm... Maybe a Warp that didn't fully form? Hmmm.
Thank GOODNESS. My nose is about to fall off!

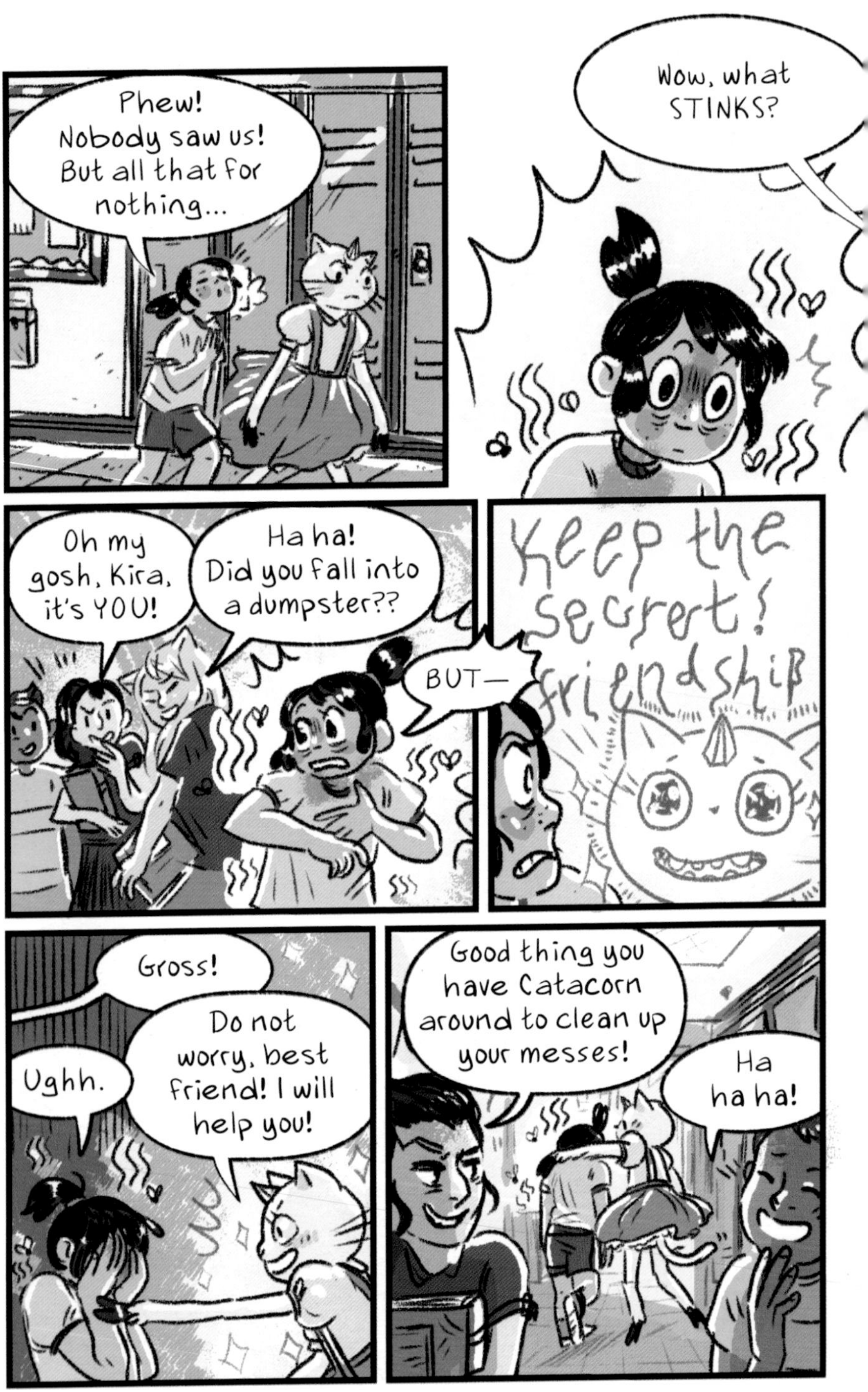

Phew! Nobody saw us! But all that for nothing...
Wow, what STINKS?
Oh my gosh, Kira, it's YOU!
Ha ha! Did you fall into a dumpster??
BUT—
Keep the secret! friendship
Gross!
Ughh.
Do not worry, best friend! I will help you!
Good thing you have Catacorn around to clean up your messes!
Ha ha ha!

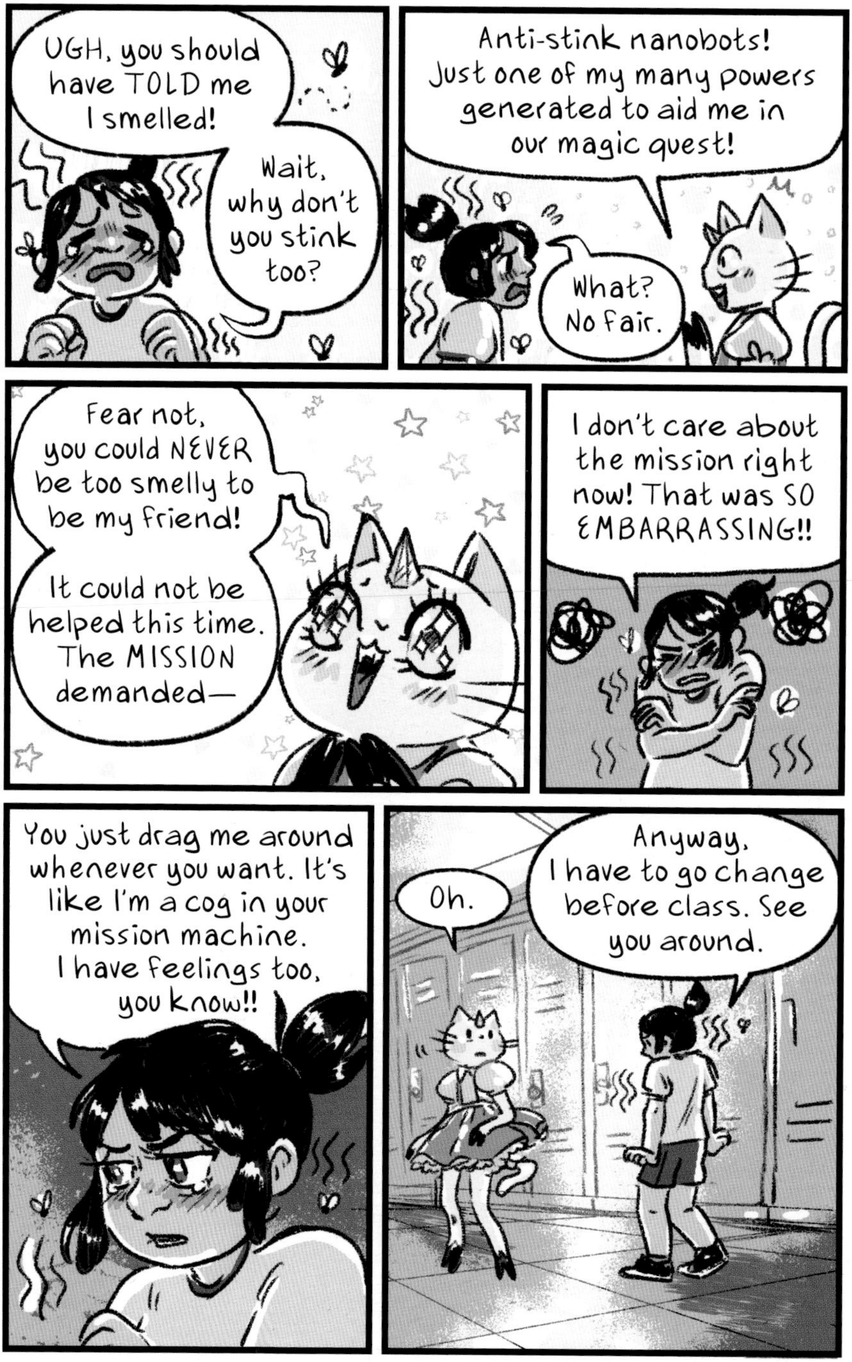
UGH, you should have TOLD me I smelled!
Wait, why don't you stink too?
Anti-stink nanobots! Just one of my many powers generated to aid me in our magic quest!
What? No fair.
Fear not, you could NEVER be too smelly to be my friend!
It could not be helped this time. The MISSION demanded—
I don't care about the mission right now! That was SO EMBARRASSING!!
You just drag me around whenever you want. It's like I'm a cog in your mission machine. I have feelings too, you know!!
Oh.
Anyway, I have to go change before class. See you around.

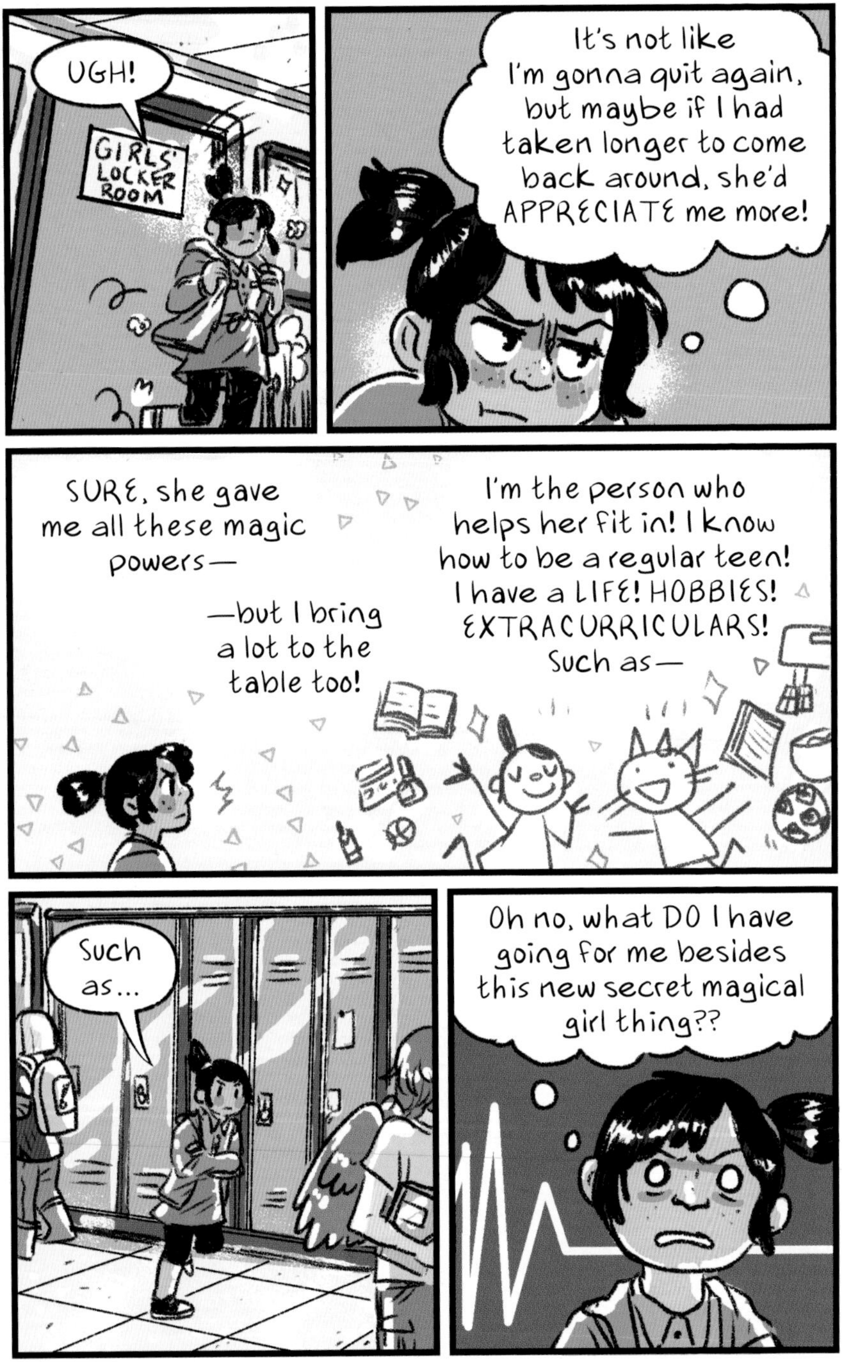
UGH!
GIRLS' LOCKER ROOM
It's not like I'm gonna quit again, but maybe if I had taken longer to come back around, she'd APPRECIATE me more!
SURE, she gave me all these magic powers—
—but I bring a lot to the table too!
I'm the person who helps her fit in! I know how to be a regular teen! I have a LIFE! HOBBIES! EXTRACURRICULARS! Such as—
Such as...
Oh no, what DO I have going for me besides this new secret magical girl thing??

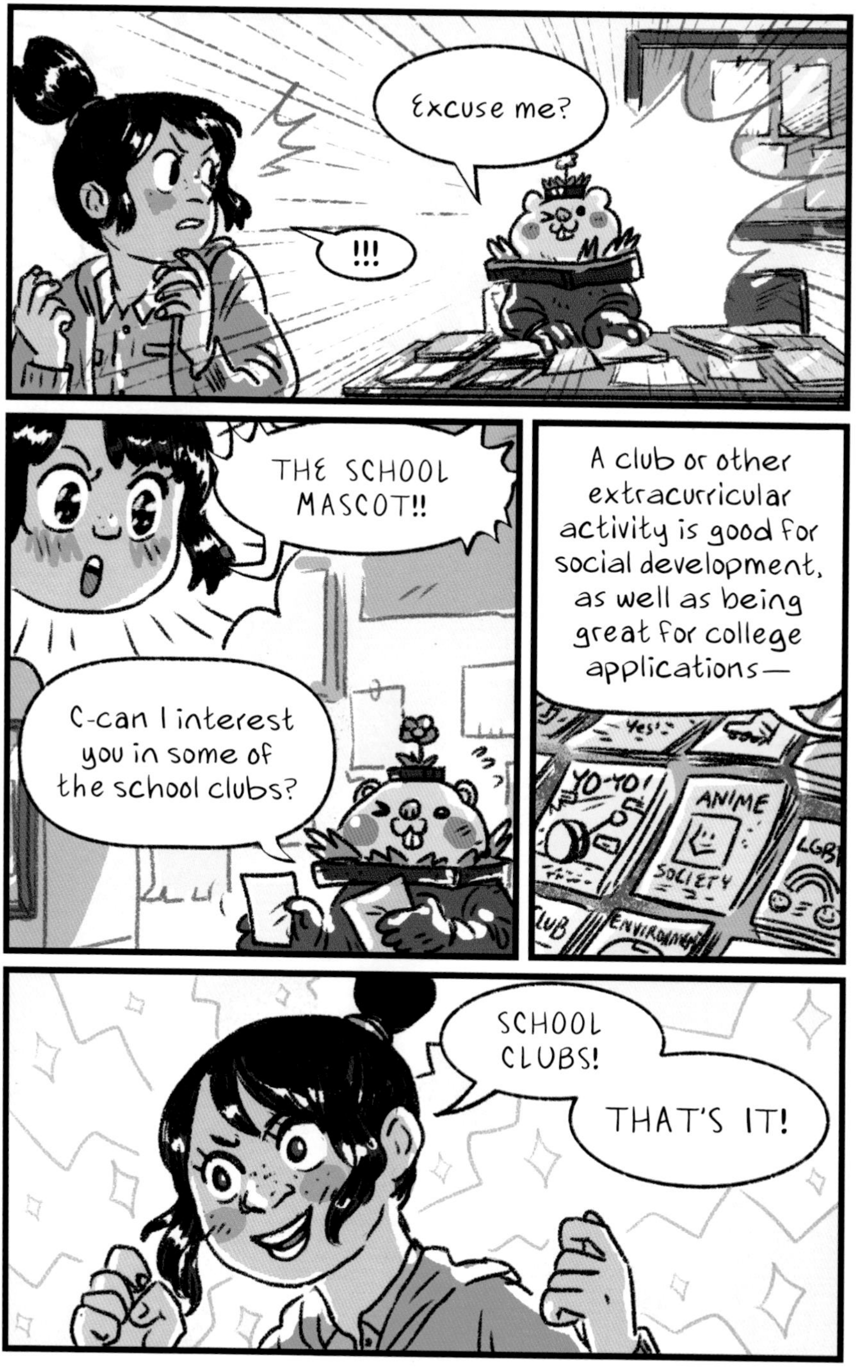
Excuse me?
!!!
THE SCHOOL MASCOT!!
C-can I interest you in some of the school clubs?
A club or other extracurricular activity is good for social development, as well as being great for college applications—
YO-YO!
ANIME SOCIETY
CLUB
SCHOOL CLUBS!
THAT'S IT!

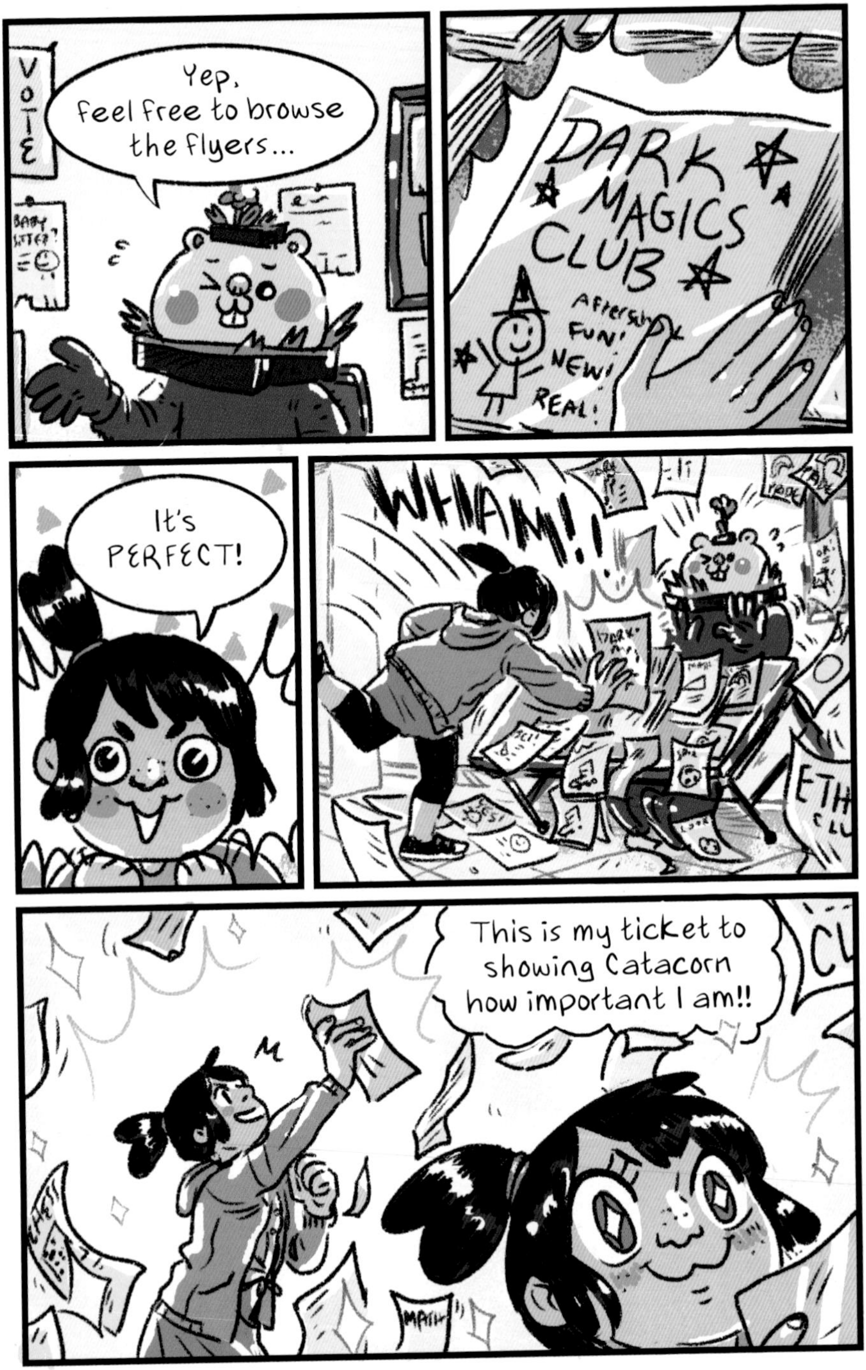
VOTE
Yep, feel free to browse the flyers...
DARK MAGICS CLUB
FUN!
NEW!
REAL!
It's PERFECT!
WHAM!!
This is my ticket to showing Catacorn how important I am!!

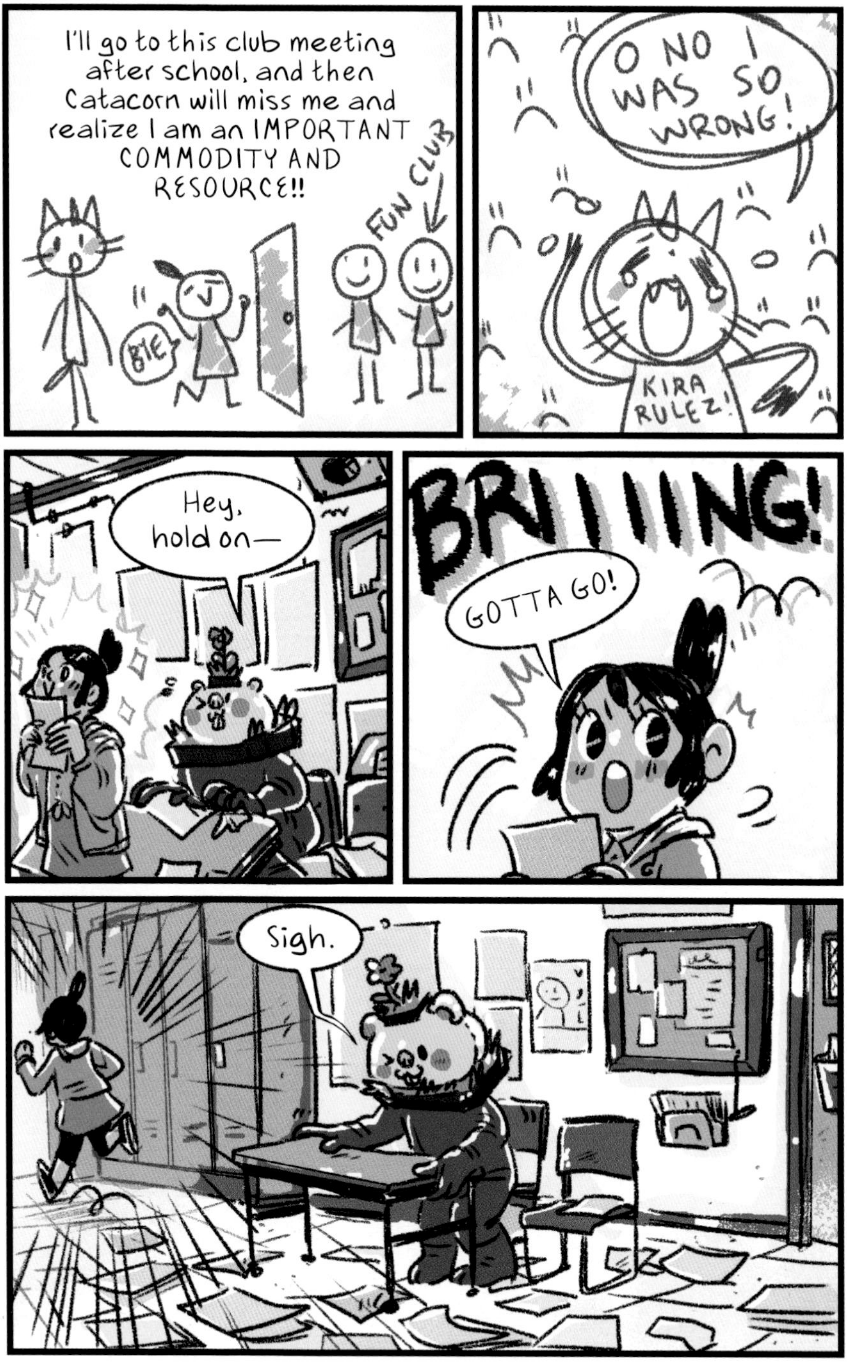
I'll go to this club meeting after school, and then Catacorn will miss me and realize I am an IMPORTANT COMMODITY AND RESOURCE!!
FUN CLUB
BYE
O NO I WAS SO WRONG!
KIRA RULEZ!
Hey, hold on—
BRIIIING!
GOTTA GO!
Sigh.

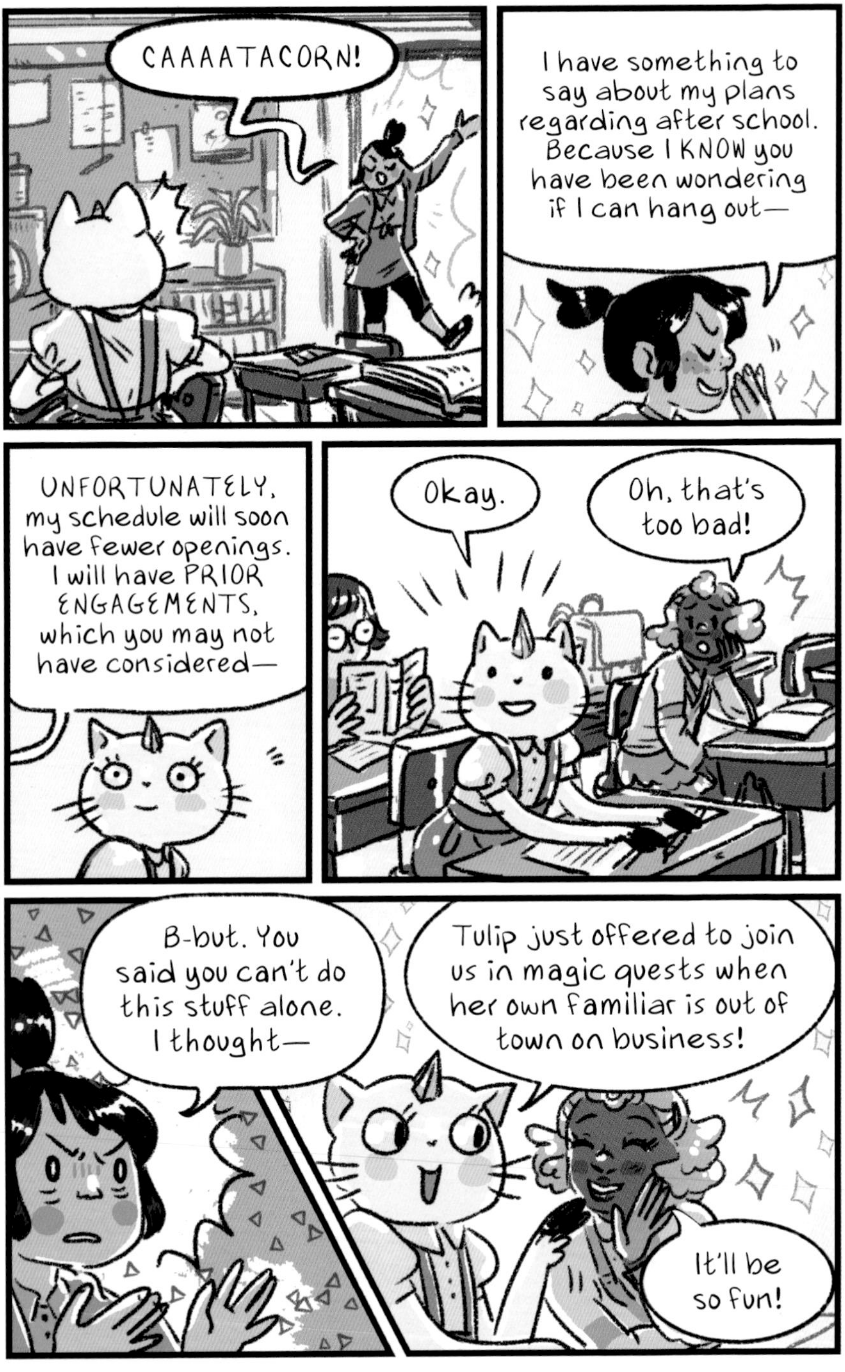
CAAAATACORN!
I have something to say about my plans regarding after school. Because I KNOW you have been wondering if I can hang out—
UNFORTUNATELY, my schedule will soon have fewer openings. I will have PRIOR ENGAGEMENTS, which you may not have considered—
Okay.
Oh, that's too bad!
B-but. You said you can't do this stuff alone. I thought—
Tulip just offered to join us in magic quests when her own familiar is out of town on business!
It'll be so fun!

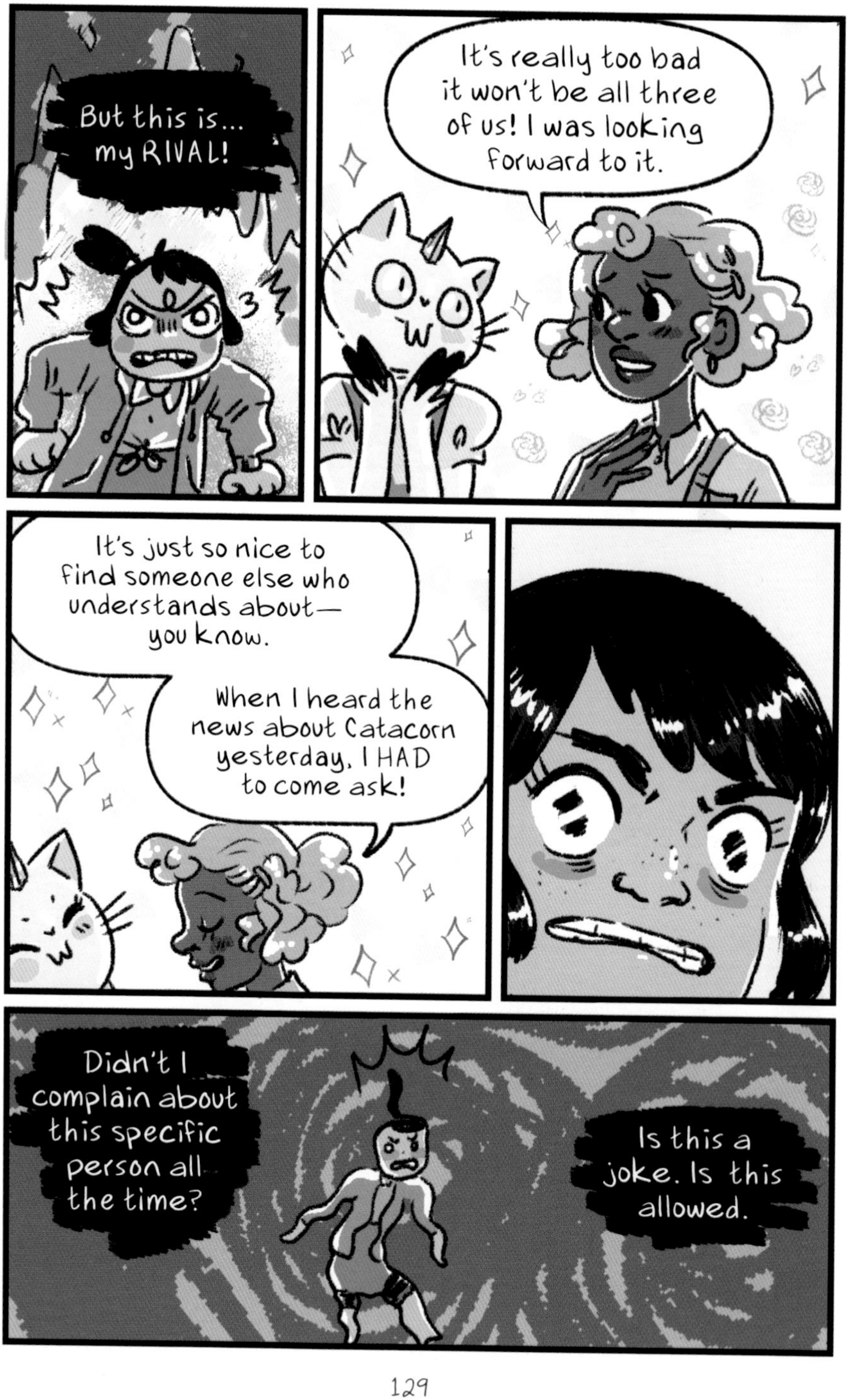
But this is... my RIVAL!
It's really too bad it won't be all three of us! I was looking forward to it.
It's just so nice to find someone else who understands about— you know.
When I heard the news about Catacorn yesterday, I HAD to come ask!
Didn't I complain about this specific person all the time?
Is this a joke. Is this allowed.

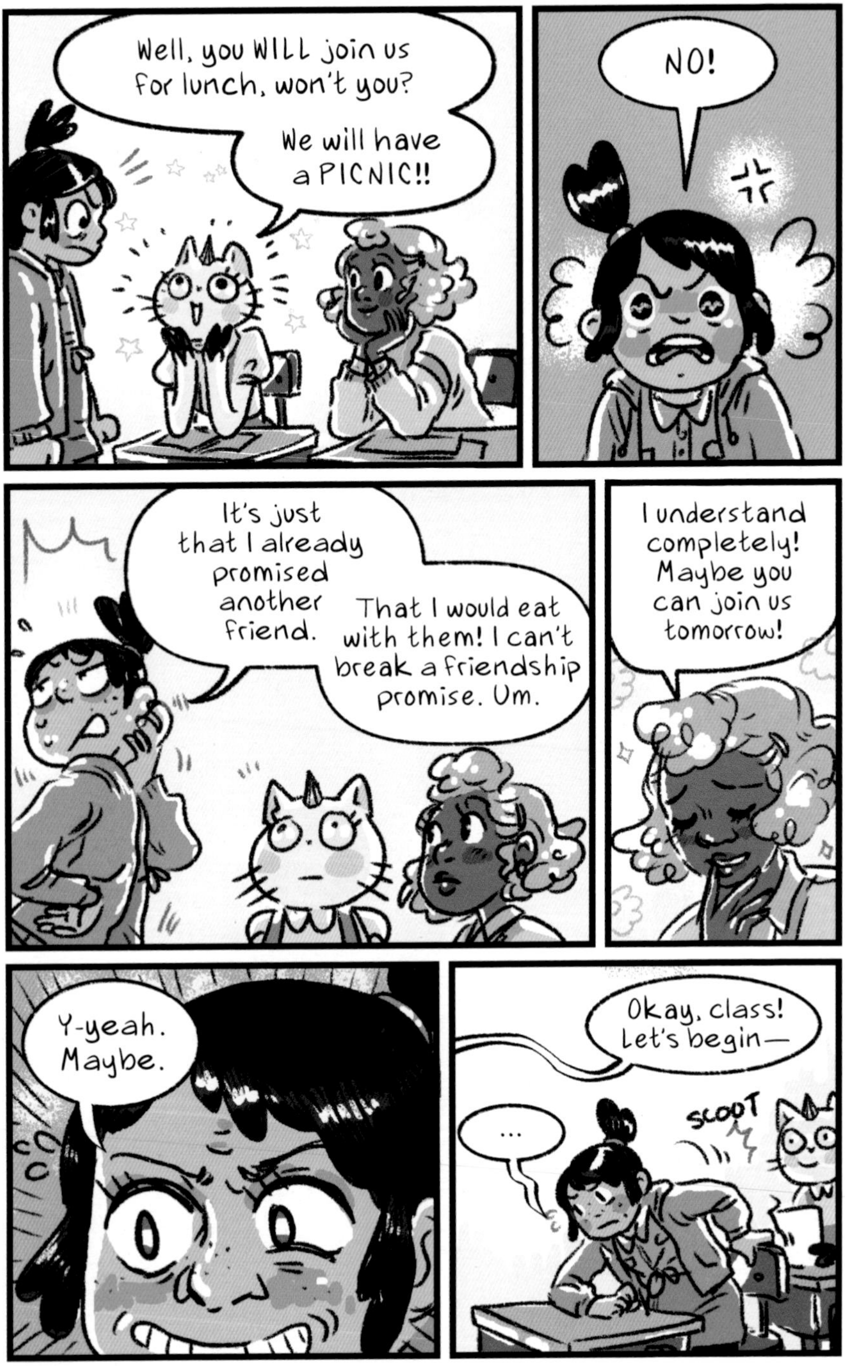
Well, you WILL join us for lunch, won't you?
We will have a PICNIC!!
NO!
It's just that I already promised another friend.
That I would eat with them! I can't break a friendship promise. Um.
I understand completely! Maybe you can join us tomorrow!
Y-yeah. Maybe.
Okay, class! Let's begin—
...
SCOOT

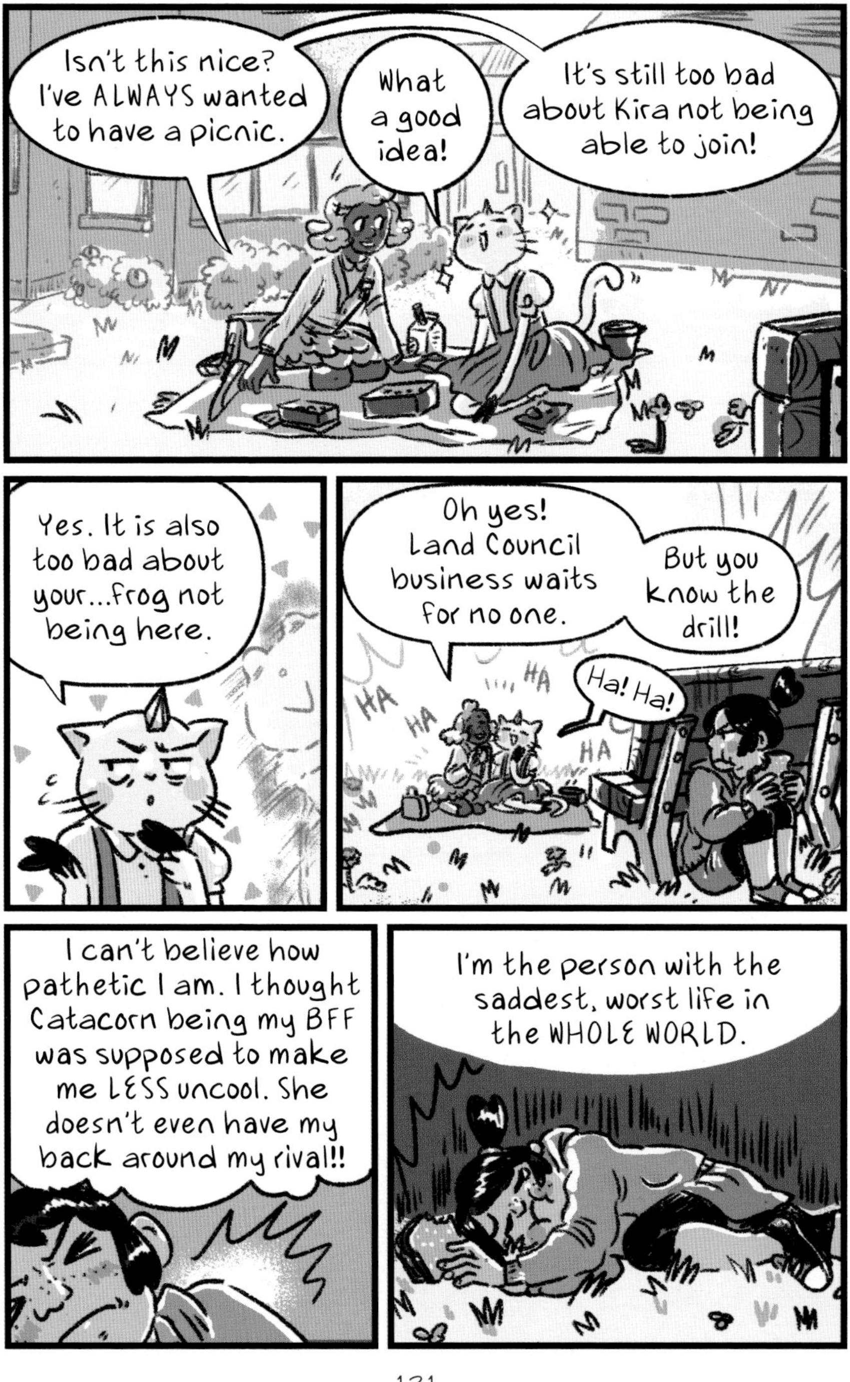
Isn't this nice? I've ALWAYS wanted to have a picnic.
What a good idea!
It's still too bad about Kira not being able to join!
Yes. It is also too bad about your...frog not being here.
Oh yes! Land Council business waits for no one.
But you know the drill!
HA HA HA HA
Ha! Ha!
I can't believe how pathetic I am. I thought Catacorn being my BFF was supposed to make me LESS uncool. She doesn't even have my back around my rival!!
I'm the person with the saddest, worst life in the WHOLE WORLD.

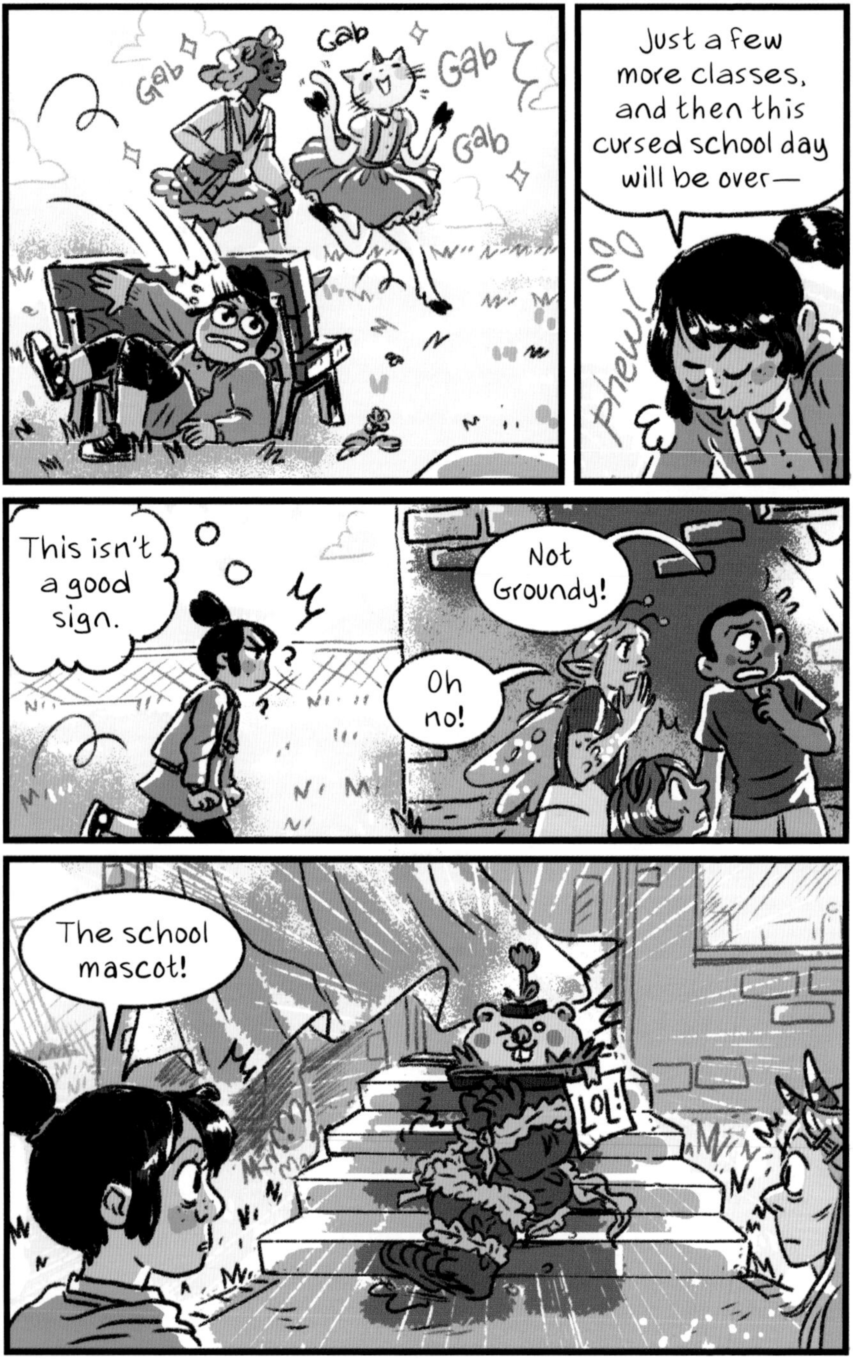
Gab
Gab
Gab
Gab
Just a few more classes, and then this cursed school day will be over—
phew!
This isn't a good sign.
Not Groundy!
Oh no!
The school mascot!
LOL!

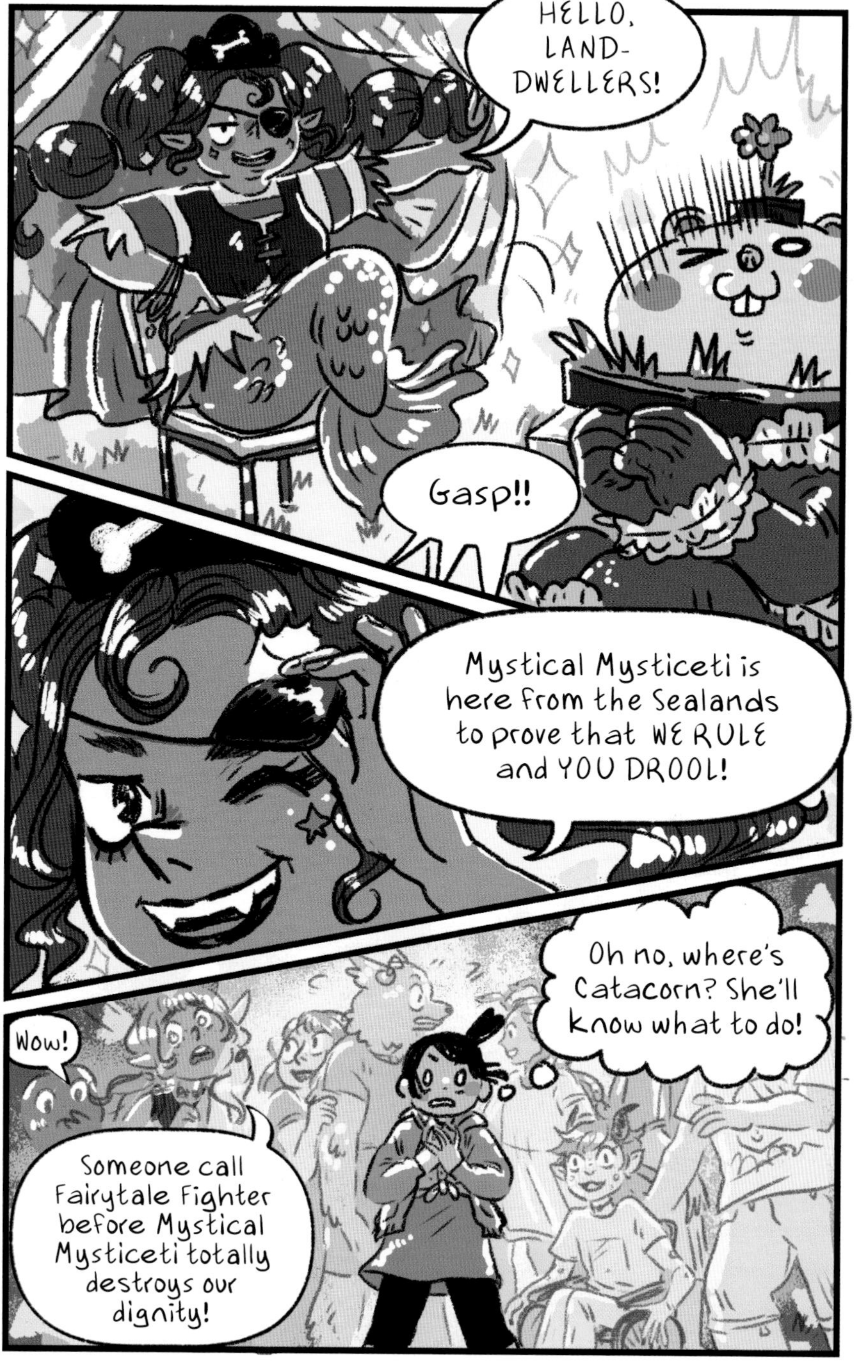
HELLO, LAND-DWELLERS!
Gasp!!
Mystical Mysticeti is here from the Sealands to prove that WE RULE and YOU DROOL!
Oh no, where's Catacorn? She'll know what to do!
Wow!
Someone call Fairytale Fighter before Mystical Mysticeti totally destroys our dignity!

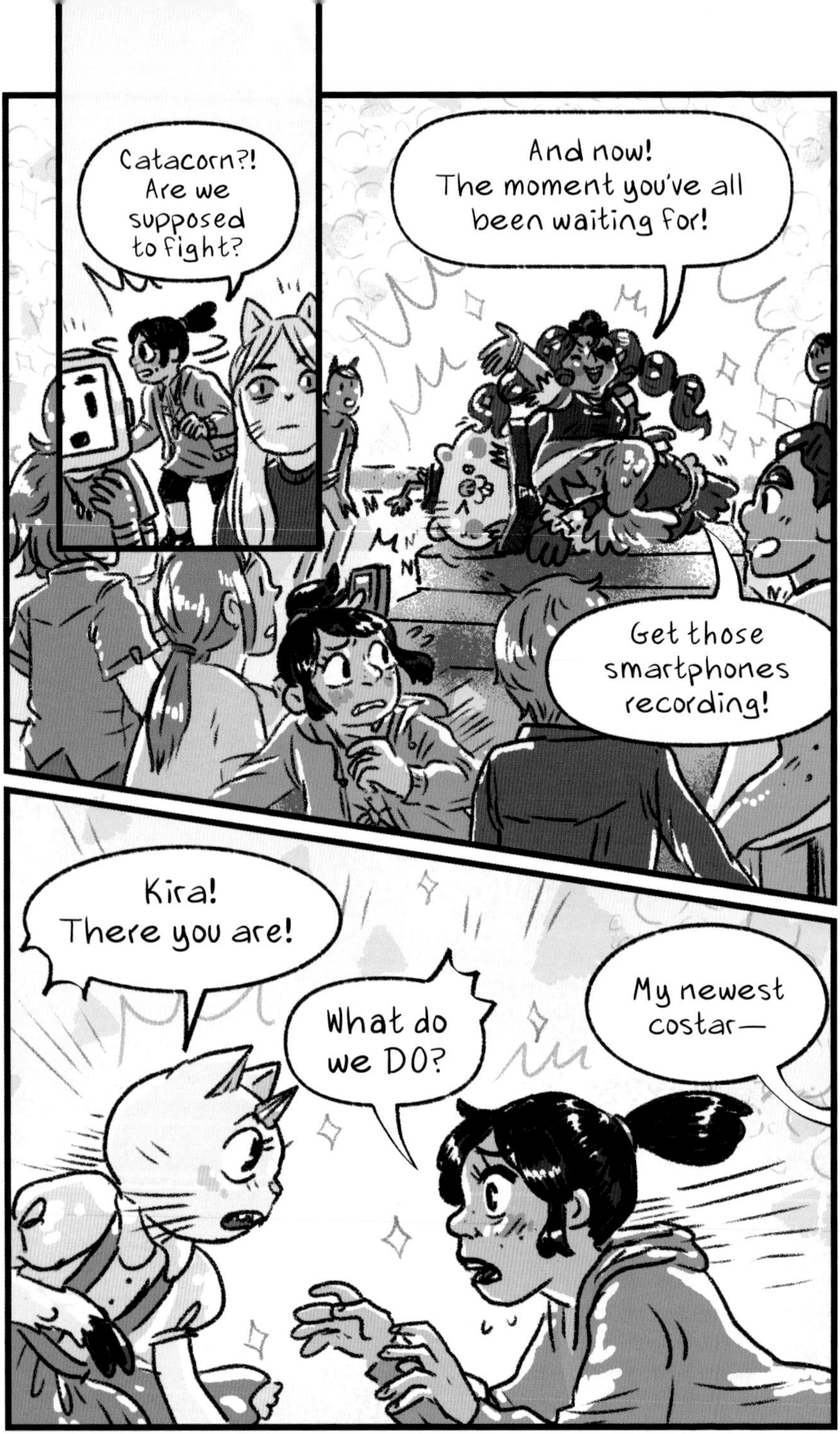

Catacorn?! Are we supposed to fight?
And now! The moment you've all been waiting for!
Get those smartphones recording!
Kira! There you are!
What do we DO?
My newest costar—

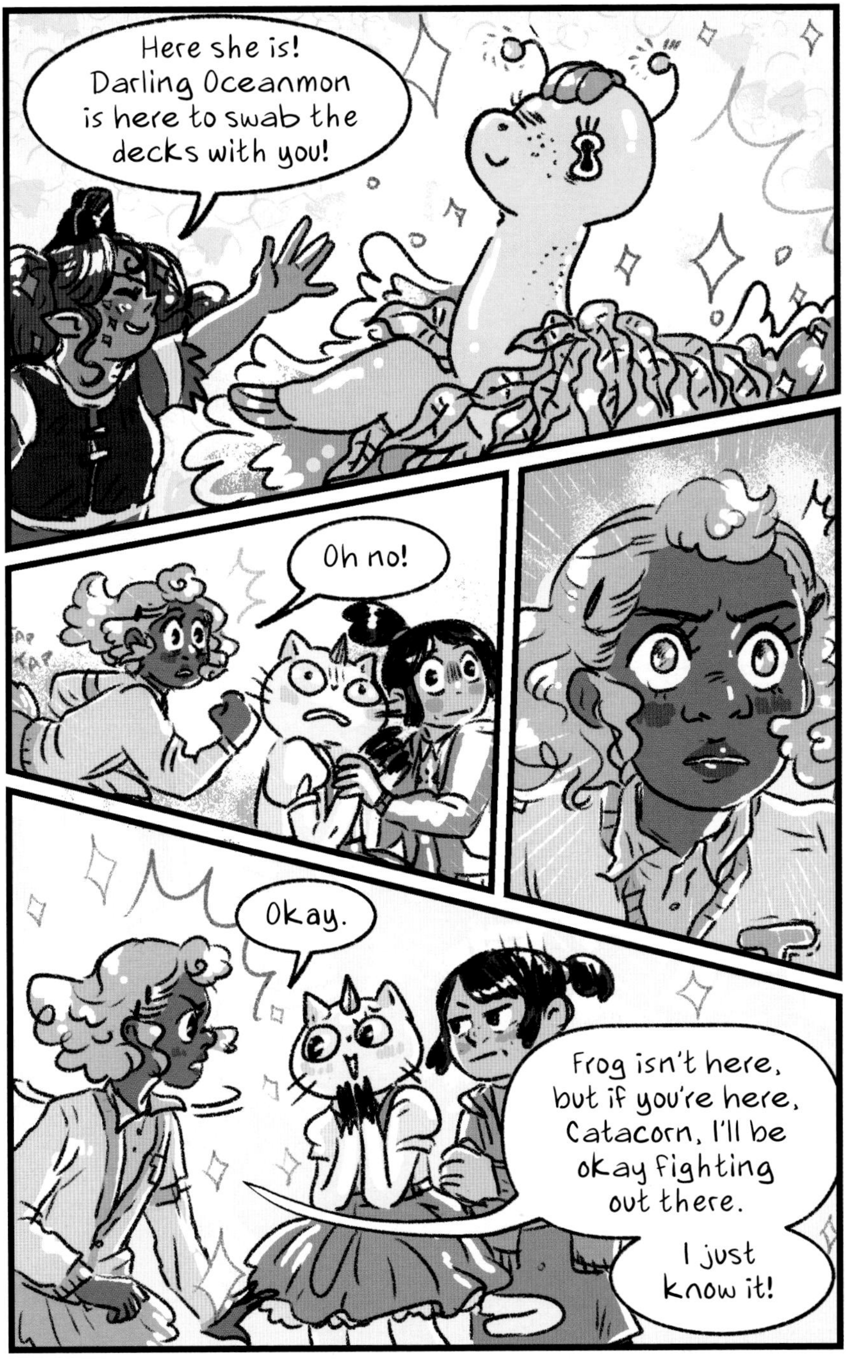
Here she is! Darling Oceanmon is here to swab the decks with you!
Oh no!
Okay.
Frog isn't here, but if you're here, Catacorn, I'll be okay fighting out there.
I just know it!

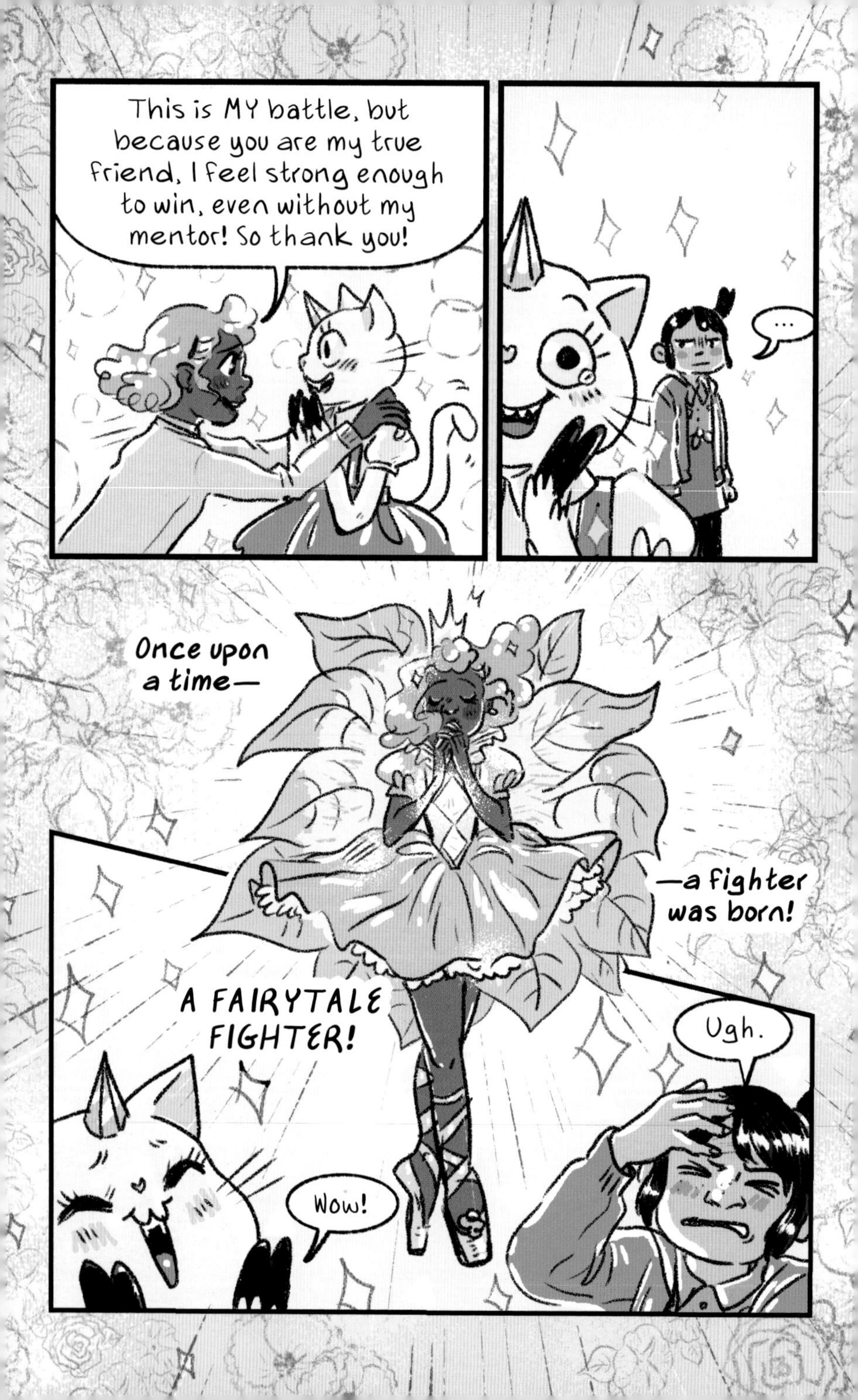
This is MY battle, but because you are my true friend, I feel strong enough to win, even without my mentor! So thank you!
...
Once upon a time—
—a fighter was born!
A FAIRYTALE FIGHTER!
Ugh.
Wow!

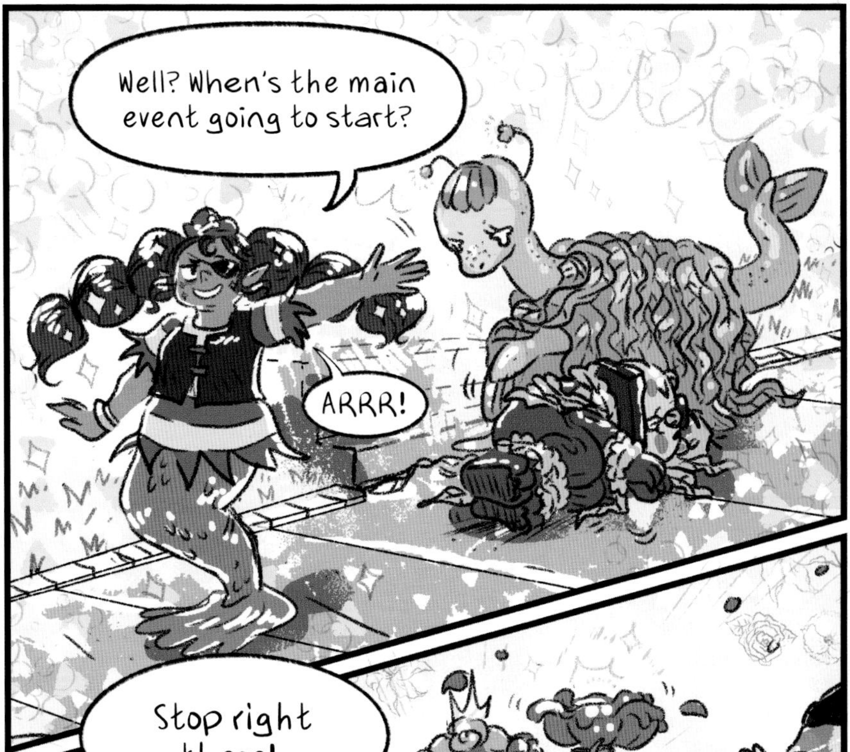
Well? When's the main event going to start?
ARRR!

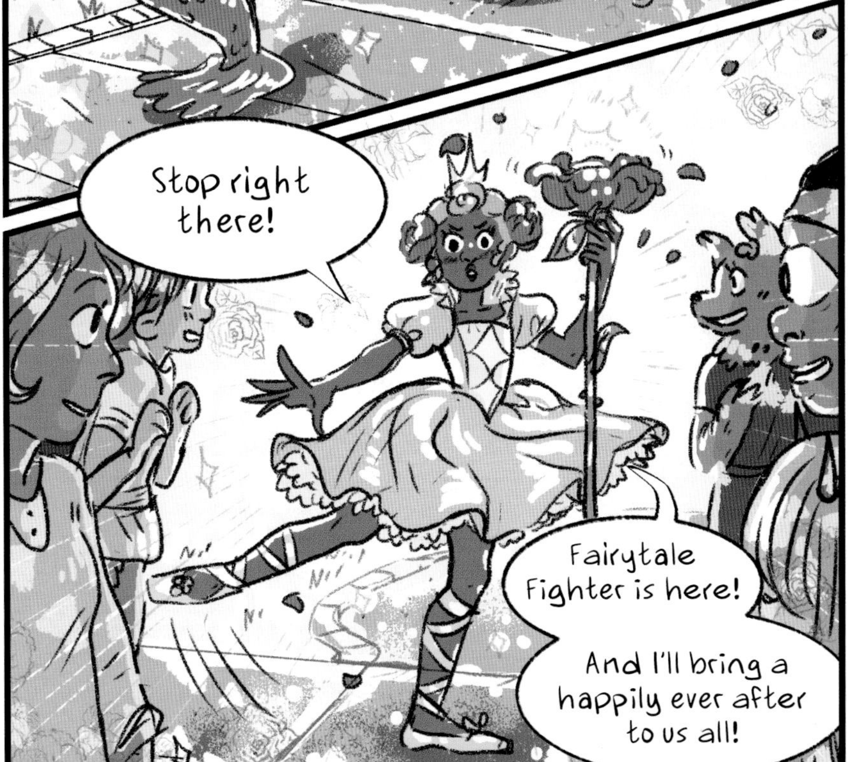
Stop right there!
Fairytale Fighter is here!
And I'll bring a happily ever after to us all!

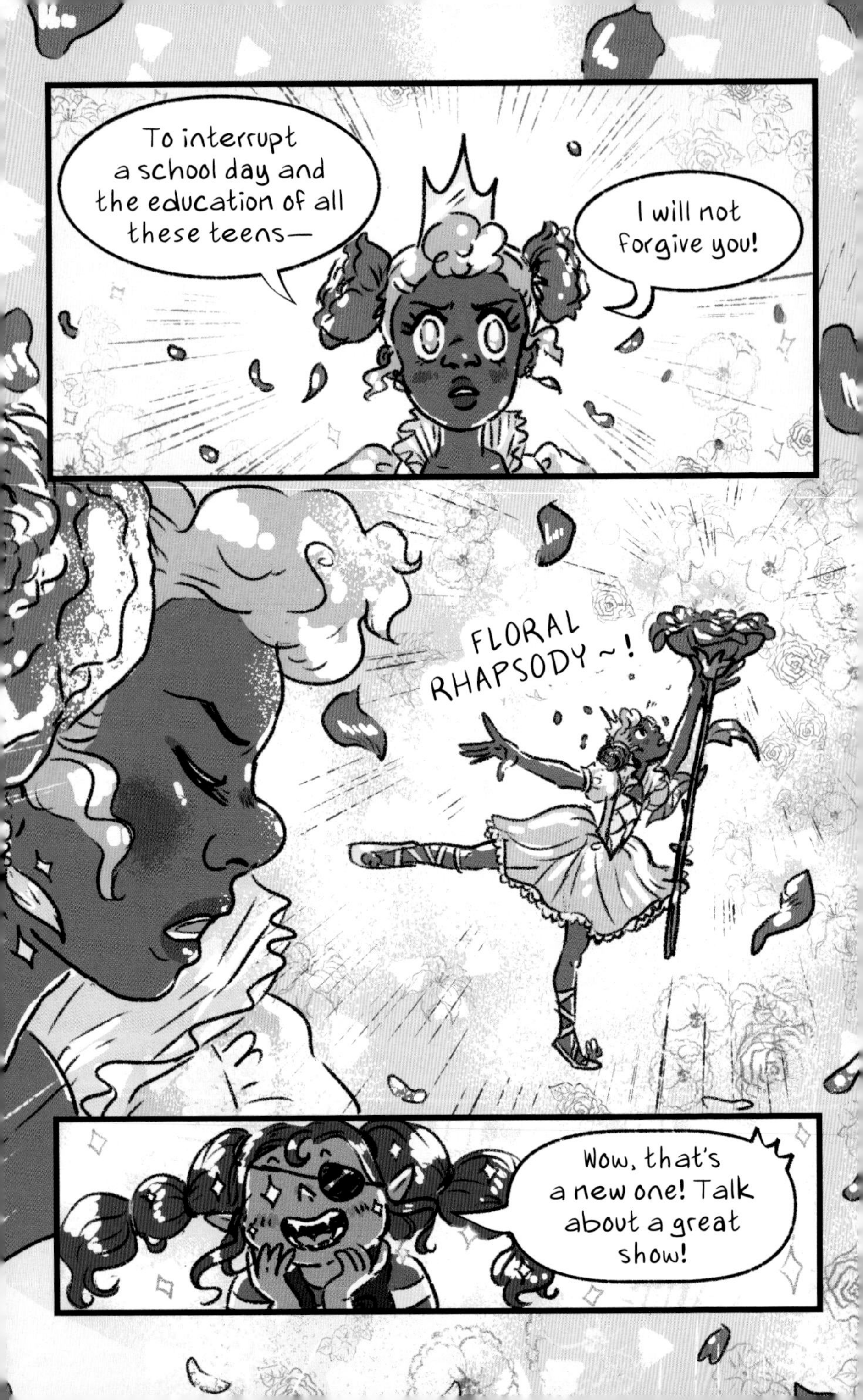
To interrupt a school day and the education of all these teens—
I will not forgive you!
FLORAL RHAPSODY ~!
Wow, that's a new one! Talk about a great show!

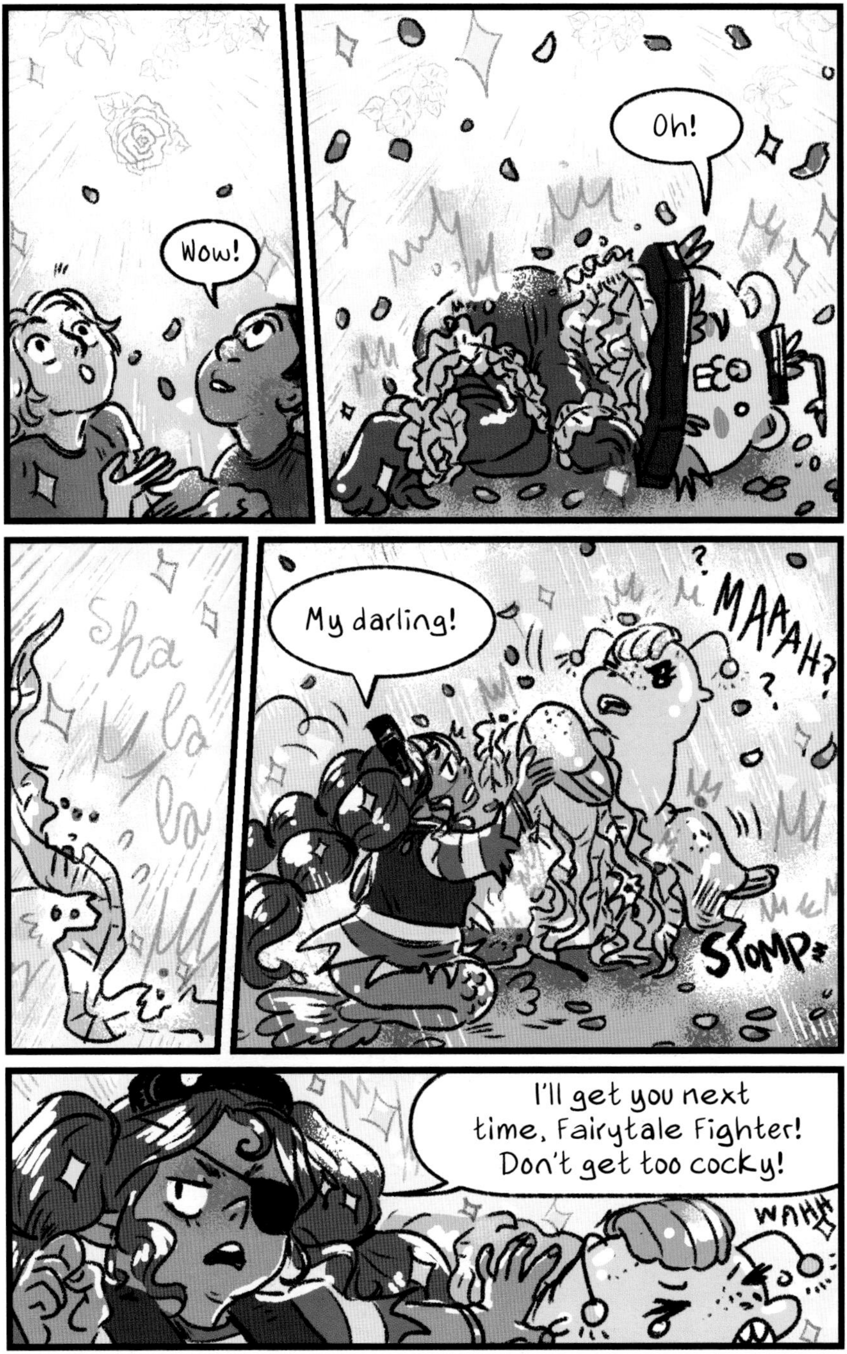
Wow!
Oh!
Sha la la
My darling!
MAAAH??
STOMP
I'll get you next time, Fairytale Fighter! Don't get too cocky!
WAHH

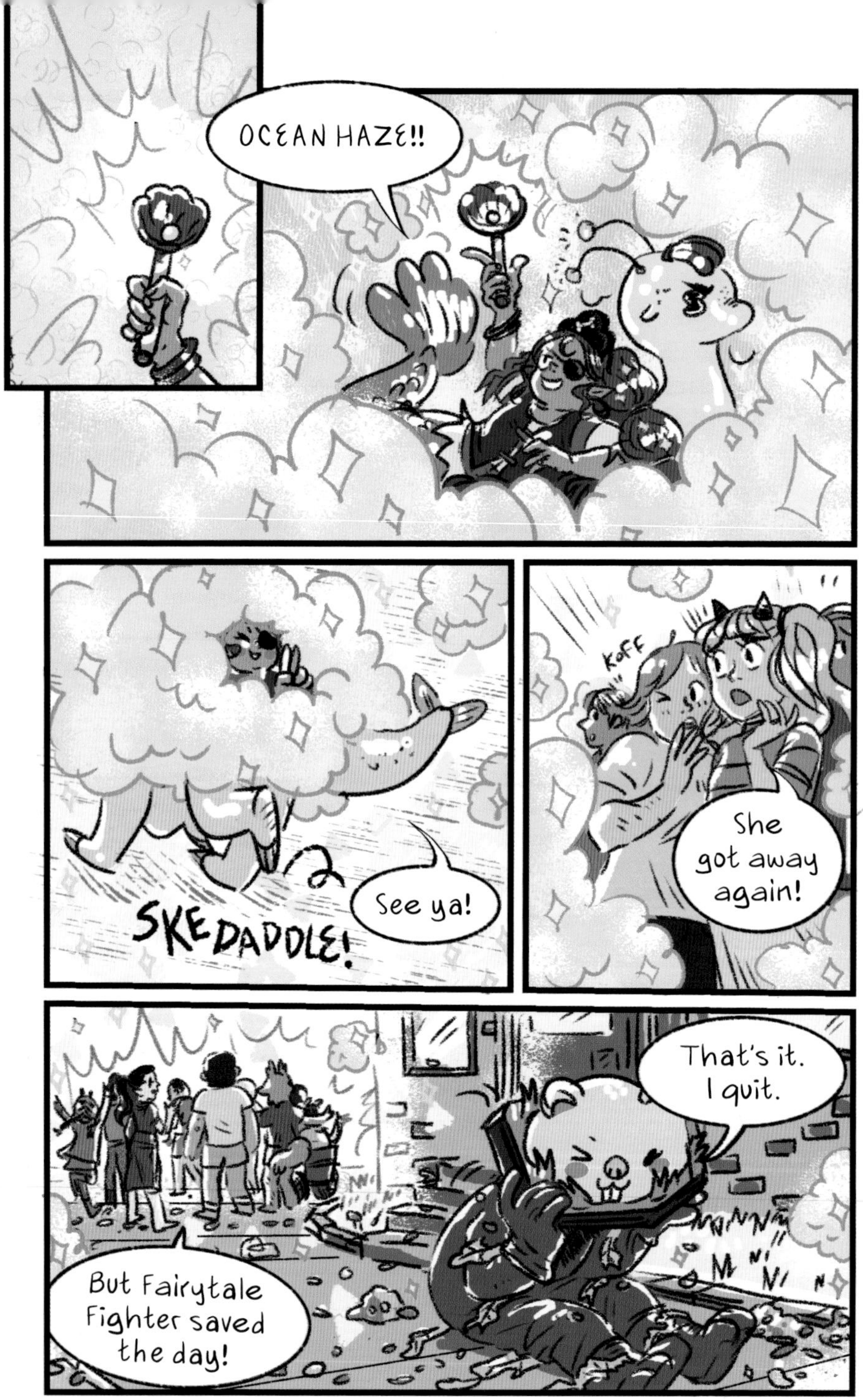
OCEAN HAZE!!
SKEDADDLE!
See ya!
KOFF
She got away again!
That's it. I quit.
But Fairytale Fighter saved the day!

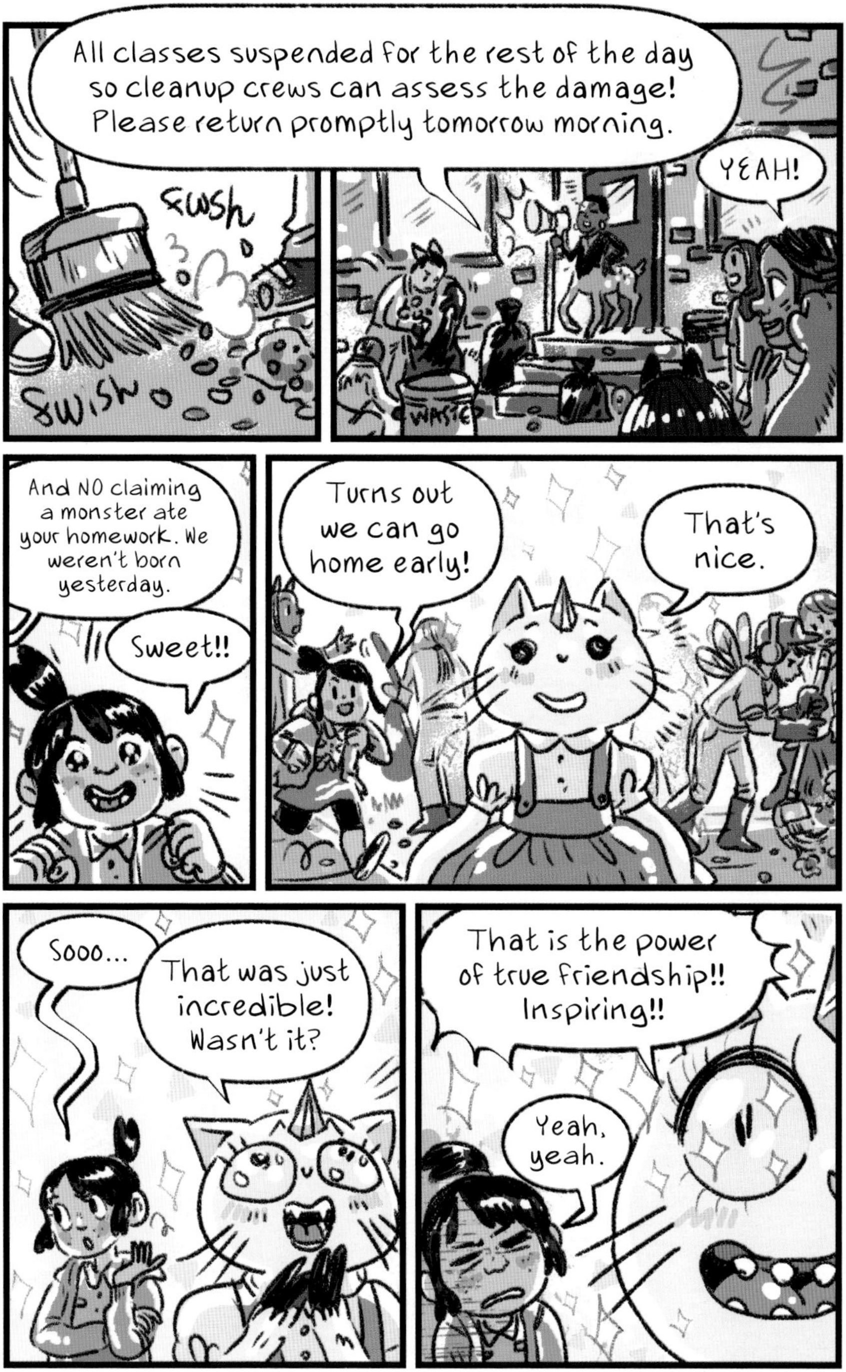
All classes suspended for the rest of the day so cleanup crews can assess the damage! Please return promptly tomorrow morning.
FWSH
SWISH
WASTE
YEAH!
And NO claiming a monster ate your homework. We weren't born yesterday.
Sweet!!
Turns out we can go home early!
That's nice.
Sooo...
That was just incredible! Wasn't it?
That is the power of true friendship!! Inspiring!!
Yeah, yeah.

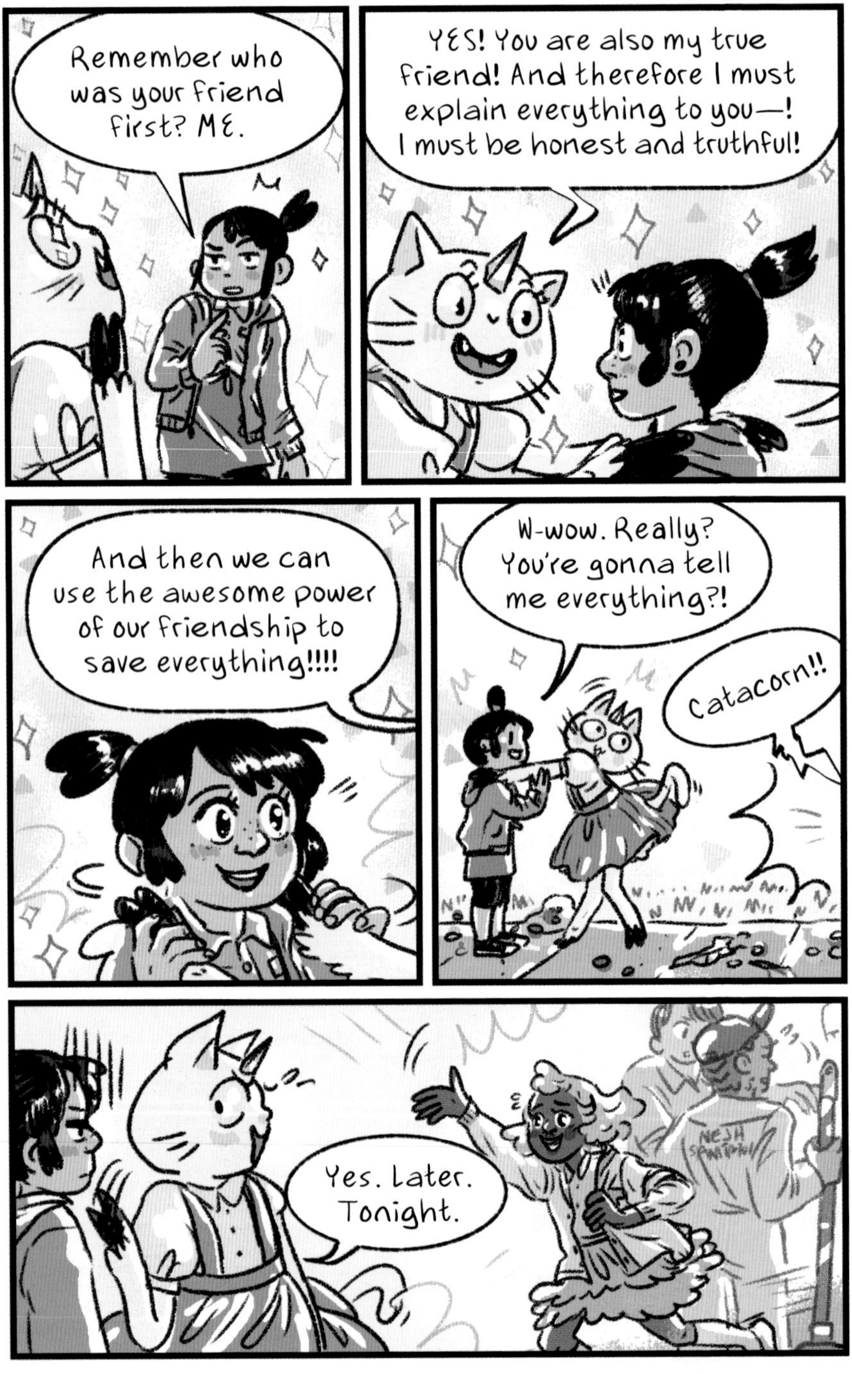
Remember who was your friend first? ME.
YES! You are also my true friend! And therefore I must explain everything to you—! I must be honest and truthful!
And then we can use the awesome power of our friendship to save everything!!!!
W-wow. Really? You're gonna tell me everything?!
Catacorn!!
Yes. Later. Tonight.

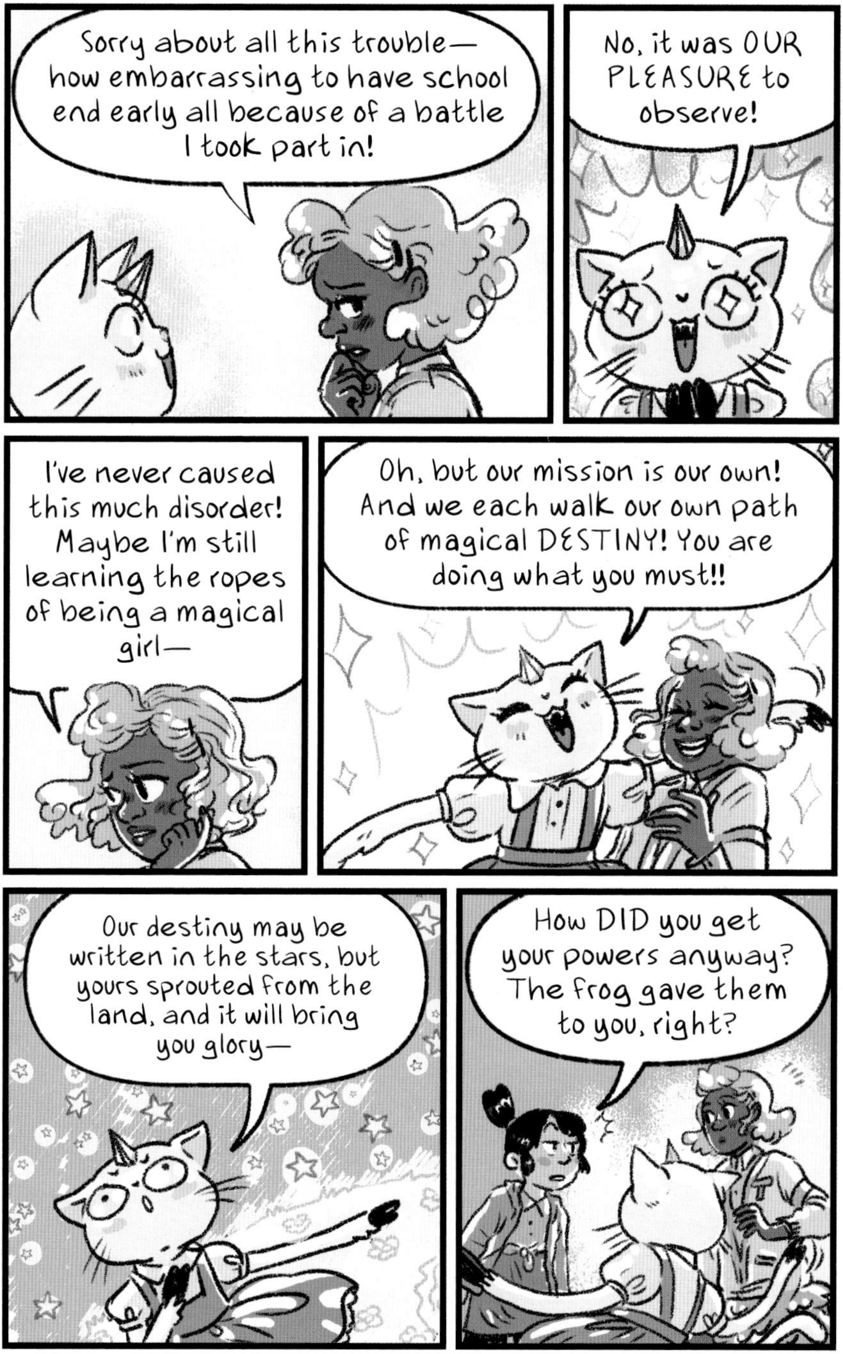
Sorry about all this trouble— how embarrassing to have school end early all because of a battle I took part in!
No, it was OUR PLEASURE to observe!
I've never caused this much disorder! Maybe I'm still learning the ropes of being a magical girl—
Oh, but our mission is our own! And we each walk our own path of magical DESTINY! You are doing what you must!!
Our destiny may be written in the stars, but yours sprouted from the land, and it will bring you glory—
How DID you get your powers anyway? The frog gave them to you, right?

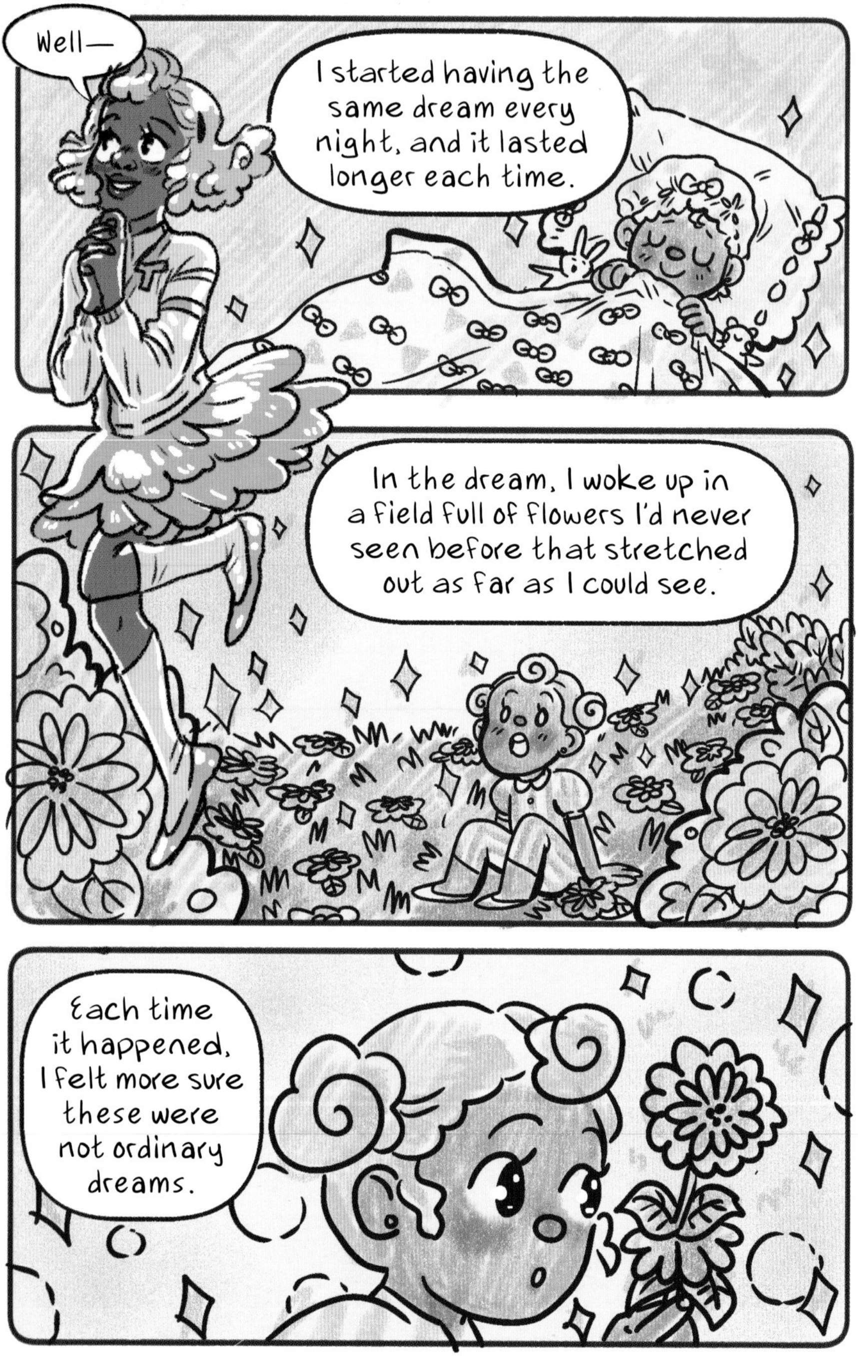
Well—
I started having the same dream every night, and it lasted longer each time.
In the dream, I woke up in a field full of flowers I'd never seen before that stretched out as far as I could see.
Each time it happened, I felt more sure these were not ordinary dreams.

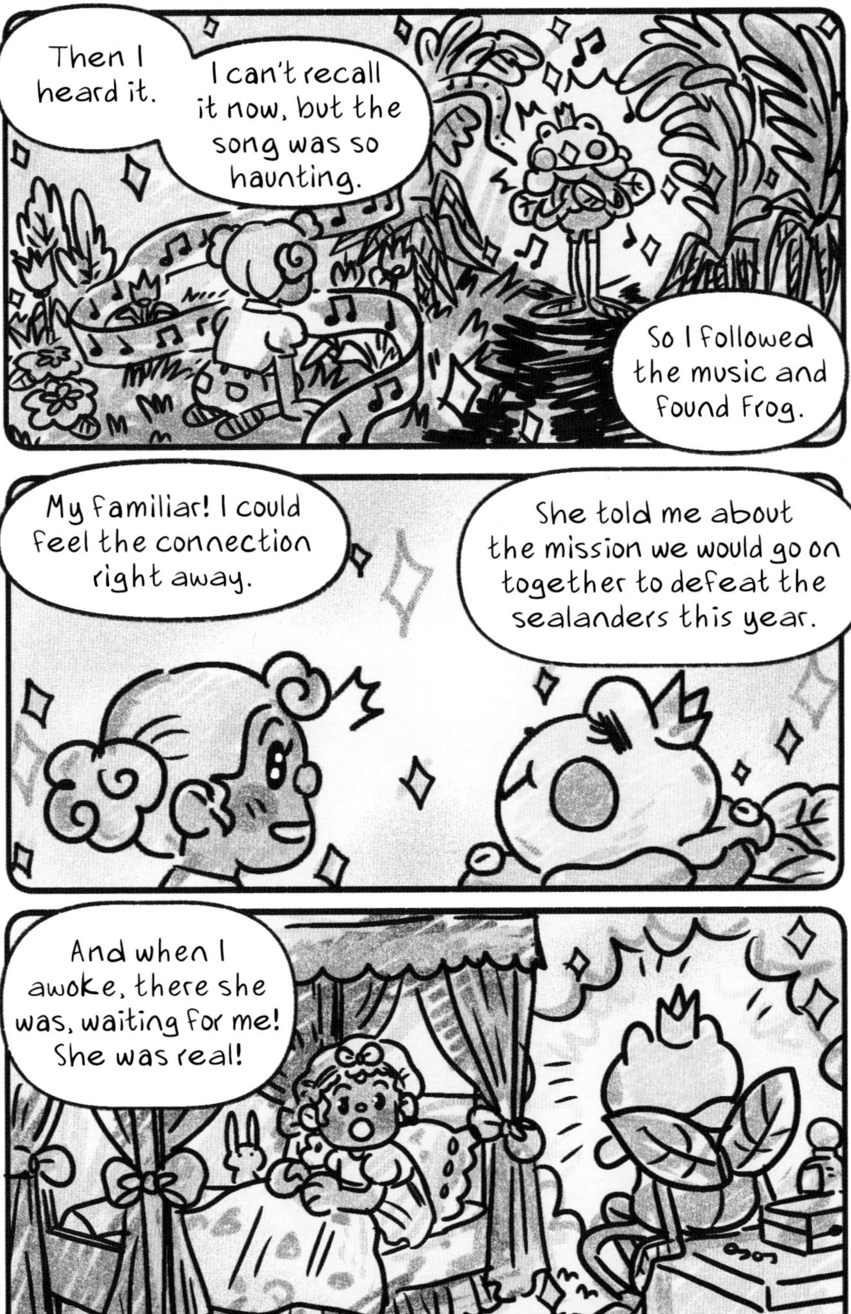
Then I heard it.
I can't recall it now, but the song was so haunting.
So I followed the music and found Frog.
My familiar! I could feel the connection right away.
She told me about the mission we would go on together to defeat the sealanders this year.
And when I awoke, there she was, waiting for me! She was real!

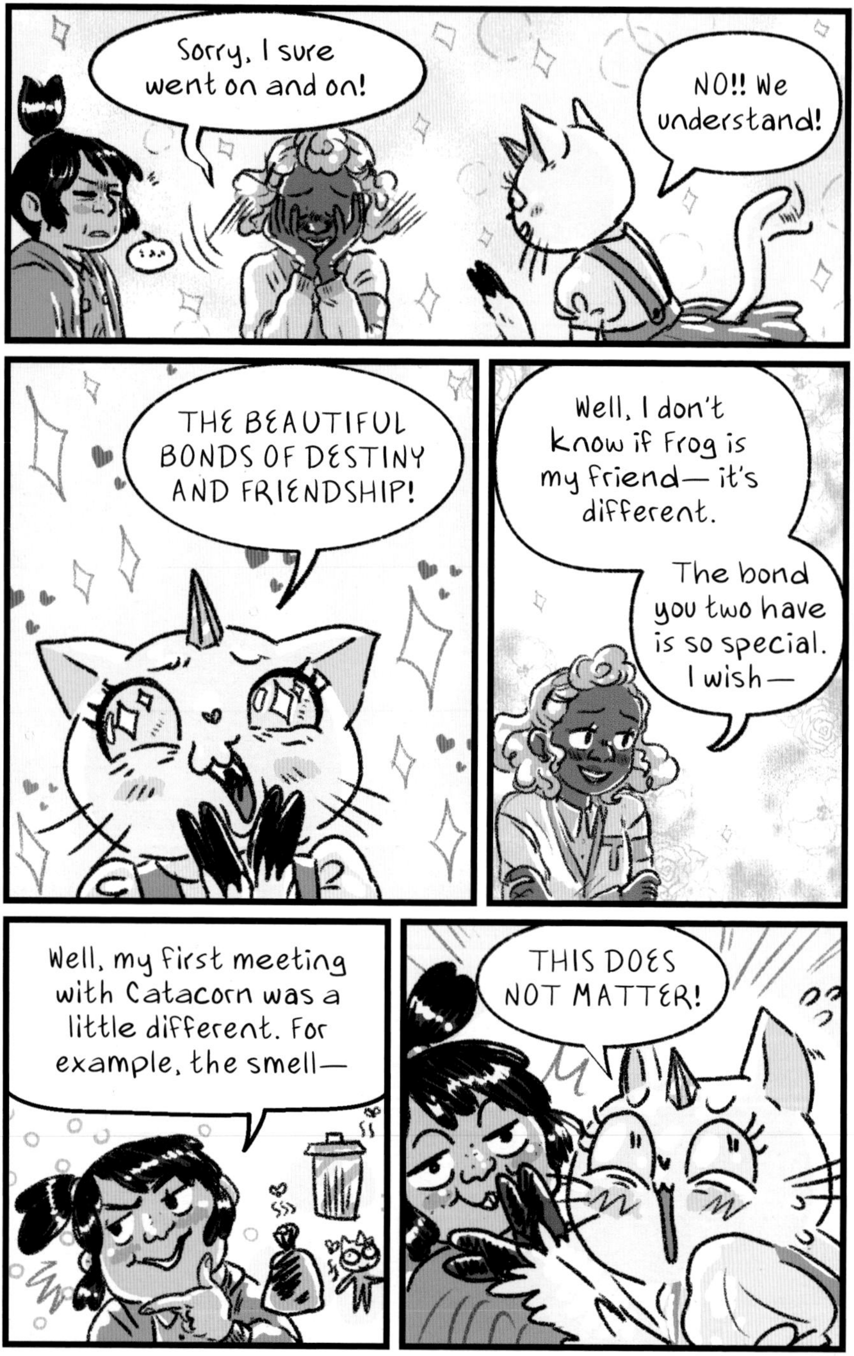
Sorry, I sure went on and on!
NO!! We understand!
THE BEAUTIFUL BONDS OF DESTINY AND FRIENDSHIP!
Well, I don't know if Frog is my friend— it's different.
The bond you two have is so special. I wish—
Well, my first meeting with Catacorn was a little different. For example, the smell—
THIS DOES NOT MATTER!

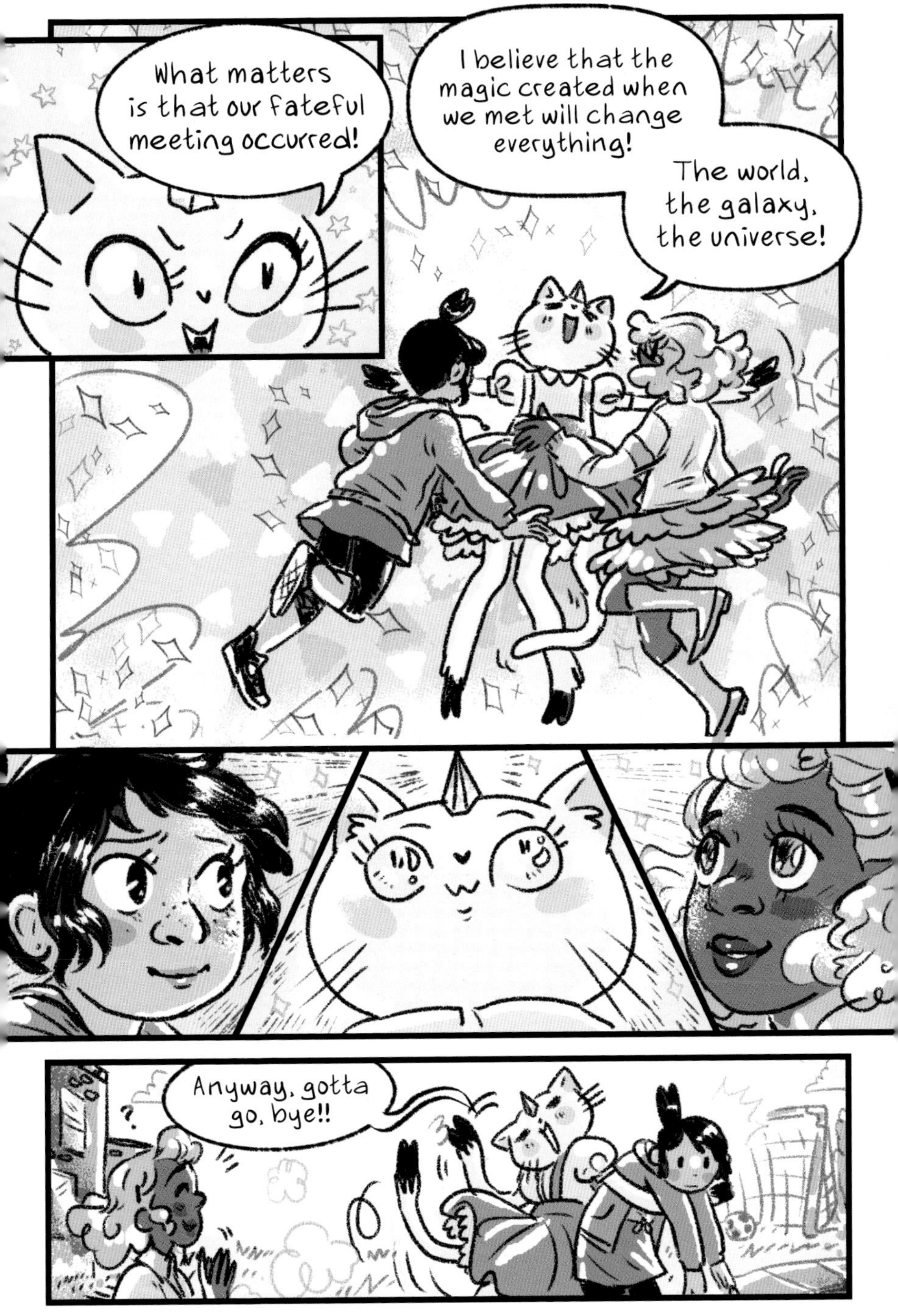
What matters is that our fateful meeting occurred!
I believe that the magic created when we met will change everything!
The world, the galaxy, the universe!
Anyway, gotta go, bye!!
?

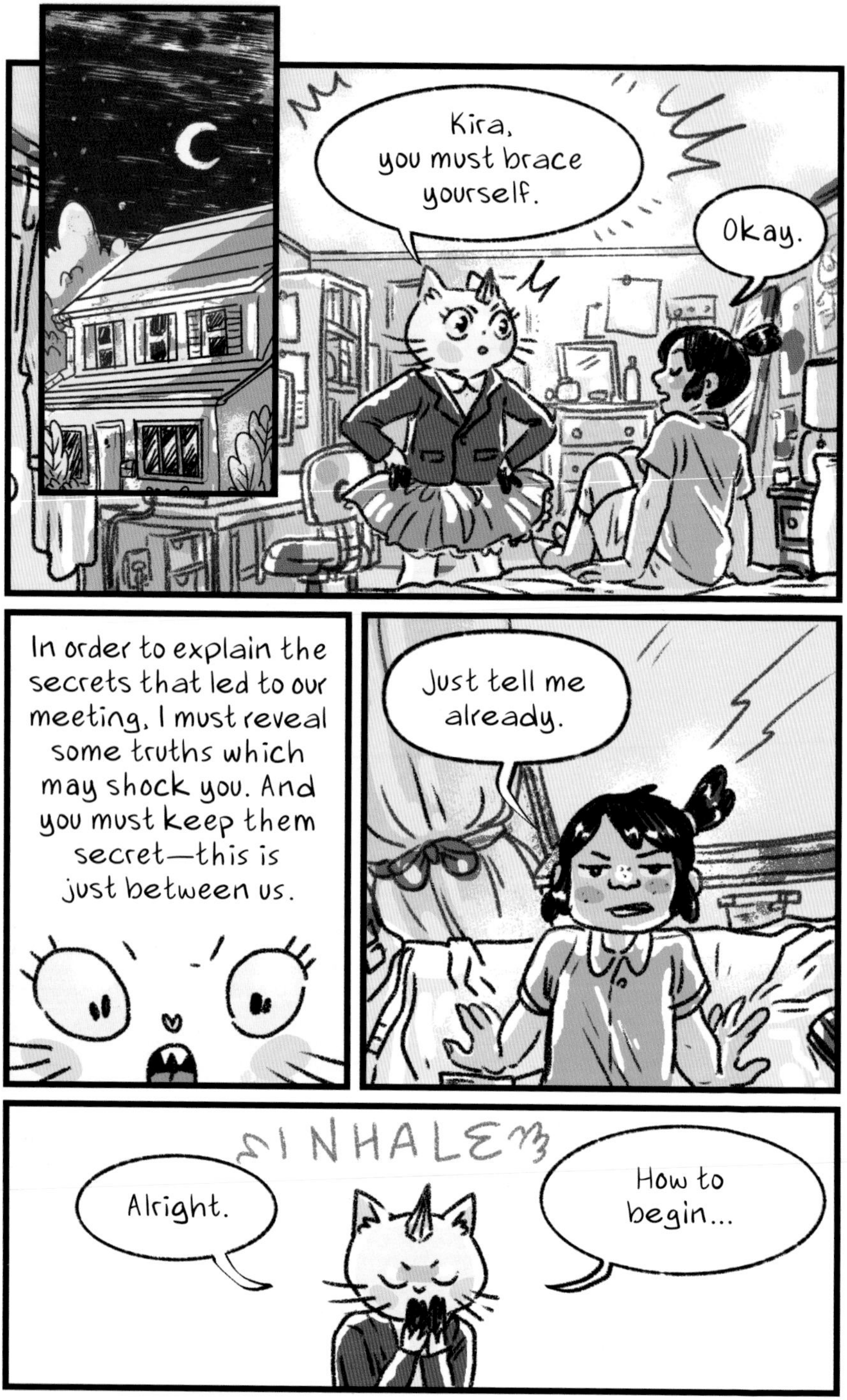

Kira, you must brace yourself.
Okay.
In order to explain the secrets that led to our meeting, I must reveal some truths which may shock you. And you must keep them secret—this is just between us.
Just tell me already.
INHALE
Alright.
How to begin...

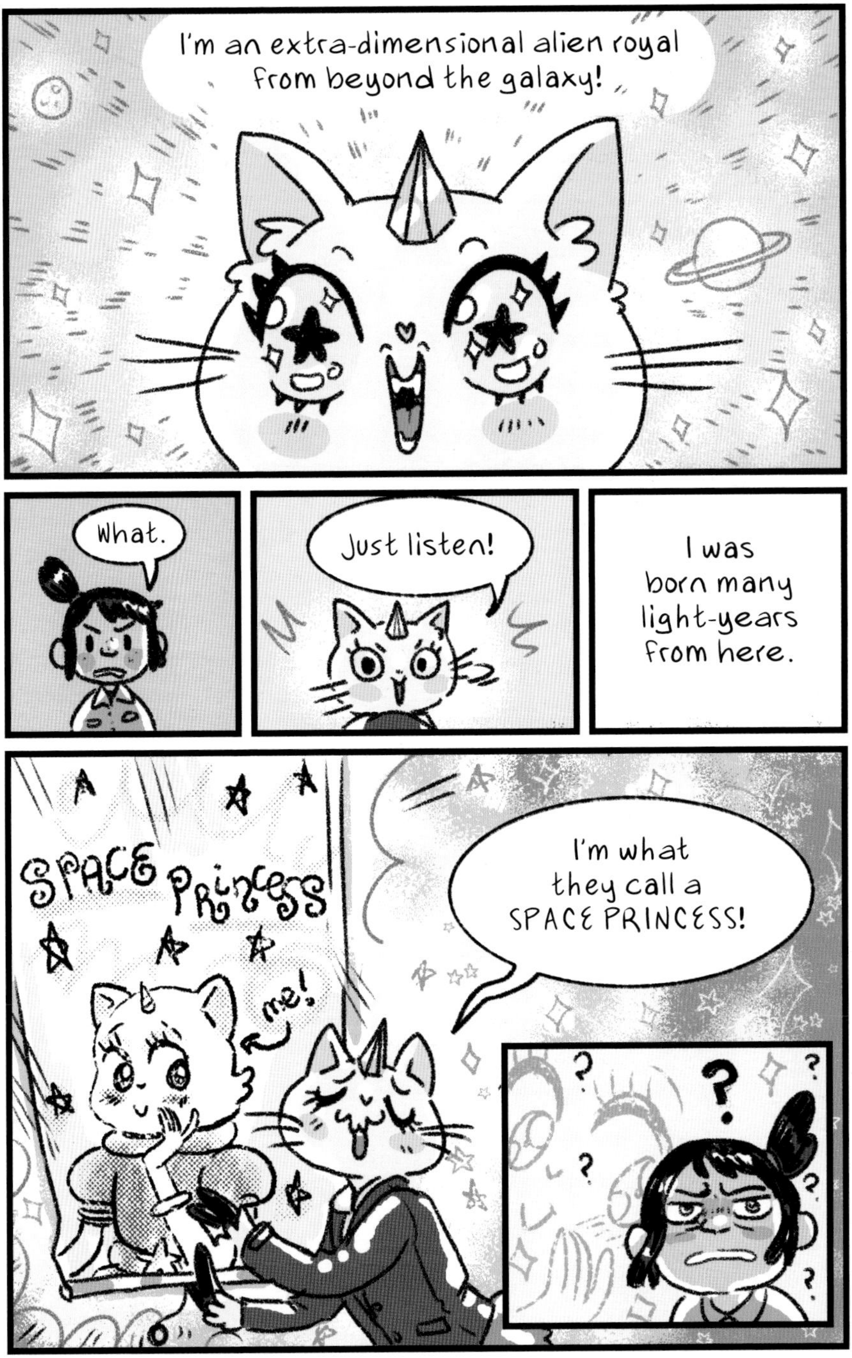
I'm an extra-dimensional alien royal from beyond the galaxy!
What.
Just listen!
I was born many light-years from here.
SPACE PRINCESS
me!
I'm what they call a SPACE PRINCESS!

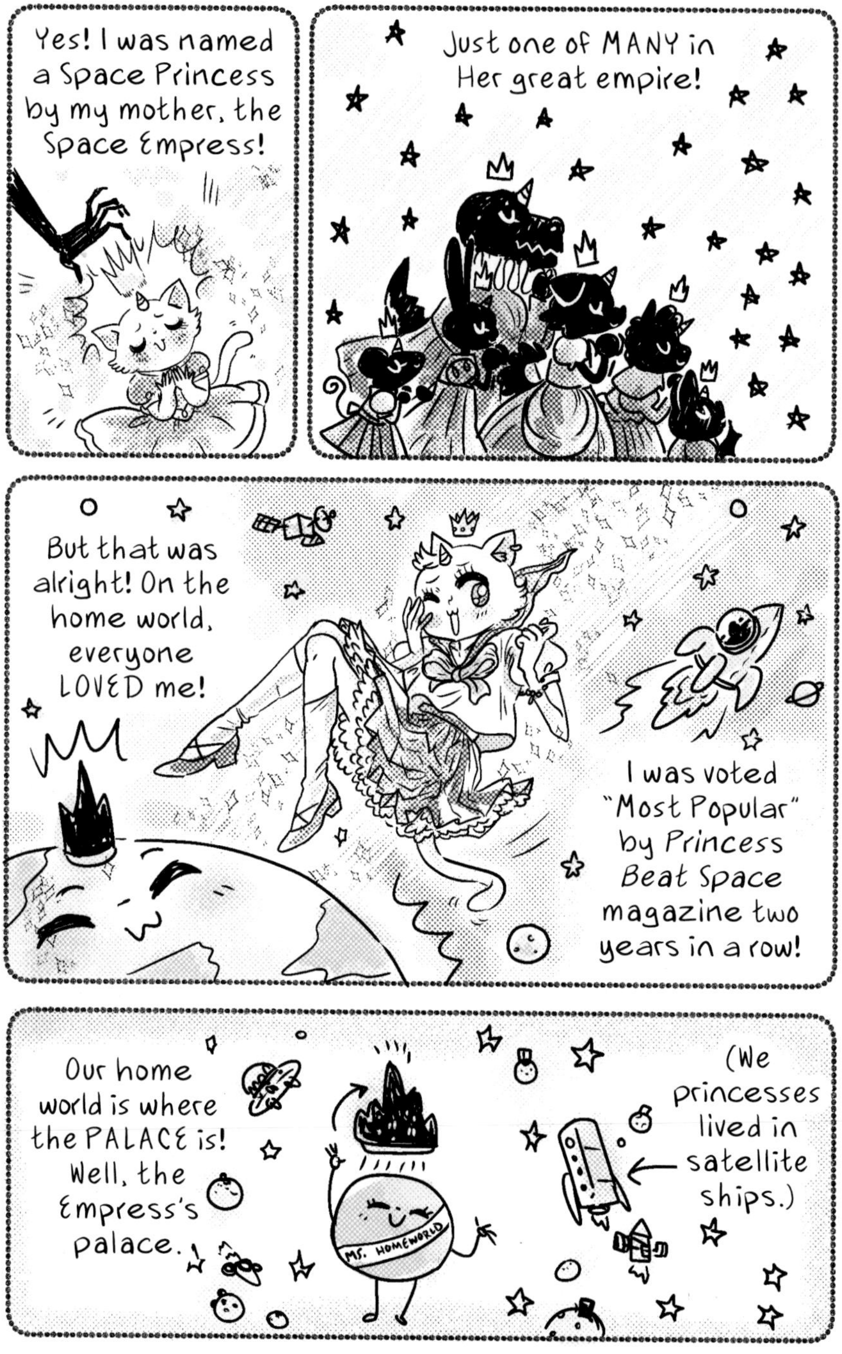
Yes! I was named a Space Princess by my mother, the Space Empress!
Just one of MANY in Her great empire!
But that was alright! On the home world, everyone LOVED me!
I was voted "Most Popular" by Princess Beat Space magazine two years in a row!
Our home world is where the PALACE is! Well, the Empress's palace.
MS. HOMEWORLD
(We princesses lived in satellite ships.)

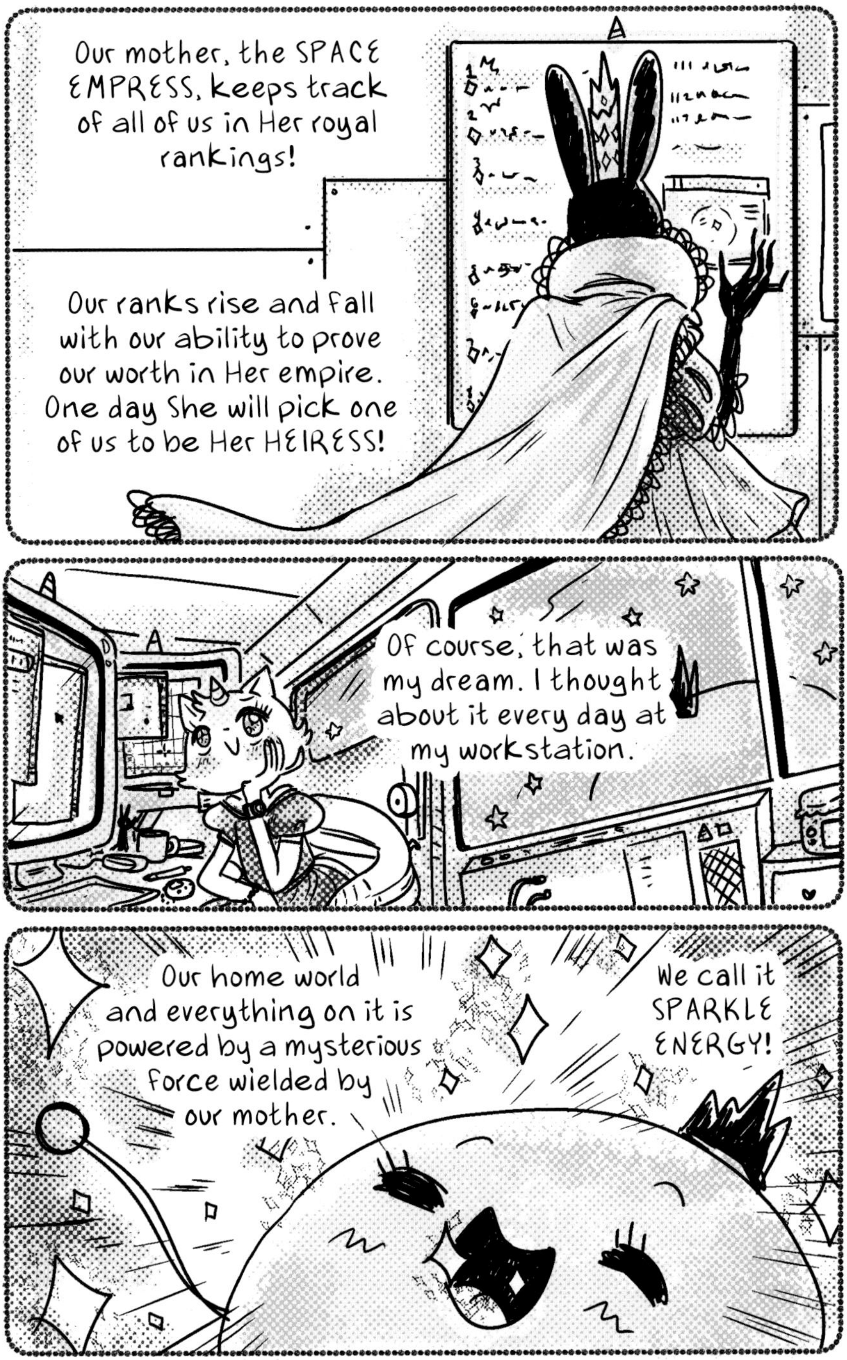
Our mother, the SPACE EMPRESS, keeps track of all of us in Her royal rankings!
Our ranks rise and fall with our ability to prove our worth in Her empire. One day She will pick one of us to be Her HEIRESS!
Of course, that was my dream. I thought about it every day at my workstation.
Our home world and everything on it is powered by a mysterious force wielded by our mother.
We call it SPARKLE ENERGY!

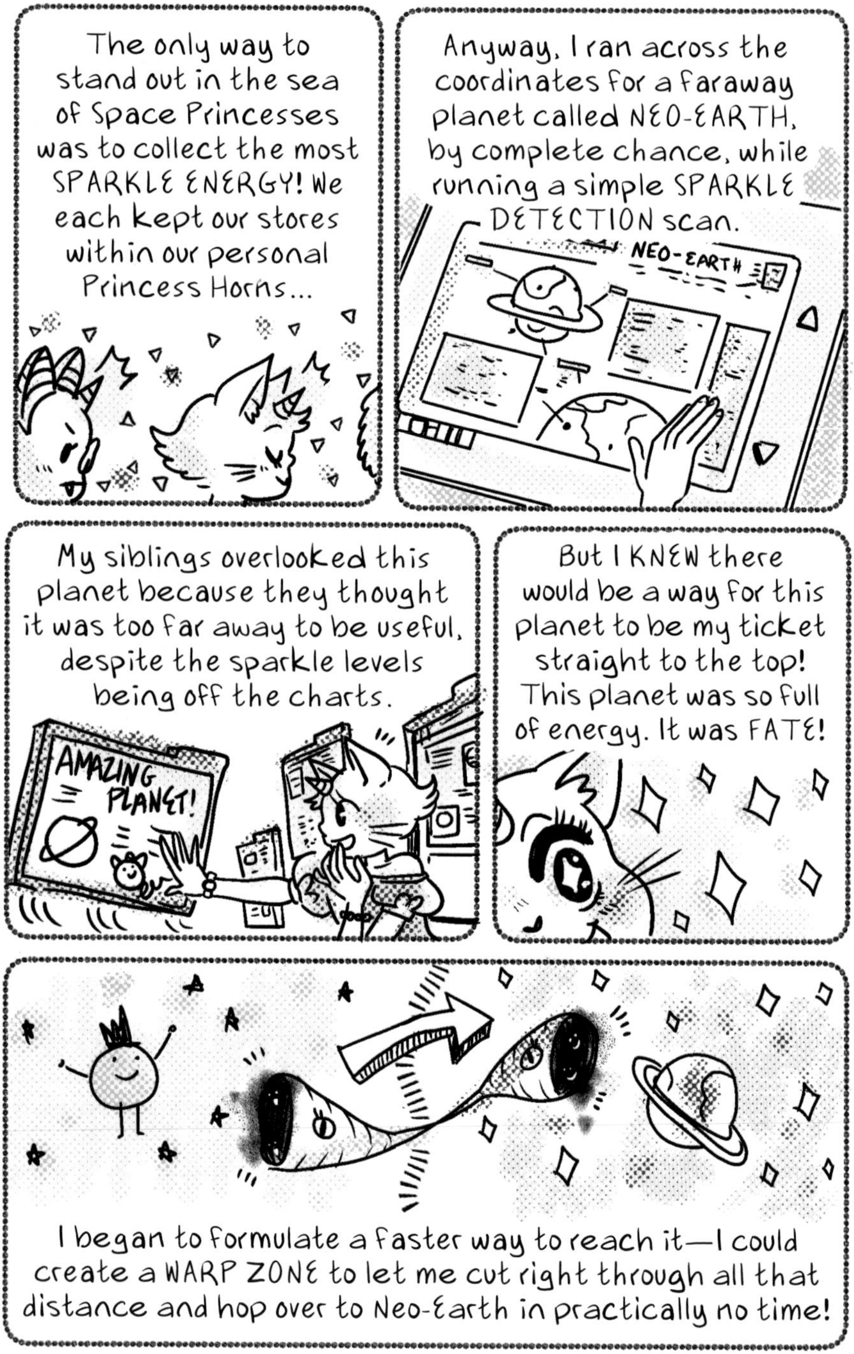
The only way to stand out in the sea of Space Princesses was to collect the most SPARKLE ENERGY! We each kept our stores within our personal Princess Horns...
Anyway, I ran across the coordinates for a faraway planet called NEO-EARTH, by complete chance, while running a simple SPARKLE DETECTION scan.
NEO-EARTH
My siblings overlooked this planet because they thought it was too far away to be useful, despite the sparkle levels being off the charts.
AMAZING PLANET!
But I KNEW there would be a way for this planet to be my ticket straight to the top! This planet was so full of energy. It was FATE!
I began to formulate a faster way to reach it—I could create a WARP ZONE to let me cut right through all that distance and hop over to Neo-Earth in practically no time!

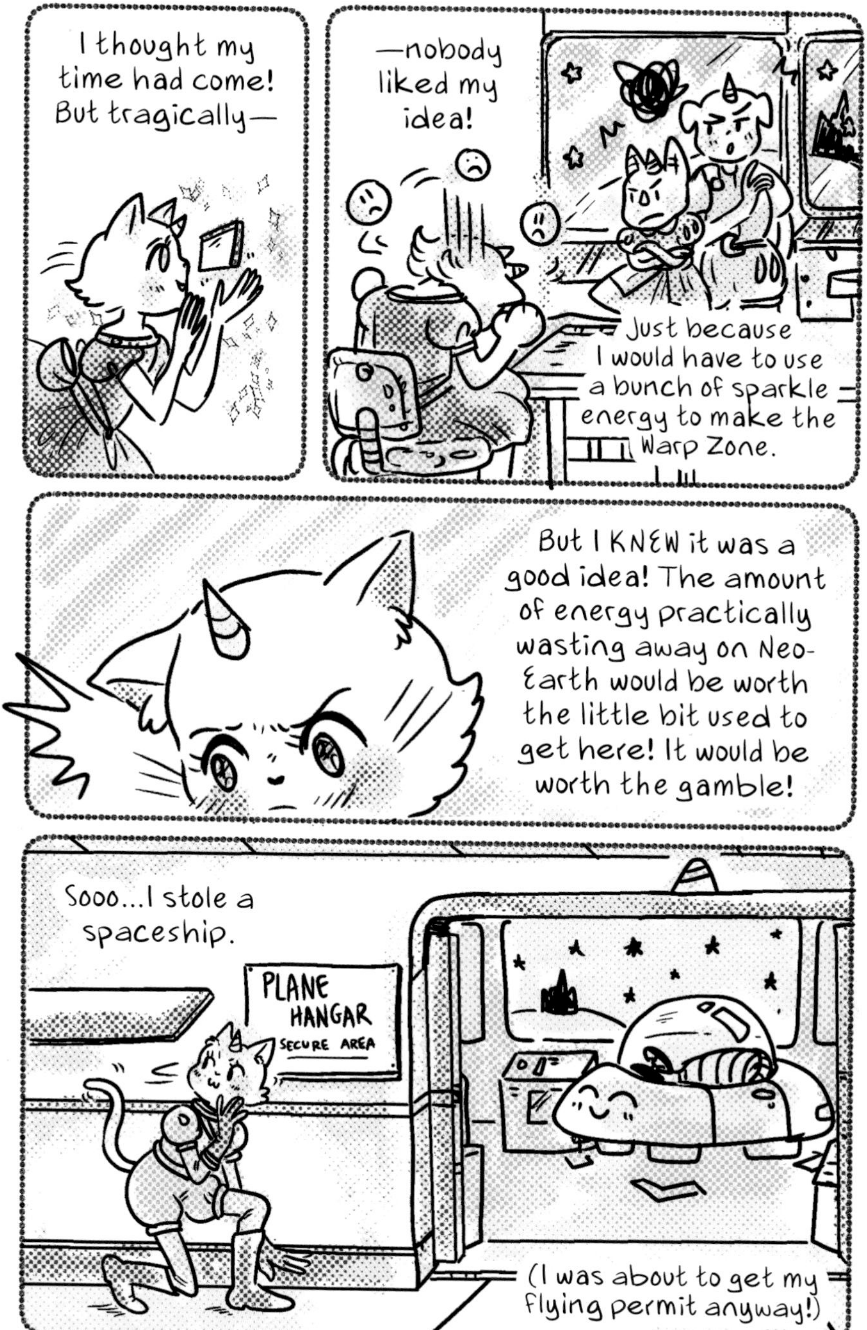
I thought my time had come! But tragically—
—nobody liked my idea!
Just because I would have to use a bunch of sparkle energy to make the Warp Zone.
But I KNEW it was a good idea! The amount of energy practically wasting away on Neo-Earth would be worth the little bit used to get here! It would be worth the gamble!
Sooo...I stole a spaceship.
PLANE HANGAR
SECURE AREA
(I was about to get my flying permit anyway!)

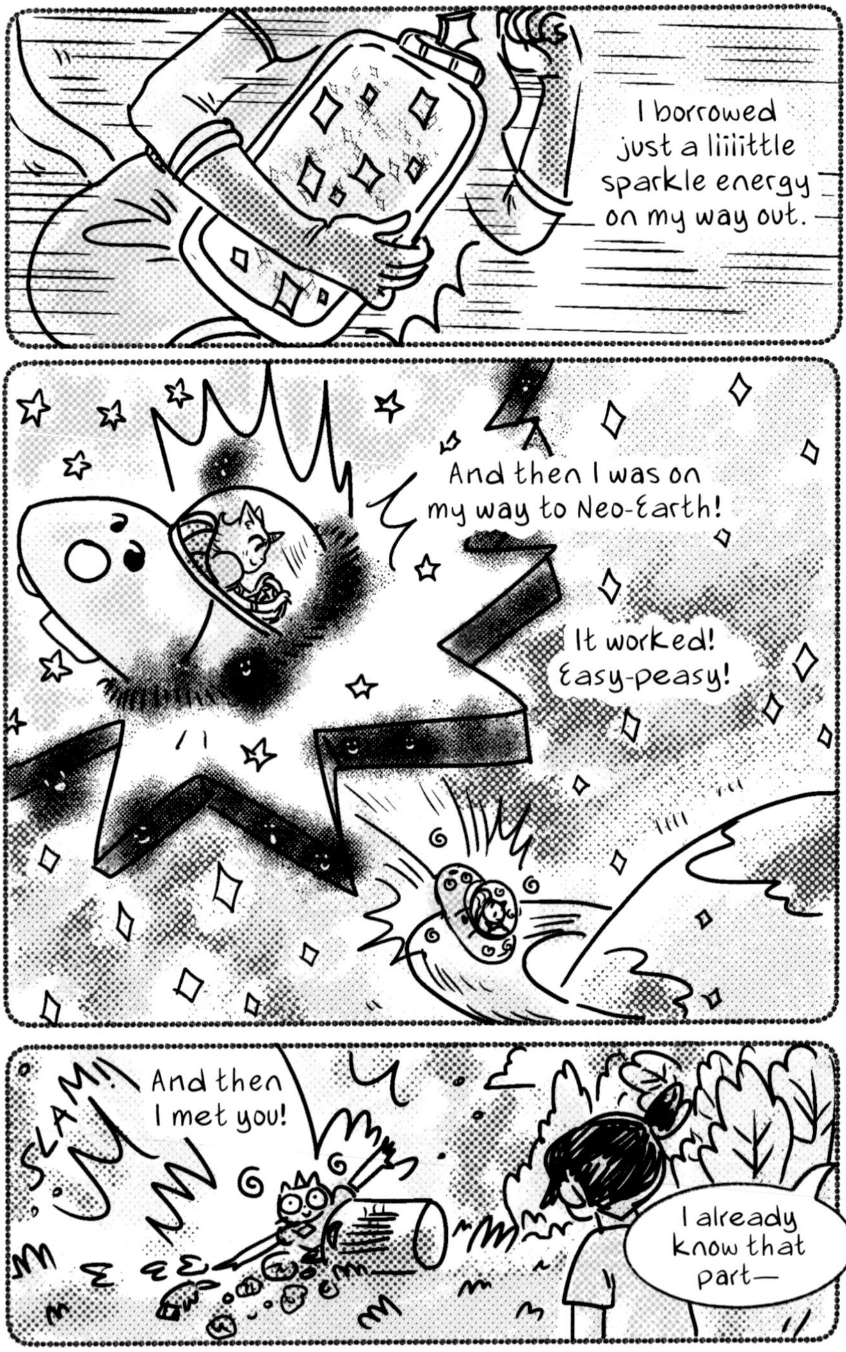
I borrowed just a liiiittle sparkle energy on my way out.
And then I was on my way to Neo-Earth!
It worked! Easy-peasy!
SLAM!!
And then I met you!
I already know that part—

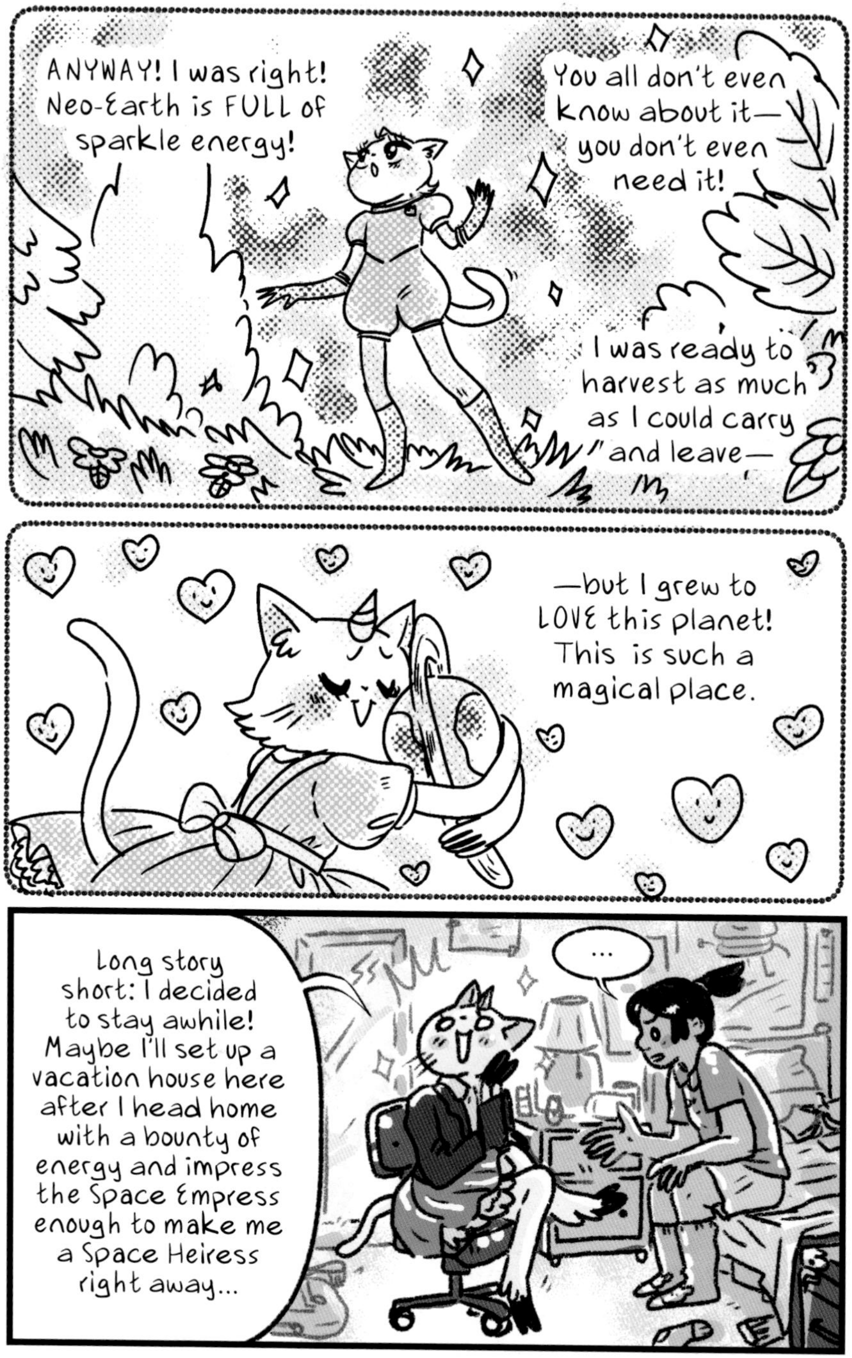
ANYWAY! I was right! Neo-Earth is FULL of sparkle energy!
You all don't even know about it— you don't even need it!
I was ready to harvest as much as I could carry and leave—
—but I grew to LOVE this planet! This is such a magical place.
Long story short: I decided to stay awhile! Maybe I'll set up a vacation house here after I head home with a bounty of energy and impress the Space Empress enough to make me a Space Heiress right away...
...

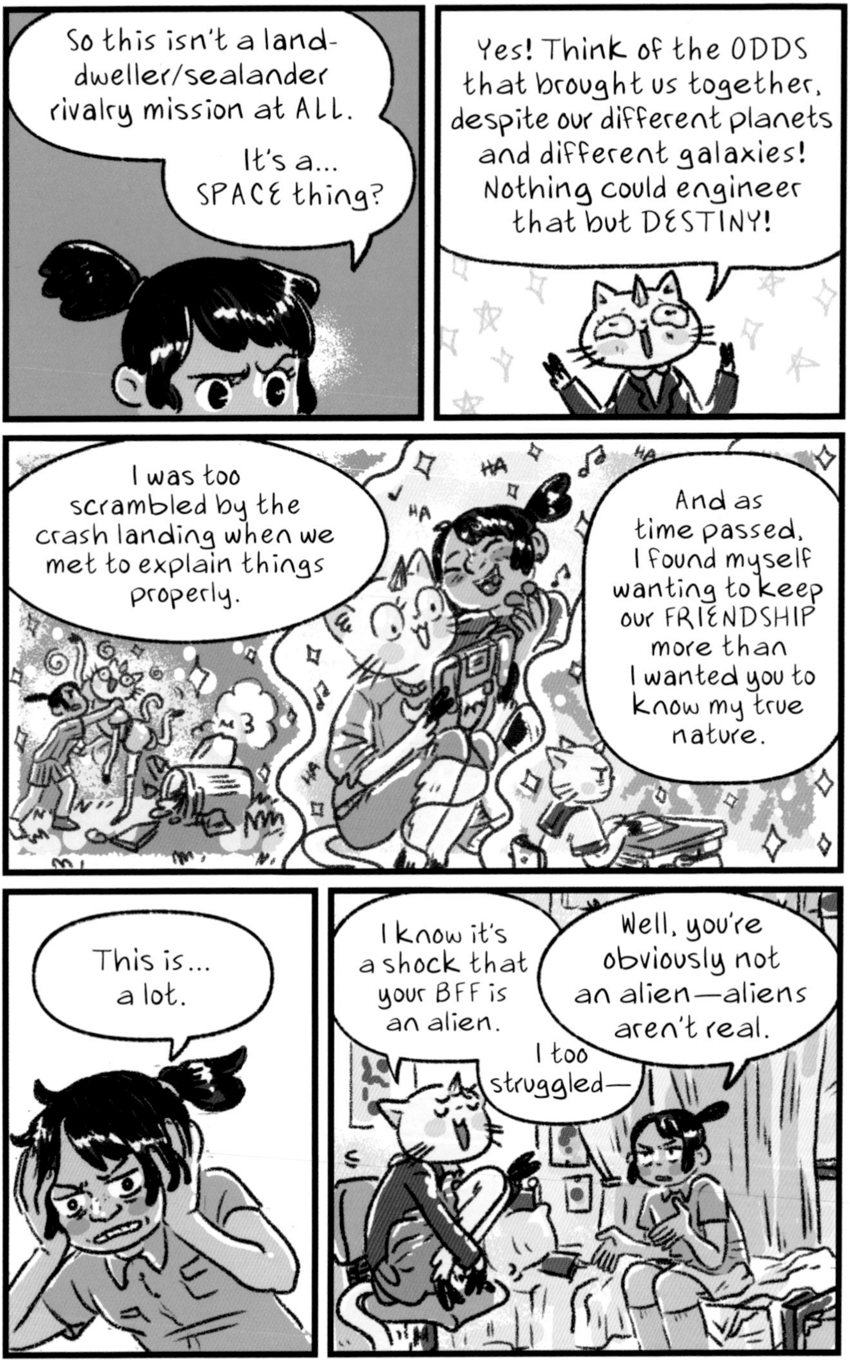
So this isn't a land-dweller/sealander rivalry mission at ALL.
It's a... SPACE thing?
Yes! Think of the ODDS that brought us together, despite our different planets and different galaxies! Nothing could engineer that but DESTINY!
I was too scrambled by the crash landing when we met to explain things properly.
HA
HA
HA
HA
And as time passed, I found myself wanting to keep our FRIENDSHIP more than I wanted you to know my true nature.
This is... a lot.
I know it's a shock that your BFF is an alien.
Well, you're obviously not an alien—aliens aren't real.
I too struggled—

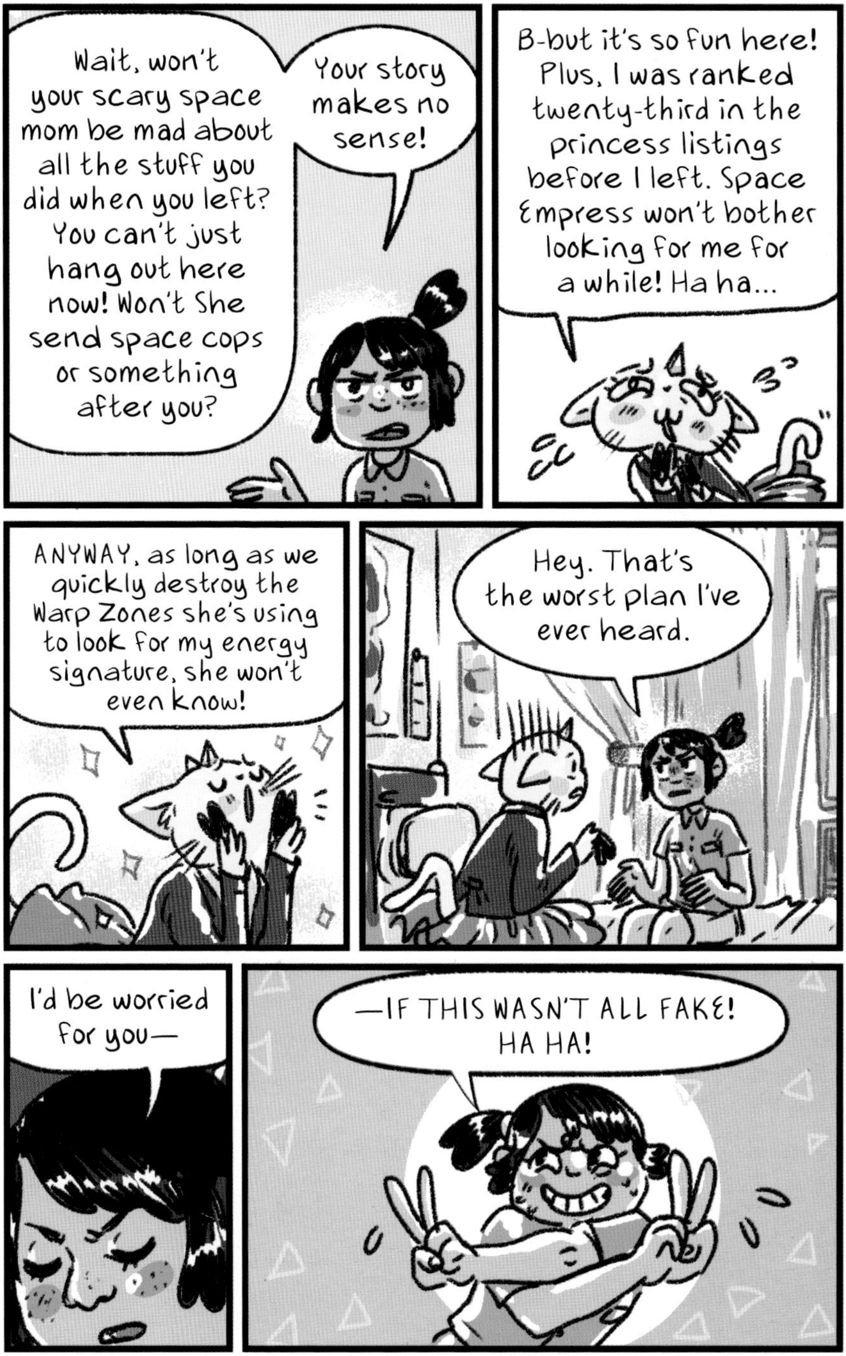
Wait, won't your scary space mom be mad about all the stuff you did when you left? You can't just hang out here now! Won't She send space cops or something after you?
Your story makes no sense!
B-but it's so fun here! Plus, I was ranked twenty-third in the princess listings before I left. Space Empress won't bother looking for me for a while! Ha ha...
ANYWAY, as long as we quickly destroy the Warp Zones she's using to look for my energy signature, she won't even know!
Hey. That's the worst plan I've ever heard.
I'd be worried for you—
—IF THIS WASN'T ALL FAKE! HA HA!

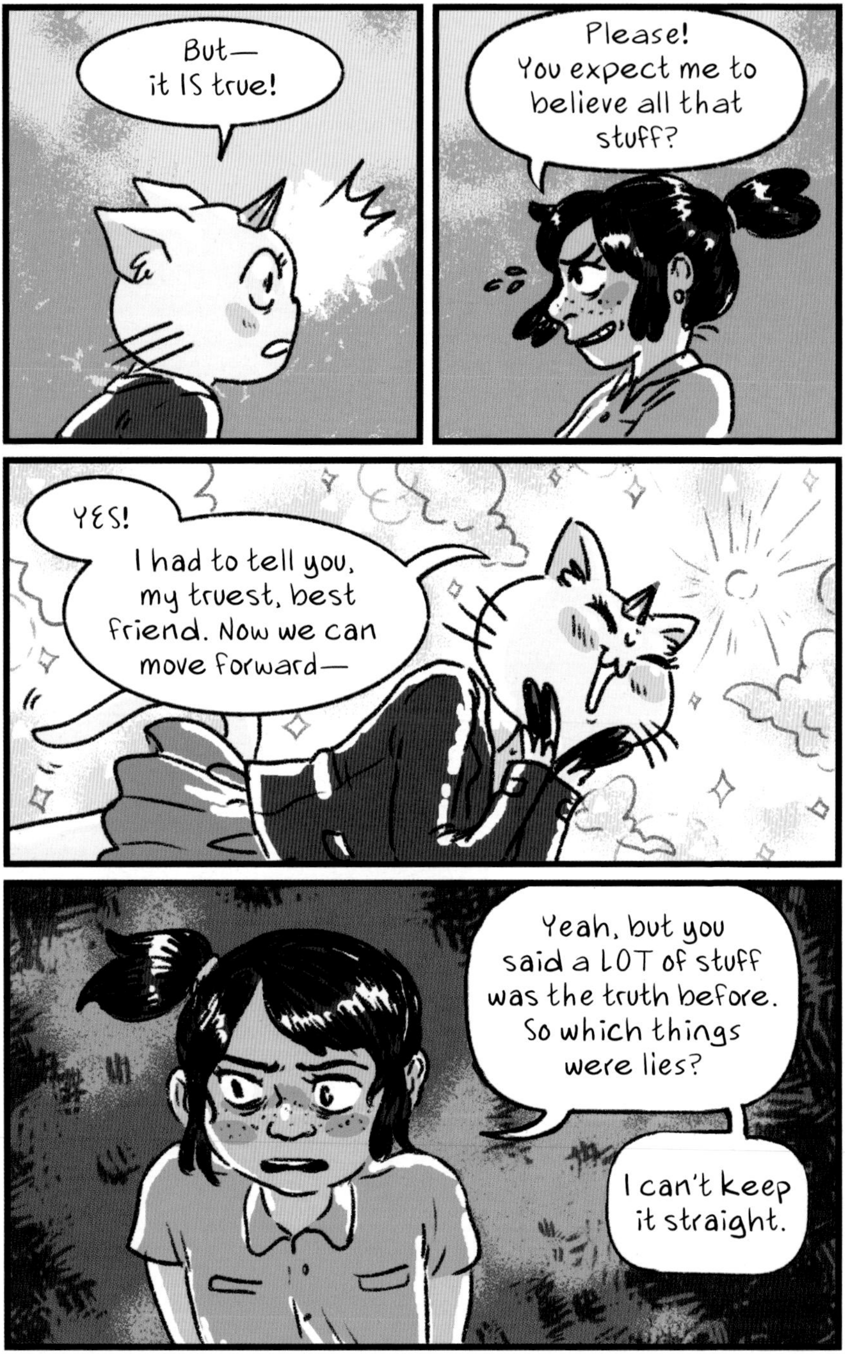
But— it IS true!
Please! You expect me to believe all that stuff?
YES!
I had to tell you, my truest, best friend. Now we can move forward—
Yeah, but you said a LOT of stuff was the truth before. So which things were lies?
I can't keep it straight.

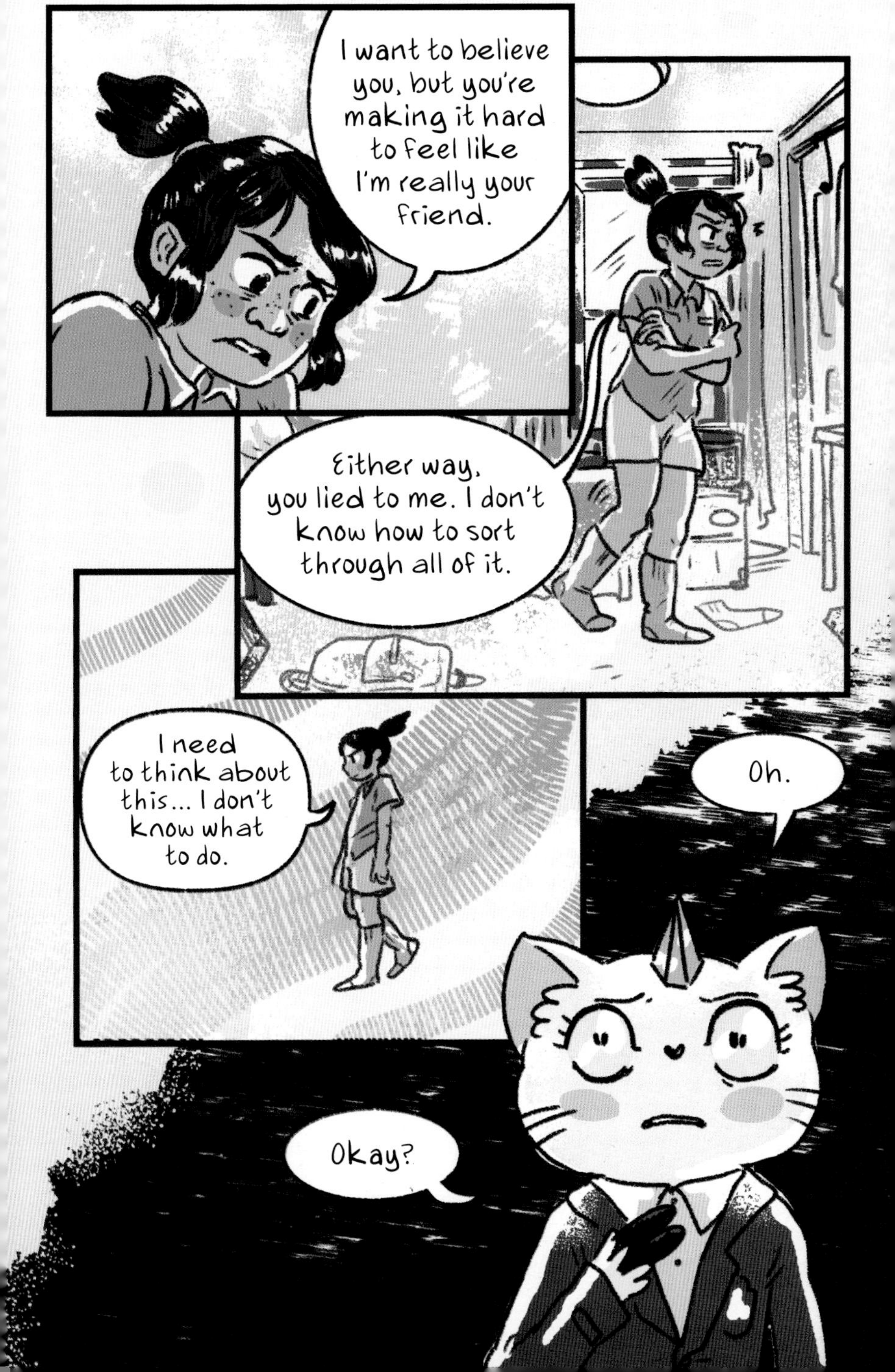
I want to believe you, but you're making it hard to feel like I'm really your friend.
Either way, you lied to me. I don't know how to sort through all of it.
I need to think about this... I don't know what to do.
Oh.
Okay?

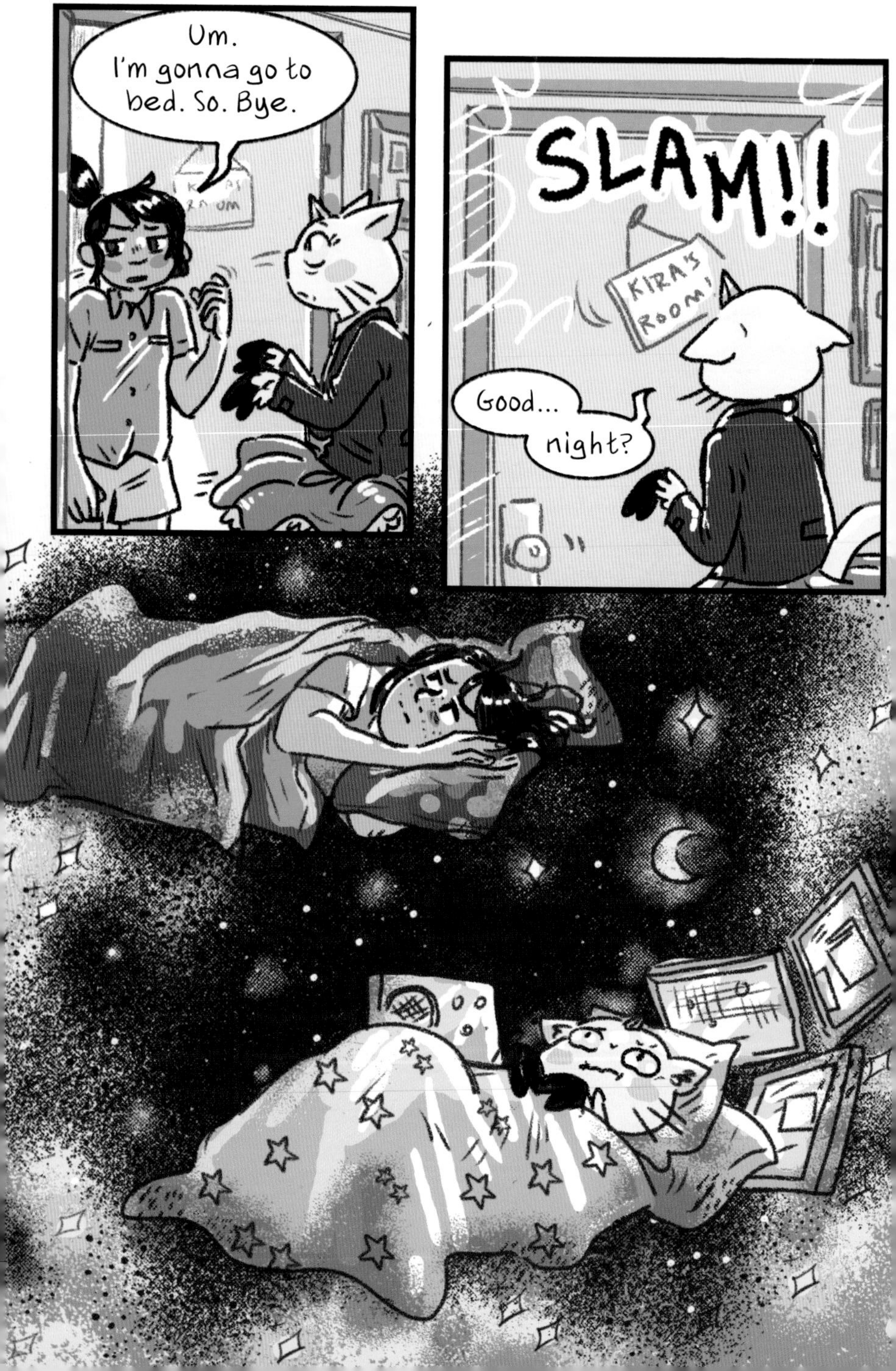
Um.
I'm gonna go to bed. So. Bye.
KIRA'S ROOM
SLAM!!
KIRA'S ROOM!
Good... night?

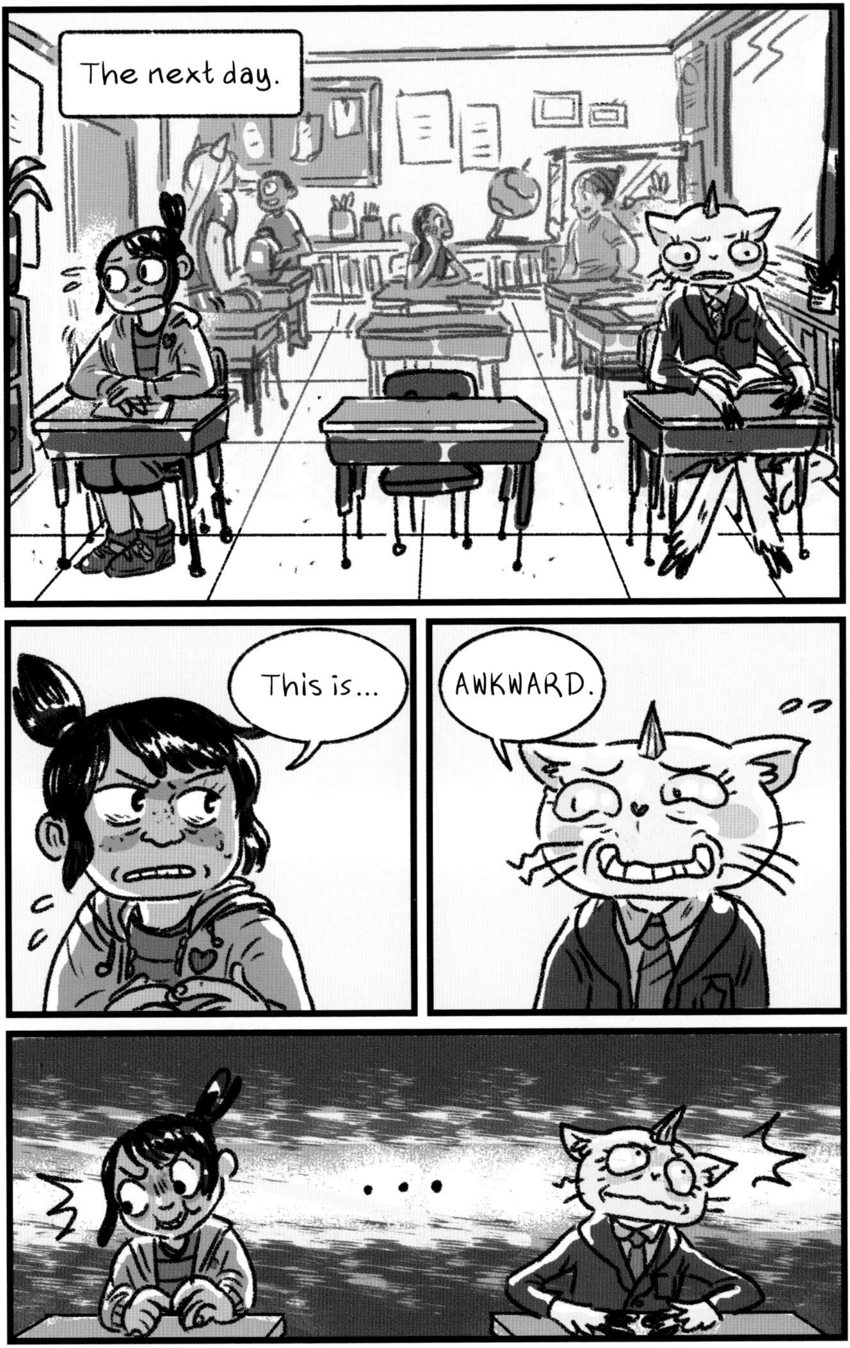
The next day.
This is...
AWKWARD.
• • •

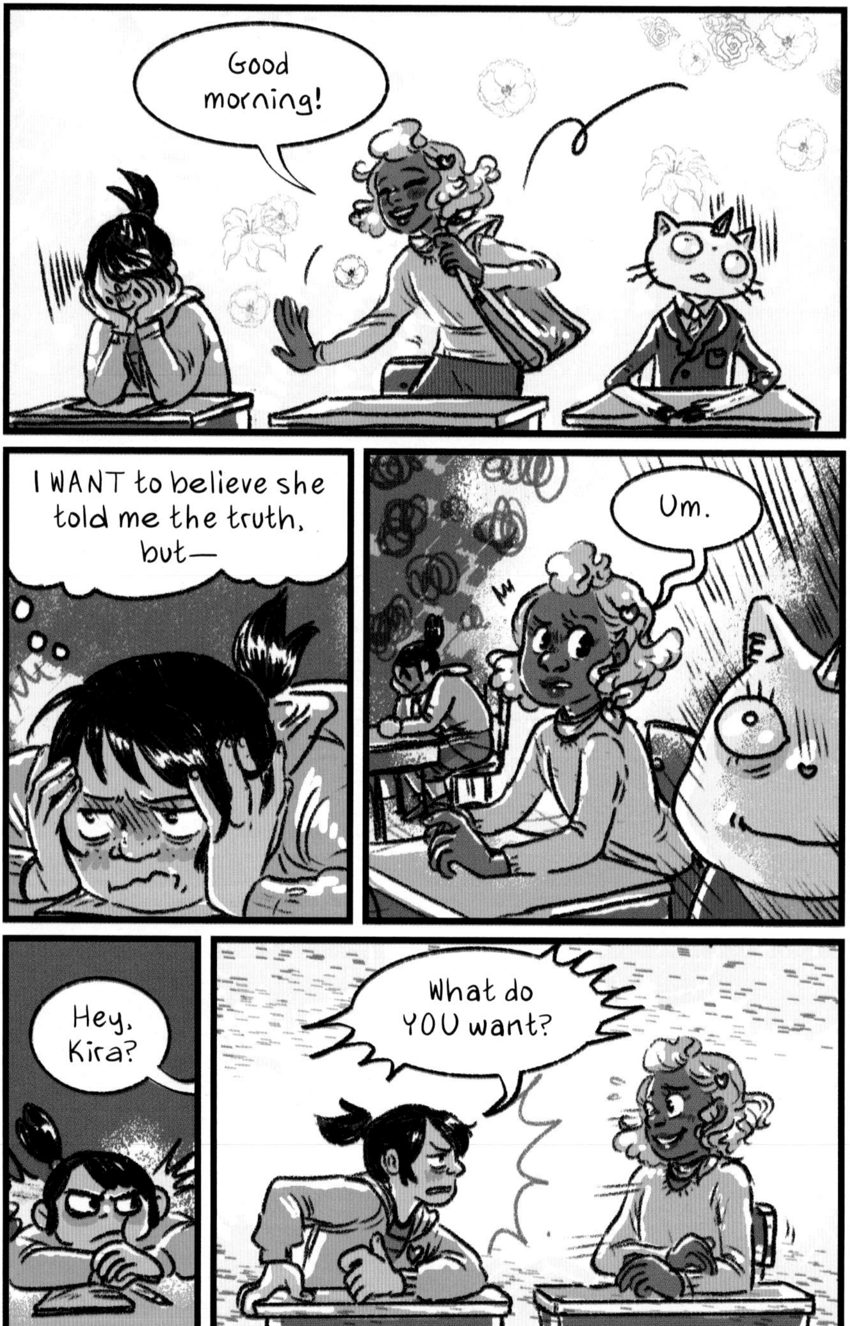
Good morning!
I WANT to believe she told me the truth, but—
Um.
Hey, Kira?
What do YOU want?

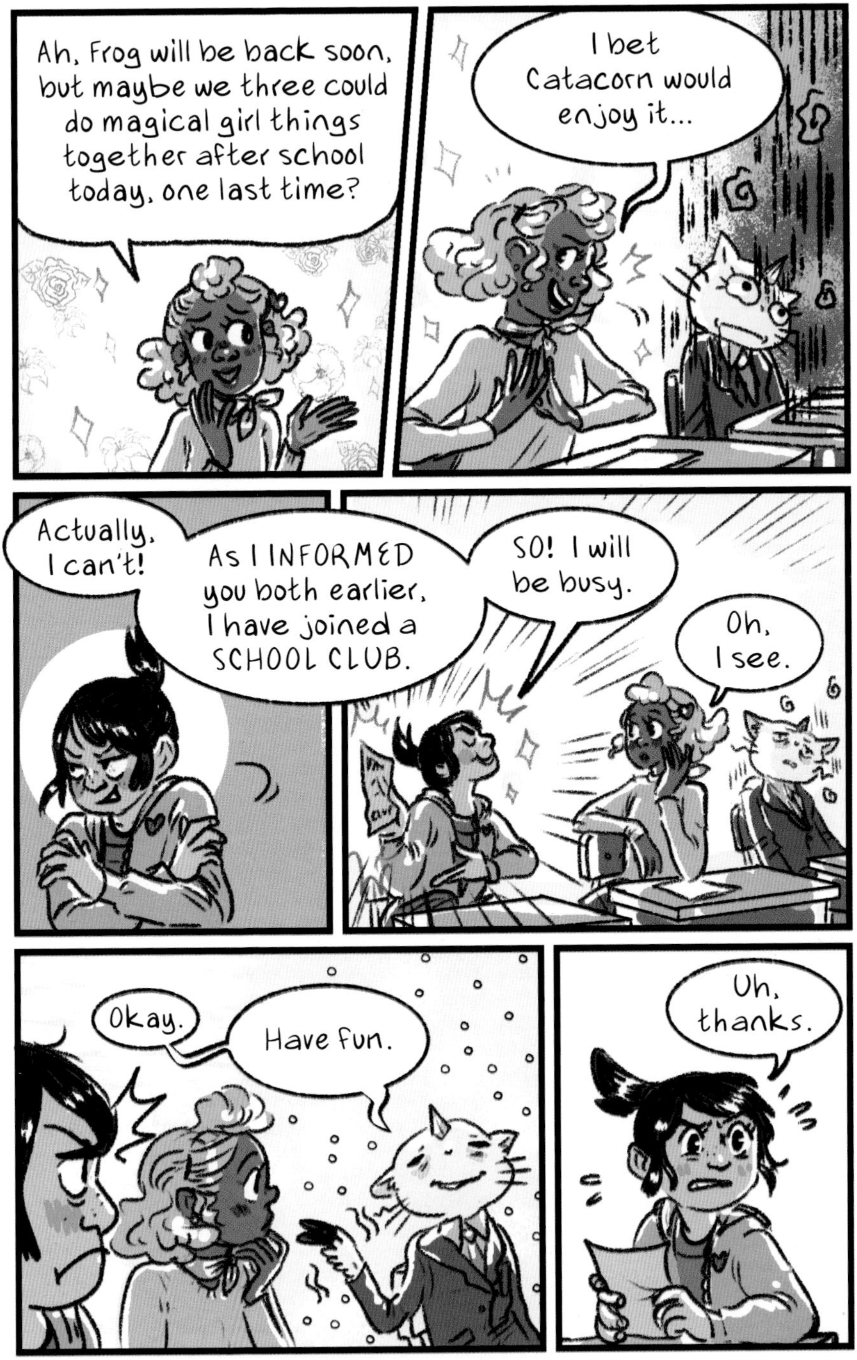
Ah, Frog will be back soon, but maybe we three could do magical girl things together after school today, one last time?
I bet Catacorn would enjoy it...
Actually, I can't!
As I INFORMED you both earlier, I have joined a SCHOOL CLUB.
SO! I will be busy.
Oh, I see.
Okay.
Have fun.
Uh, thanks.

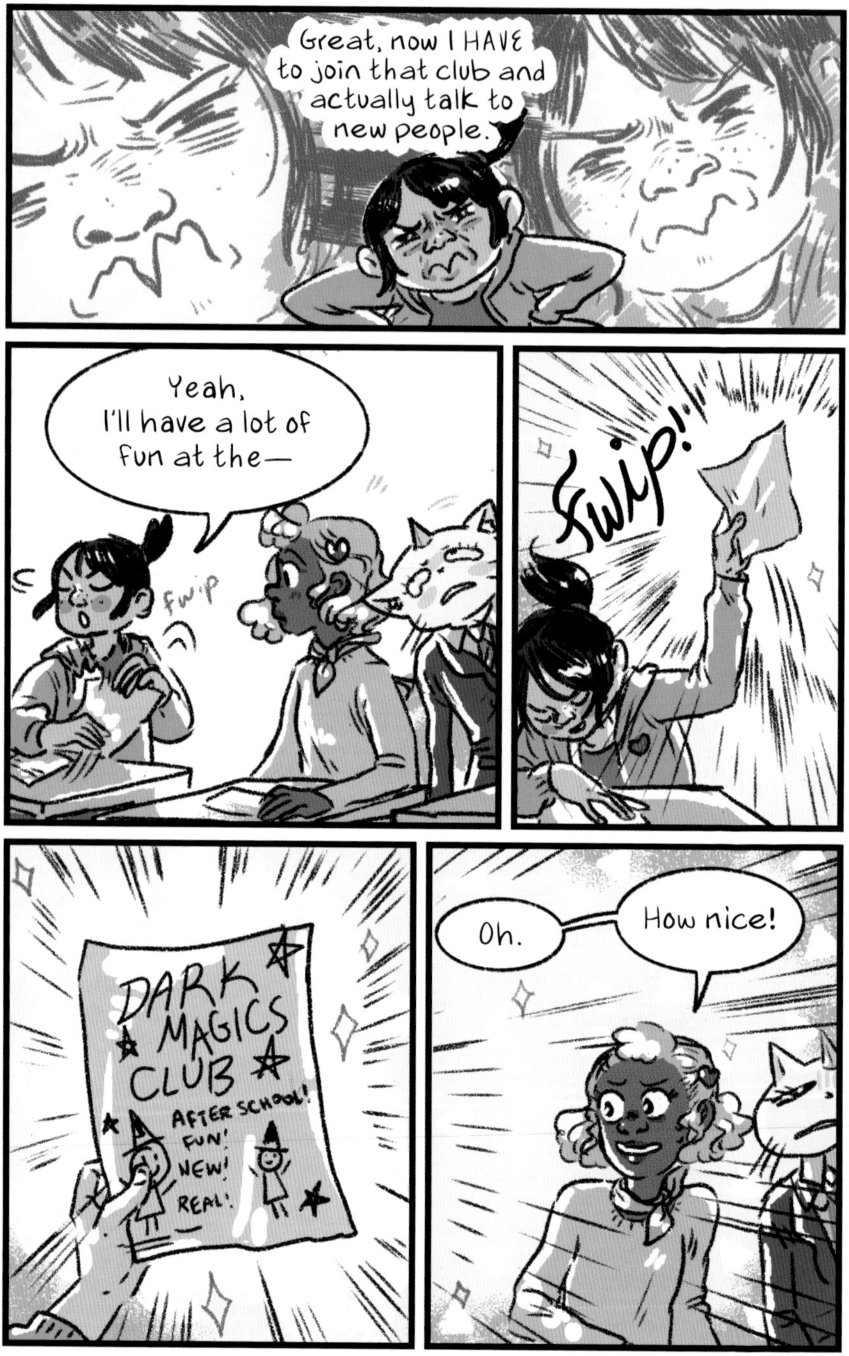
Great, now I HAVE to join that club and actually talk to new people.
Yeah, I'll have a lot of fun at the—
fwip
FWIP!
DARK MAGICS CLUB
AFTER SCHOOL!
FUN!
NEW!
REAL!
Oh.
How nice!

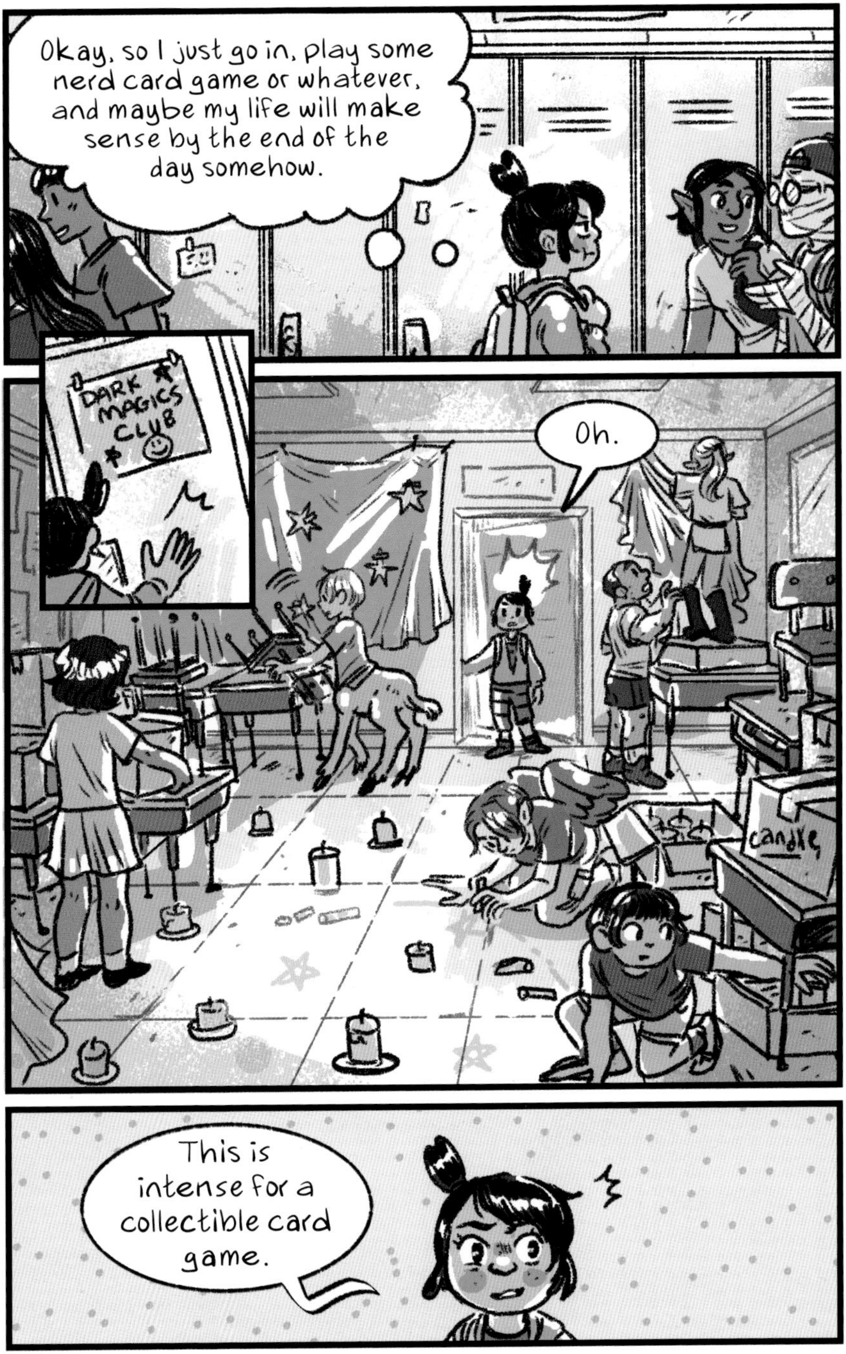
Okay, so I just go in, play some nerd card game or whatever, and maybe my life will make sense by the end of the day somehow.
DARK MAGICS CLUB
Oh.
candle
This is intense for a collectible card game.

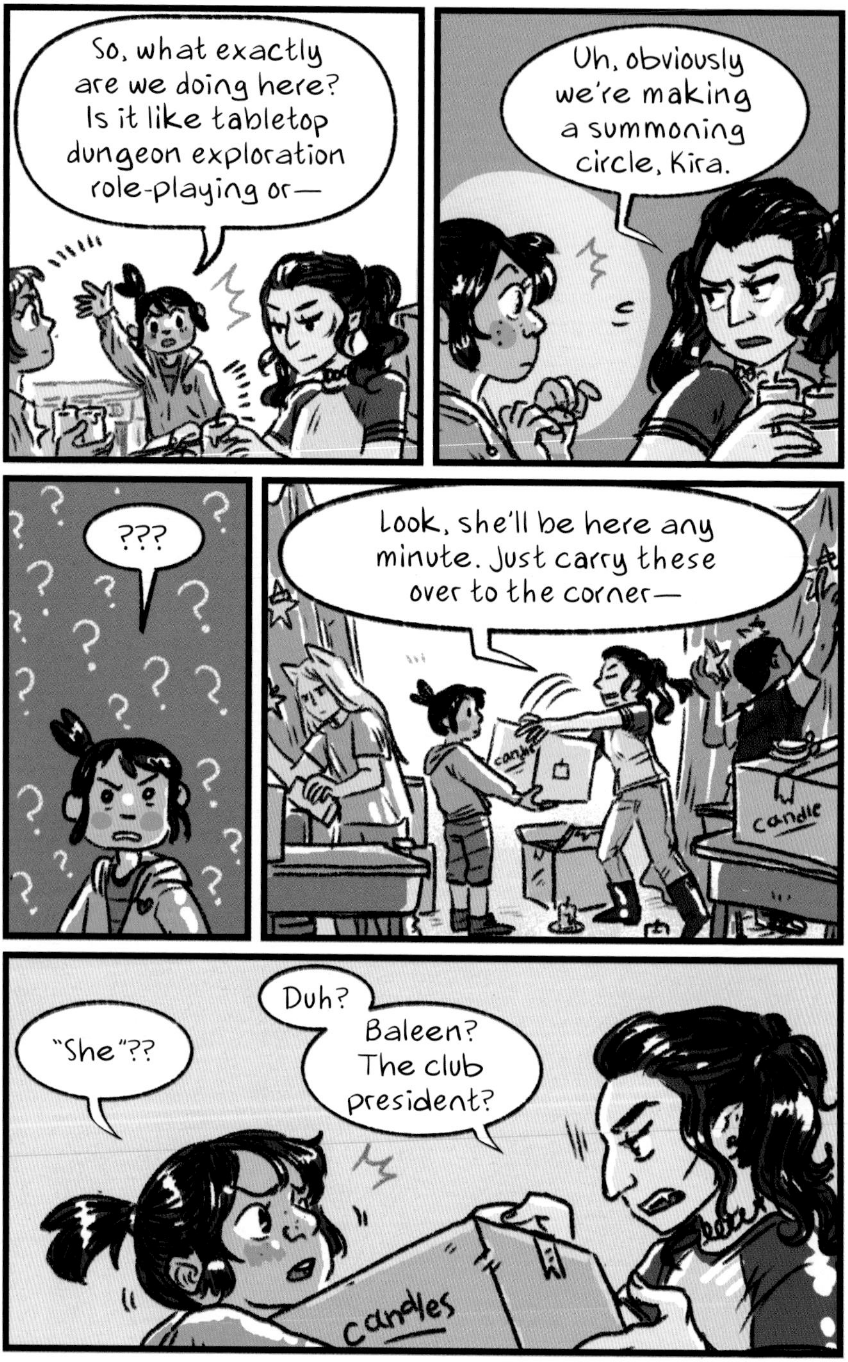
So, what exactly are we doing here? Is it like tabletop dungeon exploration role-playing or—
Uh, obviously we're making a summoning circle, Kira.
???
Look, she'll be here any minute. Just carry these over to the corner—
candle
candle
"She"??
Duh?
Baleen? The club president?
candles

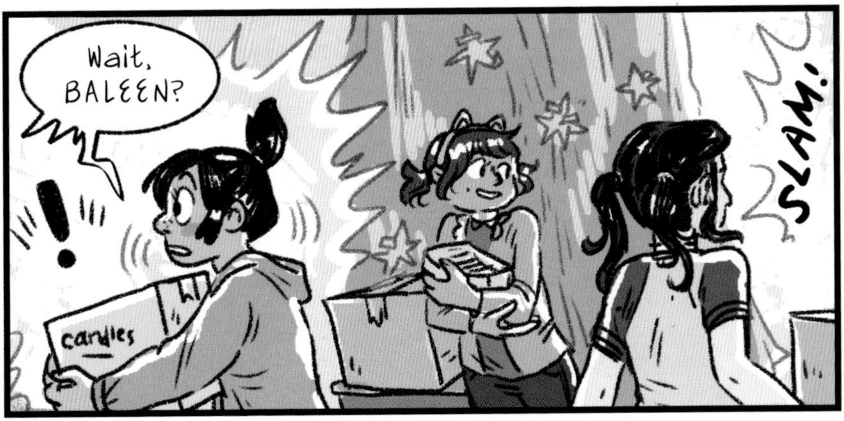
Wait, BALEEN?
!
candles
SLAM!

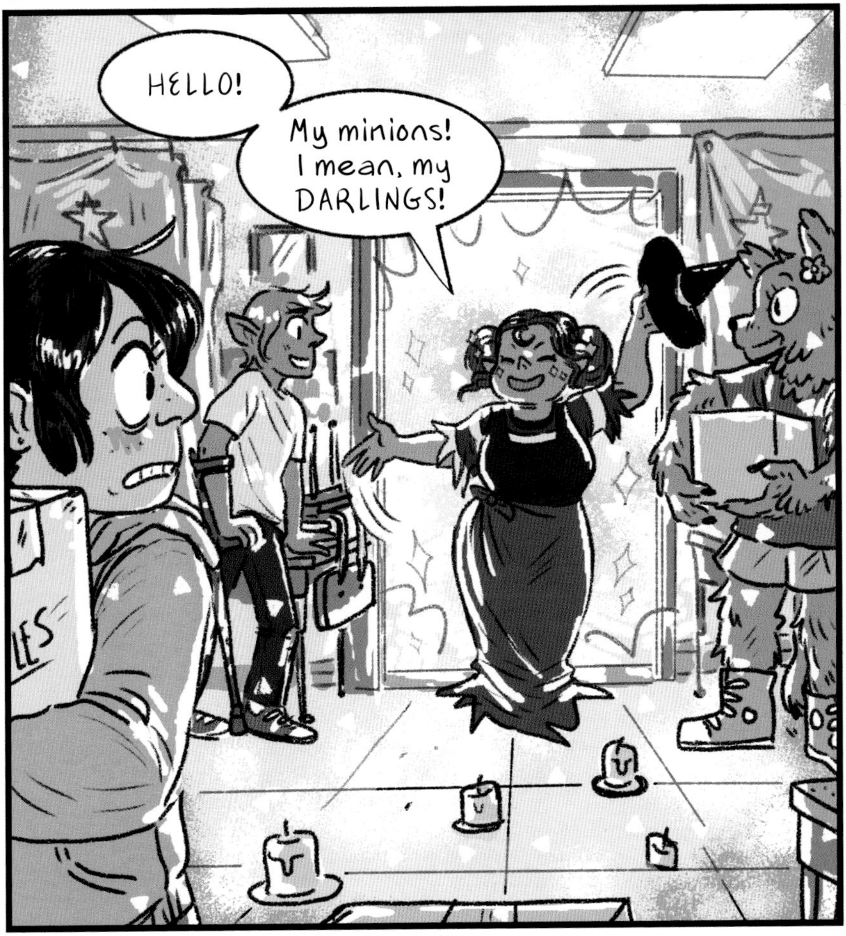
HELLO!
My minions! I mean, my DARLINGS!

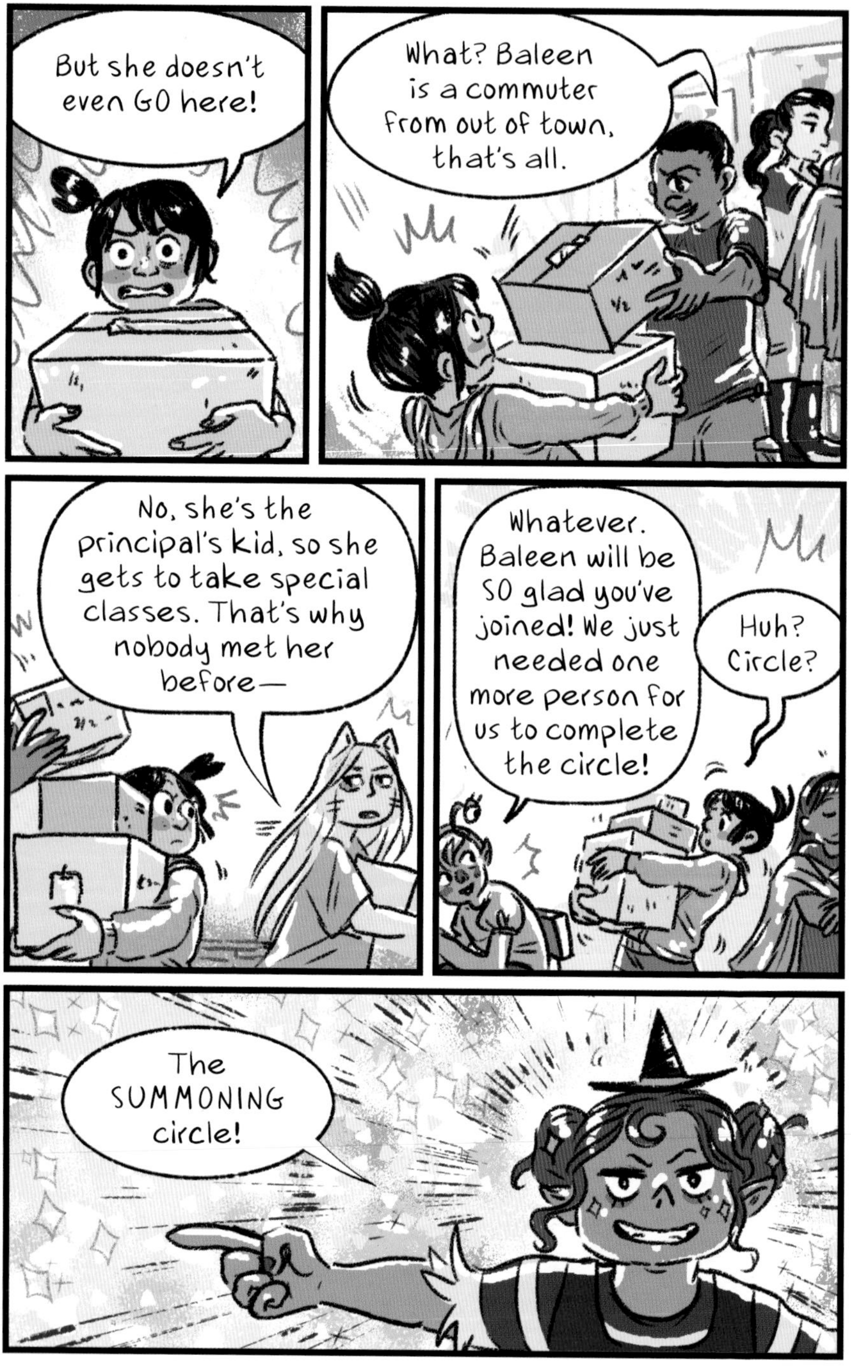
But she doesn't even GO here!
What? Baleen is a commuter from out of town, that's all.
No, she's the principal's kid, so she gets to take special classes. That's why nobody met her before—
Whatever. Baleen will be SO glad you've joined! We just needed one more person for us to complete the circle!
Huh? Circle?
The SUMMONING circle!

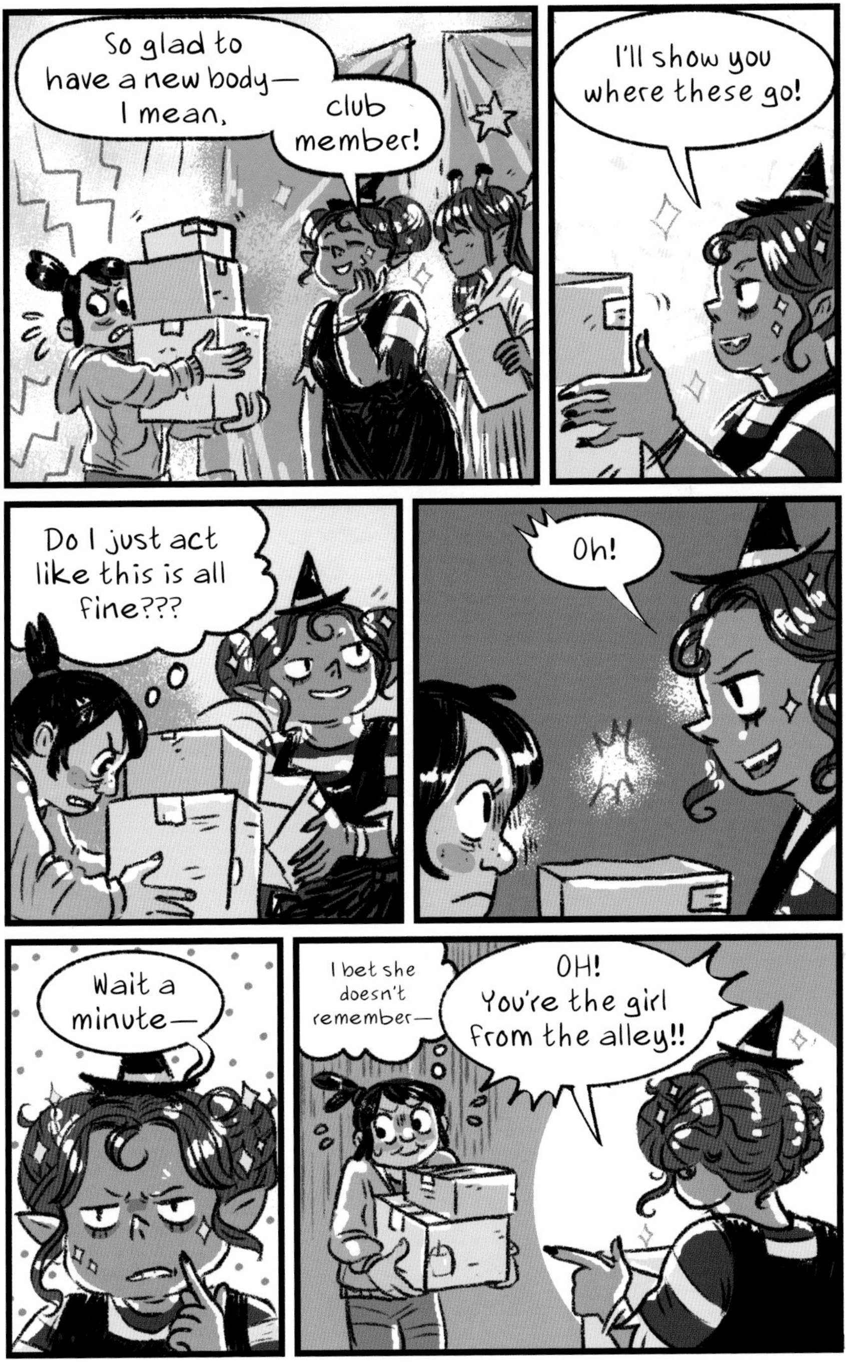
So glad to have a new body— I mean,
club member!
I'll show you where these go!
Do I just act like this is all fine???
Oh!
Wait a minute—
I bet she doesn't remember—
OH! You're the girl from the alley!!

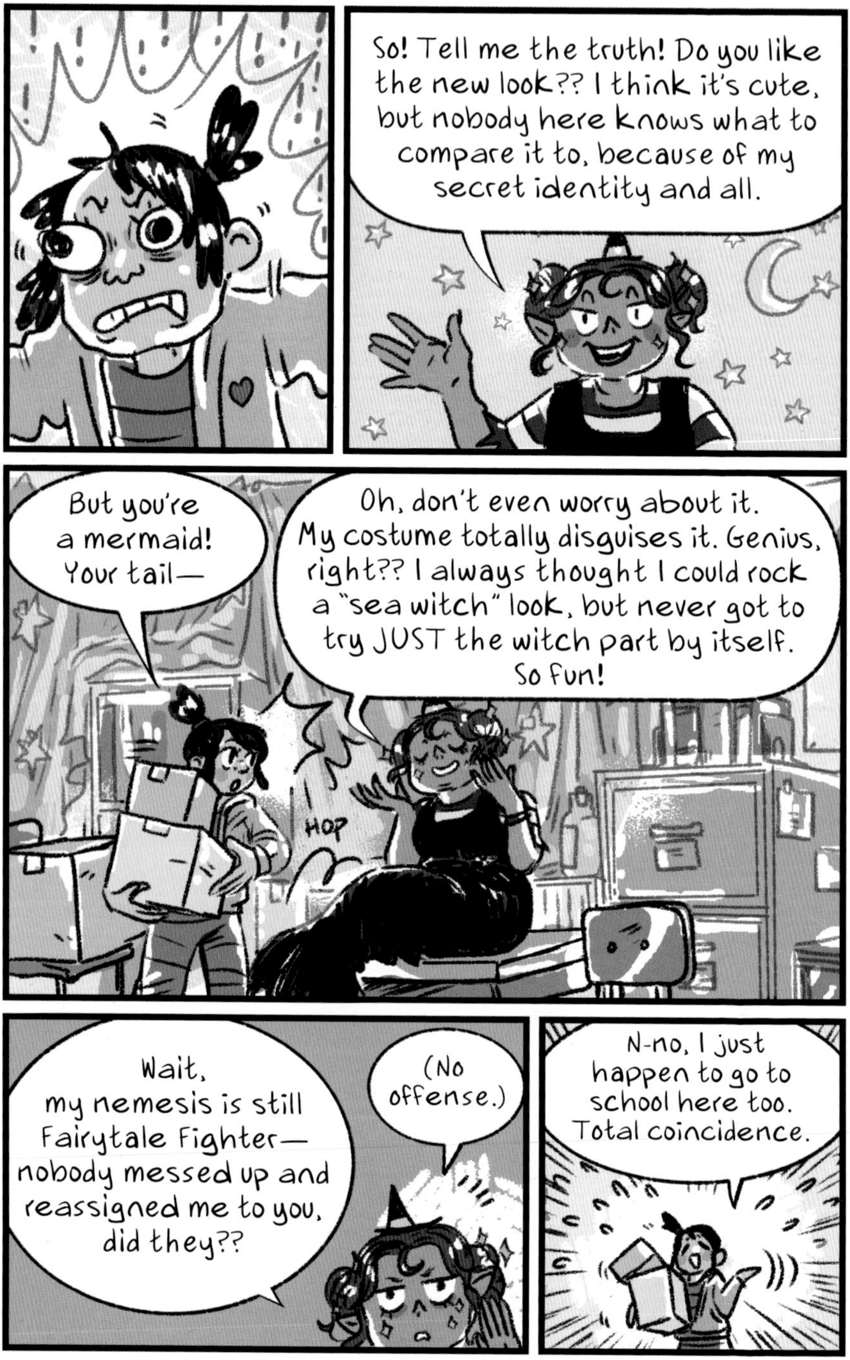
So! Tell me the truth! Do you like the new look?? I think it's cute, but nobody here knows what to compare it to, because of my secret identity and all.
But you're a mermaid! Your tail—
Oh, don't even worry about it. My costume totally disguises it. Genius, right?? I always thought I could rock a "sea witch" look, but never got to try JUST the witch part by itself. So fun!
HOP
Wait, my nemesis is still Fairytale Fighter— nobody messed up and reassigned me to you, did they??
(No offense.)
N-no, I just happen to go to school here too. Total coincidence.

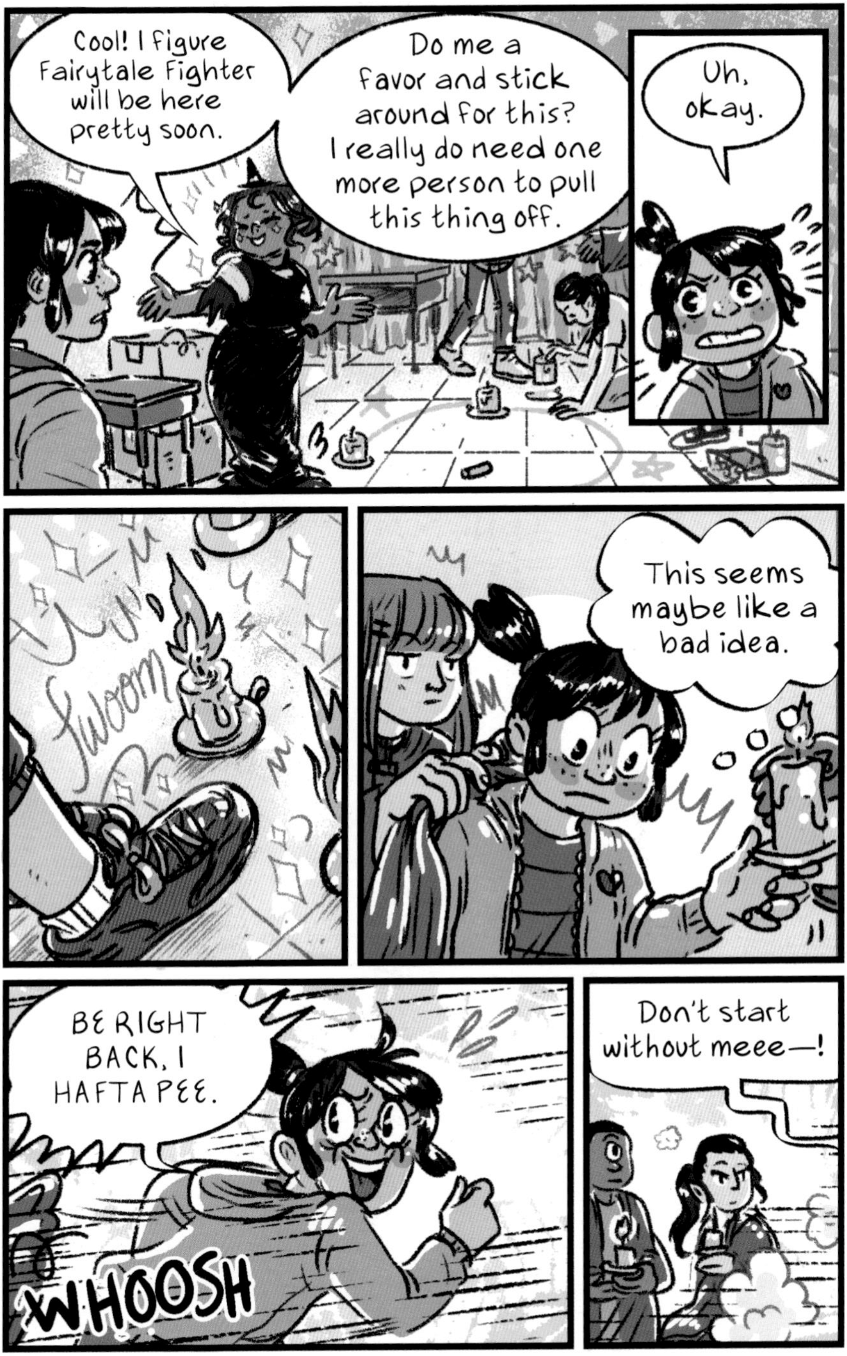
Cool! I figure Fairytale Fighter will be here pretty soon.
Do me a favor and stick around for this? I really do need one more person to pull this thing off.
Uh, okay.
fwoom
This seems maybe like a bad idea.
BE RIGHT BACK, I HAFTA PEE.
WHOOSH
Don't start without meee—!

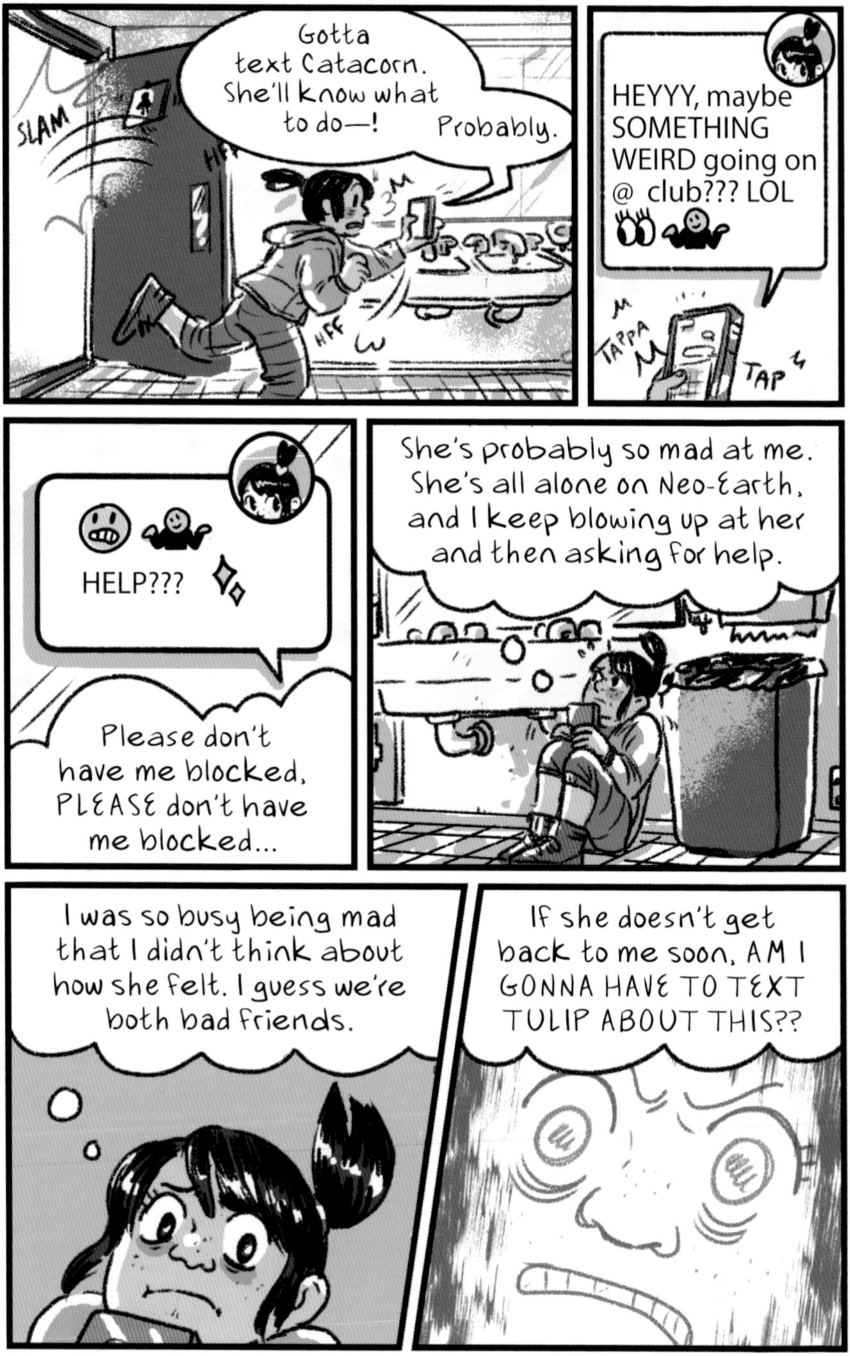
SLAM
Gotta text Catacorn. She'll know what to do—!
Probably.
HFF
HFF
HEYYY, maybe SOMETHING WEIRD going on @ club??? LOL
TAPPA
TAP
HELP???
Please don't have me blocked, PLEASE don't have me blocked...
She's probably so mad at me. She's all alone on Neo-Earth, and I keep blowing up at her and then asking for help.
I was so busy being mad that I didn't think about how she felt. I guess we're both bad friends.
If she doesn't get back to me soon, AM I GONNA HAVE TO TEXT TULIP ABOUT THIS??

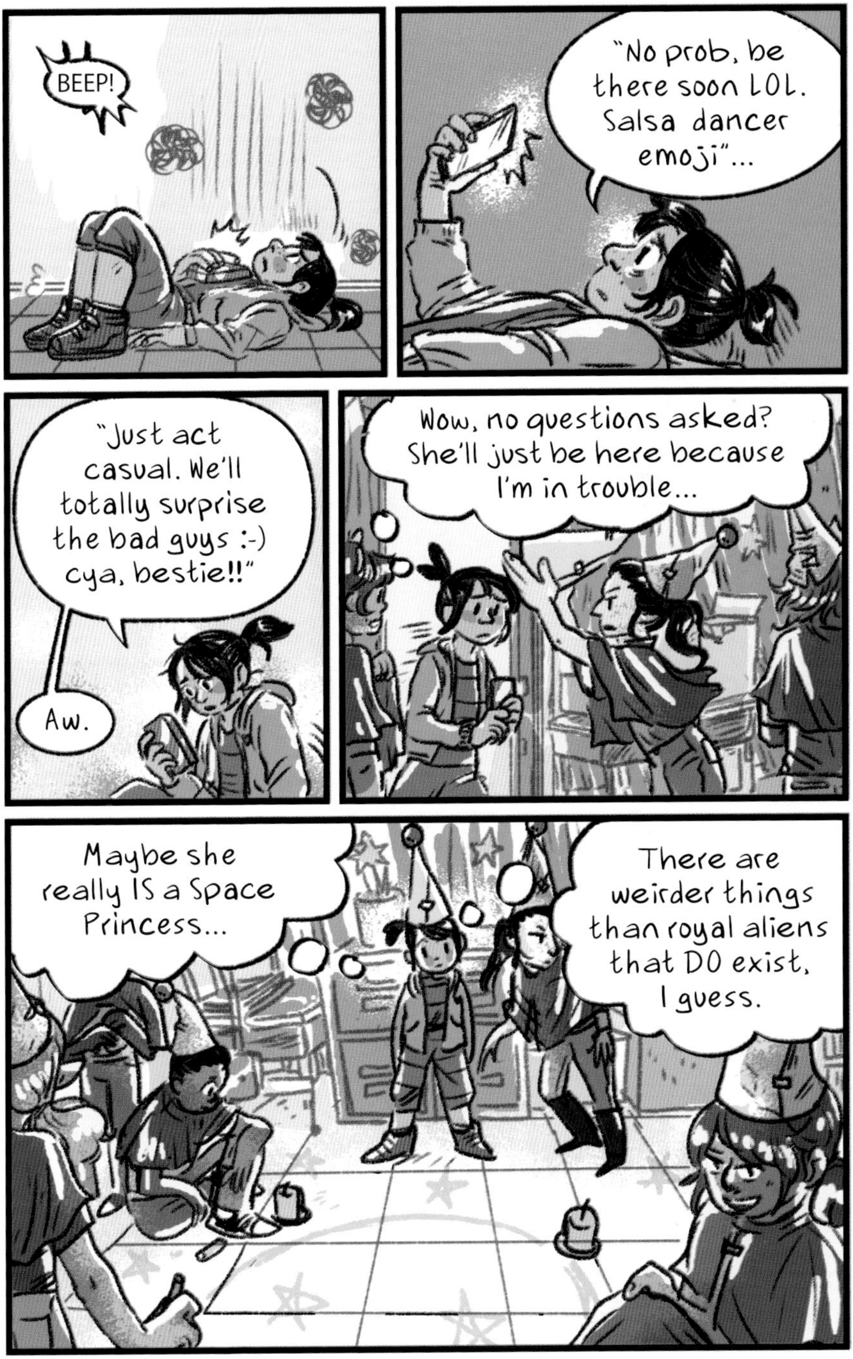
BEEP!
"No prob, be there soon LOL. Salsa dancer emoji"...
"Just act casual. We'll totally surprise the bad guys :-) cya, bestie!!"
Aw.
Wow, no questions asked? She'll just be here because I'm in trouble...
Maybe she really IS a Space Princess...
There are weirder things than royal aliens that DO exist, I guess.

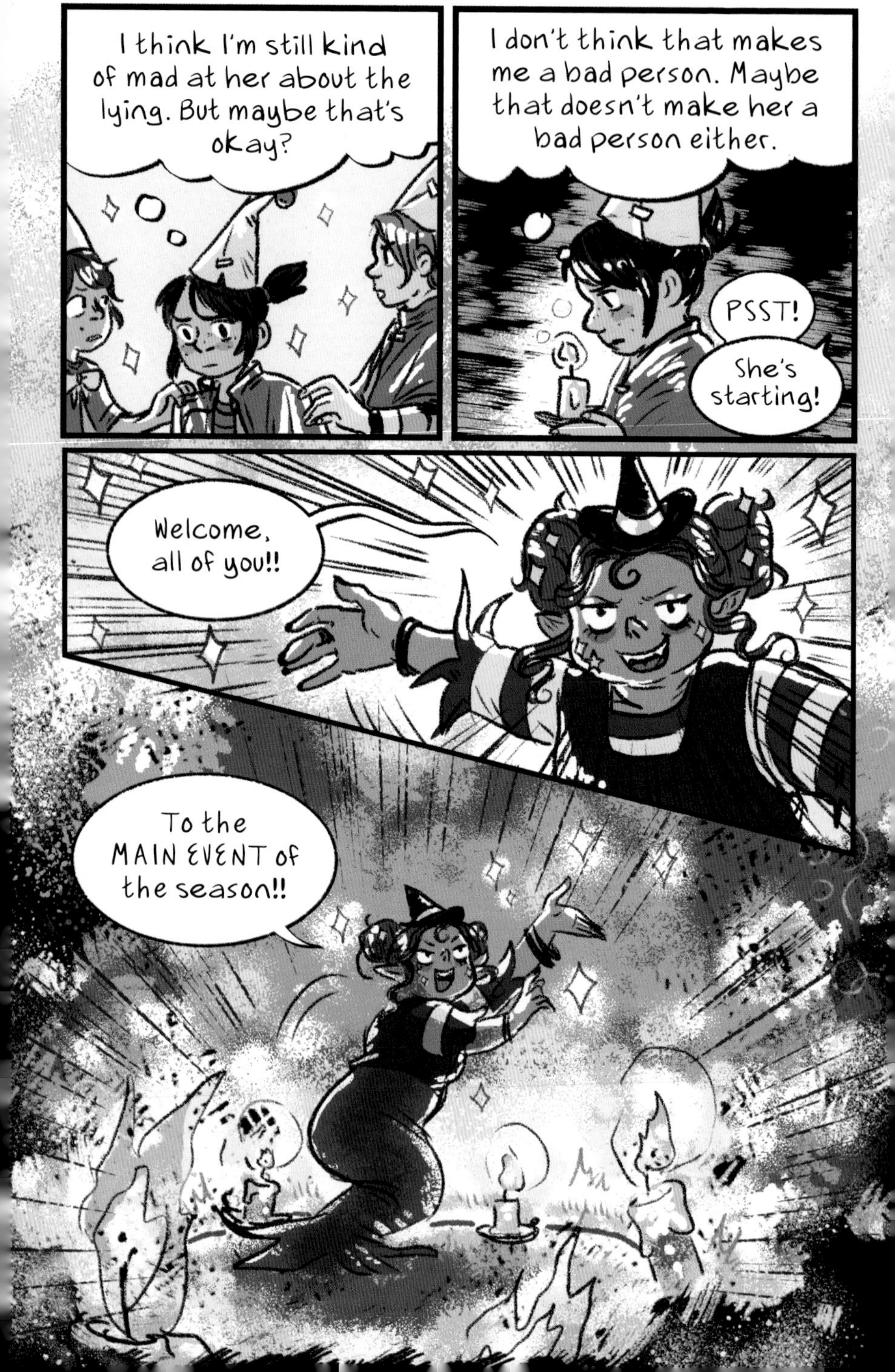
I think I'm still kind of mad at her about the lying. But maybe that's okay?
I don't think that makes me a bad person. Maybe that doesn't make her a bad person either.
PSST!
She's starting!
Welcome, all of you!!
To the MAIN EVENT of the season!!

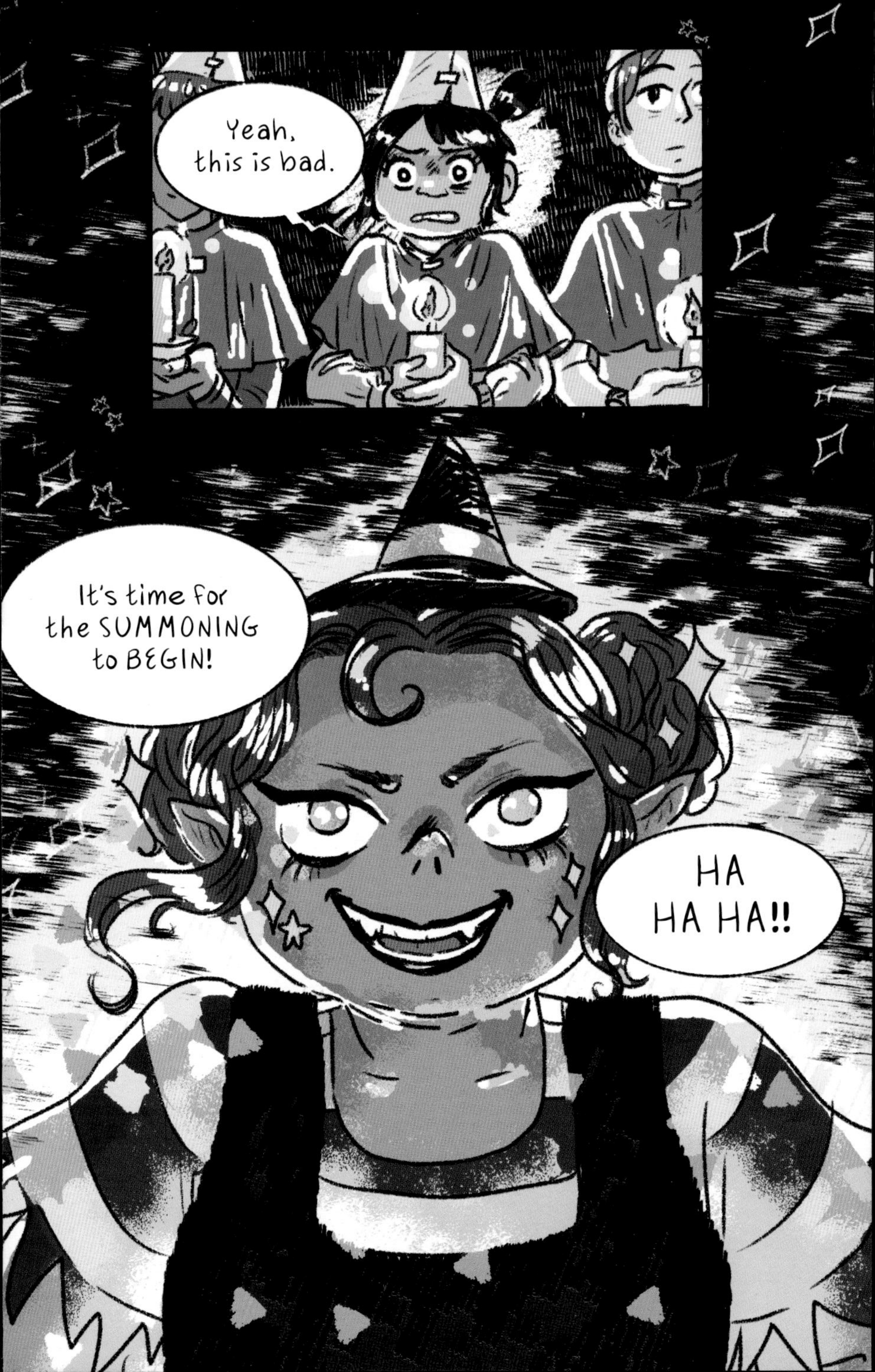
Yeah, this is bad.
It's time for the SUMMONING to BEGIN!
HA HA HA!!

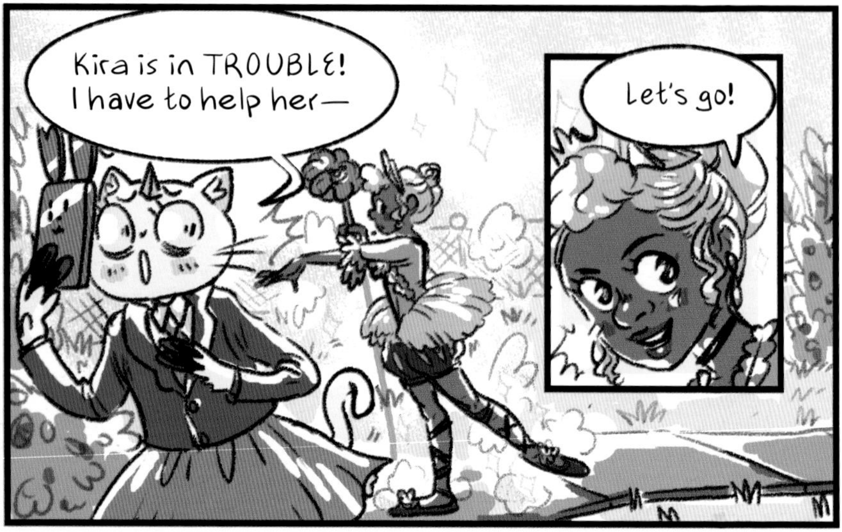
Kira is in TROUBLE! I have to help her—
Let's go!

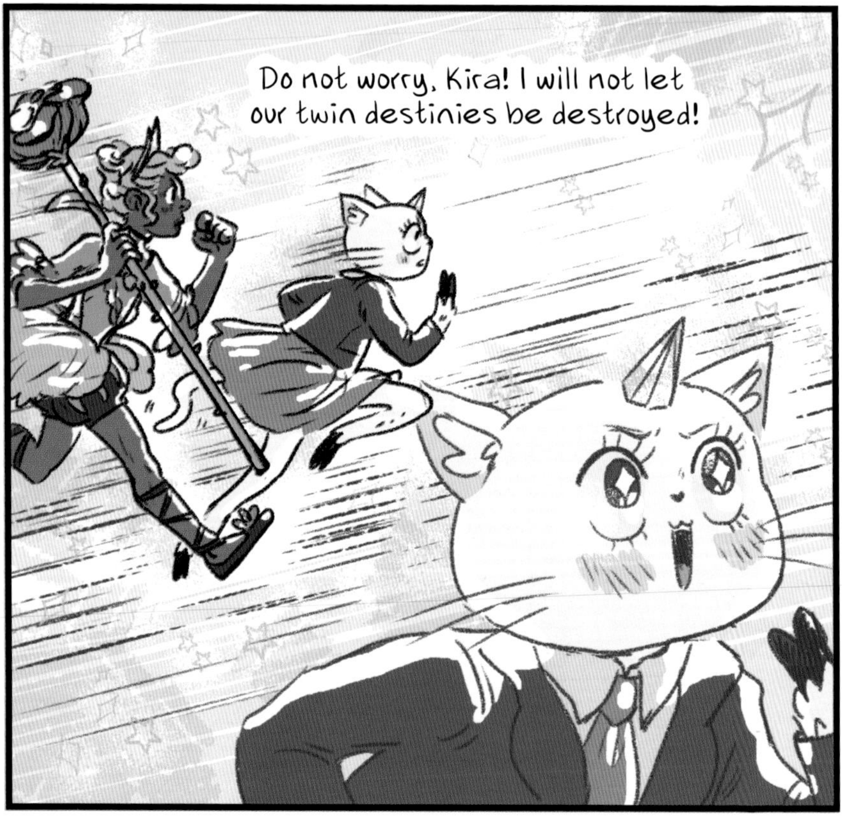
Do not worry, Kira! I will not let our twin destinies be destroyed!

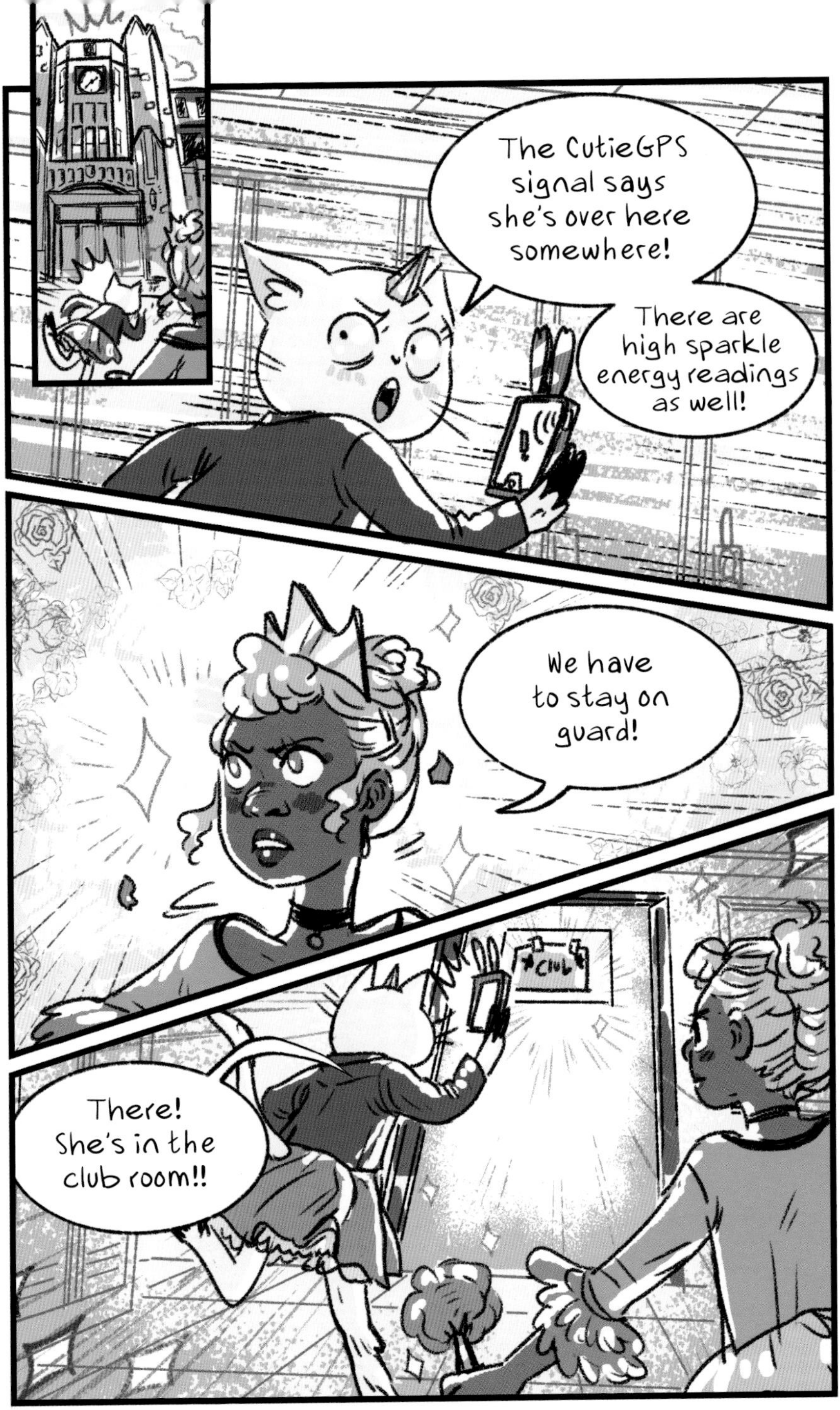
The CutieGPS signal says she's over here somewhere!
There are high sparkle energy readings as well!
We have to stay on guard!
CLUB
There! She's in the club room!!

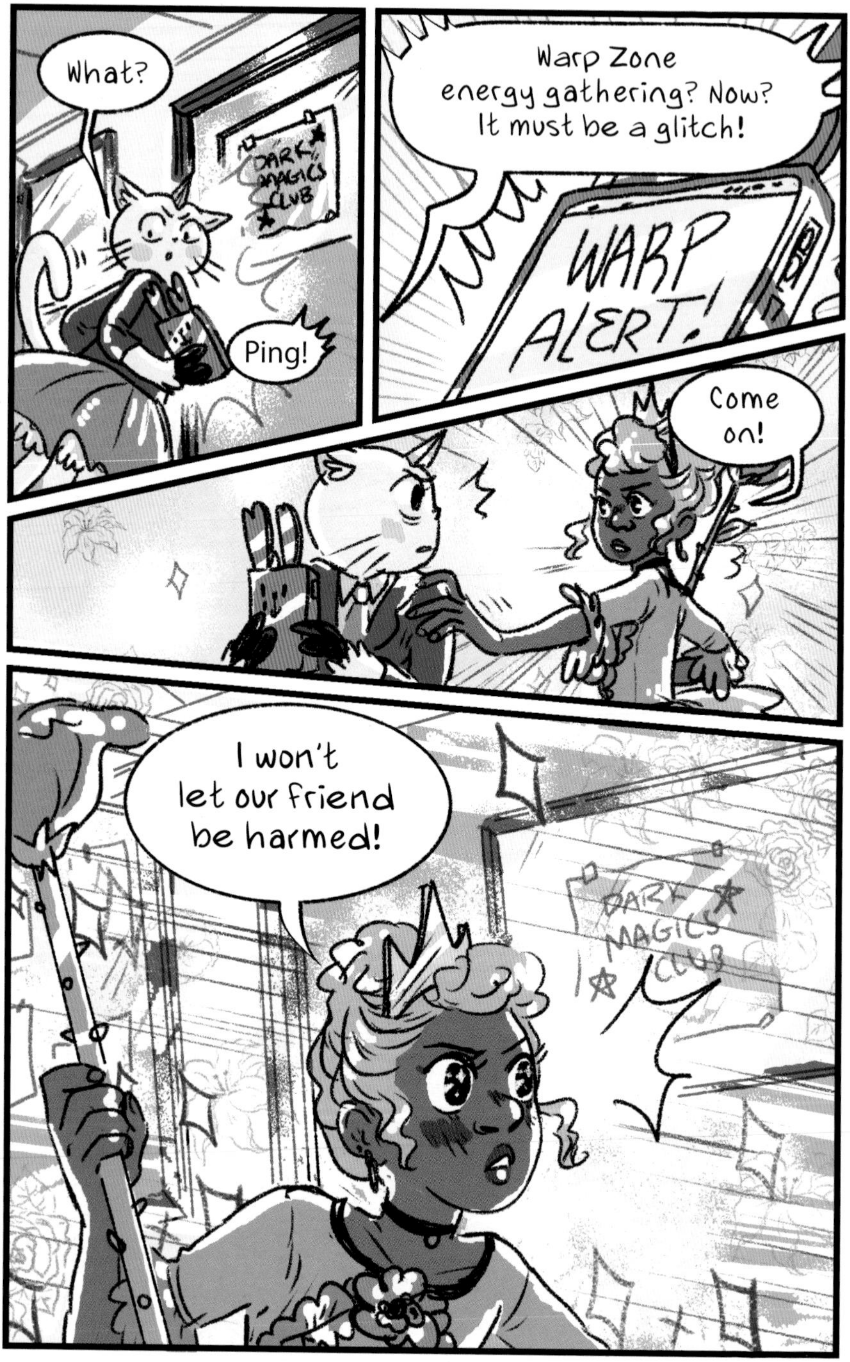
What?
DARK MAGICS CLUB
Ping!
Warp Zone energy gathering? Now? It must be a glitch!
WARP ALERT!
Come on!
I won't let our friend be harmed!
DARK MAGICS CLUB

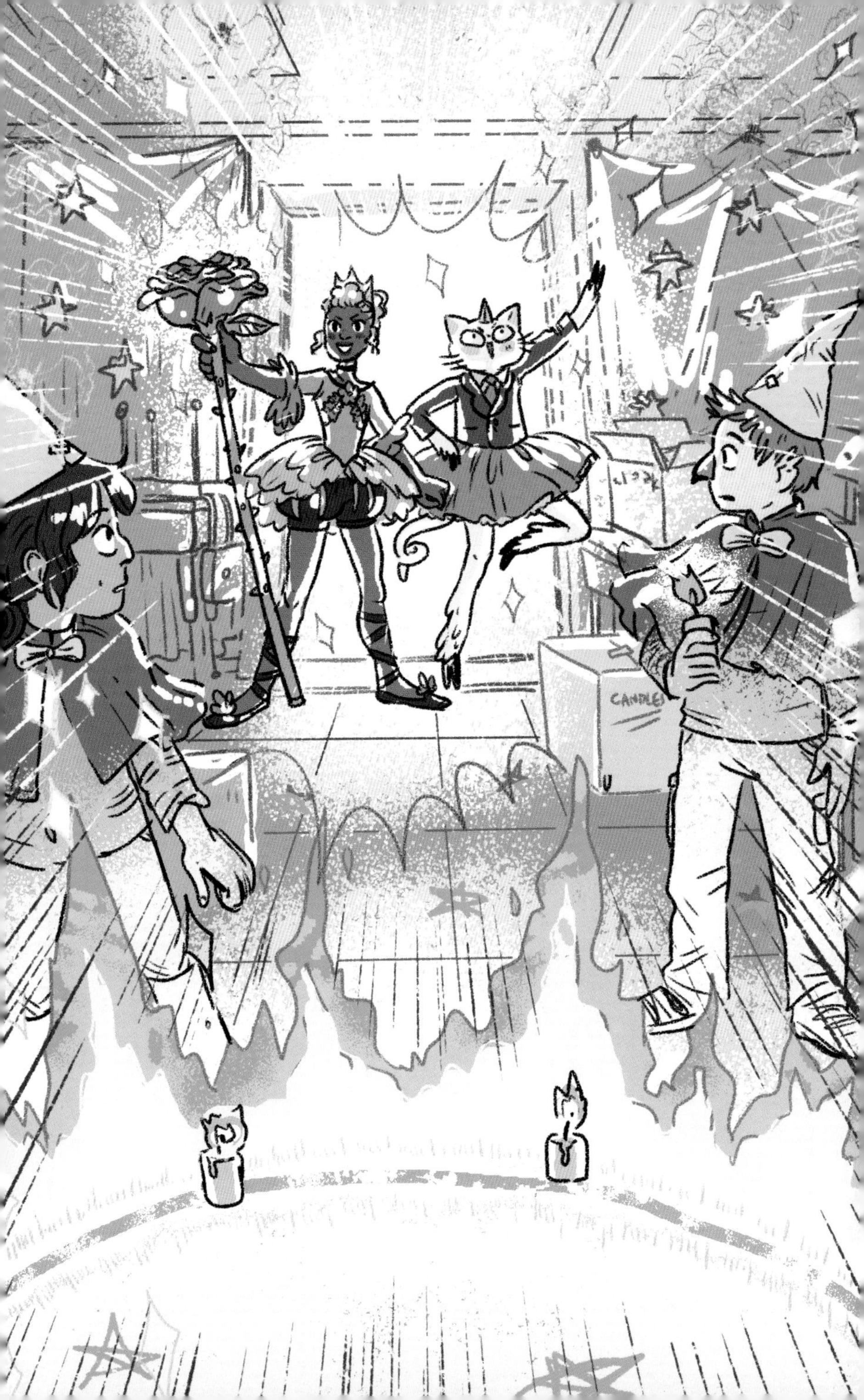
CANDLES

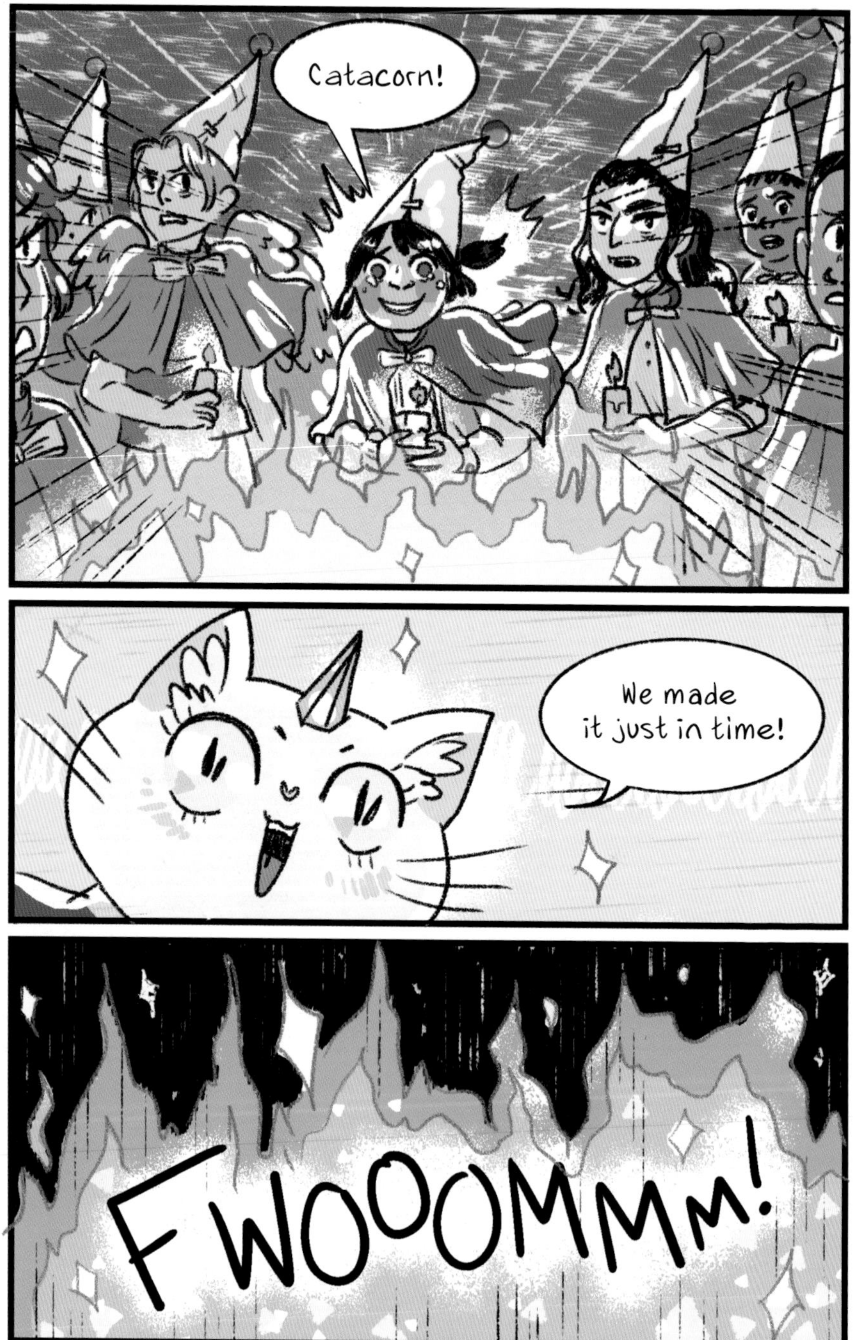

Catacorn!
We made it just in time!
FWOOOMMM!

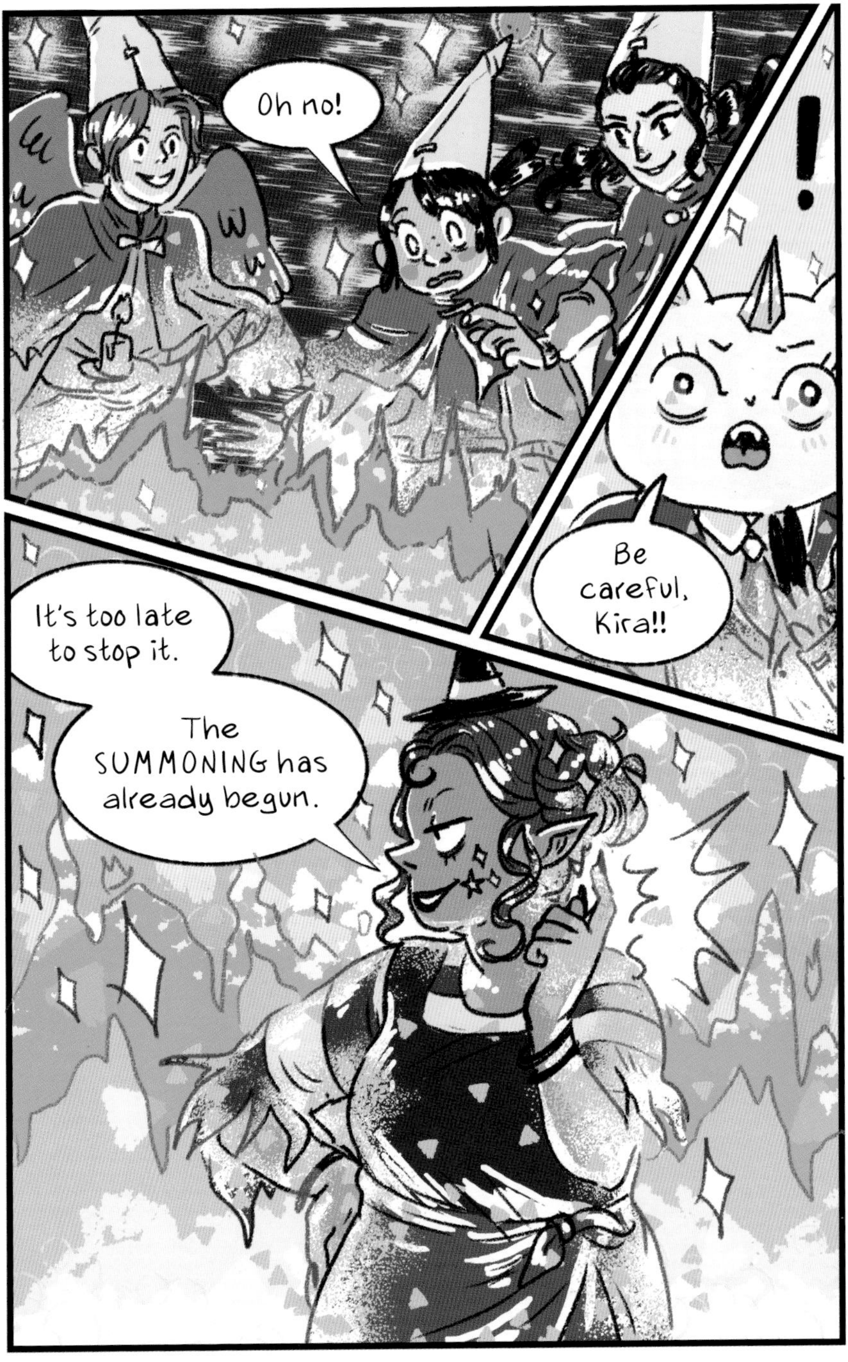
Oh no!
!
Be careful, Kira!!
It's too late to stop it.
The SUMMONING has already begun.

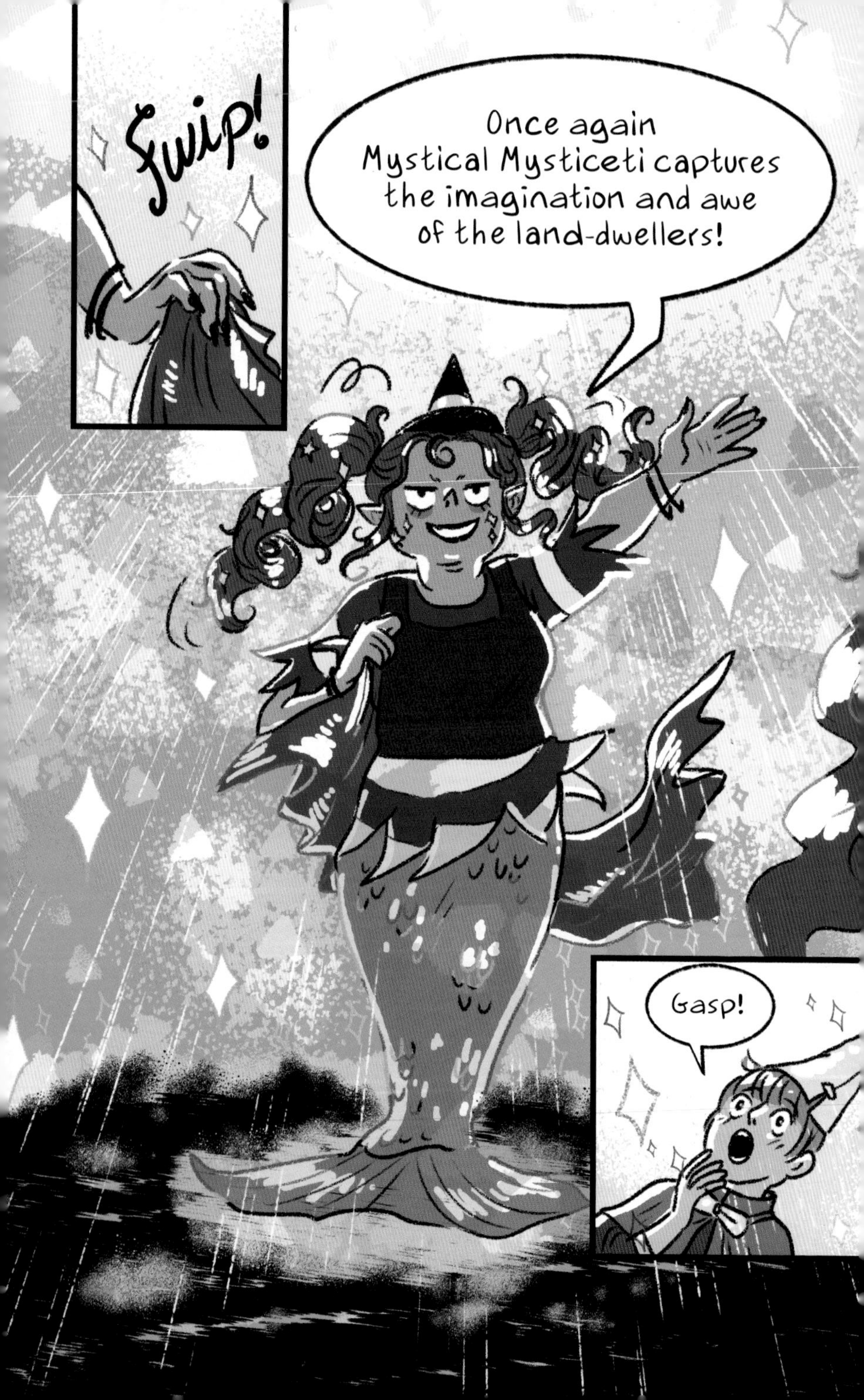
Fwip!
Once again Mystical Mysticeti captures the imagination and awe of the land-dwellers!
Gasp!

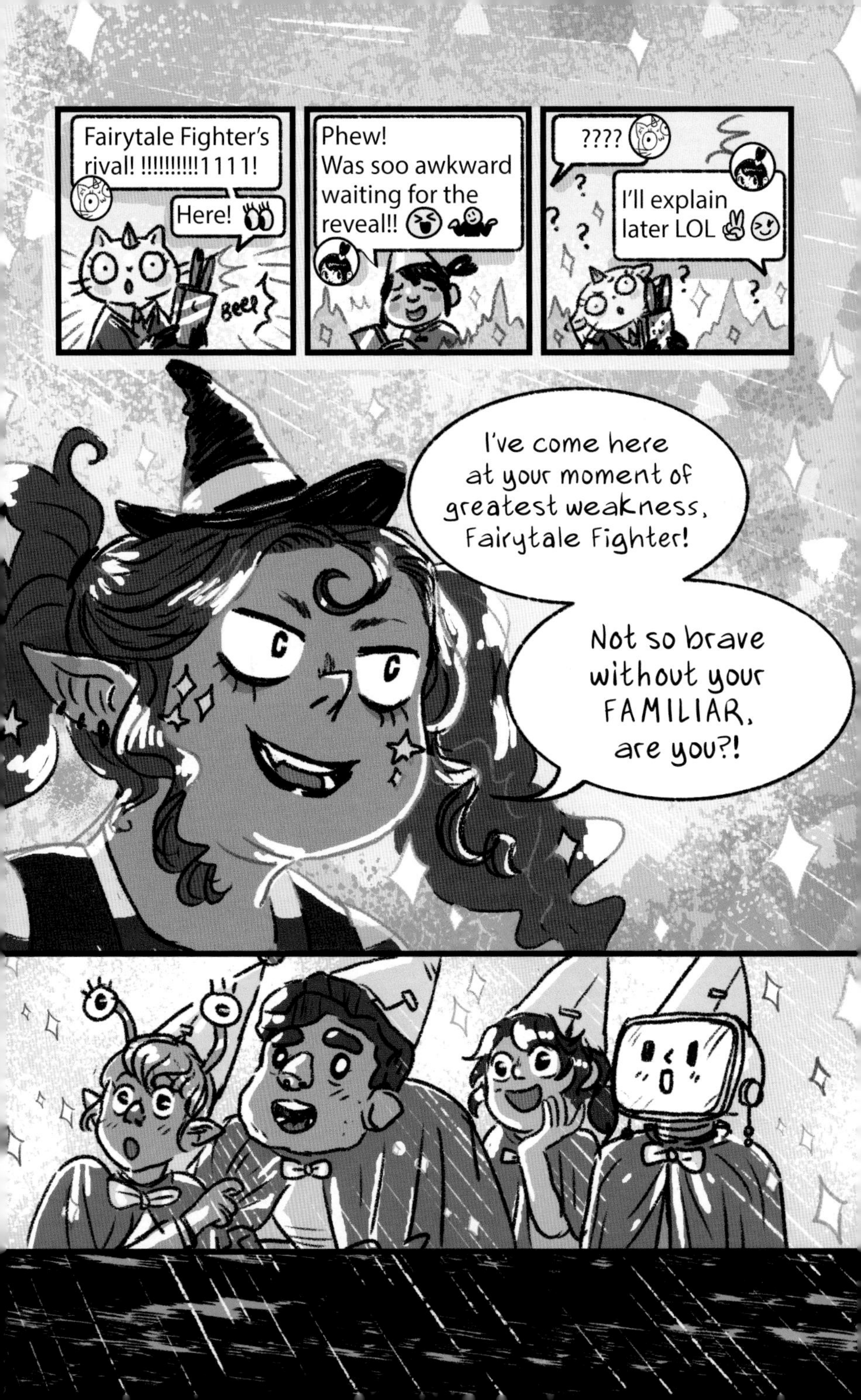
Fairytale Fighter's rival! !!!!!!!!!!1111!
Here!
Beep
Phew!
Was soo awkward waiting for the reveal!!
????
I'll explain later LOL
I've come here at your moment of greatest weakness, Fairytale Fighter!
Not so brave without your FAMILIAR, are you?!

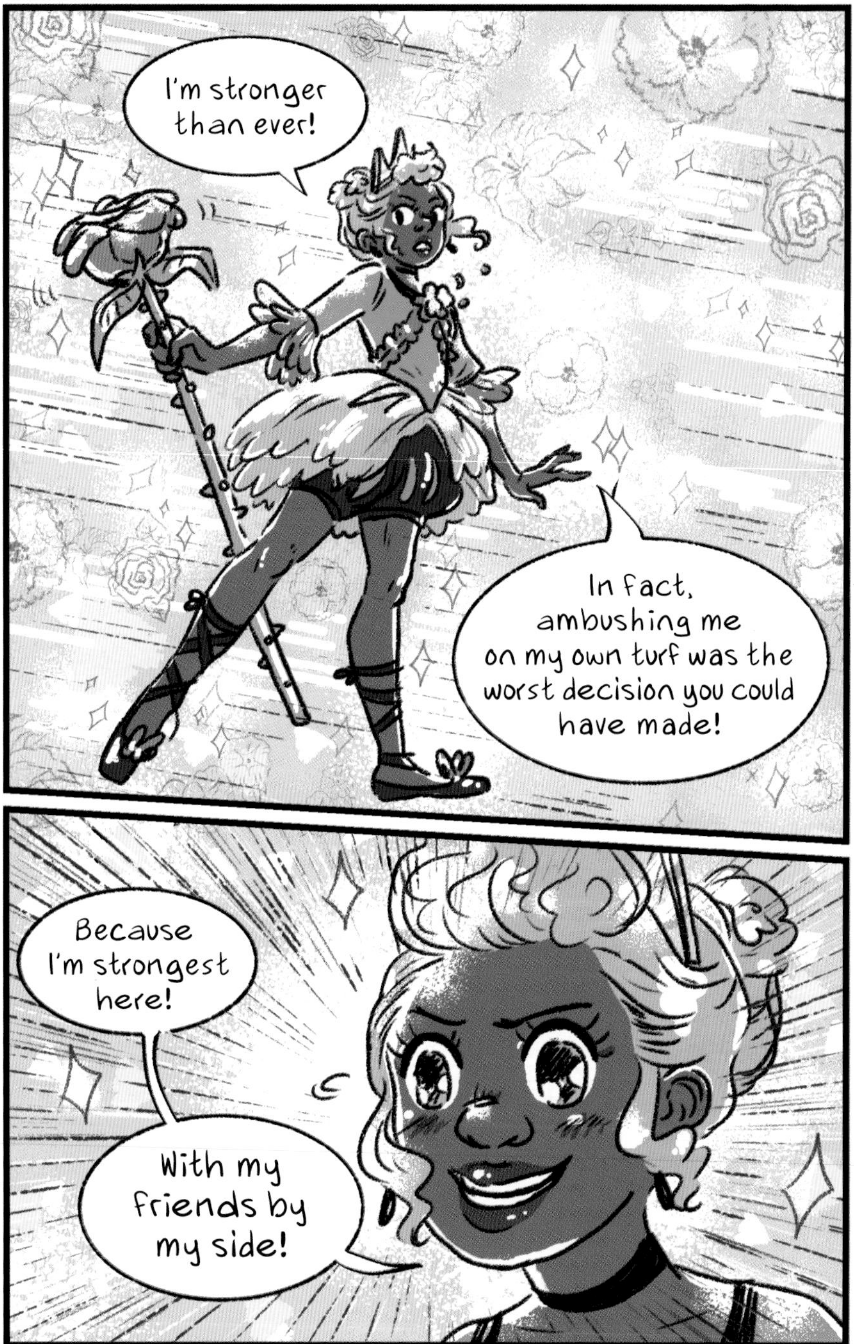
I'm stronger than ever!
In fact, ambushing me on my own turf was the worst decision you could have made!
Because I'm strongest here!
With my friends by my side!

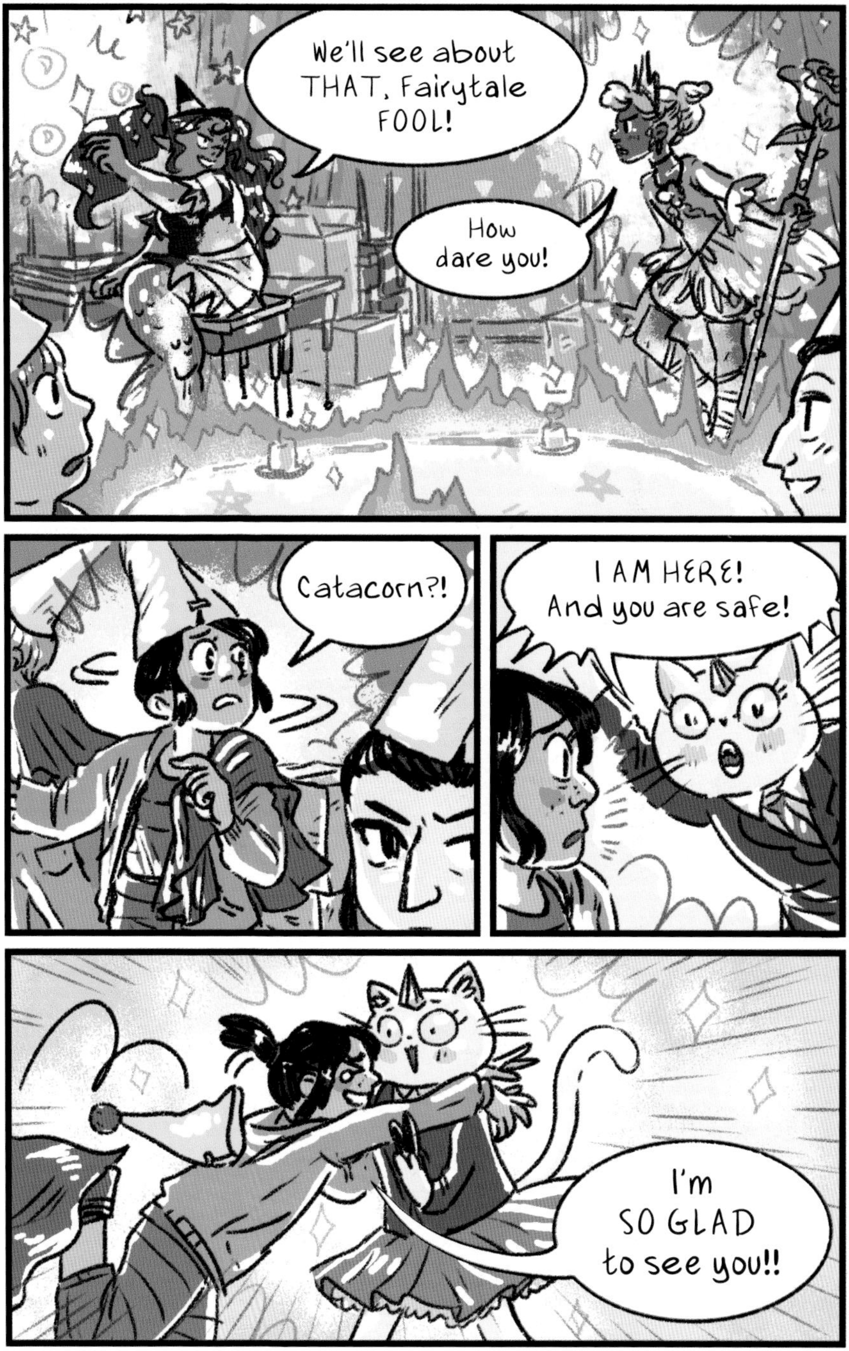
We'll see about THAT, Fairytale FOOL!
How dare you!
Catacorn?!
I AM HERE! And you are safe!
I'm SO GLAD to see you!!

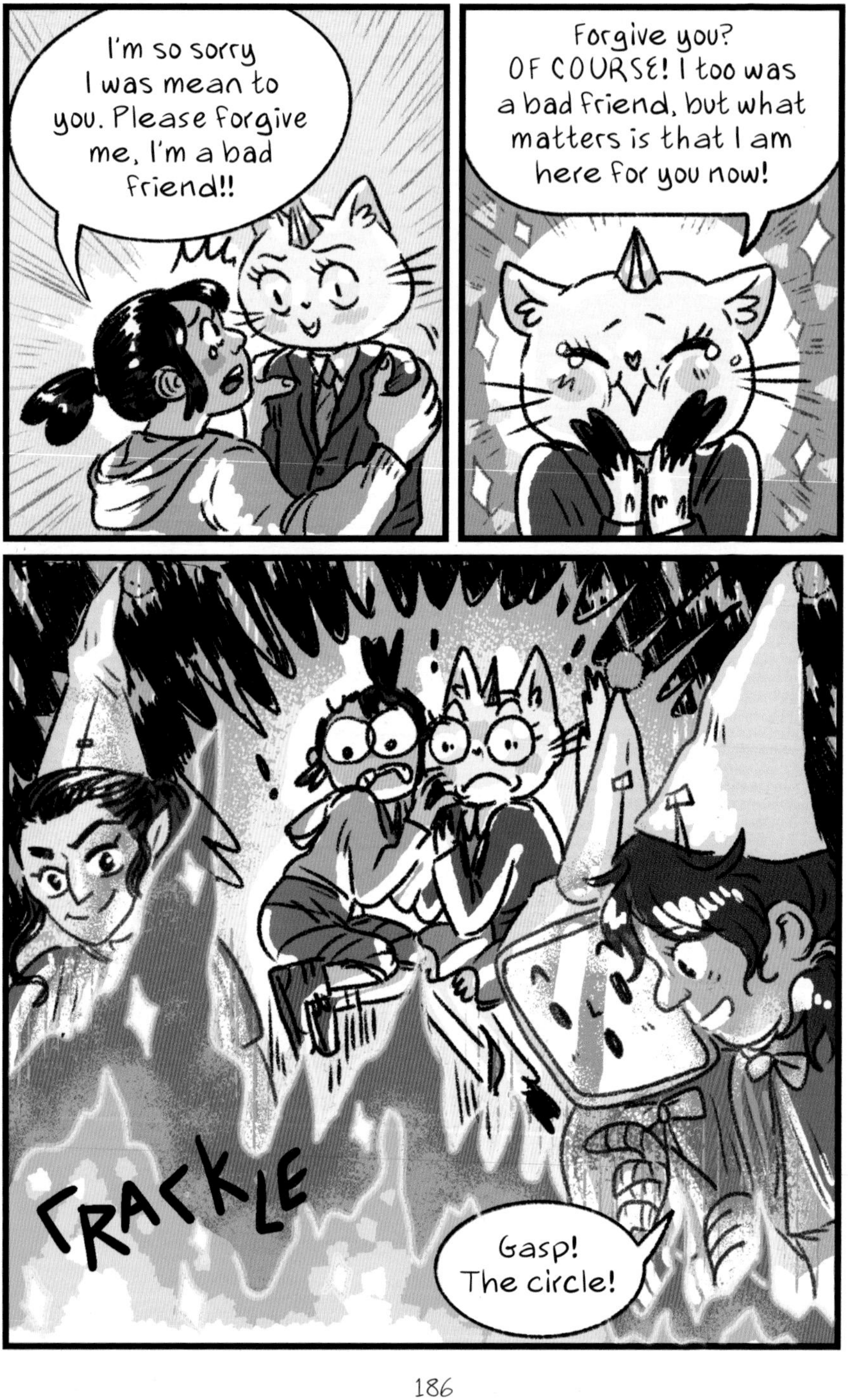
I'm so sorry I was mean to you. Please forgive me, I'm a bad friend!!
Forgive you? OF COURSE! I too was a bad friend, but what matters is that I am here for you now!
CRACKLE
Gasp! The circle!

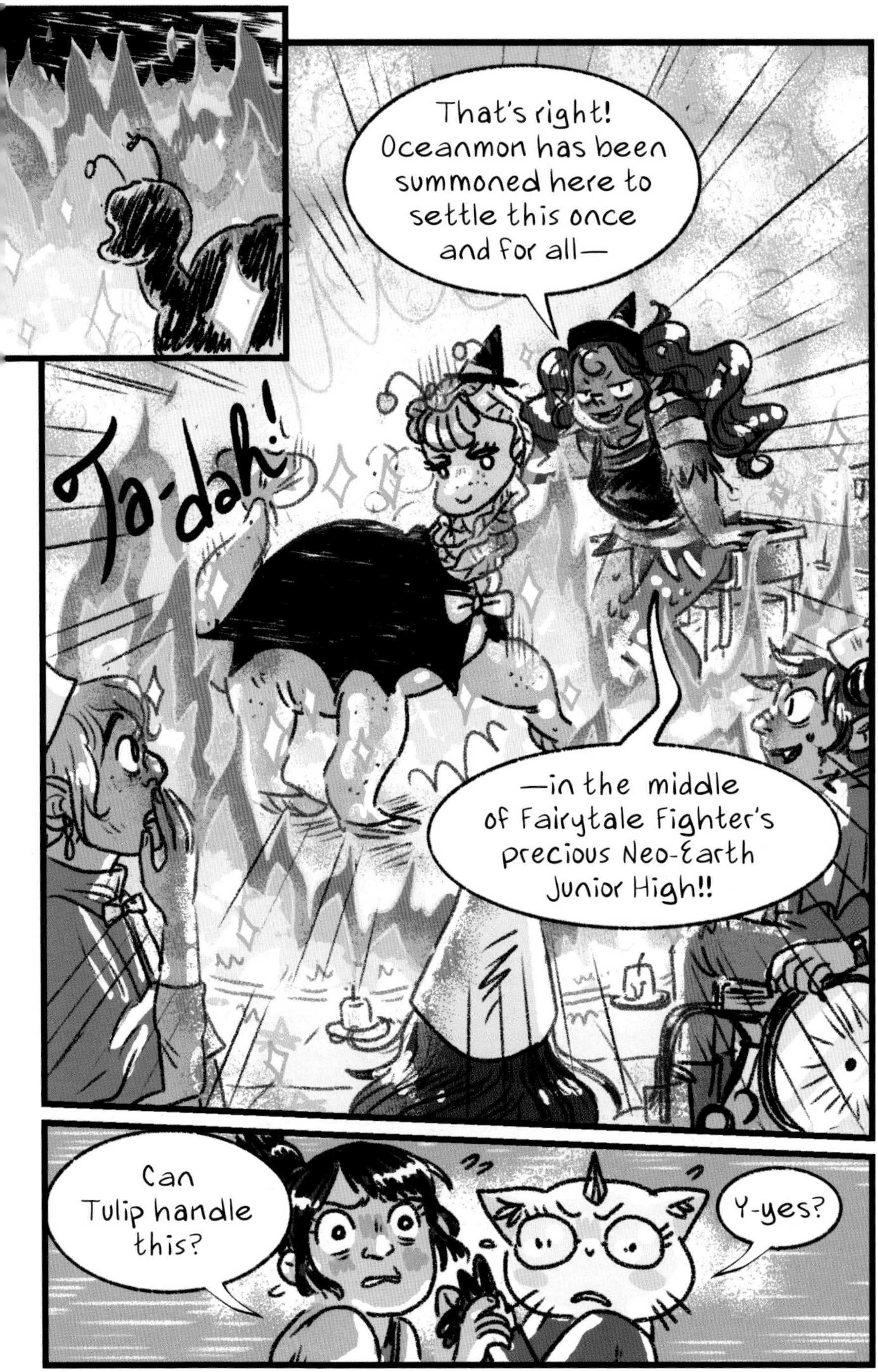
That's right! Oceanmon has been summoned here to settle this once and for all—
Ta-dah!
—in the middle of Fairytale Fighter's precious Neo-Earth Junior High!!
Can Tulip handle this?
Y-yes?

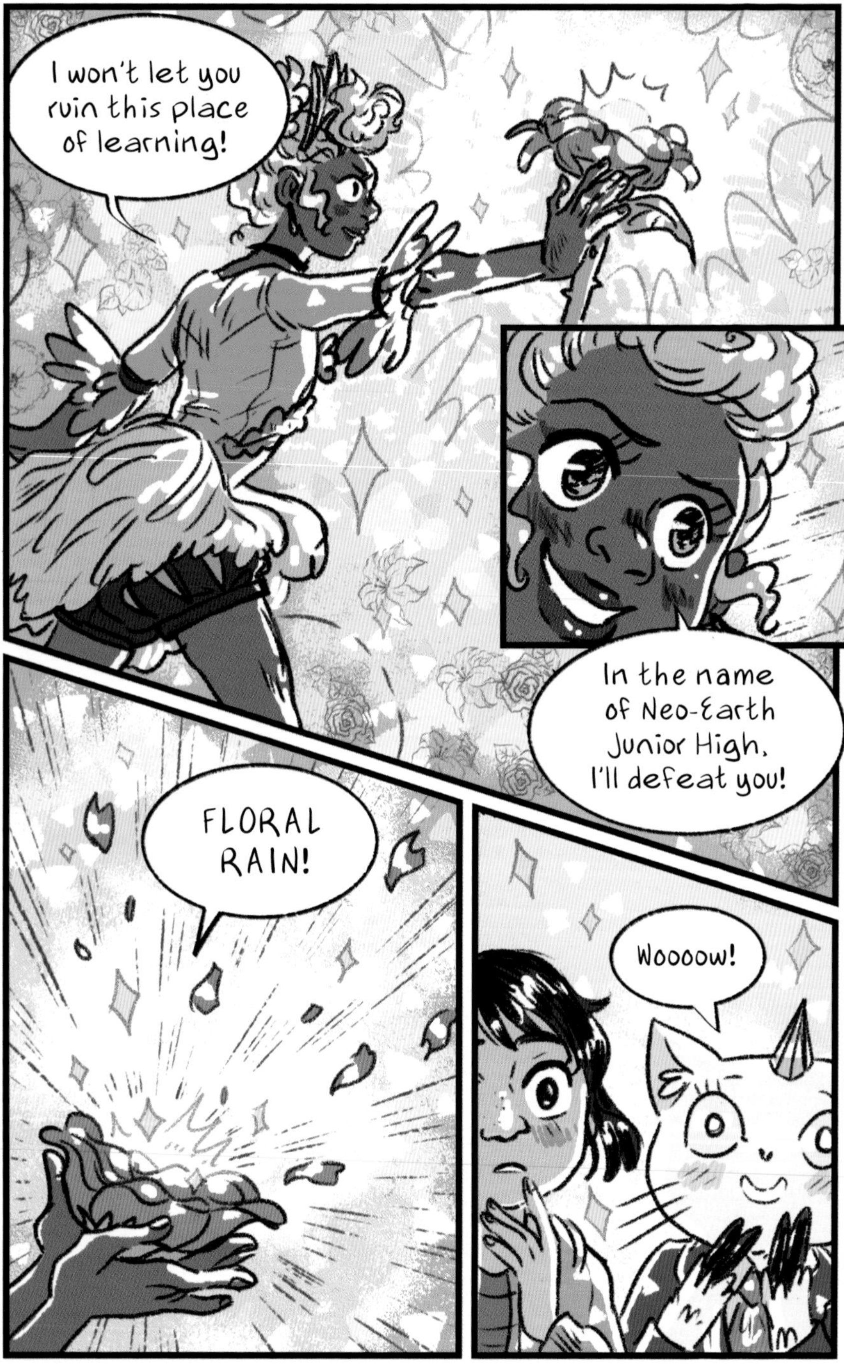
I won't let you ruin this place of learning!
In the name of Neo-Earth Junior High, I'll defeat you!
FLORAL RAIN!
Woooow!

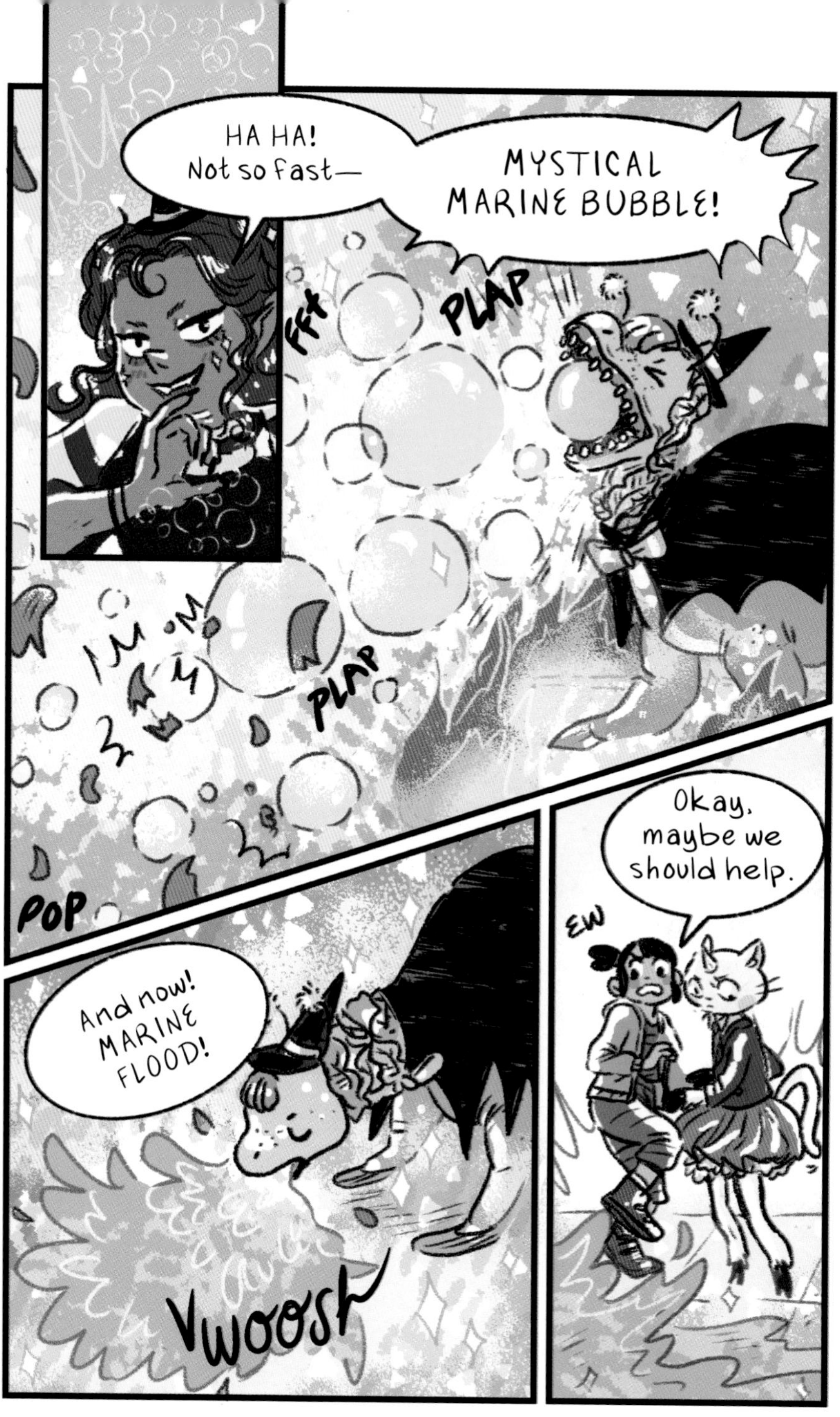
HA HA!
Not so fast—
MYSTICAL MARINE BUBBLE!
FFT
PLAP
PLAP
POP
Okay, maybe we should help.
EW
And now! MARINE FLOOD!
VWOOSH

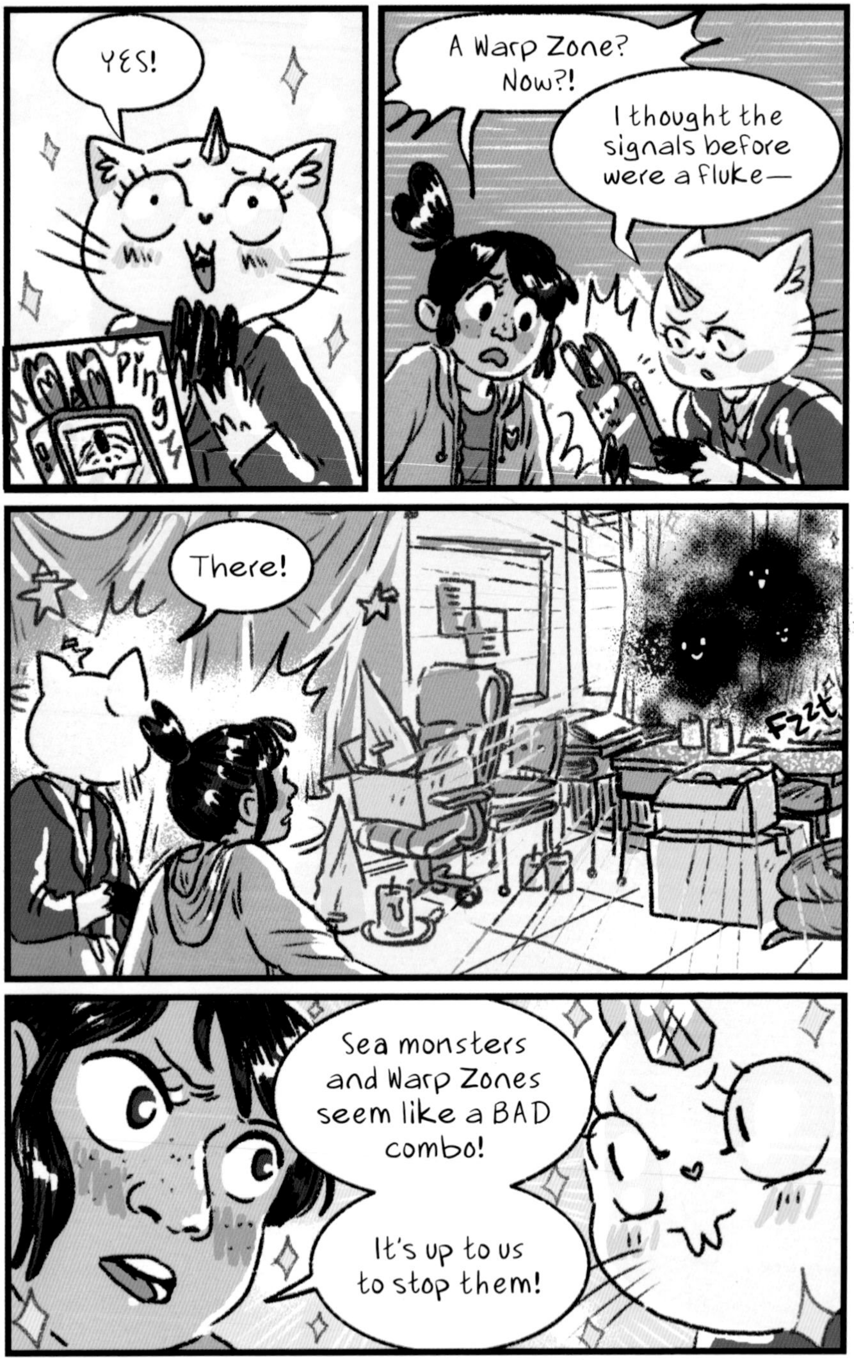
YES!
Ping
A Warp Zone? Now?!
I thought the signals before were a fluke—
There!
Fzzt
Sea monsters and Warp Zones seem like a BAD combo!
It's up to us to stop them!

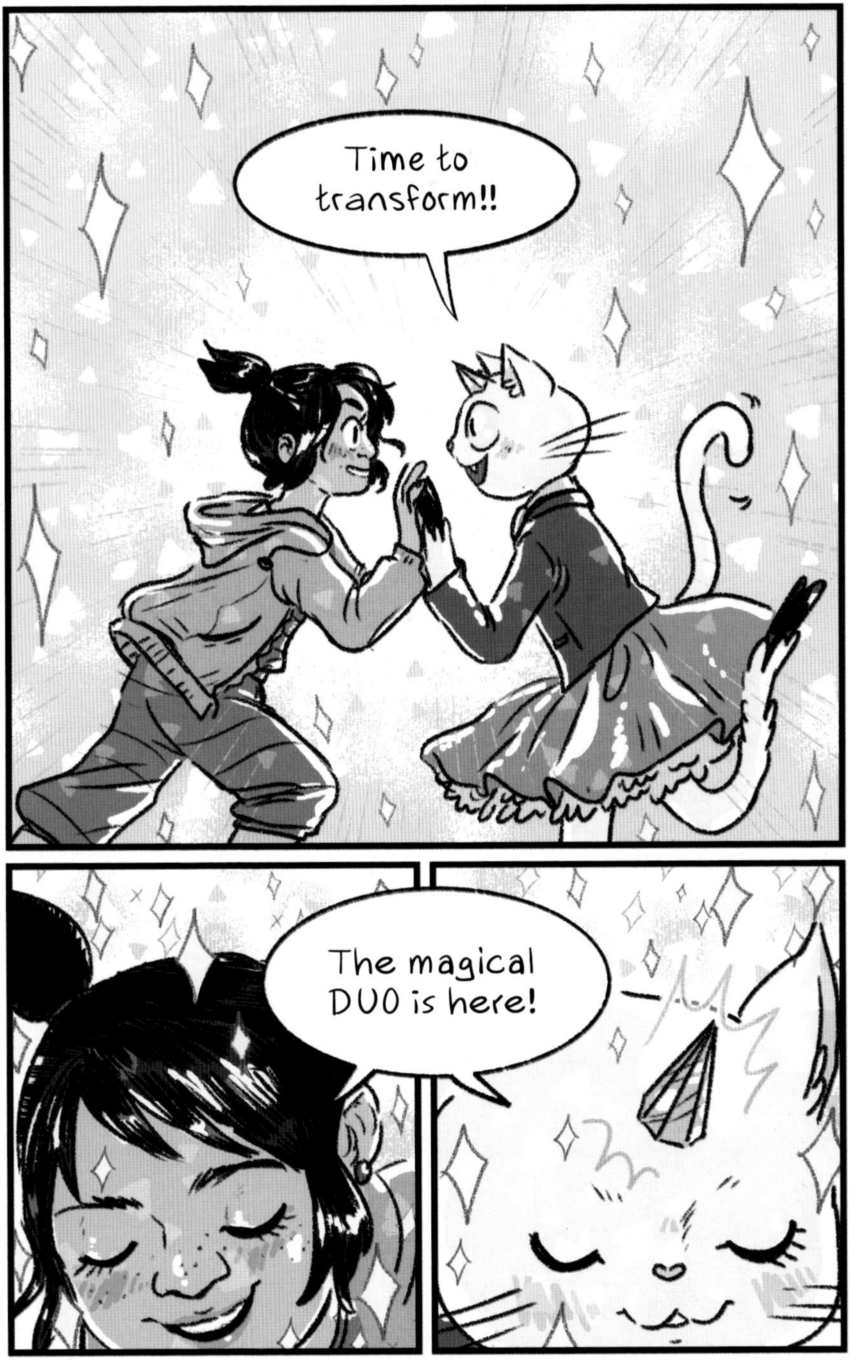
Time to transform!!
The magical DUO is here!

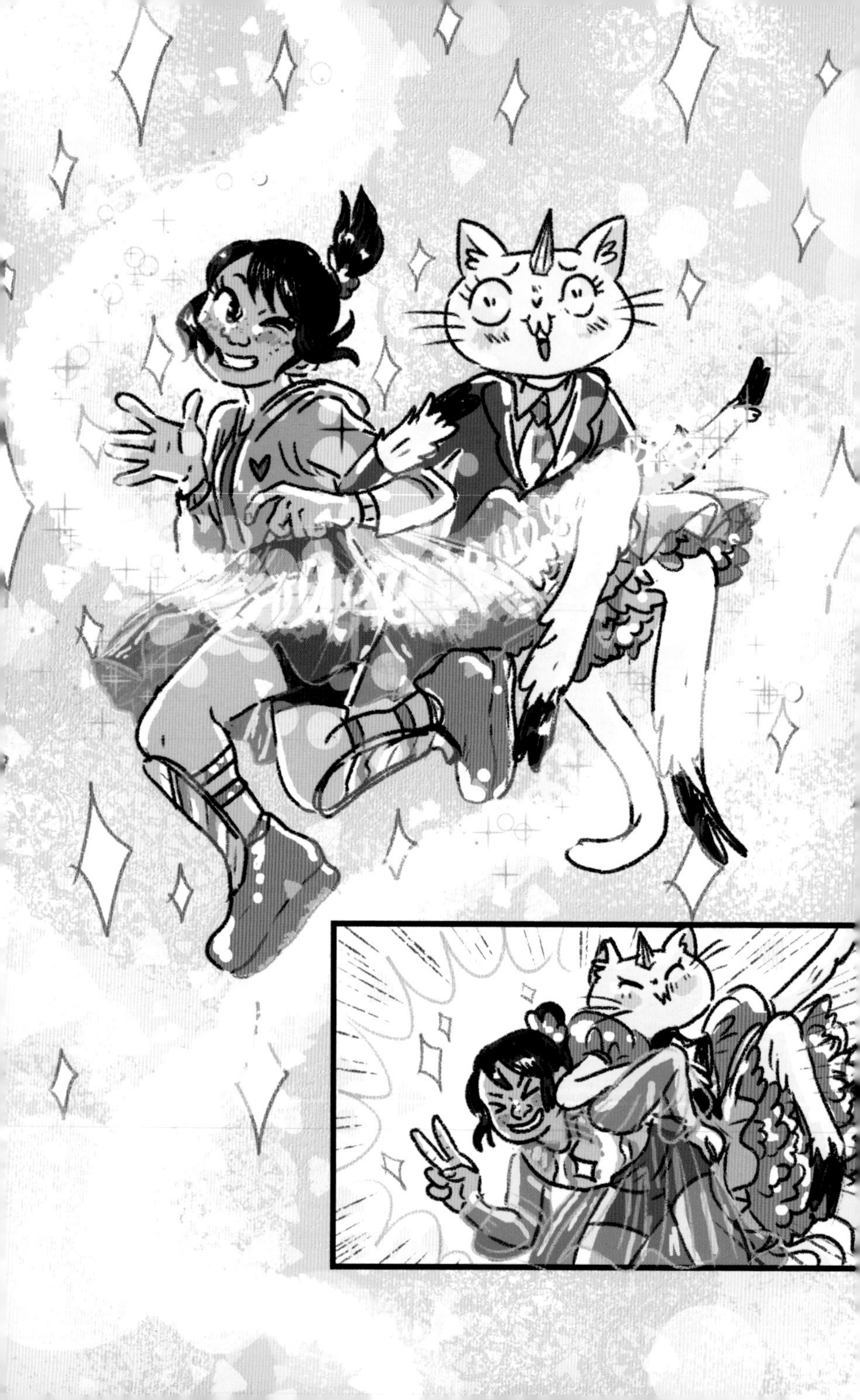

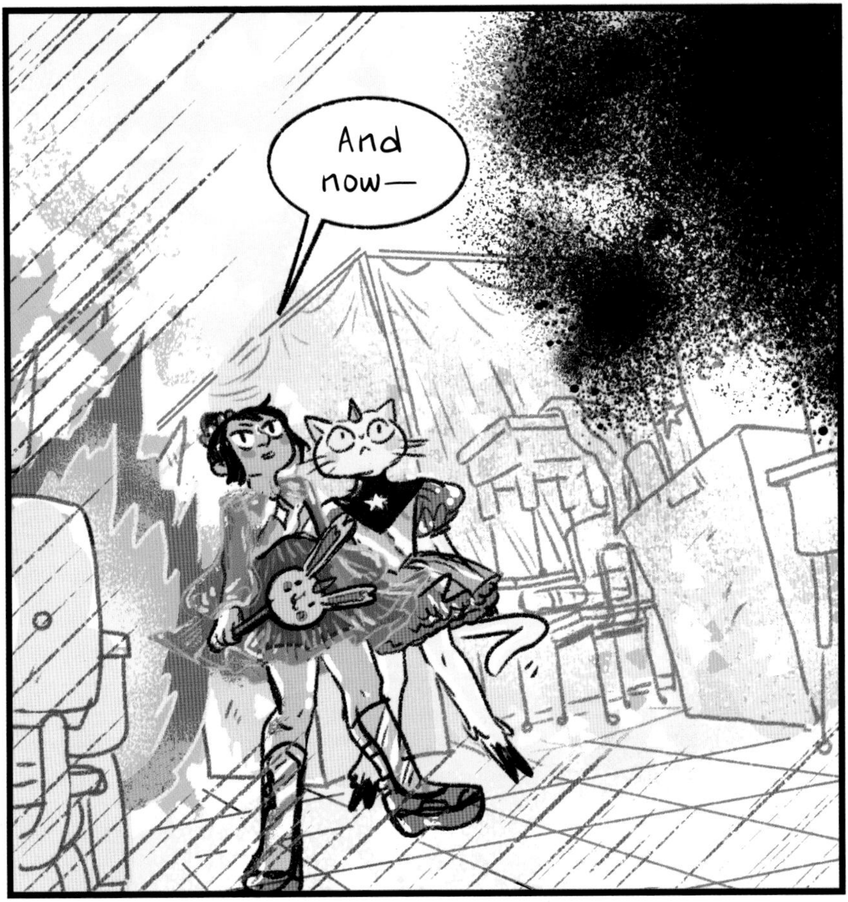
And now—

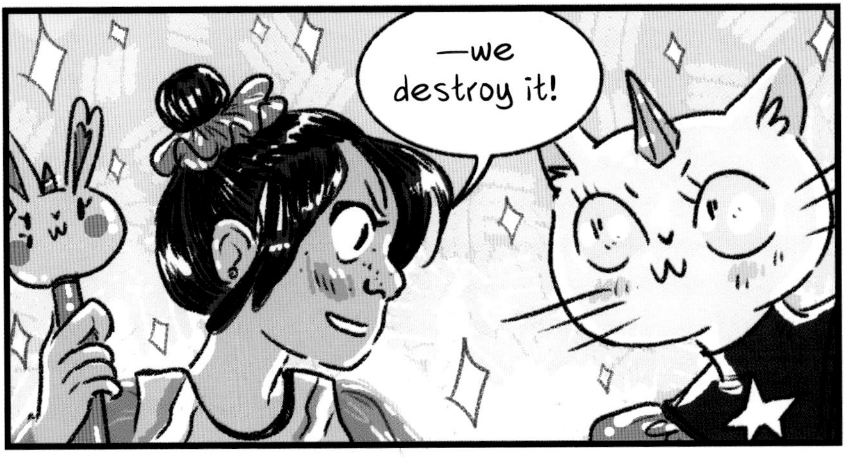
—we destroy it!

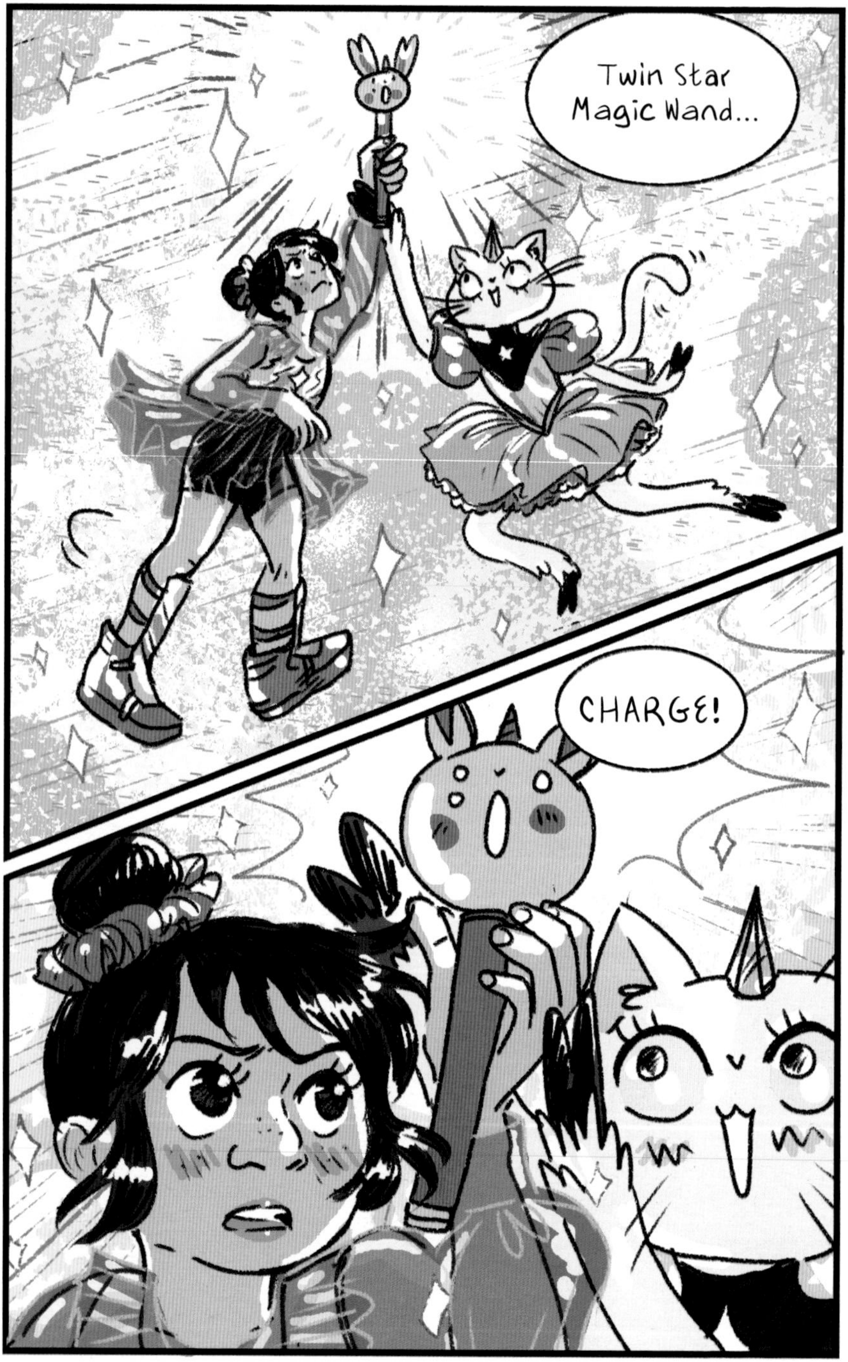
Twin Star Magic Wand...
CHARGE!

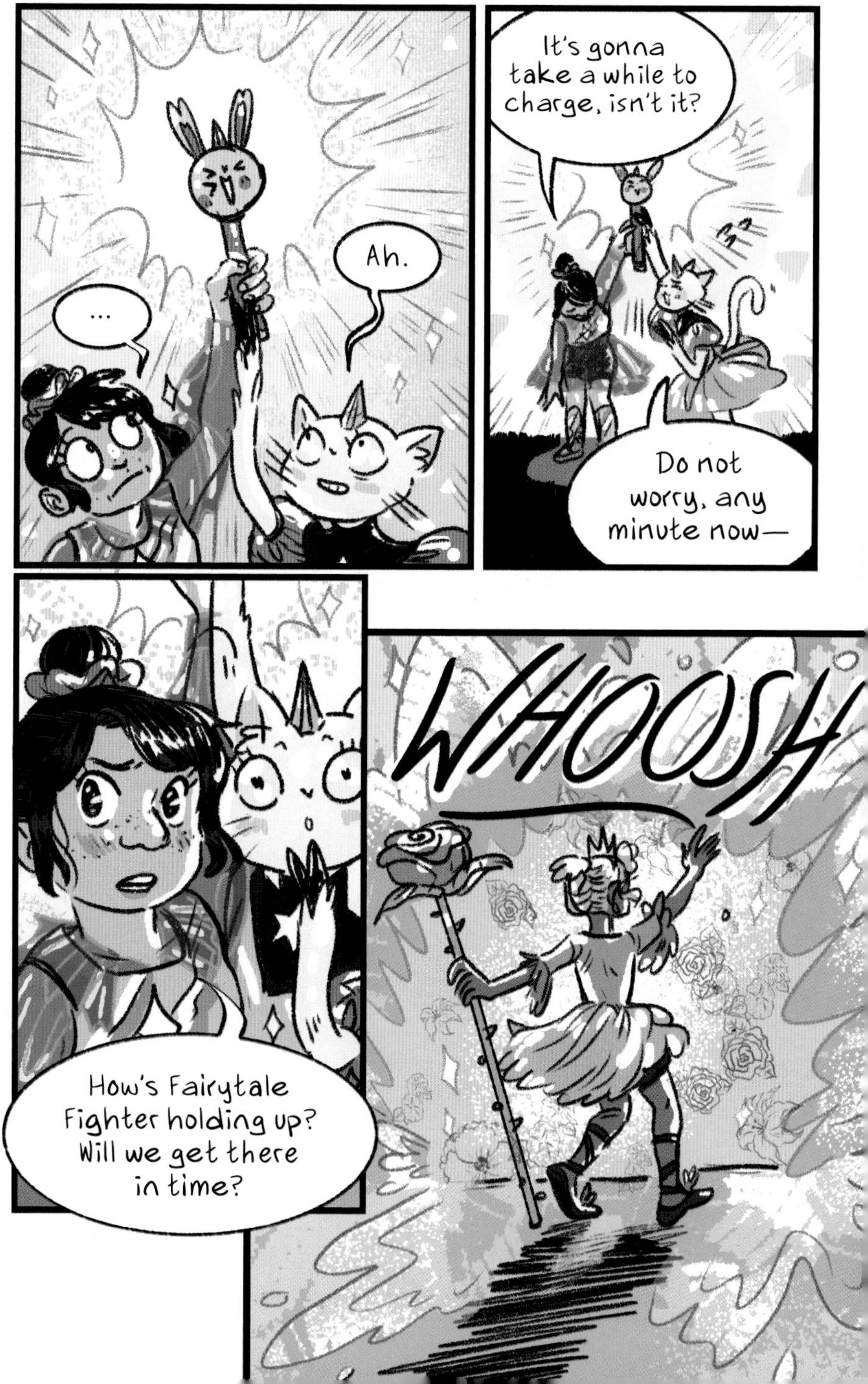
...
Ah.
It's gonna take a while to charge, isn't it?
Do not worry, any minute now—
How's Fairytale Fighter holding up? Will we get there in time?
WHOOSH

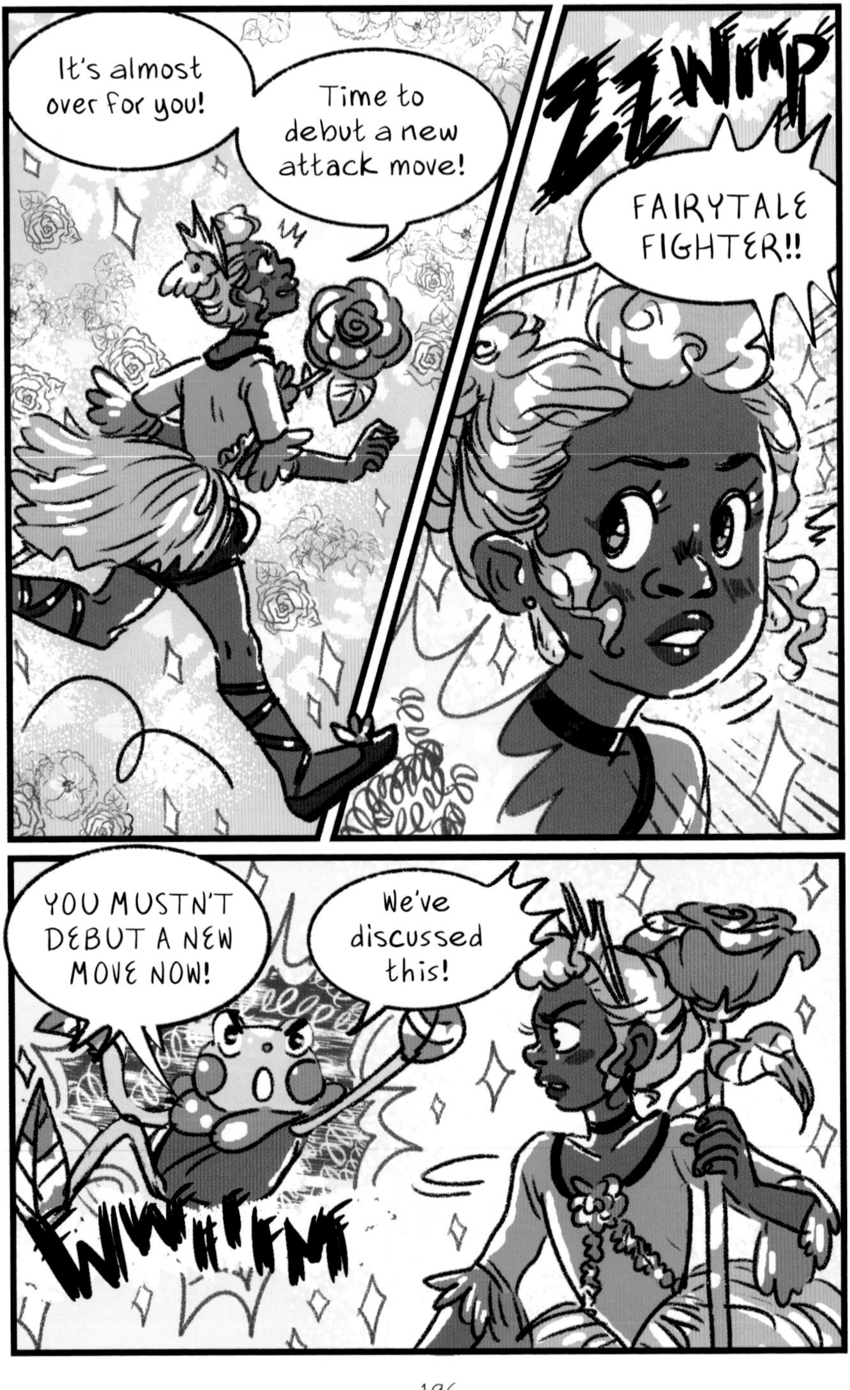
It's almost over for you!
Time to debut a new attack move!
ZZWMP
FAIRYTALE FIGHTER!!
YOU MUSTN'T DEBUT A NEW MOVE NOW!
We've discussed this!
FWWHHM

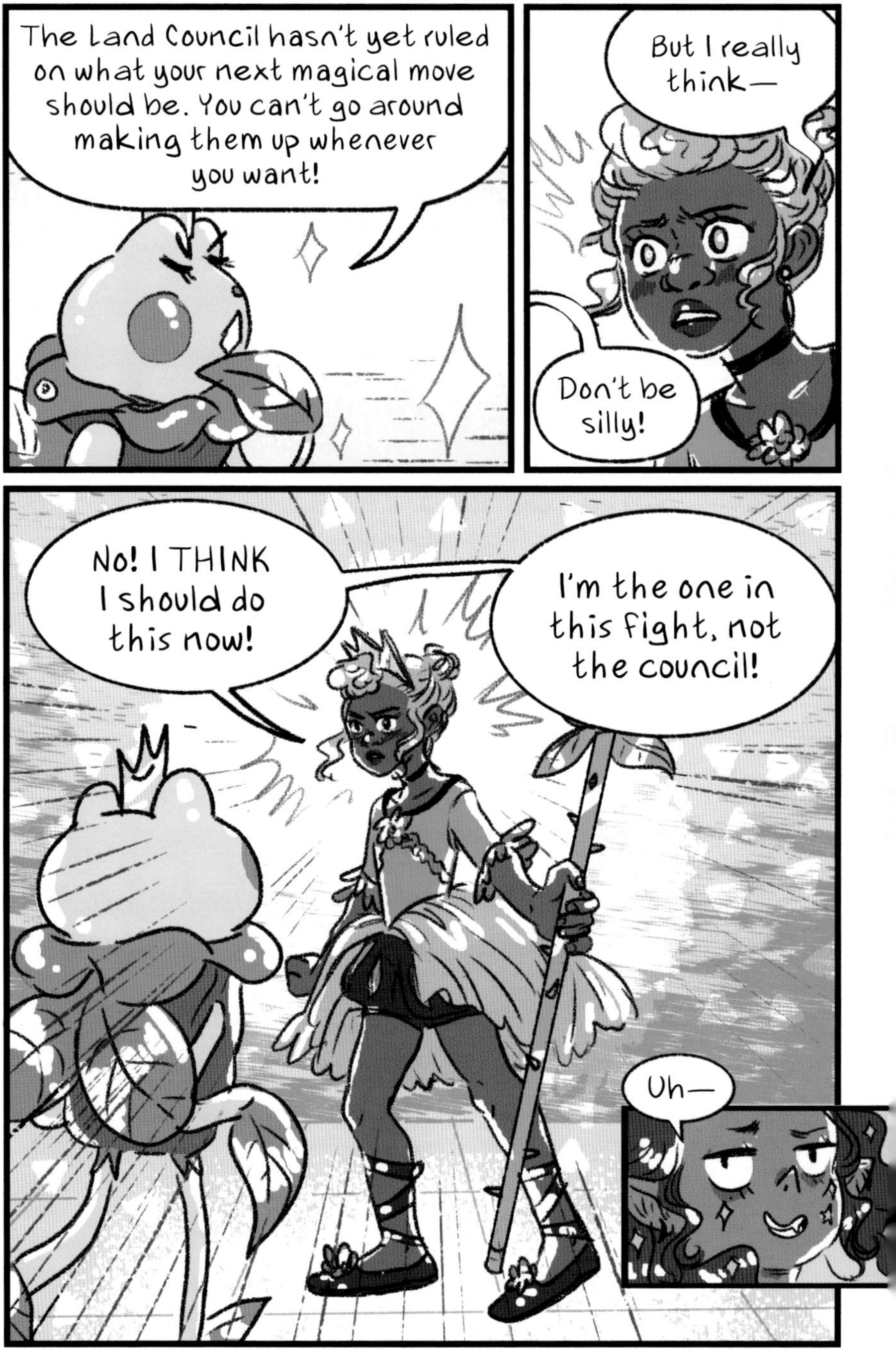
The Land Council hasn't yet ruled on what your next magical move should be. You can't go around making them up whenever you want!
But I really think—
Don't be silly!
No! I THINK I should do this now!
I'm the one in this fight, not the council!
Uh—

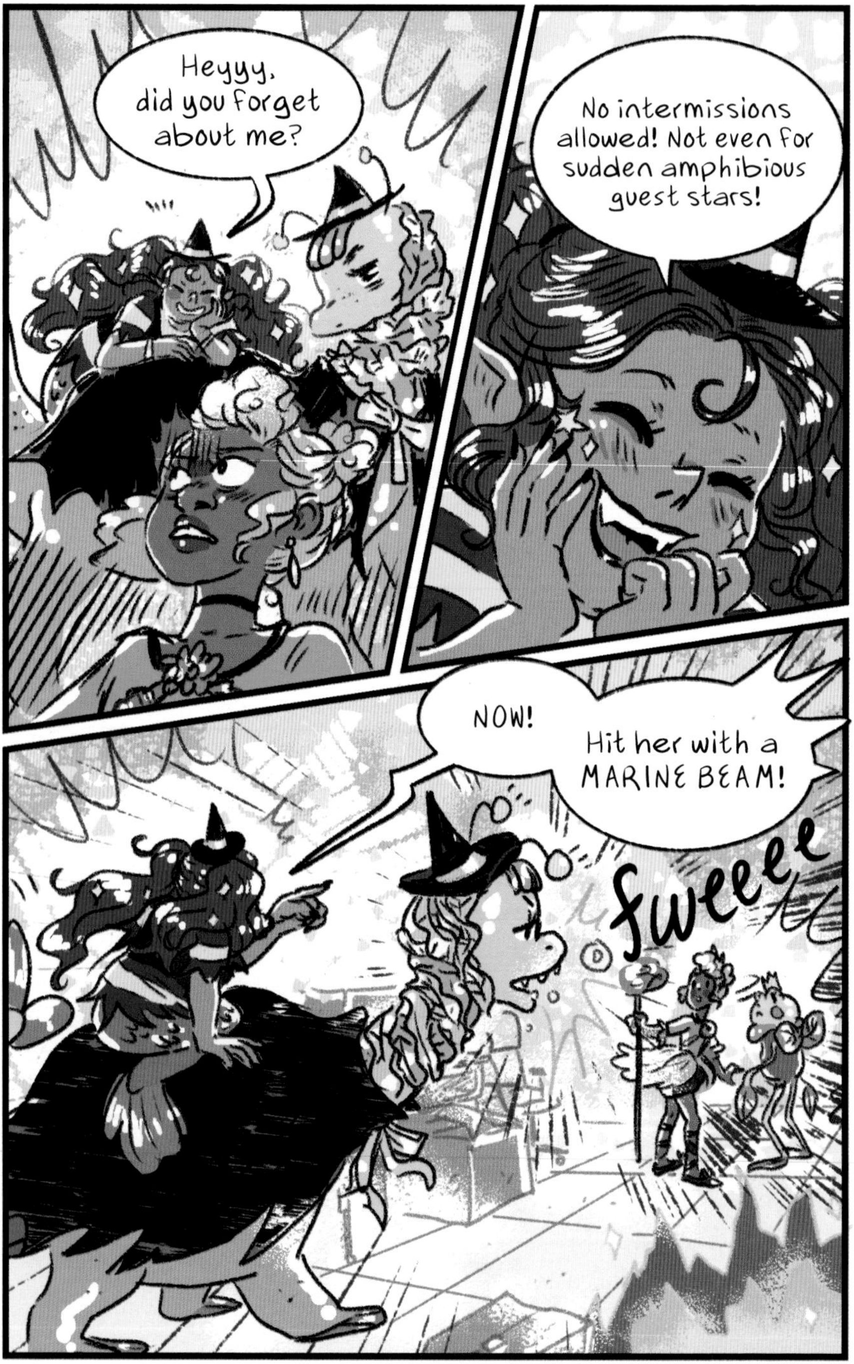
Heyyy,
did you forget
about me?
No intermissions
allowed! Not even for
sudden amphibious
guest stars!
NOW!
Hit her with a
MARINE BEAM!
fweeee

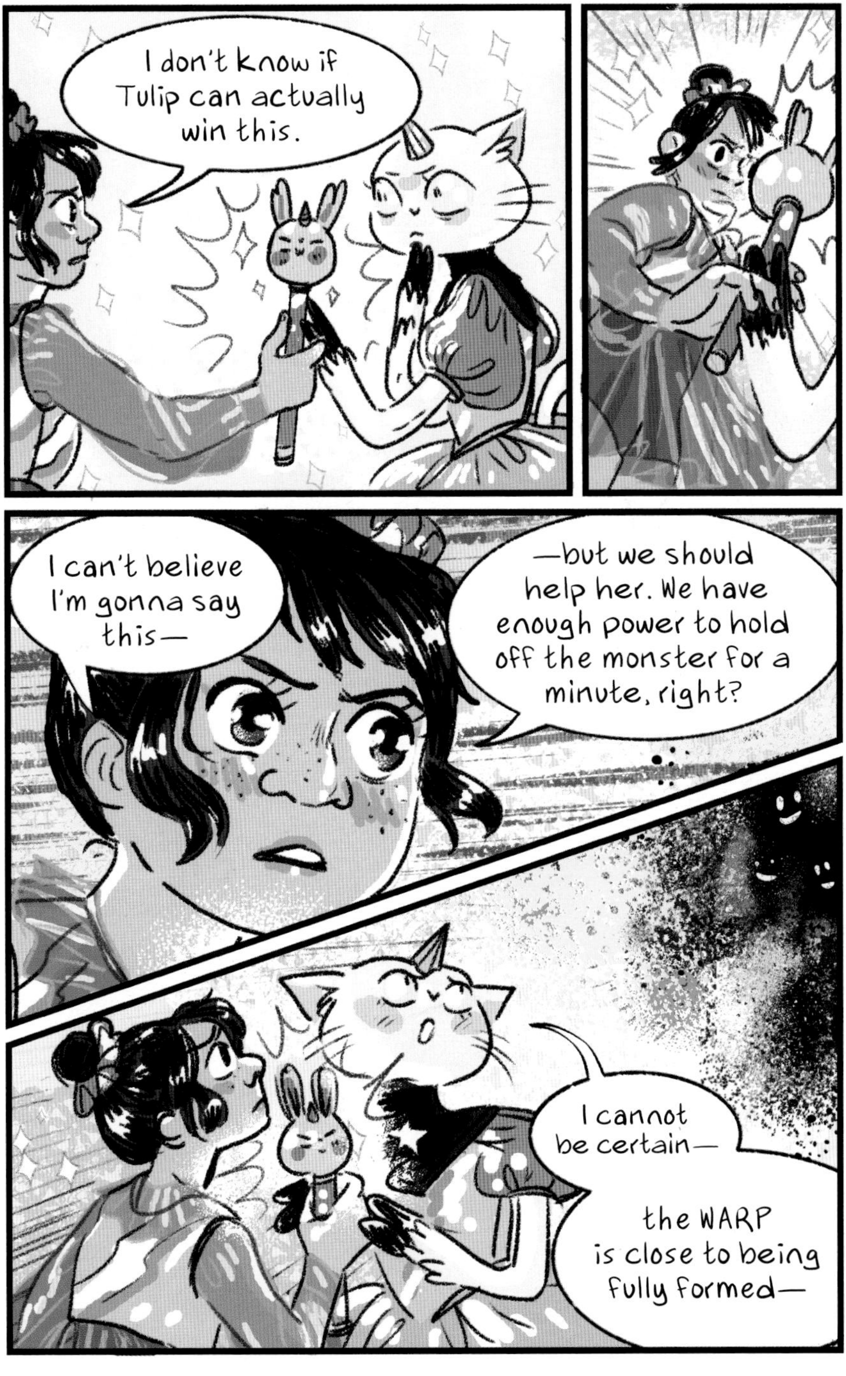
I don't know if Tulip can actually win this.
I can't believe I'm gonna say this—
—but we should help her. We have enough power to hold off the monster for a minute, right?
I cannot be certain—
the WARP is close to being fully formed—

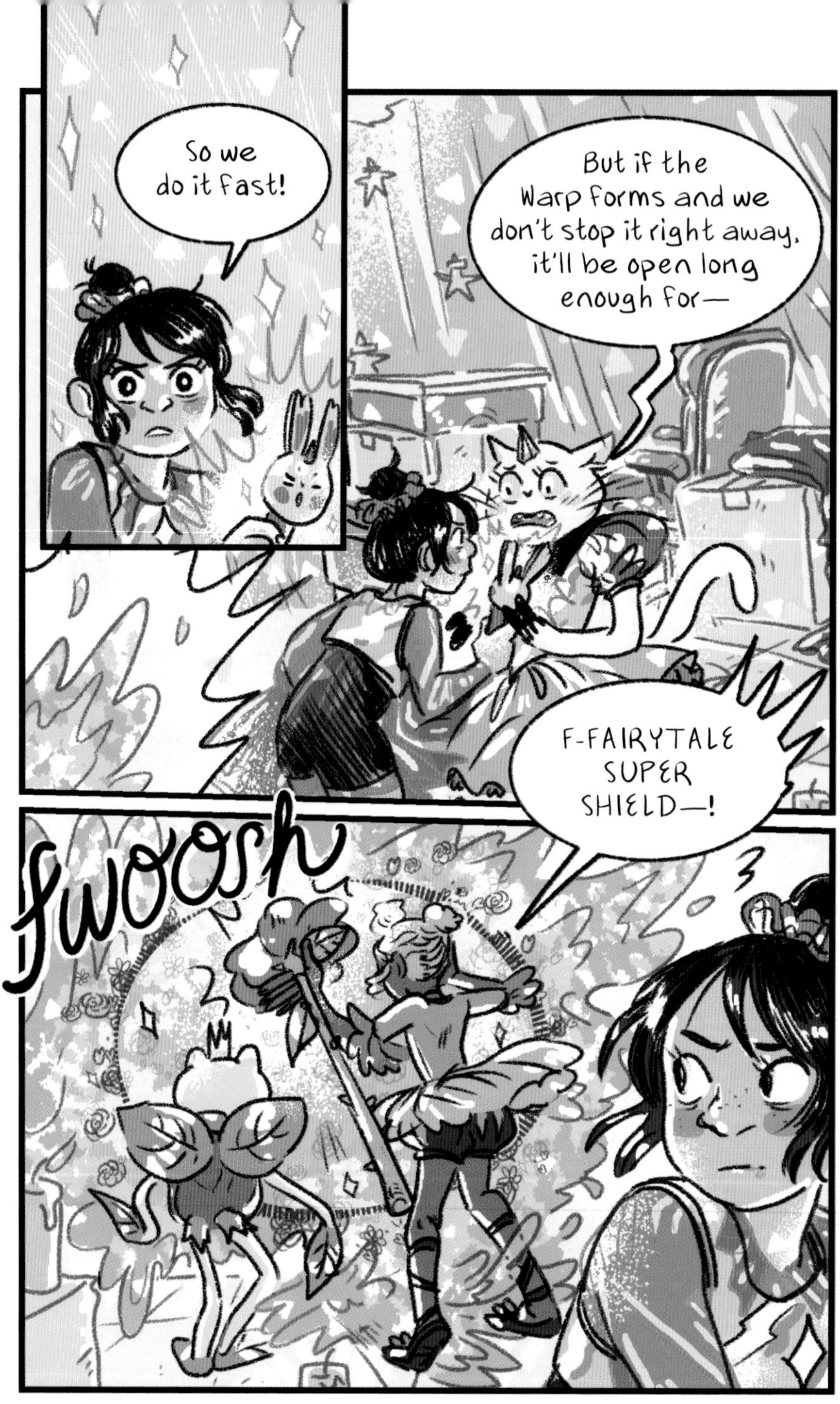
So we do it fast!
But if the Warp forms and we don't stop it right away, it'll be open long enough for—
F-FAIRYTALE SUPER SHIELD—!
fwoosh

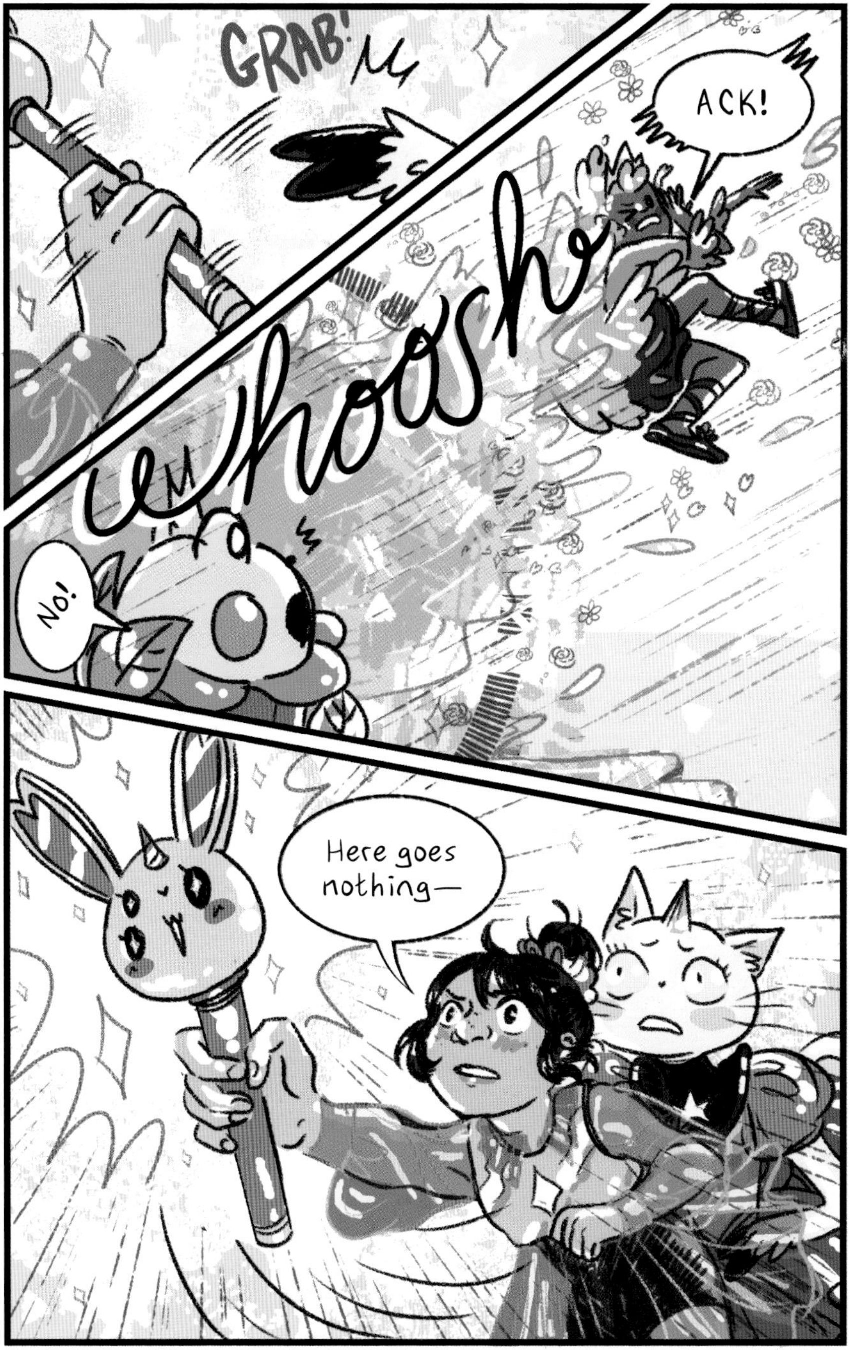
GRAB!
ACK!
Whoosh
No!
Here goes nothing—

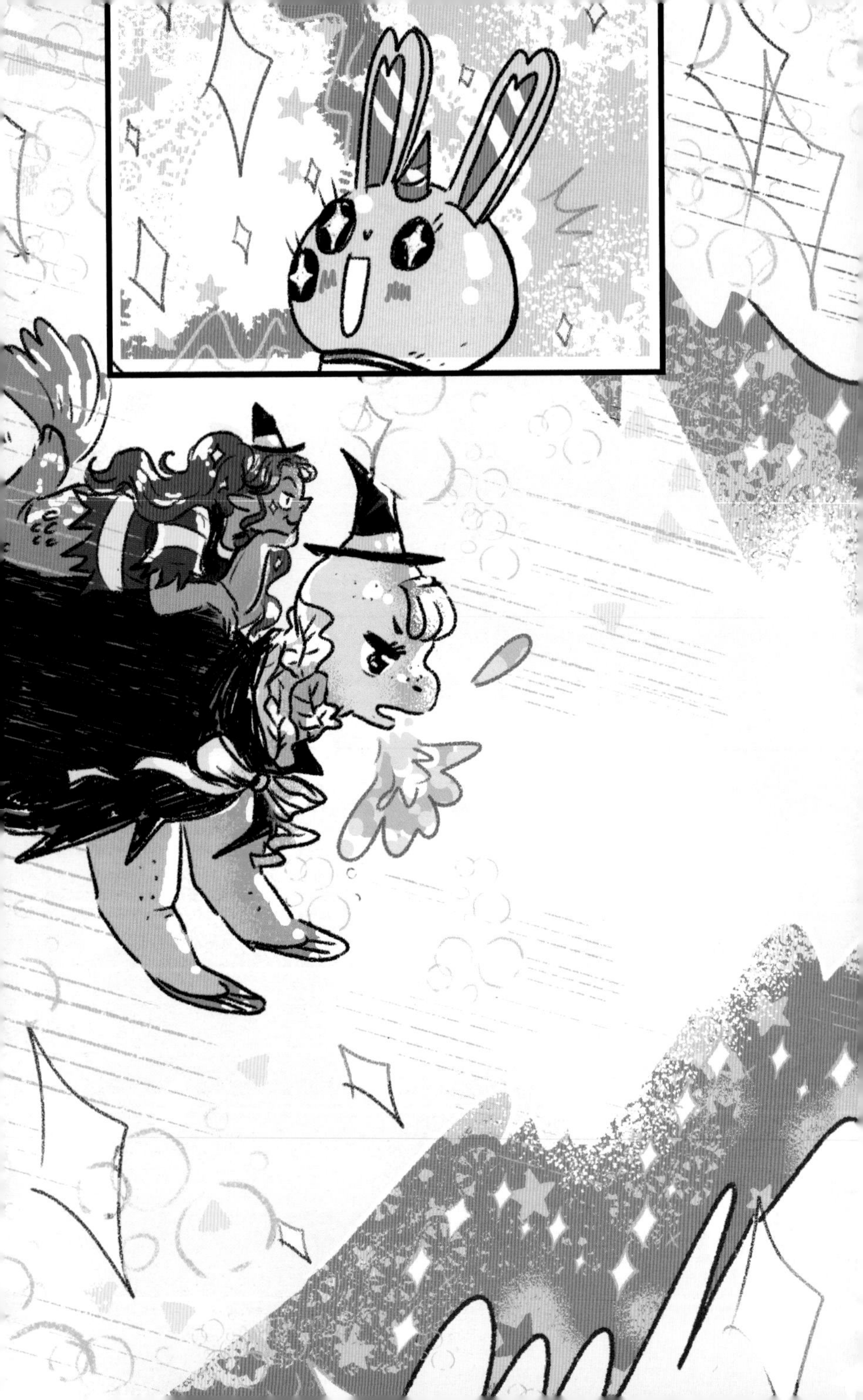

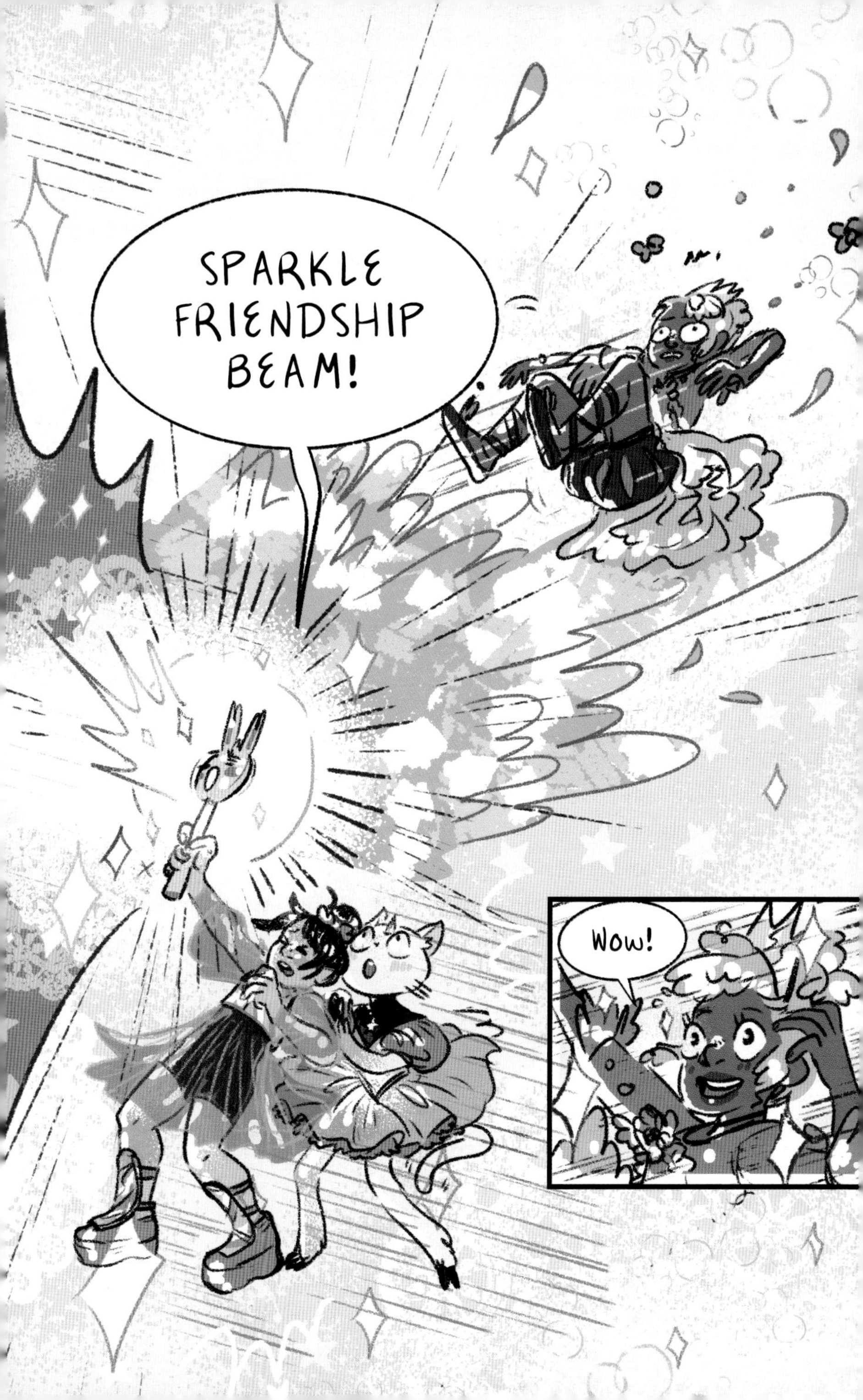
SPARKLE FRIENDSHIP BEAM!
WOW!

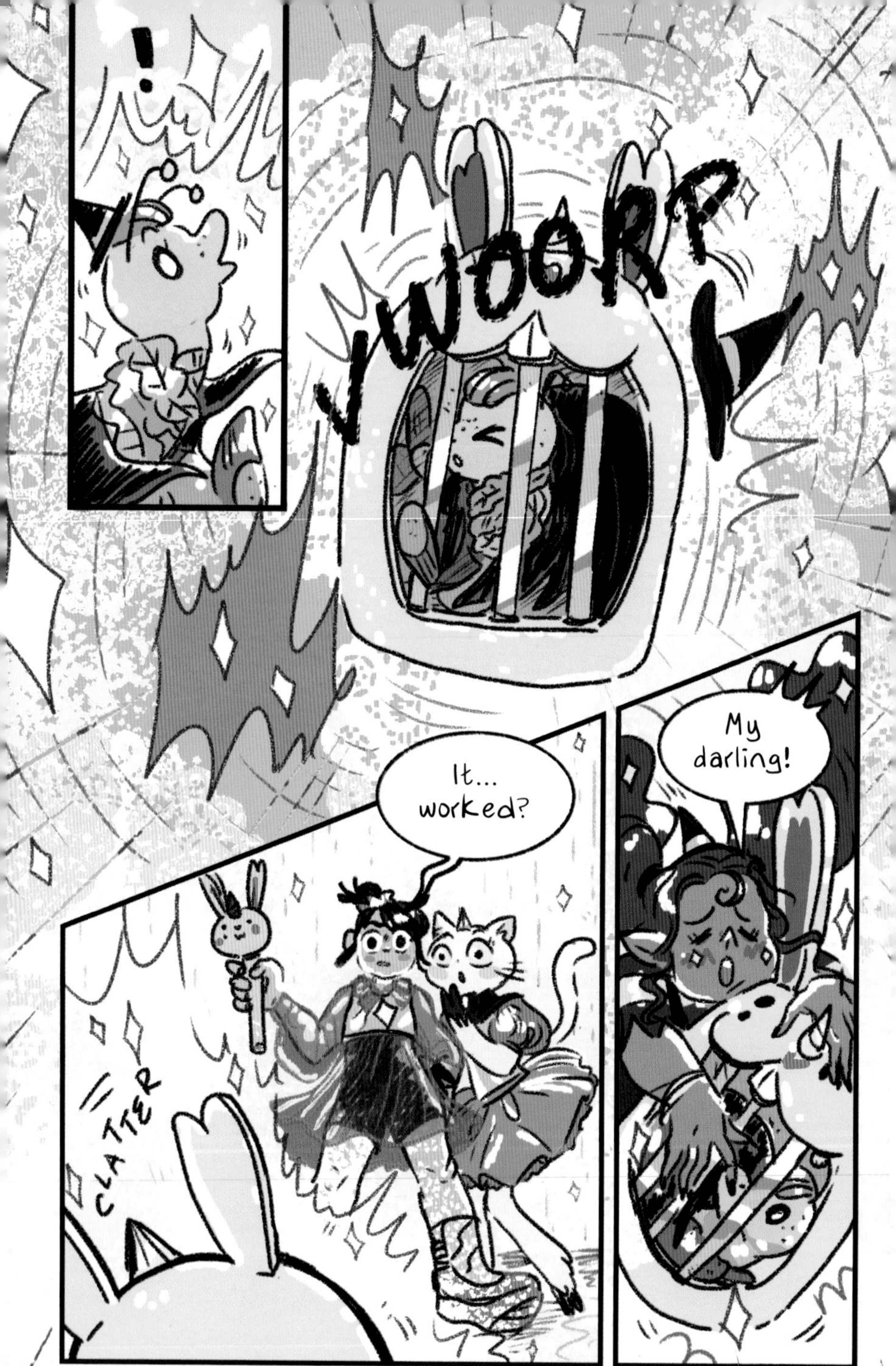
!
VWOORP
It... worked?
My darling!
CLATTER

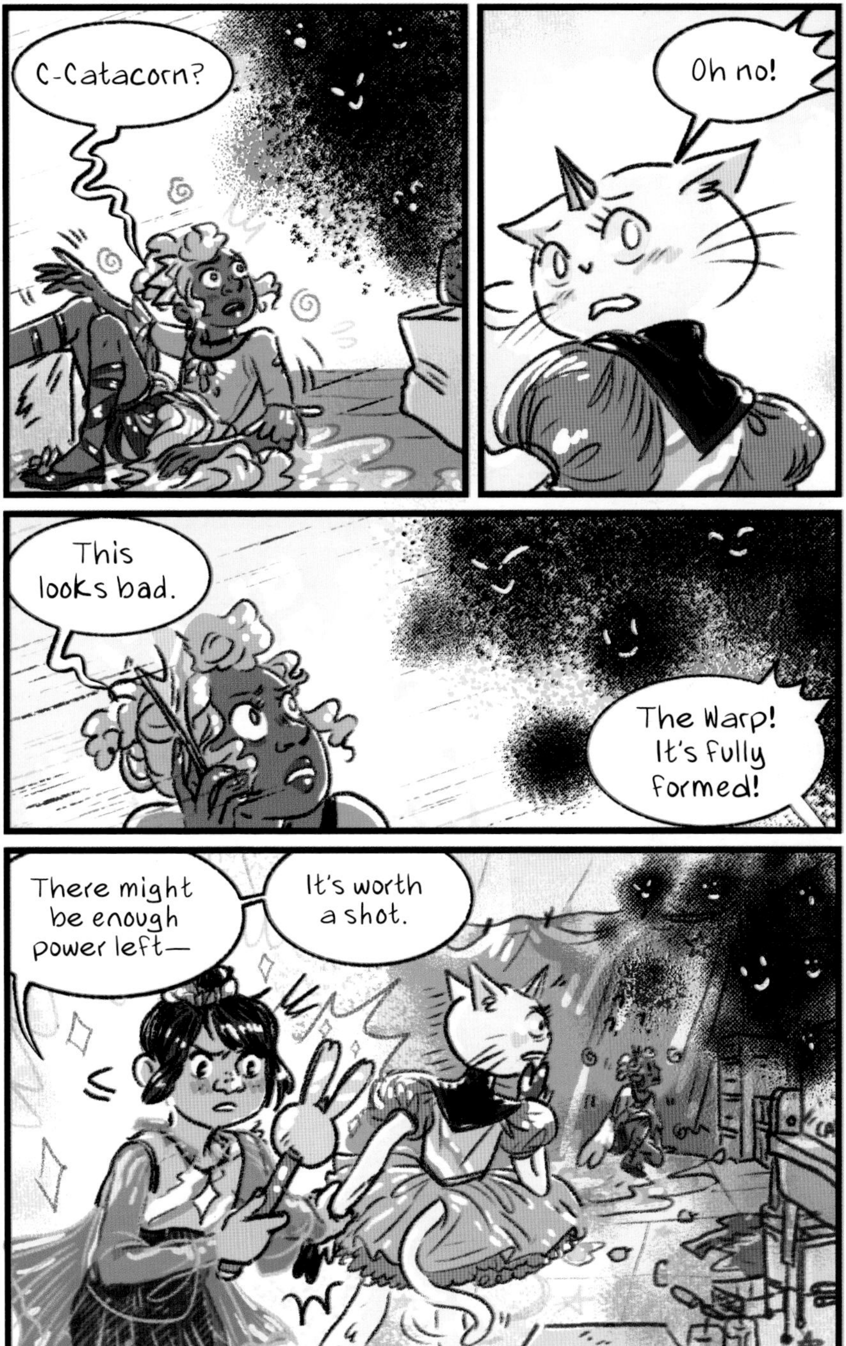
C-Catacorn?
Oh no!
This looks bad.
The Warp! It's fully formed!
There might be enough power left—
It's worth a shot.

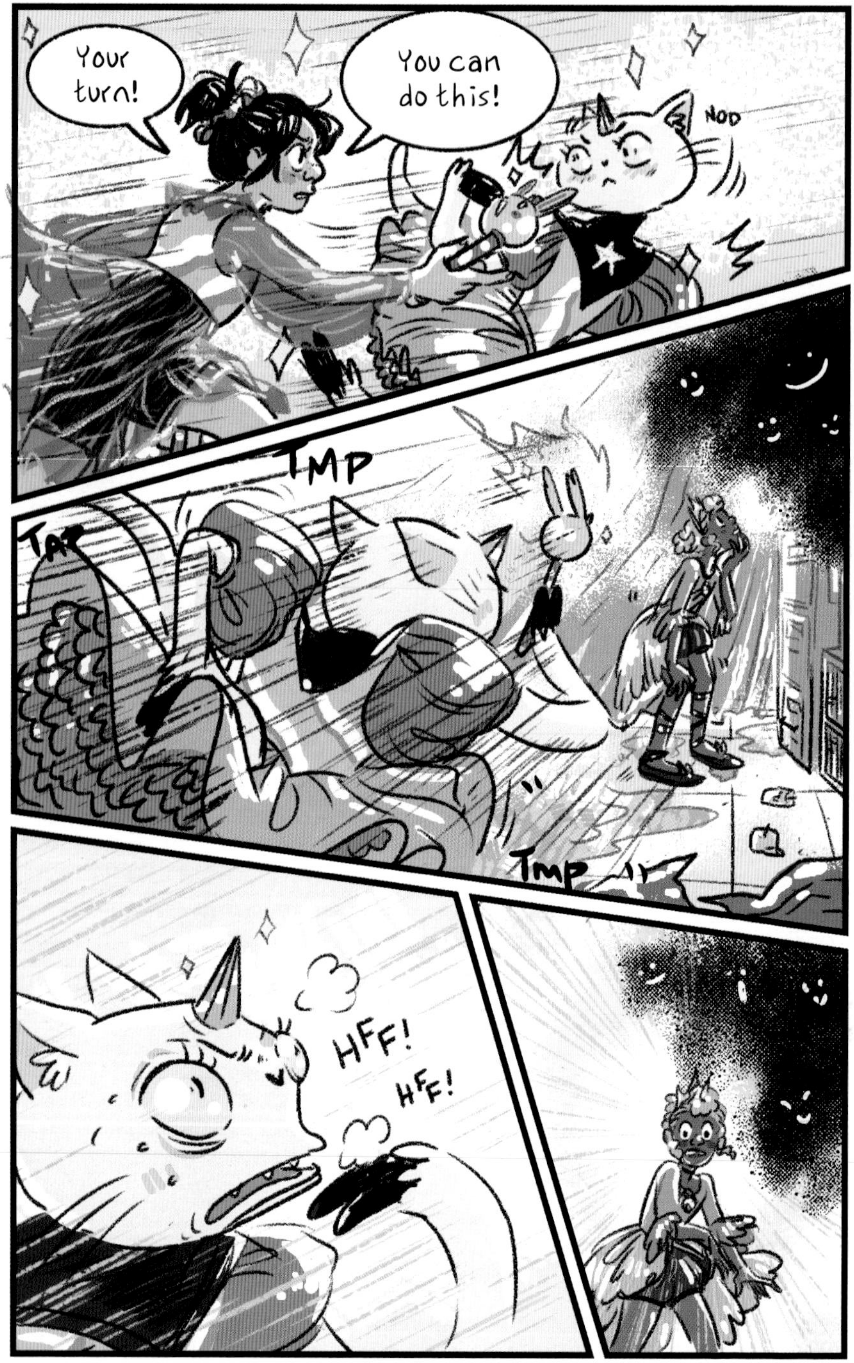
Your turn!
You can do this!
NOD
TMP
TAP
Tmp
HFF!
HFF!

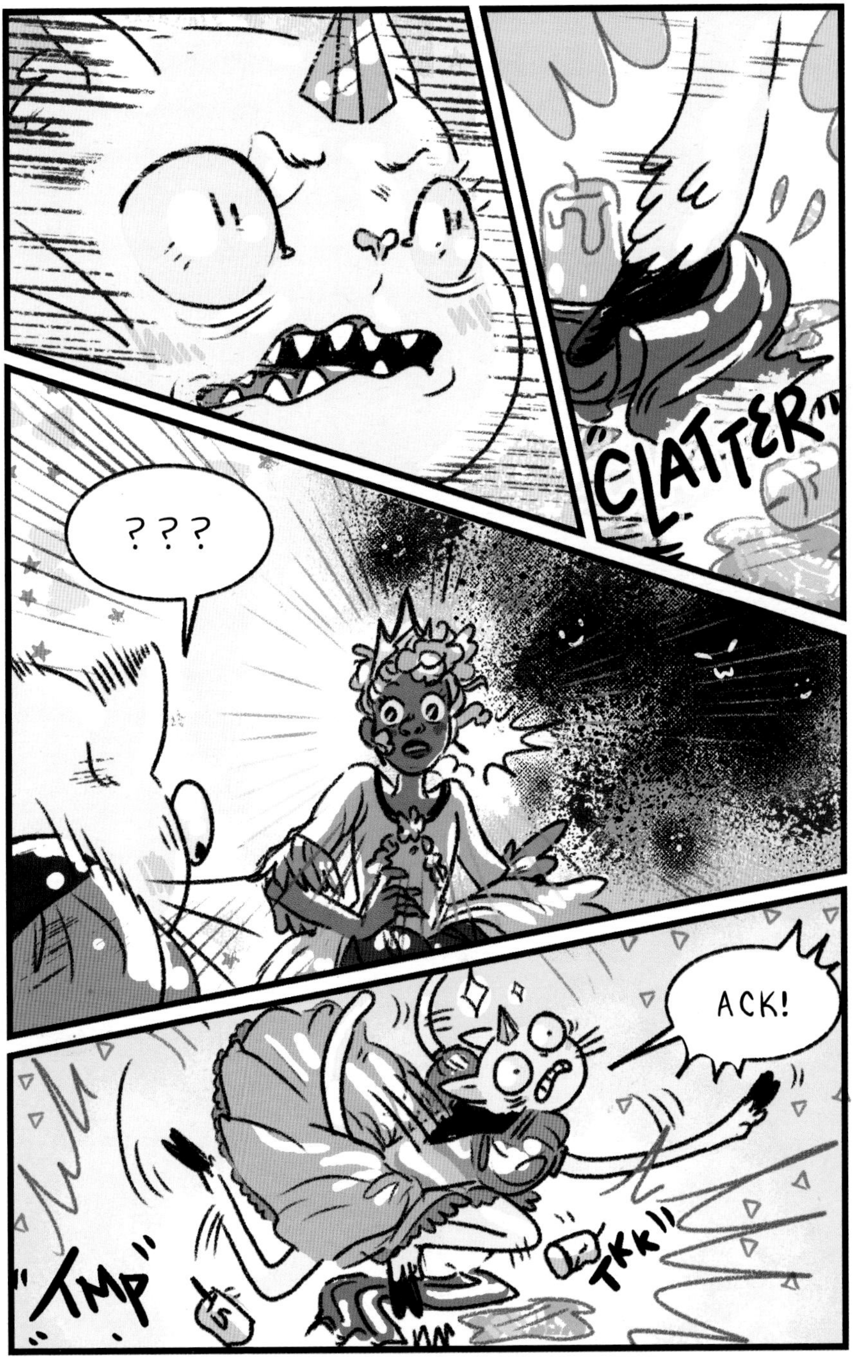
"CLATTER"
???
ACK!
"TMP"
"TKK"

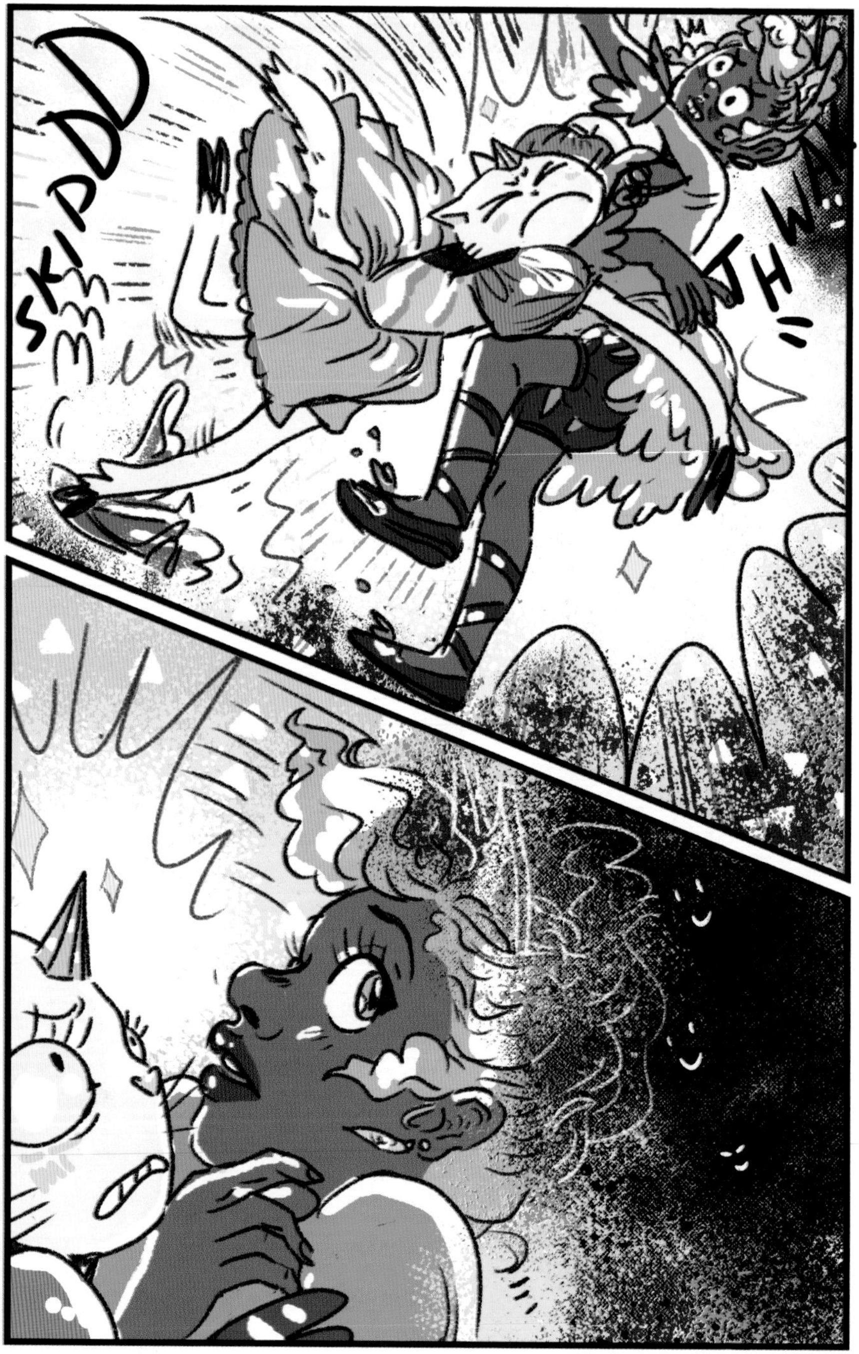
SKIPDD
THWA

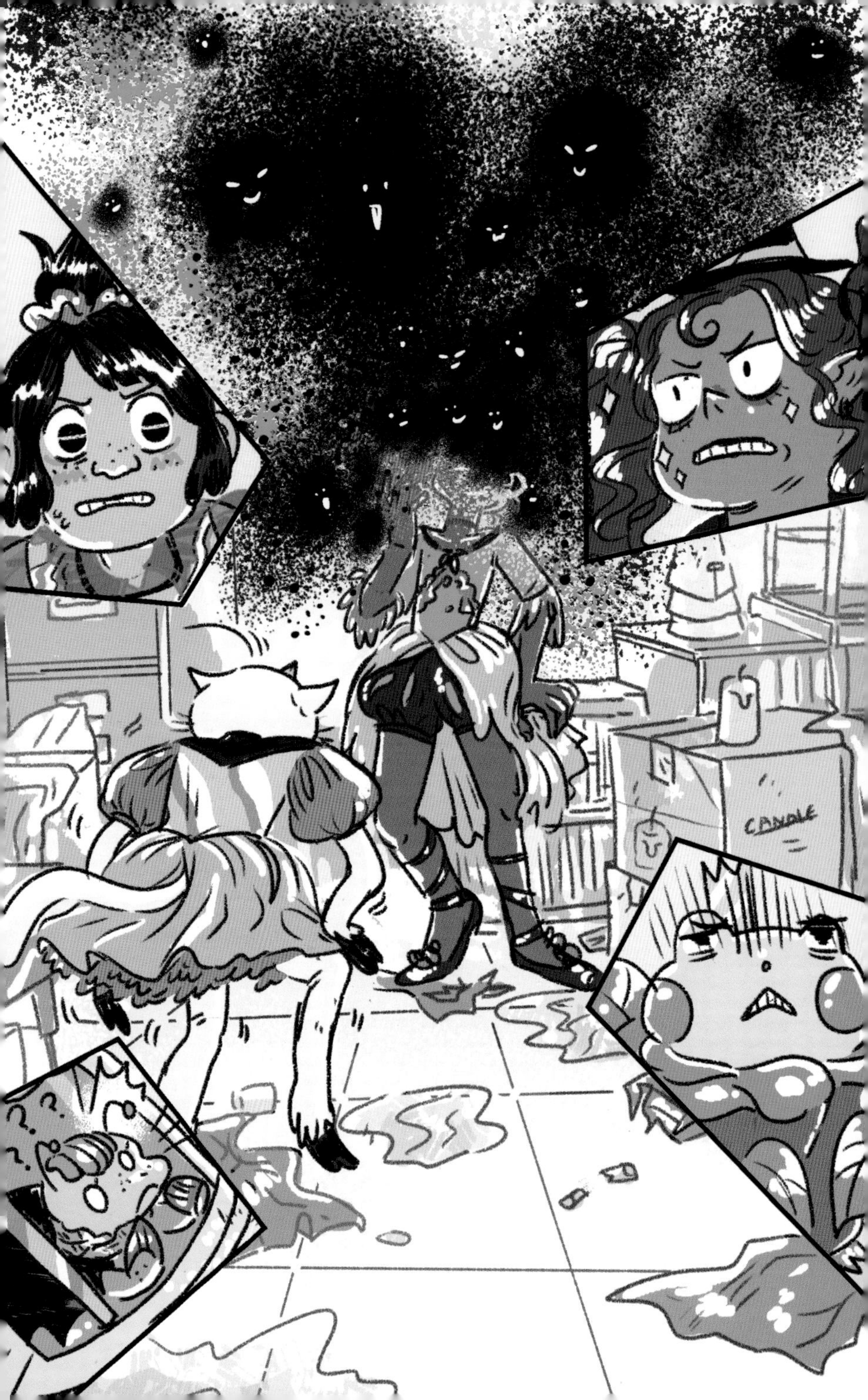
CANDLE

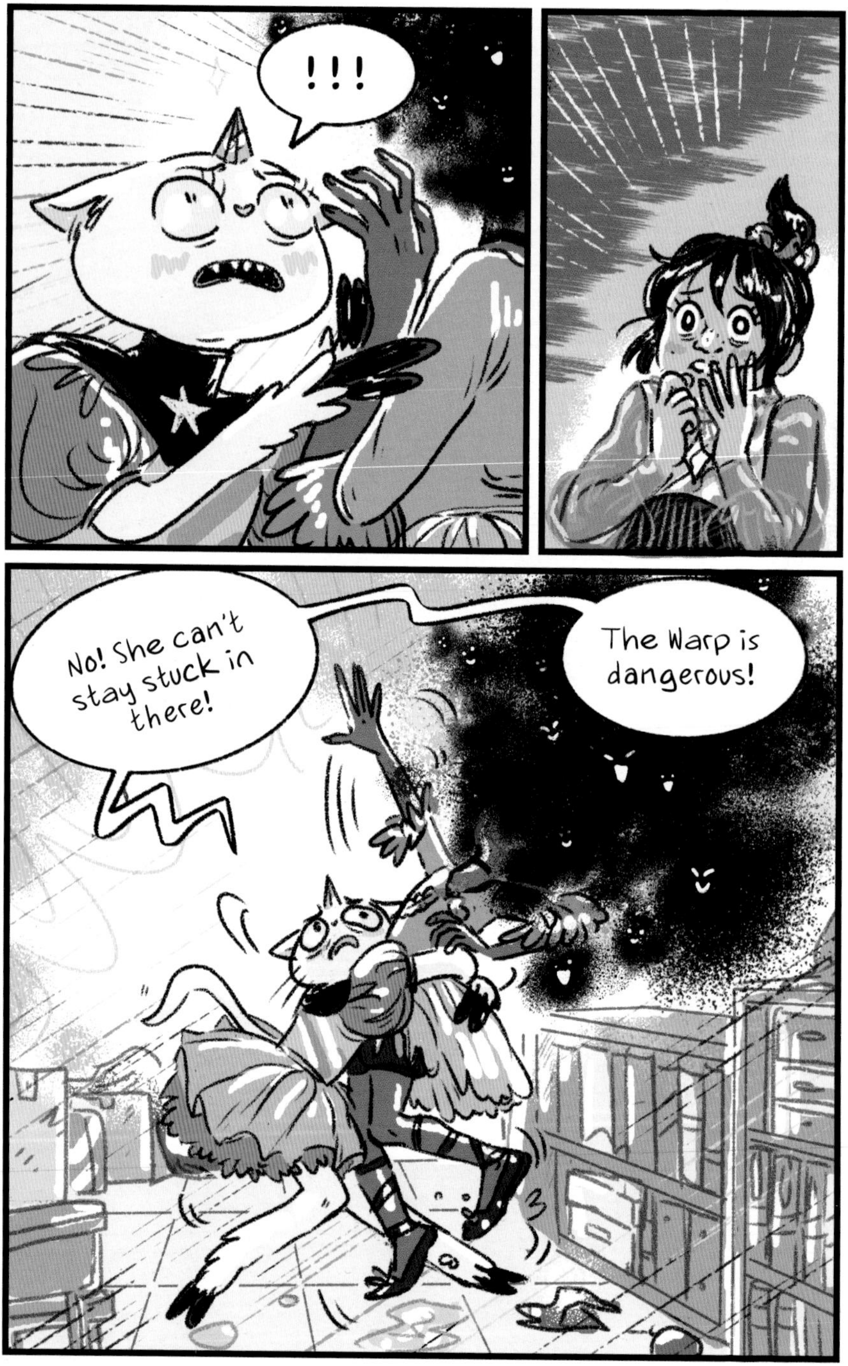
!!!
No! She can't stay stuck in there!
The Warp is dangerous!

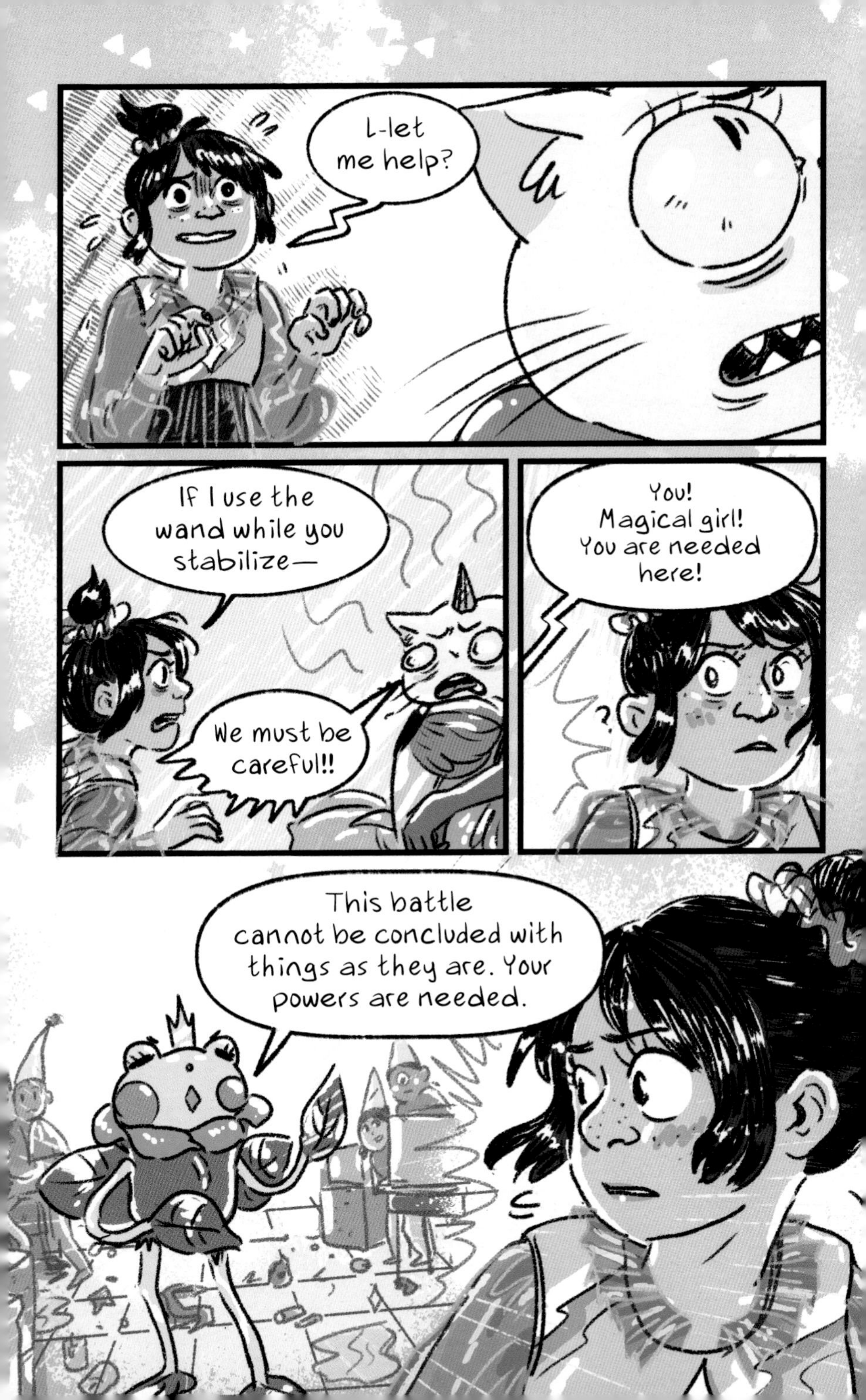
L-let me help?
If I use the wand while you stabilize—
We must be careful!!
You! Magical girl! You are needed here!
This battle cannot be concluded with things as they are. Your powers are needed.

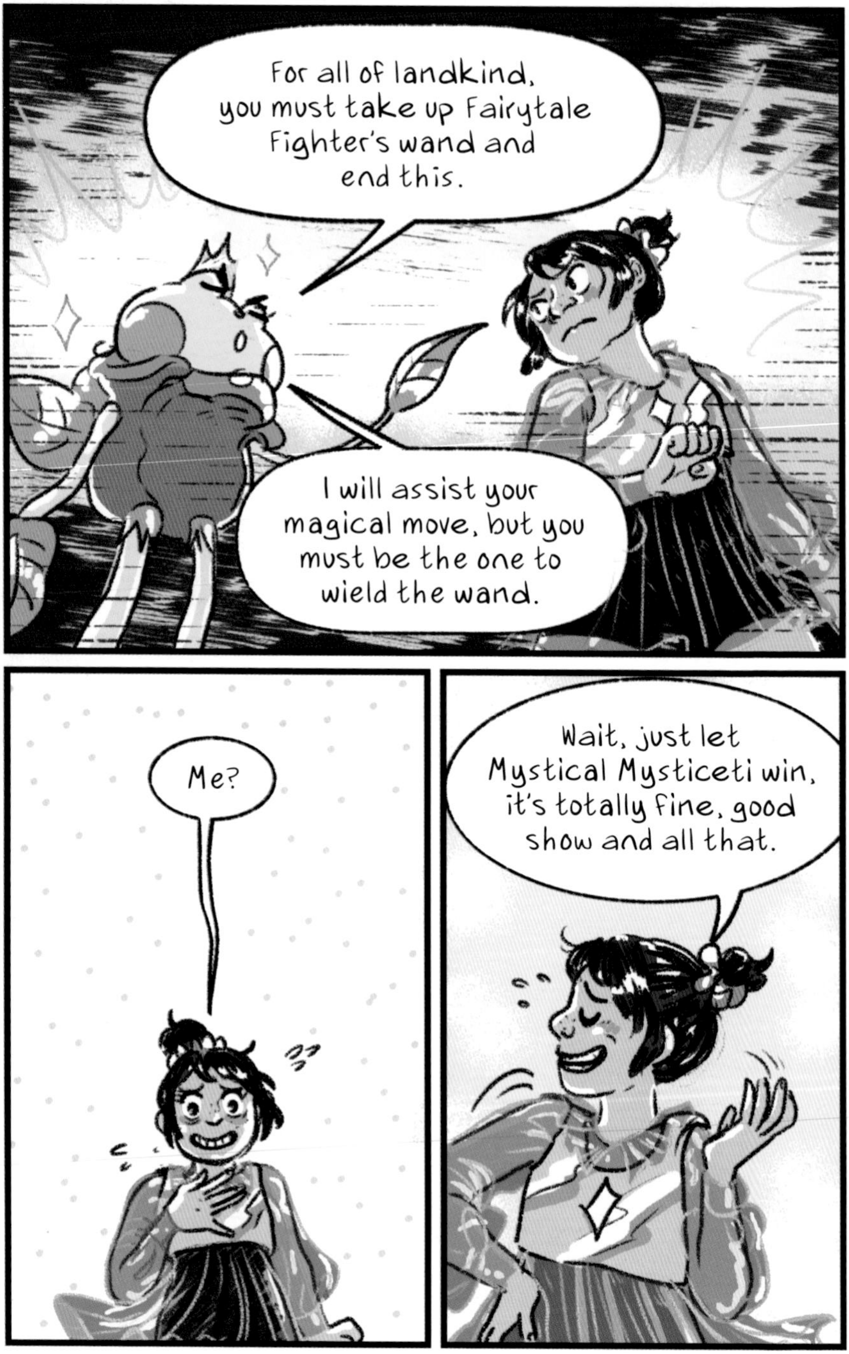
For all of landkind, you must take up Fairytale Fighter's wand and end this.
I will assist your magical move, but you must be the one to wield the wand.
Me?
Wait, just let Mystical Mysticeti win, it's totally fine, good show and all that.

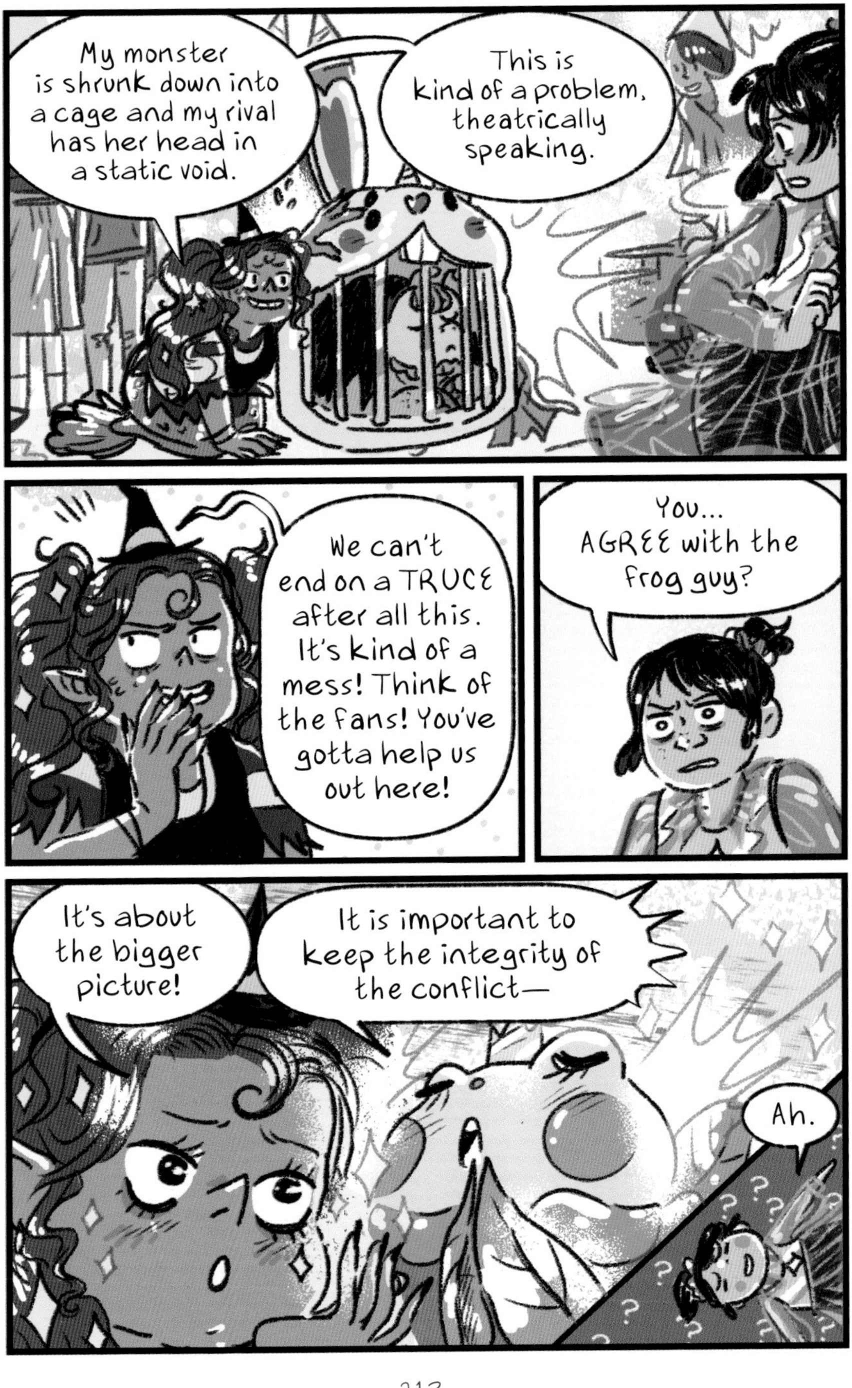
My monster is shrunk down into a cage and my rival has her head in a static void.
This is kind of a problem, theatrically speaking.
We can't end on a TRUCE after all this. It's kind of a mess! Think of the fans! You've gotta help us out here!
You... AGREE with the frog guy?
It's about the bigger picture!
It is important to keep the integrity of the conflict—
Ah.

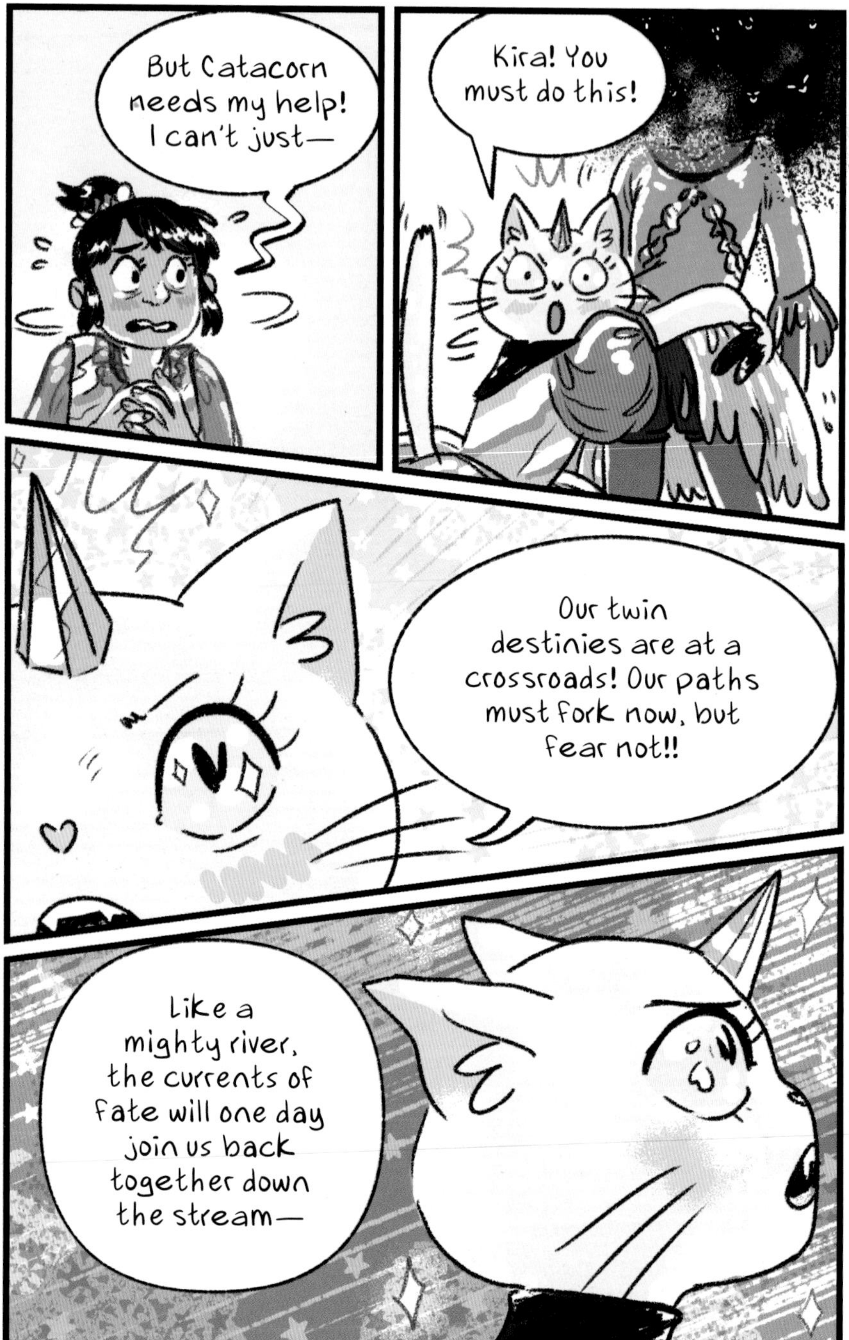
But Catacorn needs my help! I can't just—
Kira! You must do this!
Our twin destinies are at a crossroads! Our paths must fork now, but fear not!!
Like a mighty river, the currents of fate will one day join us back together down the stream—

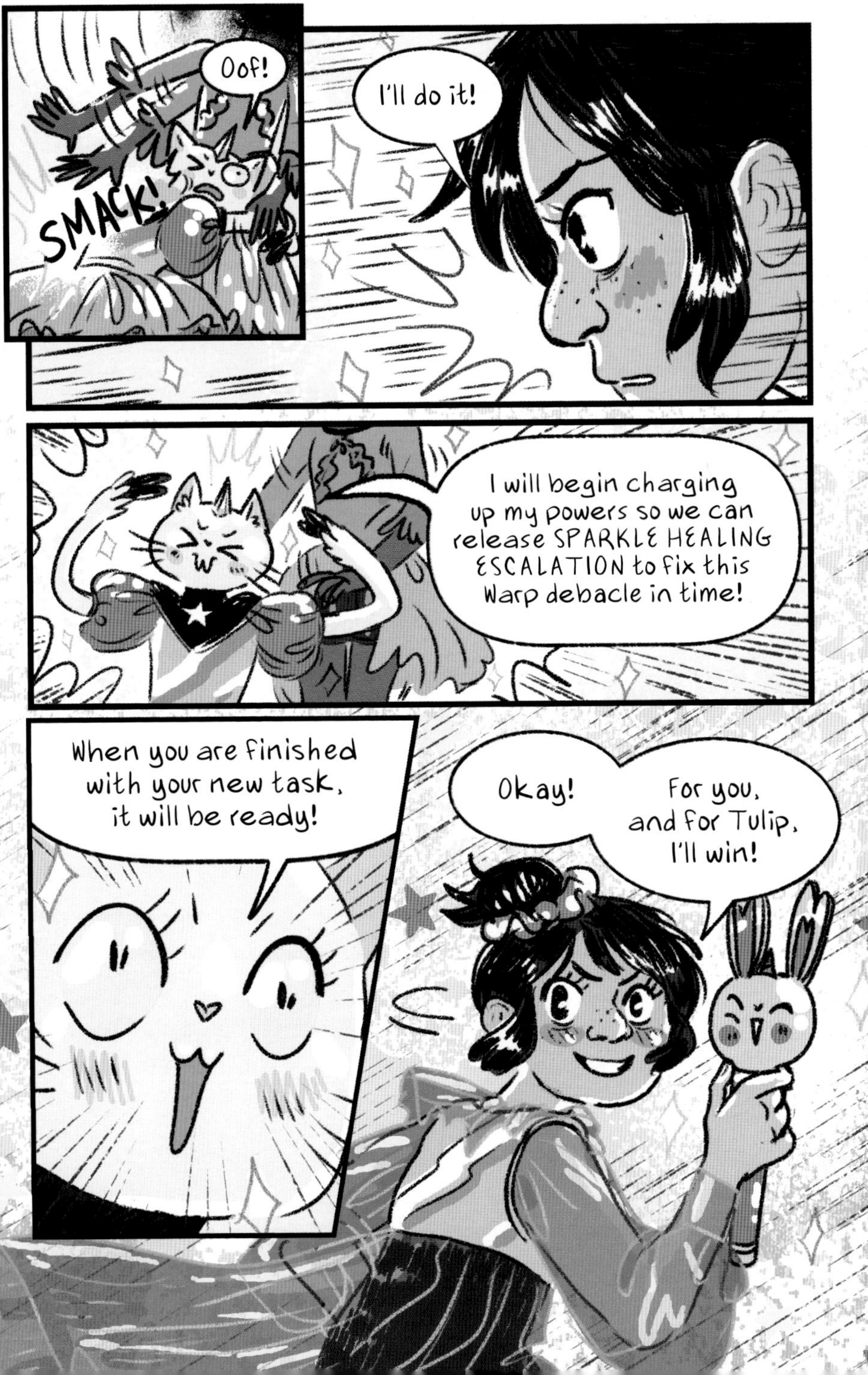
Oof!
SMACK!
I'll do it!
I will begin charging up my powers so we can release SPARKLE HEALING ESCALATION to fix this Warp debacle in time!
When you are finished with your new task, it will be ready!
Okay!
For you, and for Tulip, I'll win!

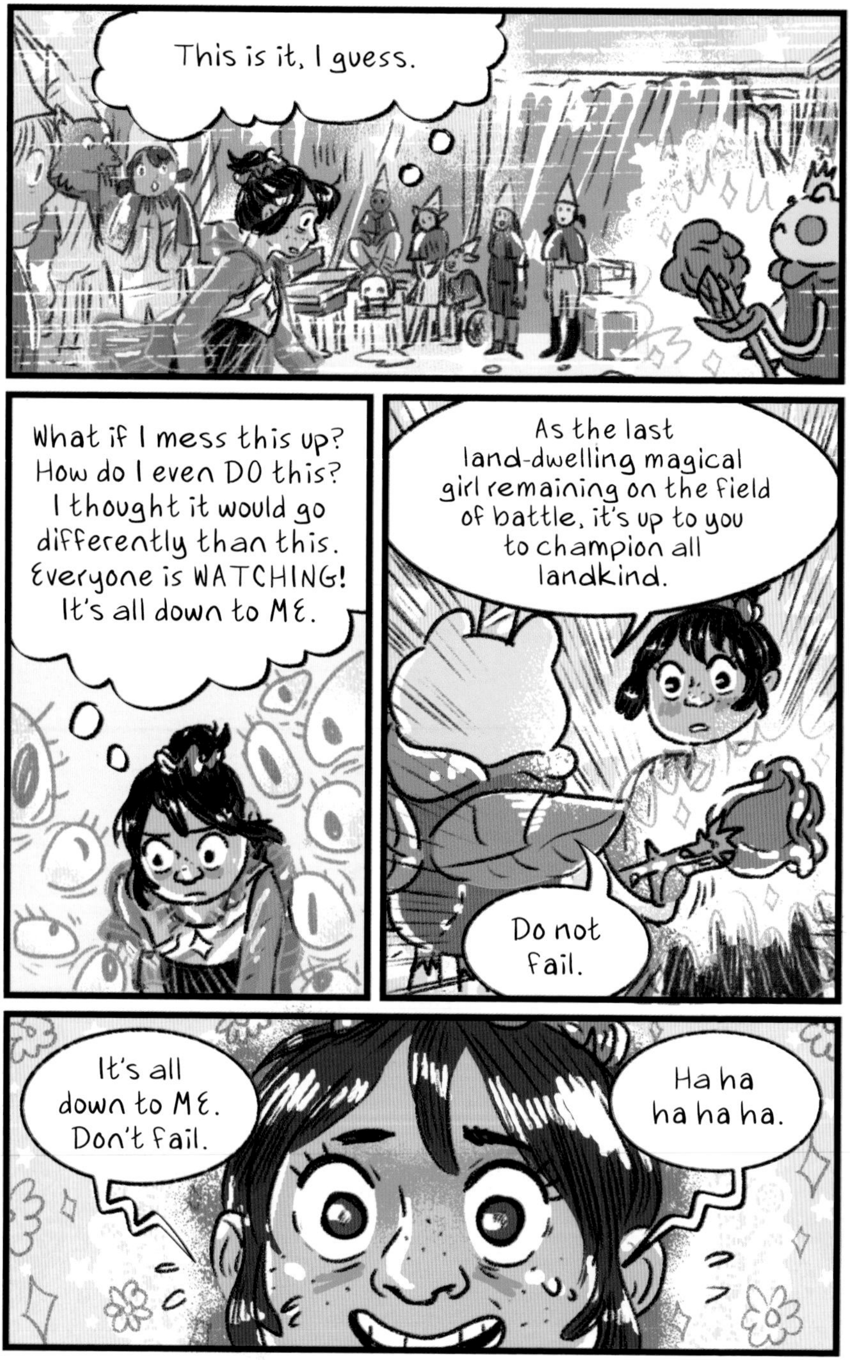
This is it, I guess.
What if I mess this up? How do I even DO this? I thought it would go differently than this. Everyone is WATCHING! It's all down to ME.
As the last land-dwelling magical girl remaining on the field of battle, it's up to you to champion all landkind.
Do not fail.
It's all down to ME. Don't fail.
Ha ha ha ha ha.

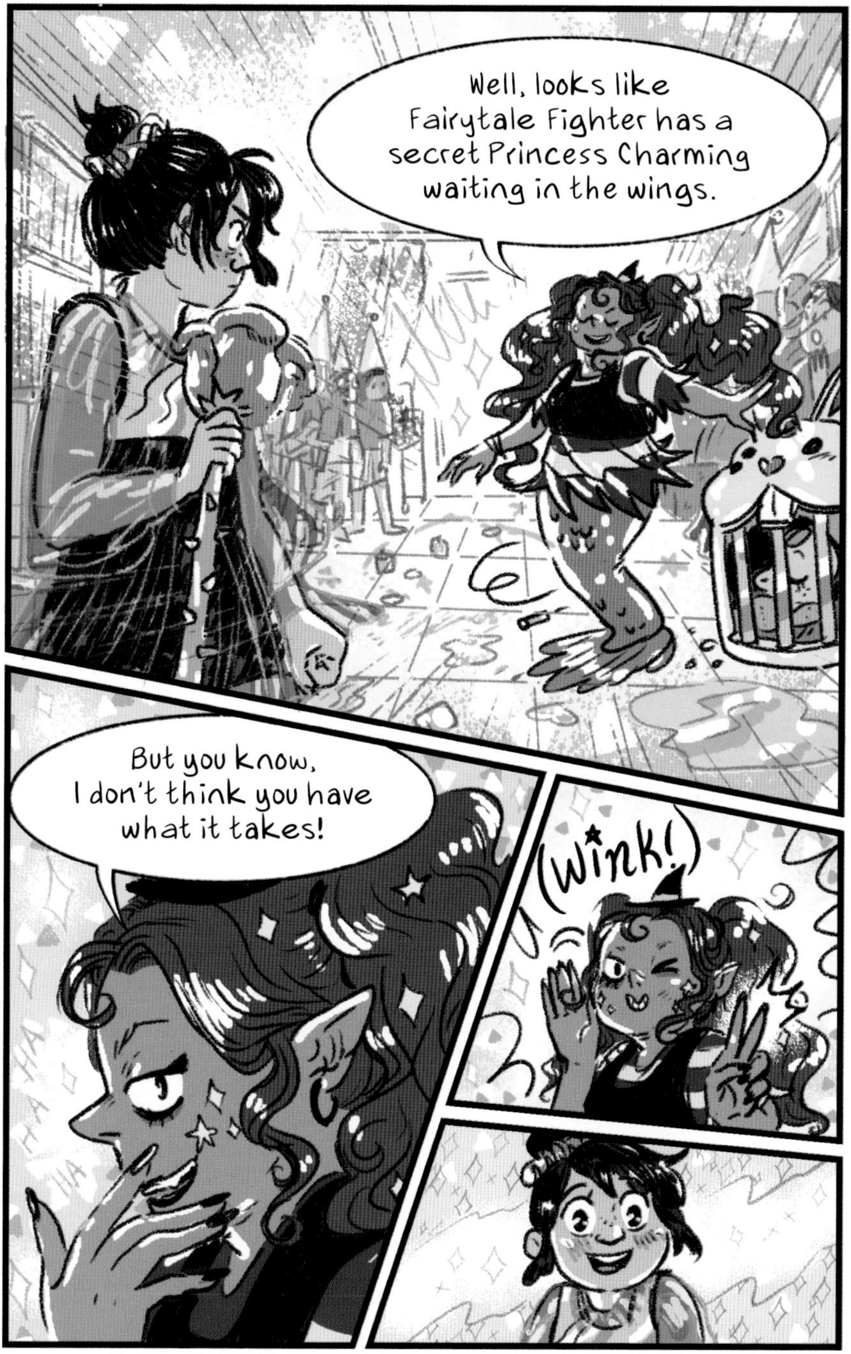
Well, looks like Fairytale Fighter has a secret Princess Charming waiting in the wings.
But you know, I don't think you have what it takes!
(wink!)
HA
HA
HA

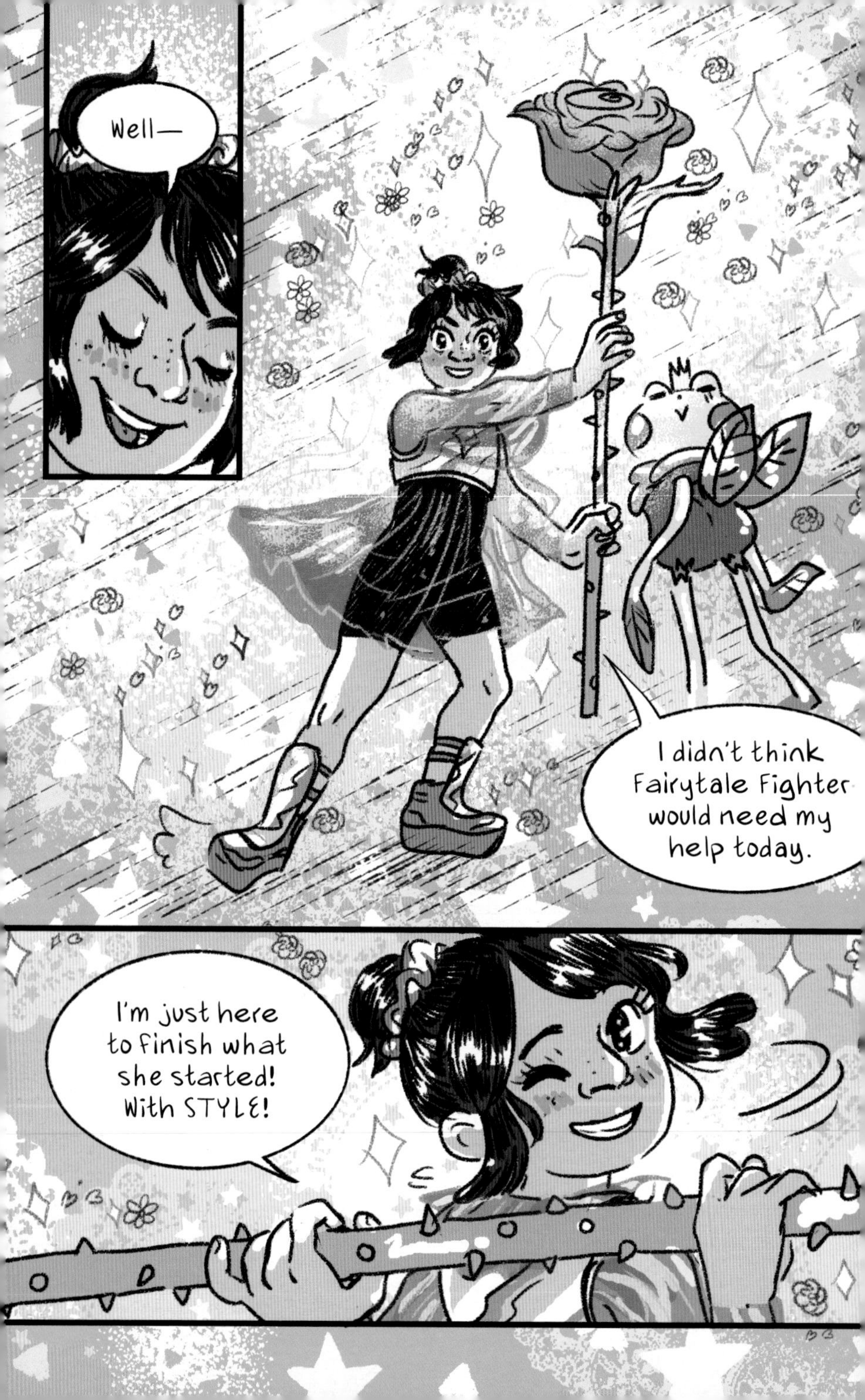
Well—
I didn't think Fairytale Fighter would need my help today.
I'm just here to finish what she started! With STYLE!

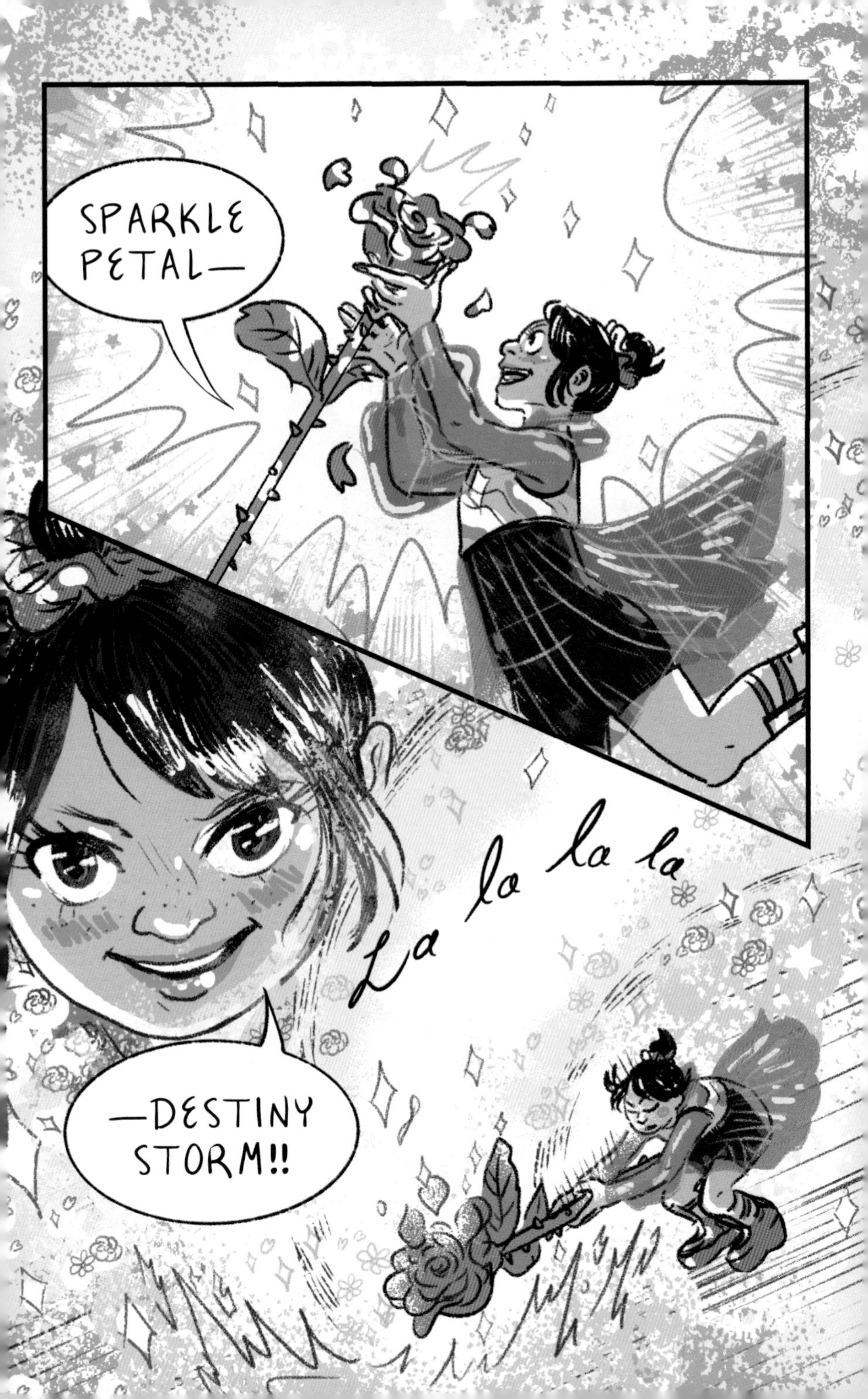
SPARKLE PETAL—
La la la la
—DESTINY STORM!!

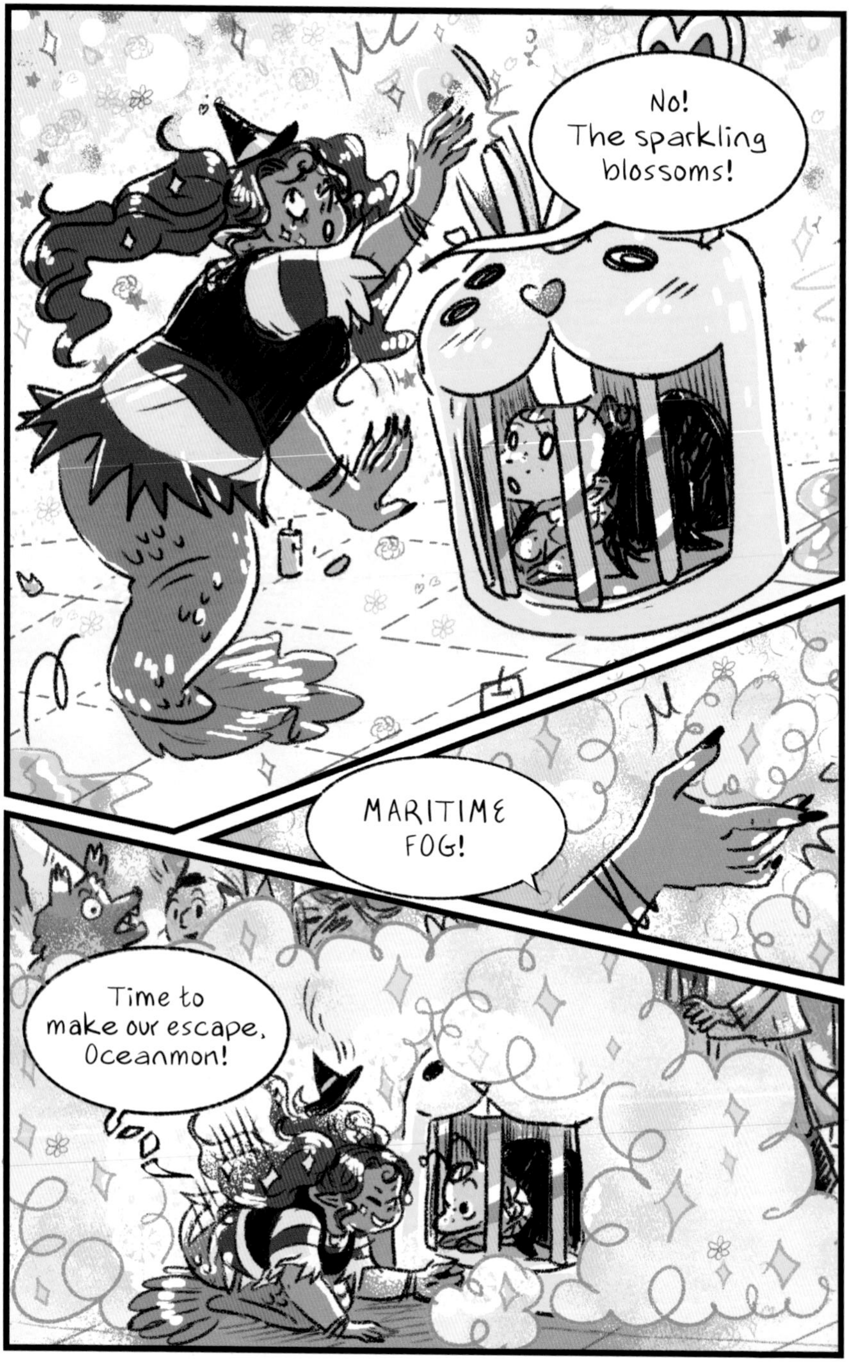
No! The sparkling blossoms!
MARITIME FOG!
Time to make our escape, Oceanmon!

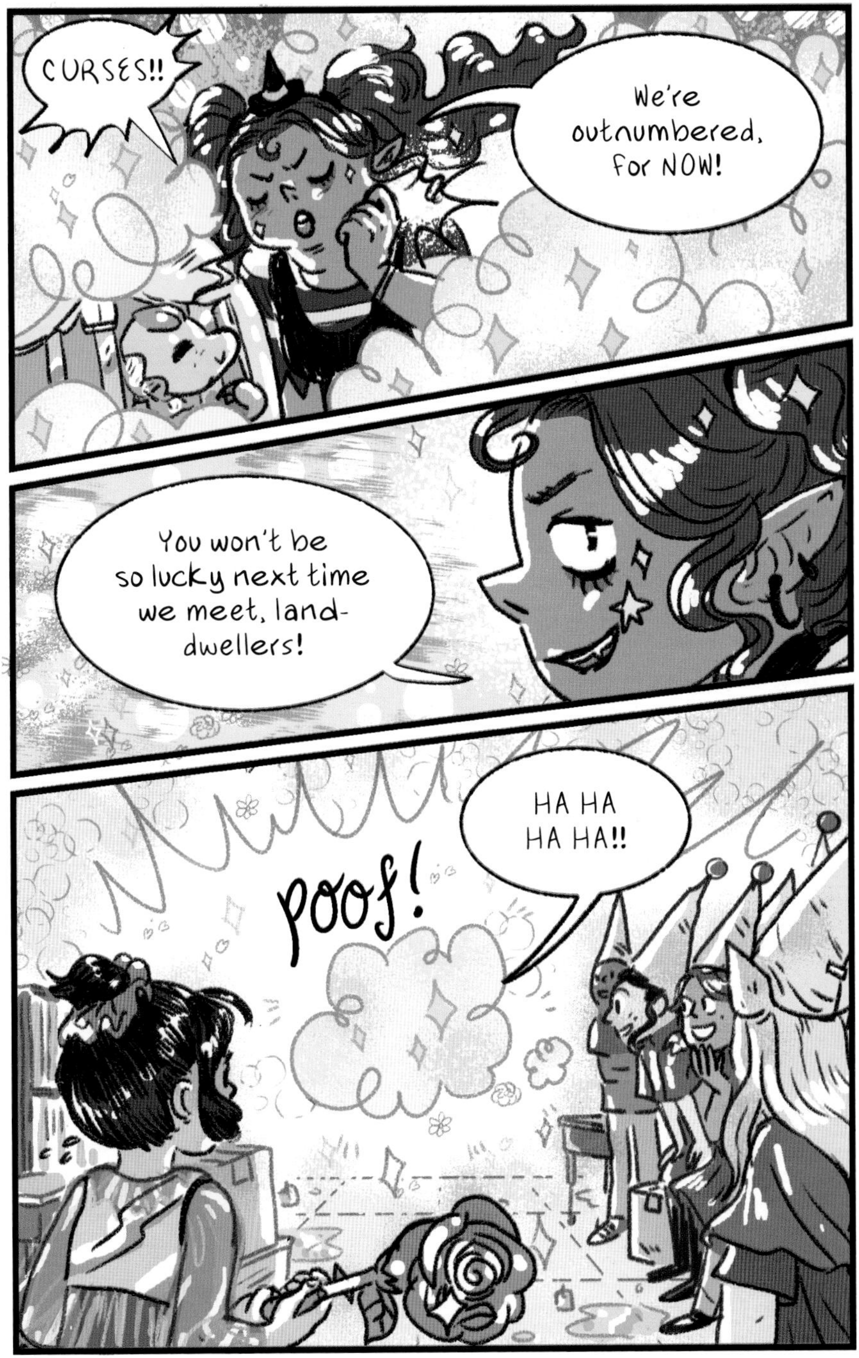
CURSES!!
We're outnumbered, for NOW!
You won't be so lucky next time we meet, land-dwellers!
HA HA HA HA!!
poof!

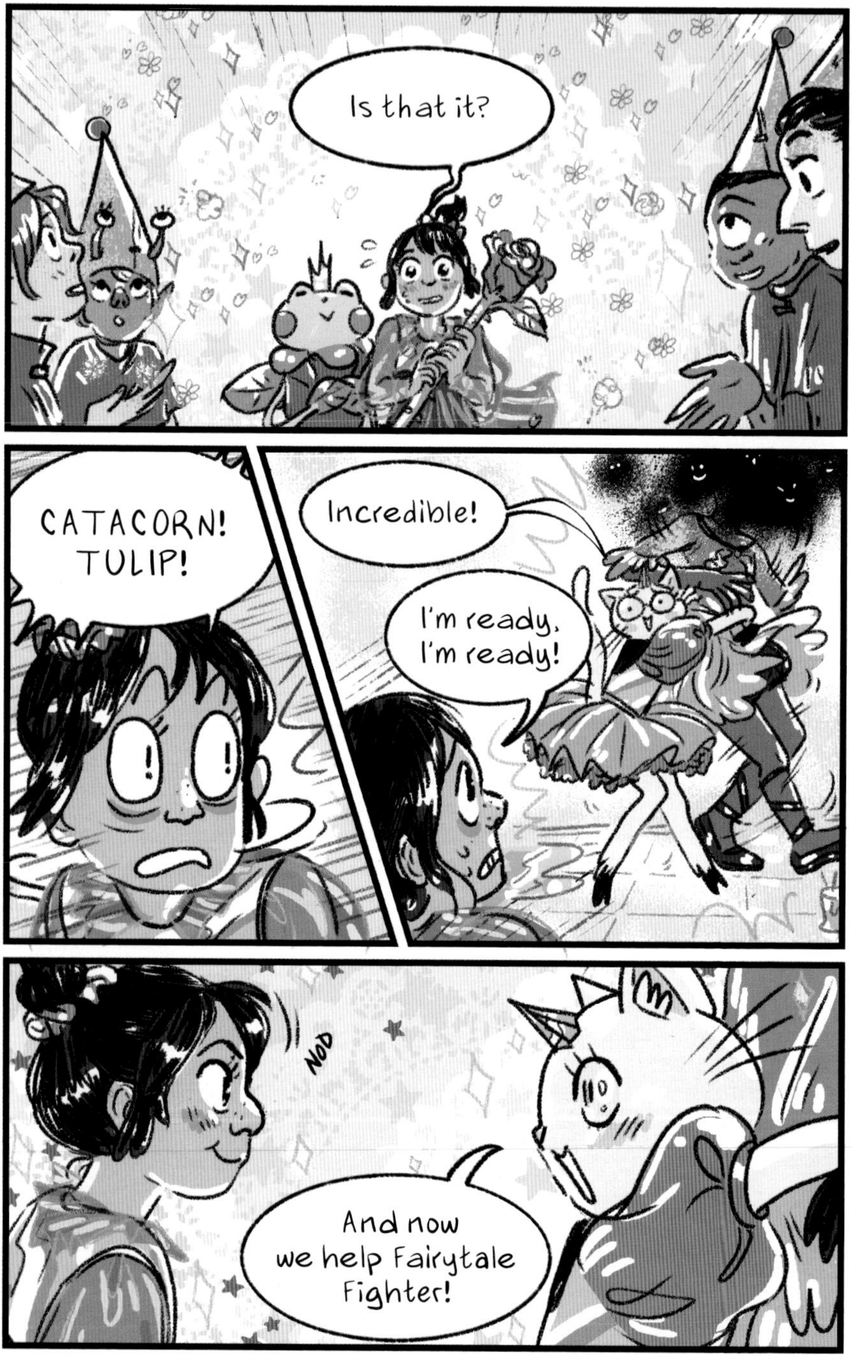
Is that it?
CATACORN! TULIP!
Incredible!
I'm ready, I'm ready!
NOD
And now we help Fairytale Fighter!

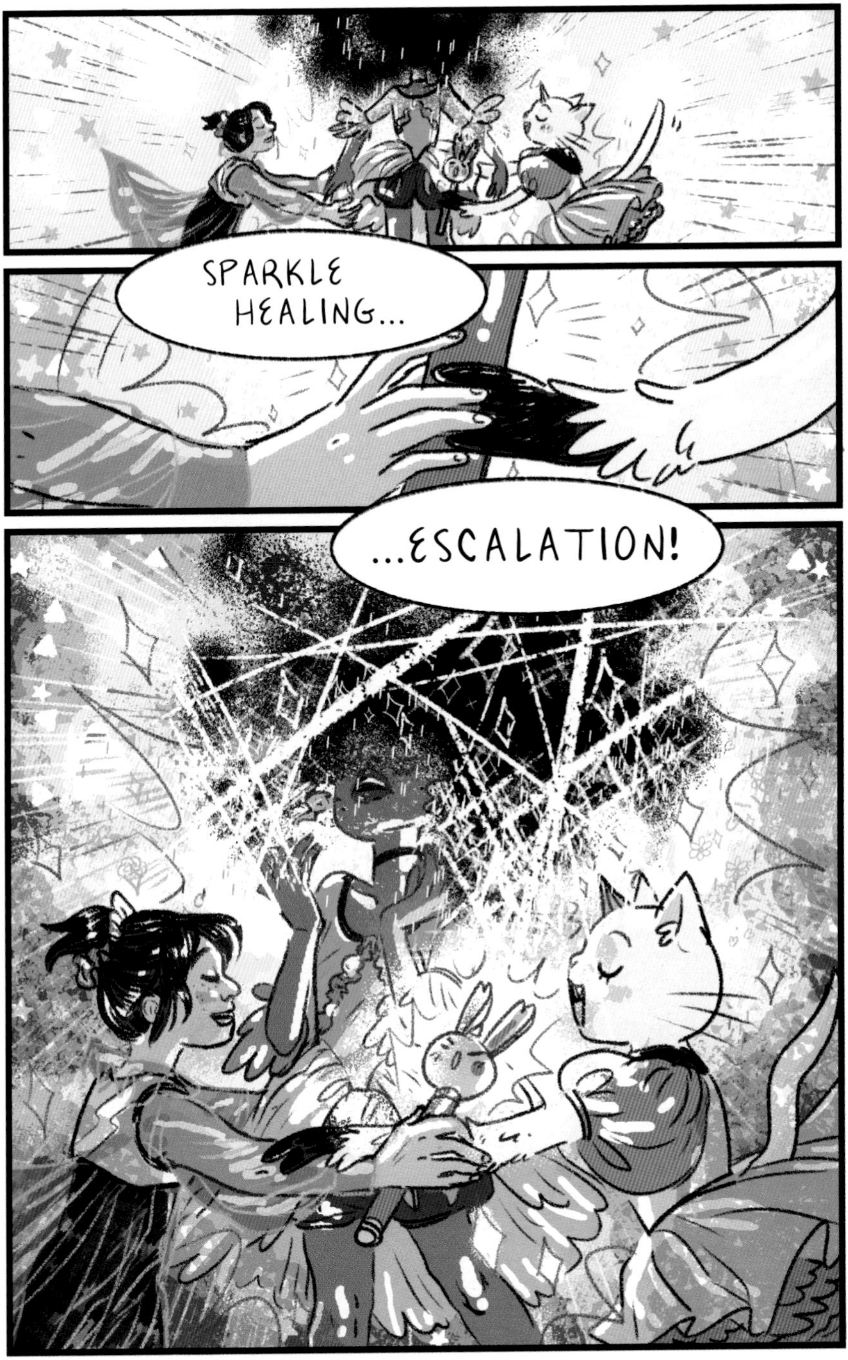
SPARKLE HEALING...
...ESCALATION!

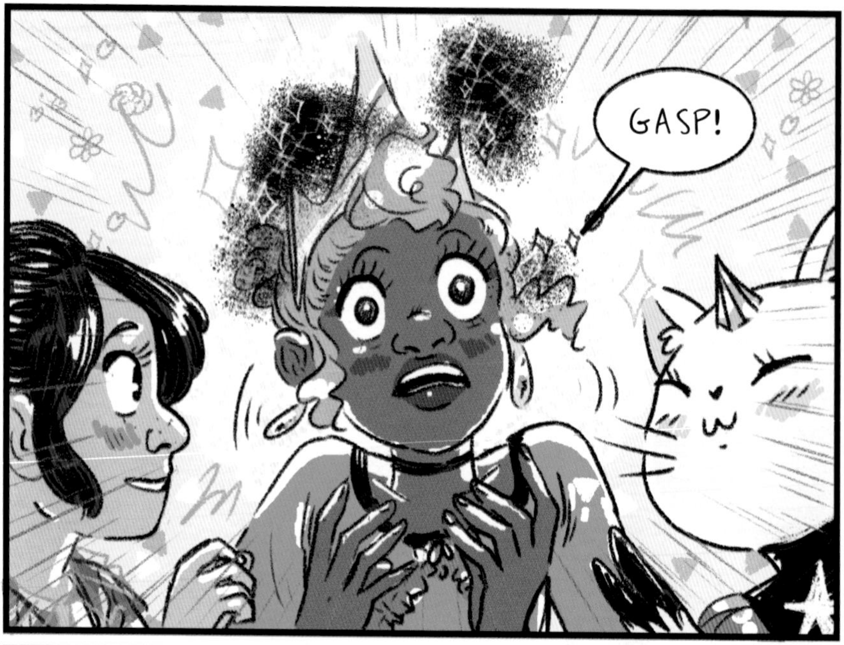
GASP!

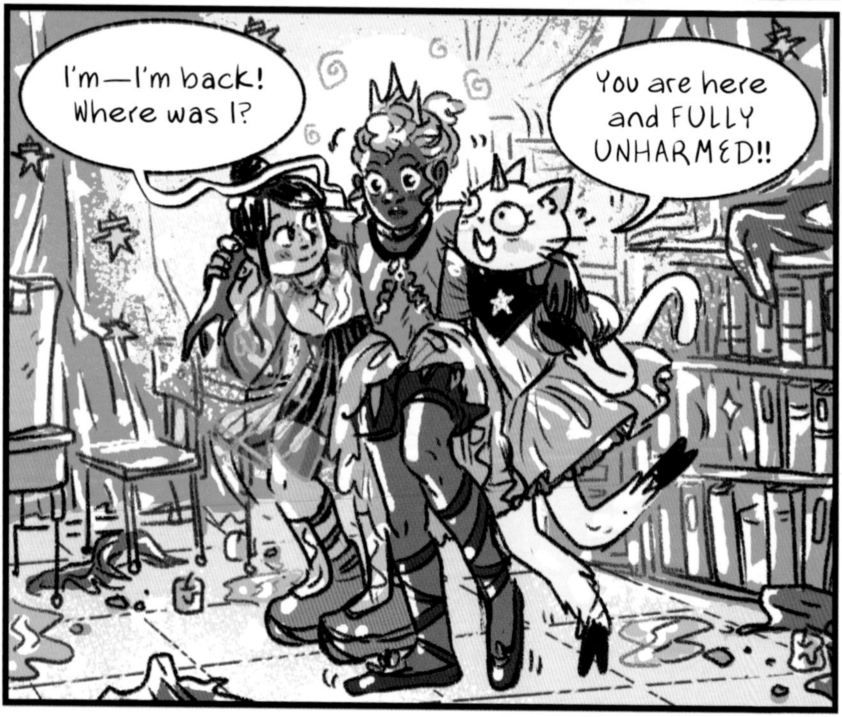
I'm—I'm back! Where was I?
You are here and FULLY UNHARMED!!

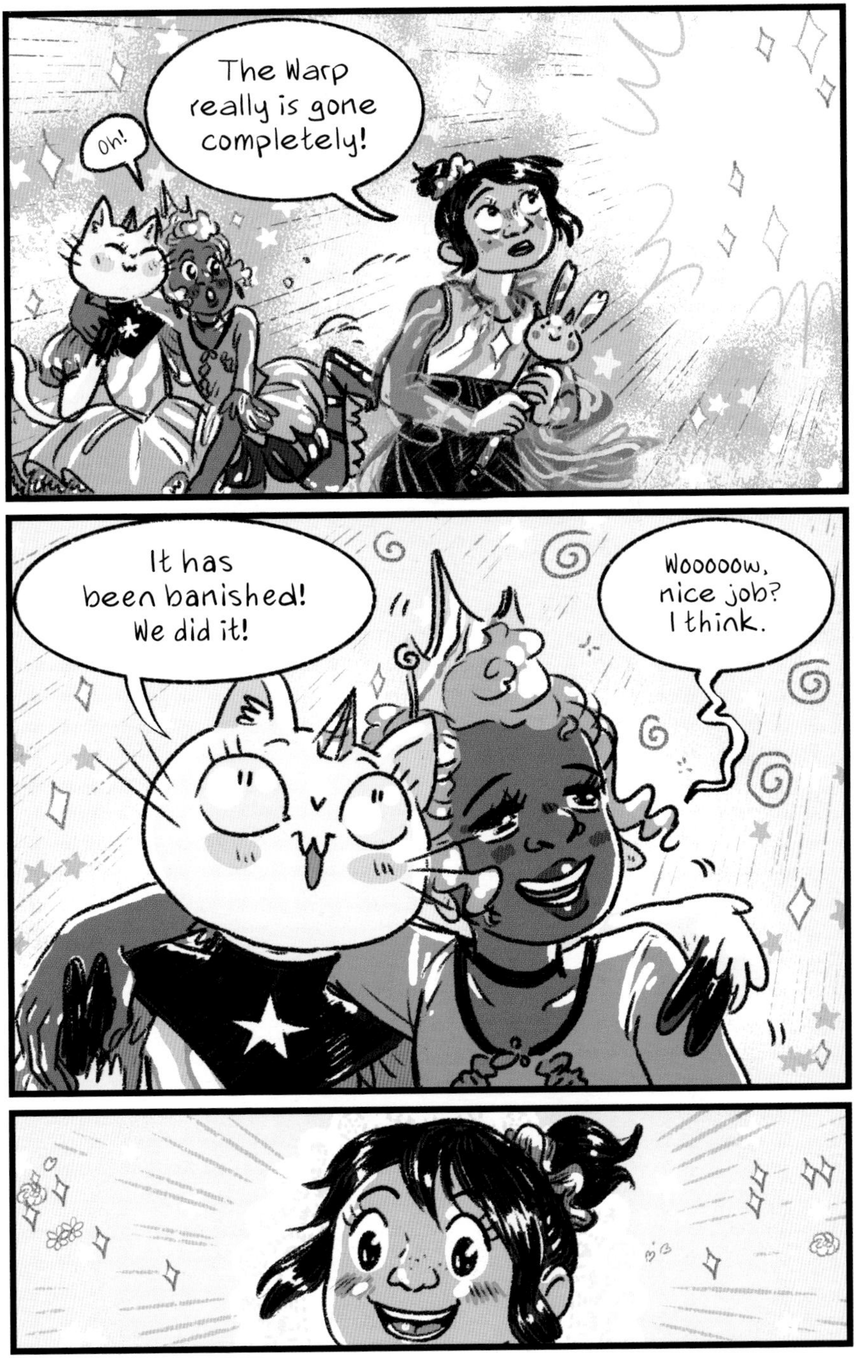
Oh!
The Warp really is gone completely!
It has been banished! We did it!
Wooooow, nice job? I think.

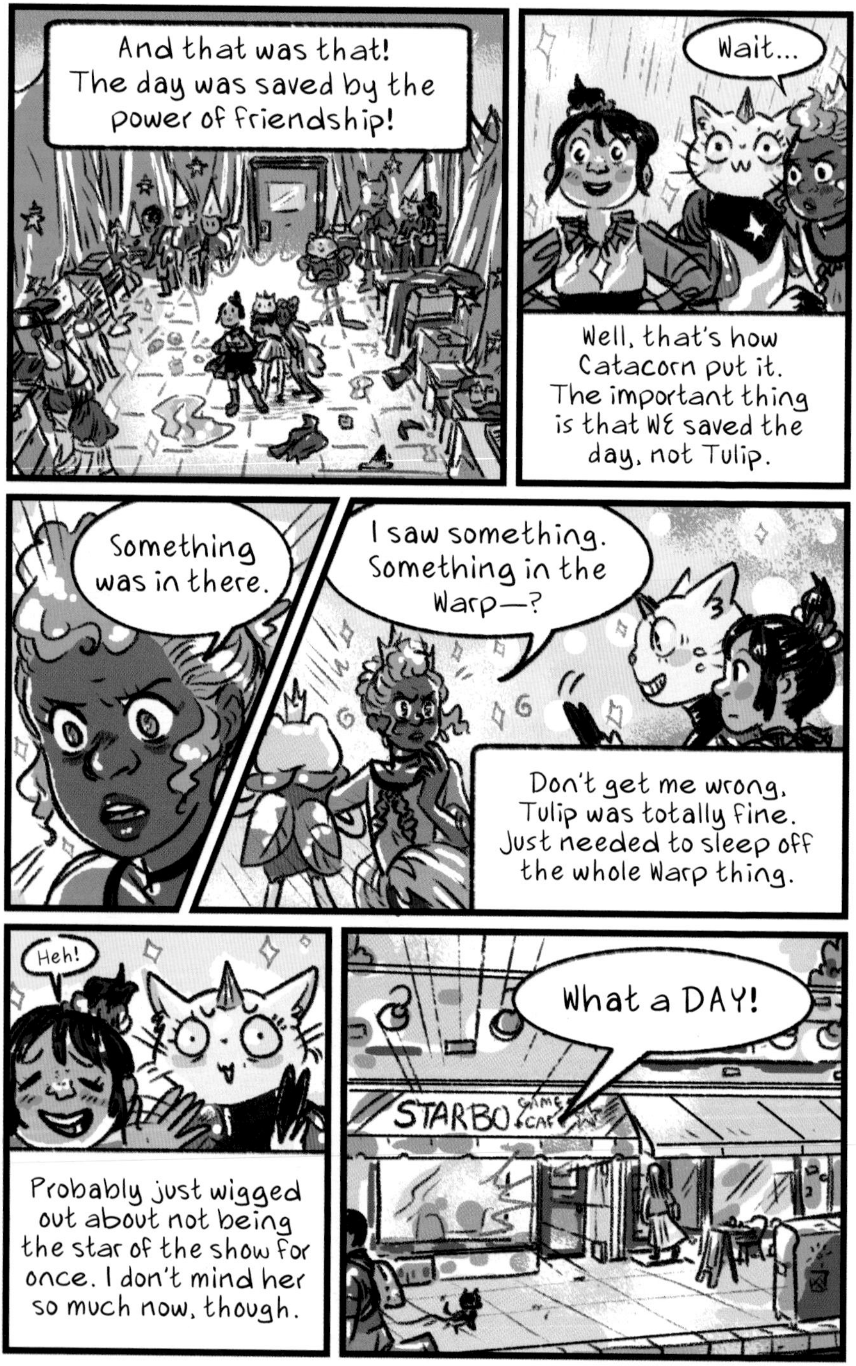
And that was that! The day was saved by the power of friendship!
Wait...
Well, that's how Catacorn put it. The important thing is that WE saved the day, not Tulip.
Something was in there.
I saw something. Something in the Warp—?
Don't get me wrong, Tulip was totally fine. Just needed to sleep off the whole Warp thing.
Heh!
Probably just wigged out about not being the star of the show for once. I don't mind her so much now, though.
What a DAY!
STARBO

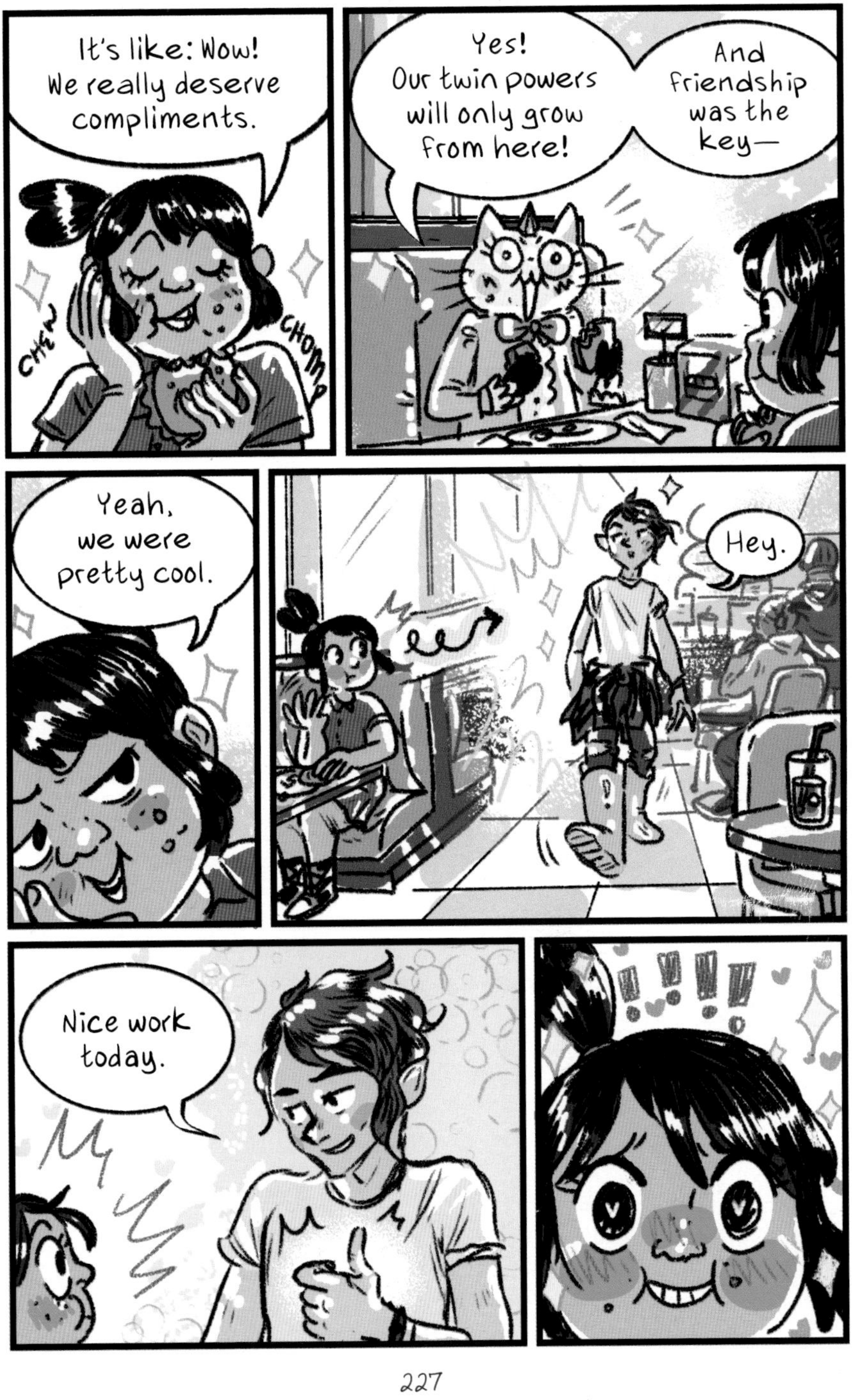
It's like: Wow! We really deserve compliments.
CHEW
CHOMP
Yes! Our twin powers will only grow from here!
And friendship was the key—
Yeah, we were pretty cool.
Hey.
Nice work today.

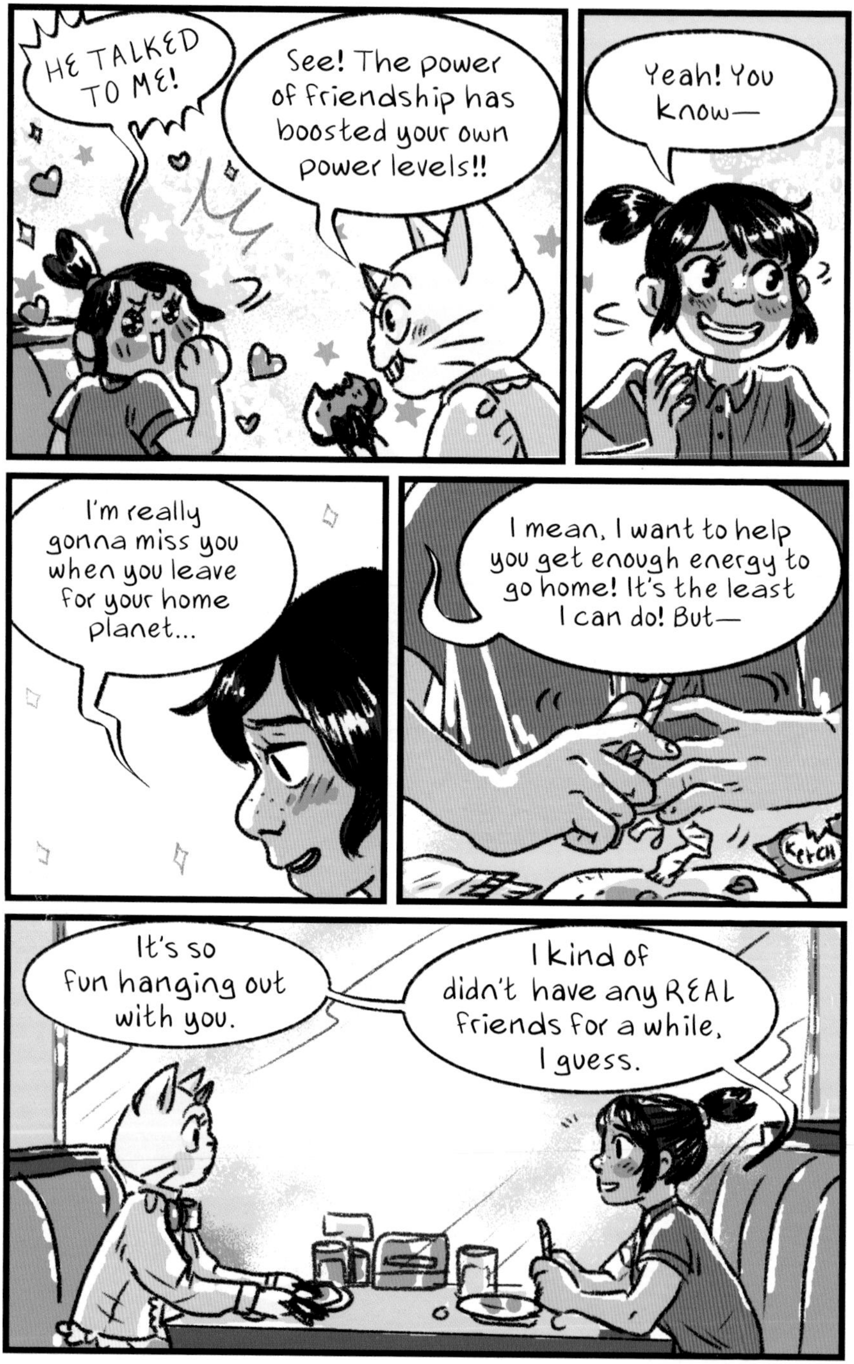
HE TALKED TO ME!
See! The power of friendship has boosted your own power levels!!
Yeah! You know—
I'm really gonna miss you when you leave for your home planet...
I mean, I want to help you get enough energy to go home! It's the least I can do! But—
It's so fun hanging out with you.
I kind of didn't have any REAL friends for a while, I guess.

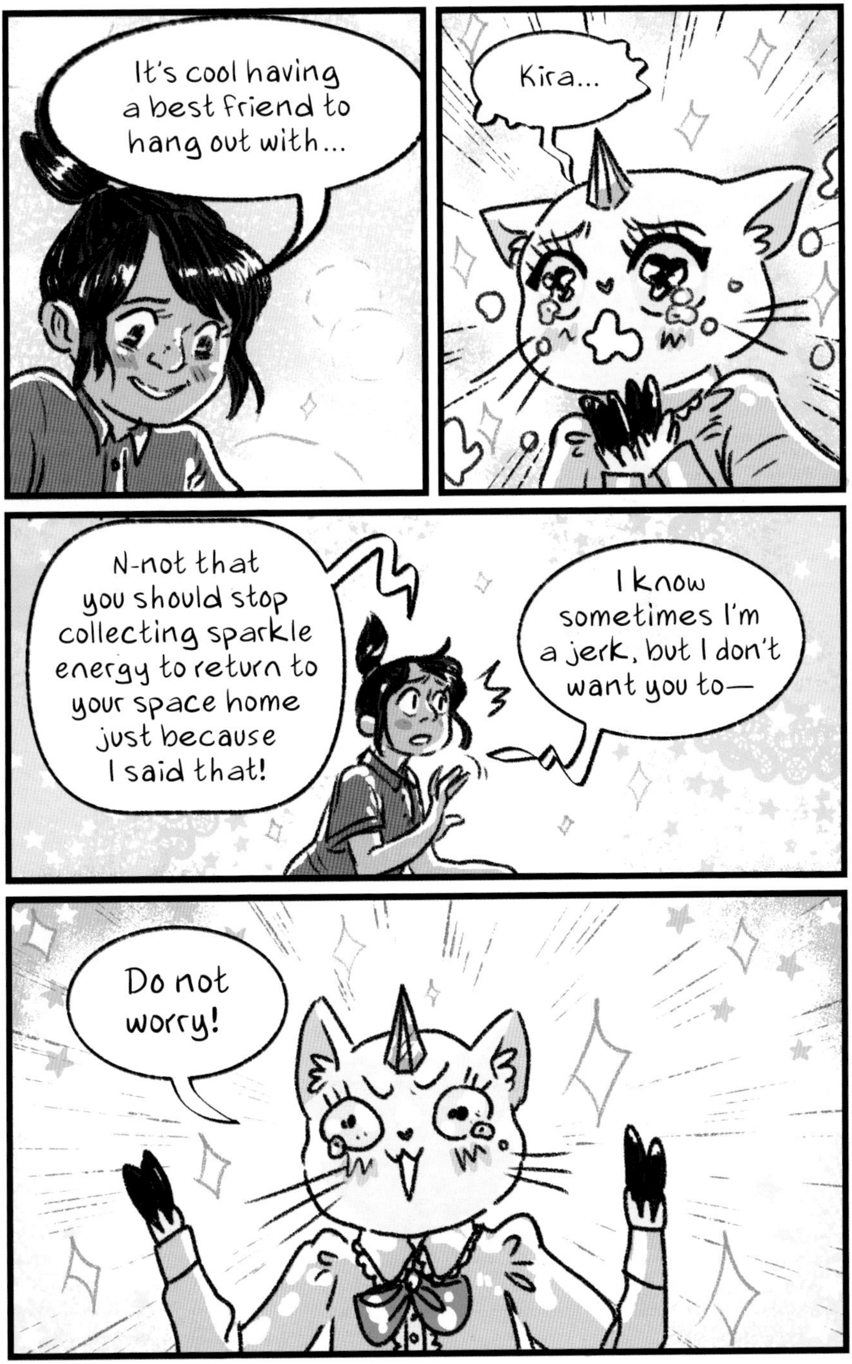
It's cool having a best friend to hang out with...
Kira...
N-not that you should stop collecting sparkle energy to return to your space home just because I said that!
I know sometimes I'm a jerk, but I don't want you to—
Do not worry!

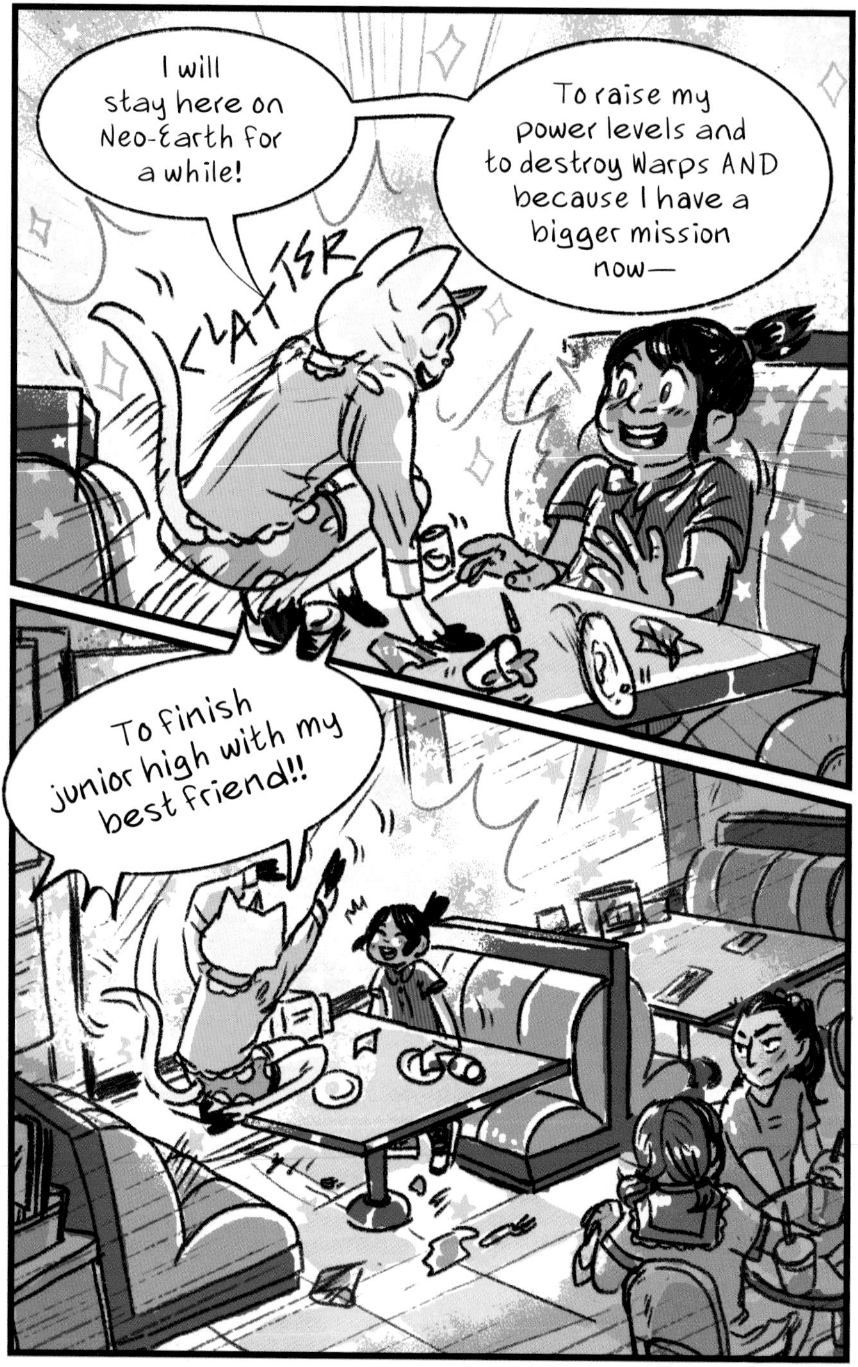

I will stay here on Neo-Earth for a while!
To raise my power levels and to destroy Warps AND because I have a bigger mission now—
CLATTER
To finish junior high with my best friend!!

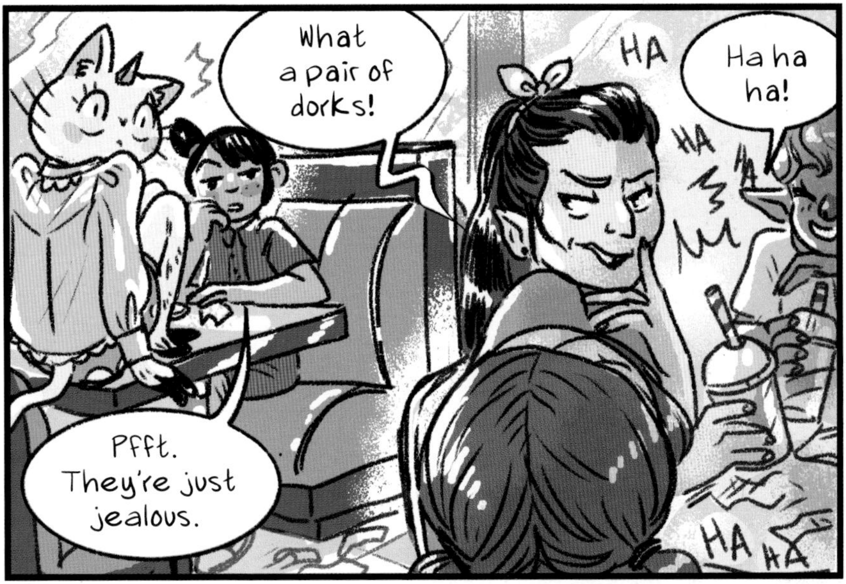
What a pair of dorks!
HA
Ha ha ha!
HA
HA
HA
Pfft. They're just jealous.
HA
HA

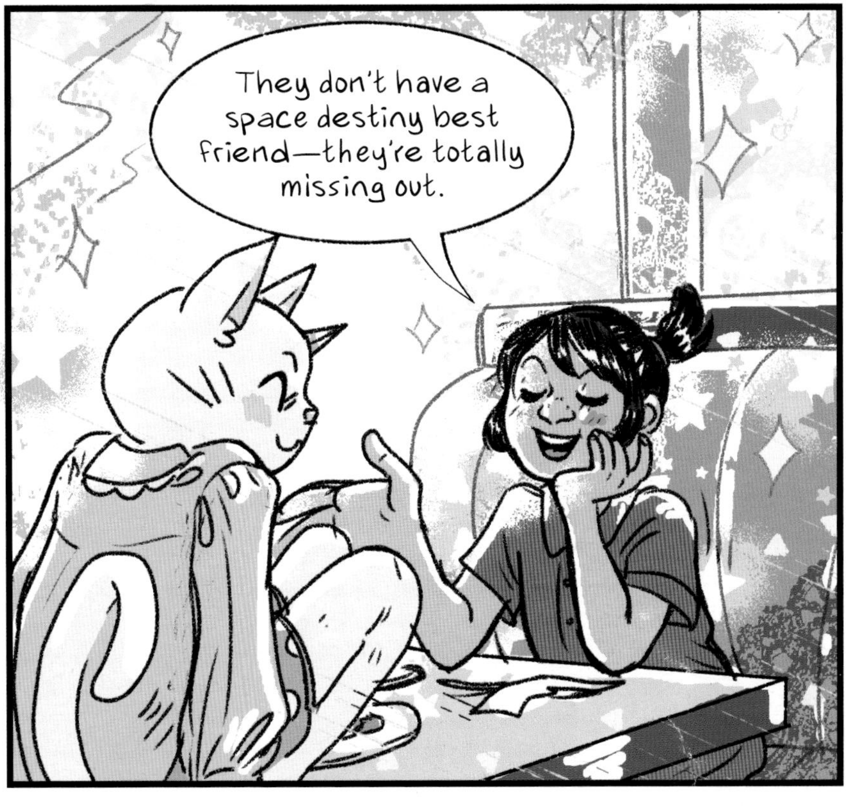
They don't have a space destiny best friend—they're totally missing out.

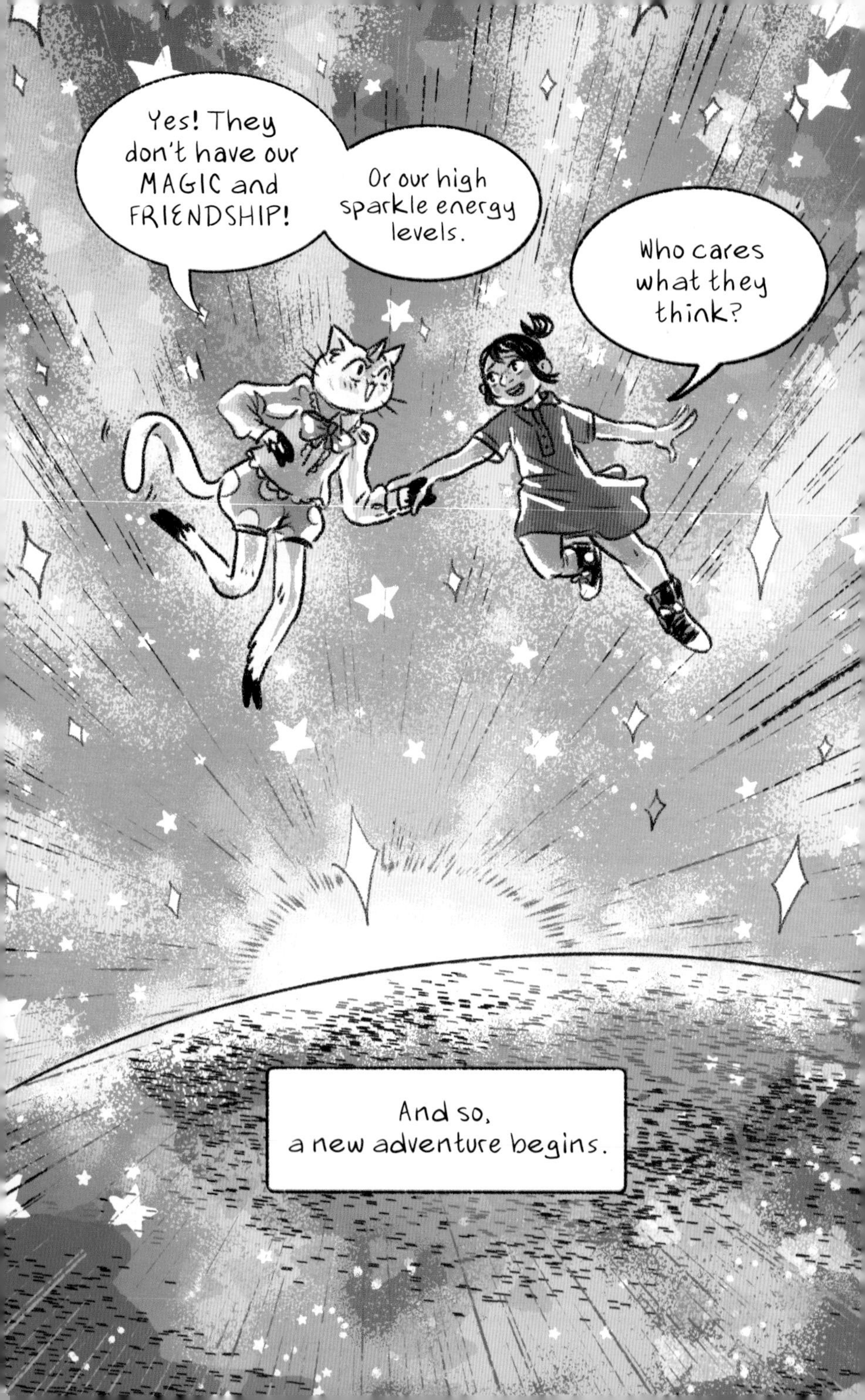
Yes! They don't have our MAGIC and FRIENDSHIP!
Or our high sparkle energy levels.
Who cares what they think?
And so, a new adventure begins.

I can't WAIT for the next book! Especially for when the Sea Prin—
Mmph
Catacorn, shhh!!! No spoilers!

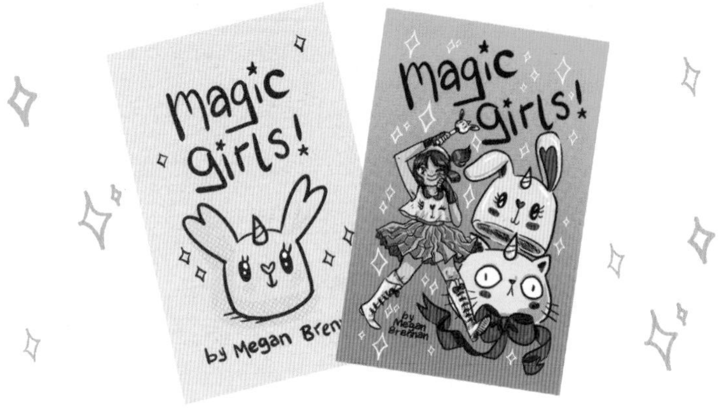
magic girls!
by Megan Bren
magic girls!
by Megan Brennan

I first made *Magic Girls* as a super-short (just a few pages total) entry for an anthology celebrating shoujo manga. In case you don't know, shoujo is a category of manga in Japan that's primarily made for young girls—and I LOVE it! Most importantly because magical girl stories are a big genre within it.

I had always liked *Peanuts* and other newspaper strips, but reading *Sailor Moon* as a kid unlocked the knowledge that comics can be used to tell big stories. And those big stories had the specific stuff I LOVED in a story: magic, romance, and friendship! So with that anthology entry, I got to reminisce about the things I loved about that genre, and especially magical girl stories. In stories like that, usually it's the messy, imperfect normal girls who get powers.

Working on that short comic reminded me why I loved magical girl stories so much in the first place, even as I made jokes about the stuff that happens in them! A little later, I went back and made some sequel pages to the original few *Magic Girls* pages, because I thought of some funny things that could happen next...and then I made a couple more issues of self-printed zines about them. Eventually, after trying to make other comics that didn't work out, I spent a while trying to figure out how to give Kira and Catacorn a bigger and better version of their story.

The version that became this book is the result of a lot of thinking and rewriting and asking my friends and colleagues what they thought of what I made, but also hopefully a result of a lot of love. I hope you had fun reading it. In case you wanted a peek at the older version of *Magic Girls*, here are a few pages:

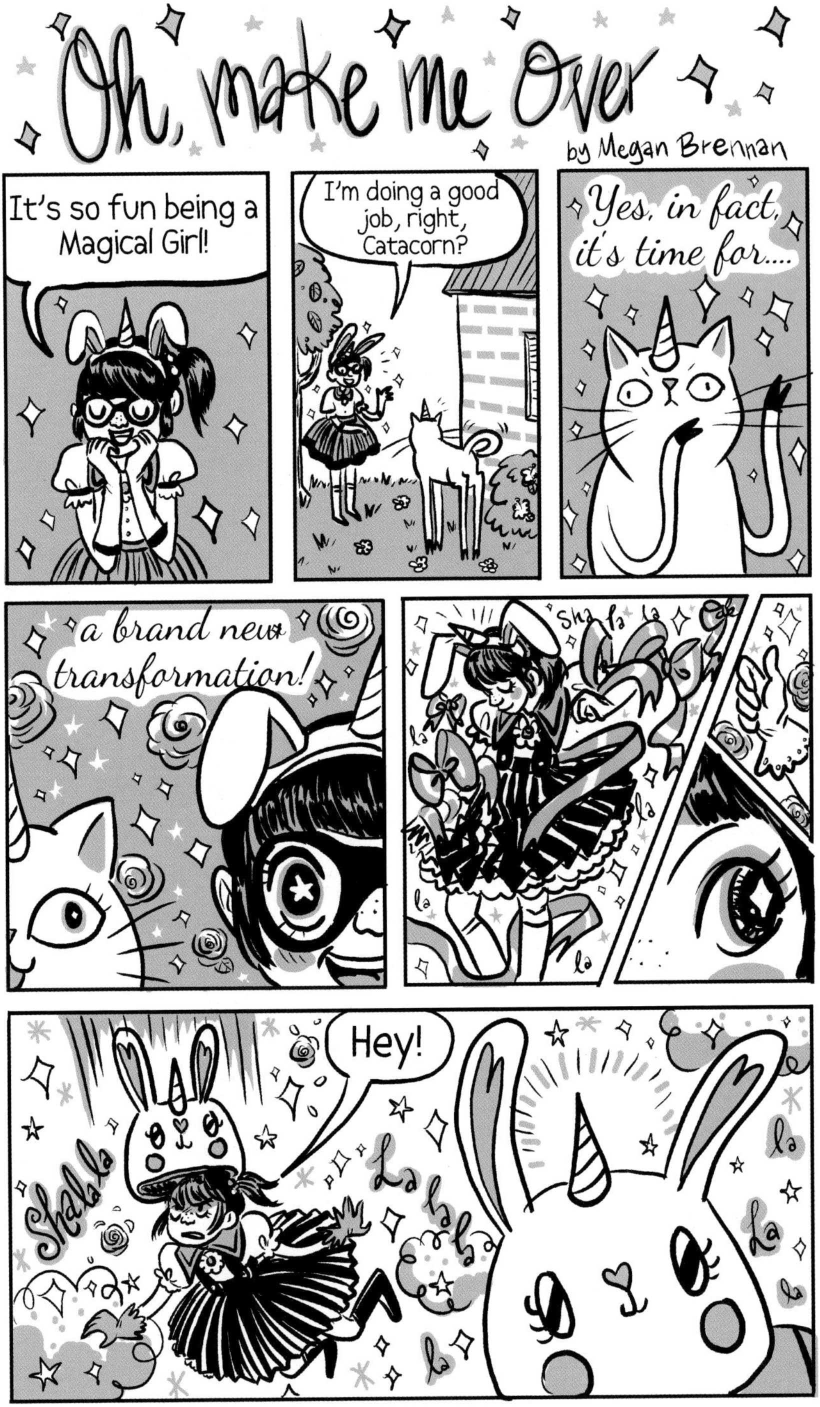
Oh, make me Over
by Megan Brennan
It's so fun being a Magical Girl!
I'm doing a good job, right, Catacorn?
Yes, in fact, it's time for....
a brand new transformation!
Sha la la
la
la
la
la
Hey!
Shalala
La la la
la
La
la
la

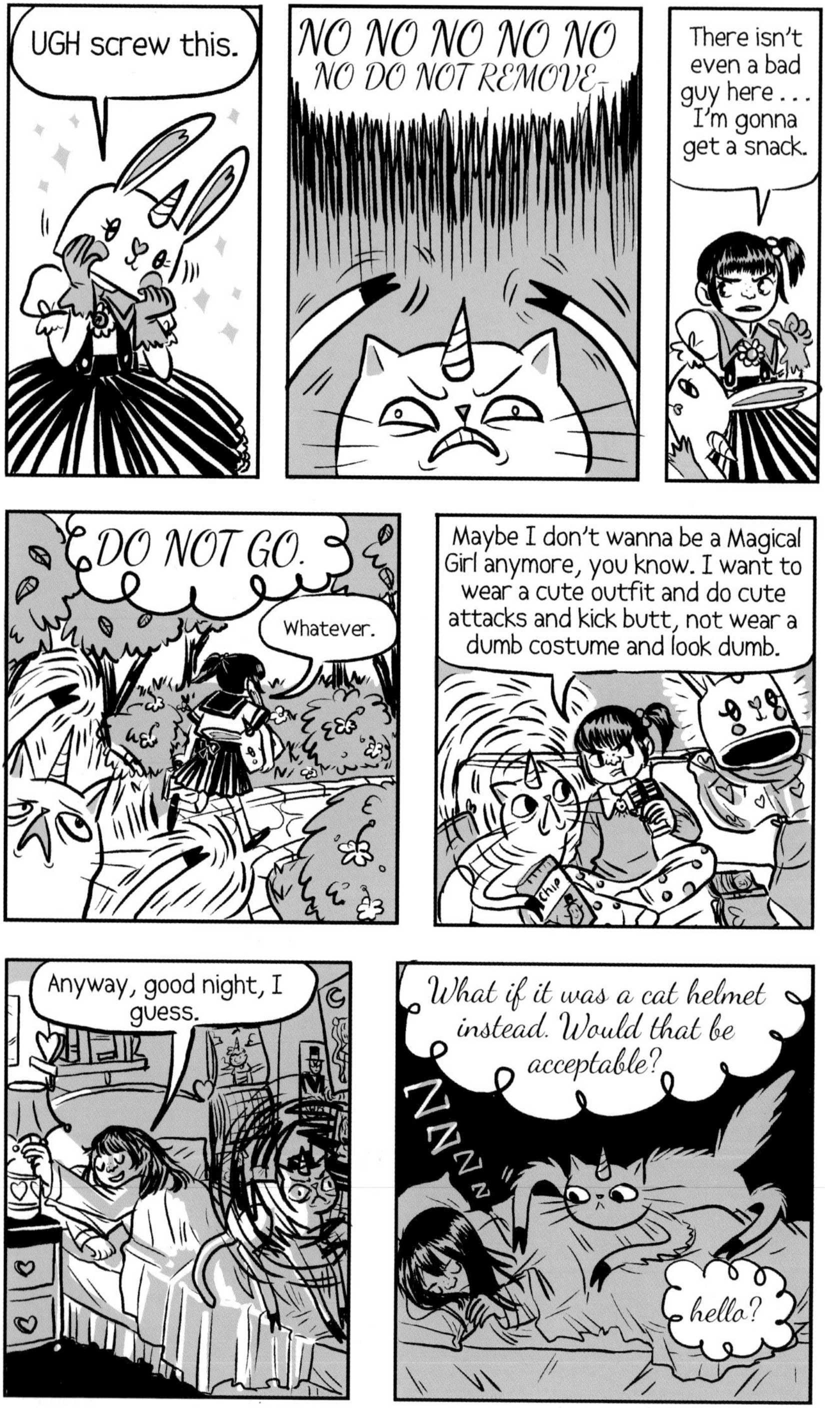
UGH screw this.
NO NO NO NO NO
NO DO NOT REMOVE-
There isn't even a bad guy here . . . I'm gonna get a snack.
DO NOT GO.
Whatever.
Maybe I don't wanna be a Magical Girl anymore, you know. I want to wear a cute outfit and do cute attacks and kick butt, not wear a dumb costume and look dumb.
Chip
Anyway, good night, I guess.
What if it was a cat helmet instead. Would that be acceptable?
ZZZzz
hello?

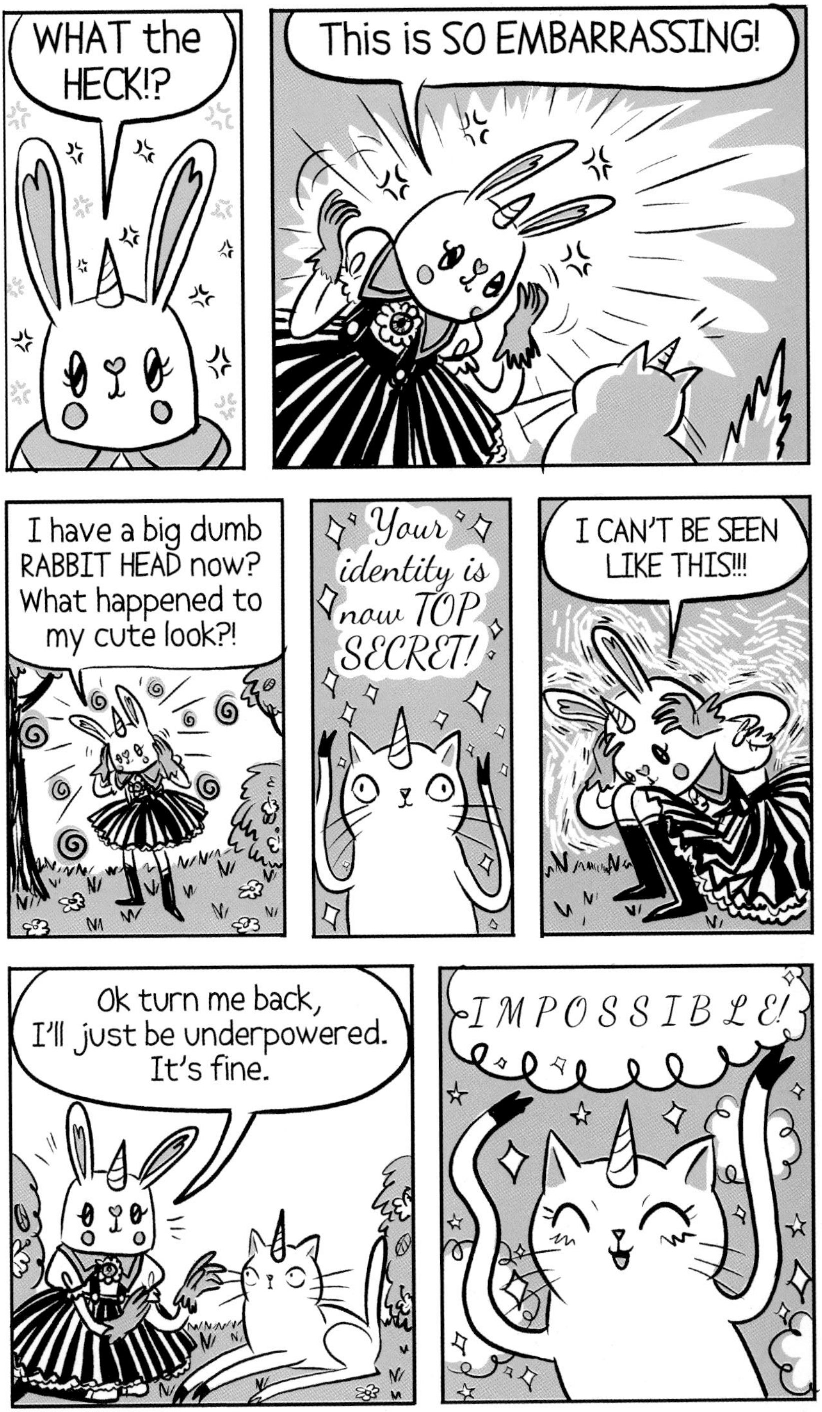
WHAT the HECK!?
This is SO EMBARRASSING!
I have a big dumb RABBIT HEAD now? What happened to my cute look?!
Your identity is now TOP SECRET!
I CAN'T BE SEEN LIKE THIS!!!
Ok turn me back, I'll just be underpowered. It's fine.
IMPOSSIBLE!

I drew this waaay back when I first got the book deal! The person on the right will make more sense after you read book 2. I just wanted to draw the girls being cute.

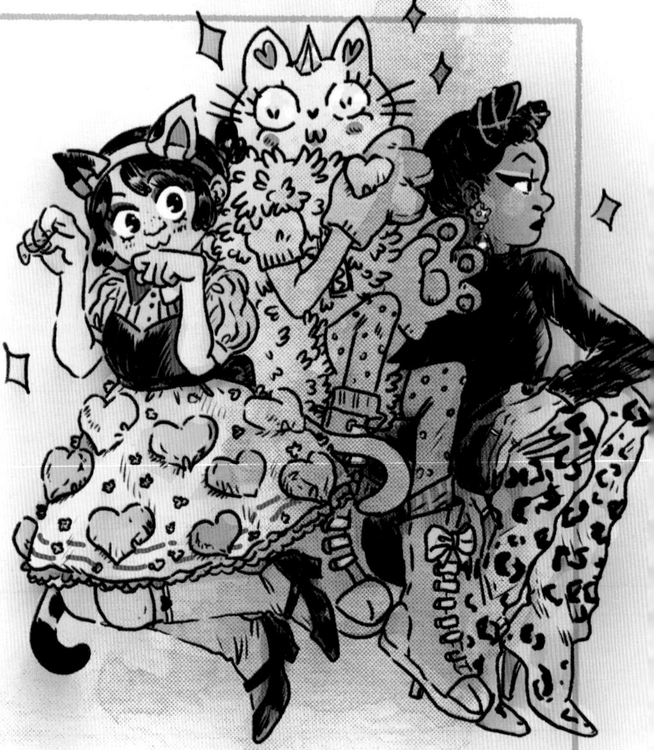

I guess at some point Baleen's monster was just gonna be a gator? Sorry I fogot about the magic wand, though, that's cute.

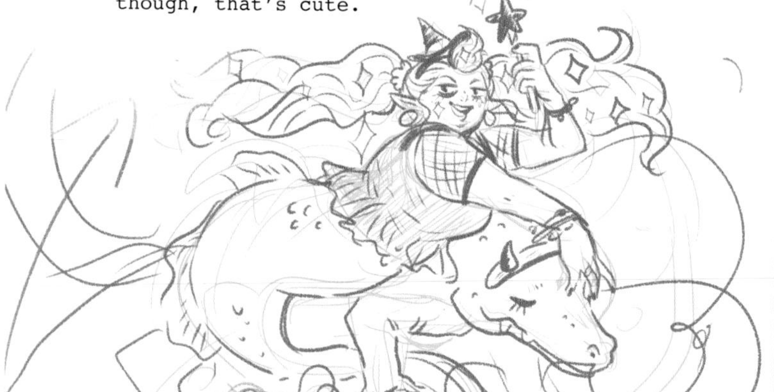

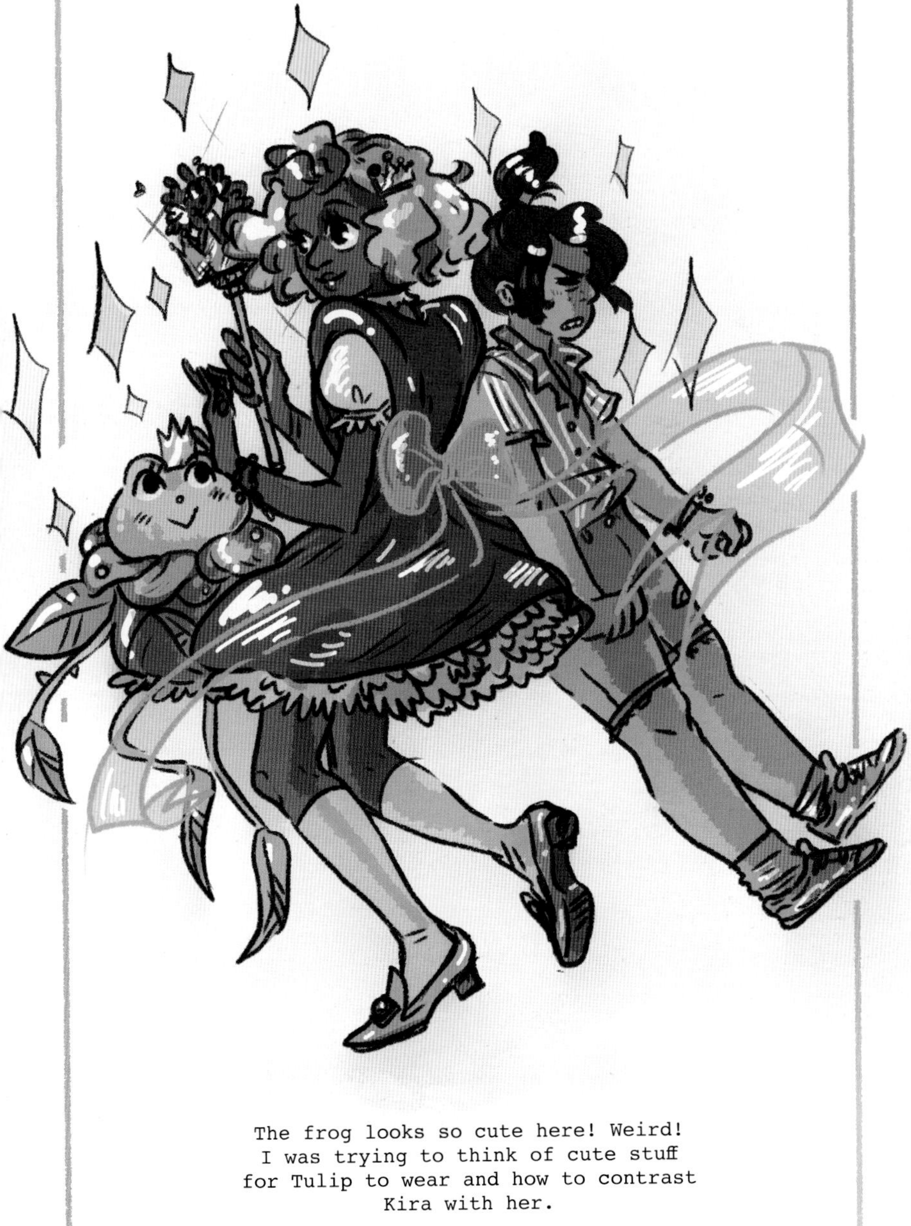

The frog looks so cute here! Weird!
I was trying to think of cute stuff
for Tulip to wear and how to contrast
Kira with her.

How I make comics!

The first part of making a new comic is: spending some time thinking about what cool things could happen to my characters... And THEN I spend a lot MORE time trying to figure out how to get to those cool points.

Sometimes this is easy and fun, and sometimes I end up staring at the wall or taking a walk or drawing something else, because it's hard!! But when it finally comes together, it's SO satisfying.

Then I write down that stuff in an outline. This helps me remember everything I spent so much time thinking about, and also helps my editor understand what my plans for the book are, so she can give me feedback.

Next, I write the script! I think this part of the book is really hard. You have to sit alone and imagine everything that happens and write it down in a way that fits into comic pages. Sometimes it feels like you're magically making thoughts into reality, and sometimes it feels like you're writing nonsense. All of that is useful in the end, especially the nonsense! Sometimes realizing what doesn't work helps you realize what you DO care most about in the story. I scrapped a LOT of stuff.

Because comics are not JUST words, I usually start to draw the thumbnails alongside the script at a certain point. (Some people do this way after the script, but for me, it helps to think about the art and the words close together!)

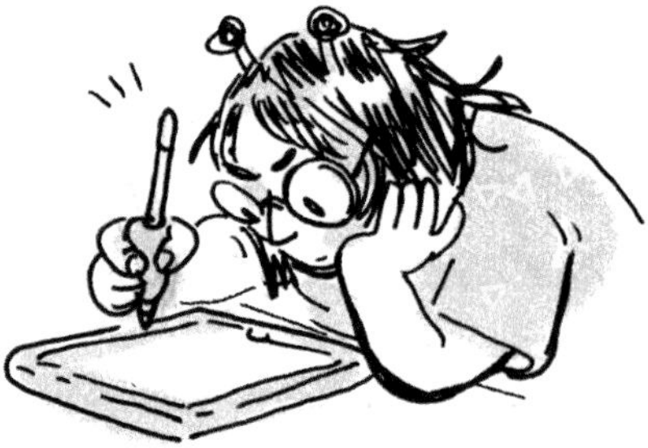

To make thumbnails, I look at the script and draw a little scribbly version of every panel and page in the comic. This way, when I sit down to draw it for real, I'll know what I want it to look like. Sometimes the scribbles are hard to decipher, but that's my own fault.

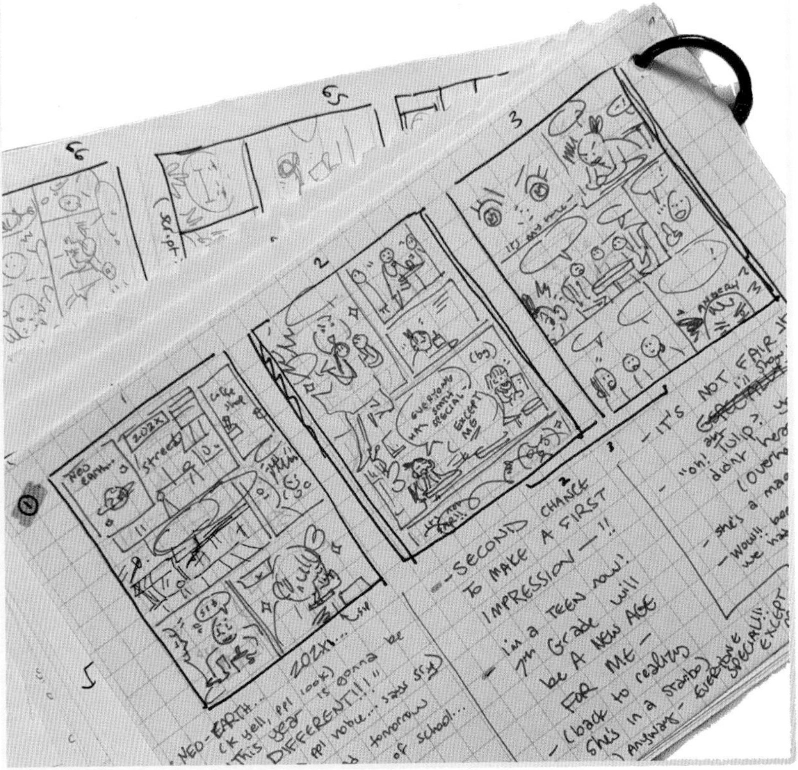

SECOND CHANCE
TO MAKE A FIRST
IMPRESSION—!!
I'm a TEEN now!
7th Grade will
be A NEW AGE
FOR ME—
IT'S NOT FAIR
DIFFERENT!!!
NEO-EARTH...

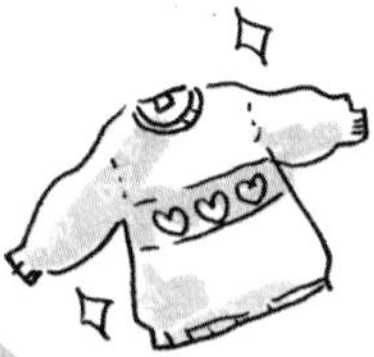

When all that is done, I spend a little time trying to make sure I know what the characters should look like, and the places they go to in the story. I end up having to collect folders of reference pictures of schools and outfits. I think for the kinds of stories I'm telling, it's important for the characters to have different outfits that really fit them. I actually made a little flip-book of all the outfits everyone wears in the book, so I could keep track of their clothing in every scene. It's kind of silly, but it worked! I only messed up and drew someone in the wrong outfit in...one scene. (It got fixed.)

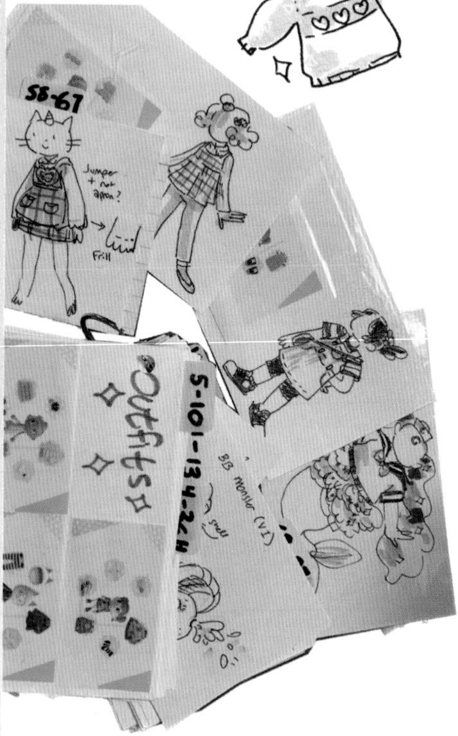

S8-67
Jumper + not apron?
Frill
Outfits

This is also when I thought up some of the other kids in Kira's class, so I'm not having to make everyone up on the spot! (See character profiles for more.)

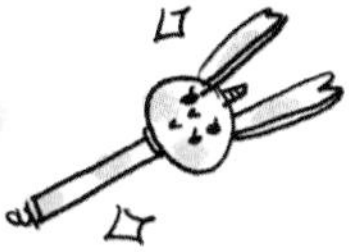

(I designed magical items around this time too! I definitely refined them while I worked on the final art though.)

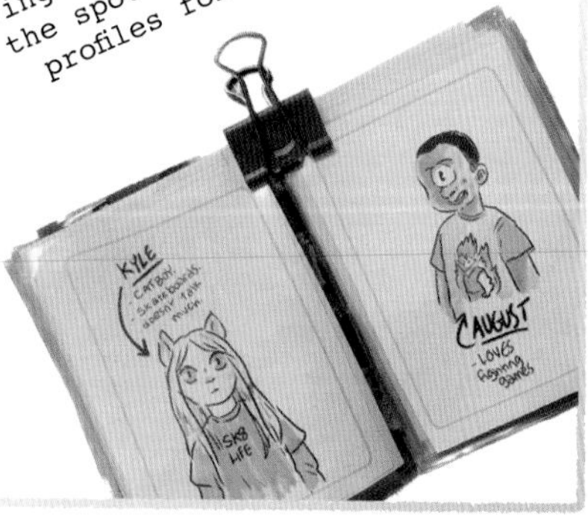

KYLE
SK8 LIFE
AUGUST

Actually drawing the comic takes the longest time! Because I'm sitting and drawing and not thinking about words, it's the hardest to explain. But here's what I do:

1.

But this year -! THIS YEAR-!
Did you hear about Tulip?
Ugh, Tulip.
It can't be true.
What can't?
Over the summer she became a Magical Girl. The Land Council sent out a familiar, and it chose her.
No WAY! It's been so long since we had a local one-
Tulip is so cool.
She is definitely going to be Jr. Prom Queen in the spring-

2.

But this year -!
Did you hear about Tulip?
Ugh, Tulip.
It can't be true.
What can't??
Over the summer she became a Magical Girl. The Land Council sent out a Familiar, and it chose her.
No WAY! It's been so long since we had a local one-
Tulip is so cool!
She is definitely going to be Jr. Prom Queen in the spring-

3.

But this year—!
Did you hear about Tulip?
Ugh, Tulip.
It can't be true.
What can't??
Over the summer she became a Magical Girl. The Land Council sent out a Familiar, and it chose her.
No WAY! It's been so long since we had a local one—
Tulip is so cool!
She is definitely going to be Junior Prom Queen in the spring.

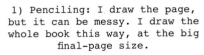

1) Penciling: I draw the page, but it can be messy. I draw the whole book this way, at the big final-page size.

2) Inking: I go back and draw a version of each page on top of the pencils, so the pages are neat and easy to read.

3) After all the inks are done, I add color!

For all of these stages you mostly just have to be patient and determined, because sometimes you get very bored, or very annoyed at how hard it is to draw a hand in one panel, or the motion of a gesture in another, or the light that's supposed to indicate what time of day it is. Other times I'm drawing stuff that is so fun, it doesn't feel like work at all! The hard parts keep me going because they mean that I'm learning and growing as an artist!
Doesn't mean I can't complain, though.

Some of Kira and Catacorn's classmates!
See if you can spot them in the background of this book! Some of them didn't appear much... maybe they were home sick.

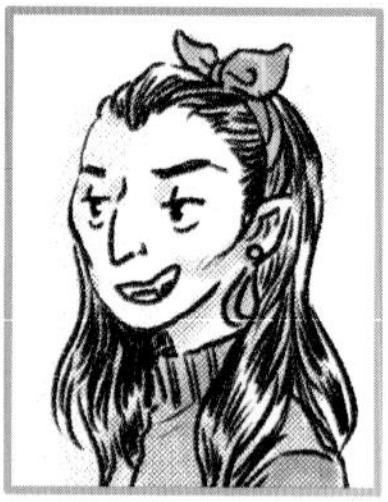

Lucretia
Born into an ancient line of vampires. She's been classmates with Kira since kindergarten. Also in the school band.

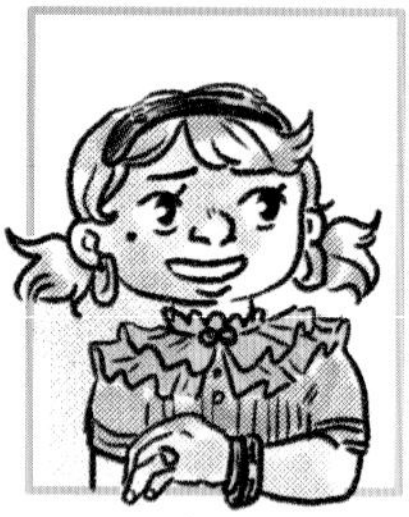

Marisol
Loves fashion! She knows EVERYBODY at school and knows all the gossip. Probably posts about her outfits online.

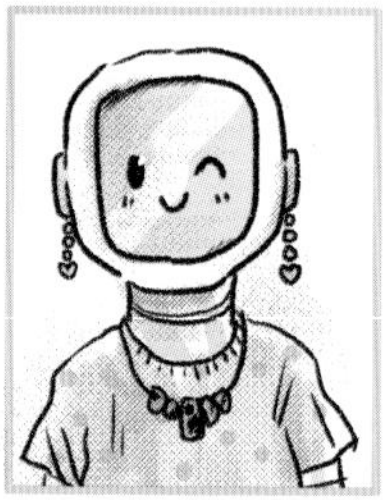

Iso
An android. Really nice, and good at crafts. Popular for knowing where all the electrical outlets in school are.

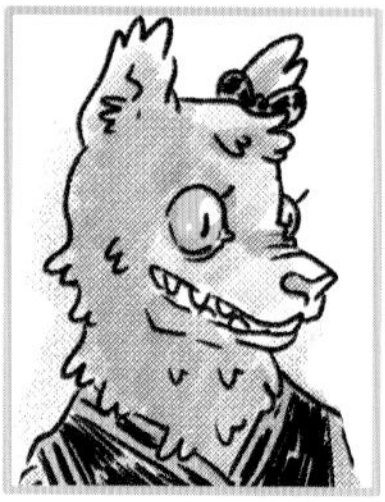

Hazel
Werewolf, but that just means she's a wolf girl all the time. On the school sports team, **she's** the MVP!

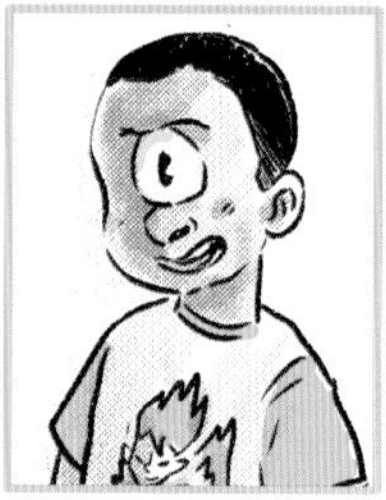

August
Loves fighting games & cartoons. Always working on a high score on whatever game is new to the arcade. His best friend is Kyle.

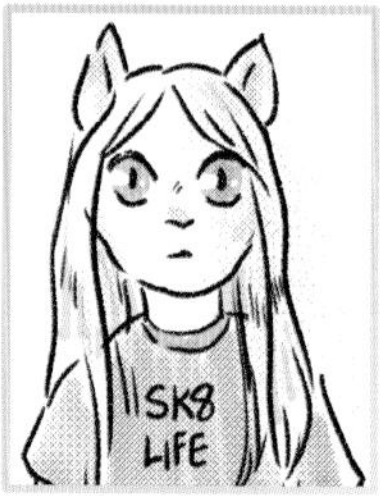
SK8
LIFE

Kyle
Catboy. He loves to skateboard. Doesn't talk much. Has great hair, which **baffles** everyone.

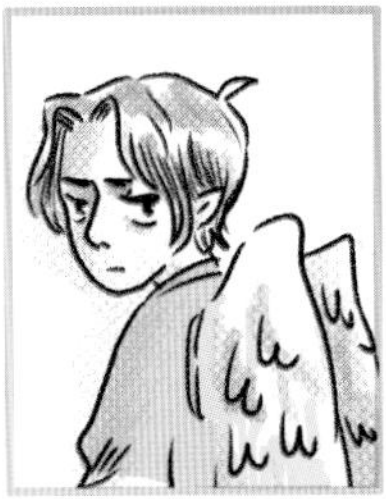

Darien
He's so moody... Object of many crushes.

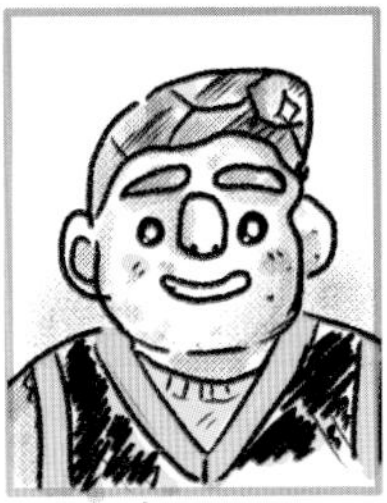

Batholith
On sports team with Hazel. Very kind. Hair is some kind of shiny crystal.

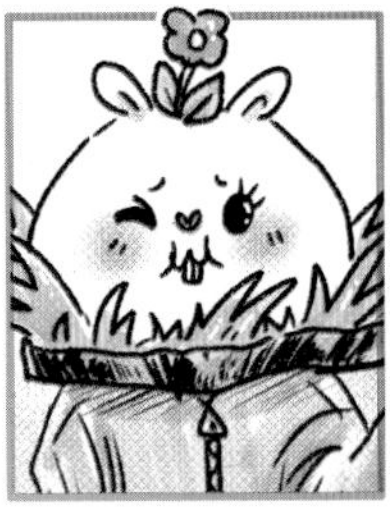

Groundy
School mascot. Whoever was inside quit after the events of this book.

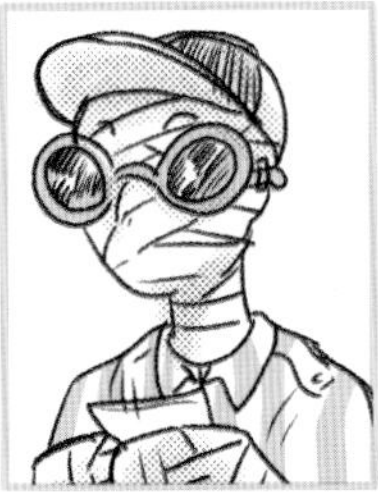

Horus
Class president, collector of sunglasses.

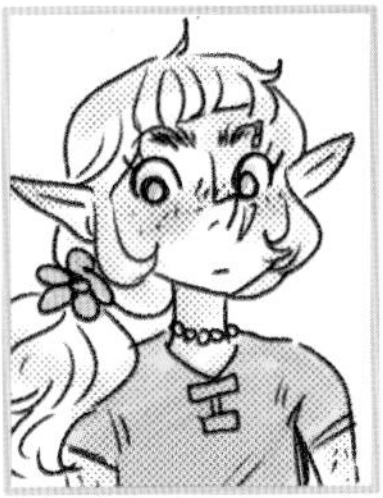

Chamomile
Loves the outdoors and summer camp. Spends weekends camping whenever possible.

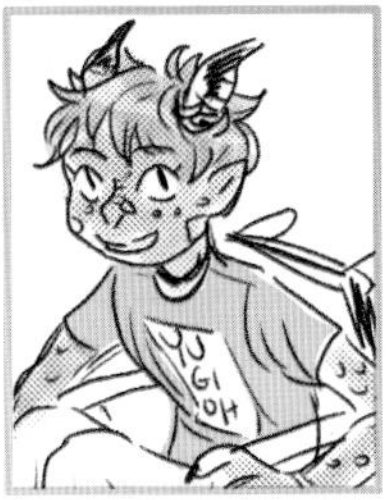
YU GI OH

Florin
All about tabletop games & trading cards.

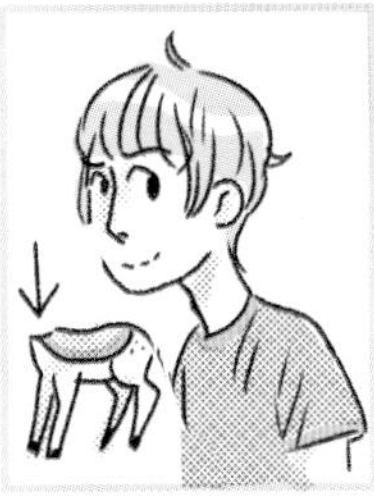

Centaur kid
Not related to the school principal.

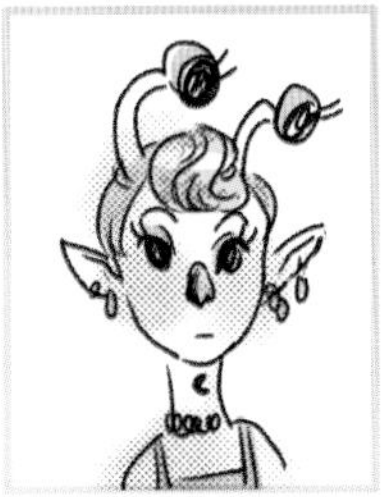

Kid who is NOT an alien, even if she looks like an alien.

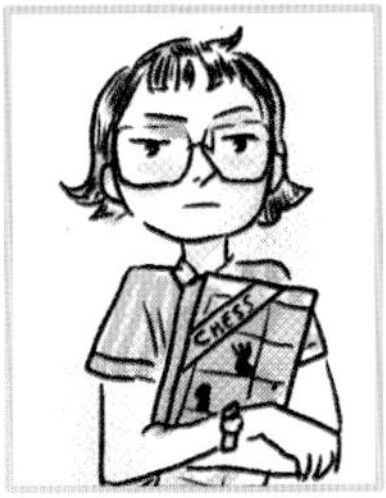
CHESS

Agnes
Not actually good at chess yet, but she's working on it.

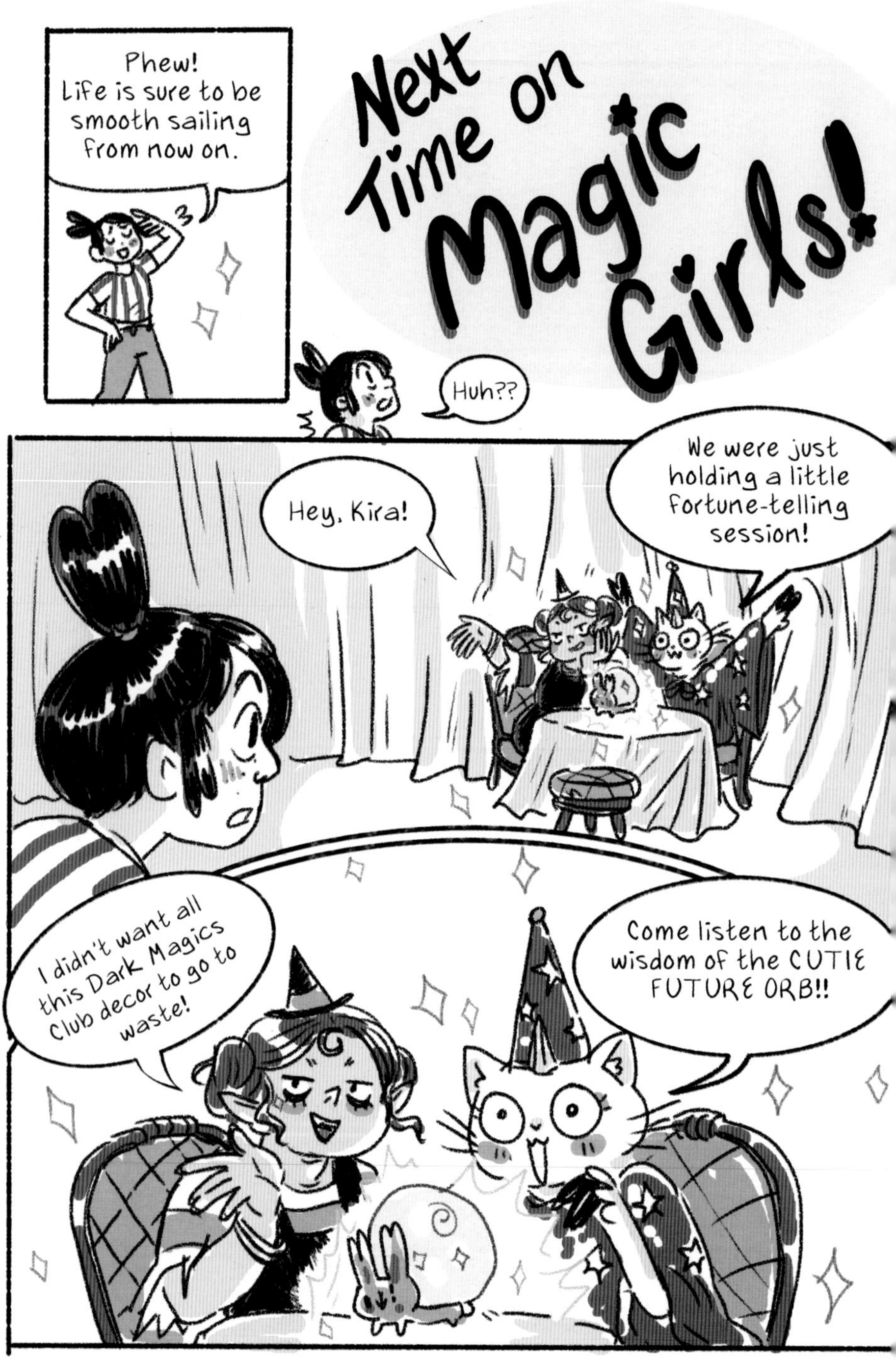
Phew!
Life is sure to be smooth sailing from now on.
Next Time on Magic Girls!
Huh??
Hey, Kira!
We were just holding a little fortune-telling session!
I didn't want all this Dark Magics Club decor to go to waste!
Come listen to the wisdom of the CUTIE FUTURE ORB!!

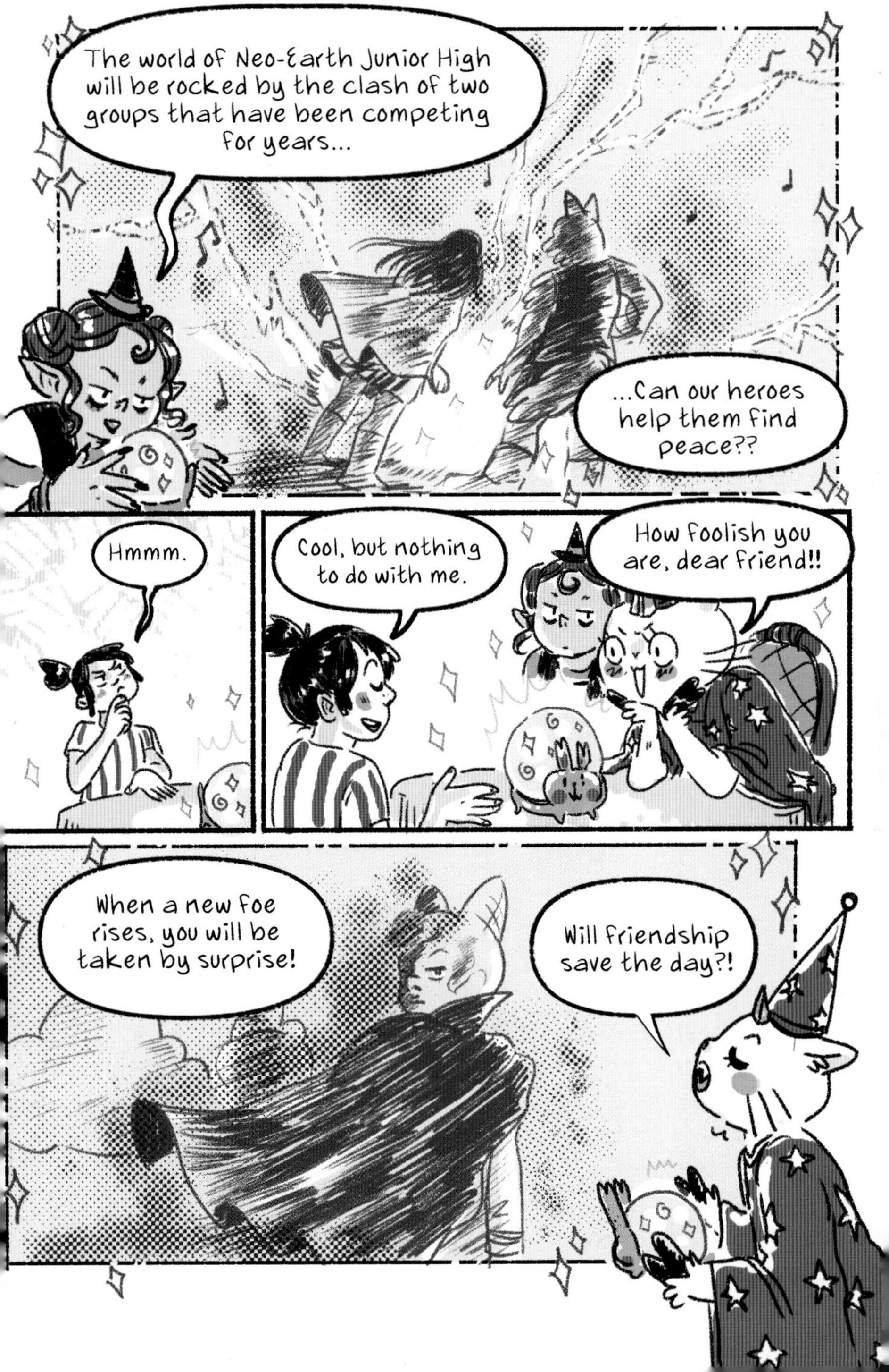
The world of Neo-Earth Junior High will be rocked by the clash of two groups that have been competing for years...
...Can our heroes help them find peace??
Hmmm.
Cool, but nothing to do with me.
How foolish you are, dear friend!!
When a new foe rises, you will be taken by surprise!
Will friendship save the day?!

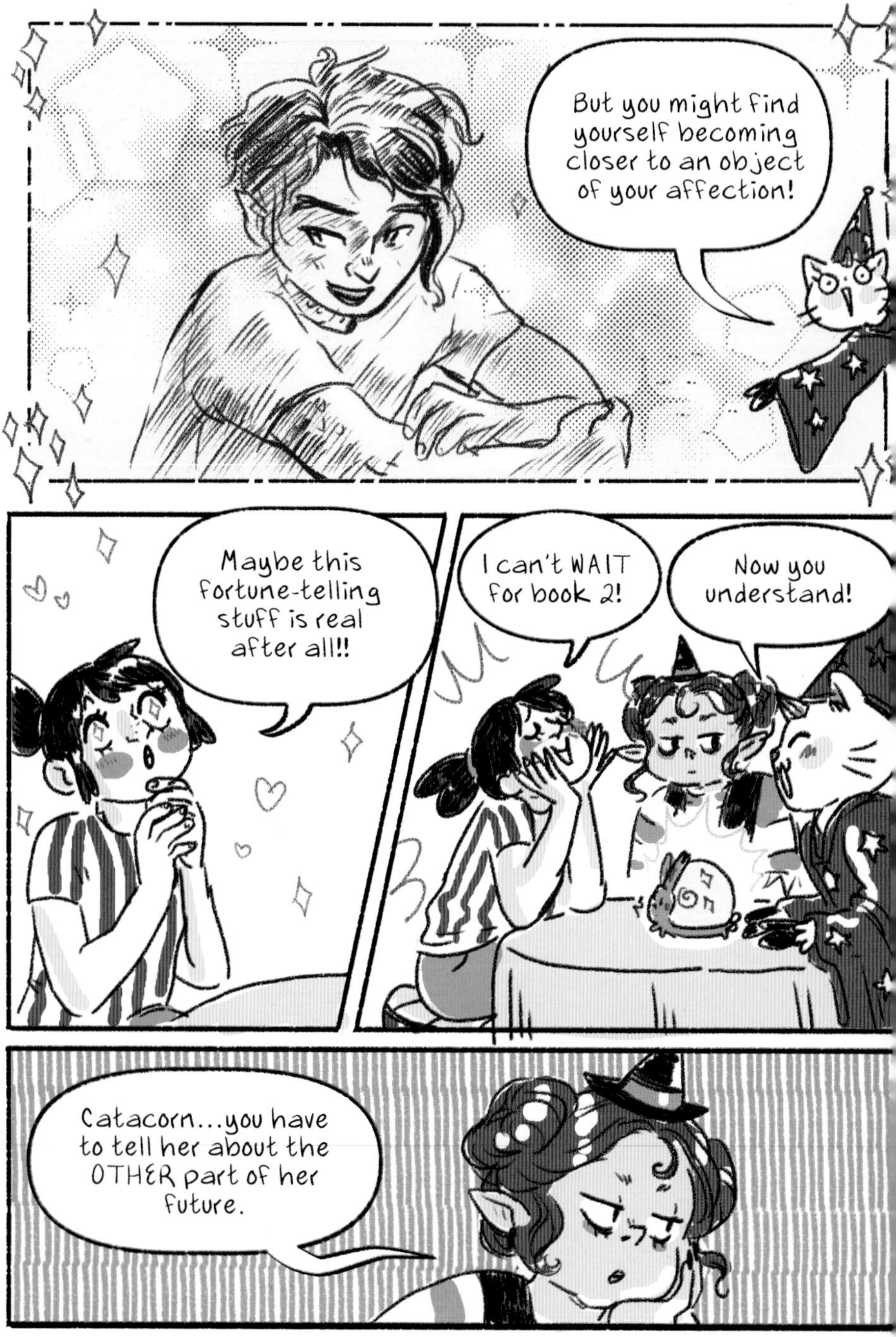
But you might find yourself becoming closer to an object of your affection!
Maybe this fortune-telling stuff is real after all!!
I can't WAIT for book 2!
Now you understand!
Catacorn...you have to tell her about the OTHER part of her future.

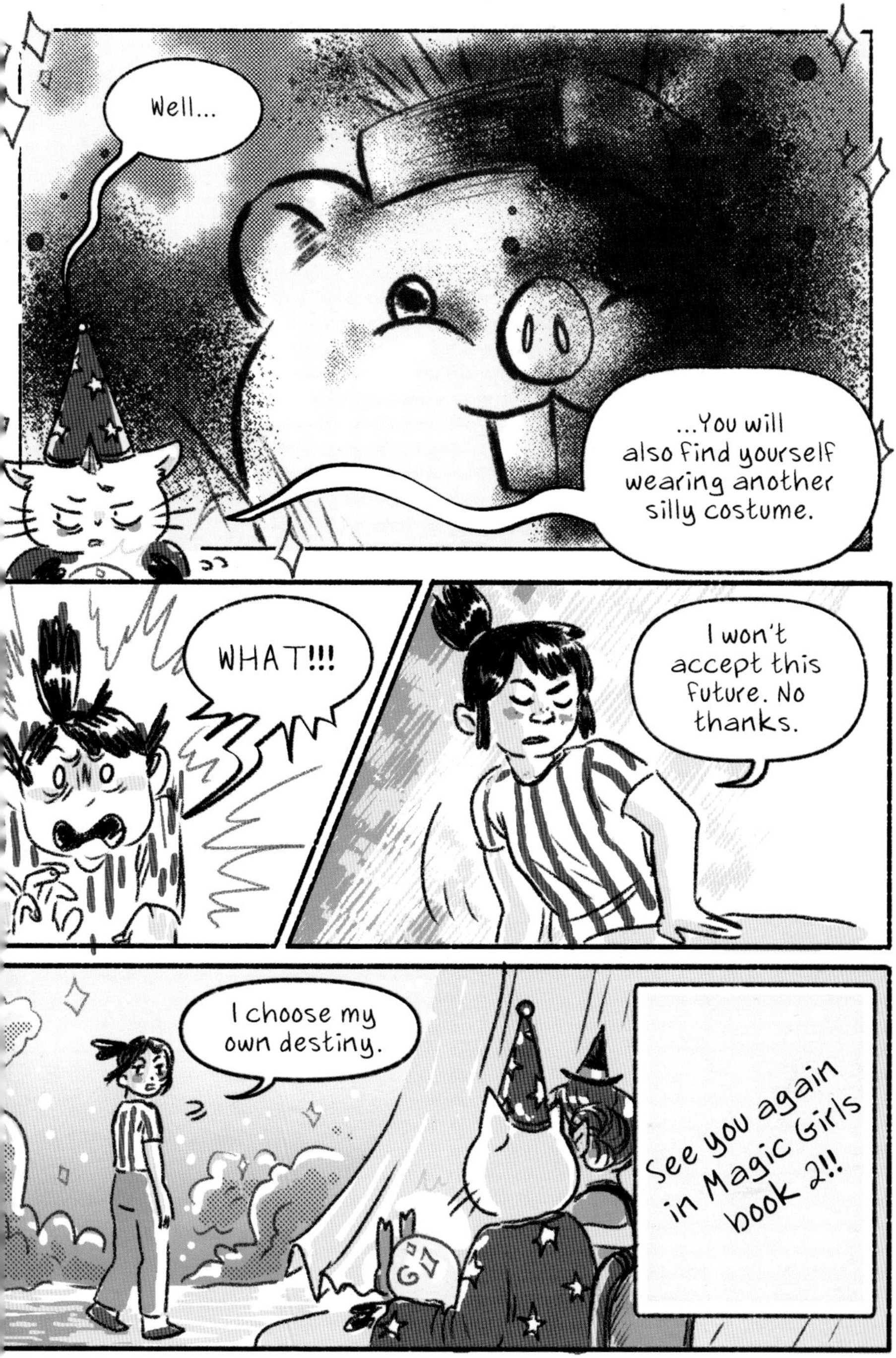
Well...
...You will also find yourself wearing another silly costume.
WHAT!!!
I won't accept this future. No thanks.
I choose my own destiny.
See you again in Magic Girls book 2!!

MEGAN BRENNAN is an indie comics sweetheart who has been publishing zines for years. She has also worked on the production side of comics on books like *Drama, Amulet,* and *The Adventure Zone: Here There Be Gerblins.* This is her debut graphic novel.

MEGAN-BRENNAN.COM
@MEGTHEBRENNAN